INVASION 14

Maxence Van der Meersch in 1936. Photograph by the Agence de presse Meurisse. Courtesy of the Bibliothèque nationale de France, département des Estampes et de la photographie, EI-13 (2916). Meurisse 36 12 61.

Invasion 14

A Novel

MAXENCE VAN DER MEERSCH

Translated by W. Brian Newsome

McGill-Queen's University Press
Montreal & Kingston · London · Chicago

© McGill-Queen's University Press 2016

First published in French as *Invasion 14*
© Editions Albin Michel – Paris 1935, 2014

ISBN 978-0-7735-4754-4 (paper)
ISBN 978-0-7735-9934-5 (ePDF)
ISBN 978-0-7735-9935-2 (ePUB)

Legal deposit second quarter 2016
Bibliothèque nationale du Québec

Printed in Canada on acid-free paper that is 100% ancient forest free (100% post-consumer recycled), processed chlorine free

This book has received support from the Institut français's Publication Support Programmes.

McGill-Queen's University Press acknowledges the support of the Canada Council for the Arts for our publishing program. We also acknowledge the financial support of the Government of Canada through the Canada Book Fund for our publishing activities.

Library and Archives Canada Cataloguing in Publication

Meersch, Maxence van der, 1907–1951
[Invasion 14. English]
    Invasion 14 : a novel / Maxence Van der Meersch ; translated by W. Brian Newsome.

Translated from the French.
Translation of: Invasion 14.
Includes bibliographical references.
Issued in print and electronic formats.
ISBN 978-0-7735-4754-4 (paper). – ISBN 978-0-7735-9934-5 (ePDF). – ISBN 978-0-7735-9935-2 (ePUB)

    1. World War, 1914–1918 – Fiction. I. Newsome, W. Brian, 1974–, translator II. Title. Title: Invasion 14. English

PQ2625.E31613 2016   843'.91   C2016-901199-2
                                             C2016-901200-X

This book was typeset by True to Type in 11/14 Minion

Contents

Acknowledgments

Many individuals played key roles in this project. Dean Fletcher McClellan and the Professional Development Committee at Elizabethtown College provided generous financial support, as did Linda Mitchell, Vivian Berghahn, and Martha Hoffman of *Historical Reflections/Réflexions historiques*. Among my Elizabethtown colleagues, I relied on the encouragement and feedback of David Brown, David Kenley, Gabriel Ricci, Patricia Ricci, Thomas Winpenny, Paul Gottfried, Carl Strikwerda, Gail Bossenga, Susan Traverso, Mark Harman, Vanessa Borilot, Douglas Bomberger, Sylvester Williams, Jesse Waters, Jean-Paul Benowitz, Stephen Burwood, Peter DePuydt, Louise Hyder-Darlington, Sylvia Morra, Elizabeth Young-Miller, and Barbara Forney. The logistical expertise of Carol Ouimet, my administrative assistant, allowed me to devote sufficient time to research. My student assistants – Allison Burkhardt, Jason Halberstadt, and Christopher Panetta – reviewed numerous drafts of the manuscript, and ITS student worker Jonathan Anderson composed the maps.

I am also indebted to a number of colleagues at other institutions. Members of the program committees at the New York State Association of European Historians and the Western Society for French History allowed me to present my work at their annual meetings. There the comments of Rick Fogarty, Jean Pedersen, Nicole Hudgins, Michael McGuire, Cherilyn Lacy, Andrew Nicholls, Lisa Cerami, Sarah Fishman, Gary Mole, Audra Merfeld-Langston, Ronen Steinberg, and Greg Parsons stimulated my thinking. James Connolly, Yves Pourcher, Vincent Grégoire, and Arthur Goldhammer corresponded with astute reflections of their own, and Raymond Hrinko provided relevant maps from the US Military Academy.

In Wasquehal, France, municipal administrators Luce Vincent, Cécile Clemmersseune, and Victor Godon made the Archives Maxence Van der Meersch available for my use and furnished additional support following my site visit. In Paris Virginie Raimbault of the Bibliothèque nationale de France facilitated acquisition of the photograph used for the frontispiece. Solène Chabanais of Les Éditions Albin Michel also kindly arranged for translation rights, which made this edition of *Invasion 14* possible.

In Canada the team at McGill-Queen's University Press brought the project to fruition. My editor Mark Abley deserves special thanks. He provided crucial feedback and shepherded the manuscript through multiple stages of review, always with grace and good humour. I am grateful for the insights of the two anonymous readers who reviewed the manuscript for MQUP. The Press's director Philip Cercone, managing editor Ryan Van Huijstee, production manager Elena Goranescu, marketing director Susan McIntosh, publicist Jacqueline Davis, exhibits coordinator Filomena Falocco, copyeditor Claude Lalumière, and editorial board members also gave generously of their time and support.

Many mentors have shaped my career as a scholar: Michael Smith, Kenneth Perkins, Gerasimos Augustinos, Patrick Maney, Brigitte Guillemin-Persels, and the late Owen Connelly at the University of South Carolina, and Hubert van Tuyll, Helen Callahan, Lee Ann Caldwell, Christopher Murphy, the late Edward Cashin, and the late Mary-Kathleen Blanchard at Augusta College (now Augusta University). They honed the skills that readied me for this project, and a number of them – particularly Mike, Ken, and Jerry – offered cogent advice regarding my work on *Invasion 14*.

As always, the members of my family sustained my scholarship in many, many respects. They read one draft after another, forced me to pause for necessary periods of reflection, and encouraged me to see the project through to completion. I am grateful to my wife Susan, my sons Braden and Barrett, my parents Danny and Ann, and my sisters Dana and Ashley. I dedicate this book to each and every one of them.

Maxence Van der Meersch's *Invasion 14*: An Introduction

W. BRIAN NEWSOME

In 1935 Albin Michel published *Invasion 14*, Maxence Van der Meersch's novel about the German occupation of northern France during World War I.[1] Van der Meersch explored the complexities of a prolonged ordeal: the material and emotional suffering of French civilians and German troops, the economic and social collaboration of French citizens with the German administration and individual soldiers, the resistance activities in which a few groups engaged, and the compassion that some people developed for ordinary German infantrymen. This was no Manichean portrait. It was a rich, varied, and highly accurate tableau, and one that differed from other accounts of the conflict. Like Henri Barbusse, the author of *Under Fire*, Van der Meersch condemned not World War I but war itself, hoping that the sacrifices occasioned by the conflict would pave the way for a better future, one without war.[2] Unlike the veteran Barbusse, however, Van der Meersch was a civilian – a child at the start of the war – who focused on the trauma of life under the occupation rather than the physical brutalities of the frontlines.[3] Van der Meersch's tale of the war and the occupation was unique, and though his novel stirred controversy in northern France – where accusations of collaboration were unwelcome – national and international critics praised it in leading journals of the day.[4]

Underpinning *Invasion 14* is the experience of Van der Meersch's own family, lower-middle-class residents of Roubaix.[5] Herlem, the fictional village in the opening pages of the novel, is based on Bondues, the native village of Van der Meersch's father Benjamin, and Herlem's lime kilns on those owned by a distant relative in the town of Hellemmes. Van der

Meersch crafted the character Judith Lacombe, a Herlem farm girl who has an affair with a German infantryman, from the model of a Bondues cousin who slept with a German soldier and turned to prostitution when her father expelled her from their house. In Roubaix and Lille the fictional Fontcroix family – Samuel, Édith, and their children Antoinette and Christophe – represent Van der Meersch's own immediate family. Like his father Benjamin and his mother Marguerite, Samuel and Édith separate because of Samuel's extramarital affairs and Édith's vexing disposition, but they survive the war by working together to smuggle and sell Belgian produce. Antoinette dies of tuberculosis, just like Van der Meersch's sister Sarah, and Christophe's Uncle Gaspard goes blind and then insane, much like Van der Meersch's Uncle Georges. The similarities between the Van der Meerschs and the Fontcroix are unmistakable and verified by the author's notes and published articles.[6]

Van der Meersch was hardly the only child to survive the occupation, but he was well positioned to write an account of it. As one of the region's few young novelists of national renown, Van der Meersch could use his reputation to draw a broad audience to the story of the occupation. Born in 1907, Van der Meersch studied literature under lycée professor Pierre Jourda, who went on to teach at the university in Montpellier. Jourda introduced Van der Meersch to the works of Émile Zola and encouraged Van der Meersch to develop his own skills as a naturalist by writing detailed descriptions of the countryside. Van der Meersch first came to national attention in 1925, when he won the Concours général des lycées et colleges de France, the country's top student essay contest. The following year Van der Meersch entered law school in Lille. He earned degrees in law and letters in 1930 and 1932, respectively, but he devoted much of his time to writing.[7]

In 1932 Van der Meersch published his first novel, a tale about tobacco smugglers whom he encountered during his brief career as an attorney. Van der Meersch's father Benjamin suggested the book's title, *La Maison dans la dune*, and served as his son's literary agent with Albin Michel. *La Maison dans la dune* was a commercial success, and in 1934 director Pierre Billon would transform it into a film. Other novels soon followed: *Car ils ne savent ce qu'ils font*, a semi-autobiographical work about a young bourgeois whose encounter with a mill girl transforms his life; *Quand les sirènes se taisent*, an account of the 1931 textile strikes in Roubaix; *Le Péché du monde*, a tale based on the life of Van der Meersch's working-class girlfriend Thérèze Denis; and *Maria, fille de Flandre*, the story of an affair set in Bruges, Belgium.[8] Critics were soon comparing Van der Meersch to Zola, particularly for *Quand les sirènes se taisent*, which bears a striking resemblance to Zola's description of a miners' strike in *Germinal*.[9] Van der Meersch acknowledged his debt not only to Zola but also to Stendhal. And though Van der Meersch aligned himself with no single school of contemporary writers, his works bear some affinity with those of Henry Poulaille's "proletarian" group, as Mary Melliez has argued.[10] With esteem for Van der Meersch increasing, he turned his attention to the conflict that had marked his childhood.

Van der Meersch completed *Invasion 14* in 1935, just after the conflict's twentieth anniversary. He had first conceptualized his war novel in 1928, the armistice's tenth anniversary, which had inspired a number of books on the occupation. Van der Meersch considered these works too narrow in scope or too panegyrical to capture the complex experiences of his family.[11] He thus set out to pen his own account of the conflict. Van der Meersch went beyond the history of his relatives, though, by examining extant documents, such as letters and newspaper articles. He also conducted interviews with people outside the family circle. The smugglers connected to his father Benjamin were a valuable source of information, as was the Abbé Jules Pinte, a resistance hero who operated a clandestine newspaper until his arrest and imprisonment in 1916. Roubaix resident Georges Pannier, who like Van der Meersch was a child at the time of the war, offered testimony on his deportation to unoccupied France.[12] Survivors of wartime labour camps described their mistreatment at the hands of the Germans. Villagers told of family members who had turned on each other in the course of the war and its aftermath. Van der Meersch's extensive notebooks are filled with such accounts.[13]

Utilizing this large resource base, Van der Meersch provided a faithful depiction of many aspects of the occupation. In the opening chapters, for example, the reader encounters snapshots of combat operations that swirled around Lille in 1914. When war erupted at the beginning of August, German commander Helmuth von Moltke devoted the bulk of German forces to the Western Front. Attempting to outflank French armies positioned along the Franco-German border, Moltke sent most of his units through neutral Belgium and Luxembourg. Though delayed by Belgian resistance at Liège, German columns began pouring across the Franco-

Belgian frontier in late August. They swept to the south of Lille, clashing with British forces at Le Cateau on 25 August. Facing defeat in Lorraine, French commander Joseph Joffre withdrew to the interior, called up reserves, and joined the British to launch a successful counteroffensive at the Battle of the Marne on 5–12 September. To the north, French troops had abandoned Lille on 24 August. German scouts had appeared briefly on 2 September, but German forces had been driving southeast and had not attempted to occupy the city. After the Battle of the Marne, Allied and German armies shifted northwest, attempting to outflank each other in a series of engagements that came to be known as the Race to the Sea. French forces returned to Lille on 3 October. German troops quickly laid siege to the city and seized control of it on 13 October, after an artillery barrage that destroyed more than 2,000 buildings. Civilians who had not fled were trapped. By November the Germans controlled all or part of ten departments in northern France, placing more than two million French citizens under German rule.[14]

Van der Meersch captured the initial stages of the war not with an overview but with select episodes, namely a skirmish in Herlem in September and the siege of Lille in October. The contaminant flight of Belgian and French refugees is also a prominent feature of the first three chapters. Van der Meersch's use of snapshots allows the reader to experience the invasion just as Van der Meersch and his compatriots did in 1914. They were civilians caught in the crossfire and attempting to piece together events at a time when accurate information was becoming increasingly scarce.[15]

In another passage, set after the trenches had evolved into an impenetrable barrier, the Roubaix youth Alain Laubigier and a renegade French soldier named Thaunier sneak into occupied Belgium and try to cross from there to the neutral Netherlands. Thaunier is killed as Alain and he are tunneling under an electric fence the Germans have built along the Dutch border, foiling the escape attempt and forcing Alain to return to Roubaix. From a literary perspective, these events symbolize danger and death. Yet the border fence was quite real, and Van der Meersch's account – gleaned from interviews with smugglers – accords precisely with the actual history of efforts to cross the barrier.[16]

Despite the accuracy of scenes like the siege of Lille and the attempted border crossing, one would be remiss to interpret *Invasion 14* as a purely

factual source. Beyond the Fontcroix family, some characters can be identified with real individuals. The Abbé Jules Pinte, for instance, was the inspiration for the Abbé Marc Sennevilliers, one of the central figures of the
novel. Often, though, Van der Meersch took components from the experiences of different witnesses and wove them together. The Laubigier family provides a good illustration. Van der Meersch fashioned Alain from the
testimony of several forced labourers. Alain's younger siblings Camille
and Jacqueline are representations of Georges Pannier and his sister
Jeanne. Van der Meersch faithfully recreated the Panniers' experience of
deportation while according them a brother they did not have. He thereby used a single family to explore themes of forced labour and exile. Even
the physical landscape reflects Van der Meersch's method of composition.
As noted above, the author based the fictional village of Herlem on the
real town of Bondues, but he gave Herlem a quarry that was actually located in Hellemmes.

Van der Meersch also drew on literary references as he crafted characters, themes, and plot structure. One example is Judith Lacombe, the Herlem prostitute who uses her connections with the Germans to help her
neighbours despite the contempt in which the community holds her. The
name "Judith" evokes the Book of Judith's morally complex heroine: a se-
ductress who saves fellow villagers through guile and deceit.[17] In addition,
Judith Lacombe reminds the reader of Boule de Suif, the title character of
naturalist Guy de Maupassant's short story about the Prussian invasion of
1870. Both Judith Lacombe and Boule de Suif trade sex for German
favours – to the benefit of fellow French citizens more than themselves –
only to be scorned by compatriots once the danger has passed.[18] Equally
relevant to *Invasion 14* is Émile Zola's naturalist classic *The Debacle*, which
explores the "savage egotism" of soldiers and civilians as both groups
attempt to survive defeat in the Franco-Prussian War.[19] Similar themes
appear in *War and Peace*, Leo Tolstoy's account of the Russian struggle
during the Napoleonic Wars.[20] *Invasion 14*'s complex plot, weaving together the stories of dozens of interconnected characters, mirrors that of
War and Peace. Van der Meersch's title also recalls the outcome of the
Napoleonic Wars. The Russians who had suffered at French hands in 1812
led allied forces into France itself in 1814, making the German invasion of
1914 the third of the preceding century.[21] The product of Van der Meersch's narrative construction is thus fictional, blending family experience

with oral testimony, documentary research, and references to other occupation narratives. Yet it is a type of fiction that provides the reader with a real sense of life under German rule.

One can best understand *Invasion 14* by utilizing the analytical framework that Jay Winter developed for Henri Barbusse's *Under Fire*.[22] According to Winter, Barbusse was a "moral witness," a truth-teller who sought to demolish romantic images of war circulating in the rear. Barbusse hoped "to set the record straight" by confronting civilians with conditions at the front. In similar fashion, Van der Meersch wanted to combat crude dichotomies between heroes and villains and to present the entire French nation with events that only people in northern France had endured. To accomplish their goals, both authors offered "fictional truth" rather than documentary truth.[23]

Van der Meersch adopted this approach, in part, to avoid lawsuits that might have arisen from accusations of collaboration. By casting his tale as fiction, he deflected charges of slander. Van der Meersch nonetheless took care to examine the intricacies of collaboration and resistance. In *Invasion 14*, not all collaborators are evil, and not all resisters are good. The Roubaix businessman Barthélémy David trades with the Germans, but he also provides employment and relief supplies to starving residents of the city. In contrast, the Lille mill owner Daniel Decraemer shutters his factory and burns his warehouse to keep the Germans from pilfering it. After the war, however, Decraemer exploits his workers just as he had before the conflict, despite a religiously inspired decision to mend his ways (a decision made while suffering wartime imprisonment alongside the priest Marc Sennevilliers).[24] The reader is left to ponder the shades of grey represented by David and Decraemer. Who was worse, the collaborator who helped others during the war or the resister who did his patriotic duty but took advantage of his employees?

Invasion 14 provides a balance between the city and the countryside, between Roubaix/Lille and the fictionalized village of Herlem, a community of farmers and artisans where relationships between occupier and occupied – and among French citizens themselves – are as complex as they are in the big city. Hector Lacombe, the village mayor, establishes a comfortable relationship with the German manager assigned to his farm, steals from the ration program that he oversees, and uses his position to settle scores with fellow villagers. His chief targets are Marc Sennevilliers's

mother Berthe and sister Lise, who run the family's guesthouse and quarry. Lacombe resents the Sennevilliers's prosperity, and he hates Berthe and
Lise because their opposition to collaboration tarnishes his image. Lacombe takes his revenge by directing the Germans to the inn for requisitions of household items and to the quarry for the industrial equipment
that German authorities are stripping from the region. At first Berthe and
Lise endure the hardships, but soon they are so desperate that Berthe re-
sorts to theft, the very type of activity in which she refused to engage at
the beginning of the occupation. In addition, Berthe and Lise come to
sympathize with the German soldiers who have been lodged with them
and who in increasing numbers are being sent to the slaughter on the
frontlines. Van der Meersch depicts Lacombe as a wicked collaborator,
and Berthe and Lise are initially noble resisters. Yet in the end even they
are brought low by the scarcities of the war.[25]

Berthe's daughter-in-law Fannie also succumbs to pressures placed on
her. Fannie's husband Jean, the brother of Marc and Lise, is mobilized in
autumn 1914 and flees the region as German troops are pouring into it.
Faced with the absence of her husband and the care of a young son, Fannie begins sleeping with Paul, a German soldier housed with her. She en-
ters this relationship not because she is lecherous but because she needs
emotional and material support. Fannie thereby elicits the reader's sympathy more than his condemnation. As in Roubaix and Lille, collaboration and resistance in Herlem are not always black and white.[26]

The same can be said of the war's aftermath. Seeking to avert criticism
for their own activities, the region's most prominent businessmen use
Barthélémy David as a scapegoat for collaboration. The state indicts him, but
the prosecution drops its case when David threatens to expose the other
merchants who used his connections to trade with the enemy. Hector Lacombe, the mayor of Herlem, suffers no reprisals. The only collaborators
punished are those too weak to defend themselves, especially the women
who established relationships with German soldiers. As for resisters, those
who served and suffered are honoured alongside those who acted for selfish
reasons and shirked their responsibilities. Marc Sennevilliers receives acco-
lades, but so does the newspaper owner Thorel, who provided printing facilities for the covert newssheet only because he hoped to boost sales of his own
paper and only until the operation became dangerous. Was justice served?
Was merit recognized? Again, the reader is left to consider the balance sheet.[27]

Despite Van der Meersch's deft handling of collaboration and resistance, *Invasion 14* provoked controversy in Roubaix and Lille, where critics accused the author of exaggerating the extent of collaboration. For Eugène Saillard, a contributor to the *Grand Écho du Nord*, Van der Meersch "placed disproportionate emphasis on certain moral lapses."[28] In one respect such critics were right. Van der Meersch was hard on the peasantry, echoing the embittered memories of his cousin in Bondues.[29] Overall, however, Van der Meersch's analysis of collaboration and resistance was balanced – a reflection of the wartime complexities that scholars have since documented.[30] Van der Meersch himself interpreted the local reaction as an indication of his accuracy. Those who protested, he thought, did so because he had struck an uncomfortable chord.[31] Van der Meersch was correct in more ways than he realized. A significant if unspoken issue for regional critics was the author's breach of a silent taboo. In the wake of the war, the French people as a whole had concentrated on honouring victims and veterans of combat, a category into which occupation survivors did not fit. Many of the latter felt a sense of inferiority and by the mid-1930s had come to remember their experience only as one of suffering and resistance. These themes, not the shades of grey depicted by Van der Meersch, were compatible with the nationwide discourse on the plight of the soldiers.[32]

Van der Meersch himself examined the gulf dividing the French who lived under the occupation from those who did not. In the novel Pascal Donadieu, the son of Herlem's blacksmith, attempts to convey his experience to interlocutors in Paris, but he gives up when he finds they cannot understand. The young man and his Parisian audience simply have no common points of reference.[33] The gap between soldiers at the front and families at home – one of the main themes of Henri Barbusse's *Under Fire* and Erich Maria Remarque's *All Quiet on the Western Front* – thus finds its purely civilian parallel in *Invasion 14*.[34] Like Barbusse and Remarque, Van der Meersch hoped that his book would bridge the divide. Drawing on the naturalist techniques of Émile Zola, Van der Meersch painted precise pictures of the turmoil occasioned by the war and the occupation. Van der Meersch wanted to memorialize the experience of his compatriots and communicate *their* war – *his* war – to the rest of the French. For the people of northern France, however, *Invasion 14* unearthed difficult memories and underscored the distinctions separating them from their fellow citizens.

On the national and international levels, some commentators echoed the sentiments of critics in Roubaix and Lille.[35] Yet overwhelmingly Van der Meersch won praise for his ability to paint an impartial picture of the occupation. To Réné Lalou, writing for *Les Nouvelles littéraires*, Van der Meersch was "scrupulously just" to French and Germans alike. "Half-history, half-fiction," stated Lalou, "*Invasion 14* is a powerful epic … a poignant testament."[36] For G.M.A. Grube, a classics professor at the University of Toronto, *Invasion 14* was a book "written with passion but without prejudice and with amazing fairness," providing "an extraordinarily vivid, intimate, and compelling picture of life in the German-occupied territory of Northern France."[37] The novel's moving images of hardship again led many reviewers to compare Van der Meersch to Zola.[38] Others argued that *Invasion 14* was simply one of the best French books on the war. In the opinion of novelist and radio commentator Pierre Descaves – himself a veteran – "*Invasion 14* is for civilians what [Roland] Dorgelès's *Wooden Crosses* was for the poilus!"[39] Louis-Jean Finot, editor of *La Revue mondiale*, placed Van der Meersch's novel alongside Henri Barbusse's *Under Fire*, and Henry Benazet of *La Tribune républicaine* ranked it with Louis-Ferdinand Céline's *Journey to the End of the Night*.[40] A number of observers considered *Invasion 14* the obvious choice for the Prix Goncourt. They were shocked when academy president J.-H. Rosny broke an unexpected tie in favour of Joseph Peyré's *Sang et lumières*.[41] Sales of *Invasion 14* nonetheless proceeded apace.

Notoriety undoubtedly contributed to the ease with which Albin Michel marketed *Invasion 14*. However, Van der Meersch stirred far less national and international controversy than he did locally because he portrayed neither the French nor the Germans as ubiquitously good or evil: a sentiment that meshed with the spirit of Franco-German reconciliation embodied in the Locarno Treaty of 1925.[42] Indeed, the novel *reflected* that spirit, indicating that postwar trends shaped Van der Meersch and *Invasion 14* as much as the war itself. Other examples abound. The novel's focus on material destruction, starting in the first chapter with an intricate account of the 1914 shelling of Lille, stemmed from frustration with state management of postwar damage claims – grievances with which the author's father Benjamin, the head of a building supply company, was quite familiar. Van der Meersch's broader emphasis on human suffering, seen in the plight of Berthe and Lise, was a reaction to characterization of the residents of the occupied territories as "Boches du Nord," a stereotype that began in free France during the war and persisted years after the conflict ended. Castigation of the business elite, visible in descriptions of Barthélémy David's associates, took shape in the midst of the Great Depression, when labour disputes intensified (as Van der Meersch himself had documented in *Quand les sirènes se taisent*).[43] Audiences at home and abroad could identify with such motifs, contributing to the popularity of *Invasion 14*.

The single best example of the interplay between past and present is Van der Meersch's focus on religion and redemptive suffering. Material deprivation facilitates a "spiritual renaissance" for Marc Sennevilliers and Daniel Decraemer as they transcend their anguish to find new purpose in life and religion.[44] When wartime deprivation stripped existence to its bare essentials, thought Van der Meersch, people could see more clearly the values and practices that gave life significance. The author's perspective reflected a real increase in wartime spiritualism and Van der Meersch's postwar interest in Catholicism. Though reared by his father as a secular humanist, Van der Meersch began to embrace Catholicism as interviews with the Abbé Jules Pinte led to a friendship between the two men. They began dining together on Sunday afternoons, and Pinte officiated in 1934 when Van der Meersch wed his lover Thérèze Denis, who had borne Van der Meersch a daughter in 1929. Van der Meersch retained an aversion for liturgical ritual, but he would convert to Catholicism in 1936, following the death of a premature baby daughter. This conversion came merely a year after publication of *Invasion 14*, and one can read the author's spiritual struggle in the pages of the novel.[45]

Invasion 14 also reveals the influence of Leo Tolstoy's spiritualism.[46] Tolstoy invested his religious ideals in the character Pierre Bezukhov, who is transformed by interactions with a fellow prisoner when both are held captive by French forces. Van der Meersch clearly drew on this scene as he depicted Daniel Decraemer's experience with Marc Sennevilliers. In contrast to Bezukhov, however, change is short-lived for Decraemer. Mirroring the nervousness that followed Hitler's rise to power, Van der Meersch concluded that the path to epiphany was perilous and that maintenance of new commitments in a corrupt world could be difficult.[47]

The message of Van der Meersch bears some resemblance to that of Henri Barbusse. Both condemned war while arguing that World War I offered hope for a better future. For Barbusse, the collective and secular sacrifice of the soldiers could pave the way for a secure peace built on socialist foundations.[48] Van der Meersch hoped that his novel, too, would help build a wall of sentiment against armed conflict. Yet for him the product of redemptive suffering was more religious, more individual, and more uncertain, leaving the reader to ponder a grey zone of ambiguity regarding the meaning of the war.[49]

In this respect, *Invasion 14* fits into the metanarrative identified by Leonard Smith in his examination of wartime and postwar accounts of combat.[50] According to Smith, the dominant theme of the memoirs and novels produced by French soldiers evolved from consent (in the 1910s) to rejection of the war (in the 1920s). Building on the work of the German novelist Erich Maria Remarque, French writers such as Roger Martin du Gard and Jules Romains were by the late 1930s developing more complex narratives of tragedy and victimization, in works such as *Summer 1914* and *Verdun*, respectively. Van der Meersch cast the occupation in much the same light, with one notable difference. Van der Meersch, though less confident in a positive meaning of the war than Barbusse, was more optimistic than either Martin du Gard or Romains. Timing explains the distinction. Barbusse wrote in 1916, Van der Meersch in 1935, Martin du Gard in 1936, and Romains in 1938. Barbusse invested his expectations for a better tomorrow in the war he was fighting. Van der Meersch, writing just as the Nazis were initiating German rearmament, could still embrace some hope that wartime sacrifices had not been in vain. Following the remilitarization of the Rhineland in 1936 and the descent to war that began in 1938, Romains and Martin du Gard were less certain that a new tragedy could be averted.

Despite the political uncertainty of the late 1930s, Van der Meersch enjoyed continued literary success. In 1936, for example, he won the Prix Goncourt for *L'Empreinte du dieu*, the tale of an incestuous love affair.[51] Van der Meersch also devoted increasing attention to religious themes with *L'Élu*, a fictionalized description of his conversion experience, and *Pêcheurs d'hommes*, an account of the struggles of Catholic workers in Roubaix.[52] For the latter novel, Van der Meersch relied on interviews with members of the Young Christian Workers (YCW), a Catholic association of labourers in their teens and twenties. Ironically, the book would soon become popular with young prisoners of war struggling to find comfort in the midst of World War II, the very conflict that Van der Meersch had longed to avoid.

The war that erupted in 1939 brought profound change for Van der Meersch and his regional compatriots. During the Battle of France in 1940, Van der Meersch and his family joined the long columns of refugees fleeing the frontlines. After the armistice, Van der Meersch returned to Roubaix.[53] There – and across northern France – memory of the previous occupation and its aftermath had a profound impact on the way inhabitants understood the new ordeal. Despite regional efforts to reintegrate with the nation, the stereotype of the Boche du Nord had persisted, stimulating local resentment of Paris and the south. In 1940 rumours quickly circulated that southern politicians had betrayed northerners, that the former had concluded the armistice to save themselves from the hard fighting the latter had endured. The Germans also drew on past experience by separating the administration of northern France from the rest of the country and placing it under the military governor of Belgium. The commandant of Roubaix in 1940 filled the same position that his uncle had in 1914, and a familiar list of requisitions followed. This time, though, the Germans did not ransack industrial facilities as they had in the early stages of World War I. Instead they encouraged production to support the local economy and the wider German war effort. Given the apparent inevitability of German victory over Britain, most of the area's businessmen complied.[54]

For many residents of northern France, the unoccupied zone in the south appeared distant, and few in the region's professional and working classes looked to Marshal Philippe Pétain, the head of the Vichy regime, as a saviour. The aging general's call for a new moral order nevertheless enticed the business elite, Catholic prelates, and much of the peasantry. It also appealed to Van der Meersch, who embraced Pétain's triptych of family, work, and fatherland. Politically as well, Pétain's denunciation of the Popular Front fit with Van der Meersch's own position, which tended to the right of the spectrum. In 1942 Van der Meersch wrote a short biography of Saint Jean Vianney, the Curé d'Ars, with profits benefitting a government relief agency called the Secours national. Van der Meersch's 1943 bestseller, *Corps et âmes* – an endorsement of the regimen of diet and exercise prescribed by the author's physician, Dr Paul Carton – also accorded with the "return to nature" promoted by Pétain's officials.[55] As the war dragged on, however, the occupation grew more repressive and the Vichy regime more overtly collaborationist. Such conditions sparked active resistance, which ultimately became more widespread during World War II than in World War I. Van der Meersch himself engaged in some limited resistance activity. He contributed articles to underground newspapers like the communist *Nord-Libre*, allowed resistance agents to use his house as a stopover, and passed a few clandestine messages. Like many of the characters he had described in *Invasion 14* – and like many of his countrymen during World War II – Van der Meersch's attitudes and actions were evolving and complex, not black and white.[56]

The postwar era proved even more difficult than the war years. In 1945 Van der Meersch began spitting up blood, signalling the onset of active tuberculosis – the same disease that had killed his sister Sarah and which he may have contracted as early as 1937. Van der Meersch retreated to the highlands of Savoy. His lungs seemed to clear, and he returned to Roubaix. In 1946, however, tragedy struck when his father Benjamin, with whom he had remained close, suffered a series of strokes and died. The following year, in which a new book produced new controversy, was still worse for Van der Meersch.[57] In 1947 he published *La Petite Sainte Thérèse*, a biography of one of France's most popular saints, Thérèse de Lisieux, who had been canonized in 1925.[58] In an approach not unlike that of *Invasion 14*, Van der Meersch attempted to cut through the hagiography and humanize Thérèse. *La Petite Sainte Thérèse* is a testament of the extent to which Van der Meersch had evolved into a Catholic novelist. Clergy bristled, though, at Van der Meersch's portrait of Thérèse de Lisieux as a flawed individual whose saintliness lay not in a form of holy perfection but in acknowledgement of her weaknesses, and who was thus redeemed primarily by faith in God's grace rather than faith, hope, and charity.[59]

The controversy over *La Petite Sainte Thérèse* distressed Van der Meersch far more than the disputes over *Invasion 14*, particularly as his health began slipping again in 1948. Tubercular symptoms reappeared, but this time Van der Meersch did little to effectively treat the disease. After the death of Dr Carton in 1947, Van der Meersch had refused medical treatment, preferring to care for himself through diet and exercise alone. His health worsened, and renewed debate over *La Petite Sainte Thérèse* further dampened his spirits. In 1950 a new collection of essays condemned the book.[60] Van der Meersch was devastated. He maintained communication with a few clerical friends, but the controversy over *La Petite Sainte Thérèse* led to a mounting disenchantment with the Church. Van der Meersch retreated to a villa in Touquet and grew increasingly depressed. He struggled to complete projects, never finishing *Invasion 40* – a novel on the occupation of World War II – and died in 1951.[61]

In subsequent years, the works of Van der Meersch became the subject of individual studies focusing on themes of religion, suffering, and love.[62] Examination of his novels also appeared in general works on modern French literature. Pierre de Boisdeffre situated Van der Meersch among other Catholic novelists, such as Georges Bernanos, François Mauriac, Julien Green, and Daniel-Rops, while Pierre-Henri Simon positioned Van der Meersch between Fyodor Dostoyevsky and Émile Zola, describing Van der Meersch as a "Christian Zola."[63] Zola analyzed the impact of environmental factors on his characters, and although Van der Meersch did likewise he also devoted far more attention than Zola to the inner lives of his creations, indicating a kinship to Dostoyevsky's approach to character psychology.[64] For Maurice Fraigneux, Van der Meersch thus "fulfilled the promise of naturalism" by moving beyond materialistic determinism to explore the spiritual dimension of human beings.[65] René Lalou praised the detailed panoramas in which Van der Meersch set his characters, and Maurice Rieuneau compared the author's meticulous research to that of Roger Martin du Gard and Jules Romains.[66]

In the some respects, though, Van der Meersch's works came to seem dated. In the 1930s Van der Meersch had been competing with surrealists like André Breton. In the 1940s and 1950s, with the growing popularity of existentialists like Jean-Paul Sartre, Van der Meersch's naturalist prose appeared increasingly antiquated, an impression reinforced by the accessible style in which Van der Meersch had intentionally written.[67] A good example of this straightforward form is Van der Meersch's use of names and physical attributes to mark certain characters for the reader, in the style of Honoré de Balzac. Judith Lacombe stirs images of the Biblical figure Judith. Patrice Hennedyck, one of Marc Sennevilliers's partners in the resistance, bears a first name meaning "noble." Étienne Duydt – a Belgian refugee who traffics gold on behalf of the Germans – is cast as a hunchback. And most redheads – including a thief nicknamed "Red" – are malevolent characters. Van der Meersch hoped to reach a wide audience. He sought to craft a text that the public could read with ease, and he did.

But for some critics such obvious metaphors were a bit too black and white, even melodramatic, despite the other respects in which Van der Meersch emphasized shades of grey.[68]

As Christian Morzewski has argued, a few of Van der Meersch's "moral and ideological considerations" came to seem dated as well, like hallmarks of a different era.[69] Most of these positions, such as the author's approach to women and same-sex relationships, stemmed from his commitment to Catholicism. Some of *Invasion 14*'s female characters are strong figures. Berthe and Lise Sennevilliers are good examples. But even Berthe stumbles in contrast to her son, the priest Marc Sennevilliers. From Van der Meersch's Catholic perspective, women were more prone to succumb to temptation than men. Occasional moralizing, including the sporadic homophobic barb, is also evident in *Invasion 14* and became more pronounced in the author's later works. The most striking instance of this moralizing tendency is the novel *Masque de chair*, which focuses on the struggles of a gay character, Manuel Ghelens, to end his relationships with other men. Written in the midst of World War II, the story is based on conversations Van der Meersch had with an individual conflicted about his sexual identity. While expressing revulsion for persecution of gays, Van der Meersch depicted homosexuality as a vice redeemable by God's grace alone. Acting on the counsel of clerical friends, Van der Meersch decided not to publish the manuscript, which risked alienating gays more than reconciling them to Catholicism. As Mary Melliez has indicated, Van der Meersch also fell into disputes with his informant over the primacy of the Eucharist, which the ritual-averse Van der Meersch downplayed in the life of the main character. Against Van der Meersch's express wishes, his wife Thérèze and his daughter Sarah released the book in 1958, seven years after his death. In their search for financial stability, Thérèze and Sarah published a book that stigmatized Van der Meersch as a reactionary.[70]

This reputation was in many respects unmerited. Van der Meersch had determined not to print *Masque de chair*. Over time, Van der Meersch had also modified his position on labour relations, moving away from the enlightened paternalism that he had at first envisioned as a solution to economic strife. In *Invasion 14*, Daniel Decraemer's vision for a model factory – with a generous "family" wage to support stay-at-home mothers and subsidized housing to promote healthful living – provides evidence of the welfare capitalism that Van der Meersch initially favoured. By the late

1930s, however, Van der Meersch had come into contact with the Young Christian Workers. As Van der Meersch cultivated friendships with members of the YCW, he concluded that workers could and should take the lead in their own spiritual and social renewal.[71] Like his friends in the YCW, though, Van der Meersch remained suspicious of the Popular Front, whose overt support for secular labour unions seemed to threaten Christian ones, and he continued calling for a "family" wage even after World War II. Van der Meersch was thus a conservative – but hardly a reactionary – whose position is perhaps best described as "a Christian non-conformism of the right."[72]

Beyond stylistic and socioeconomic concerns, scholars and the public willfully ignored *Invasion 14* after World War II, when national discourse focused predominantly on heroes of anti-Nazi resistance movements.[73] Van der Meersch's nuanced examination of collaboration and resistance during World War I created considerable discomfort for those who wanted to believe that most French citizens had resisted in one way or another during World War II, and that only a few politicians like Pierre Laval had been deliberate collaborators. In the 1960s and 1970s, pioneering historians such as Eberhard Jäckel, Robert Paxton, and Jean-Pierre Azéma deconstructed concepts of widespread resistance and examined trends of both collaboration and resistance between 1940 and 1944.[74] Many Vichy officials, similar to Herlem's Mayor Lacombe, had worked willingly with the Germans, and most people had simply tried to survive, much like the characters in *Invasion 14*. Given the dangers involved, only a small minority, less than 2 percent of the adult population, had engaged in active resistance during World War II. As this interpretation of the second war prevailed, scholars began examining *Invasion 14* afresh.[75]

Stimulating this trend was historical interest in the invasion and occupation of 1914-18, not only of France but also of Belgium. Like *Invasion 14*, study of the occupation was long overshadowed by other subjects: the battlefields and homefronts of World War I and the occupation of all of France, rather than part of it, during World War II. In the 1970s and 1980s Louis Köll, Marc Blancpain, and Richard Cobb began exploring the occupation of World War I.[76] As late as 1998, however, scholarship remained limited enough that Annette Becker entitled a book *Oubliés de la guerre* in reference to the war's "forgotten" – civilians living under occupation, forced labourers, and prisoners of war.[77] Much has since changed, with

Francophone and Anglophone researchers devoting increasing attention to the occupation of 1914-18 and its impact on subsequent trends, including attitudes and behavior as the French endured another occupation between 1940 and 1944.[78] In the process, historians have come to value *Invasion 14* as a crucial lens onto the occupation of World War I.[79] Literary scholars now appreciate it as Van der Meersch's best novel – with its intricate plot, complex characters, and nuanced discourses on collaboration, resistance, and faith.[80] And researchers have recognized the book's impact on other twentieth-century writers, particularly Irène Némirovsky, who like Van der Meersch published with Albin Michel and who almost certainly drew on *Invasion 14* as she crafted the structure and themes of *Suite française* – her acclaimed account of the occupation of World War II.[81]

Despite renewed interest in *Invasion 14*, the only English translation has long been that of Gerard Hopkins, a nephew of the English poet Gerard Manley Hopkins and a prolific writer and translator in his own right.[82] Hopkins completed the translation of *Invasion 14* for Viking Press, making Van der Meersch's novel available to English audiences in 1937, just two years after its original publication.[83] This contribution was considerable, but the speed with which Hopkins translated the book led to substantial errors.[84] Most serious is the misattribution of passages, which corrupted dialogue and confused readers. In one such instance, Hopkins attributed words spoken by Marellis, Hector Lacombe's chief opponent on the Herlem ration board, to Lacombe himself.[85] In more subtle ways as well, Hopkins failed to convey the full meaning of Van der Meersch's text. A good example is a scene in which the German soldier Albrecht seduces Judith Lacombe. Describing Judith's emotions, Van der Meersch wrote, "Une espèce de défaillance, de langueur délicieuse et perfide l'envahissait."[86] Hopkins translated this passage as, "A swooning, an insidious sweetness, drugged her senses."[87] Van der Meersch chose the verb "envahir," meaning "invade," to draw a parallel between Albrecht's conquest of Judith and the Germans' conquest of northern France. The reader begins to see this connection at the start of the paragraph, in which Judith is described as falling into a "thick, treacherous bed of hay" and Albrecht's body as "crushing" that of Judith. "Traîtresse" ("treacherous"), "écraser" ("crush"), "envahir" ("invade"): all three words convey a military metaphor. To complete the triptych, one must use the verb "invade" rather than "drug." In the present translation, the sentence has thus been rendered as, "A sort of faintness, a delicious and perfidious languor, was invading her."

In still other instances, Hopkins needlessly dropped phrases and entire sentences. Listing the products with which Herlem's farmers were failing to compete, Van der Meersch included "Russian flax, German beets, American wheat, Algerian potatoes, Moroccan eggs, [and] Danish butter."[88] Hopkins removed the latter, thereby depriving readers of the complete range of the original.[89] A few pages later, after Marc Sennevilliers tells his mother of Jean's demise, Berthe puts away her supper. Marc urges her to persevere. Berthe then shakes her head and says, "It's no longer worthwhile, dear … It's no longer worthwhile …"[90] Hopkins included no description of Berthe shaking her head, thus eradicating the physical action accompanying Berthe's statement.[91] Though seemingly minor, such problems occur dozens of times, marring Hopkins's rendition of the novel. The new translation, which is based on the same 1935 French original that Hopkins utilized, facilitates a more accurate and nuanced understanding of *Invasion 14*.

By the early 2000s Van der Meersch and his oeuvre had become the subject of academic conferences and new articles, books, and dissertations.[92] More than any other of Van der Meersch's texts, *Invasion 14* has become the object of scholarly investigations – and for good reason. *Invasion 14* allows the reader to understand life under the German occupation between 1914 and 1918. Scholars have come to recognize the significance of that event and Van der Meersch's accomplishment in conveying its complexities. May the present translation stimulate further work in this growing field of research and remind readers of the pain and sacrifices occasioned by the first great war of the twentieth century.

NOTES

1 Maxence Van der Meersch, *Invasion 14* (Paris: Albin Michel, 1935). Albin Michel released a reprint edition of the book in 2014.

2 Henri Barbusse, *Under Fire*, trans. Robin Buss, with an introduction by Jay Winter (London: Penguin, 2004), originally published in French in 1916. On Barbusse's attitude toward the war, see also Jay Winter, *Sites of Memory, Sites of Mourning: The Great War in European Cultural History* (Cambridge: Cambridge

University Press, 1995), 178–86, and Leonard V. Smith, *The Embattled Self: French Soldiers' Testimony of the Great War* (Ithaca: Cornell University Press, 2007), 69–72.

3 Bernard Alluin, "*Invasion 14*, un 'roman-fresque,'" *Nord*, no. 1 (June 1983): 57; Laurent Drapier, "*Invasion 14*: genèse d'une solitude," in *"L'Empreinte du dieu" et "Invasion 14" de Maxence Van der Meersch*, eds Christian Morzewski and Paul Renard, published by the journal *Roman 20–50* (2007), 65.

4 For an example of a negative local review, see Eugène Saillard, "Invasion 14," *Grand Écho du Nord*, 7 December 1935, 1–2. For an example of a positive local review, see Paul Schaepelynck, "Invasion 14," *Revue de Flandres*, 5 December 1935, n.p., in the Archives Maxence Van der Meersch (hereafter AMVDM), Hôtel de Ville de Wasquehal, I14 3/3 Revue de presse, no. 24. For examples of national and international reviews, see Louis-Jean Finot, "Au jardin du livre," *La Revue mondiale*, 15 November 1935, 26–7; René Lalou, "Invasion 14," *Les Nouvelles littéraires*, 7 December 1935, 5; A.V. de Walle, "Un jeune Maxence Van der Meersch," *Chronique sociale de France* 45, no. 2 (February 1936): 110–26; Harold Littledale, "Drums and Destruction," *Saturday Review of Literature*, 23 January 1937, 5; Louise MacNeice, "Fiction," *The Spectator*, 19 February 1937, 330; Stuart Streeter, Review of *Invasion 14*, by Maxence Van der Meersch *Books Abroad* 11, no. 1 (winter 1937): 70. See below for further discussion of reaction to *Invasion 14*.

5 The best biography of Maxence Van de Meersch is Térèse Bonte, *Van der Meersch au plus près* (Arras: Artois presses université, 2002). See also Paul Renard, ed., *Maxence Van der Meersch, auteur et témoin* (Villeneuve-d'Ascq: Éditions Ravet-Anceau, 2007).

6 See, for example, notes on the smuggling activities of Van der Meersch's father and the illness of his sister Sarah in AMVDM, I14 1/3, Notes sur les personnages, "Samuel Fontcroix," 2, 4, 5, 7. For articles, see "Il y a vingt ans les Allemands occupaient Roubaix," *Paris Midi*, 12 December 1935, n.p., in AMVDM, I14 3/3, Revue de presse, no. 35; "Souvenirs d'un petit bonhomme en blouse de marin à col bleu," press clipping without journal title, 12 December 1935, in n.p., AMVDM, I14 3/3, Articles de V.D.M. sur la guerre de 1914. See also Bonte, *Van der Meersch au plus près*, 123–4; Francis Nazé, "Présence des racines bonduoises dans l'œuvre de Van der Meersch," in *Maxence Van der Meersch: "écrire le Nord, écrire le monde*," eds Christian Morzewski and Paul Renard, published by the journal *Roman 20–50* (2001), 23–6; Mary Barbier, "La guerre," in *Maxence Van der Meersch, auteur et témoin*, ed. Paul Renard (Villeneuve-d'Ascq: Éditions Ravet-Anceau, 2007), 42–5.

7 Drapier, "*Invasion 14*: genèse d'une solitude," 72; Bonte, *Van der Meersch au plus près*, 31, 70–3, 78–80, 103.

8 Maxence Van der Meersch, *Car ils ne savent ce qu'ils font* (Paris: Albin Michel,

1933); Maxence Van der Meersch, *Quand les sirènes se taisent* (Paris: Albin Michel, 1933); Maxence Van der Meersch, *Le Péché du monde* (Paris: Albin Michel, 1934); Maxence Van der Meersch, *Maria, fille de Flandre* (Paris: Albin Michel, 1935). For succinct plot summaries and critical analyses of these novels, see William Wheat Bailey, "Maxence Van der Meersch: The Man and His Works," Ph.D. diss. (University of Virginia, 1961), 22–106. See also Bonte, *Van der Meersch au plus près*, 101, 112–21, 125.

9   See, for example, J. Ernest-Charles, "Livres tristes – *Quand les sirènes se taisent*," *L'Opinion*, 13 November 1933, 7–8; Louis-Jean Finot, Review of *Quand les sirènes se taisent*, by Maxence Van der Meersch, *La Revue mondiale*, 15 November 1933, 32. For summaries of these reviews and others, see Bailey, "Maxence Van der Meersch: The Man and His Works," 68–77. On Zola's novel *Germinal*, see Émile Zola, *Germinal*, trans. Roger Pearson (London: Penguin, 2004).

10 Mary Melliez, "Maxence Van der Meersch, héraut du peuple," Ph.D. diss. (Université d'Artois, 2008), available through Books on Demand (2010), 10, 25, 62, 75–6, 234.

11 Maxence Van der Meersch, "Pourquoi j'ai écrit *Invasion 14*. Manuscrit inédit transcrit par Mary Barbier," in "*L'Empreinte du dieu*" *et* "*Invasion 14*" *de Maxence Van der Meersch*, eds Christian Morzewski and Paul Renard, published by the journal *Roman 20–50* (2007), 59–63. Van der Meersch did not designate the books by name. However, he was likely referring to Pierre Boulin's *L'Organisation du travail dans la région envahie de la France pendant l'occupation* (Paris: Presses universitaires de France, 1927), Paul Collinet and Paul Stahl's *Le Ravitaillement de la France occupée* (Paris: Presses universitaires de France, 1928), and perhaps Georges Gromaire's earlier work on *L'Occupation allemande en France (1914–1918)* (Paris: Payot, 1925).

12 To prevent infection among the troops and to preserve supplies for themselves, German authorities started "repatriating" the ill, the old, and the young to unoccupied France. For purposes of military security, the army forced the refugees to travel slowly through Belgium and Germany to Switzerland and from there to France.

13 AMVDM, I14 1/3, Notes sur les personnages, Samuel Fontcroix, 2–4; AMVDM, I14 2/3, Cahiers, l'Abbé Pinte, Divers; AMVDM, I14 1/3, Notes sur les personnages, Au dehors, no. 189, 194, 205–6; AMVDM, BRA 1/1, Recits recueillis sur la guerre 1914–18, no. 1–37; AMVDM, I14 1/3, Notes sur les personnages, Village d'Herlem, no. 47, 68–9. See also Michel David, "*Invasion 14*. La peinture et la photographie," *Nord*, no. 20 (December 1992): 50–1.

14 R. Ernest Dupuy and Trevor N. Dupuy, *The Harper Encyclopedia of Military History*, 4th ed. (New York: HarperCollins Publishers, 1993), 1017–29; James E. Connolly, "Encountering Germans: The Experience of Occupation in the Nord, 1914–1918," Ph.D. diss. (King's College, London, 2012), 28–30.

15 Van der Meersch, *Invasion 14*, chaps 1–3. On the flight of refugees, see John Horne and Alan Kramer, *German Atrocities, 1914: A History of Denial* (New Haven: Yale University Press, 2001).

16 Van der Meersch, *Invasion 14*, 52–60; Alex Vanneste, "Sur un passage de Maxence Van der Meersch: Histoire romancée ou roman historique?" in *Maxence Van der Meersch, écrivain engagé*, eds Christian Morzewski and Paul Renard, published by the journal *Roman 20–50* (2008), 69–96.

17 Linda Day, "Judith," in *The New Oxford Annotated Bible*, ed. Michael D. Coogan, 3rd ed. (Oxford: Oxford University Press, 2001), 32 Aprocrypha.

18 Guy de Maupassant, "Boule de Suif," in *More Stories by Guy de Maupassant* (London: Cassell & Co., 1950), 395–440. See also Drapier, "*Invasion 14*: genèse d'une solitude," 66.

19 Émile Zola, *The Debacle*, trans. Leonard Tancock (London: Penguin, 1972), 363. See also 408. In addition, see Luc Rasson, "L'élu et la bête. Le sens de la guerre selon Maxence Van der Meersch," in *"L'Empreinte du dieu" et "Invasion 14" de Maxence Van der Meersch*, eds Christian Morzewski and Paul Renard, published by the journal *Roman 20–50* (2007), 93.

20 Leo Tolstoy, *War and Peace*, trans. Louise and Aylmer Maude, ed. George Gibian (New York: W.W. Norton, 1966), 1045–6, 1128.

21 Special thanks to Professor Christine Haynes, who reminded the author of the allied invasion of France in 1814. See also Bonte, *Van der Meersch au plus près*, 74.

22 Jay Winter, "Introduction: Henri Barbusse and the Birth of the Moral Witness," in *Under Fire*, by Henri Barbusse, trans. Robin Buss (London: Penguin, 2004), vii–xix. Note that Winter drew the concept of the "moral witness" from Avishai Margalit, *The Ethics of Memory* (Harvard: Harvard University Press, 2002), chap. 5.

23 On the concept of fictional truth, see Winter, "Introduction," xiv.

24 Van der Meersch, *Invasion 14*, 294–300, 312–14, 464–74.

25 Ibid., 23, 29–31, 34–9, 114–16, 383.

26 Ibid., 39–41.

27 Ibid., 450–1, 457–64, 486–96.

28 Eugène Saillard, "Invasion 14," *Grand Écho du Nord*, 7 December 1935, 1–2. Translation by W. Brian Newsome. See also André Douriez, "Invasion 14," *La Dépêche*, 26 November 1936, 1; David, "*Invasion 14*. La peinture et la photographie," 56. All local reviewers were not negative. See P.-H. Simon, "Invasion 14," *Le Journal de Roubaix*, 26 November 1935, 1–2; Paul Schaepelynck, "Invasion 14," *Revue de Flandres*, 5 December 1935, n.p., in AMVDM I14 3/3, Revue de presse, no. 24.

29 Alluin, "*Invasion 14*, un 'roman-fresque,'" 58–9.

30 Connolly, "Encountering Germans: The Experience of Occupation in the Nord," Part I. Connolly's analysis stands in some contrast to the dichotomies posited by

other historians, particularly Annette Becker. See Becker, *Oubliés de la Grande guerre* (Paris: Noêsis, 1998), 40, 48; Annette Becker, *Les Cicatrices rouges, 14–18: France et Belgique occupées* (Paris: Fayard, 2010), 240–70, 295–7. The work of Philippe Nivet is somewhat more nuanced than that of Becker, but Nivet's focus remains on forms of resistance. See Philippe Nivet *La France occupée, 1914–1918* (Paris: Armand Colin, 2011), chaps 10–12.

31   Van der Meersch, "Pourquoi j'ai écrit *Invasion 14*. Manuscrit inédit transcrit par Mary Barbier," 60.

32   James E. Connolly, "*Mauvaise conduite*: Complicity and Respectability in the Occupied Nord, 1914–1918," *First World War Studies* 4, no. 1 (2013): 10. See also Connolly, "Encountering Germans: The Experience of Occupation in the Nord, 1914–1918," chap. 9; Becker, *Oubliés de la Grande guerre*, 14, 359–60.

33   Van der Meersch, *Invasion 14*, 441–5.

34   Barbusse, *Under Fire*; Erich Maria Remarque, *All Quiet on the Western Front*, trans. A.W. Wheen (New York: Ballatine Books, 1982), originally published in German in 1928.

35   P. Loemel, "La vie littéraire," *L'Ordre*, 30 December 1935, n.p., in AMVDM, I14 3/3, Revue de presse, no. 47; Charles Bourdon, "Invasion 14," *Revue des lectures*, 16 January 1936, 35–6. Less harsh than Loemel and Bourdon, but arguing that Van der Meersch was a little too pessimistic, were the following: Maurice Clavière, "Livres récents," *Comoedia*, 10 December 1935, n.p., in AMVDM, I14 3/3, Revue de presse, no. 32; Jean Morienval, "L'Aube littéraire," *L'Aube*, 20 December 1935, n.p., in AMVDM, I14 3/3, Revue de presse, no. 42; Julius Adelberg, "Invasion 14," *Boston Evening Transcript*, 23 January 1937, 2.

36   René Lalou, "Invasion 14," *Les Nouvelles littéraires*, 7 December 1935, 5. Translation by W. Brian Newsome. See also "Invasion 14," *Le Matin*, 8 December 1935, n.p., in AMVDM, I14 3/3, Revue de presse, no. 30; Amélie Fillon, "Littérature," *La Revue mensuelle* (January 1935): 171–2; Regis Seron, "En marge du Prix Goncourt," *Minerva*, 12 January 1936, n.p., in AMVDM, I14 3/3, Revue de presse, no. 65; A.V. de Walle, "Un jeune Maxence Van der Meersch," *Chronique sociale de France* 45, no. 2 (February 1936): 110–26; Milliet, "Invasion 14," *Adam*, 15 March 1936, n.p., in AMVDM, I14 3/3, Revue de presse, no. 77.

37   G.M.A. Grube, "Behind the German Guns," *The Canadian Forum* 17 (July 1937): 141. For other English language reviews, see Harold Littledale, "Drums and Destruction," *Saturday Review of Literature*, 23 January 1937, 5; M.W.S., Review of *Invasion 14*, by Maxence Van der Meersch, *Christian Science Monitor*, 26 January 1937, 16; "War and Childhood," *Commonweal* 25 (5 February 1937): 424; Louise MacNeice, "Fiction," *The Spectator*, 19 February 1937, 330; Stuart Streeter, Review of *Invasion 14*, by Maxence Van der Meersch, *Books Abroad* 11, no. 1 (winter 1937): 70; Mary W. Colum, "Life and Literature," *The Forum* 47, no. 3 (March 1937):

159–64; Hamish Miles, Review of *Invasion 14*, by Maxence Van der Meersch, *New Statesman and Nation* 13 (10 April 1937): 606.

38   Charles Laval, "Chronique littéraire," *Le Populaire*, 25 November 1935, n.p., in AMVDM, I14 3/3, Revue de presse, no. 9; Paul Lombard, "Nouvelles têtes," *L'Homme libre*, 15 December 1935, n.p., in AMVDM, I14 3/3, Revue de presse, no. 40; Lucien Descaves, "Invasion 14," *La Chronique filmée du mois*, 12, 15–16, in AMVDM, I14 3/3, Revue de presse, no. 61a–62a.

39   Pierre Descaves, "La Vie littéraire," *L'Avenir*, 7 December 1935, n.p., in AMVDM, I14 3/3, Revue de presse, no. 28. Translation by W. Brian Newsome.

40   Louis-Jean Finot, "Au jardin du livre," *La Revue mondiale*, 15 November 1935, 26–7; Henry Benazet, "Le Mouvement littéraire," *La Tribune républicaine*, 24 November 1935, n.p., in AMVDM, I14 3/3, Revue de presse, no. 8.

41   "Le livre du Var," *La République du Var*, 23 November 1935, n.p., in AMVDM, I14 3/3, Revue de presse, no. 12; "Prix littéraires," *La Vie toulousaine*, 14 December 1935, n.p., in AMVDM, I14 3/3, Revue de presse, no. 39; P.-H. Simon, "Autour des prix," *Esprit*, 1 January 1936, 610–12; Michel Corday, "La Critique," *La Griffe littéraire*, 5 January 1936, n.p., in AMVDM, I14 3/3, Revue de presse, no. 63a; "Invasion 14," *Annales africaines*, 15 January 1936, n.p., in AMVDM, I14 3/3, Revue de presse, no. 68; S. Fages, "Invasion 14," *La Vie bitteroise*, 1 February 1936, n.p., in AMVDM, I14 3/3, Revue de presse, no. 76.

42   Drapier, "*Invasion 14*: genèse d'une solitude," 74.

43   Robert Vandenbussche, "*Invasion 14*: quelques pistes de lecture," in *Maxence Van der Meersch: "écrire le Nord, écrire le monde,"* eds Christian Morzewski and Paul Renard, published by the journal *Roman 20–50* (2001), 107–16.

44   Christian Morzewski, "(Re)lire Van der Meersch?" in *"L'Empreinte du dieu" et "Invasion 14" de Maxence Van der Meersch,* eds Christian Morzewski and Paul Renard, published by the journal *Roman 20–50* (2007), 9. See also Rasson, "L'élu et la bête," 97.

45   On wartime spiritualism, see Annette Becker, *La Guerre et la foi. De la mort à la mémoire* (Paris: Armand Colin, 1994). On Van der Meersch's spiritual path, see Maxence Van der Meersch, "Postface" to *Car ils ne savent ce qu'ils font*, new edition (Paris: Albin Michel, 1941), 235–51; Maxence Van der Meersch, "L'Élu," in *Nouvelles et chroniques*, eds Mary Melliez, Christian Morzewski, and Francis Nazé (Arras: Artois presses université, 2014), 1:267–8; Bonte, *Van der Meersch au plus près*, 96, 110, 126–9, 137, 142–4; Bailey, "Maxence Van der Meersch: The Man and His Works," 4, 134–6, 194.

46   Bonte, *Van der Meersch au plus près*, 74. On Tolstoy's spiritualism, see Isaiah Berlin, "Tolstoy's World View in *War and Peace*," in *War and Peace*, ed. George Gibian (New York: W.W. Norton, 1966), 1451–5.

47   Rasson, "L'élu et la bête," 94–7.

48 Winter, *Sites of Memory, Sites of Mourning*, 182–3.

49 Luc Rasson, "L'élu et la bête," 97.

50 Smith, *The Embattled Self*, 185.

51 Maxence Van der Meersch, *L'Empreinte du dieu* (Paris: Albin Michel, 1936).

52 Maxence Van der Meersch, *L'Élu* (Paris: Albin Michel, 1937); Maxence Van der Meersch, *Pêcheurs d'hommes* (Paris: Albin Michel, 1940). See also Bailey, "Maxence Van der Meersch: The Man and His Works," 170–242; Bonte, *Van der Meersch au plus près*, 145–6.

53 Bonte, *Van der Meersch au plus près*, 161–2.

54 Helen McPhail, *The Long Silence: Civilian Life under the German Occupation of Northern France, 1914–1918* (London: I.B. Tauris, 1999), 8; Richard Cobb, *French and Germans, Germans and French* (Waltham, MA: Brandeis University Press, 1983), 30–1, 41–56.

55 Maxence Van der Meersch, *Corps et âmes* (Paris: Albin Michel, 1943); Francis Nazé, "La position de Maxence Van der Meersch pendant la Seconde Guerre mondiale," in *Maxence Van der Meersch, écrivain engagé*, eds Christian Morzewski and Paul Renard, published by the journal *Roman 20–50* (2008), 126–7; Robert Vanderbussche, "Écrire et publier sous les regards d'Hitler et de Pétain," in *Maxence Van der Meersch, écrivain engagé*, eds Christian Morzewski and Paul Renard, published by the journal *Roman 20–50* (2008), 148–50.

56 Maxence Van der Meersch, "Ceux de la Résistance" and "L'homme traqué," in *Nouvelles et chroniques*, eds Mary Melliez, Christian Morzewski, and Francis Nazé (Arras: Artois presses université, 2014), 2:225–7 and 229–31, respectively; Nazé, "La position de Maxence Van der Meersch pendant la Seconde Guerre mondiale," 113–27; Bonte, *Van der Meersch au plus près*, 162–6.

57 Hughes Melliez, "La tuberculose vécue par Maxence Van der Meersch," in *Maxence Van der Meersch, écrivain engagé*, eds Christian Morzewski and Paul Renard, published by the journal *Roman 20–50* (2008), 242; Bonte, *Van der Meersch au plus près*, 180–1, 186, 199–206.

58 Maxence Van der Meersch, *La Petite Sainte Thérèse* (Paris: Albin Michel, 1947). See also Maxence Van der Meersch, "Il y a cinquante ans Thérèse Martin" and "Dieu m'a fait la faveur d'être lu," in *Nouvelles et chroniques*, eds Mary Melliez, Christian Morzewski, and Francis Nazé (Arras: Artois presses université, 2014), 2:247–50 and 251–4, respectively.

59 André Combes, "La critique historique," 26–7, André Combes, "La critique doctrinale," 36–7, and M.-M. Philipon, "En lisant Van der Meersch: réflexions d'un théologien," 78–9, all originally published in 1947 and included in André Combes et al., *La Petite Sainte Thérèse de Maxence Van der Meersch devant la critique et devant les textes* (Paris: Les Éditions Saint-Paul, 1950). See also Bailey, "Maxence Van der Meersch: The Man and His Works," 447–8, 454–5, 501, 594.

60 The book was Combes et al., *La Petite Sainte Thérèse de Maxence Van der Meersch devant la critique et devant les textes*. This collection included articles from the late 1940s alongside new and even more virulent ones. See also Bonte, *Van der Meersch au plus près*, 207, 224–5, 229–31; Bailey, "Maxence Van der Meersch: The Man and His Works," 517.

61 Van der Meersch's daughter Sarah did not deposit the manuscript of *Invasion 40* with the rest of her father's archives. Based on the notes that do remain, one can conclude that Van der Meersch planned to focus on deportees. See Barbier, "La guerre," 48–50; Bonte, *Van der Meersch au plus près*, 176–7.

62 Bailey, "Maxence Van der Meersch: The Man and His Works"; Mary Clarence Bolger, "Le Thème de la souffrance dans les romans de Maxence Van der Meersch," Ph.D. diss., Université Laval, 1965); Jan Verachtert, *L'Amour dans les romans de Maxence Van der Meersch* (Louvain, 1969). Van der Meersch himself was the subject of Robert Reus, *Portrait morpho-psychologique de Maxence Van der Meersch* (Aurillac: Pierre Clairac, 1952).

63 Pierre de Boisdeffre, *Une histoire vivante de la littérature d'aujourd'hui*, 7th ed. (Paris: Perrin, 1958): 359–67; Pierre-Henri Simon, *Histoire de la littérature française au XXe siècle, 1900–1950*, 8th ed. (Paris: Armand Colin, 1965), 2:98.

64 Bailey, "Maxence Van der Meersch: The Man and His Works," 596–7.

65 Maurice Fraigneux, "Maxence Van der Meersch ou le naturalisme chrétiene," *Revue générale belge* 25 (November 1947): 49. See also Maurice Fraigneux, *Littérature de l'homme: Dostoïevski, Rilke, Bernanos, Saint-Exupéry, Kafka, Undset, Plisnier, Breton, Van der Meersch* (Brussels: Goemaere, 1953), 147–8.

66 René Lalou, *Histoire de la littérature française contemporaine (de 1870 à nos jours)* (Paris: Presses universitaires de France, 1953), 787; Maurice Rieuneau, *Guerre et révolution dans le roman français, 1919–1939* (Paris: Klincksieck, 1974), 418. See also J.R. Foster, *Modern Christian Literature* (London: Burns & Oates, 1963), 88–9.

67 Boisdeffre, *Une histoire vivante de la littérature d'aujourd'hui*, 366–7; Bailey, "Maxence Van der Meersch: The Man and His Works," ii, 12. See also Francis Nazé, "Le monde ouvrier," in *Maxence Van der Meersch, auteur et témoin*, ed. Paul Renard (Villeneuve-d'Ascq: Éditions Ravet-Anceau, 2007), 28–9; Morzewski, "(Re)lire Van der Meersch?" 8–9.

68 Paul Renard, "Le corps," chap. in *Maxence Van der Meersch, auteur et témoin* (Villeneuve-d'Ascq: Éditions Ravet-Anceau, 2007), 61–72; Mary Barbier, "Corps et âme dans *Invasion 14*," in *"L'Empreinte du dieu" et "Invasion 14" de Maxence Van der Meersch*, eds Christian Morzewski and Paul Renard, published by the journal *Roman 20–50* (2007), 78–9; Alluin, "*Invasion 14*, un 'roman-fresque,'" 60–1.

69 Morzewski, "(Re)lire Van der Meersch?" 9. See also Jacques Duquesne, "Préface" to *Maxence Van der Meersch: Gens du Nord* (Paris: Presses de la Cité, 1993), vi.

70 Maxence Van der Meersch, *Masque de chair* (Paris: Albin Michel, 1958); Bonte, *Van der Meersch au plus près*, 171–2; Melliez, "Maxence Van der Meersch, héraut du people," 119–21; Hélène Dottin, "*Masque de chair*: l'écriture d'une rédemption," in *Maxence Van der Meersch: "écrire le Nord, écrire le monde,"* eds Christian Morzewski and Paul Renard, published by the journal *Roman 20–50* (2001), 185–94. Bonte, Melliez, and Dottin have emphasized the tolerance expressed in *Masque de chair*. For a critical contemporary reaction, however, see Pierre Nedra (penname of André Gaillard), "Un marécage," *Arcadie*, no. 59 (November 1958), available at ddata.over-blog.com/0/05/17/99/DOSSIER1/UN-MARECAGE-par-PIERRE-NEDRA-ARCADIE-59-MASQUE-DE-CHAIR.pdf, consulted 15 January 2015. On Van der Meersch's reputation as a Catholic polemicist, see Richard Cobb, *Promenades: A Historian's Appreciation of Modern French Literature* (Oxford: Oxford University Press, 1980), 14; Michel David, "Relire Maxence Van der Meersch aujourd'hui," in *Maxence Van der Meersch, auteur et témoin*, ed. Paul Renard (Villeneuve-d'Ascq: Éditions Ravet-Anceau, 2007), 5.

71 Élie Bordes, *Le Drame spiritual dans l'œuvre de Maxence Van der Meersch*, 3rd ed. (Tourcoing : Éditions Georges Frère, 1944), 87; Bruno Béthouart, "La conscience sociale de Maxence Van der Meersch et la réalité sociale: du constat à l'engagement," in *Maxence Van der Meersch, écrivain engagé*, eds Christian Morzewski and Paul Renard, published by the journal *Roman 20–50* (2008), 172–6; Bailey, "Maxence Van der Meersch: The Man and His Works," 213, 528.

72 Michel David, "Entre expérience personnelle et réforme de la société : le non-conformisme de Maxence Van der Meersch," in *Maxence Van der Meersch, écrivain engagé*, eds Christian Morzewski and Paul Renard, published by the journal *Roman 20–50* (2008), 221. Translated by W. Brian Newsome. See also Christian Morzewski, "Préface" to *Nouvelles et chroniques*, eds Mary Melliez, Christian Morzewski, and Francis Nazé (Arras: Artois presses université, 2014), 1:9–10.

73 Laurent Drapier, "Invasion 14: Une écriture à contretemps, une lecture à rebours," in *Maxence Van der Meersch, écrivain engagé*, eds Christian Morzewski and Paul Renard, published by the journal *Roman 20–50* (2008), 97–112.

74 Eberhard Jäckel, *Frankreich in Hitlers Europa* (Stuttgart: Deutsche Verlags-Anstalt, 1966); Robert Paxton, *Vichy France: Old Guard and New Order, 1940–1944* (New York: Alfred A. Knopf, 1972); Jean-Pierre Azéma, *De Munich à la libération, 1938–1944* (Paris: Éditions du Seuil, 1979).

75 Alluin, "*Invasion 14*, un 'roman-fresque,'" 57–64; Gérard Vindt and Nicole Giraud, *Les Grands Romans historiques: l'histoire à travers les romans* (Paris: Bordas, 1991); David, "*Invasion 14*. La peinture et la photographie," 49–57; Annette Becker, "Mémoire et commémoration, les 'atrocités' allemandes de la Première Guerre mondiale dans le nord de la France," *Revue du Nord* 74, no. 295

(April-June 1992): 342, 344; Annette Becker, "D'une guerre à l'autre: mémoire de l'occupation et de la résistance: 1914–1940," *Revue du Nord* 76, no. 306 (July-September 1994): 456.

76 See for example Louis Köll, "La population civile d'Auboué durant l'occupation allemande," in *1914–1918, l'autre front*, ed. Patrick Fridenson (Paris: Les Éditions ouvrières, 1977), 35–63; Marc Blancpain, *Quand Guillaume II gouvernait de la Somme aux Vosges* (Paris: Fayard, 1980); Marc Blancpain, *La Vie quotidienne dans la France du nord sous les occupations (1814–1944)* (Paris: Hachette, 1983); Cobb, *French and Germans, Germans and French*.

77 Becker, *Oubliés de la Grande guerre*.

78 McPhail, *The Long Silence*; Horne and Kramer, *German Atrocities, 1914: A History of Denial*; Stéphane Audoin-Rouzeau and Annette Becker, *Understanding the Great War* (New York: Hill and Wang, 2003); Leonard V. Smith, Stéphane Audoin-Rouzeau, and Annette Becker, *France and the Great War, 1914–1918* (Cambridge: Cambridge University Press, 2003), chap. 2; Larry Zuckerman, *The Rape of Belgium: The Untold Story of World War I* (New York: New York University Press, 2004); Becker, *Les Cicatrices rouges,* 14–18; Nivet, *La France occupée, 1914–1918*; Jay Winter, ed., *The Cambridge History of the First World War* (Cambridge: Cambridge University Press, 2014), 3:chaps 10–11. Regarding the impact of the occupation of 1914–18 on subsequent trends, see especially Thomas Grabau, *Industrial Reconstruction in France after World War I* (New York: Garland, 1991); Hugh Clout, *After the Ruins: Restoring the Countryside of Northern France after the Great War* (Exeter: Exeter University Press, 1996); Cobb, *French and Germans, Germans and French*, 30.

79 See, for example, McPhail, *The Long Silence*, 10; Vanneste, "Sur un passage de Maxence Van der Meersch," 69–96; Connolly, "Encountering Germans," 100, 110, 248; Michel Winock, "Les classiques: 'Invasion 14' de Van der Meersch," *L'Histoire*, no. 388 (June 2013): 96; Nicole Hudgins, *Hold Still, Madame: Wartime Gender and the Photography of Women in France during the Great War* (Edinburgh: Centre for French History and Culture of the University of St. Andrews, 2014), 1. Philippe Nivet has also indicated that *Invasion 14* is "très bien documenté." See Nivet, *La France occupée*, 339. Annette Becker, who has argued that relatively few French citizens collaborated with German forces, has been more critical of Van der Meersch. See Becker, *Oubliés de la Grande guerre*, 48.

80 See, for example, Drapier, "Invasion 14: Une écriture à contretemps, une lecture à rebours," 97–112; Morzewski, "(Re)lire Van der Meersch?" 9; Barbier, "La guerre," 42–5; Barbier, "Corps et âme dans *Invasion 14*," 79–80; Rasson, "L'élu et la bête," 89–97.

81 Irène Némirovsky, *Suite française*, trans. Sandra Smith (New York: Vintage Books, 2006). *Suite française* remains unfinished. Némirovsky, who was of

Russian Jewish ancestry, perished in the Holocaust. For details on the influence of *Invasion 14* on *Suite française*, see Yves Baudelle, "'L'assiette à bouillie de bonne-maman' et 'le ratelier de rechange de papa': ironie et comique dans *Suite française*," *Roman 20–50*, no. 54 (December 2012): 121.

82 On the relationship between Gerard Hopkins and Gerard Manley Hopkins, see Helen Vendler, "I Have Not Lived Up to It," *London Review of Books* 36, no. 7 (April 2014): 13–18. Among Gerard Hopkins's own works are the following: *A City in the Foreground* (London: Constable & Co., 1921); *An Unknown Quantity* (London: Chatto & Windus, 1922); *The Friend of Antaeus: A Comedy of Fantastic People* (London: Duckworth, 1927); *Seeing's Believing: Variations on a Theme* (London: Victor Gollancz, 1928); *Something Attempted* (London: Victor Gollancz, 1929); *An Angel in the Room* (London: Victor Gollancz, 1931); *Nor Fish nor Flesh* (London: Victor Gollancz, 1933); ed., *The Battle of the Books* (London: Allan Wingate, 1947). Hopkins ultimately translated more than a dozen books, among them the following: François Mauriac, *Verdun* (London: Peter Davies, 1939); Jules Romains, *Men of Good Will* (London: Peter Davies, 1940); Marcel Proust, *A Selection from His Miscellaneous Writings* (London: Allan Wingate, 1948); Gustave Flaubert, *Madame Bovary: Life in a Country Town* (London: Hamish Hamilton, 1948); Jean-Paul Sartre, *Iron in the Soul* (London: Hamish Hamilton, 1950); François Mauriac, *That Which Was Lost* and *The Dark Angels* (London: Eyre & Spottiswoode, 1951); Henri Bosco, *Barbache* (Oxford: Oxford University Press, 1959).

83 Maxence Van der Meersch, *Invasion 14*, trans. Gerard Hopkins (New York: The Viking Press, 1937).

84 Lydia Davis, who has translated Gustave Flaubert's *Madame Bovary*, noted similar problems with Hopkins's 1948 translation of this novel. According to Davis, Hopkins routinely added material to Flaubert's text. See Lydia Davis, "Introduction," in *Madame Bovary*, by Gustave Flaubert, trans. Lydia Davis (New York: Viking Adult, 2010), xxiii.

85 Van der Meersch, *Invasion 14*, trans. Gerard Hopkins, 36–7. Compare to Van der Meersch, *Invasion 14*, 30.

86 Van der Meersch, *Invasion 14*, 22.

87 Van der Meersch, *Invasion 14*, trans. Gerard Hopkins, 26.

88 Van der Meersch, *Invasion 14*, 36. Reference is to the French original. Translation by W. Brian Newsome.

89 Van der Meersch, *Invasion 14*, trans. Gerard Hopkins, 46.

90 Van der Meersch, *Invasion 14*, 41. Reference is to the French original. Translation by W. Brian Newsome.

91 Van der Meersch, *Invasion 14*, trans. Gerard Hopkins, 52.

92 Conferences devoted entirely to Van der Meersch were held in Arras in 2001 and
2007, leading to the publication of two volumes of articles by conference partici-
pants: Christian Morzewski and Paul Renard, eds., *Maxence Van der Meersch:
écrire le Nord, écrire le monde*, published by the journal *Roman 20–50* (2001); and
Christian Morzewski and Paul Renard, eds., *Maxence Van der Meersch, écrivain
engagé*, published by the journal *Roman 20–50* (2008). A 2007 issue of *Roman
20–50* is also devoted to Van der Meersch. It is collectively entitled *"L'Empreinte
du dieu" et "Invasion 14" de Maxence Van der Meersch*, eds Christian Morzewski
and Paul Renard. Recent books and dissertations include the following: Bonte,
Van der Meersch au plus près; Renard, ed., *Maxence Van der Meersch, auteur et
témoin*; Melliez, "Maxence Van der Meersch, héraut du people." Analysis of *Invasion 14* also appears in Connolly, "Encountering Germans: The Experience of
Occupation in the Nord, 1914–1918," and in "From Occupation to Liberation:
Northern France in the Great War," a panel at the 2013 meeting of the Western
Society for French History.

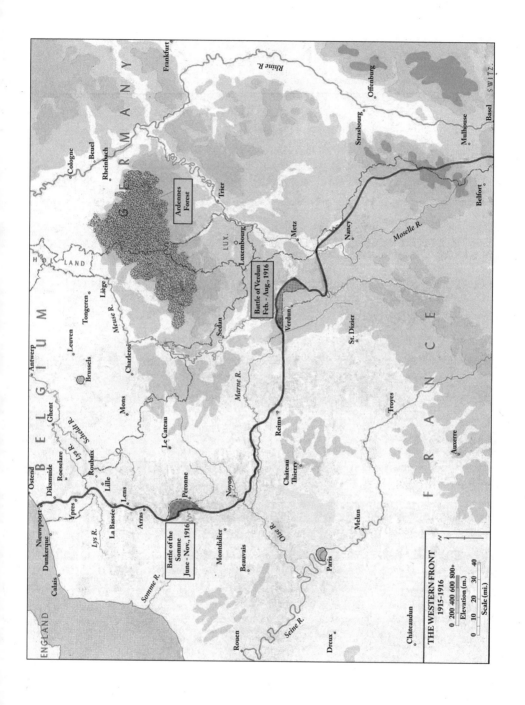

THE WESTERN FRONT
1915–1916

Elevation (m.)
0 200 400 600 800+

Scale (mi.)
0 10 20 30 40

Battle of the Somme
June – Nov., 1916

Battle of Verdun
Feb. – Aug., 1916

Ardennes Forest

ENGLAND

BELGIUM

GERMANY

FRANCE

HOLLAND

LUX.

SWITZ.

Calais
Dunkerque
Ostend
Nieuwpoort
Ypres
Diksmuide
Roeselare
Roubaix
Lille
Lens
La Bassée
Arras
Péronne
Noyon
Montdidier
Beauvais
Dreux
Rouen
Châteaudun
Paris
Melun
Auxerre
Troyes
Château Thierry
Reims
St. Dizier
Verdun
Sedan
Charleroi
Mons
Le Cateau
Ghent
Brussels
Leuven
Tongeren
Liège
Antwerp
Cologne
Beuel
Rheinbach
Frankfurt
Trier
Luxembourg
Metz
Nancy
Strasbourg
Offenburg
Mulhouse
Basel
Belfort

Rhine R.
Moselle R.
Meuse R.
Marne R.
Lys R.
Schelde R.
Somme R.
Oise R.
Seine R.

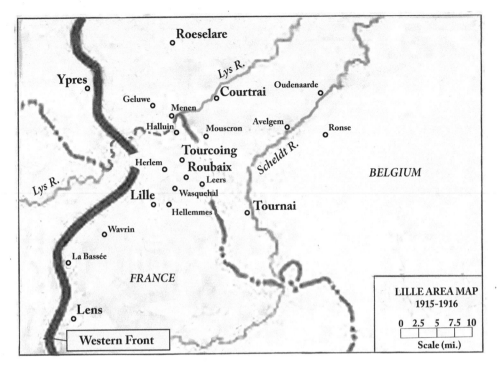

Based on a map of the stabilized front in Northwest Europe prepared by the History Department at the US Military Academy and available through Google Images and Wikimedia Commons to use, share, or modify, even commercially. The map has been rendered in greyscale and in greater detail than the original. Also, please note that Herlem is the fictional name attributed to the real town of Bondues.

Opposite   Based on a map of the stabilized front in Northwest Europe prepared by the History Department at the US Military Academy and available through Google Images and Wikimedia Commons to use, share, or modify, even commercially. The map has been rendered in greyscale and in less detail than the original.

INVASION 14

Here therefore are men tried as gold in the furnace.

Thomas à Kempis, *The Imitation of Christ.*

To my wife

Main Characters

Albrecht: German soldier stationed in Herlem
Brook: policeman in Herlem
Clavard: typesetter in Roubaix
David, Barthélémy: businessman in Roubaix
Decraemer, Daniel: manufacturer in Lille
Decraemer, Adrienne: wife of Daniel Decraemer
Decraemer, Jacques: adolescent son of Daniel and Adrienne Decraemer
Decraemer, Louise: young daughter of Daniel and Adrienne Decraemer
Donadieu, Simon: blacksmith in Herlem
Donadieu, Pascal: adolescent son of Simon Donadieu
Duydt: Belgian miner, refugee in Roubaix's Épeule neighbourhood
Duydt, Mrs: wife of Duydt
Duydt, Étienne: eldest, adult son of Duydt, trafficker in gold
Duydt, Léonie: eldest, adult daughter of Duydt
Duydt, Isidore: adolescent son of Duydt, boxer
Duydt, Armande: youngest daughter of Duydt
Duydt, Marcel: youngest son of Duydt
Feuillebois, Jean-Louis: teacher in Roubaix
Fontcroix, Samuel: coal merchant in Roubaix's Épeule neighbourhood
Fontcroix, Édith: estranged wife of Samuel Fontcroix, shopkeeper in
    Lille and Roubaix
Fontcroix, Antoinette: adolescent daughter of Samuel and Édith
    Fontcroix
Fontcroix, Christophe: young son of Samuel and Édith Fontcroix
Fontcroix, Gaspard: brother of Samuel Fontcroix

Foulaud, Félicie: widow of a Belgian soldier, refugee in Roubaix

Gaure: chemistry professor at the Tourcoing lycée

Gayet: manufacturer in Roubaix

Georgina: mistress of Isidore Duydt

Hennedyck, Patrice: manufacturer in Roubaix

Hennedyck, Émilie: wife of Patrice Hennedyck, founder of a Roubaix hospital

Hérard: landowner in Herlem, member of the Herlem ration board

Humfels: deputy mayor of Herlem, member of the Herlem ration board

Ingelby: brewer in Roubaix

Krems: German soldier stationed in Roubaix

Lacombe, Hector: farmer in Herlem, mayor of Herlem, member of the Herlem ration board

Lacombe, Mrs: wife of Hector Lacombe

Lacombe, Estelle: eldest, adult daughter of Hector Lacombe

Lacombe, Judith: youngest, adolescent daughter of Hector Lacombe

Laubigier, Félicie: housewife in Roubaix's Épeule neighbourhood

Laubigier, Alain: eldest, adolescent son of Félicie Laubigier

Laubigier, Jacqueline: adolescent daughter of Félicie Laubigier

Laubigier, Camille: youngest son of Félicie Laubigier

Leuil: member of the Herlem ration board

Limard: priest in Herlem, member of the Herlem ration board

Mailly, Albertine: mistress of Barthélémy David

Marellis: tax collector in Herlem, member of the Herlem ration board

Mouraud, Henri: mechanic in Roubaix

Mouraud, Joséphine: wife of Henri Mouraud, sister of Gaspard and Samuel Fontcroix

Mouraud, Annie: adolescent daughter of Henri and Joséphine Mouraud

Mouraud, Georges: young son of Henri and Joséphine Mouraud

Paul: German soldier stationed in Herlem

Pauret, Gilberte: typist in Roubaix

Pélegrin, Françoise: leader of a spy ring in Lille, Roubaix, and Tourcoing

Premelle: town secretary in Herlem, member of the Herlem ration board

Sancey, Juliette: adolescent daughter of a Roubaix drapery merchant

Sennevilliers, Berthe: innkeeper in Herlem

Sennevilliers, Marc: eldest, adult son of Berthe Sennevilliers, chaplain of the Tourcoing lycée

Sennevilliers, Jean: youngest, adult son of Berthe Sennevilliers, lime burner in Herlem

Sennevilliers, Fannie: wife of Jean Sennevilliers

Sennevilliers, Pierre: young son of Jean and Fannie Sennevilliers

Sennevilliers, Lise: adult daughter of Berthe Sennevilliers

Sérez: teacher in Herlem, member of the Herlem ration board

Thaunier: French soldier

Théverand: clerk in Lille

Thorel: newspaper publisher in Lille

Van Groede, Flavie: housewife in Roubaix's Épeule neighbourhood

Van Groede, François: adolescent son of Flavie van Groede

Van Groede, Abel: young son of Flavie van Groede

Van Groede, Cécile: young daughter of Flavie van Groede

Villard: manufacturer in Roubaix

Von Mesnil, Rudolf: German army doctor stationed in Roubaix

Wendiével: manufacturer in Roubaix

PART I

Chapter One

Jean Sennevilliers, the lime burner, left home for the quarry.

His house stood at the summit of Herlem Hill. To the east, one could see the entire village of Herlem, a ragged cluster of red and white houses crowded round a tall brick belfry with a slate-roofed spire. Beyond the village lay a sumptuous mass of tawny leaves, the splendour of a large forest, gilded by autumn, from which the regal towers of a château rose into view. This mansion belonged to the Baron des Parges, the owner of nine tenths of the land and farmsteads in the area. To the south, on a spur of the hill, was Fort Herlem: an old citadel with grassy embankments bordered by tall lines of poplars. Beside the fort, thick-set and huge, all bare walls and pointed roofs, Lacombe's farmhouse sat nestled among barns, cowsheds, and stables. Lacombe was a rich farmer and the village mayor. Behind the farm and the fort, in the hazy distance and shadowed by a sinister cloud of soot, the cities of Roubaix and Tourcoing spread toward the horizon, fuming and bristling with smokestacks, reservoirs, and gasometers.

To the north, at the foot of the hill, the white rock was cleft by a large and steep ravine, a sort of gaping rift, which stretched and widened into the form of an enormous seashell. This was the Sennevilliers' quarry. Hidden in its depths were the still waters of an emerald green pond, set in the white stone amid a confused mass of little willows and sturdy rushes serried along the banks. Halfway up the hill, one could see the kilns, types of square towers capped by extinguisher roofs, from which smoke rose gently into the tranquil air. The view, from this side, opened onto the endless

Flemish plain. In the far reaches, one could just make out the hills of Messines and Kemmel, barely perceptible ripples set against the misty, bluish sky, and finally two white and almost indiscernible silhouettes – the tower of Cloth Hall and the steeple of the cathedral in Ypres.

This landscape was peaceful and showed no marks of war. But the villagers had already seen the Germans in September: a troop of Uhlans clothed in huge grey cloaks, with embossed shapkas of black leather on their heads; long lances, adorned with red and black pennons, resting in stirrup boots; and revolvers at the ready. They had advanced slowly, restraining their slender, spirited horses with new harnesses of tanned leather. The men were big, strong, young, with fine, ruddy complexions and athletic shoulders. Beneath their capes, long horizontal epaulettes further magnified their commanding appearance.

The Germans had locked all the men in the church and ransacked the house of Marellis, the tax collector, to find his cash box. Reservists from Lille had driven off the Germans, killing two of them. Lacombe, the mayor, had nailed the cloaks of the dead men to the door of town hall and divided the bloody tunics among the crowd.

Since then, the Uhlans had not returned.

Jean Sennevilliers went down to the quarry. Mobilization orders had just arrived from Lille. It was now the beginning of October. This time, the Germans were overrunning the entire department of the Nord. Since the first of September, the prefect of the Nord had been asking the General Staff in Boulogne for instructions about recruits, but in vain. He had been told to wait. Finally on 6 October the General Staff had sent the order to evacuate all available men. This order could have been delivered by car, dispatch rider, or telegram. It was put in the mail. The prefect in Lille received it three days later. By then the Germans were at the gates of the city. The prefect sent policemen, cyclists, and volunteers in all directions to announce the mobilization. People hesitated, sensing peril, but most men started off. Thus began a new exodus – after the one in September toward Dunkerque – of thousands and thousands of men toward the south of France and the unknown.

Jean had to leave the next morning, but first he wanted to finish his work in the quarry. He laboured at the kilns until nightfall. His younger sister Lise was helping him. He loaded the ovens so they would finish firing the lime while he was gone, arranging layers of limestone and coal by turns. Stifling, white, carbonic fumes were rising from the furnaces. Lise was sorting the blocks of stone with a pitchfork.

"You need to empty this kiln first," said Jean. "That'll give you twenty tons of lime. Pay attention to the firing. With this batch, you can get by till I return. If you find some men, you can keep on loading the kilns. Take advantage of the dry weather to get chalk from the bottom of the quarry. The water in the pond's low, so there's more rock to be had."

"Don't worry," said Lise.

"I'm also putting you in charge of Fannie and the child. You know she isn't strong, that she needs to take it easy. Make sure neither of them goes hungry ... We'll settle up after the war ..."

They continued loading the kilns until midnight, by the light of oil lamps.

Jean went back up to his house in the darkness. Fannie was waiting for him and crying as she packed his bags. He could already see signs of grief and anxiety on her face. How would she withstand the ordeal if she were already so upset?

He had split the money from the cashbox with Lise and his mother. He gave Fannie 600 francs.

"You mustn't spend more than twenty francs a week," he said. "Lise'll give you a hand if you have trouble."

Jean was in the habit of treating her like a child. He was the one who managed the household. What would become of her with him gone? He would have preferred to have gotten everything ready in advance so she could have kept on living like before. While waiting to depart, he cleaned the goat stable and the rabbit hutches. He felt bad that he was leaving so many things to be done: the beets to harvest, the ceilings to whitewash, a windowpane to fix in the laundry room. He was working on the most urgent things first – bringing up sacks of coal from the basement, splitting kindling, sawing logs – and rattling off words of advice: "You won't be able to wash the wool blankets. They're too heavy to wring out. While I'm thinking about it, I'll rinse the sheets in the wash tub ... Above all, never lift the laundry cauldron by yourself. Look after Pierre. Make sure he goes to school and behaves ... If you can't manage him, Lise'll help."

Jean worked till two o'clock in the morning. Then, exhausted, he stopped. To have worked so hard, to have seen again how useful – indispensable – he was, reminded him just how much he would be missed.

"We really ought to rest for an hour," he said.

They went upstairs. Pierre was sleeping. Fannie and Jean went to bed. Jean could hear his wife crying. He had neither the courage nor the desire to enjoy a last moment of carnal pleasure before he left. Somehow he sensed he would have tarnished the purity of his grief, his suffering, which was that of a father more than of a husband. They stayed awake till dawn.

Jean rose early. Before setting out, he went once more to see the quarry. It was bathed in a lovely, bluish October mist. He looked for a long time at this white gully, this ravine widening into the shape of an immense, resonant seashell, where the sound of the winter winds would soon roar. At the bottom, steam was rising off the water of the pond, and thin veils were clinging to the golden foliage of little willows and bushes.

The quarry, this big hole, this deep furrow, was largely his creation, the mark of his passage on Earth. It had need of him, too – his expertise and his strength. He knew every corner of it, every seam. He recognized the good parts and the bad, the resources and the dangers. It only lived by him, through him. No one could replace him here without long experience, patient study. If he did not return, would the quarry pass into someone else's hands and suffer? Or worse, would it cease to exist, remaining there like an inexplicable and useless fissure, a hollow of wild rock slowly invaded by brambles and flooded by rain and springwater? The thought saddened him like the death of a living being. He went back toward his house.

Jean left at nine o'clock. He travelled with Marellis, the tax collector, who did not know if he should leave his post and was going to Lille to seek instructions.

At the train station in Lille, amid incredible chaos, Jean suddenly came across his older brother, Marc Sennevilliers, the chaplain of the lycée in Tourcoing. Marc had rushed over to Lille to say goodbye to his brother. They embraced, and since they could not bear to part, they went to the tracks together. The entire station was in uproar. A single steaming locomotive waited. Hundreds of men had invaded the carriages, squeezing together like cattle. An enormous crowd besieged the train. Railway conductors were pulling down men who were hanging from the doors, standing on the bumpers, or perched on the roofs. There was not, however, a single trace of enthusiasm left in these men. Quite the opposite: the scene reeked of panic.

Suitcase in hand, Jean ran alongside the train with his brother, trying in vain to get onboard. He went all the way to the engine and was about to give up when he heard a voice calling: "Jean!"

He was surprised to see his friend Simon Donadieu, Herlem's blacksmith, sitting on the tender. Donadieu and many others had spent the night in Lille, sleeping on the sidewalk in the open air. And by chance he had run across a pal who happened to be the stoker on the locomotive. Thanks to this fellow, Jean was able to climb onto the tender with Simon.

The exodus from Lille was the starting point of the grisly adventure of 40,000 recruits whom the Germans would massacre or imprison, for the enemy already held the countryside. Once again, innocents would pay with their lives for the carelessness and negligence of their masters.

II

The Germans had been firing on Lille for three straight days. Each evening the flames of the inferno could be seen from Roubaix. Samuel Fontcroix, like many others, rushed to the outskirts at nightfall to watch this dancing, bloody line at the edge of the horizon, silhouetted against the black chasm of the sky. This hell seemed all too near. Huge red flames spurted into the air, like the product of some distant ironworks, and in the noise of the crashing metal one could almost hear a desperate cry.

Samuel Fontcroix thought of his wife and daughter, who were being subjected to this terror, and the prospect filled him with anguish.

Samuel was in his forties and lived in Roubaix's Épeule neighbourhood, where he ran a coal business. His wife and he had been separated for two years.

They had married foolishly. Samuel had been working for his father. Édith was a dressmaker. A commonplace encounter had brought them together. He was rather naïve. Édith, in an odd way, combined slyness and sentimentality. They had mistaken sensual passion for the most beautiful love. Samuel was by nature cheerful, optimistic, a poet in his spare time, prone to enthusiasm. She was materialistic and bitter. Constant fighting would have led them to separate before long had it not been for the birth of two children, though the presence of youngsters did nothing to restore harmony to the marriage. The household continued to struggle. Édith's sourness and maliciousness exasperated Samuel. There was no happiness at home. He made the mistake of looking for it elsewhere, getting involved in several passing affairs, and relations between husband and wife worsened decidedly.

Then Samuel fell in love with a young woman who considered herself unhappy and was truly as forlorn as he was. The affair lasted three years. The lovers hid themselves well. The whole neighbourhood of Épeule remained in ignorance. They were living for the future – Samuel envisioned divorce and happiness down the road. But one day Édith discovered the affair. She exacted a cruel and ignoble vengeance, going straight to the husband of the miserable woman, and in one stroke destroyed the home of another along with her own.

It was then that the Fontcroix separated. Battered, disheartened, Samuel preferred to put an end to the stupid charade their marriage had become. They parted by mutual consent. Édith took the girl, Antoinette, who was thirteen, and opened a grocery store in Lille. Samuel kept the boy, Christophe, who was five. Once a month, Samuel would go to Lille to see his daughter and take her a little money.

And now Édith and Antoinette were over there, in the thick of the bombardment. Samuel was surprised to find that concern for his wife was such a large part of his distress. Fifteen years of marriage, whatever the misunderstandings, cannot be lived entirely in vain.

The siege of Lille lasted three days. The inhabitants took refuge in their cellars.

On the morning of the fourth day, Samuel Fontcroix raced toward Lille and managed to get into the city, where the Germans had made their entrance among the ruins. He was overwhelmed by what he saw.

The burning and destruction were drawing to a close. Neighbourhoods in the city centre, and near the train station, had been laid waste. But the residents were starting to come out again, emerging from cellars, rushing to see the fires and the wreckage. The city was full of smoke, steam, and enormous clouds of red dust produced by the toppling buildings. Toward the station and the theatre, one could now see a huge empty space, like a battlefield, where big, black skeletons of stone and iron stood scattered about, ominous, with windows open to emptiness and fire. The streets were buried under mountains of bricks, beams, and powdered glass. In some areas the fires still crackled, even roared, filling the air with falling sparks, embers and ashes, and stifling clouds of smoke. People walked around with their hands over their eyes – crying, coughing, choking on the fumes. Volunteer firefighters formed bucket brigades, and on occasion one would discover the black face of a friend beneath a helmet. Long lines of refugees were fleeing, bewildered, laden with misshapen packs, the men half-clothed, the women with nothing but shifts beneath their coats, the naked children wrapped in blankets. Many looters, impudent men in espadrilles, were lugging sacks and wading through the ruins. Here and there, bystanders evacuated stores threatened by the lapping flames – the shopkeepers distributing groceries, toys, fabrics, suitcases, and other merchandise, to be returned when the danger had passed. A ubiquitous stench of burned wool and charred wood filled the air. Men emptied pails of water onto the flames, or onto ruins that were still smouldering, the water making a shrill cry as it vapourized into dirty clouds of steam. Disemboweled houses, cut in two, exposed little rooms, their furniture hanging over gaping chasms, their beds dangling above the abyss. The ground was covered with heaps of bricks, glass, iron, mangled furniture, saucepans and dishes, chunks of plaster. Neither the sidewalk nor the street was visible; one had to climb over hills of rubble. In several spots, great groups massed round fallen houses, watching volunteers who were removing the debris, trying to reach the poor wretches swallowed by their shelters. The rescuers pulled out the wounded, the suffocating, the dead. From one basement window, cleared with great difficulty, a big white dog escaped. Mad with fright, it fled and disappeared among the ruins, the only creature left alive in this location. People gathered rifles, French uniforms, and Arab burnouses littering the roadway. To escape from the enemy, Major de Pardieu's cavalrymen had cast aside their weapons and clothing and sought refuge in civilian homes, where they remained hidden. The goumiers, the auxiliary Arab horsemen, had slit their chargers' throats in the street.

White rags, signs of defeat and capitulation, still fluttered on the steeple of Saint-Maurice and the belfry of the Chamber of Commerce. And above them already hung the German flag, an enormous and motionless symbol.

People pointed to it, cried, and moved away. Vast patches of reddish fog – huge clouds of dust kicked up by the tumbling buildings, like the smoke of a cannonade that lingers on a battlefield – still floated over the roads blocked with ruins, the open wounds of brick walls, the white cracks in the stone, the black and dirty fumes of the fires, the swarming crowds and fleeing victims, the agitated firefighters and rescue workers, the teetering skeletons of buildings, the heaps of twisted iron.

Suddenly, in the midst of a throng at the corner of rue Saint-Sauveur, Samuel ran into his wife and daughter, who were wandering through the devastation. They fell into each other's arms, unable to utter a word.

Chapter Two

In Herlem, as in all the occupied villages, the German authorities attempted a curious experiment in collectivism. The endeavour was all the more interesting since they were applying it to rural areas, which are typically considered the most resistant to such ventures.

Scarcely had he set foot in the village than Colonel von Glow, charged with governance of the Herlem district, summoned all the mayors, deputy mayors, town secretaries, school teachers, tax collectors, doctors, and priests. Thus assembled in Herlem's town hall, the representatives of eleven communes received the colonel's orders and were made responsible for their fulfillment. Within two months, the Germans had gradually brought all rural life under their sway.

Each week the colonel convened a meeting. He thereby maintained control over the entire region, issued commands, listened to complaints, and made his remarks. He would say roughly, "I order," and he was obeyed.

The mayors first had to draw up an inventory of land in each commune. Lacombe, the mayor of Herlem, toured the area distributing leaflets to all the farmers. The papers were questionnaires, and they were lengthy. How many hectares have you planted in wheat, oats, clover, etc.? How much stocked wheat do you have? How many horses, cows, sheep? How many carts, tools, harnesses? How much leather? How much oil and gas?

After the questionnaires were returned, Lacombe and the colonel were seen taking a horse-drawn carriage around the village. The result was new commands: to repair and pave the roads, dredge the ponds and the ditches, clean and spread ashes around the wells and keep the nearby ground clear within a radius of ten metres. The sick were ordered to report their illnesses to the Germans and everyone to work for them ten hours a day: to put sand on icy roads, dry fruit for preserves, thresh and bag the wheat, harvest and store the beets, keep their kitchens clean, work the fire pump once a month. Never had Herlem been so tidy.

In the meantime, a team of chemists analyzed the soil. Starting in January, the farmers were given manure and forced to plant certain crops. They were forbidden to cultivate sugar beets; Germany already produced enough. They were told to grow wheat here and alfalfa there, to finish plowing in February and sowing in March, to harrow, irrigate, and roll the hay. Lacombe was ordered to cut his hedges, Humfels to clear his ditches, Bozin to fix his reaper. The farmers had to remove weeds from their ponds, keep registers of livestock, tell German headquarters about the birth and death of animals as well as the amount of milk, butter, and eggs produced on a daily basis. They had to hand over so many litres of milk for each cow and three eggs per chicken each week. The German authorities paid five pfennigs an egg and seven for each litre of milk, but deducted ten pfennigs for every litre or egg that was missing. The villagers were forbidden to kill rabbits, chickens, or pigs. And they had to bring to the town hall the carcass of any animal that died by accident.

At first people laughed, but fines, searches, and seizures quickly broke down resistance. They had to give in, to submit, but with an anger tempered by a degree of admiration. The Germans certainly were powerful!

One afternoon in February 1915, Pascal Donadieu, the blacksmith's son, headed for Lacombe's farm.

Simon Donadieu had left with Jean Sennevilliers in October 1914. Nothing had since been heard of either one. Pascal, who was seventeen, lived with his mother at the blacksmith shop and had had to give up the courses in mechanics and electricity that he had been taking at the Tourcoing Institute. Their money was gone. Pascal wanted to work. He had set out to find a job.

Snow had fallen the day before. A pale sun, almost invisible, was whitening the mist as Pascal walked briskly across the fields. The farms were buried under snow. Only the black specks of scattered walls and a thin network of wild trees interrupted the universal whiteness. It was almost luminous, like an enormous blank page. In the white sky, the white ground dotted with but a few dark spots – in the pale and overwhelming uniformity – Pascal found something gentle and pure, filling him with a vague satisfaction despite the sadness of the hour. He breathed easily.

The idea of once again seeing Judith Lacombe, the farmer's daughter, stirred his emotions. In the past, Pascal had flirted a little with the young girl. They had taken two or three strolls along the avenues of the château des Parges and exchanged a few confidences. Before leaving, Simon Donadieu had taken his son aside and had a word with him: "You're young. You don't yet have a job. I'm asking you to be serious. The Lacombes' daughter isn't for you, not now. Later on, we'll see ..."

Since the departure of his father, Pascal had tried to forget about Judith. Under such circumstances, disobeying the missing man had frightened him, as if doing so would have brought his father bad luck. But at present things were different. He had to go to Lacombe's, where he hoped to find a job. The Germans were insisting that everyone work. Pascal himself had been forced to work for them, making horseshoes in his father's shop. He had only been able to get out of it by intentionally wounding his hand with a hammer. Now that he was better, he was trying to avoid working for the Germans again. He had thought of Lacombe, the mayor, whom he knew well and for whom he had repaired reapers and plows many times.

In the early days of the war, Lacombe had made lots of money. Hordes of refugees, fleeing from the enemy, had passed through Herlem as they descended upon France. These people, mostly tenant farmers and peasants, led enormous herds of cumbersome, starving cattle, which slowed them down. Lacombe and some other big farmers bought these cows at despicably low prices and then sold them for three times as much to butchers in neighbouring towns.

When the Germans returned to Herlem, Lacombe was at first terrified and went into hiding. He felt uneasy about the appropriation of the dead Uhlans' capes and could easily see himself imprisoned or shot. He was so scared that he made himself sick, thinking he was developing jaundice. Luckily, the Germans did not get wind of the incident. Since he was the village mayor, Lacombe was quickly summoned to headquarters. Trembling with fear, he promised the Germans everything they wanted, demonstrated exemplary docility, showed them where supplies were before they even asked, gave them a list of able-bodied men. He took his servility to the point that the village government itself sent men orders to work for the enemy. Lacombe set a precedent for submission, agreeing to lodge a German farm manager and three workers to replace his missing day labourers.

Now that Lacombe had calmed down, he was again beginning to see the sunny side of things, working his land with the Bavarian farm manager and swindling most of the produce in complicity with him.

Pascal found Lacombe in the kitchen, his back to the door, standing in front of the window and smoking his pipe as he watched over the fields. Lacombe was a great big fellow, as strong as an ox. Judith, his younger daughter, her arms bare, was bent over a tub washing butter in cool water. A sour odour filled the room.

"Hello!" said Lacombe, "So, Pascal, what's going on?"

Pascal explained his business: "You see, Mr Mayor, I don't like working for the enemy. I have a little education. Couldn't you find me a job at town hall?"

"Well ..." said Lacombe, "That is to say ... I was actually thinking of replacing the remaining staff with women. The Germans need men ..."

"Oh, okay. Very well," said Pascal, dumbfounded. "Thanks anyway ..."

He made such an odd expression that Old Lacombe realized he had made a mistake and sought to redeem himself.

"Of course, I don't like playing their game. But they're stronger, you know ... You have to make do the best you can ..."

"Yes, I understand," said Pascal, keeping his anger in check. He told himself that he needed Lacombe and had to handle him with care. He started over, in an almost tranquil voice: "At the very least, Mr Mayor, couldn't you ... forget to write my name on the list? Or perhaps not put it down right away?"

Lacombe laughed: "Not bad, Pascal! Listen, my boy, I'll work something out ... I'll put the Larmigets' son in your place ... They refused to sell me their cow. That'll teach them ... Goodbye, now."

Lacombe went back to smoking his pipe in front of the window.

Outside, Pascal found Judith on the footpath. She had dragged her tub under the pump and was rinsing the yellow butter in a stream of cool water. Her bare arms seemed to be in flight as they raised and lowered the long, creaking iron handle.

Pascal stopped in front of her.

"Good evening, Judith."

Judith was seventeen. Slender and high strung, with a long, pale face and black hair, she had a striking expression: willful and tense, something romantic too, revealing a hot-headed disposition, a quick-tempered and whimsical nature in this daughter of wealthy but common farmers.

"Good evening," she said.

Pascal thought he could sense in her the same awkwardness he felt himself.

She seemed both pleased and a bit uncomfortable in his presence.

"How've you been?"

"Okay."

"It's been a long time since we've seen each other," said Pascal, immediately regretting his careless words, which evoked the past.

"Yes ..."

"I came to get a job at town hall, but it's impossible."

"And your father?"

"No news."

"Is it true the Germans are cutting down the linden trees on avenue du Château?"

"Yes, it's true ..."

They fell silent. In spite of themselves, every word brought back the memory of their short and innocent romance, the two or three brief and timid strolls they had taken as sweethearts along the pathways of the great château.

At that moment, a muscular young man in his early thirties walked into the yard. He had curly blond hair, a ruddy complexion, blue-grey eyes, and was dressed like a farmhand. He came straight to the pump. With a strong German accent, he said, "Hello, hello ..."

"Hello, Albrecht," said Judith.

Pascal realized that this was the German manager running Lacombe's farm. He was foolishly surprised that a German in workclothes so resembled a Frenchman. The man did not look like an enemy, dressed as he was, with his fine, curly head and big, good-humoured smile.

"Dirty," said Albrecht. "Much dirty! And hungry! Have worked a lot."

He showed his grubby hands, waving them in Judith's face in a familiar manner. She pulled back swiftly.

"Go on, Albrecht! Behave!"

She seemed uneasy in front of Pascal.

"Wasser?" asked Albrecht, pointing to the pump handle.

And he gripped it, moving it with one hand, without effort, with unbelievable strength, making the water gush onto the yellow slabs of butter in
a powerful, continuous stream.

"That's enough, that's enough, thank you."

Judith went back to rinsing her butter. Blushing, she turned her back to
Pascal, almost as if she were trying to hide. Albrecht, for his part, looked
at Pascal and gave him a wink. Laughing, revealing a set of square white
teeth, he made gestures and funny faces, pretending he was about to pump
water on Judith's head.

"Goodbye," said Pascal.

"Goodbye," replied Judith, still bent over her tub.

Pascal set off. He headed back toward the village square along a path
that went behind the fort and cut across the fields. It was still misty, the
light pale and hazy, diffused from a cloudless sky onto the snowbound
earth. There were no shadows, only a white and still vastness. This time
the silence caused his heart to sink. The whole landscape now seemed
filled with a crushing sadness.

Pascal hurried toward the blacksmith shop, feeling old and bitter. He
thought of his father, finding in his last words of advice a profound wisdom he had not gleaned before. Within Pascal was a confused sense of
grief, which he had no desire to explore.

• • •

That evening, after they finished in the fields, the German workers came
back to the farmhouse with Albrecht. It was almost dark. Judith was heating a cauldron of rainwater so they could wash outside on the little brick
footpath, in spite of the cold.

They undressed, merely keeping on their pants belted round the waist.
Judith brought them hot water. They began to wash, splashing themselves,
scrubbing their bodies. Judith and her sister Estelle watched.

"Soap?"

Estelle went into the kitchen, returning with the black soap. She was a
tall girl, flat-chested and thin, who resembled her mother, feigned piety,
and maintained a hypocritical air of humility. But she loved men, and sev-

eral times Judith had found her in the barn with one or another of the Germans. Estelle was a licentious woman who concealed her true ways and whose husband Louis Babet – now in the French army – had without knowing it been the laughing stock of the village.

Leaning against the door, Estelle eyed the three men as they bathed. Night had fallen. On the wall hung a lantern whose red glow carved out a circle of light, caressing and gilding the naked chests – the rosy, oily, healthy flesh of these three strapping, broad-shouldered lads.

"Estelle!" shouted her mother from the kitchen.

Estelle had to go back inside. Judith remained alone, but she did not leave. She was always amused by the sight of these three robust men, impervious to the cold and seemingly accustomed to a fuller, purer life than the people of her village. Such courage, such scrupulous cleanliness, surprised her a little. Among her father's farmhands, she had never seen anything but smelly filth, superficially removed on Sundays.

The men dried off. They went into the kitchen, shaking themselves and smacking their backs. The only one left outside was Albrecht, who was washing his hair, transforming his head into an enormous frothy ball. He could be seen moving about, a distinct silhouette in the darkness.

"Wasser ..."

He had come up to the pump.

"Pump, Judith, pump a lot, hard ..."

He bent down, presenting his head and exposed chest to the stream of cold water, which spilled onto his healthy skin.

He stood up, ran to the doorway of the barn to take shelter from the wind, and dried himself with an old towel, in big rapid strokes. From afar, he held out the rag to Judith.

"Rub! Like horse! Hard, hard, like horse!"

Judith took the cloth. With all her strength, she scrubbed the huge back, to the point that she scratched it. Albrecht laughed: "Harder, harder!" He turned to face her, his arms outstretched, offering his front. Each stroke left a mark. All of a sudden, Judith felt bashful in front of this great naked chest. She started to laugh. It had a hollow ring. Her movements slowed.

Albrecht's arms closed roughly around her. She fell into the thick, treacherous bed of hay. Albrecht's massive body was on top of her, crushing her. She was intoxicated by a heady smell of hay, dry grass, soap, sweat, by the soft, warm touch of his bare skin. She felt powerless ... A sort of faintness, a delicious and perfidious languor, was invading her. Suddenly she remembered her sister Estelle, whom she had discovered like this in the straw ... Judith was caught by the wanton desire to indulge herself, too ... Without even realizing what she was doing, she embraced the man freely and fully and put her mouth to his in an animal abandonment, as if she thirsted for him ...

A heart-rending pain made her moan. She gave a start, instinctively try-ing to free herself. In a flash, without warning, the memory of Pascal passed through her mind, filling her with an unexpected horror. She stiff-ened in a reflex movement of defense, in an attempt to escape. But she felt trapped. Albrecht paralyzed her ...

Now that he was satisfied, he was speaking to her, whispering in her ear, German expressions – soft words that she did not understand, words that hurt her. She felt hot beneath him. He dug his lips into her hair, nibbling at her ear, playing like a puppy. She gave herself to him again, holding onto him almost in despair. He did not notice that she was crying.

· · ·

Judith clung wildly to Albrecht. She was mad about him, absorbed by a passion that went beyond the physical, expressing a need to dedicate herself, to give of herself. She instinctually accorded him all the devotion, all the unused possibilities that until then had lain dormant within her, though he had done nothing to merit this splendid gift. The young woman no longer recognized herself. In the past Judith had thought of herself as rather selfish, preoccupied mostly with her own needs. Suddenly, she felt capable of making any sacrifice for Albrecht. As for him, he did not even realize she was giving him her soul. He was a boy who lacked any real idealism and saw in love only an opportunity for happy and frequent diversions. Nor did he did consider himself deprived in this regard. She was a sensuous mistress, ready to please him. In fact, he thought her rather lecherous. He never understood that it was all for him, not for herself, and that she would have been content with nothing more than his presence, his voice.

She had hoped to find in him all that she had glimpsed of love during her brief idyll with Pascal – long shared reveries, ennobling thoughts, the tender and heavenly understanding of two souls ... But Albrecht did not share such a dream. And she accepted him, courageously, the way he was. He had violated her soul as he had done to her body.

Judith found it natural to be seen with him in the village. Since she loved him, she thought it useless to hide their relationship. After all, was she doing anything wrong?

Straight away Estelle, the elder of the two girls, guessed what was happening. Estelle said nothing, though, content to have an advantage over her sister.

Their mother also noticed the affair. She too kept her silence. Afraid of her husband and of scandal, she chose not to intervene.

As for Lacombe, it was impossible to tell if he understood or not. Albrecht and he were good buddies, thick as thieves when it came to looting the produce of the farm. Starting an argument would have been disastrous. So long as no one began rubbing Lacombe's nose in this mess ...

Besides, there was nothing to prove he had any suspicions. Always preoccupied with himself, inordinately tyrannical and selfish, Lacombe went through life as if the whole world revolved around him. He alone mattered. Perhaps knowledge of the terror he inspired in his family also allowed him to dismiss the possibility of his daughters committing the least fault.

II

One night at the end of March, Judith, who slept with Estelle in the bedroom above the kitchen, was startled awake by the sound of moaning. She listened for a second. The moaning began again. It was coming from Estelle's bed.

In one bound, Judith leapt to the floor. Barefoot, in her nightshirt, she ran to her sister's bedside.

"Estelle! Estelle!"

Horribly pale, eyes closed, bathed in sweat, Estelle groaned painfully. Judith, terrified, frantically tore off the covers. In the middle of the bed was a large dark stain, almost black. It was blood.

At first Judith did not understand.

"Estelle, Estelle! My God!"

She screamed, panic-stricken.

Estelle opened her eyes. With immense effort, she managed to speak. Very softly she whispered, "Shut up! Mamma ... Go find mamma ..."

She closed her eyes again, fell back onto the bed, and with a final effort said, "Don't wake father ... Oh, I'm dying ..."

Judith ran to her parents' bedroom. They were sleeping. She touched her mother's arm to rouse her.

"Estelle? What? Oh ... yes. Oh, my God!"

She got up, put on her slippers, and begged, "Not a sound ... Father, don't wake father ..."

She followed her daughter in the darkness, only lighting a candle when they were in the hallway.

They revived Estelle with vinegar. By the faint light of the candle, they could see a grimace on her wan, pinched, haggard face ... She reopened her eyes, recognized her mother and sister. Her mother had taken her under the arms to sit her up. She lifted her gently. Estelle seemed exhausted. A torrent flowed beneath her, in a horrid stream.

"Ah, là, là! Estelle, what have you done!" wailed her mother.

"It's you," whispered Estelle. "It's you who wanted it ..."

She spoke these words with an expression of unspeakable hatred, the terrible hatred of one who thinks she is dying and blames another. Then she let herself fall back again, as if dead.

Slaps, vinegar, cool water revived her a second time. Judith went down to the kitchen, lit a fire, and made coffee with gin. Estelle drank some, regained a little strength. They changed her underclothes and put her in Judith's bed. She fell into a deep sleep.

"Where's Estelle?" asked Lacombe the next morning.

"She's taken some medicine, she's still in bed," said her mother.

"Good."

He did not dwell on the matter. In the countryside, one fasts and stays in bed when recovering from an illness. Lacombe took his pipe and staff and went to make his daily rounds through the fields.

Judith and her mother remained alone in the kitchen. One could sense that the elder woman had something on her chest. She was pacing back and forth, trying awkwardly to find a way to begin, but shame prevented her from expressing herself openly. At last she said, "Did you hear what Estelle said last night? She must've been feverish ..."

Judith did not look up.

"Because, of course, I didn't tell her to do that. I only said I didn't want 'it' ... A bastard! What would your father have said? And Babet, when he comes back from the war?"

In her mind, her son-in-law had remained "Babet" and not "Louis," as if he had never become part of the family. She continued, "We certainly don't have room for that kind of trouble! It's okay ... It's okay to fool around. I understand. The men just have to take basic precautions, you know. In any event, it's certain your father would never have accepted it."

The word "it" reminded her of the thing, in a precise and brutally concrete way. She left the pile of laundry she was sorting for the wash and went up to the bedroom.

Estelle looked worn, lying in bed thinking, staring straight ahead. She turned toward her mother and murmured, "Are you looking for something?"

"The ... the pail ..."

"Under my bed ..."

Her mother bent down.

"You can dig a hole in the dung heap," whispered Estelle.

"In the dung heap? Oh no! That won't do! I'm going to put it in a little box and make arrangements with the sexton. He'll bury it with another body ... It must be put in consecrated ground. That's what must be done ..."

She disappeared down the stairs with the bucket in hand. She was a woman mindful of propriety and respectful of holy rites.

III

On 9 April 1915 Lacombe and the other mayors of the region were called to a meeting by the Committee for Relief in Belgium, or CRB, which wished to help the population. It had finally obtained the Germans' permission to bring food and coal into the occupied areas of France.

Each commune had to have a ration board. In Herlem, it was composed of the mayor, Humfels the deputy mayor, Premelle the town secretary, Marellis the tax collector, Limard the priest, Sérez the schoolmaster, and Mr Hérard, a wealthy villager named directly by the Committee to represent it. This board would receive the provisions, sell them to the inhabitants, and send the revenue to the Committee.

For those unable to pay, the ration board would open special accounts which the commune would liquidate after the war. Any profit on the sales was forbidden, and none of the positions was to be salaried.

. . .

Henceforth, Marellis and Sérez handled the distribution of foodstuffs, a duty in which Marellis took great pride. He drew a naïve element of satisfaction from his position as a civil servant and fulfilled his duties as a tax collector with solemnity. His favourite phrase was, "Officials like me ..." Marellis was scrupulous, almost a nitpicker, but his rigid honesty, his concern for fairness, and his zeal to defend the interests of the State made him a valuable guardian of the public good. At the time of the invasion, everyone had advised him to flee as many of his colleagues had done. "An official," Marellis had responded, "cannot leave without an order." The order had never come. Marellis had stayed.

Stranded though he was in the department of the Nord, he had nonetheless carried out his duty, hiding his cashbox and records and, unlike certain of his colleagues, refusing to collect taxes on behalf of the enemy. The behaviour of the villagers sickened Marellis. They bowed obediently before the Germans. The farmers had not even thought of resistance, isolated as they were, too eager to make a profit, too attached to their land and livestock to risk losing them. They had submitted, adapted with a humiliating resignation. And since Marellis had begun dispensing rations, his indignation had grown all the more. Lacombe, Premelle, and Hérard abused their positions. Marellis saw invoices for 300 sacks of coal, or fifteen tons, while the village received only seven or eight. Board members divided leftover goods. And so that the amount would be larger, the share allotted each resident was reduced. Lacombe and his pals "forgot" to announce the arrival of rare articles, like milk and cheese, with the result that many people did not think to ask for them, leaving such items for the distributors. There were shady deals reselling cards and tickets. The destitute did not have to pay for their supplies. Lacombe took advantage of the situation by giving indigent cards to all his friends. Most of the workers who laboured for the Germans – and who were paid seven francs a day at the expense of the commune – received their provisions for free just like the poor. Lacombe kept no record of the money received. It all went into the town treasury. And these funds were used not to reimburse the Committee but to pay fines and war taxes levied by the Germans. Lacombe thus helped his fellow farmers avoid such expenses as a matter of course. Army headquarters forced the communes to buy German flour, called KK, for the baking of bread. Two bakers each received half. Baille's bread was edible. Orchon's was revolting. Orchon sold part of the flour on the sly and underbaked his bread to make up for the lost weight. Since he was Lacombe's friend, nothing could be said, and he poisoned half the population with impunity. Each time rations were dispensed, there were battles to be the first in line, to get Baille's bread.

For a meticulous and scrupulous man like Marellis – obsessed with accurate scales, well-kept books, clear and ordered accounts – such a mess was a constant source of bewilderment and exasperation.

This Saturday, as always, the members of the ration board were meeting with the colonel, after which they would discuss measures to be taken the following week. Marellis, who had spent his afternoon counting sacks of coal and again noticed a scandalous discrepancy, was late to the meeting with the colonel.

As usual, they received orders for the administration of the village. The atmosphere was that of vassals gathered to hear the will of their lord. The colonel arrived, set his unsheathed sword on the table, and commanded: "Silence, gentlemen!"

They stopped talking, and he began: "I order ... I order ... I order ..."

These demands fell like the blade of a guillotine.

First he questioned the mayor about the quality of the German KK flour, which was used to make the notorious "caca" bread. Lacombe naturally declared that it was excellent.

The colonel listed the prices headquarters would pay farmers for their butter, eggs, and milk. He imposed fines on the commune for delivery shortfalls, dirty toilets, unprotected wells. He issued commands for the cultivation of land and the gathering of nettles. They listened obediently. Lacombe would have to slaughter a calf, Humfels place props under the branches of his apple trees, Bozin tie up his troublesome bull. Then came some new edicts, which astounded those present. "I order:

"Given the number of infectious illnesses that German soldiers have been contracting, henceforth all the village men will undergo a medical exam.

"From now on, the women named on this list, and suspected of poor morals, will be inspected each week by the army doctor. The list is to be posted on the door of town hall.

"Within a week, the mayor of each commune will have to draw up a list of the sick, the elderly, children, and generally useless people, in preparation for their evacuation to France ...

"Gentlemen, the meeting is adjourned. You are to gather here again next week. Good evening."

He picked up his sword, bowed, and departed. Even in his manner of leaving, he retained the air of a master.

• • •

"So," said Marellis an hour later, "the farmers have a running account with German headquarters! They buy from the Germans, sell to the Germans, accept money from the Germans! And now the town government's going to give them a list of people to banish!"

The Herlem ration board was meeting after the visit of the colonel. Marellis represented the opposition.

"We're here to talk about rations," said Premelle, the town secretary.

"Okay, then, let's talk about them," exclaimed Marellis. "First of all, I'm still waiting for the accounts we're supposed to send the Committee. Where do we stand with the matter? Is there a register of expenses, of receipts? Nothing of the sort! Everything we get from the villagers goes into the town treasury to pay fines and people working for the enemy. Where's the Committee's money and the separate accounts it's demanding?"

"For what we make!" said Lacombe. "It's really a pain to consider keeping the books!"

"Of course! Half the people in the village don't pay for their rations! The workers recruited by the enemy don't pay! The shopkeepers don't pay! Guégain, the barber, has an indigent's card! The Baron des Parges doesn't pay on the excuse that he no longer receives his farm rents! The little bit of money contributed by those naïve enough to pay, you put into the town treasury, and the Germans take it. The relief program is playing into the hands of the enemy! It's as simple as that!"

"We can't force people to pay if they don't have the money," said Premelle.

"Money for supplies could at least be withheld from the wages of the workers, since we're the ones paying them. Besides, there're plenty of people who could pay ..."

"Does Mr Premelle pay for his goods, or Mr Hérard?" interjected Sérez the schoolmaster, who supported Marellis.

"That's none of your business!" shouted Hérard, who was a man of independent means. "We work, we give our labour ..."

"And take the butter and the cheese and the packing crates for firewood," concluded Sérez.

"And the coal?" continued Marellis. "Mr Mayor, I counted 420 sacks. I found an invoice for 740. What happened to the 320 sacks we didn't receive?"

Lacombe had turned purple. He had not seen Marellis counting the bags of coal. He stammered, "The rail car ... on its way ... I ... I don't know ..."

"And the butter and cheese?" said Sérez again.

"It's extra. I've already told you that," protested Premelle. "We can't weigh everything down to the last centigram!"

"You're light-fingered, in any event. And you could distribute the left-overs to the elderly, the children. Six extra kilos of butter, four of cheese – I think that's a lot ..."

"Now, Mr Mayor," Marellis continued, "how dare you tell the colonel the KK bread is good?"

"I think it's good," said Lacombe.

"You don't eat it! You have your own wheat!"

"It really could be improved," said the priest. "Baille's bread is a lot better than Orchon's."

"Nothing surprising there! Orchon's underhanded. He hardly bakes his bread, mixes in too much water, sells the flour on the side ..."

"Well then you prefer favouritism?" said Premelle. "You'd rather give an advantage to one baker over the other? Fine, we'll give all the flour to one of them, since you so desire. Is that everything?"

"No," said Sérez. "There's something even worse. There's this question of the evacuees. The town government's already drafted people to work for the enemy. Now is it going to help drive out our children and old people, and again make itself an accessory of the Germans? Mr Mayor, are you going to hand over this list of evacuees?"

"You certainly don't want me to let myself be thrown in prison, do you?

Damn it, it's me, the mayor, who'll pay the price if I don't obey, not you. Do what you want. As for me, I'm going to obey."

"Speaking of lists," interrupted Hérard, "what about this list of women suspected of disease?"

"Oh, yes," said Lacombe, thankful for the diversion. "I'd forgotten."

He took the list from his pocket and read aloud: "Each week the following will be subject to medical examination: Augustine Godeaux's daughter ..."

"Not surprising," said Sérez.

"The two Debraine sisters ..."

"The drapers! You don't say!"

They laughed, for they found it very funny.

"Houez's wife, Lacombe's daughter, Norel's daughter ..."

He had been reading mechanically. He stopped amid stunned silence. He lifted the paper again, reread it, let it slip from his hand, gazed at the others with a distraught expression. His face was crimson. He put his hand to his collar, breathing like a man who was choking. They thought he was about to have a stroke. All of a sudden, he rushed toward the door, and through the window the others saw him hurrying toward German headquarters.

• • •

In the kitchen of Lacombe's farmhouse, the two sisters were kneading dough for bread. They picked up the heavy white mass and let it drop by bits into the mixing trough. Their bare, flour-coated arms were sticky with dough up to the elbows. A thin layer of flour lay like powder on the blue flagstones of the floor. At the stove, their mother stirred buttermilk. The only sounds were the steady scraping of the ladle on the bottom of the pot and the dull thud of the dough falling back into the trough. Outside, there was a strong wind. Night was coming, and a cold rain was falling.

Suddenly the door flew open. Lacombe stormed in. He took off his hat and threw it to the floor in a furious gesture.

"Jesus Christ!"

The women jumped. He had obviously been drinking.

"Jesus Christ! God damn it!"

He marched up to his wife, thrusting his flushed, angry face into hers.

"So! Which of your two bitches of daughters let herself get knocked up by the Boches?"

Lacombe's wife had turned deathly pale.

"What're you saying, Hector? Are you crazy? You're saying what now ..."

"Which one has to go for an exam? Which one's had an abortion? Huh? Huh? I ran to German headquarters! They made a fool of me! They told me all the Boches knew about it from the sexton! Huh! Huh!"

She had not heard a thing. Lacombe's yelling was not reaching her. She thought frantically of a way to rescue the situation, of an excuse to find, quickly ... Estelle was married! What would her son-in-law Babet say when he returned? Scandal! Dishonour! The other was still a girl, unattached ...

"Are you going to answer!" roared Lacombe, raising a threatening hand.

She murmured, "It's ... It's ..."

She looked at Estelle, then Judith. The three of them understood one another. Each had had the same thought. Honour ... This bizarre and grotesque notion of family honour.

"Who is it?"

"Judith ..."

"Judith?"

He was shocked. He had had faith in his younger daughter. As a result, his fury grew all the worse.

"Judith! Bitch! Dirty woman!"

He flew at her. She took cover, shielding her face with her dough-covered hands. She uttered a cry of terror.

"Which German, you bitch? Which one? Which one? Answer, or I'll wear you out!"

"Albrecht ..." whispered Judith.

For her at that moment, it was almost true. She felt a sombre joy, an inexplicable pleasure, in confessing to a crime she had not committed.

"Get out of here!" yelled Lacombe.

Judith glanced first at her mother, then her sister. They looked dumbfounded, stunned, and said not a word.

"Go! Off with you! Get out!" Lacombe shouted again.

"Hector!" whimpered their mother.

"You ..."

He had turned toward her, the backside of his hand poised to strike. She shrank from him and said nothing more.

Judith steadily wiped the gluey dough from her fingers. Like a servant, she slowly untied her apron, put it on the back of a chair, and left the kitchen. It was impossible to tell what stopped Lacombe, but he did not dare hit her.

• • •

Judith went to live in a little house that she found to be vacant. It was on Herlem Hill, across from the Sennevilliers' quarry, about a hundred metres from Fannie's cottage. Albrecht helped her. He had furniture that had been stolen from abandoned houses brought to her. Almost every evening, he came to see her after work, for he had remained on Lacombe's farm, naturally. Lacombe was not so bold as to say anything to him. With these German scoundrels, one could never tell what might happen. Above all, if Albrecht left, who would replace him? Lacombe knew what he would lose, not what he might gain. Albrecht ran the farm with a sure hand, and Lacombe and he got along admirably regarding the division of small profits. Besides, his honour was intact. The culprit had been driven out, the dishonour expunged in the eyes of the village. Lacombe, the mayor of Herlem, once again walked with his head held high among his constituents.

He was also in the process of drawing up the list of the disabled, the sick, and the undesirable whom the Germans wanted to deport to France. This threat of exile, far from home and family, was a sword of Damocles that he held over the entire community. Lacombe could smite anyone he wanted, and he was merciless. As a result, the villagers showed him the greatest consideration.

IV

The prosperity of Lacombe, Humfels, and the other big farmers stood in contrast to the distress of the Sennevilliers.

The Sennevilliers suffered from the general hostility of the villagers. Old Sennevilliers was only a humble mason. He had had the impudence – committed the crime – of perceiving and taking advantage of a source of riches that everyone else had ignored.

The limestone quarry had been in existence for a long time. Vauban had made use of it in the seventeenth century, mining rock for the fortifications at Menen.* The quarry had remained in operation until the Revolution. Subsequently abandoned, it had turned into a deep, useless pond, full of fish but seldom visited because of the dark tales surrounding it. These still waters, hidden at the bottom of a wild ravine, stirred the imaginations of the villagers.

Old Sennevilliers bought this hole from the Baron des Parges, telling him that he wanted to use it for a fishpond. He paid 25 percent in cash, took out a mortgage for the rest, and with his own hands constructed a lime kiln out of bricks and a shack in which to live. Within ten years, he had paid off the mortgage, built the inn, and bought enough land around the quarry to incur the lasting enmity of all the local farmers. In the midst of the extraordinary industrial development of French Flanders, Herlem, where the vast majority of the land belonged to the Baron des Parges and the rest to a few rich farmers, had remained a backward, reactionary island where the outsider, the new, the unknown had been completely shunned. The Baron des Parges, the owner of an enormous landed fortune slowly accumulated over the years, took on the prideful bearing of an old country squire, despising industry and the occupation of a man like Sennevilliers. The farmers watched with hatred as the lime burner attracted manpower from the city, paid good wages, demanded electricity and a rail line, and installed machinery, pumps, winches, and light rails. They tried to strangle him, refusing to sell him land, the extension he needed each year to continue mining more of the deposit. But Old Sennevilliers, a man with no formal education in the law, could be shrewd, even malicious, characteristics that helped him gain through cunning what the farmers would not sell him willingly. He resorted to all manner of stratagems – anonymous purchases, closed-ended leases, options, maneuvres through third parties – and was soon famous among local notaries. He lent money on mortgages, bought parcels of land here and there to trade for the ones he really needed, and throughout his life waged a kind of silent, patient war, a feudal strategy of growth, acquisitions, alliances, exchanges, encirclements. When he died, he left Jean, the younger of his

*Vauban was Louis XIV's famed military engineer.

two sons, who took over the business, a sophisticated industrial establishment, enough land for almost unlimited mining, and the firm hatred of
nearly all the powerful families in the village.

After Jean's departure, the Sennevilliers had spent three or four days in
anguish. Jean's mother and his sister Lise lived at the inn. His wife Fannie
and their little son Pierre occupied the humble cottage, on the crest of
Herlem Hill, where the Sennevilliers family had once lived. From there,
the women had watched Lille burn. Herlem itself was submerged by the
flood of German legions as they rushed toward the sea. Hordes of Bavarians and Saxons arrived one night, invaded the inn, and sacked it, burning
tables and chairs, laying waste to the wine cellar and the bar, killing the
chickens, pillaging the cupboards, then headed farther west, leaving in
ruins the quarry's big house, which had been so neat and pleasant just the
day before.

Old Berthe and her daughter Lise had hardly finished clearing the rubble when a second wave poured in. The pillage and destruction began
again. This time, the Germans did not leave. Herlem was permanently
occupied.

It was then that Lise and her mother truly began to suffer from the
hatred of the big farmers. Lacombe the mayor and Humfels the deputy
mayor were jealous of the Sennevilliers, whose prosperity offended them.
Just before the war, the state of agriculture had been disastrous. Lacombe,
a rich farmer in the style of yesteryear – drinker; patron of card games,
cockfights, and pigeon races; mad lover of the horse track; hunter; smok-
er; skirt chaser – had long led a coarse and hedonistic lifestyle that had
slowly driven him toward ruin. Marellis the tax collector knew it well.
Lacombe had trouble paying his taxes. He had deeply mortgaged his land
and squandered two oil presses, a small wood, and a chicory roasting concern that his wife had received as a dowry. Humfels, brought down by his
very love of profit, had stupidly invested his money in the fallen stars of
the stock exchange. He had lost most of his assets in a refinery and the rest
in a lawsuit. He had rented some land and put it in good shape, enriching
it with long-term artificial fertilizers. Then the owner had refused to
renew the lease. Humfels had lost his lawsuit and his money. Nine of ten
farmers were in similar condition. Russian flax, German beets, American
wheat, Algerian potatoes, Moroccan eggs, Danish butter – the produce of
countries where agriculture was beginning to be practiced along scientif-

ic lines and was conducted on a vast scale – were plowing the furrows of dark days for Herlem's farmers. The Sennevilliers, the lime kiln with its chimneys and their thin trails of white smoke permanently etched in the heart of sky, seemed in the eyes of all these people to be the incarnation of progress, the machine, the very developments that were killing them.

The war was for them a type of revenge. The kilns were dead. The earth continued to live. The Germans had taken it, no doubt, but the farmers still managed to make a decent living from it.

This vengeance was not enough for Lacombe. As mayor of the village, he had to find lodging for the troops. He marked down the Sennevilliers' inn for fifty men. Fifty soldiers invaded it, chasing Lise and her mother into the kitchen, using the basement as a latrine, vandalizing everything, building fires with the bedroom floorboards, the doors, and the wainscoting. They bullied Old Berthe and stormed into the small room where Lise slept at night – upsetting her, humiliating her, offending her virginal sense of propriety to the point that she had to run and ask their officers for protection. Army headquarters sent a constant stream of policemen, known as "green devils," bearing imperative orders: to hand over ten sheets, twenty bottles of wine, two mattresses for the wounded. The officers needed a thousand things for their amusement or their comfort. They asked Lacombe where to get them. He directed them first to the Sennevilliers' inn. And if the Sennevilliers refused, if it were impossible for them to produce what they were supposed to have, they were thrown in prison for a few days or slapped around at the hands of a policeman known as "Beanpole," so long and thin was he in his green gendarme's uniform.

At the same time the quarry was wrecked, methodically and incredibly quickly. Lacombe had pointed it out as a precious source of equipment, though in this matter the Germans had not needed his advice. Motors, rails, winches, tip trucks, sheds, carts, horses, harnesses, dynamos, power lines, tools, cables, buckets, jacks, lumber, girders ... everything was taken.

Lise and her mother, however, continued to resist. Jean had not left them much money. The Germans had taken the quicklime, leaving a requisition voucher as the only payment. All around them, Lise and her mother witnessed bargains, compromises, capitulations. Lacombe and the farmers openly associated with the enemy. Some workers laboured for the Germans, making seven francs a day paid by the commune. Young girls and women welcomed the soldiers into their beds. Those who cooperat-

ed with the Germans found enough to eat. Isolated, obstinate, intransigent, the Sennevilliers refused to surrender. In the village, they came to
symbolize resistance, commitment to duty and the lost fatherland. Beanpole, the tall "green devil," sensed this fierce stubbornness. He chose them
as his victims, raining fines and perquisitions down on them. At all hours
of the day and night, he would come and search the house from top to
bottom, carrying off whatever fell into his hands. To keep anything, to
hide anything, was impossible. Like the other villagers, the poor women
received their share of rations. Beanpole, who knew when these goods
were distributed, would come the next day and make off with the packages. He went as far as checking saucepans on the stove, taking the food
that was done, or – with a sarcastic expression – swallowing it right in
front of them. Once he imposed a fine of a hundred marks for a loaf of
army bread found under a mattress. Walking through the yard on his way
out, he saw six big rabbits at the back of the hutch. He took them by the
ears and put them in a sack.

"I take rabbits," he said. "You no pay fine."

Lise consented, half-pleased by the turn of events. The following day
she nonetheless received an order to pay the fine, and there was no possibility of dodging it.

Out of spite, Lacombe had thought it clever to put Lise on the list of
people capable of working in the fields. One morning Beanpole came to
look for her. Lise resisted. Not for a fortune would she have agreed to
betray her country that way. Old Berthe rushed to her daughter's assistance, and Beanpole hit her with such force that he sent her crashing
against the wall. Lise spent three weeks in a Roubaix prison.

Upon returning, she found her mother in the stable of the quarry. A
hundred and fifty men were living at the inn and had driven out Berthe.
Mother and daughter could not go home until two weeks later, only to
find a wrecked and empty house: a cellar flooded with excrement, bedrooms without floorboards, windows without frames – the whole pervaded by filth, squalour, and a dreadful smell. Barely had they managed to
clean this mess up a little when Lise received an order to prepare for evacuation. Lacombe had designated Lise Sennevilliers as a woman of loose
morals who would threaten the virtue of German troops. The Germans
expelled such dangerous elements to France as expeditiously as possible.
Only desperate pleas, innumerable appeals to German headquarters, the

support of the local priest, and the testimony of a few villagers of good faith saved Lise from being shipped off to France, which would have left Old Berthe alone in the midst of the devastation.

• • •

In all of the chaos that affected the Sennevilliers, Jean's wife Fannie suffered the least. Her house was rather distant from the quarry. The Germans had not targeted it in their punishment of Berthe and Lise. Besides, Fannie lived in a small, old cottage whose humble appearance had helped in this regard. Only one German had been boarded with her. Paul, a good boy in his thirties, worked at Donadieu's blacksmith shop shoeing horses and repairing the iron fittings of baggage-wagons and caissons. He was tall, blond, good-natured, and pleasant right from the start. He took a liking to little Pierre, who was soon friendly with him. Paul had quickly abandoned his uniform for blue workclothes and a big leather apron, his blacksmith's outfit, which he had had sent from Germany. He was living in France as he would have lived in his own country: going regularly to work, coming back to Fannie's at noon and night, doing odd jobs for her, raising the chickens, working in the garden, chopping the wood – replacing the man. In the evenings, he would smoke his pipe on the threshold or near the fire, while Pierre sat on his knee and watched him puff away. Fannie and Pierre soon grew completely accustomed to him. He would have been missed. They would not have thought of eating without him, of not waiting for him.

Lise soon noticed that Fannie was avoiding her. She seemed ashamed not to share in the misfortune and sufferings of her family. She no longer went down to the quarry. She even kept away from people in the village. Apparently she felt guilty for being less miserable than the others, for Paul brought many things to the house.

Then it was little Pierre's turn. At first Lise did not understand why he was no longer coming. Until then, the quarry and the pond had been his domain, his universe. There he had found mountain, plain, and ocean, jungle and adventure. Suddenly, he abandoned it. The same boy who used to appear at the inn every day came no more to see his aunt and his grandmother. He became surprisingly unsociable, almost wild. One morning, Lise caught sight of him in the village lane and beckoned to him. But as

soon as he recognized her from afar he ran away like a hare and disappeared. She was pained. Some time passed, though, before she could understand his behaviour and grasp the real reasons for it.

· · ·

In August 1915 the Abbé Marc Sennevilliers, the older brother of Lise and
Jean, came to Herlem. He had seen Pascal Donadieu. The young man had
brought him a letter from his father Simon. It had arrived by way of a
Flemish smuggler, whom Pascal had paid a hundred francs. The letter
provided news of Simon's health and told of the death of Jean Sennevilliers. He had been killed on the train of evacuees from Lille in October
1914. At Wavrin, the convoy had been attacked by Uhlans and most of the
recruits massacred.

Pascal had been afraid to take the letter to the quarry himself.

The abbé found the inn in a frightful state of disrepair – without windowpanes, doors, floors. Mountains of garbage, charred remains, burned
planks ... the universal devastation could well have symbolized invasion
and war.

In the kitchen, barricaded like a fortress with boards and beams, Lise
and her mother were sorting lentils for supper. Berthe was eating bread
with milk as she worked.

The abbé broke the bad news to his mother. He had thought of telling
only Lise, leaving his sister the burden of revealing the tragedy. But he
understood that he did not have the right to shirk his responsibility.

Berthe Sennevilliers received the blow passively. To have been so long
without news had in a way prepared her. She had already suffered so much
that nothing now surprised her. She pulled out her handkerchief of rough
linen, dried her tears, and slowly emptied back into the sack the lentils she
had begun sorting in her apron. She returned the bag to the cupboard,
along with her bread and her milk.

"Oh, Mother," said the abbé, "what are you doing? You have to eat, you
have to carry on ..."

But Old Berthe shook her head. "It's no longer worthwhile, dear ... It's
no longer worthwhile ..."

Now that her son was dead, she did not seem to have a reason to keep
going, to keep struggling, to continue living.

Lise escorted her brother halfway up the hill.

"I'll tell Fannie, too," said the abbé. "Or would you have the courage ..."

"There's no point," said Lise.

She explained what she knew, what no one had yet been able to fathom. What could Fannie have given in to? Neither to sensual pleasure, certainly, nor to a need for escape and liberation, as was the case for many women suddenly freed from the overweening domination of their husbands. Perhaps she had succumbed more to a slow familiarization, to the constant, peaceful, almost haunting presence of one man replacing another, to the need for support, in her moment of weakness ...

In the end, it was almost better that Jean Sennevilliers was dead.

Chapter Three

Samuel Fontcroix lived in the Épeule district, at the end of a cul-de-sac behind the convent. Across the street from his home was a row of sordid little houses, half-sunken hovels with mansard roofs and subterranean entrances flooded by the rains in wintertime. Much of Roubaix was built on this pattern. A few months after the arrival of the Germans, a Lille family called the Laubigiers came to live in one of these holes.

They hailed from the Faubourg des Postes. There were four of them: the mother Félicie, a woman old beyond her years, thin and withered, her face worn; the eldest son Alain, who was almost seventeen; Jacqueline, who was ten; and little Camille, who was six. The torrent of miseries suffered in Lille – particularly in the Faubourg des Postes, where the Germans exacted terrible reprisals – had led the Laubigiers to take refuge in Épeule, where Félicie's sister-in-law lived on the cul-de-sac adjacent to the convent.

The first Germans attempting to penetrate Lille approached through the Faubourg des Postes. There, at the beginning of October 1914, they ran up against a brigade of armed firefighters who attacked them with carbines. A few gunshots also rang out from the windows of the Faubourg. The Germans retreated, leaving half a dozen dead on the pavement.

But the next day thousands of men invaded the Faubourg. The siege of Lille began, and the prince of Bavaria authorized the sack of the Faubourg by way of reprisal. The Germans took it by storm, as if it were a fort, firing on anyone standing at doorways or windows. Folks heard bullets shattering windowpanes and roofing tiles round about them. Puzzled, failing to grasp the danger, thinking it was a shower of pebbles, they stepped out to see what was happening and were killed. It is hard to imagine how poorly these people understood war. Hordes of drunken soldiers broke into the houses, using rifle butts to drive out the women and children and taking the men prisoner. The troops pillaged and sacked, sprinkled petrol on furniture and floors, and throughout the neighbourhood released cats soaked in gasoline and set ablaze. Within moments, much of the Faubourg des Postes was in flames. The terrified population, innocent for the most part of the events of the previous day, embarked haphazardly along the roadways, taking fire from the canons of Lille's defenders and wading through the indescribable congestion of the German armies flooding the city, flowing toward it like the sea.

For three days the Laubigiers wandered through the countryside, from farm to farm, along with the four children of a dead neighbour. Doors slammed in Félicie's face because of the rabble of kids accompanying her. The Germans hurled insults. The farmers unleashed their dogs. The Laubigiers spent two nights in the open fields. The third evening they found a farmer who let them stay in his barn but who threw them out the next day at four o'clock in the morning because he did not want any trouble. Exhausted, consumed by hunger, their clothes muddy and torn, they trudged back through the gunfire toward Lille and the Faubourg des Postes, preferring – if they had to die – to starve to death in their own home.

The siege continued. In their house the Laubigiers found dead soldiers and a crying child. They gathered a little food and ran to seek shelter in the church, like all the residents who had remained in the Faubourg. For these unfortunates, the church instinctively became a place of refuge. It is above all in times of trial that man is a religious animal. The Laubigiers stayed there under the shellfire until the end of the bombardment.

After the surrender of the city, the Faubourg des Postes suffered merciless repression. The Germans wanted to make the local population pay for the murder of their soldiers. Curfew at three o'clock in the afternoon, troops to billet, humiliations of every sort – nothing was spared them.

Félicie's difficulties were exacerbated by a situation in which she had put herself of her own accord. Lots of French soldiers who had taken part in the siege had not surrendered. The inhabitants had hidden them as best they could, giving them civilian clothes and new identities. The vicar of the Faubourg des Postes, where Félicie lived, assumed responsibility for finding many of these fellows more permanent homes. He asked Félicie if she would lodge three. She agreed and welcomed three French soldiers to the second storey of her little house.

It was a curious situation. The men had arrived without revealing their names, their ages, or anything about their real persons or past lives. That was the plan: to disclose nothing, so that in the minds of the hosts there could be no confusion between the refugee's old identity and the new and fictional one created for him. The soldiers had to burn their uniforms, their papers, even their service records. The vicar of the Faubourg des Postes had gotten them work certificates, falsely dated before the war. It was a difficult task. Many employers feared the forgery would be discovered and refused to produce the papers. But enough certificates were collected for the fugitives. With great difficulty, they had been taught their stories. New families and jobs, a whole imaginary past had been invented for them. They had learned these tales by heart. They were under orders to tell the Laubigiers nothing about themselves, or anything else for that matter, with the result that Félicie never knew their true identities. They received their allowance of coal and lived in their room. After several weeks of mutual goodwill, the first conflicts began to occur. These individuals had no real ties to the Laubigiers. They suffered from the painful seclusion, thought of their own families, and were irritated that – as much to keep them occupied as to earn some money for their food – they were forced to take up new trades: to become cobblers, harness-makers, chair-menders. Quarrels with the Laubigiers soon began. They argued about the division of coal and foodstuffs. The carelessness and messiness of these three men drove Félicie, a good housekeeper, to the verge of despair.

The men had never imagined that the enemy might remain in the Nord for years. And now the fear of punishment – of the death penalty which the Germans were imposing on fugitive French soldiers – pinned them down in spite of themselves. The risks were real. And though the folks who harboured these men were not to blame – were in fact putting their own lives on the line – they were expected to show the soldiers every respect for their supposed courage, to serve them, to spare them any danger. Félicie, already distressed enough by the responsibility of feeding her children, did not see it that way and left her boarders to fend for themselves. There was none of the beautiful harmony, the joyous heroism, such as has since been described, just people chained together who grew to hate each other. Only one of the three, who gave his name as Thaunier, showed proof of sure courage and might well have refused to surrender out of patriotism. The others were nothing but cowards. These two also had girl-friends in the Faubourg des Postes. Their love affairs chanced one day or other leading to an anonymous denunciation by a jealous woman or an ousted rival ... Félicie had lectured them in vain. They told her they were not in a monastery.

Thus it was that Félcie decided to move. To her great relief, the soldiers found housing elsewhere, and she went to live in Roubaix on the cul-de-sac behind Épeule Convent, in the house next door to her sister-in-law, Flavie van Groede.

Flavie had four children. The eldest was in the war. They had had no news of him. The second, François, became the Pylades* of his cousin Alain. He was two years younger than Alain and admired him. The youngest children were close friends with Camille and Jacqueline.

It was around this time that identity cards became a problem for Alain. The moment the Germans arrived, they had conducted a census of the entire population. People were photographed in groups of twenty. Identity cards were distributed, and each house received a roster that was supposed to list every member of the family and be posted in the hallway. Many men did not put their names on the rosters or report for the census and the photographs, and so did not get identity cards. Some acted out of patriotism; others thought that enemy rule would be of short duration.

The rebels were found mostly among the young – hotheads, zealots still full of their school lessons. Alain, who was not yet seventeen, refused to be registered. He dreamed of heroism, and for him the unadulterated idea of duty had not yet been distorted by the compromises imposed by life and the spectacle of mankind. Unfortunately, the renegades were forced to conceal themselves at home. In the street, in their houses, anywhere, at any hour, a policeman – a green devil – could ask for their papers and arrest them. To lead a life that was remotely bearable, one had to have a fake card.

*In Greek mythology, Pylades is the cousin and good friend of Orestes, the son of King Agamemnon of Mycenae.

Luckily Alain, who had no friends in Roubaix, got help from his neighbour Isidore Duydt, a boy his age who came from Belgium, where he had worked in the mines and whence the German advance had driven him and the rest of his family at the time of the Battle of Charleroi. A blond lad, nice, a little rash, a bit of a braggart, a tad naïve, proud of his muscles, ready for any piece of foolishness that would generate shock and admiration, Isidore had become pals with Alain and François. Isidore was not registered on the German lists either. He resisted neither for the sake of patriotism nor to fulfill an ideal. In his home, he had received no instruction of the sort. The Duydts were a wretched family. They quarreled with each other, beat each other, stole from each other. The father drank, the eldest son trafficked on the black market, the daughter led a wild existence. Left to his own devices, Isidore turned bad, frequented cabarets, hung out with a gang – a dangerous association at an age when one is equally prone to good and to evil and when a certain boastfulness, the desire to astonish, leads boys and adolescents to foolishly adopt the lifestyle of the bandit. But during the war most of the rebels came from these very circles. They were revolting against the French cops as much as the German ones. They refused to accept any source of authority. A certain taste for risk, the habit of living beyond the law, the recklessness of those who have nothing to lose – all these factors inclined them to rebellion. Many of these rogues acted heroically.

Isidore Duydt, nicknamed Zidore, had managed well enough. Among the renegades, the culture of a secret society had quickly developed. They recognized each other, sought each other out, helped each other. Zidore was familiar with all the means of evasion. He taught them to Alain. By way of Zidore, Alain obtained the address of a printer on rue des Arts who made fake cards. Alain bought one and set his mind at ease. But a month later the Germans, having gotten wind that fake cards were circulating, altered the format and the paper and demanded the addition of a photo of the card holder, along with the seal of German headquarters.

This time Alain procured a real card thanks to the courage of a municipal employee who stole one from the Germans. This man did it for nothing, refusing to take a cent. No one even knew his name. Alain glued his photo to the card, forging the imperial seal with a German coin featuring the double-headed eagle. And for a couple of weeks he was safe again.

At this juncture the Germans established a new requirement: biweekly reviews. All the men had to go to Grand-Place, submit to a headcount, and have their identity cards checked. Alain found another printer and paid a hundred francs for a fake card. Henceforth, every other week, he went to the home of a former businessman who had set himself up as a petty scrivener and was now making a career out of forgery, charging two francs to duplicate the sign and seal of headquarters on the cards of fugitives. This chap raked in a fortune.

All these maneuvers were quite expensive, and the Laubigiers lived in perpetual distress. First one friend was caught, then another. They continued to hope for deliverance, but the war dragged on interminably. On the slightest pretext, the Germans conducted searches far and wide, looking for mattresses, linen, food, copperware. Each time Alain had to flee or hide. Going for a walk and getting fresh air became complicated affairs. Green devils were everywhere, asking for papers, inspecting them scrupulously. Alain was not listed on the roster for his house either. As a result, he had no claim to rations. It was a terrible loss. Fortunately Jacqueline and Camille had small appetites, and Félicie knew how to do without. But the situation upset Alain, who felt guilty for adding to the misery of his family. Using various stratagems, he managed to get out, to work, to earn a little money. He bought some wine from rich folks and resold it. Remembering his job as a foundry worker, he smelted mixtures of lead and tin in a ladle, making ash trays and paper knives, which he sold for three francs apiece. Next he learned of a mineral water firm that was still operating by giving kickbacks to the Germans. He worked there for a few weeks. Then his friend Isidore Duydt got him a permit for the trade in rabbit hides. The Germans needed rabbit skins. Yarn from the fur was used to make textiles. They paid top dollar for the pelts and gave pass cards to people willing to gather them street by street. With this card, Alain almost felt safe.

Zidore's friendship was dear to him. Félicie worried about it. Alain himself sensed the danger in such a relationship. But necessity obliged him. During the war, thus did one see many young men step almost willingly beyond the law. Forced into a new and dangerous existence, compelled to associate with bad company, confined for demoralizing terms in German prisons, they were corrupted, in the end lowering themselves, debasing themselves beyond recovery, even though the starting point of their adventure had been an act of heroism.

The Duydts were refugees from the mines of Charleroi. They had stayed with Samuel Fontcroix for several days. Then Old Duydt had found a vacant hovel on the cul-de-sac and moved in. There he did business in anything one could possibly buy or sell. He beat his wife and two youngest children, forcing the latter to roam the streets as petty thieves, exploiting them like a form of capital. But the older ones escaped his grasp. Zidore rebelled, trading blow for blow. He earned money by boxing in the cabarets and kept it for himself. Léonie, the daughter, slept elsewhere for weeks at a time, returning with dresses and sumptuous jewellery that she guarded savagely. She ended up leaving home and moving to the second floor of a neighbouring house. Truckloads of furniture were brought to her from a looted mansion, and officers came to see her openly.

The eldest of the children, Étienne, was a strange boy well into his thirties, a hunchback nicknamed Humpty: short, thin, his head all askew between his shoulders, his face pale and pointed like a rat's. From his father, this fellow had inherited his insatiable desire for money. He had been married and had arrived in the Nord with his wife. But he beat her, kept her confined to the house, exhibited a jealousy that bordered on obsession. In the main, he was unbalanced. The wretched woman eventually saved herself and hid somewhere in Roubaix. Étienne the hunchback was consumed by the idea of finding his wife.

Deformed, feeble, his eyes hollow, his limbs frightfully thin, his hands skeletal and enormous, with a bad heart and a weak stomach, affected by a pulmonary lesion that he held in check by some miracle of willpower, this former tailor was an influential man. It was rumoured that he trafficked in gold. The Germans paid dearly for gold coins. Étienne bought them from the peasants, from anyone who had hidden a stockingful before the war, and sold them to the enemy. From his old profession, he had retained the idea that the clothes make the man. He was always well dressed, always very neat, wearing polished shoes and clothing of the finest material. He astounded his family. He had rented a huge home on rue de l'Épeule and turned it into a counting house, a bank of sorts. For him the authority and laws of the Germans were no longer problems. His residence was never searched. He came and went at any time of day or night, a leather briefcase always tucked under his arm, and the green devils saluted him with respect. He scorned his family, maintaining contact only with Zidore, whom he suspected of knowing the whereabouts of his wife. For amid the riches he did not know how to enjoy, Étienne the hunchback was miserable, haunted by memories of his estranged bride. A thirst for vengeance – as much as a determination to reconquer her – animated his mad desire to find her again. Léonie and Étienne were the most prominent members of the family. All the gold that Humpty collected, and from which his father could not profit, enfuriated the old man. He was so greedy that he paid his children visits just to pilfer them, taking whatever he could from their homes: a garment, a trinket, a bottle ... For the Duydts stole from each other – and food above all else. Hardly were rations brought into the house before they were parcelled out. As in many families, they cut up bread, lard, bacon – anything that could be divided – into as many pieces as there were mouths. Each portion was carefully weighed on the shop scales, and each individual took his allotment to live on the rest of week, in fierce selfishness. They hid their provisions in unlikely corners. Toward the end of the week, the big eaters had nothing left. Then they would search, rummage, and steal – when one discovered the hiding place of another. The youngsters, Marcel and Armande, had an extraordinary ability to sniff out their father's bread. Old Duydt, when he was hungry, never left his wife's side, watching her, spying on her to uncover the provisions she had saved for the youngest and grab them. Zidore pilfered tools or rags from the shop and sold them, resulting in horrible family fights that drew crowds from the entire neighbourhood.

Zidore was nonetheless Alain's only friend, aside from his cousin François. Everyone else in the neighbourhood hated Alain because he had not submitted to the Germans. This general hostility was painful and dangerous. Men subject to the headcount had quickly noticed that Alain was not there. He was the object of jealousy, escaping as he did the vexations, the humiliations, the perpetual fear of deportation that the German authorities instilled in the others. They never considered if his freedom were not offset by perpetual apprehension, a state of watchfulness that had continued since October. They only saw that he did not come to be counted, did not have to fear being one day or another recruited for a team of forced labourers, and could thumb his nose at the Germans. The women resented him even more than their husbands. They scolded him when he passed. They insinuated that he must have been on good terms with the Boches to have gotten off in such fashion. In this as in much else, the civilians did each other more harm than did the Germans. Alain ended up wondering if he had not been denounced. For the searches at his mother's house became incessant: day and night, at every hour, on any pretext. The Germans interrogated Félicie, asking how many sons she had, then questioned Jacqueline and little Camille slowly and meticulously.

"But you have a second son," they said. "We know it. We have his name: Alain ..."

"Yes ..."

"He's here, admit it!"

"He's in the war," replied Félicie.

The Germans scoured the house once more, determined to uncover a false wall, some little hole.

Thereafter Alain had to stay in his garret, keeping a rainjacket under his bed and a ladder against his window, always ready to take flight, to seek refuge on the adjacent rooftops. Two or three times he had to escape in this manner, crouching between two chimneys, an old sack over his shoulders, anxious and trying to keep still, while from the windows of surrounding dwellings the Germans attempted to spot him on the housetops. One day, as he was squatting in the corner of a flat roof, Big Semberger's wife noticed him. She held a grudge against Alain for refusing to submit to German orders like her husband. Walking on the gutters, the Germans tried to find Alain. She signalled to them, pinpointing his whereabouts. It was only by a miracle that he was able to slide down a rainspout and flee without being seen. Nor could he dream of exacting revenge for this betrayal: it would have attracted the attention of the German police.

Alain began to realize that he was involving his family in his troubles. The perpetual anxiety was wearing on his mother, poor Félicie, who was not very strong. He could not leave without her living in fear till his return. One day he came back in the midst of a search. His mother appeared in the doorway, her face livid and distorted, her eyes wild. She did not say a word but silently made a terrified gesture with her hand, motioning for him to go. He ran away before the officers rummaging through the house could get to the threshhold. Another time, as he was being pursued, he crossed the railroad tracks, flew as fast as he could toward the Créchet neighbourhood and the fields, and hid in a stand of wheat. The Germans, who had followed him all the way there, furious at seeing him disappear, decided to watch the field and shoot him as soon as he emerged. By one of those chances beyond belief, a second runaway happened to be in the same field, having hidden there for several hours to escape other policemen. Thinking the danger had passed, he came out and was killed. The triumphant Germans requisitioned a cart, loaded the corpse, took it to Félicie's house, and announced, "Here's your son, we caught him this time. He's dead ..." For a moment she thought the body was Alain's and nearly died of shock. This incident convinced Alain. Men were setting out, taking their chances, trying to cross the Dutch frontier to get to France. He decided to head off, too. He had already found a travelling companion, Thaunier, one of the soldiers whom the Laubigiers had housed in Lille, and who, unlike most of the hidden troops, decided to do whatever it took to return to France. Since the beginning of the occupation, he had jealously guarded four gold coins as a precious resource, with this purpose in mind. Alain and Thaunier began looking for a way to cross the Dutch border.

II

The invasion had ruined the coal business of Samuel Fontcroix. Two of his three horses had been taken, along with his entire stockpile of goods. Since Samuel only had a little money saved up and had been obliged to split it with his brother Gaspard, who was his business partner, he anxiously wondered how he would be able to survive in several weeks, when this modest reserve would be exhausted. His brother Gaspard had more resources, but he was ill and spent a lot on cures. And a sizeable part of his fortune was tied up in Russian bonds.

As Samuel had wandered around Lille in the first days after the bombardment, he had been struck by the virtual famine that prevailed. There was nothing in Édith's shop. Bare shelves and empty stores were the norm. Street peddlers with merchandise loaded in wheelbarrows, carts, or baby carriages were demanding huge prices – five or six times more than usual – for eggs, butter, and poultry brought in from the countryside. This sight made an impression on Samuel. He knew Belgium well. He decided to set off on foot, to make a circuit through Flanders in the vicinity of Courtrai and see if he could find some food to sell in Lille.

He combed the area for an entire Sunday, encountered many Germans – of whom folks were terrified but who did him no harm – and came back with twelve kilos of butter. So the next day he hitched up the veteran of his stable, Sultan, an old horse that even the Germans had scorned, and headed to Courtrai to look for a wagonload of food.

Nowadays he had two horses and a big tarp and went to Ghent in search of sugar, butter, ham, eggs, flour, and coffee. He sold these provisions to Édith, whose shop in Lille was always stocked, and who herself sometimes ventured as far as the front to deliver groceries.

Little François van Groede, Alain's cousin, often accompanied Samuel. He led the horses, helped load the wagon, received a bundle of groceries for his mother, and considered himself fortunate. Thanks to François, Alain and Thaunier got Samuel to take them across the Belgian frontier and drop them off in Ghent.

• • •

They reached Ghent on a Monday night. They had crossed the French border hidden behind big crates at the back of Samuel's wagon. Fontcroix used an old permit for Tournai, which he showed to the Germans. Poorly versed in geography, they thought it perfectly reasonable that one would pass through Ghent on the way to Tournai. Besides, Samuel was known at the customs stations. He bought the local currency in which the soldiers were paid, exchanging it for marks that they could send home to their families.

Ghent surprised Alain and Thaunier. The huge Flemish city was merry and lively, the war seemingly forgotten. The wagon rumbled across the city, halting under the porch of a big, decrepit cabaret. They unhitched the animals and stepped into an enormous kitchen, low-ceilinged and dark, where a red fire was glowing. There they found the owner, Van Oosterkerke, with his two daughters.

Van Oosterkerke's establishment was welcoming. Each man received a pair of slippers and took a seat by the fireside. They passed the time till supper flirting with the two young women, who giggled at the attention. The place was full of Germans who seemed quite at home. They came, went, and ate their fill. One German was doing the cooking, another tending bar in the tavern. Still others were bringing in sacks of merchandise. Since the beginning of the war, Van Oosterkerke had amassed a considerable and startling fortune. Alain was astonished to see the abundance of commodities of every sort – destined for sale to the French – filling the warehouses and the granaries. Few talked of the war. They hardly thought about it. The Germans told stories and dined royally. The German cook, truthfully or not, claimed to have served in the Emperor's kitchen. So he was the one making supper. He whipped up boiled fish with capers and set it out on a napkin – a style of presentation that Alain had never seen – then roasted goose with currant jelly and, lastly, served a strange marmalade made with pumpkin, carrots, and honey. Everything was exquisite. They washed it all down with a frothy pale ale and a decent red wine. Alain forgot about Roubaix, the danger, the coming day. He felt as if he were immersed in an adventure, a grander, freer existence ... Since the morning, he seemed to have gotten a glimpse of a meaningful life, one worth living. Never again would he want to be a foundry worker now that he had tasted these things: the journey, the pure air of mornings and evenings, the open road, the tavern, the chance friendships, in short the adventure ... Later he would have a wagon and a good horse like Mr Fontcroix and would roam freely across the countryside, buying and selling. That was the good life.

Alain and Thaunier were escorted to a little room, where the feather bed swallowed them at once. They slept soundly till dawn.

• • •

"A light," said Thaunier, stopping in the darkness.

"Sentries?"

"No, it's a house."

Since nightfall they had been walking through a flat district, a land of wheat, beets, and pastures intersected by ditches, canals, and drainage works, that depressingly humid and monotonous region which stretches from Ghent to the mouth of the Schledt and cuts across the Dutch frontier.

It was raining. The darkness was impenetrable. The two men had gotten lost. Twice they had almost stumbled into a guardpost. Surely the border was not much farther. But they were exhausted.

"Let's try to reach that house," said Alain.

They threaded their way through the trees toward the cottage. The wind made the branches about them groan, drowning out the sound of their footsteps. A cold mist fell, a light rain, as if the evening fog had turned to icy water. They stepped into a vegetable garden through a gap in the hedge and found themselves facing the house. Frozen, paralyzed with fear, they stopped in front of the window they had seen from afar. They glanced inside. It was a quiet, shabby little room. There was a coal fire, a lamp on the table, and a woman knitting by the fireside. They looked at each other.

"Should we go in?"

"Yes."

Thaunier tapped on the door. They walked inside.

"Good evening, Madam," said Thaunier, showing her a gold coin.

The woman looked panic-stricken. She stammered protests in Flemish, with frantic signs, clearly indicating that she wanted them to leave. She seemed prey to a genuine terror. Suddenly she rushed out, closed the shutters, came back, bolted the door. She stood there panting, watching them.

"Cognac?" asked Thaunier, making the motion of emptying a glass.

"No, no ... mumbled the woman, putting together the bits of French she knew. "Must leave, must leave at once."

"Why?" said Alain, annoyed. "We're tired ... Hungry, thirsty ..."

"No, no ... Germans shoot me. Forbidden ... Border three kilometres ... Forbidden ... Must leave now ..."

"Three kilometres ... What's she talking about?"

"I think we're in the forbidden zone ..."

"Ja, Ja," wailed the woman, who was listening.

"All right. We'll go. Even so, she could tell us the way! Holland, Madam? Nederland?"

"Nein, nein," repeated the woman in distress. "Shot, electric wires, sentries. You go back to France." She put her hands together, almost begging them to abandon their plan.

"Confound it!"

They glanced at each other, uncertain.

"I really think we ought to stop," said Alain. "We'd be better off heading back, making surer plans for another attempt. I've heard talk of special 'smugglers.'"

"Turn back now, when we've come so far!"

"What if we at least returned to Ghent, to get information, to look for a smuggler? It seems they have wooden contraptions for getting through the electric wires."

"I'd rather risk it. Three kilometres. It's nothing."

"And the electric wires?"

"We'll slip under them. With a shovel, we'll get through."

Thaunier lit a taper, went out, rummaged through a shed, and came back with a rake and a spade, which he showed to the woman. She made a sign for "yes." He tried to give her a gold piece. But she refused, crying "Nein, nein" with indications of real fear. She would be shot if the Germans discovered the coin. Using a big knife, Thaunier cut the handles of the tools to a third of their original length. They thanked the woman and stepped out into the night and the rain. The locks immediately turned behind them.

They paused on the roadside, hesitating, probing the darkness, and dejected in spite of themselves; then they resumed their journey north. Instinctively, they now held their tools like weapons. All of a sudden they noticed a sentry close at hand, walking beside a hedge. They turned east, crawling on the ground. It was raining hard now. They lost their way amid the dripping gloom, in a huge field of beets whose unbelievably wet leaves drenched them like a cold shower. They went along on hands and knees, afraid to stand up, sinking into the clay, extricating themselves, all sweaty and frozen, with great difficulty. Without warning, the ground beneath them gave way. They almost rolled into a deep canal, whose bank they had reached unawares. They stopped for a moment, breathing hard, looking at each other, reticent to admit their fear. Alain wrung out his soaking handkerchief and wiped his face. Suddenly they made a frightful start, throwing themselves against each other. Something had stirred nearby. They remained glued together, sick to death, their hearts racing. But nothing happened. It was only an animal. They rested side by side, their chests heaving.

"We shouldn't have ..." murmered Alain.

"No, no ... It's my fault."

"It's our fault, both of us."

Thaunier thought for a second: "Hey, pal ..."

"What?"

"If something happens to me ..."

"Yeah?"

"You should at least know my name ..."

"It's true," said Alain, in amazement. "I don't know your name."

"It isn't Thaunier. It's Gaudebert, Paul Gaudebert. I'm from Chalon-sur-Saône. If I don't make it, write to my mother in Chalon ... You won't forget?"

"I promise."

"Thanks. That makes me feel better. Now let's go."

They climbed back to the top of the bank, checked their compass, then crawled toward a group of trees, which they could see dribbling in the darkness. Alain grabbed his buddy abruptly.

"Lightning!"

"No, it's a searchlight. The bastards are lighting up the line!"

They waited. At the edge of the horizon, a reddish star appeared every twenty seconds. In the inky blackness, it cast a faint, blurry light on the watery fields, revealing trees, hedges, boundless open spaces.

"Lucky they're so far off!" whispered Thaunier. "We won't be seen."

They started creeping toward the stand of trees again. And then in front of them, so close that they almost ran into it, was a thin, wet maze, a sort of giant spider web – a network of barbed wire dimly visible in the murky depths of the night. Thaunier had seized Alain's arm, holding him back: "Look, old chap, it's the frontier."

In his voice was a wild excitement, barely restrained. It was as if he were already in Holland. They waited a moment, listening in the darkness. Then Thaunier quickly grabbed his spade and started digging under the wires; they worked frantically, drawing deep breaths, groaning under the strain. Thaunier dug furiously, like a miner. Alain pulled the dirt back with his rake. "Mind the wires," said one or the other instinctively, from time to time.

Water quickly invaded the muddy trench as it began to take shape. They sloshed about heedlessly. In a few minutes, the skin of their hands was raw, such determination were they putting into their work. But they were already under the barrier and began clearing the other side.

All of a sudden, Thaunier threw down his spade and straightened up: "I can't go on ..."

"I'll switch with you," said Alain. "Hand it to me ..."

A huge blue flash blinded him, making a sharp crack. Muscles contracted, back arched, all contorted and dreadful, Thaunier made a terrible leap and was flung backward, his arms bent, his face turned skyward, his hands hooked like claws. He fell to the ground with a thud. A moment later, from afar, came shouts and gunshots ...

Alain stood there for a couple of seconds, too stunned to move: "Thaunier! Thaunier!"

He threw himself on Thaunier, pulling him up without even thinking about the danger of being electrocuted himself.

"Thaunier, Thaunier, for pity's sake, answer me!"

He pleaded with him, as if the other could hear him. Alain had taken the two rigid hands in his own, probing the face, looking for signs of life. But the eyes were white, the countenance black, frozen, dead. Instantaneously, throughout the whole of the paralyzed body, rigor mortis seemed to have set in. Horrified, Alain released the victim's hands. Far off, in the night, silhouettes and torch lights were approaching.

Alain rushed headlong into the darkness.

· · ·

He found Fontcroix and little François at Van Oosterkerque's inn. He told his story. And the next day they began the painful trip back to Roubaix. Until Mouscron, the journey was uneventful. When they ran across Germans, the celebrated permit for Tournai did its duty. Then, a little before Mouscron, Fontcroix pulled out three German berets, like the ones worn by Bavarian soldiers. They put them on.

"The Belgians from the borderland won't let us pass," explained Samuel. "They claim the French are starving them by coming to look for food, and they wait for the wagons to attack them. As long as it's light, with these caps they'll take us for Germans. We won't be bothered."

And in fact they travelled through Mouscron without a problem, sporting the grey caps on their heads and concealing the wagon rear with covers.

They stopped at the wayside cross overlooking the edge of Mouscron facing Tourcoing. It was dark. Samuel lit the lanterns. Then he climbed back onboard.

"The bars?" he said to François.

And from beneath the seat the latter retrieved three rolls of elegantly bound tissue paper. Alain took one. It was surprisingly heavy.

"It's iron," explained Samuel. "It doesn't look like a weapon, so we never have a problem. And it works when people from Mont-à-Leux and the borderland try to block our way. My wagon's been attacked many times ... There's little love between neighbours along the frontier ..."

But they traversed the hamlet of Mont-à-Leux without difficulty.

At the Belgian customhouse, a Flemish officer ran out. Since the invasion, these civil servants had no authority, no role. Those who remained – no longer paid by their government – levied a toll of their own. It was totally illegal, but they managed to live from the proceeds. Fontcroix gave the man forty cents. And they returned to Roubaix without incident.

Chapter Four

I

That morning Thorel, the Lille publisher, was waiting at the headquarters of his newspaper *The Lantern*, anticipating the arrival of Patrice Hennedyck, the mill owner from Roubaix, and the Abbé Sennevilliers, chaplain of the lycée in Tourcoing.

Since October 1914 the Abbé Sennevilliers had been embarked on a perilous enterprise. At the start of the war, he had wanted to enlist, to do something. Like many folks, he was fired by patriotic enthusiasm, unable to imagine what the war would really be like. He went to ask his ecclesiastical superiors for permission. They reminded him that the Church might tolerate military service but cannot encourage it, and that the word of the Gospel – "All that take the sword shall perish with the sword" – applies to a priest even more than to others.* The abbé did not enroll. Nevertheless, consumed by the need to be useful, to act, he volunteered to help military offices, hospitals, the prefecture. He was jostled about, sent rudely from one service to another, but in the end found a position as chaplain in one of the hospitals that manufacturers were establishing at their factories in Roubaix.

It was thus that the Abbé Sennevilliers and Patrice Hennedyck had come to know each other. On the premises of the factory in Épeule, Hennedyck's wife Émilie had emulated her peers by setting up four spacious wards – clean, white, enlivened by flowers, almost stylish – where 150

*Matthew 26:52. For this and subsequent quoted passages, the Douay-Rheims Bible (Challoner translation) has been used.

beds awaited the French wounded. All Roubaix had streamed through the hospital to admire the facility. The only problem was that it never saw a wounded Frenchman. The first to receive care were German soldiers. They arrived in October 1914, retreating after the Battle of the Marne and marching toward the sea. And so Mrs Hennedyck's hospital, like all others, was in that way invaded by foreign troops.

Since then there had been no news from France. An iron barrier had fallen between the occupied territories and the rest of the world. What had become of French forces? Why had they let the German army stay? How many days would it remain? No one had a real understanding of the Battle of the Marne and the Race to the Sea. It was believed that the occupation of Lille, Roubaix, and Tourcoing only marked a step in the German retreat and that the French would soon be hard on their heels.

The Germans occupied the lycée in Tourcoing. Classrooms, hallways, courtyards: all were overrun by a tumultuous crowd of the invaders, their horses, and their equipment. The abbé's room, behind the chapel, was practically besieged. Soldiers slept in front of his door. They had requisitioned his office for bed space. He witnessed the spectacle of troops coming and going, enormous masses of merry fellows, strong and well equipped, setting off in the evening only to return a few days later exhausted, muddy, consumed by vermin, famished and dazed, with broken artillery covered in clay and horses on their last breath. They told the abbé about the "Front." They named towns: Ypres, Diksmuide, Péronne ... But the abbé did not believe them. People were convinced that the Germans in Roubaix were in some sort of pocket, stretching in one direction toward Antwerp, in the other toward Liège, and that one day soon the French would break through.

In this uncertainty, however, imaginations ran wild. People invented all manner of stories, envisioning victories and resounding defeats. The mind needs truth. Ignorance was clearly demoralizing the civilians, throwing them into confusion – and such was undoubtedly the intention of the enemy. The Germans had taken measures to this end: pigeons, telephones, radios, anything that could be used to communicate with France had to be handed over or destroyed, along with rifles, bicycles, cameras. So it was that the idea germinated in the brain of the Abbé Sennevilliers: to build a little radio set using his knowledge as an amateur wireless operator and make contact with France. In the beginning, it must be said, his project had entailed no concern for heroics. Often circumstances, more than conscious will, lead one to become a hero. The abbé was primarily satisfying a personal need to know; it also seemed amusing to attempt the ruse and thumb his nose at the enemy. He never imagined that it might go further. He simply wanted to get the news for himself and a small circle of friends.

The abbé had the crystal made by his friend Gaure, a chemistry professor at the lycée. Gaure melted and crystallized a bit of sulfur and some powdered lead in a test tube. The mixture produced an excellent sulfide. For an antenna, the abbé used a telephone wire. One night he climbed onto the roof and cut his line. He spliced each end of the severed wire to insulating material so that the line still appeared intact to the naked eye. He found an old telephone receiver and made a coil with a cardboard cylinder and a copper wire that he varnished himself. A curtain rod gave him his slide tuner. A ceramic insulator served as a base for his detector and crystal. Except for the coil and the crystal, which he carefully hid, all the parts could be left in plain sight. They were only pieces in general use for electrical equipment, and no one would be surprised to find them in his home. Very quickly, this rudimentary receiver allowed him to pick up the Eiffel Tower, a good many ships, and especially the big English station in Poldhu, whose transmissions were particularly strong and regular, broadcasting a communiqué at one hour past midnight.

The first intelligible communiqué he received – it took him a while to get used to Morse code and to translate English – left him in astonishment. Antwerp and Liège indeed! Poldhu named Nieuwpoort, Ypres, La Bassée, Arras, Albert, Montdidier, Noyon, Reims, Verdun, and Nancy as towns along the front. All of Belgium occupied! All the Nord except Dunkerque! Much of the east! The German soldiers had not been lying.

Like the abbé, Gaure and Hennedyck the manufacturer were shocked. They began to await the communiqués with eagerness. They spread the news clandestinely and noticed the relief that people felt just knowing, having some certainty for better or worse. Hennedyck had the next idea: to disseminate the news, to inform the citizenry. Unfounded rumours threw people into enthusiasm one day, despair the next. And the Germans were not averse to spreading false information. In the midst of this confusion, people were losing heart. The task of enlightening them, of giving them at least a general sense of the truth, came immediately to Hennedyck's mind. He had a mimeograph machine in his office. He worked in concert with the abbé. They agreed that each evening the abbé would bring the communiqués from the Eiffel Tower and Poldhu to Épeule. Patrice Hennedyck mimeographed them, and they put the precious little sheets into circulation. Sixty copies were made. The abbé gave them to priests in the main parishes, Hennedyck to other manufacturers. The little pink leaflets were soon known across the city as messengers of hope.

Then Hennedyck's ambition grew. He pulled along the abbé, who was a little frightened. Hennedyck persuaded him that they should produce a real newspaper, using a press and type. Their common friend Decraemer put them in touch with Thorel, the Lille publisher.

Thorel was a man of fifty. Starting from nothing, he had married the daughter of the Dumesnais, the owners of a big printing works. Thorel was a handsome boy with whom the daughter had been smitten. They had been obliged to marry. And by the law of the first night Thorel had become manager of the Dumesnais press.

The firm's best client was the *The Lantern*, a weekly periodical printed by the Dumesnais. This old, orthodox publication was widely popular among the bourgeois clientele of the region. And its advertising pages were well read. Skilled at judging opportunities for profit, Thorel took an interest in the business and soon came to run it. *The Lantern* turned into a daily, and at Thorel's urging the respectable periodical – traditionalist and dignified, a little prudish even – was transformed into a thick, copious newspaper, abundantly illustrated, filled with ads and provocative photos, sprinkled with simple, light-hearted articles highlighting sensational crimes, profiting from scandal and filth, adopting a shallow conformism with respect to all ministers and all parties. "A government paper," said Thorel: one of those organs that debases readers by its listlessness, its ease, its disgusting readiness to flatter their tastes, their weaknesses, to spare them the very effort of reading by use of illustrations, to discuss only what they like – sports, shows, actresses and celebrities, crimes, sex scandals, and police business ... A paper that maintained a hypocritical loyalty toward the Republic, the army, and even the clergy, with whom it attempted to live on good terms because of the Church's influence. A newssheet that promoted boisterous patriotism, hatred of Germany, a thirst for revenge ... Anything that sold well and which in reality Thorel could not have cared less about. *The Lantern* – or the art of making a million a year by subscribing to the French news agency Havas, his colleagues said, and not without reason. For *The Lantern* grew, upsetting the great regional dailies, which were loath to resort to the same means. Over all its competitors, *The Lantern* had the considerable advantage of being devoid of opinion and accessible to everyone because it flattered the masses, and profitted by it.

II

The offices of *The Lantern* had been closed since the start of the war. On the premises of all the Lille dailies, the Germans had installed military services and laid waste to the equipment, taking the presses and type from the print shops. Miraculously, *The Lantern* had been almost completely spared.

Thorel was wandering through the big newsroom while waiting for Hennedyck and the Abbé Sennevilliers. The windows overlooked the mouth of Grand Boulevard, where a squad of Bavarians was passing by, leaving for exercises. Thorel had just grabbed a cigar, a mediocre German one that had been exceedingly expensive. He lit it when the bell rang. He descended the grand staircase, went himself to open the door, and brought the two men up to the newsroom. Thorel apologized; his executive office, devoid of heat, was ice cold.

"Mr Thorel," said Hennedyck, "our friend Decraemer has undoubtedly explained the reason for our visit. We need you to sell us printing paper and type ... A newspaper in our city has loaned us a press. We lack type and paper ..."

"For your underground print shop?"

"For our newspaper, yes," said the abbé, for whom the word "underground" made a disagreeable impression.

"You're amazing fellows," said Thorel, throwing himself into his chair. "Really, I admire you!"

He smiled at them, giving his big, ball-like face an expression of sympathy. Clean-shaven, his nose short and enormous, with blood-red lips, small black eyes glistening behind gold spectacles, and a round, low scalp almost completely denude of hair, his features – beyond a kind of surly mirth – reflected the cunning, the suspicion, the skepticism of a businessman accustomed to all manner of knavery. Thorel was strong-backed, barrel-bellied, broad-shouldered, stupendously robust and flushed.

"Yes, yes, what you're doing here's wonderful! It's courageous! And I only want the privilege of helping you. By George! You need type, paper? You'll have them!"

"I expected no less of you, Mr Thorel," said Hennedyck, "and I can assure you ..."

"But are you ready? Do you have a place, first of all? Obviously, the paper can't be printed here. The Germans would soon be suspicious."

"I'll install the press in my factory," said Hennedyck.

"And the transportation of the type and the rolls of paper?"

"We have someone, a driver on the Mongy tram."

"And the typesetters?"

"Here again, we've thought of you. Perhaps some of the old workers from *The Lantern* ...?"

"I'll find some, yes. And now, the name of our paper?"

"That's not very important ..."

"Oh yes, I want something reminiscent of my *Lantern* ... Because it's agreed that I'll be one of the editors, right?"

Hennedyck and the abbé looked at each other. They did not yet grasp his meaning.

"You understand," continued Thorel, "that *The Lantern* can't be left out of an activity as vital as the production of an underground newspaper. It must play its role. It will, of course, since its type and its paper will be used, its workers provide the labour. Given the circumstances, I think it reasonable to ask for the right to compose the editorials, under a pseudonym, of course."

"The editorials!" said the abbé in astonishment.

"Mr Thorel," said Hennedyck, "I think you've misunderstood our aim. This is certainly not a newspaper in the ordinary sense. We want to disseminate our little communiqués, spread the truth, that's all. Neither profit, nor publicity, nor glory. We'll remain anonymous."

"Of course, of course ... But you can't keep this whole project from having enormous value, a major influence after the war. The French government can't ignore those who've contributed. You must look ahead, Mr Hennedyck. For my part, I need my *Lantern* to be connected to this business."

Hennedyck had stood up.

"Frankly, Mr Thorel, none of that matters to me. I don't like to hear talk of the future and self-interest in these sorts of concerns!"

A sign from the abbé quieted him. He did not finish.

"As you wish," said Thorel. "I thought you wanted my equipment."

"But we do," interjected the abbé. "It's agreed that you'll write the editorials and take part in the paper as you see fit. Help is what we need. We certainly don't want" – he glanced at Hennedyck – "for anyone to think that we've made this project into a 'cause célèbre,' that we want to monopolize the credit. Supply us with the type, the paper, the typesetters, and help us as you're inclined."

"Well done," said Thorel. "Spoken like a true Frenchman. The equipment's yours."

They went down to the workshops to pick out what they would need to get started.

III

It was Pascal Donadieu who handled transportion. The abbé often saw him on the Mongy tram. They knew each other from Herlem, having met at the quarry from time to time. Pascal, who had a rudimentary knowledge of mechanics, had found a job as a streetcar driver. After curfew he piloted the tramcars from Lille or Roubaix to the depot, or occasionally made two or three more trips for German officers. Taking advantage of the darkness, he strapped the rolls of paper to the roof of a trailer and deposited them in Roubaix, in a café from which Hennedyck had them moved to the factory. The press, which had arrived a few weeks before, was installed in a small room concealed at the far end of the main suite of offices.

The partners met there every day. Hennedyck's wife had a delicate constitution, and he had told her nothing of what he was doing.

The abbé's life was henceforth divided between the lycée and the factory. Although his existence at the lycée was exhausting, split as it was between lessons to teach the children and communiqués to intercept with his receiver, it was the few hours he spent at the factory in Épeule that were the most difficult for him. Very often he found Thorel the publisher there. This man truly repulsed him, now that he had gotten to know him better. Thorel arrived with the mentality of both the upstart and the journalist. Behind his mask of sincerity, the skeptic quickly came to light. He pretended to "churn out" articles in the newsroom much like his old

reporters – ready with a joke, toying with his prose. Thorel's thoughtlessness and cynicism disgusted the abbé, the same as the man's theories on
religion, morality, social questions. No one was in more complete dis-
agreement with the abbé, on every point, than Thorel. The abbé, who
dreamed of Christianity regenerating the world, bringing a noble solution
to the problem of human selfishness, found in Thorel the very model of
the enemy, the type who regarded the priest as a policeman or a fortune-
hunter, who attended mass and gave to charity but put a water-tight barrier between religion and business, who proclaimed morality on Sunday
morning and abandoned it during the week. The two men were in every
way antithetical, opposites. The abbé dreamed of sacrifice and austerity,
Thorel of the good life, fine cigars, and women. The abbé believed in sincerity, in the essential goodness of mankind. Thorel laughed at such
notions, called honourable men hypocrites, and suspected the priest of
having a secret affair with Gilberte Pauret, the little typist who worked for
the paper. After the war, the abbé wanted all their efforts to remain anonymous, wanted them to disappear, leaving only a symbolic memory – the
paper, an image of the devotion of an unfortunate people to their fatherland. In this spirit they had named the newssheet *Loyalty*. Thorel dreamed
of the Legion of Honour and the fame from which *The Lantern* would
benefit. Several times the pair had gotten into arguments, the abbé outraged and furious, Thorel equally beside himself at the thought of letting
such an opportunity for publicity slip away. In the eyes of the priest, this
mercenary mentality was ruining all their work.

He recognized the same spirit, even more disfigured and debased, in
Clavard the typesetter. Thorel had recommended two employees who
would agree to work on the newspaper: Gilberte Pauret, the little typist,
and Clavard the typesetter. Both lived in Roubaix. They came to the factory of Hennedyck, who paid their salaries. Each day Gilberte Pauret
arrived quietly, as she had at her old office, doing her job without preten-
sion, modestly, humbly, pleased that she could still draw her weekly wages,
and filled with an unconscious heroism, the discreet, self-effacing courage
of the meek. The abbé liked and admired the character of this dear girl.
He told her so from time to time. She laughed. She found it funny that she
could be considered brave because she came to earn her daily bread, just
like she had before the war. The attitude of Clavard seemed all the more
irritating in comparison. Like Thorel, Clavard dreamed of the postwar

era. He gathered all the papers, everything that was lying about, swiped old communiqués and radiograms from the abbé, assembled a complete collection of the newspaper *Loyalty,* put together an entire packet of documents. In vain had Marc warned him of the risk he was running by keeping these dangerous records. Clavard shrugged his shoulders: "There's no danger, Father, they're well hidden."

Clavard disguised his goal no less than Thorel: the Legion of Honour after the war. He came each day, fully aware of his courage, so proud that he spoiled it. "Heroes like us ..." he liked to say. It seemed as if this young man were conscious of writing a page in history. He was posing for posterity, to the point that he quickly became hostile toward the abbé, who had two or three times criticized him for his ambitions. Clavard and Thorel secretly laughed at the abbé. Clavard claimed to have proof of an affair between the priest and little Gilberte. The affection of the abbé for this poor girl was turned, twisted in their minds into something shameful ...

Though ignorant of the slander, the abbé suffered in this environment. He could sense that these men undermined his moral synthesis, his certainty of the truth and the higher purpose for which he strove as a priest. One does not live in the midst of ugliness and skepticism without losing one's own assurance of an ideal, a noble mission. These surroundings, these quarrels were disheartening. Such confrontations left him disgusted, filled with the distressing notion of man's vileness. The situation was so bad that – in contrast to arguments with men who proclaimed essentially the same faith as him, calling themselves Catholics – he infinitely preferred invigourating battles with Gaure, the chemistry professor: an atheist, a believer in the supremacy of matter, but in whom a nobility of spirit prevailed and who, determinist, unbeliever, pessimist though he was, unaware of it himself and even denying it, retained a generous fund of idealism, rendering this unbeliever quite similar to the Abbé Sennevilliers.

• • •

Gaure was a chemistry professor at the lycée in Tourcoing. The lycée's laboratory – a solitary retreat sheltered in a deserted and silent corner of the vast building, behind the uncultivated gardens of the infirmary and the chapel – also served as the municipal research facility. In addition to teaching students about Joule's law and the derivatives of coal tar, Gaure analyzed well water and the calcium level of soil in the city, conveniently increasing a budget that often suffered from rash purchases of books and instruments for optics and chemistry.

Gaure was fifty-five years old. He was a tall, bilious fellow with a large moustache and the face of a Gaul. Long, straight hair fell to each side of his naked scalp. His yellow eyes glistened. A nervous type, he was constantly chewing on his moustache or biting his nails or fidgeting with his false teeth. Untidy, often dirty, he lectured in his shirtsleeves, a bowler on his head, one hand in the back of his waistband, the other sweeping in big majestic gestures, confirming the gravity of the formulas he proclaimed with such intensity. Extraordinarily absent-minded, distracted, and whimsical, neglectful of his appearance beyond all imagining, hands corroded by acid, fingers brown with nicotine, always on the verge of losing his handkerchief or mechanical pencil, the knot of his tie hanging loose, vest unbuttoned, shoes unpolished, clothes unbrushed, hair rarely combed, and always running late, he passed through life like a big kid, forever the child, the dreamer, usually ignorant of either the joking or the affection his behaviour could elicit from his students. He had never married, rather naïvely and generously restrained by the desire to spare his mother grief. She had kept him under her tutelage for forty years. Now dead, she had left him alone and aging, in a solitude filled only by the friendship of the Abbé Sennevilliers.

Hundreds of students had passed through the hands of "uncle" Gaure, without any recalling him ever assigning an hour of detention. Only when they taunted him too much would he fly into a frightful rage and run off, swearing, abandoning his laboratory to the rebels, as if he were afraid of committing a crime. For he knew himself to be prodigiously fierce and strong. Mocked by most, secretly loved by a few for the absolute devotion that he brought to his job, he jogged along in complete oblivion. Undoubtedly he would never know what sweet, melancholy, warm-hearted memories some of these boys, become men in their turn, still had of their old-fashioned schoolmaster, who had worked like a horse for them, chalk in hand before the blackboard, enamoured with knowledge and satisfied by the sole joy of diligently transmitting it to others.

Two months after the arrival of the Germans in Tourcoing, Gaure had established a spy centre, taking advantage of his appointment as director of the municipal research facility and the numerous visits this job occasioned. He had started as he had been able, with information gathered at random, and conveyed it by way of Belgians paid to cross the Dutch frontier. Then came French envoys, dropped by plane in the occupied territories, who undertook the organization of a network. And so Gaure had become the head of a section, his laboratory the assembly point of a group of agents from whom he received missives and to whom he transmitted instructions from France. Marc Sennevilliers, on his end, received messages by wireless. Soon they were acting in concert with British Intelligence. By radio from Poldhu, and following a special code that a spy had brought to the abbé, the latter received regular dispatches indicating the day, hour, and place where English planes would deposit spies and pigeons. The abbé conveyed the information to Gaure, and Gaure took the necessary measures. Thus did the abbé, in addition to the newspaper, step into the world of espionage. Of all the peculiar types one encountered in this milieu, the most sincere was Uncle Gaure, the zealot who considered himself a skeptic. His perspective was the subject of interminable quarrels with the abbé. The old mathematician believed in nothing, affirming the insignificance of mankind, the vanity of all his efforts. Matter, matter! It was his favourite word, and the source of his conflict with the abbé, who – while refraining from "preaching" – could not easily accept theories so opposed to his own conception of man and the world.

"Even so," said the abbé, "your science doesn't explain everything! Love, charity, devotion, they're not a sum of calories."

"Begging your pardon," objected Gaure. "They're a product of glandular secretions. Remove your adrenal glands, my dear friend, and you'll lose that beautiful logic you're so proud of. Enlarge or shrink your thyroid and you'll fall into premature senility ... And you can't imagine how this moral austerity, this chastity imposed on you priests, influences your vision of the world, glorifies it, spiritualizes it. Oh yes, Father."

"So be it!" said the abbé. "Eat, drink, be merry, and die, since that's your ideal."

"Eat? Be merry? Ah! There's the arrogance of the Catholic. Virtue is not yours alone!"

"And what's the basis of your virtue? What foundation, what underlying reason do you have? A morality without rewards or punishments? I hardly believe it!"

"And why not? Yes, yes, morality without punishment. It's much better that way! Morality based on nothing at all, or rather on pride, on the consciousness of human dignity."

"Virtue is not built on vice ..."

"Pride a vice? The prime mover of human activity?"

"But pride bends. It's fine before a large audience, a crowd, a witness. But alone with your conscience, tempted to do something bad that no one will know about, carried away by passion, do you claim that pride will sustain you then?"

"I do," said Gaure. "And the man of tomorrow will build his new Church on it!"

"Illusions!"

"Truths!"

Such arguments lasted hours between these two men, for whom chance had cast idealism in two different veins.

Gaure, such as he was, galvanized the heterogenous band around him – the generous sorts, at least. For a good half of the secret agents did this dangerous job like any other, without faith or devotion, out of pure self-interest, individualistic motives, the same way they might have handled smuggling or trafficking in foodstuffs. Men like Théverand, who came from Lille each week, undoubtedly gave themselves to their mission like the apostles, body and soul, without asking for a cent more than necessary, often paying out of their own pockets, doing their duty without counting the cost. Françoise Pélegrin, a young woman of twenty, and Félicie Foulaud, the widow of a Belgian soldier, also exhibited a real patriotic mysticism. But alongside these folks were nothing but half-hearted, selfish, dishonest types ... Fired by the enthusiasm of her twenty years, Françoise Pélegrin forged ahead, laughed at the Germans, thought of the whole thing a little like a big amusing game, took wild, foolish chances for which Gaure reprimanded her in vain. And since she was the head of the women, the leader of the whole movement, in fact, she risked bringing the entire group down with her if she were caught. Félicie Foulaud, for her part, did her duty like a religious obligation, going on faith, neglecting any precaution, making her colleagues shudder. But at least these women were sincere, motivated only by their love of country. The others – Pauline Bult, Jeanne Villien, Mauserel – speculated, haggled, got as much money as they could for each trip. Pauline Bult smuggled letters. She started by asking for ten francs a letter, then twenty, then thirty as the danger increased. Jeanne Villien, a specialist in Parisian newspapers, carried forty of them on her person, wrapped around her body, and sold them for twenty-five francs apiece. There were Belgians, too, "runners," sometimes old smugglers, a bunch of scum on whom one was forced to rely, who knew the frontier well and could serve as guides. Some of the women were outright crooks, like Mauserel, a smuggler of letters, who one day "borrowed" Gaure's wallet, along with all the money from the cashbox, and was never seen again. Greed, lies, bragging, boasting, heroic stories disguising fear and a grasping spirit – that is what one discovered, next to the few earnest souls, in these circles where one would have thought to find the purest, the most ardent love of France ...

Chapter Five

I

Every five minutes, Antoinette Fontcroix went to the corner of rue Saint-Sauveur to see if her father's wagon had arrived. She was quite concerned. Samuel was supposed to be bringing goods back from Belgium for Édith's grocery store. He was running late. Standing in the middle of the road, Antoinette peered toward the other end, at the mouth of the broad avenue between the tall grey buildings of the Saint-Sauveur neighbourhood. There was no sign of him!

Since the beginning of the war, Édith and her daughter had been doing brisk business selling the butter, eggs, and coffee that Samuel delivered. Édith had pulled Antoinette out of school and put her in the shop, despite Samuel's objections. They had to support themselves. And Édith held education in low esteem. Antoinette, for that matter, was delighted with the situation. Whimsical, impulsive, undisciplined, she got along poorly with her teachers and much preferred her mother's store: the gossip with suppliers and customers, the maneuvring, the wrangling, the bargaining, all the lively traffic – and which at least brought in something. Samuel had to give in. He was forced to recognize that his daughter no longer belonged to him, now that he was separated from his wife.

All the same, Antoinette still loved her father. She was particularly aware of it at this moment, when she was waiting for him. She could see him taken by the Germans, carried off to prison! Her overactive imagination ran wild with the idea. Her guilty conscience reminded her, accused her of everything bad she had thought of him. Suddenly she resented her mother. Never again would she tolerate such slander. She herself had been ungrateful and wicked. Her father should not be judged! Leaning against the wall, eyes turned toward rue du Molinel, Antoinette fought back tears and swore to do better.

Édith had long since taken her daughter as a confidante. She honestly believed that her husband had ruined her life. One easily forgets one's own faults. Édith had proof of the affairs, the mistakes of her husband: letters that she showed to her daughter. Édith exhibited these items without reserve, without regard, oblivious of the impact that abrupt revelation of the sadly carnal side of man can have on the delicate and tender spirit of a young girl. She thought to secure the love of her daughter thereby, and also to prepare her, to warn her of life's dangers. Édith only succeeded in mingling all sorts of mistrust and shame with Antoinette's fondness for her father. As for the rest of men, Antoinette despised and hated them. She had a fear, a disgust for men that approached terror, with the added desire to make them suffer, to exact a type of vengeance if possible.

The noon bell tolled. There was still no sign of her father. Antoinette began crying in the middle of rue Saint-Sauveur.

Samuel was winding his way through the narrow streets of Wasquehal, heading toward Lille. He went on foot, 500 metres ahead of the wagon that little François was driving. Whenever Samuel caught sight of a green devil, he would ostentatiously pull out his handkerchief and blow his nose. Behind him, François would see the signal and turn around or else direct the horses to a farm where he would shelter the wagon till the danger had passed.

On this trip, one of the wheels had lost a cotter pin along the way. It was almost one o'clock when the wagon finally turned onto rue Saint-Saveur. Antoinette ran, wild with joy, laughing and crying. She threw herself on her father's neck, kissing him frantically. Samuel, surprised and a little touched by this welcome, tried to calm her down.

"What a crazy girl, what a crazy little girl!"

He held her at arm's length and looked at her, examining his daughter's clothes with surprise and even a certain dissatisfaction, which he had difficulty concealing. She was wearing an enormous bright yellow apron with red flower prints, blue slippers with red pompons, and a garnet ribbon in her hair – a whole strange, vivid outfit which reflected Antoinette's fanciful personality quite well. He said nothing, not wanting to upset her by a

comment when he had just arrived. And without delay he began unloading the wagon with little François. He had brought cheese and packs of
brown sugar from Courtrai. They hurried. The Germans could not see a
sack being moved without confiscating it.

Then he followed Édith and Antoinette into the Grande Bourloire, the
neighbouring cabaret, where the women had a room on the fourth floor,
overlooking the courtyard.* Struck by the musty smell of mould and
burned fat that the little room gave off, Samuel immediately opened the
window. And he reiterated a point he had made on previous occasions:
"This isn't good, Édith. You really don't have enough room."

"Bah! Bah!" said Antoinette.

She found it exhilarating to live here amid the cancans, the arguments
of the old busybodies, the whole teeming, motley, wretched, entertaining
crowd of the poorer districts.

"It won't last forever," said Édith.

"Thank goodness!"

He said nothing more, sat down at the table, and shared their meal of cold
bacon, pickles, and fries: items easy to cook and easy to set out, with which
mother and daughter – absorbed by their shop and equally "bohemian" in
lifestyle – often contented themselves.

"And Christophe?" said Antoinette, who passionately loved her little
brother.

"He's fine. He told me to give you a kiss."

Samuel looked at her, thought she seemed tired, but held his tongue. He
resented Édith for the life she was dragging their daughter into: the excessive work, the furnished room where the bed, the stove, and the table
butted ends, the eccentric clothes, the libertine, almost unbalanced lifestyle in which he, a conventional man, no longer recognized his daughter.
He had more discretion than Édith. He did not want to say anything in
front of Antoinette, concerned to leave maternal authority intact. Even so,
he resolved to chastise his wife about the situation. He worried over par-
ticulars, asking his daughter what she had been up to, what she was eating, if she were sleeping. And Antoinette, remembering the confidences of
her mother, was astonished not to find her father similar to the image she

---

*A *bourloire* is a place where one plays *bourle*, a type of bowling game specific to northern France.

had constructed of him from afar. No, decidedly, the two images did not agree, were not compatible. Such a man – calm, serious, stern – a father preoccupied to such an extent with his daughter, could he also be the hedonist, the brute, the womanizer whom Édith described? Antoinette suffered from this uncertainty. She had the impression of committing an injustice each time she saw him again. But then a reprimand or warning from Samuel – very strict on the subject of proper dress – was enough for Antoinette to immediately rebel. Why the concern for appearances, the perpetual preoccupation for a certain respectability in the eyes of the world? Provided one did no harm, the rest was no business of others. When an argument like this broke out between Antoinette and her father, he instantly lost the ground gained, and she became hostile and foreign to him again.

II

At two o'clock in the morning, Gaure's comrade Théverand roused from his half-sleep. He had spent the night deep in the countryside, awaiting an airplane. Édith's wagon had dropped him off here the day before. He stood up, chilled, stiff, more tired than if he had not slept at all. He looked around, seeing nothing but the darkness, the fields, the emptiness filled only by a savage wind. Behind him was the ruined mill on whose thresh-old he had been resting.

Théverand had been drawn into espionage almost instinctively. He was a simple soul. The arrival of the Germans had inflamed his patriotism, his anger at defeat. He immediately took in eighteen French soldiers.

A few days later the problems began. These men had to be fed, clothed, hidden. Then, as volunteers became scarce with the increasing danger, Théverand started looking for a way to send the men back to France. He knew some "smugglers," specialists in the passage through Holland. He made arrangements for fake passports, clothes, and money. He entrusted each departing soldier with information on the nature and number of German troops stationed in the region, the traffic in supply and hospital trains. He gathered these tidbits rather naïvely, sending pell-mell a little that was valuable with a lot that was useless, at the risk of being shot to no great end. Then a French spy – a former customs officer who had come from France by plane and who knew the area well – paid Théverand a visit. An extraordinary number of these spies had worked in customs. This one's mission was to reestablish a broken network. Each agent received information from another and conveyed it to a third person, never knowing anyone besides these two colleagues. That way the enemy could not dismantle an entire chain. Théverand agreed to help. He was designated Molinel 114 (a number and a place name were always combined in this manner). He would pass his information to Gaure, the professor in Tourcoing, and retrieve French pigeons when told of their arrival. Only the day before yesterday, by means of a radio message, Gaure had learned that some pigeons would be dropped to the south of Pont-à-Marcq, near the old mill. He had sent Théverand to get them.

Théverand was waiting for the plane. Daybreak remained far off. There was but one thing to do: walk. At this point he could no longer fall asleep quite so easily. And he could not stay still in the frozen silence. He plunged into the darkness haphazardly, forcing his numb limbs to move, pulling along chunks of clay stuck to his shoes, dragging about like a sleepwalker, his body heavy and his spirit restless. He closed his eyes a few times, even as he walked.

How strange life was. He, Théverand, a peaceful little clerk, a steady man, a father, here he was deep in the countryside, in the freezing cold, at two o'clock in the morning, stumbling around waiting on an English plane – at the risk of getting himself shot if he were by chance discovered. It was hardly believable, almost fictional. As he trudged along, Théverand mulled the situation over in his head. Was this really him, Théverand, the man who had a wife and children, whose horizons in times past had been limited to the grey walls of the Saint-Sauveur neighbourhood, who deemed an excursion to Malo-les-Bains a big trip and considered going home after midnight a great danger? To think that he was here and risking his life! No, it was preposterous, unimaginable, an improbable dream. How could he have dared commit to such a cause?

It was only in these moments of solitude and inactivity that he examined himself, amazed to be actively involved. The remainder of the time he was swept up in the action. He had never had time or inclination to reflect deeply on the commitment he had made. The whole adventure merely seemed like a game, an amusing pastime.

Théverand walked. Increasingly weary, he dragged his feet, bumbled, leapt clumsily over ditches. He would have given anything to find a decent place to sit and rest.

Dawn broke, a thread of grey light on the eastern horizon, a dim glow invading the flat, windy, desolate space. It reminded him a bit of the sun rising over the sea. Leaning against an elm, huddled up to keep warm, his collar on end, Théverand watched as the infinite stretch of land gradually appeared: dark and misty, wet, glistening faintly under a low, dull, stormy sky swept by squalls. He could make out the black silhouette of a tree, the tawny mass of a dreary thicket: a dreamscape of sorts. Théverand continued waiting.

From afar, a subtle drone reached his ears, like the buzz of a distant insect carried by the wind. Théverand gave a start, raised his head, and looked. He could see nothing, only a dim half-light at the edge of the sky. The murmur grew louder, nearer. Suddenly, close behind him, Théverand heard it clearly. He turned round. A shape was gliding toward him, a big grey bird nearly level with the ground, so low that Théverand ducked his head. The plane rushed up, descended, skimmed the earth. It passed beyond Théverand with the motor cut, in a long, harmonious glide. One could hear the rustling of the propeller caught by the wind. Two, three, four black masses dropped, tumbling to the ground at random. In a triumphant roar, the motor restarted, the plane regained altitude and climbed, turned, and sped like an arrow toward the south.

Théverand ran to pick up the baskets. He found two right away, the third in a ditch. One was missing. He searched for a long time. He had to find it. If the basket fell into the hands of the Germans, they would be alerted. Several networks had been uncovered in such fashion, as a result of pigeons discovered by the enemy.

The sun was rising. Théverand beat the bushes, scoured the ditches, turned in circles, and grew anxious. It was getting brighter. The sun was really up now. One could see quite far. What would the Germans think if they noticed a man busying about like this, deep in the countryside? Sweating, nervous, exhausted, Théverand lost his composure, could no longer remember exactly where the plane had passed. He went back to the elm, tried to remember, searched again ... And as he was starting to lose hope and panic, he suddenly spotted the basket two metres away, hidden in a tuft of grass.

Théverand set off with the four baskets joined by a cord and dangling from his arm. He went two kilometres before resting. He stopped in a little wood and opened the first basket. It was a rather large wicker cage, inside of which was a smaller one connected to the first by types of wicker springs, to absorb the shock of the fall. In the second cage was the pigeon and a scrap of corn. Théverand pulled out the bird and examined it. Not a mark: the darling creature had not been hurt. Théverand kissed it on the head. He looked at the dispatch tube attached to a tail feather. Then he rolled the pigeon up in a fragment of newspaper and put it in his pocket. Thus secured, the animal could be carried without danger. Théverand also gathered the corn since no more was to be had in Lille. Next he crushed the basket and threw it into a ditch overrun with grass. He did the same with the other cages.

Two hours later the Fontcroix's wagon picked him up along the highway, where he had been waiting for them. Édith and Antoinette had gone to peddle their groceries in a village near the front. For amid the ruins some inhabitants still remained, held in place by the love of home or the lure of profit. One could sell anything one wanted to the German soldiers, and the locals exploited them ruthlessly. Édith sold everything she had brought. Mother and daughter slept on the seats, suffering from cold and hunger all night long. They came back exhausted, still frozen. Antoinette was completely worn out. But Édith's satchel was full of bills.

They headed for Lille. Édith had purchased five hundred kilos of wheat from a farm. The return trip was always easier than the outbound journey. Antoinette talked about the money they had made and the pretty purple dress she so desired. She knew her mother, knew her to be at once very stingy and very vain when it came to her daughter. Antoinette manipulated her accordingly. At heart Antoinette was a sly girl. She stoked her mother's love of money, fed it, cultivated it. Of the two, Antoinette proved to be the greediest, the most avaricious. She reckoned figures, made arrangements, handled business better than her mother. Then, to satisfy her latest whim – a dress, a toy, costume jewellery, novels, any old trinket – she struck other chords: vanity, jealousy, maternal pride. Or, by use of a little flattery, she brought her mother round to the desired mood. She played her mother much like a musical instrument. Antoinette was extravagant and totally ignorant of propriety and fashion. And her impulses reflected this lack of balance. She would do without woolen stockings to treat herself to a pretty hat, or survive for two weeks on sausage and cheese so she could take a construction set to her little brother Christophe in Roubaix. Édith, who had been reared carelessly, let her daughter do as she pleased and, herself in good health, of sound constitution, never imagined that this strange existence could have any result other than making her daughter stronger. Among the working classes, rearing children the hard way has always been considered best. In true good faith, Édith let Antoinette push herself and waste her vital energy, convinced that the ordeal would steel and toughen her. Besides, was Antoinette not satisfying her every caprice? How could she not be happy?

III

The Grande Bourloire cabaret, on rue Saint-Sauveur, was one of Old Lille's veteran establishments: a long, low, smoky room opening onto a courtyard by six narrow windows trimmed with half-curtains. The yard was big, deep, and obstructed in the middle by an enormous heap of pestilential manure. To the right stood the cabaret, to the left were the stables and the storehouse for straw. All around, very high up, the innumerable filthy dormers of Saint-Sauveur's cheap hotels overlooked the enclosure.

During the first years of the war, Jouvet, the owner of the Grande Bourloire, made lots of money. Traffickers from the entire region came to stay at his place, store their merchandise, and livery their horses. These people spent money freely, as fast as they made it.

Upon returning from Pont-à-Marcq, Édith had gone to the Grande Bourloire to sell her wheat. She had stationed herself at a table near the front door, alongside two or three traffickers in foodstuffs. And she was holding her own, not letting go of a cent as they tried to talk her down. The atmosphere was smoky, sweltering. Folks were drinking, laughing, singing, and arguing amid the haze. The Grande Bourloire was the meeting place for a load of venturesome fellows. Anyone who had had some prewar experience in the grocery, butcher, or feed businesses – traders of butter and potatoes, farmers, butchers, horse slaughterers, poultry merchants – had naturally continued to deal on the black market. Times were good; Lille was short of just about everything. And these people shamelessly took advantage of the situation. With such "regulars" mingled the dregs: adventurers, speculators, gamblers, smugglers, men and women who grew rich in troubled waters and whose impudence, whose habit of living beyond the law, made them particularly fit for "business" in difficult times. This brutal, earthy crowd, their ranks swelled by the constant traffic in meat and victuals, formed a tumultuous, uncivilized, and wanton clientele for the Grande Bourloire. Germans came here too, selling food from the commissariat or drinking and playing cards. Farmers used barrels designed for the transport of liquid manure – covered with dripping sacs in an ultimate effort at realism – to bring in wheat and potatoes. And then there were the speculators and profiteers of this type of wholesale market, the ones who operated like parasites, buying only to sell again and enriching themselves without dirtying their hands.

Édith played her part in this performance quite well. At the moment she was arguing with a strange little fellow named Mr Clovis – a hunchback with a worn face and an unbelievably bold and cunning air. He was a speculator in foodstuffs, one of the people starving Lille by buying up provisions and holding them in a miniature trust of sorts.

Big Léonard Jouvet – a real simpleton, the son of the Bourloire's owner – was listening to them with a naïve expression on his face. The two could not come to terms. Édith wanted 105 francs a hectolitre. Clovis was offering eighty.

It was then that Antoinette arrived. She was sporting the famous purple dress, which she had just bought, and giggling to herself, unable to restrain her glee. She passed triumphantly through the crowd – the clusters of men teeming round the bar, the gaggles of women about the stove. For there were lots of women here: farmers, traders like Édith, prostitutes or mistresses of the men, along with old market women who had become important wholesalers. Pleased with her success, incapable of containing her naïve vanity at hearing whispers of admiration and jealousy, Antoinette came to her mother's table, sat down on a bench, and absorbed everyone's attention with an impertinent and supremely satisfied look. Édith had broken off her discussion and was eyeing her daughter with pride.

"Oh, Clovis, isn't she pretty!"

"Yes, yes ... Chic, very chic!" said the little hunchback, his eyes alight. He cast a longing glance at the neckline of the young girl. His nostrils made a bit of a twinge, and in his gaze was a glimmer of foul desire.

"Oh, yes, Toinette, you're really smashing!" exclaimed the big fool Léonard. And from every side of the café came calls.

"Hey, Toinette! Toinette! Come here! Come! Over here!"

The men laughed. The women, jealous, gave her an evil look and sniggered maliciously, saying to one another, "She's made up like an ace of spades again! What a figure for you! A real clown!"

And Antoinette, insolent, triumphant, showed off her purple dress and her head of hair, unbelievably styled in colossal loops. Comical, almost ridiculous, she nonetheless remained insuperably charming, for behind the dreadful attire one could sense her spontaneity, sincerity, and naïve purity.

"Hurry up," she said. "Go on, Clovis, finish haggling. You know I owe you a chance to beat me at backgammon. I promised the other day. Wind it up quickly. This fuss over wheat's annoying."

Big Léonard was already bringing the set and the dice.

"All right," said Clovis the hunchback, "I'll settle for ninety-five." He pulled out his wallet, paid Édith, and went to sit by Antoinette, taking the box and rolling the dice. He laughed, told jokes, got worked up. His thin hands were visibly shaking. Antoinette mimicked his wry face, his grin, ridiculing him piteously, in the cruel thoughtlessness of youth. Round about them, a whole group was poking fun at the hunchback. Antoinette got him to lift his eyes, looking for something, and right under his nose she changed the dice and moved the pieces on the triangles. He had lost within a quarter of an hour. She forced him to buy drinks for the whole cabaret. He paid without batting an eyelash, satisfied, pleased to be seen playing dice – him, the hunchback – with this pretty girl. He was oblivious to the laughter directed his way. People were also laughing at Antoinette. She did not recognize it either, delighted as she was, proud of her pretty dress and her success.

But she was starting to feel a little tired and agitated. She had squandered all her energy in the course of the nighttime journey, resulting in a weariness that she did not comprehend but that had gradually left her sad and ready to cry for no apparent reason. She wanted to get away, find peace and quiet somewhere, or else try to forget, dance, dispel the fatigue in a new bout of excitement. She felt a light, irritating sweat moisten her forehead and her hands. Suddenly she caught wind of an argument between Léonard and another big blockhead. Léonard bet that he could walk around the cabaret on his hands. He asked for space, stepped back, dashed forward, landed on his hands, and began trudging along with his feet in the air. He made a laborious circuit of the room and stood up, flushed, to the sound of applause.

Antoinette immediately rushed into this foolishness: "A real feat! I can do as much!"

"You!"

"Yes, yes, me!"

In the thick of shouting and laughter, Édith intervened: "Antoinette, I forbid you ..." But a clamour arose: "Do it! Do it! Bet she can't make the lap! What a laugh! This brat's a fast talker!"

Eyes caught fire at thought of the spectacle. Antoinette, in a supple pirouette, threw herself on her hands. But the crowd was disappointed: she had pinned her dress securely. Only her sinewy knees and a flash of thighs were visible. She made the circuit without difficulty, waddling on her hands, and jumped up amid the applause, to find the dirty, half-inebriated gaze of Clovis the hunchback directed her way. She was almost afraid and retreated from her triumph, withdrawing behind her dissatisfied mother.

Antoinette's head felt heavy and her cheeks aflame. At the far end of the cabaret, an argument broke out between two men holding white sacks. They were cockfighters, energized by the atmosphere of the cabaret. They pulled out the birds. A circle immediately formed. An arena – a pen – was improvised with overturned benches. At the centre of the crowd, the roosters clucked and glared at each other with round, wild eyes. Antoinette abhorred these violent and barbarous spectacles. Unobserved in the confusion, she stepped into the courtyard, went to find her horse in the stable, and gave him a handful of brown sugar.

Elbow on the manger, she stood there resting and daydreaming, watching the movement of the animal's jaws as it ground the sugar with the low hum of a millstone. Then a voice startled her.

"Is something the matter?"

It was Clovis the hunchback ...

"Yes," said Antoinette, coming out of the mild reverie to which, in her weariness, she had unconsciously abandoned herself.

"Why'd you come out here?"

"I don't like to watch cockfights..."

"Ah."

He could find nothing else to say. She turned her back to him again, returning to her horse, who was blowing his nostrils as he reached for her. Suddenly she felt an arm round her body, squeezing her high on the chest, a gluttonous mouth laying hold of the nape of her neck. She was strong. With a twirl of her skirt she freed herself and the same second gave Clovis an enormous smack.

"Dirty little hunchback! I don't know what holds me back ..."

And she smacked Clovis again.

"Christ!" he swore. But Antoinette had already disappeared. Furious, ashamed, beside herself, she had taken refuge in the barn. The day's events now seemed clear to her, only at this instant realizing the foolish things she had done. She was consumed by anger and humiliation, as if she had learned a lesson she deserved, as if she had been handed abrupt proof of her naïvety regarding men and the world, she who had thought herself knowledgeable and mature, the poor dear ...

She reasoned with herself, tried to tell herself: *Why're you surprised? You know what men are like, all dirty animals ...* But she could sense that she had still not accepted this bitter philosophy, that in spite of everything she was still more innocent, more trusting than she would have preferred, revealing an indestructible youthfulness of spirit. All of a sudden, she thought of her father ... What would he say if he knew? A blast of heat and shame seared her forehead. At this instant, she felt disgust for those around her, for her mother, and for herself.

Then she heard the sound of rustling straw at the back of the barn. She went to look and found little Raymonde, Théverand's young daughter, who was playing with a doll and old rags, the remnants of a torn sheet.

"Is that you, my dear?"

"Oh, Antoinette, you've come to play with me, eh?"

"I'd like that very much. What're you playing?"

"I'm dressing my doll. For first communion ..."

"Oh, good. Well, let's play ..."

She took the ribbons, the rags. They dressed the doll. Then Raymonde adorned herself with a big veil. They had a grand time.

"My God, am I happy! How I'm having fun!" cried Raymonde.

"Yes, indeed," said Antoinette.

She fastened paper flowers to Raymonde's forehead and wove a crown of plaited straw for her.

"How beautiful you are like that, Raymonde. And me? Am I beautiful, too?"

"Yes, you're beautiful!" said Raymonde.

They wrapped themselves in their big veils.

"How pretty! I love white! I love it better than anything. I'd like ... I'd like to always wear white. It inspires me. It's beautiful ... It's pure ..."

"You're crying! Why're you crying, Antoinette?"

"Nothing ... It's nothing ... I don't know. I really don't know ... Enough ... Enough ..."

She dried her eyes.

"I'm silly, eh? ... I don't know what's wrong. I must be going crazy, but it's over now ... Come on, let's play. Let's play, Raymonde ..."

Chapter Six

No one ever learned just who had betrayed Gaure and Théverand. In any event, Gaure was surprised by five German policemen as he was getting out of bed one morning. They said they were arresting him for involvement in the theft of some meat. They began searching the house and found a fresh steak.

Gaure was not alarmed. It was not a serious charge. He had indeed just bought ten kilos of beef from three German soldiers who had gone to a stockyard one night and killed the animal. Troops from the front took what they pleased in the rear. Gaure had allowed his neighbours to profit from his stroke of luck. They were arrested alongside him and carried off to headquarters. Gaure was interrogated for a long time. He explained how he had purchased the meat from the soldiers.

"That's not true," responded the policemen, "our soldiers aren't thieves. Tell us who killed the animal. Give us the name of the civilian."

"That's impossible."

"Very well, you'll be condemned as a cattle thief."

"As you wish," said Gaure. "I'd only point out that I couldn't so much as kill a rabbit."

He was tossed back into prison, as were the others found in possession of the meat.

But Gaure soon discovered that one by one everyone else had been released while he continued to be held. He began to worry. He had quit his house without being able to hide anything or pack anything, not even a jacket. He was wearing trousers and a nightshirt, draped in an old grey overcoat he had just had time to grab in the hallway on his way out. He had had to leave the "onion skin" papers and the avian message tubes in the base of a plaster bust on his mantle. If the Germans found this cache, he would be done for. Surely they did not suspect him. But then why keep him after letting the others go?

He spent ten days in the cellar of town hall before the Germans came to get him again. Gaure, who had been in bed with his overcoat wrapped round him in place of a blanket, followed the soldiers outside. He noticed they were guarding him closely. They handcuffed him and forced him up into a covered transport.

The journey was long. Two or three times, in bad German, Gaure questioned his keepers; they did not respond. After going about fifteen kilometres, the wagon stopped. Gaure stepped down into the bare and sinister courtyard of a prison; it must have been Loos. They pushed him toward an office. He went into a corridor where his cuffs were removed, then entered a little room where two German officers and a plainclothes policeman were seated at a desk. Behind them, on a stand, sat an old phonograph with a copper horn. On a bench, at the back of the room, were six gendarmes.

"Sit down."

Gaure took a seat.

"Have you decided to tell us the truth about the cattle?"

"I've told you the truth right from the start."

"So, you insist on claiming it was our soldiers who killed the steer?"

"There's nothing else to say."

They bombarded him with questions for an hour but only got the same response.

Behind the two officers, the policeman listened, his eyes fixed on Gaure and a deprecating look on this face. He walked round the office, took a chair, came to sit in front of Gaure. And calmly, with a wry expression, playing with a short, flexible riding crop that he had retrieved from the table, he said in a familiar voice: "So tell me, old man, how long have you been a spy?"

Gaure was visibly shaken. He had not eaten since the day before. The cold, the fatigue, the exhaustion of the long, tormenting interrogation had worn him out. He did not know how to respond. He stammered: "Me? A spy?"

"Yes, yes, precisely. Don't play dumb. Go on, admit it, confess. You did something stupid. Try to help yourself out. Tell us what you know. We'll take it into consideration. Go on, spill it ..."

He spoke French as well as Gaure, with a hint of an accent from the Paris suburbs. Gaure had already pulled himself together: don't confess, deny everything, it's the only way. In a firm voice he said, "I don't understand."

"You think my head's stuffed with cotton! You'd better look out, or this won't go well for you! I'll say it again: we know everything. You receive pigeons by airplane. Some officers stayed at your place two weeks ago. We found 'onion skin' papers and message tubes in your house ... Yes, yes, under Beethoven's head, in your parlour. That shocks you, eh! And we know plenty of other things, too. Go on, don't play the fool. Come clean and blurt it out. I tell you it'll go better for you ..."

He had reeled all of this off very quickly, stunning Gaure, leaving him little chance to think.

"Go on, go on, answer, answer quickly!"

"I have nothing to say," repeated Gaure.

The policeman was still playing with the horsewhip, bending it, stretching it. Suddenly he struck Gaure across the eyes, giving him no time to anticipate the blow ...

Gaure jumped up, cried out, hands over his face. A punch to the stomach threw him to the floor. And this was the signal for a terrible mêlée. The six gendarmes rushed at him, trampling him, hammering him with their boots. Curled in a fetal position, covering his eyes, flayed, bloody, bruised, Gaure was pummeled with chairs and steel toes – in the stomach, on his head, his chest, and his limbs. In the midst of this uproar, one of the officers had calmly gone to turn on the old phonograph, whose nasal din muffled Gaure's screams.

They stood him up. He could no longer see – blind, bloody, stunned. A gendarme threw the old grey overcoat on Gaure's shoulders, brutally bound his hands behind his neck, and pushed him toward the door as if he were a big, tottering, sobbing child. He had had no opportunity to defend himself.

The hallway was dark. Two gendarmes had taken him by the arms. As he was going down the stairs, still reeling, he came upon a figure heading up, his wrists fastened with chains. This shadow stopped for a second.

"Mr Gaure!"

Gaure opened his bloody eyes.

"Théverand!"

What, Théverand too! And because of Gaure's mistake! The "onion skin" papers, the message tubes ... He was seized by a fit of terrible despair.

"Théverand, Théverand, forgive me, forgive me, it's my fault ..."

The gendarmes were already dragging him away, swearing as they carried him off.

• • •

Théverand had been arrested one morning when he had come to see Gaure. The professor had not been at the lycée for several days. Théverarnd had wanted to check on him and had fallen into the trap.

Like Gaure, he underwent several interrogations before the committee. And each time the start of the sinister phonograph gave the signal for a display of brutality and extraordinary violence. Afterward the guards returned the men to their cells. Gaure and Théverand were subjected to the regimen for severe cases, known as Streng arrest, which meant three days of confinement in total darkness, with bread and water their only fare. The fourth day they were put on the ordinary prison diet and given light. This treatment was unbelievable debilitating. And every two or three days, toward evening, after a day of fasting and anxiety, at the hour when the weary spirit weakens and feels more depressed with the approach of nightfall, the Germans came to look for them, subjecting them once more to the frightful ordeal.

Several times, in the hallways, Théverand crossed paths with Gaure – a Gaure grown old and hollow-looking, grisly, his hair long and white, his expression bewildered, tormented, with his enormous, dirty, threadbare overcoat flowing round him like a huge rag. And Théverand was shocked, not realizing that he himself had arrived at the same state of physical decrepitude as a result of the blows and the suffering.

The German police put Gaure under terrible pressure. They suspected he was one of the leaders, wanted to extract names from him. Ten times he was returned to his torturers. In the end they brought him face to face with dogs, understanding the terror that vicious ivory jaws can instill in a naked and defenseless man. Théverand, for his part, knew nothing, could tell them nothing. For Gaure, a superhuman energy was necessary. He put all his pride to the task, the pride that he had once told the abbé could replace faith in the heart of mankind. He was fighting again, and – though unaware of the emotions stirring within him – Gaure loved the battle. Against the will of his tormentors, his own stiffened. As early as the first encounter, he had noticed that beyond a certain point the blows no longer affect you, or at least no longer make you suffer. When ten men beat you relentlessly, the brutalized body no longer reacts. It is reduced to inert matter. The waiting was more painful than the trial itself. Gaure retained only his dread of dogs, but he masked his fright so well that the Germans never set them loose on him.

By the time Gaure passed from the hands of the policemen to those of a German magistrate, he had become little more than a machine made to suffer. He no longer reasoned, no longer sought the motives for his resistance, his desperate silence. It had become instinctual. Of his country, his friends, his ambitions, and his dreams, of all that his existence had been, nothing remained but a fierce stubbornness, an obstinate and invincible zeal for silence, something that resembled the willfulness of an exhausted animal. Gaure was already far from the pride, the self-confidence, the consciousness of human dignity upon which he had believed he could rely.

The magistrate's preliminary inquiry was quite routine. There were no blows, no insults, only simple, almost polite questions. Gaure recovered a little strength and managed to regain control of his faculties before the trial began.

The court martial convened in grand style in Lille's Palais de Justice. Gaure and Théverand had been brought by transport from Loos. Upon entering the vast, solemn, oak-panelled chamber, Théverand felt as if he were being crushed. A colonel presided, flanked by four captains in dress uniform, studded with decorations. On the bench lay swords and golden-spiked helmets. To the left were the public authorities, represented by an imperial prosecutor. Behind Gaure and Théverand, their lawyer sat at a desk. Théverand had never seen him, this German officer. And yet, because man will cling to any shred of hope, Théverand had confidence in the enemy who was supposed to defend him, who had accepted this responsibility. A defense attorney was something after all!

The presiding judge read the indictment: spying, possession of carrier pigeons, assistance given to men of military age crossing the Dutch border. Then the imperial prosecutor began to speak. Théverand listened in terror. One by one, the imperial prosecutor took up the counts of the indictment. After each, he called for the death penalty. Five or six times, in this long speech in German, Théverand recognized the word "death," repeated like a leitmotif. Seated on the bench beside Théverand, Gaure was dozing, indifferent and exhausted, buried in his overcoat, which hid his dirty nightshirt and his ragged old trousers. It was as if the proceedings were not about him. He did not even stir when the imperial prosecutor sat and their lawyer rose.

Théverand had turned round to watch his attorney. He gazed at him eagerly. He felt as if his life hung on the words this man was about to say. Never before had he fully understood the magnificent mission of a lawyer defending his client. At this moment, Théverand was ready to snatch at anything. There was still hope since he had an attorney, since he was allowed this support. In his heart he almost felt gratitude toward the judges, dreadful in their way, but who still retained respect for equity. Mustering all his attention, all his faculties, he pieced together the address of his defender:

"Gentlemen, the case is clear. I do not have much to add ... There is a law of war. Did these men violate it? If so, they can only be condemned to death."

He took his seat again.

Théverand remained sitting there, staggered, looking at this man – his attorney. What, that was it, his defense? This grotesque and sinister comedy? It was undoubtedly a joke. He was dazed, paralyzed ... He could not admit that such a travesty of justice could be anything but a farce. He waited for the proceedings to start over, for there to be something else, a genuine trial ... He watched in astonishment as the judges rose and retired, while at the rear of the chamber soldiers at attention presented arms, with a clap of metal. A gendarme touched his shoulder. He followed Gaure and walked slowly away.

Five days passed before Théverand learned the verdict. Still subject to Streng arrest, he waited anxiously in the darkness, thinking of his loved ones, of Gaure, of the life he had left behind. The noise of steps in the hall-way would make him spring up in fear and hope. These five days lasted an eternity. Finally one evening, gendarmes and officers entered his cell. Among them was his lawyer. Théverand, who was seated on his straw mat-tress, got to his feet.

"Your judges have just pronounced your sentence," said an officer in French.

"Oh, yes?"

"Death."

Théverand sat down. He felt as if he had received a vicious blow to the stomach. His mouth dry, his temples moist, he looked at the men around him. He repeated, "Death ... Death ..."

"You still have one hope, however, a petition for leniency ..."

The mind of man will jump enthusiastically at any possibility of salva-tion! This sufficed. Théverand felt alive again. For the days to come, his mind would have sustenance, a ray of light. A petition for leniency ...

The Germans departed, leaving him pacified, comforted by this new and fragile hope to which he now clung frantically.

II

Gaure was sitting in his cell amid the shadows. It must have still been light outside. But his skylight was boarded up. Feeling his way, Gaure slowly made the rounds of his room, moving his long, weakened legs with diffi-culty. He found his straw mattress and let himself fall upon it, indifferent to the vermin. He fished a scrap of paper from his pocket, rolled it into a tube, unhurriedly, as he would a cigarette, and inhaled as if he were smok-ing. The smell of his hands, the remnant of nicotine permeating his index finger, went to his head and intoxicated him. Since his imprisonment, he had suffered terribly from the absence of tobacco.

There was neither day nor night, only undifferentiated time, flowing like an eternal river; a single meal of bread and water, which he made last for hours; a dreadful boredom, a maddening intellectual void.

It had been two weeks or more since Gaure had signed his petition for leniency. He no longer knew exactly how long it had been.

Slowly the cold came. Outside, night was no doubt falling. The cold sig-nalled nighttime for Gaure. He groped for his old grey overcoat, slipped it on. He coughed long and hard. Though winded, he could finally breathe. He said aloud, "I don't think I'll pull through, even if pardoned ..." This made him think of Théverand. It was Gaure's great sorrow, his remorse. He had always understood Théverand, his naïvety, the element of obliviousness, of childishness that had thrown the man into this drama. *I should have warned him, enlightened him, dissuaded him,* thought Gaure. After all, it was a little his fault if Théverand had been caught. He had come to Gaure's; he had been arrested there. Gaure should not have let himself be taken in by that story about the meat. In his mind's eye he saw Théverand – thin, sad, feverish and distressed, awaiting the verdict of the tribunal, listening to his lawyer. He could envision Théverand's good, somewhat naïve face: the childlike look of the youngster who cannot accept, cannot understand ... And then there were wretched Théverand's wife and daughter ... Gaure cried, holding his face in his hands. For a while now, he had been crying readily, sometimes for no reason at all. The simple memory of certain of his students, even the ones he had considered indifferent, the idea that he would never see them again – it cut him to the core, without his quite understanding why. Everything had become precious to him ...

There were footsteps, a halt in front of his door. Gaure raised his head. The lock creaked. A pale light invaded the cell. Lifting his dazed and sick eyes, Gaure recognized human silhouettes ... Gendarmes. They approached him, seized his huge arms. Something cold bound his wrists ... Handcuffs. "No need," he said weakly. But the guards put them on forcibly. They took him under the arms and dragged him into the corridor, toward the outside. The cold, pure air affected him like a shot of hard liquor.

In the courtyard was a covered transport. They pushed him toward it. He climbed up laboriously. From inside, two Germans grabbed him by the shoulders, hauling him up. He sat down on a plank, a soldier to each side of him. They slid clips into their Mausers with a great flourish and cocked them with a snap. The tarp closed over the men. The vehicle started moving.

Gaure let himself be tossed about, dozing, almost indifferent. Weariness stupefied him. He was not troubled by this change of prison, so often had he been transferred from one cell to another. The swaying lulled him. A slowly dimming light filtered through the gaps of the tarp. Evening was coming. His strength gone, Gaure wavered, leaning toward one or the other of the guards. With a strong grasp, but without brutality, they sat him up again. By the time the vehicle stopped – after turning suddenly and passing under a sonorous archway – he could not tell if they had been travelling for an hour or merely ten minutes.

The guards opened the canvas tarp. Gaure stepped down. He was in a vast courtyard paved with cobblestones and framed by tall, sinister old buildings: barracks. The sight of the entryway through which he had just passed roused a specific memory: the citadel in Lille ... Soldiers encircled him. They removed his chains and led him toward an office whose lamp shone through the window like a bloody star in the grey twilight. He moved slowly, sustained by a remnant of pride, the desire to not let these men see him stumble. They pushed him gently. The evening cold bit through his shirt and his worn overcoat. The warmth of the office, where a little stove was roaring, did him good.

Inside were four or five scribes working at dark wooden tables. They cast curious glances at him. An officer came from a second room. He gave Gaure a military salute. To be polite, by way of response, Gaure raised his thin hand before his drawn face, whose drooping moustache seemed to have become disproportionately large.

"Sir," said the officer in good French, "I'm sorry, but your request for leniency has been denied. You'll be shot tomorrow morning."

Gaure did not utter a word. He cocked his head a bit, though he could not tell if it were from weakness or emotion. His lips stirred, but he did not speak. The Germans looked at him for a second.

"Take the gentleman away," said the officer.

Gaure departed, flanked by four men. They forced him up a dark stone stairway. He skirted a building that looked vaguely like a barn. Then he entered a large frozen passageway. At the end was a heavy grey door. The guards drew the bolts and pushed him into a cell. He went down four or five stone steps. Two candles, cigarettes, ink, and paper had been left on a table. The door shut behind him.

He was in a room three metres by four, with walls of rough-hewn rock and flagstone pavers. It contained a table, a stool, and in one corner a few stone steps rising toward the door. A doleful austerity pervaded the entire chamber.

Gaure coughed. His hacking created a hollow echo in the crypt. He said aloud, "So, I'm going to die tomorrow ..." His voice sounded strange. The circumstances stirred no thought in him. His mind seemed blank.

He walked around the cell. Once more the eternal, obsessive idea of the prisoner came to him: escape ... With a gesture that had almost become a habit, he cast a glance about. He went up to the door, the window. There was no possibility. He whispered again, "What am I going to do from now till tomorrow morning ..."

He sat down on the stool. He no longer had a single idea in his head. The minutes ticked away slowly. Time crept by. How long it would be to wait till tomorrow! The end seemed like it would never come. He repeated, "What boredom till tomorrow!" And all of a sudden, the idea that one could be bored like this, just a few hours from death, seemed unimaginable and grotesque. He suddenly realized that the time he was wasting, letting escape into the void, was all of his life, all there was left for him to live. And he was bored! He gave a start, stood so abruptly that he sent his seat tumbling to the floor. To think that time was flying away, that he only had a few hours ahead of him! He must live! Live! Use the remaining hours, avail himself of them like a treasure, greedily, savouring the seconds, enjoying them drop by drop ... But how? What to do? How to spend them best? How to relish them till the last moment? A thousand ideas beset him, a thousand mad, incoherent ideas. There were so many things to do, so many memories to recall, so many different perspectives on the world and on himself! So many thoughts, so many ways to make use of this poor remnant of life that he was submerged, suffocated, unable to choose ... And this with the awareness, the fury, the despair of feeling time elude and escape from him, like precious blood ebbing away ... He had a fit of insane delirium. It took all his might to keep from throwing himself against the door, the window, lashing out, howling, one way or another unleashing his passion to live, to defend himself and fight. He turned in his prison like a tiger, foaming with rage. Then he got control himself and sat on the stool. He heard his heart pounding in his clammy chest. He caught sight of the white paper on the table. He averted his eyes in disgust. Write? To what end? Tomorrow morning he would be dead, annihilated. Did it matter what the future held for the others since he would no longer know, no longer exist? And again the horror rose in him, a savage upsurge of instinctive selfishness ...

Beside the candle was a pack of cigarettes. He stretched out his hand, grabbed it, retrieved a cigarette, and lit it. It sickened him, filling him with true disgust. He furiously threw the whole pack on the floor, nauseated by the thought of this solitary gratification – animalistic and useless – only a few hours from death. Time was too precious, too infinitely precious to lose smoking a cigarette! Smoking, wasting such seconds in a childish gesture! He who had wanted to take advantage of these moments like a treasure, to be useful one final time, at the last, in one stroke complete his human task, the mysterious labour to which we all are called – which he knew was slipping away, unfinished, and which he had wanted to conclude, fulfill in one night, so he could die with a peaceful spirit. And once more the recognition of his powerlessness to accomplish anything, of the situation in which he found himself – waiting and growing bored, thinking of the seconds which were now so precious and solemn as slow to pass – threw him into fury and despair ... For a few minutes he was like a madman. He feared being forced, in spite of himself, to face the idea he wanted to avoid at all costs: annihilation. He could feel the presence of this idea – obsessive, ready to spring up, to impose itself. He pushed it aside with all his might, spent the rest of his energy pacing to and fro, wringing his hands, cursing heaven ... Exhausted, bathed in sweat, he sat back down on his stool.

He was cold. Over his nightshirt he rebuttoned his old woolen overcoat – worn, shapeless, more blanket than clothing – in which he was going to die, for weeks his companion in agony and which would go with him to the grave ... Everything, decidedly, brought Gaure back to this ultimate horror. He suddenly stood, ran to the door, haunted by the frenzied desire to cry out, beg, implore ... Men were on the other side, men like him. They could not let him die. They would have pity on his lamentations, his groans, his outcries, his dismay. In front of the closed door, the enormous grey panel covered in iron plate, he raised his fists to shout, bellow like an animal. Only a final flash, a remnant of pride, kept him from his mistake ...

"Gaure, Gaure, you mustn't."

He returned to the stool, sat down, and put his head in his hands.

"But what? I don't have the heart, then! I don't know how to look death in the face!"

He recalled his parents, their peaceful end, their serenity when he had witnessed their final breath ... What a contrast with the rebellion, the insanity which he hurled at this door, moaning and blaspheming. Yes, but they had believed. For them death was nothing but a radiant awakening. For him ... The memory of the Abbé Sennevilliers and their old and pleasant friendship came to mind, bringing tears to his eyes. His heart grew tender as he cried. He seemed to become a man again, escaping insanity. He leaned his arm on the table, burying his emaciated head in it, with his hair, now white, falling in long, stiff strands over his ears and his neck. He sobbed uncontrollably, shamelessly, for a long time.

Comforted, he straightened up. From the pocket of his wretched overcoat, he took the bit of lining that served as his handkerchief and wiped his eyes. With an instinctive gesture, he stretched his hand toward the pen and paper, to address a melancholy greeting one last time, from beyond the grave, to the only friend he would miss ...

Father Sennevilliers,

I am going to die tomorrow morning. I write to inform you. And I cannot accept that nothing will be left of me when you read these lines. I am overwhelmed by terror. If I were to let myself go, I would fall at the feet of my executioners and humiliate myself piteously ...

Take heart, I will hold out. But I do not know what I would do if a cowardly act could save me at this moment ... Do not let anyone portray me as a hero later on. I am ashamed of myself, of my miserable weakness as a man. You were right, before ... Morality cannot be built on oneself, on the consciousness of one's human dignity, on pride ... Pride bends.

Farewell. My death makes no sense. It's illogical, since I believe in nothing. Why am I going to die? For nothing. I will die without knowing what bid me act. And yet I have the inexplicable certainty of having done well ... But why did I embark on this adventure? What impelled me? And why do I have the feeling that I would do it all again, if I had to start over. Yes, I will die without having understood myself ...

I think of you, my house, my work. Nothing is more beautiful than life! How I would like to live ...!

He wrote the address. Expressing his moral anguish had brought him some relief. With the letter finished and set on a corner of the table, his renewed inactivity – the sudden cessation of mental work – again gave rise to an impression of emptiness and horror. Over – tomorrow it would be over! The mass of knowledge, memories, affection, tenderness that comprised his being, the consciousness of living, the inward gaze of his mind's eye, none of it would exist anymore, as if the world were coming to an end ... And why? For nothing. Sennevilliers had his God, Théverand his country. For Gaure the chemist, these words stood only for a slow atavistic development. He had nothing, had searched in vain for something. Why then had he heeded this deep, illogical impulse which reason alone could not explain? Nothing should have been more precious to him than the pleasure of living. Yet at this final hour, he was startled to sense that, inexplicable though it may seem, he could not have acted more logically, and that he was ready, had it been possible, to do it all again ...

Oddly, abruptly, it was at this instant that he remembered the prophetic saying, the words he had never wanted to understand, which he still spurned with all the power of his mind but which forced themselves upon his heart, softening it, and which suddenly took on immense meaning, leaving him at once frightened and overcome by a sweetness he had never known, a vague unbounded hope ...

*Be of good cheer. You would not seek me if you had not found me ...**

• • •

Around five o'clock in the morning, a squad of soldiers reached Théverand's cell. They opened the door. He stepped into the corridor. There stood a priest whose services Théverand had accepted the day before. He was German. He had put his cassock over his uniform. Beneath the hem, his army boots could be seen.

The passageway was dark, poorly illumined by a lantern. The soldiers were waiting. Théverand stumbled into something, looked down, and saw two long boxes made from thin planks of white pine. He gave a frightful start and went livid.

The officer approached him: "You're afraid?"

"No," said Théverand, trembling, his teeth clenched.

"Come," said the officer, "don't be stupid. In ten minutes, you'll be lying in that box. You have accomplices, we know it. Give us their names and we'll pardon you ... Think of your wife, your child, life ... Look here, consider it, I'll give you three minutes."

---

*A quotation from Blaise Pascal's *Pensées* (1669).

"I won't consider it!" Théverand shouted hoarsely. And he pushed the officer aside, quickly walking of his own accord toward the exit.

It was cold outside. The morning wind was blowing. It was only the very beginning of spring. The citadel slept in silence. The long buildings rose in sinister masses. A pale glow lit the grey sky. The group skirted one side of the immense courtyard. They went out through an arched doorway and crossed the drawbridge. Then they immediately turned to the left and descended a naked staircase hung upon the side of a sloping wall and leading to the bottom of the citadel's large moats. At this moment, turning round, Théverand saw Gaure following behind, tall, emaciated, and ascetic-looking in his old grey overcoat. His long, white hair floated in the breeze. The two men spoke not a word.

They walked along the bottom of the huge moat, cut into small, barren gardens, which the soldiers cultivated in summertime. At present nothing was left but rigid cabbage stems, a few dead hedges, a cask of liquid manure, and some heaps of dry leaves. Winter had clearly passed through. In the middle of the moat, dividing the shallows in two, was a narrow stream of green water filled with rushes. Tall, pitched, gloomy walls enclosed this wild ravine, whose damp soil clung to the soles of their shoes.

They arrived at the corner of a long wall. Two soldiers had detached from the squad, taking Théverand by the arms and dragging him toward the wall with a rough gesture that undoubtedly masked their anxiety. The rest of the squad had formed a line.

Théverand stood at the foot of the wall. The officer stepped forward, a blindfold in hand. Théverand pushed it away, refusing with an almost unconscious shake of the head. He buttoned his jacket, slowly, instinctively, with the childlike and automatic gesture of a man who wants to remain proper. He looked at Gaure ... Up to that point, Théverand had lived as if in a dream, far from reality. Last night he had written three letters, three brave letters to his wife, his little girl, and a friend, three letters in which he had called on them to take heart, to regret nothing, to think of France, for which he would cheerfully die. Now he had no explanation for all of this, it no longer made sense. And he gave Gaure a bewildered look, almost infantile, which seemed to question Gaure, asking him if it were really true, really possible that he would be killed here, that it would all end this way ...

"Théverand! Théverand!" sobbed Gaure, stretching his arms toward him ...

Gaure's turn had come. He made the same unconscious gesture as Théverand, buttoning his old grey overcoat over his shirt ... He looked around, absorbing this last terrestrial sight, this wild scenery, in a single glance: the long, sad walls of the rifle-pit topped by a grassy embankment, the huge moat – with its sharp corners – cut into small, pitiful gardens ravaged by winter, and the sky above, high, clear, a very pale blue, dappled with rose-coloured clouds, where dawn was breaking ...

III

It must have been Gaure's death that frightened the publisher Thorel. He had not been to the factory in Épeule for several weeks now. Hennedyck and Marc were glad of it, quite pleased to find themselves delivered from such a pretentious and disagreeable fellow. Then, through the medium of Clavard the typesetter, Hennedyck received a letter from Thorel. It was awkward and decidedly convoluted. It explained that there had been a number of searches in Lille, at the headquarters of *The Lantern*. The Germans must have noticed the disappearance of a portion of his equipment. To avoid the risk of trial and imprisonment, Thorel found himself obliged to ask his friends to return the machinery he had loaned them, for the time being.

Hennedyck, beside himself, rushed to Lille that very day. He found Thorel at home, seated in a vast Empire-style office hung with green velvet wallpaper. In this artistic setting, amid an accumulation of knickknacks and museum pieces, Thorel was smoking his usual cigar while reviewing some personnel accounts. Since it was rather dark in the room, Hennedyck could not see the unease on the publisher's face.

"I received this letter, Thorel."

"Ah, yes, yes ..."

"And I've come to ask what it's supposed to mean ..."

"Nothing more or less than what I wrote to you, Hennedyck. The Germans are taking an inventory of my equipment. I'm afraid that ..."

"You're afraid? And you're leaving us in the lurch! You're forgetting your commitments, the interest of our country, our work? It's unacceptable."

"I have my position," said Thorel. "And I'm diabetic. The prison diet ... I can't get by on pleasantries."

"Sell us the type and the paper, if you want to pull out."

"I tell you again, the Germans will notice these things are missing!"

"If it's a question of money, name your price. I'll buy the equipment. I'll draw up a draft payable after the war, in fabric, in whatever form you'd like ..."

"It's not a question of money," said Thorel.

Hennedyck flew into a rage.

"So, you really want to put an end to the paper?"

"Me? Me?"

"You don't suppose it can continue without you or your *Lantern*? Is that it?"

"No, that's not what I meant! I ..."

"Very well, keep your equipment. I don't want it anymore! Tomorrow you'll have your type, and the newspaper will carry on!"

"But you're talking nonsense, Hennedyck! You've lost your head! Such words!"

Frightened, dismayed, he ran behind Hennedyck, grabbed him by the arm. The manufacturer wrenched himself free and left.

Hennedyck took the tram back to Roubaix. He was very concerned. No more paper, no more type. How would they keep going? Where would they find new equipment? At present they could not dream of interrupting a project that had become so vital for so many people. The issues of *Loyalty*, the wonderful little pages that passed from hand to hand, that brought news, the truth, that sowed a bit of hope – Hennedyck could understand their enormous significance, the unbelievable influence they had on the morale of his fellow citizens. No one, apart from a few insiders, knew who published the paper. Most thought it was a French production dropped by airplane or smuggled across the Dutch frontier. No one suspected Hennedyck or the abbé, to the point that several times people had told *them* about *Loyalty*, even bringing them copies, in total ignorance of their role: "Look here, read, see!"

Hennedyck and the abbé took the pages with emotion and put them back into circulation, as messengers of hope. They were encouraged and rewarded by the sight of such joy, such comfort among those who read the paper and passed it along. Yes, it was necessary work, a task they could not just abandon, since without it their lives would have seemed empty and purposeless.

I'll make the rounds of all the publishers in Roubaix and Tourcoing, thought Hennedyck. *I'll find paper and type all right. As for Thorel, his equipment must go back this week. I won't use even one piece of his type, by God!* The difficulty lay in returning items to Lille. Thorel was insisting on it. Hennedyck had seen through Thorel: he was afraid, and, furthermore, he did not want the newspaper of the occupied territories to survive without him, to escape the *The Lantern*'s tutelage. Thorel was consumed by limitless ambition. He had foreseen huge rewards after the war, in compensation for his heroism. Now that the prize was slipping from his grasp, others must not reap the benefits. Behind all this, at bottom, was perhaps the fear that this cursed little underground rag would persist in the wake of the war, this time above board, and with a successful launch – profiting from the enormous popularity attached to its name and the identification of its creators – topple *The Lantern* outright. On certain occasions, Thorel looked extremely far ahead. Obviously, the best way to ruin *Loyalty* was to demand his equipment. Without type, Hennedyck would be left with nothing but a useless printing press.

His pride at stake, Hennedyck put all his energy to the task at hand. Thorel would have his goods, but the paper would continue. The problem was returning the equipment. Pascal Donadieu, exasperated by the demands of the Germans on the tramway, had abandoned his job as driver. Walking down boulevard de Paris, toward his house, Hennedyck suddenly had an idea: the ambulance.

The hospital he had established at his factory in Épeule remained in operation. Hennedyck and his wife got along much better with Major von Mesnil, the new head doctor who had arrived several months ago, than with his predecessors. This von Mesnil was still young and of high culture. At the beginning of the occupation, the hospital in Épeule had been a source of great stress for Émilie Hennedyck. She had had to deal with savage, hateful, tyrannical majors, men who made poor wounded Englishmen – occasionally brought in pell-mell with the Germans – suffer real torture. These physicians went as far as refusing to administer chloroform and operating on patients who were fully conscious. And they left them alone among wounded Saxons and Prussians, resulting in fresh battles between the dying.

Von Mesnil proved to be much more humane. He had completed his medical studies in Paris. He spoke French as fluently as his own language.

Through his offices, Émilie had obtained a notable improvement in the treatment of English prisoners. He put his duty as a doctor first, tolerating gifts, packages, even the occasional letter for the Englishmen. Émilie had been able to set up a clean and healthy ward for them, have them given almost the same daily fare as the German wounded, and ensure them fresh linen, strolls in the courtyard, conversations and readings in the company of fellow countrymen. Several times von Mesnil had spared Hennedyck significant requisitions by giving him advance warning of pending searches. Then Émilie had fallen ill. She was a nervous type constantly on edge, drained by hospital work, by worry, by the unending sight of the misery around her. She had always been prone to sickness. Von Mesnil, who lived in a room at the Hennedycks', looked after her. He was an odd doctor in the opinion of Hennedyck, who, perfectly healthy himself, was in a poor position to judge the all-too-common impotence of classical medicine.

Von Mesnil prescribed neither drugs nor stimulants nor injections. A detailed calculation of dietary intake, a strict supervision of expenditures of heat and work, of physical and mental strength – a treatment more psychological than physiological – restored Émilie to health rather quickly. To her great astonishment, Émilie gradually realized that just by living, working, and going about her business, dispensing with shots and remedies, sticking to an almost normal pace of life, she no longer had reason to consider herself sickly, and this for a woman who had been watching for death ever since childhood. Émilie accorded von Mesnil boundless gratitude, and the doctor had since become a real friend of the Hennedycks.

Hennedyck's plan was simple. He would ask the doctor for an ambulance to move some textiles on the sly, and instead load Thorel's material. A hundred mark bill to the driver would do the trick. Hennedyck went home quite pleased. As he was hanging up his overcoat in the hallway, he saw von Mesnil's big grey cloak and realized that the major had returned.

Von Mesnil was on the verandah with Émilie. As Hennedyck was entering, he stopped in the doorway, surprised, vaguely captivated by the charm of the sight that lay before him.

Positioned behind an easel, pencil in hand, von Mesnil was sketching Émilie's silhouette. She was posing, seated on a high ebony stool in front of the large open piano, her motionless fingers brushing the keys, her face turned three quarters toward the doctor. Seen like this from behind – back arched, thin, fragile, in a long black dress whose train spread beneath her, swallowing her tiny feet – she looked surprisingly elongated and almost immaterial. Her black silhouette merged into the shadows. The only feature illuminated, in a sort of chimerical twilight, was her delicate face – pointed, sharp, triangular – a face almost without cheekbones or cheeks and seemingly overwhelmed by an enormous head of dark, heavy hair. Toward von Mesnil she turned her huge, deep black eyes. These fixed and vaguely uneasy eyes – vast eyes, like those painted by English portraitists – consumed her whole face, giving her the anxious and frightened expression of a sick child ...

Without daring to move, she murmured, "Good evening, Patrice," in response to her husband's affectionate gesture. And her eyes returned to von Mesnil. The soft tone of her voice always trembled, somewhat like a poorly restrained internal vibration. Hennedyck was madly in love with Émilie, his "child-wife," as he called her, in remembrance of Old Dickens.* He spared her every trouble, watching over her just like a child. He had hidden the entire the business with *Loyalty* from her. She knew nothing of the risks he was running.

Von Mesnil promised the ambulance. His skepticism willingly accommodated itself to this entertaining little conspiracy with a French manufacturer. Von Mesnil believed in nothing, not even the country he served – loyally, to be sure, but more from a deep-seated instinct than from reason. He returned to his sketch.

Émilie had resumed her pose. A bit weary, apparently lost in thought, she looked at the doctor and, without realizing it, gave him a smile, a vague, dreamy half-smile...

• • •

Thorel had his equipment three days later. Clavard and the Abbé Sennevilliers dismantled it. And an ambulance from the German army transferred it to the headquarters of *The Lantern*. Hennedyck still had the press that a local newspaper had provided him. A brave ironmaster cast some type for him. And he managed to purchase a supply of butter paper on

---

*A reference to Dora Spenlow, a character in Charles Dickens's novel *David Copperfield* (1849).

which it was just possible to print. After a two-week hiatus, *Loyalty* resumed production. Hennedyck treated himself to the petty revenge of sending Thorel a copy. It was unwise. The response was not long in coming. Seeing the paper continue without him made Thorel furious. Since Clavard the typesetter and Gilberte Pauret, the little typist, were his former employees, he summoned them to his house. He made it known that he would not take them back after the war if they kept working on *Loyalty* for Hennedyck. Clavard obeyed and asked Hennedyck for his remaining pay. Little Pauret stayed on with *Loyalty*. She had learned to set type and replaced Clavard as best she could.

"You're a heroine!" Hennedyck told her.

"Me," said Gilberte Pauret, amazed, "a heroine? You're joking, Mr Hennedyck. You pay me. I'm earning a living. That's all. No, no, it's ludicrous to say such things. Since you're paying me, I'm no heroine at all ..."

And the dear girl believed it.

Chapter Seven

I

Amid a savage winter wind that nipped at her face and pierced her threadbare clothes, Old Berthe Sennevilliers was going for rations. Her daughter Lise was ill. For three days they had not eaten. For two days Old Berthe had trudged from farm to farm, vainly seeking an egg for her daughter. She had roamed the entire village, from street to street, house to house, across the plowed fields, the slimy paths, the broken and greasy roads, her last forty-cent bill in her hand, with a blanket over her head and old men's ankle boots on her feet. Drained by privation, Lise had come down with pneumonia and was running a fever. Neither medicine nor money, nor even a fire or a fresh egg, was available for her care. The Germans had taken everything. Berthe had combed the countryside, offering her paltry forty-cent note. No one had helped. The farmers kept their eggs for the Germans and sold the ones they managed to hide at enormous prices in Tourcoing.

In several spots – at Lacombe's, at Humfels's – Berthe had seen relative ease, well-being, the tranquility of these men of the earth who were not suffering from hunger. At Humfels's bread was baking, a golden loaf of almost pure flour, whose smell had made her head swim with want. At Lacombe's there was a roaring fire in the hearth, a bright, red-hot fire fed by packing crates from the ration program. Berthe had intentionally protracted her stay to warm herself a tad longer.

She had finally returned home, wet, frozen, her feet bloody, her back iced over. In a kitchen without food or fuel, she had found her daughter tucked in a bed of straw, her speech rambling. And nothing could be done but wait for the next day, when rations were distributed, when Berthe would go to look for bread and perhaps a little milk ...

The Sennevilliers were too envied, too hated in the village to hope for an ounce of pity from anyone. And they were intransigent, inflexible types who did not argue or debate matters of principle. One did not steal, one did not associate with the enemy. These rules were inviolable. Neither Berthe nor her daughter would have thought of going into the fields to steal a beet or a sheaf of wheat from the stack. They even kept their hands off the goods of the enemy. The Germans stole, pillaged, plundered? So much the worse for them. A bad example is not to be followed. In the midst of the general degradation, the Sennevilliers remained representatives of morality, of dignity, and as a result suffered, bore the weight of the war more than the rest. For them there was no compromise: neither trafficking, nor theft, nor exchange with the enemy. Embittered, weakened and sick, obstinate in their rigidity, in their stubbornness as French citizens and upright women, they witnessed with disgust the ignominy, the prostitution, the capitulation of the others and, to reestablish balance and justice, hoped for nothing more than an ultimate, distant, belated French victory, which they might never see ...

The blessed day of the distribution had finally arrived. Still covered in her blanket, carter's shoes on her feet, nose red, face pale, eyes bleary, skin bitten by the cold, Old Berthe approached the schoolhouse, where a crowd had gathered, and entered the classroom in which the food was dispensed. The space was packed with folks smelling of wet wool, sweat, and poverty. A black, cast-iron stove warmed the middle of the room, and people were scrambling to get close to it. Toward the back, the space was cordoned off by a partition behind which the distributors sat. There were two windows. At one, Marellis was dispensing bread and canned goods. At the other, Leuil – Lacombe's friend, who had replaced Sérez the schoolmaster – was handing out rice, peas, and dried vegetables. But his window was built in such a way that he could not see those to whom he was passing the food. And behind him a big, complex machine, contrived by Pascal Donadieu, distributed the rations automatically, weighing and measuring them to the nearest half-gram. Before Donadieu had devised this mechanism, Leuil's measure had consisted of a tin can in the bottom of which he put wooden disks to determine the shares. But Marellis had noticed that

Leuil removed the disks for his friends. And Marellis had demanded a method of mechanical distribution and a window through which Leuil could no longer see the people he served.

Marellis had begun the distribution of bread and honey. The crowd pressed round his window, grabbing the bread – balls of blackish putty. Many immediately took a bite, tore off a mouthful. Families parcelled it out, divided it on the spot, each jealously carrying away his morsel. They argued, asked Marellis to split it up and weigh the ration for each individual, one at a time. Hunger killed the spirit of family, of tenderness. A certain level of well-being is needed for man to remain man. Inside the round loaves, beneath a stony crust, one found a ball of dough – unbaked, sticky, separated like a yolk in its shell. This ball was oftentimes mouldy, sprinkled with crystals of red salt which had a bitter and almost rotten taste. The villagers showed them to Marellis: "Isn't this rubbish disgusting?" And Marellis raised his hands toward the ceiling: "What'd you want me to do? I can only give what I'm given!"

He had no desire to spread bitterness and rebellion in the village. But he could see how the quality of bread had become even worse since Orchon alone had been baking bread for the ration program. Baille, by far the better baker of the two, had been ousted on the pretext that having two bakers complicated the distribution. Orchon, who bought firewood for his bakery from Lacombe and who agreed to make a hundred kilos of bread from eighty kilos of wheat, had obtained a monopoly from the ration board and abused his advantage. To the already inedible KK flour, he added powder from ground kidney beans and roasted potatoes. And since he then kneaded poorly and did not follow German instructions for the rising and baking of the dough, his bread was revolting. Salt was in short supply. The Germans had had the idea of using crystals from the brine left in casks of American meat. Instead of soaking and dissolving the crystals in water which would later be used in the kneading trough, Orchon tossed them into the dough as they were, solid and specked with blood. They did not dissolve and were to be found, intact and disgusting, in the middle of the insipid and tasteless bread. But Orchon was Lacombe's buddy.

Marellis pressed on with the distribution. He collected the local currency, handing out loaves of bread in exchange. Many folks timidly asked for credit because often they did not even have enough to pay for this meager allotment of food, and Lacombe only gave indigent cards to his friends. Some villagers, having run out of currency but still possessing a little gold, a jewel, or a ring, brought it and gave it to Marellis: "Sir, keep it for me till next week, I'll pay what I owe."

Others brought a gold coin, a ten-franc piece – a distant memory of the old days – preserved like a talisman.

"Mr Marellis, please don't put it in right away, hold onto it for a couple of days ... Perhaps we can redeem it."

Thus did he see a louis d'or* brought to him ten times and ten times recovered, like a precious token, in a miracle of stubbornness and attachment. Certain people as well, bereft of everything but too proud to admit it, asked for just one loaf and a cube of honey for a family of four, a paltry ration that would not even sustain them for a couple of days: "We don't have much appetite, since we're not working anymore ..." And these types became more numerous from week to week. For the last louis, the last bit of cash, always ended up being spent. This war, it was lasting too long.

The townspeople were thin and pale. Hunger and suffering had wasted away at their faces. One would have thought oneself among a nation of ascetics. There were signs of frightful physiological distress: sties, carbuncles and spots, jaundice, ringworm, scabs between the fingers, scurvy of the gums, strumous abscesses in the neck and behind the ears. Coughing, wheezing, a moaning murmur filled the room. People warmed themselves with delight and discretion. It seemed that they were no longer accustomed to fire. Near Berthe, a twenty-year-old woman carrying a baby quietly swooned and fell, seized by a fainting fit upon feeling the warmth. She was set on her feet again, without causing a stir. It was a common occurrence. Each week, two or three collapsed in like fashion.

Berthe's turn had come. She approached Marellis's window. He recognized her: "How's it going, Mrs Sennevilliers?"

"Not too bad ..."

He set three loaves on the counter. She pushed them back and asked: "No milk? Lise's sick ..."

"Sick? Her, too? Alas, no, Ma'am, no milk today."

"Well, I'll take the bread at least."

*A coin worth 20 francs.

But she only took two loaves. Awkwardly she explained: "We just need a couple. No sense to waste, right?"

And she set off. She had warmed up a little. The cold now seemed less harsh to her. She thought of Lise, who could not take advantage of the fire. Fortunately, she was bringing her the bread. Berthe sniffed the grey ball, which smelled of sour rye. She was salivating. She wanted to run.

As she reached the corner of the square, a big transport arrived, a huge wagon with sideboards drawn by two sweaty and fuming horses. Perched on the seat, a German was driving them forward. When the wagon passed Old Berthe, she saw an urchin jump off the back and roll to the ground holding onto an enormous bloc of coal wrapped in his arms. He got up and disappeared at full speed.

Coal! In three seconds, an ethical dilemma played out in Berthe Sennevilliers's mind.

A long history of honesty, an inflexible line of conduct, sixty-five years of rigid principles ... One does not steal. It was a great barrier. But before her lay doubt ... Lise was sick, burning with fever, lying on an icy bed, her teeth chattering, without milk, without bread, without heat ... And then there was the example of the others, the general collapse of values and consciences. Stealing from the Boches, it served them right. And the suffering endured because of them! And the devastated quarry, the ruined inn ... And Jean who was dead ... To do like the others, like everybody else ...

She suddenly made a dash, as if something had hurled her toward the wagon. She ran behind it, raised her arms, stretched two greedy old hands toward the load of coal, pulled out a bloc ...

"Hey! Hey! It's ours."

The voice froze her. She remained motionless, hesitated a second before daring to turn toward the person who had just yelled. She recognized Hérard, the delegate on the ration board. He was red with fury. He shouted: "Little old thief, have you no shame! Rich people like you, stealing coal from the rations! Oh, this'll cost you dearly!"

Berthe Sennevilliers looked at him with her big, grey, haggard eyes. She was shaking. She had dropped the bloc of coal, which lay broken at her feet. People were already flocking together, surrounding her. She surveyed them with a bewildered look. Lacombe the mayor, Marellis, Donadieu, Guégain the barber: they were all there. But she recognized no one. She had only one thought in her head: her infamy, her dishonour. She had stolen, she had been caught stealing. Sixty years of honesty and courage to come to this ...

In front of her, swollen with anger and self-importance, filled with the ready indignation of the man of honour faced with a crime, Hérard continued to berate her: "Stealing coal from the poor! The mother of a soldier! The mother of a priest! There's an example for you ..."

"The Germans ..." whispered Berthe Sennevilliers.

"What! The Germans?"

She murmured, "I thought it was the Germans' ... There was a German ... I assumed ..."

Hérard was not listening. He shouted, "What? What're you babbling about?"

She said no more. What was the point? It was over now, she was a thief. In everyone's eyes, she was a thief. Instinctively, in a last miserable desire for decency, she unconsciously brushed the front of her blue apron, sweeping away the coal dust, while Hérard stormed, "You'll pay dearly! I'm cutting you off from all rations for a month! You'll have to manage on your own! Get moving!"

She pushed through the crowd and headed out, a little redness in her pale cheeks and her hands trembling. She heard an indistinct murmur around her, a hubbub of sorts, without knowing if the crowd reacted from shock or pity, without daring to fasten her eyes on a single face. She was afraid of dropping dead on the spot before getting away from all these people. She was finally able to extricate herself, to take off on the road to Herlem Hill, her head buzzing, her cheeks hot, her legs unsteady. She no longer thought of the cold, the hunger, the bread she was taking to her sick daughter. She had only one thought, one obsession: she was a thief ... It seemed to her that she had still been immensely happy, in her wretchedness, a short time ago. To think that the crime was irreparable, indelible, that till her last day she would carry this shame before the world and within her being! ... For a moment she hesitated to return to the quarry, to confess to Lise, "I stole." It took the thought of her sick daughter, the sight of the bread – the life she was carrying – for her to muster the courage to go home again.

In the square, the villagers had watched in consternation as she departed. They were afraid to touch the coal she had let fall. They looked at the black dust, the fragments, like things accursed. It was Leuil who, with a broom and a bit of cardboard, swept up the mess and took it away, while Lacombe, Marellis, and the others went back to the ration room to serve themselves after the public distribution. The clerks always got their rations last. Marellis took his bread and collected his share of kidney beans and dried peas like the others. He was more than a little surprised to see Hérard give him a can of condensed milk in addition to his allotment.

"Where'd this come from?" asked Marellis.

"What ... You don't want it? As you please. It's optional. Two francs twenty a can today."

"I didn't know there was milk," said Marellis. "I didn't offer it to anyone. I even refused some folks who asked. Why was I not told?"

"We must've forgotten."

"And why wasn't a sign put up to tell people there was milk for two francs twenty a can?"

"We must've forgotten," repeated Hérard.

"And besides, we couldn't have," interjected Leuil, who had come back for his rations. "There wasn't enough for everyone, and all the villagers would've wanted some."

"It ought not to have been forgotten," said Marellis. "Instead the milk should've been kept for the sick ... I don't see any reason why we should get to take advantage of all the things in short supply, on the grounds that rationing them is impossible."

"'Taking advantage'!" Who's talking of taking advantage?" yelled Lacombe. "We're paying for this milk, we're not stealing it."

"We're paying two francs a can, yes, when it costs eighteen in the grocery stores. It isn't honest."

"You're free to refuse," sneered Premelle the secretary.

"I do refuse, to be sure!"

But upon reflection, Marellis suppressed his outrage and bought four cans of milk to take to the Sennevilliers.

II

Berthe and Lise Sennevilliers had to do without rations for a month. They suffered cruelly from hunger. They spent most of the time in bed, huddled together for warmth, keeping hunger at bay by sucking on a ball of bread wrapped in a piece of cloth, such as little children are given. Marellis shared what he could with them. Meanwhile, when Berthe could pull up a stake or an old stump from some hedge or in a meadow, she would make a fire. She cooked green cabbage stalks, the tall stringy stems still to be found in gardens after winter. Red cabbage stalks had to be eaten raw: they took too long to cook.

But, had it not been for the Germans, the two women would have starved to death. It was the Germans who saw them through. They had discovered – how no one knew – that the two wretches had been cut off from rations in the village. The Germans themselves were starting to understand what hunger was. Berthe, who had given up all pride since her downfall, collected scrapings from the bottom of their bowls, remnants from the canteen. At nighttime, soldiers sometimes brought a can of leftover grub, which the women found frozen at their doorstep in the morning.

The case of the Sennevilliers was a source of great debate for the ration board. At the preliminary session, the commanding colonel announced his departure. The officer who would succeed him was requisitioning the town hall in its entirety. A house had to be found for the archives and for Premelle, the town secretary. The colonel also levied a war tax of 30,000 francs – it had become a customary practice – and a fine of 4,000 francs for insufficient deliveries of milk and eggs by the farmers.

The ration board conducted its business as soon as the colonel left. Marellis argued, protested vehemently. Events had proven him right: the Committee for Relief in Belgium, tired of receiving no money, informed of the waste and the total lack of bookkeeping, was insisting on accounts and regular payments, separation of the commune's receipts from those collected for the ration program. The latter were to be deposited in full with the Committee. Marellis had been demanding these measures for a long time. He also protested the monopoly on bread awarded to Orchon.

"You yourself asked for only one baker," objected Lacombe.

"That's no reason for choosing the worst! Baille's bread was at least edible. Were straws even drawn before giving the monopoly to Orchon? It's just like this punishment inflicted on the Sennevilliers, and which the enemy itself finds dishonourable! By what right do you assume authority to judge and punish, Mr Hérard? The case should've been submitted directly to the Committee. And now, Mr Mayor, who's going to pay this 4,000-franc fine that the Germans are imposing on us?"

"The fine? But ... Who do you expect to pay, if not the commune?"

"So, you sell your eggs and your milk, your butter and your cheese to the Germans, you get three pfennigs an egg, five pfennigs a litre for milk, you take this money. And when it's a matter of settling accounts for an insufficient delivery, it's the commune – that's to say everyone – who pays! And you consider this just! It's dishonest!"

But they let him bluster. They met his anger, his efforts, with the quiet, stubborn obstinacy of the farmer, the peasant, whose great strength is inertia. Against their sluggish and crafty natures, Marellis fumed in vain. By way of petty vengeance, Lacombe, who managed to gain the favour of the new district commandant right away, suggested that he designate Marellis's house as the new locale for the offices of the municipality, which had been forced out of town hall. Marellis had to move and went to live with his wife and little girl in a hovel at the edge of the village, while Premelle set himself up in his house, from which Marellis had not even been able to retrieve the furniture.

Marellis nonetheless won a point of principle. He had complained to the Committee about the punishment inflicted on the Sennevilliers. The Committee informed its delegate Hérard that it was prohibiting any punishment of this sort in the future, and that all such cases had to be submitted directly to it, for the Committee to take timely measures of its own choosing.

It was about this time, a little after the March thaw, that the big rains came. The pond that hemmed in Lacombe's farm overflowed, flooding the basement of the farmhouse. Round the village, the German soldiers who helped pump it out told folks that they had heard cans of food and condensed milk floating in the water and knocking into each other, and that they had seen the farm dogs lapping water dumped in the ditches, because it was sweet.

But no one dared repeat such rumours.

• • •

The entire complement of German troops occupying Herlem departed with the old district commander. Albrecht, the manager on Lacombe's farm, set off like the others, leaving Judith behind.

She learned of the news a week in advance and lived in anguish. It was over, everything was falling apart. She had no future ahead of her. Albrecht was leaving Herlem for Belgium. He would never return. After the war, perhaps ... But how would a German dare come back to France following the war? She nevertheless tried to imagine such a return. She dreamed of an impossible path to citizenship, or the flight of both toward America, the unknown. Or she saw herself crossing the border, rejoining Albrecht in Germany under a false name, becoming German like him and for him. They were chimeras, absurd dreams, with which she numbed her despair as with a drug.

Albrecht, for his part, said nothing. This big strong boy, with impudent and irritating poise, continued his quiet life, his plowing and his sowing, coming back to Judith's in the evening neither more nor less cheerful, losing neither a bit of appetite nor a minute of sleep. This impassiveness tortured Judith and, occasionally, reassured her. Such monstrous indifference was impossible. He must have been certain of returning. She questioned him. He laughed, "Yes, yes, I'll return. You know I'll come back before the end of the war. And we'll be together for good."

"And if you're beaten?"

"We won't be beaten." He believed in the destiny of his Kaiser.

"And if you're beaten anyway?"

"I'll take you back to Germany with me."

The final evening he asked her to cook some cabbage and a pork loin, which he had brought home. He had hunted down some beer and four bottles of vintage wine. He returned with two buddies and two village women of ill repute whom Judith recognized. They all had dinner together. Judith served them. She did not eat. Time and again she stepped out to choke back her tears. Albrecht amused himself with the others and sang songs in German. The two soldiers and their mistresses left the house very late and rather drunk.

Albrecht set off the next morning, with a peaceable air, as if he were leaving for work on a typical day. He kissed Judith. She felt herself dying. She clung to him in despair.

"You'll write?"

"Yes, yes ..."

"You'll come back? Swear, swear ... I'll die if you don't come back ..."

"Yes, yes, I'll come back ..."

"Send me letters, send your friends my way, so I'll know you're alive, that you're thinking of me, that you love me ..."

Albrecht laughed as he pulled her arms from his neck.

"Yes, yes, I'll send my friends. Go on, goodbye, goodbye, I'll be back soon ..."

• • •

Judith went three months with no news of Albrecht. He had left in February 1916. She was still waiting in May, day after day, gradually losing hope of seeing him again, and growing no more accustomed to her grief. She did not suffer in regard to material goods. Albrecht had brought her plenty of provisions from the farm – dried peas, green beans, potatoes, rye and wheat, smoked bacon, broad beans, turnips and cabbage – so that she had a full basement and a full larder when he left. Besides, she was a woman who could get by on her own. She knew German tolerably well now, could make herself understood, and had established connections with the officers and clerks at headquarters. Well known as the mistress of the farm manager, she had at her disposal her preferred means for going into the city – to Lille or Tourcoing. There she went to sell her vegetables, rum, and "Goldwasser," which she got from the soldiers' mess and which went for top dollar in town. Goldwasser was a variety of liquor quite popular with the Germans. From the city, Judith brought back soap, cloth, coffee, things not to be found in the village. And this dual exchange allowed her to make lots of money. People came to her, respectfully, to ask if she could go to Lille and find some medicine for the sick, a shirt for communion. She was hated and feared. The villagers knew that, protected as she was by German headquarters, she could do much good and much harm. They asked her to get a pass so they could visit parents, to help reduce a fine or secure permission to move or to slaughter a pig. Judith's mother and her sister Estelle Babet came like the others and more often than the others. And Judith brought back whatever they wanted from the city and charged them nothing. Old Lacombe said not a word, feigned ignorance. But one day even he ended up sending his wife to ask for a pair of ankle boots his size. Judith had become a power.

She did not pride herself on it. She gave help to everyone liberally, without counting the cost, as if it were a type of atonement – as if she hoped to earn public pardon thereby. She had watched week after week go by. She continued to hope for a letter or for Albrecht's miraculous return. She could not accept the thought that it all had to end like this, in nothingness. Each time new units arrived or passed through Herlem, she ran to question the men. Perhaps they knew something, could at least tell her which district Albrecht's regiment had headed for. During the war, one saw so many people, each life crossed paths with so many others ... But no one ever knew anything.

Judith lived through this period as if it were outside reality, in a perpetual state of waiting, removed from the others. Her obsession seemed to isolate her. Travelling, working, buying and selling – this was not her life. She did it all as in a dream. She only found herself again in the evenings, in her house, in lone conversation with her haunting thoughts. She endured an immense expiation. She had made Albrecht her deity, had almost recreated him – purified and transfigured – in her own mind. Never had love been more willingly blind. She had refused to accept his flaws, his blemishes, magnified his good qualities and his virtues, loved him as she wanted him to be and not as the big boy, fond of a good table and a good bed, sensual and merry, a bit of a braggart and matter of fact, neither good nor bad, that he really was. For many people, such blindness is unconscious, almost naïve. For Judith, it was almost intentional. With all her being, she wanted to transform the adventure in which she had foundered, this downfall, into an ascension, so that her ideal, the pure aspirations of her youth toward nobleness and beauty, might still be attained.

One evening – nearly a hundred days after Albrecht's departure – Judith was in her little house making supper. It was the end of May. It had rained and was muggy. Through the window, Judith could see the huge, flat, monotonous plain bathed in trailing vapours, and the vast, congested, murky sky, a stormy sky in which the sun was sinking, completing its descent amid majestic golden reflections, the black masses of clouds, and great shafts of light slanting across the expanse.

Judith heard footsteps on the roadway. She lived in a forgotten corner of Herlem Hill, not far from the quarry. Few people came this direction. She listened. The footsteps stopped in front of her door. There was a knock. She ran, filled by the same mad hope as always. She opened the door. Three Germans stood before her.

"Mein Herren ..."

"Madam ..."

They had a pleased expression. They had not come for a billet. They had neither bags nor rifles. They were neat, clean, tidy. One of them held a bottle, a loaf of bread, a sausage. They laughed rather foolishly and said nothing.

"You've come for a room?" asked Judith.

"Ja, ja," said the one holding the sausage and the bottle. "We sleep, ja, ja ..."

He gave her a wink.

Judith looked at all three in astonishment. They must have been drunk. She did not understand. They had certainly not come from the front. They were too spotless. And the bottle! The food they seemed to offer! And the strange expressions. They were still laughing, shoving each other with their elbows. One of them pulled a paper from his pocket, held it out. She recognized Albrecht's handwriting ...

It had undoubtedly happened as the result of a binge. Men like to boast. Somewhere or other, Albrecht must have had a drinking bout with these three men setting off for Herlem and the front. To look clever, to brag, he must have told them, "I'm going to give you a billet, I am, a good one, a good bed and all the rest ... When I myself was there, in Herlem, I knew how to manage ..." When a fellow is drunk, he does not consider the consequences and sees things in a different light. Memories are distorted under the influence of alcohol. To make a joke, to have a chuckle, to pose as a sharp guy, for no good reason, he had given them this paper. They must have laughed about it long and hard, all four of them, slapping their thighs. For that matter, it was all the rage with the Germans to put these sorts of messages on vouchers for requisitions or billets. But perhaps the next day, sobered up, Albrecht had remembered and felt something akin to remorse.

Good for one night with Madam ... [signed] Albrecht.

Judith stood motionless, looking at the three men on her doorstep. She felt her mind reeling. Insulted, ridiculed, miserably treated like a creature to be sold, she found herself brutally demeaned, fallen from the height of her ideal, degraded by the total degradation of the man she had loved.

Debased, he had debased her along with himself. The horrible and distinct memory of all she had done for this man suddenly came to her – their nights, the mad love, the adoration of a contestable body to which she had humbled and prostituted herself. For what had she not renounced her decency and dignity, to what debauchery had she not stooped to arouse the thrill of pleasure in him, to merit a word, a gesture, a contented and satisfied look as her reward? He was paying her today ... He was paying her according to her deeds, like a harlot deserving of an insult ...

She was still holding the paper in her hand. Awkward and dull, the three men in front of her shifted on their feet and laughed stupidly, ill at east and almost embarrassed. She fixed them with a black look as she stood there, dreadfully pale, tall and thin, an immobile statue that was rather frightening. She raised her long, bare arm and pointed inside, with a gesture that, though they understood not why, seemed almost tragic. And she whispered, "Come in ..."

PART II

Chapter One

I

Since the beginning of the war, a number of the region's factories had shut down. But some mills were still running under German management. They produced cloth using what was left of their stock of raw materials. Toward the middle of 1915, the Germans decided to force all the manufacturers to work for them. Very cleverly, they approached the owners separately, one by one, to overcome resistance more easily.

It was thus that Hennedyck, who was at his factory in Épeule one afternoon, received notice that an officer from headquarters would come see him at ten o'clock the next morning.

The following day Hennedyck was waiting at the factory. At ten o'clock two officers and a sergeant arrived by automobile. They introduced themselves in the courtyard and came straight to the point.

"Sir, your factory isn't running. It must be started up."

"To make what?"

"What you make now."

"I manufacture cotton goods, fancy stuffs and heavy fabrics ..."

"You'll reduce the number of threads in the warp and the woof."

"My looms can only produce heavy-weight material ..."

"Let's take a look."

Hennedyck led them into the mill. The German officers were a bit surprised by the huge, sturdy English looms with their double rollers. The men argued in German. The sergeant, who seemed to be an expert, was apparently trying to dissuade the officers from their plans. They came back to Hennedyck. The tallest declared: "It doesn't matter. You'll set to work anyway. We keep hearing the same line over and over, and we're getting sick of it!"

"Very well," said Hennedyck, restraining the anger which caught hold of him, too. "But I can't operate without coal!"

"You'll have it."

"Without oil, without pickers ..."

"You'll have them."

"Without money ..."

"You'll have it ..."

"And the workers?"

"You'll have to find them, but you'll be up and running within a week."

"You're joking!" exclaimed Hennedyck. "And what'll you pay, anyhow?"

Their response left him speechless.

"Whatever you please. You can name your price."

"But my engine," cried Hennedyck, "my steam engine's broken!"

Because he had himself damaged the cylinders a few weeks before.

"Let's take a look."

They went down to the engine room. Hennedyck showed them the cylinders that had to be rebored. He explained that the engine came from Ghent, that the cylinders had to be sent there, that the work would take months.

"We'll send you some mechanics. In a month you'll be up and running."

"Impossible."

"We'll see."

They left him, went back to the courtyard, climbed into the automobile, and disappeared.

Hennedyck was greatly perplexed. He hesitated. To work for the enemy was a type of treason. But to refuse was to break with those who had continued to operate under enemy orders. It was also to expose the working population to reprisals. In the event of refusal, the Germans were threatening to cut off all provisions from the city. A dreadful famine would ensue. To refuse would finally – and this mattered too, after all – mean exile for Hennedyck, far from his wife Émilie, the destruction of the factory, perhaps ruin.

Hennedyck weighed the pros and the cons, and vacillated. It was the people, the common people, who showed him the way.

Hennedyck was at his office again the next day. He was examining his list of employees, justly worrying what would become of these good people, deprived of resources in the event of conflict with the German authorities. At this very moment his elderly doorkeeper came to tell him that some folks were asking for him.

"Who?"

"The workers, sir."

"Here?"

"Yes, Mr Patrice."

"Show them up, Césaire ..."

"They're a good forty of them, Sir."

"I'll go down."

He found a crowd of men, women, and children waiting on the stairway.

"Good day, my friends. Well, what's going on?"

He saw their uneasy and enigmatic expressions.

"Something's wrong? Come into the lobby."

They followed him, squeezing inside the lobby.

"Well?"

Then Lerue, an old foreman, began to speak. He had been at Hennedyck's for twenty years. "Mr Patrice," he said, "it's not to hurt you, you've been a good boss, and I myself've worked here some twenty years. But still, we've come to ask for our leaving certificates ..."

"Your certificates?"

"We know the German are going to start production again. And we don't want to work for them."

"But I'm not going to work for the Germans!" cried Hennedyck.

"We know, Mr Patrice, we know ... But there're mills where folks are working, you see ... And we ... we won't have any of it."

"Well, come in one at a time. I'll give you discharge forms dated July 1914. And after the war, of course, you'll come back regardless ..."

"Thank you, Mr Patrice."

He returned to his office, more moved than he let on. He received them one at a time. Trying to laugh, he said to Lerue, "I never thought I'd have to give you your papers one day, my old man ..."

"Me neither, Mr Patrice," whispered the foreman. And there was almost a vague reproach in his voice.

Upon receiving her certificate, Flavie van Groede, the sister-in-law of Félicie Laubigier, asked boldly, "Is it true, Mr Patrice, that you're going to start making great coats for the Boches?"

Another, a good hearted woman, timidly showed him a letter from her son, by way of excuse: "You see, Mr Patrice, he's the one who wants it. Here's what he sent me."

The son was at the front. On the other side of the lines, he had heard the news. He had written, "It's been reported that Roubaix's making sandbags for the German trenches. If you're doing this, if it's true, I'll never come back again."

Then the indignation grew. Some factories were known to be operating for the enemy. One must consider, without preconceived notions, the situation of manufacturers who had agreed to stay open. There was no Chamber of Commerce, no guiding organization. The Germans had sown confusion. Each employer, approached separately from the beginning of the occupation, felt himself unarmed, powerless. It had started with requisitions, the order – under threat of pillage and deportation – to finish the work underway, to exhaust the stockpiles. Then the Germans had blatantly imposed the job. But all of this had not happened without producing a certain discontent among the labour force. Suddenly, all the rumours running round Roubaix were coming true. The threat of widespread work orders – and the word that factories still in operation were making uniforms and sandbags for the enemy – fuelled a wave of resentment. And now there was talk of making everyone work to the same end! They would not do it, and they would stop the ones who still were from cooperating. The men and women employed in these factories were accosted in the alleyways. Enormous crowds went to wait for them in the evening at the factory exits. Brawls erupted. The guilty workers received a terrible thrashing at the hands of the indignant populace. German sentries at the factory gates had to run and hide. A police commissioner who attempted to calm things down was himself dealt with as a traitor and treated to a heady dose of the anger. Elsewhere, workers till then obedient to the Germans spontaneously rebelled, having realized they were producing material for sandbags. They wanted no more of it. They went on strike. The factories had to shut down. An explosive revolt spread across the occupied territories, all the way to Lille.

Hennedyck found inspiration in this movement. The path? Why, he had been shown, they had shown it to him, these good, coarse, unsophisticated people, with their rigid and unwavering sentiments. One did not work for the enemy. It was that simple. Toil, suffer, undergo persecution, hunger, perhaps exile? Well! Had not all Roubaix accepted the risk without hesitation? Without counting the cost?

In one stroke he composed a letter to his colleagues – a sharp letter, categorical and frank. He concluded it by stating, "It's the people of Roubaix who are setting an example for us ..." Deep down, he regretted that the initiative had not come from them, the employers. He was convinced that they had failed in their role, their duty as leaders of men. Oh yes, it was the workers who had taught them a lesson!

The letter exploded like a bombshell, just as Hennedyck had anticipated. Anyone whose mill was running felt implicated. The next day, a meeting of manufacturers was scheduled to discuss the situation and figure out what to do.

• • •

Gayet, the eldest member, called for quiet and stood up.

"Gentlemen, you have all received a letter from one of our colleagues, asking our intentions regarding the present strife occasioned by the question of continued operations. We have met to decide upon a response to this letter."

The gathering was at the Cercle Pierre in Roubaix. From Lille, from Tourcoing, from near and far, manufacturers had hastened to participate in the debate.

All eyes had turned toward the determined, willful, energetic face of Patrice Hennedyck. He did not bat an eyelash, looking at each attendee one at a time, with a tough and frank expression. Next to him was his friend Daniel Decraemer, the Lille industrialist, a tall man, wan and stooped, with the air of a dreamer, a long distended nose, pensive grey eyes, and a receding hairline, leaving bare a high, sloped forehead. Next to them, forming a hostile nucleus, were several Lille manufacturers whose factories were still running. Also evident was an informal grouping by disposition, between representatives of each city first of all, and then between those who were in operation and those who were not.

"This letter, gentlemen," resumed Gayet, "contains some rather incendiary language ..."

"That's right," agreed Wendiével, a friend of Gayet and of one mind with him concerning the matter.

"So explain yourself, Hennedyck. You talk of treason against the nation! Those are serious accusations!"

There was an approving murmur.

"We don't supply the enemy," persisted Gayet, encouraged, "either munitions or means of action. We're subject to the laws of war, which we can't evade. The enemy is master. He takes our goods from us. We've no means of protest. We're ordered to work, there's nothing more we can do. Hennedyck, did you close your door and grab your gun when the Germans came to 'requisition' your cloth? No, right? You had no choice but to let them take it. Well, between giving your cloth to the enemy and making it, I don't see the difference!"

There were whispers, sounds of "I beg your pardon! Right! Basically ... No, all the same!"

"Letting your goods be taken is a passive act," retorted Hennedyck. "Making them is an active gesture. That's the difference."

"In the next place," continued Gayet, "I tell you we've only been working in self-defense – under threat of imprisonment, of deportation – for ourselves and our employees. I myself've seen certain of my employees imprisoned forty-eight hours for refusing to work. The Germans threatened to burn my factory, to deprive my workers of rations. What could I do? I asked around. I conferred with bank directors, lawyers. I was told: 'Your factory mustn't be destroyed. Your duty as a Frenchman is to preserve your factory intact, so that after the war it can contribute to national prosperity again.'"

And all of this was strictly true. Gayet had sought such advice.

"We have the law on our side," responded Hennedyck. "I'm sorry to seem harsh, to implicitly condemn the behaviour of a good many of my friends. But it isn't difficult to see that the Hague Conventions forbid the enemy from demanding any more of civilians than the bare minimum for the army of occupation. There you have it!"

"Fine words, Hennedyck, but who'll enforce this law? What we don't want to give, the enemy takes. We refuse to work? He'll occupy the factories, pillage, plunder. He'll cut off all rations, he'll force the population to work under his orders. Besides, what're the people doing? They're already working. Everyone's working. There're orphanages in Lille where the Germans' underclothes are being mended!"

"What! It's come to that!" cried Hennedyck. "But it's our fault, all of us! We've failed in our task, no one's done a thing ... But wait! That's not true! And the proof is that the people of Roubaix are rebelling and giving us the example that we should've given them. Gentlemen, pull yourselves together, I beg you, so that recognition of your material interests, at the very least, will bring you to your senses ...

"Material interests?" asked Wendiével.

"Do you think that after the war, with our stockpiles destroyed, our cloth and supplies requisitioned, the French government'll see fit to help, to provide assistance for people who've betrayed it? Who's to say that tomorrow English planes won't come and drop bombs on our factories, the ones producing cloth for the enemy?"

"Oh, oh!" protested Gayet and others, chuckling. "Patrice's idea is laughable ... English planes bombing Roubaix!"

"Hennedyck, you're exaggerating!"

"He's so morbid."

"Don't be so quick to kill us, old man!"

Villard, the spinner from New Roubaix, objected: "You're looking at it from too narrow a perspective, Hennedyck. You're forgetting that we also have to think of the working class, of its suffering and its well-being. Listen to me. A number of mills have been shut down for a while. If the war keeps dragging on, I can't imagine what'll become of the workers. Unemployment paralyzes them, dulls their minds. In a year they'll be incapable of returning to their trade. The old ones get rusty, the young ones run wild. We have to consider the moral welfare of our population."

An indistinct sniggering, coming from the direction of Barthélémy David, was lost in an approving hubbub. The men whose factories were in operation latched onto this reasoning with pleasure, giving them an excuse in their own eyes. For the others, the sincere ones, the argument also carried weight. Even in Hennedyck's corner, Daniel Decraemer was impressed, nodded in agreement and admitted, "All that's quite true. I hadn't thought of it ..." His conscience, scrupulous in the extreme, weighed pros and cons with a thoroughness that occasionally irritated Hennedyck, himself a man of strong and passionate action.

"It mustn't be forgotten," went on Villard, "that in Belgium the manufacturers are working."

"No, they aren't!"

"Yes, they are!"

"We don't know ..."

"That has nothing to do with us."

And in a short, chance silence, the voice of Wendiével could be heard all
too clearly, "Basically, we'd be blockheads ..." He stopped immediately, surprised his voice had carried so far.

In the fierce discussion, the voice of Hennedyck again resounded, "If you
do it, you're no longer true leaders! You betray your trust! We're not employers just so we can fill our pockets ... We actually have a cure of souls."

"Gentlemen," grinned Gayet ironically, "here we have the unexpected –
some sort of industrial mysticism. Hennedyck's about to philosophize."

But others cut in: "Gayet, that's not fair. You're going too far."

Hennedyck hesitated, looking at Gayet, and wondering if he should
respond. He restrained himself. It was not the time for such disputes.
Besides, from all around came cries, "Go on, Hennedyck, go on." He continued, "I say that, in return for the advantages of our position, we – as
employers – have an obligation to provide our workmen a livelihood first
and an example second. Well, who's setting the example today? The people. We're failing. Don't speak of profits. Forget material interest, which is
never easy to identify. You want to protect your factories for the nation?
What a joke. True duty here demands sacrifice. You fear your workers will
be victimized? If they refuse to suffer, they'll be yielding on their own
account. It's not for us to lead them there."

"But in Belgium the factories are running," cried Gayet.

"Not anymore," retorted several voices, "they've just stopped."

"And what did the enemy do?"

"Nothing at all."

"You see! Now you've been warned. Yesterday the ones operating could
claim ignorance of treason. Today you've all been put on notice."

"It's easy for you," shouted Wendiével, "to talk of shutting down when
you've nothing to lose. You never started, your steam engine's in tatters ..."

"You need only do the same, and straightaway!"

There was applause, "Well said, Hennedyck! Long live Épeule!" They
surrounded Hennedyck, patted him on the shoulder, laughed. "What a fel-

low! One of the old school! Hennedyck and his principles! Very good, old man! Let's vote! Let's vote!"

• • •

"Victory!" exclaimed Decraemer, as he left with Hennedyck, Barthélémy David, and the Abbé Sennevilliers, who had come to wait for them at the door of the Cercle. "Unanimous approval! It's splendid. And thanks to you, Hennedyck."

"You should've supported me more in there, Decraemer. You didn't help by approving some of their ideas. Moral welfare of the workers ... Saving them from dangerous idleness ... Those are the most perfidious arguments."

"I was being sincere ..."

"I know. But you mustn't split hairs to such a fine point. That's not how great things are accomplished. Your conscience is too subtle, Decraemer. You have to look at the big picture, pass over the small things, and quickly."

"Like you, eh? It's true ..."

"In any event," said David, "the business is settled. Roubaix won't be working."

"Even Gayet, whose factory is running, voted to stop!"

"It's splendid," exclaimed the Abbé Sennevilliers. "Almost like the night of August 4th!"*

"Yes, yes," said Hennedyck pensively. "But all the same, this famous night of August 4th seems much less noble to me today. It mustn't have been quite what we imagine, old chap ..."

II

The next day each manufacturer sent German headquarters a letter signalling his refusal to work for the enemy. The first to be arrested were those whose factories were in operation before the general protest. From the ranks of the others, among the richest, fifty odd hostages were taken at ran-

*In reaction to provincial uprisings known as the Great Fear, the National Assembly voted on 4 August 1789 to abolish many of the nobility's privileges.

dom – old, sick, and healthy alike. An unfortunate weaver, afflicted with the name of Villard, was shipped off with the real Villard despite his desperate pleas. They were dispatched to Germany for several months. Hennedyck, whose engine was in pieces, was miraculously excluded from the list. He did not complain about his good fortune. The battle that the Abbé Sennevillers and he were waging on behalf of the newspaper absorbed his entire attention.

Daniel Decraemer was carted off to Germany with the other manufacturers. He was detained for several weeks. It was not the first time. He had already served a six-month term as a hostage. He was freed before the others because his health, already shaken by the first period of confinement, had finally collapsed. He came back quite ill, only to find a business and a home in ruins.

Daniel Decraemer was married and the father of two children. His was a charming, singular nature. This man, who could have devoted himself to a worthy cause and seen it through, had instead demeaned himself in a mediocre love and the pursuit of riches. In the eyes of the world, he was undoubtedly successful, accomplished. In his own eyes, he was nonetheless a failure.

Decraemer loved his wife with an almost touching devotion. He was constantly talking about her, quoting her, openly displaying his admiration and fondness for her. Bashfulness no doubt prevented him from ever saying that he loved her. He had, in this regard, retained a surprising degree of innocence. But he demonstrated his love so well! To his wife he attributed every virtue, infinite goodness. Above all, he constantly gave her the kind attention, the solicitude, the steadfast gaze, the pleading eyes that demonstrated the obsessive influence of his wife, the unwitting tyranny that she exerted over him. She herself was thereby extolled and almost deified. For one could tell that this fellow Decraemer was not just anyone – with his long thin head, his high, sallow brow, his shining, perpetually forlorn eyes, the melancholy and disenchantment of the man who feels he has still not lived up to his ideal, however far he may have come – to the point that one was led to wonder about the exceptional qualities of the woman who had so completely captivated such a soul. She was tall, tranquil, with an ample figure and an admirable, firm, elegant bust. Her long pale face, her straight nose, her enormous, black, lingering eyes, her smooth forehead beneath two dark and heavy headbands, and something imperceptibly disdainful in the bend of her full and sensual lips irre-sistibly evoked the image of the goddess Juno. She allowed him to adore her, serenely, as a woman sure of her power. She sometimes rewarded her husband with a glance, a half-smile. Beyond this sentimental affection, one could sense the deep, supple, and potent bond, the sort of happy grat-itude, the steadfast expectation and hope, generated by love of the flesh. There was a strong sensual side to their affection.

Daniel, it seemed, cherished even his children for the traits of his wife that he found in them. Happy? No doubt he ought to have been. Before the war, he had made lots of money. He had two lovely, talented, affec-tionate children, a darling wife, the unanimous respect and consideration of Lille. He delighted in a luxurious, comfortable home, enjoyed travel, had his villa in Ostend, led a grand, gilded life. And yet, those who had known Decraemer in his youth – the tall, quick-tempered boy, chimerical, idealistic, full of crazy and magnificent projects – were forced to wonder if this man had really found true happiness in materialism, if it were really what he had hoped for, asked for, expected from life. Decraemer had been a noble youth, fanciful and peculiar, endowed with a brain marvelously constructed and equipped, an intelligence that surprised his teachers, and a rare, sincere, divining sensibility. He stood out from the crowd thanks to an unexpected mysticism hidden beneath that type of fake schoolboy reserve – beneath the cynical joke, the grin, the sarcasm – but which could nonetheless be seen so obviously, so candidly in his eyes, his gestures, his passions, his generosity, his intransigence ... And then there was his taste, his passion for devotion and heroism, his secret love of rebellion, of battle, of the flag planted on the barricades ... He already had the long face, distended from top to bottom, that defined his features, the noble head with thin, light-blond hair, the eyes with the green tint of fresh water, the colour of melting glass, and the slanting, misshapen mouth with tight, narrow lips in perpetual strain. And for this tall, thin, chimeri-cal youth, one instinctively imagined a grand destiny, an existence beyond the ordinary ...

And now, of all these possibilities, what remained? Not much. Daniel Decraemer had become a businessman, a mill-owner and a merchant. He had come to know his colleagues, had had to fight, finesse, deceive to avoid deception, take what he could, and lie ... Such was the world of busi-ness. The frequenting of this brutish, voracious, unrelenting humanity, the love of money which inevitably comes to those who handle it, spend it, and gradually begin to understand its power, all these experiences had slowly extinguished in Dccraemer the elevated thoughts of his youth. It was impossible, Daniel had sensed, to love money and, at the same time, one's fellow man.

Adrienne Decraemer had also exerted a destructive influence, of which she was completely unaware, on the husband she loved both wholly and loyally. In good health, realistic, descended from a family of robust individuals who enjoyed the good life, she loved luxury and easy living, sensual pleasures, a certain happy indolence. Without intending to, she had captivated her husband, conquered him, bound him to a carnal love in which he quickly lost his independence and the nobility of his aspirations. Nothing is worse than the power of sex to dull the spirit and lead one toward other pleasures of the flesh. Daniel Decraemer began to indulge more willingly in good wine, a fine table, in plentiful and discriminating fare. He took pleasure in the comforts of his private life, sought them out – ready comforts and, to a certain extent, enervating ones. He found blissful charm in light, soothing, easily digestible music, in facile reading, in relaxing performances to which one listened without effort in a cozy armchair. Everything held together. By way of a love in which the flesh had too liberally encroached upon the spirit, Daniel arrived at Epicureanism – the search for an exclusively material well-being, a certain skepticism regarding the purpose of existence and the mission of man on Earth, the neglect and repudiation of the exalted aspirations of his youth, a real injustice with respect to the idealist and mystic that he should have been and had certainly failed to become.

He occasionally realized what he had missed and wished he could redeem himself. But these flashes of insight were brief and increasingly rare. He admired from afar the ascetic or the hero, all those whose nobility and majesty aroused a hollow, vaguely sad echo in him. But admiration no longer elicited the need for imitation. An exclusive, excessive passion for his wife and a certain natural laziness in the dreamer little inclined to action – ultimately the fear of change, of trouble – disposed Daniel to leave things as they were, to content himself with a quasi-happiness completely impregnated by materialism, casting a veil of indolence and forgetfulness on the shadows, the painful moments ... In sum, he was a good example of the splendid possibilities that life itself stifles and paralyzes for certain men.

When he returned from Germany, Decraemer found his affairs in disarray. The factory was in a distressing state, ruined by thefts, requisitions, a senseless destruction without purpose or profit. Decraemer had refused to remain in operation, and the Germans had methodically laid waste to his mill. The only remaining employee was his accountant, Mayet, a frail man in his sixties who had vainly objected to the searches and depredations of the Germans. Hardly had Daniel set foot in his factory than he met with real dismay. How to repair all this? How to recover from such a disaster? He set these concerns aside until later, turning all his attention for the moment to his home, his family, which were also threatened.

Adrienne, his wife, had suffered bitter anguish during Daniel's absence: Jacques, the eldest of their children, had come down with scarlet fever. Quarantined too late, he had transmitted the illness to his little sister Louise. Jacques was the more robust of the two, would soon be eleven years old, and had inherited his mother's strong and sanguine temperament. He had thus recovered rather quickly. But Louise, who was only seven, who had a frail constitution and her father's nervous and rather lymphatic nature, did not improve. Nighttime fevers, emaciation, accelerated growth, sadness, loss of appetite – all these symptoms alarmed her mother. Decraemer loved his youngest child to the point of distraction. Finding her in this condition threw him into a terrible state of anxiety, which he could not even articulate. His condition had discouraged and distressed his wife, who had already been affected by his absence and who, alone in Lille, responsible for a wrecked factory and an endangered child, had lost her senses and resigned herself to grief.

Decraemer sent for doctors, asked friends for money to get by, toiled, defended himself and his own. With all his energy, he sought to protect what remained of his factory, to preserve intact this final resource for the postwar years. But he confronted a powerful adversary. After the manufacturers of the Nord, under Hennedyck's courageous influence, had refused to work for the enemy, the latter had undertaken the methodical destruction of working-stock, openly seeking to forever ruin the textile industry of the Nord. The Germans started by removing raw materials – wool and cotton in unprocessed condition – then washed wool, then spun thread, and last finished cloth. On a quite regular basis, they also issued a receipt signed by the two parties, after an honest weighing and numbering of the lots taken. With this paper, one repaired to the Bank of France, which delivered a final, official document declaring weights, quantities, prices, the number of freight cars loaded and their destinations.

But the Germans did not stop there. From the factories they successively removed wires, dynamos, everything in the way of electrical equipment; then all the copper from the machines; then the machines themselves; next leather, belts, felt, rubber; afterward drive trains, pulleys, shafts, anything iron or steel; and finally pig iron. At that point, the factory stood empty.

Near his spinning mill, several years earlier, Daniel Decraemer had equipped a plant for dressing and weaving flax. In this branch of industry, the Germans were behind their French competitors. Daniel had to watch in fury as the enemy made incessant searches, long visits round his machines. Germans in civilian dress – manufacturers – came to inspect, study, get a clear understanding, take notes and make sketches. He recognized certain of his prewar rivals. Finally, to complete their research, they carted off every single machine and loom, pasteboard model, and cloth pattern, with the greatest care.

All that remained of the factory were huge, sonorous, dismal rooms, encumbered with scrap iron, debris, and twisted beams.

But Decraemer continued to resist. In his basement he had an enormous stockpile of woolen and cotton cloth, walled off, blocked by rubble. None but he, his accountant, and the latter's son knew of this hiding-place. A lot of the material would undoubtedly be damaged by moths and rats, worthless by war's end. But the Germans would not have it. To this task Decraemer applied his pride, a frenzy of patriotism that the persecution, the suffering, the unimaginable oppression of the enemy had aroused in the people of the Nord. For this crushing of spirits, this regime of tyranny stimulated love and longing for France. They became more French than the French, a little like the Alsatians after 1870. Patriotism became a mystique. A tricolour ribbon brought tears to the eyes. People calmly performed acts of heroism of which they would have been incapable before the war. There was an atmosphere of fever, exaltation, rage, and fervour, which those who did not experience it can hardly understand.

In Decraemer, with his generous spirit, this sentiment of patriotism rose to the point of fanaticism. This man, who had let his idealistic side wither when confronted with the spectacle of life, began once again to believe in at least the nation. He made of it a religion, a faith. He willingly sacrificed his fortune for it, as he would have his life. He no longer reasoned, he simply devoted himself. And for him this commitment fostered a kind of moral philosophy. He became better, nobler. His entire conduct changed, a bit like that of a new convert. A great idea, whatever it may be – a religion or an art or a grand purified love – elevates the soul. To raise itself up, the spirit will make use of almost anything as a foundation.

Besides, Decraemer felt himself sustained by the environment, the atmosphere. Self-sacrifice and sincerity abounded in those days. The most skeptical were roused. The general level of patriotism had risen incredibly. No doubt there were also renegades, traitors, folks who came to terms, sold cloth to the enemy, used stolen fabric to make sacks and clothing for the Germans. But in reaction to this group, in disgust at their behaviour, Decraemer and the others developed a deeper hatred of the enemy, a deeper love of dear old France.

It was thus that Decraemer's acquired skepticism quickly faded, dissolved. He had suffered too much in the German camps. Philosophizing, acceptance, a certain tranquility easily accord with well-being, a comfortable life. Grief, trial, suffering less readily allow for universal indifference. On the contrary, they engender rebellion, assertion and resistance, conflict. And Decraemer felt that to resist he had to cling to something, at least for the moment, to accept – true or false – a reason to fight, and not to undermine his own defensive energies with the perpetual and sterilizing thought: *What's the point? The righteous, the good will be the victims …*

The examples around him – the vitalizing influence of the multitude accepting suffering to remain loyal to the lost nation – propelled Decraemer along his path. And then, there was no more manufacturing, no more of the terrible and demoralizing fight to the death called business. Ferocious struggle, rivalry, jealousy, betrayal, lies: this daily scene embitters mankind. Who has ever dreamed of becoming a saint in the realm of commercial affairs? Business is a perpetual compromise with the conscience, a world apart in which moral sentiment no longer applies … Even the best folks can recover their humanity only by escaping this environment from time to time. He who would apply the Gospel to business would go bankrupt. Nowhere does one learn better to confuse profit and theft, to develop an instinct for greed, cruelty, and domination. Freed from this combat, this degrading scramble, Decraemer gradually felt his humanity returning.

The atmosphere had changed in his home as well. It was far from the luxurious, easygoing, and carefree lifestyle of antebellum days. The receptions, the parties, the concern for comfort, a certain sensuality – all had been swept away by the war. There were no more servants. The family spent their time in the kitchen where Adrienne herself prepared the meals. They had closed the big reception halls that, bereft of chandeliers, bronze figures, and ornaments, had a disconsolate and melancholy appearance. A monachal sobriety in meals and entertainments, a life of toil and sadness revolving around little Louise, who was not improving, brought the couple closer together, taught them to understand and value each other more. Over the course of two years, Adrienne had lost her stateliness. She was no longer Juno with the ample bust, the majestic stature, the slow step of a queen, accepting the tenderness of her husband with a serene expression. Arrogance, pride in her station, her wealth, her beauty, her culture – all had disappeared. There remained only a suffering wife, an anxious, overworked mother. She had grown thin. Her light and flawless complexion was discoloured. Her smooth forehead was wrinkled, her eyes dull, her mouth drooping. She carelessly put up her splendid black hair in a quickly made bun, wore kitchen aprons over old dresses, ruined her long, delicate hands in greasy water. Thereby rendered unattractive and aged, she had in Daniel's eyes become someone different, at once less exhilarating and more human – more of a wife and a mother. And Daniel's love for her was purified, slowly losing the fierce and sensual character that, up to then, had always made of him, at one and the same time, an eager, servile, and anxious lover. It seemed that their mutual affection had become calmer and more reasoned – and more assured.

An incident also confirmed Decraemer in his courageous tenacity and gave him heart. One at a time, the region's manufacturers were called to headquarters in Lille. "We're going to acknowledge our war debt to you," said the Germans. "Agree to the amount, and we'll guarantee payment. If not, you'll never touch a cent." Not a single manufacturer took the bargain. "We don't want to deal with the enemy," said first one and then another, and without having discussed the matter in concert.

Decraemer was encouraged, pleased by the turn of events. He knew these colleagues of his. Nine of ten had refused out of fear, remembering Hennedyck's warning. But it made no difference. It proved that one could still do something, that a single courageous act could galvanize a crowd, that providing an example was not useless. And Decraemer recalled the striking passage in the Scriptures, one he had not understood as a child, and whose profound meaning was finally revealed. *The leaven in the lump* ...* Leaven, yes, the exceedingly small seed, the living germ cell that stirs the amorphous masses. He understood that – even apart from religion – it is good for man to have a moral principle and that – lost, isolated, weighed down by selfishness and universal indifference – he can act, inspire, transform the indifference, become the leaven in the lump.

So life had a purpose! Decraemer, who till then had always felt burdened by pessimism, by the notion that any effort toward the greater good was pointless, could find a mission, a role here on Earth! Struggle – struggle for the common good – was not pointless! This thought provided relief, a feeling of exaltation and immense happiness. And already, instinctively, he went further, looking beyond these ideas for a principle, a cause, a spiritual power whose existence could explain and illuminate this enthusiasm, this noble force he felt within himself. He lived through these days in perplexity. He sensed that his beliefs, inside of him, were crumbling in order to be reconstituted – all his knowledge, all his precepts rearranged in another form. Thus is the nymph, within its thin shell, reduced to a liquid mass, given over to a mysterious, obscure, fantastical process, to emerge, perfected, as a winged insect ...

• • •

Louise, the little girl, recovered slowly. She began going out again, getting a bit of air and sunshine. But she remained sober and rarely cheerful, though she was only seven years old. One morning she began coughing. Her parents treated her without undue alarm. Toward evening the cough worsened. In the middle of the night, she deteriorated so dramatically that they ran to the doctor's. He was busy with a delivery, could not come till morning. Louise had croup. She died two days later.

Decraemer kept watch over the little body. He wanted to be left alone. One morning Mayet, his accountant, infringed upon these orders, "Mr Daniel, the Germans have come to the factory ..."

*A reference to Matthew 13:33 and Galatians 5:9.

"Do you think I care, Mayet ..."

"They've found the hiding-place ..."

"The hiding-place?"

"And ... I'm no longer your accountant, Mr Daniel ..."

"Mayet, have you lost your mind?"

"Sir, forgive me ..."

The wretched man started crying.

"I had my suspicions, they couldn't have found it by themselves ... My son has been spending money for several days now ... I discovered 7,000 marks in his jacket lining!" He burst into sobs.

Decraemer did not move, stunned by dismay, disgust, and fury all at once. Suddenly he grabbed Mayet by the arm. "To the factory!"

"Mr Daniel ..."

"Quick, Mayet, to the factory! They'll get none of it!"

For a moment he looked at the bed of his little daughter, ran weeping to kiss her, and dashed off like a madman. Mayet raced behind as fast as his legs would carry him.

That night a fire broke out in Decraemer's factory. Everything burned – buildings, the remainder of the equipment, and millions of kilos of cotton and wool. The fire lasted three days. All Lille smelled of charred wool.

The Germans came to arrest Decraemer at the bedside of his dead child. Then and there he was led away to Germany, not even permitted to complete the vigil.

Chapter Two

Heading back toward his house in Barbieux, Barthélémy David passed through the densely populated neighbourhood of Épeule. He was pleased. He was returning from Wendiével's factory in Fontenoy, where he had purchased a thousand bolts of cloth for 300,000 francs. He laughed to himself, thinking of Old Wendiével's trepidation, his bits of knavery, the thousand precautions he had taken to avoid trouble after the war. For anyone who did business with Barthélémy David was well aware that everything David bought went straight to Germany. Wendiével bore the name of an old branch of the Roubaix aristocracy. He had once filed for bankruptcy, a legitimate case that had left his reputation intact and his head held high. It had happened some thirty years ago: a matter of 700,000 francs. Wendiével had reached a settlement, agreed to pay 40 percent – irreproachable behaviour in the eyes of the world ... And as the great families were concerned for the honour and dignity of their names, Wendiével had been "set aright," helped to open a new mill which had gone on to prosper. He lived in a stylish little mansion on boulevard de Paris, but his "good fortune" had not permitted him to liquidate the remainder of his debt.

The coming of the war had left Wendiével mired in self-pity. Production was no longer possible. That blasted Hennedyck had forbidden it. At present, working would mean blacklisting oneself. There was no more money coming in. He had to live on savings: no good cigars or vintage wines or fine meals at Divoire's or the Rocher du Cancale in Lille, or at the Cathédrale in Tournai, or the Châtellenie in Ypres, or the Damier in Courtrai ... Alas! All the gaiety of the world had suddenly disappeared. On top of everything else, the Germans poisoned the life of the simple man.

Searches, seizures, bullying, petty annoyances! It never ended! He had to watch them take away his two carriage horses, then all the copperware from his house, the bronze chandeliers, the charming statues, the heavy bronze candlesticks, the knickknacks, the inkwells, the chalices, the vases, the mantle clocks. Then it was his wines. His cellar, an incomparable collection, was carted off in the space of a single day. Then the mattresses, the bedding, the linen, his piano – destined for a dance hall – and his masterpieces of art. The cost of living shot up as well. Wendiével counted each penny. Pauline, his old servant, came every other day, ashamed and teary-eyed, as if it were her fault, to tell him that she needed money ... He gave her a bill to the accompaniment of lamentations and endless reproaches. A prudent man, Wendiével had gone to the bank right after the mobilization to convert 60,000 francs worth of bills into gold. This treasure lay idle in his basement. He disposed of it judiciously, selling his coins four or five at a time to a so-called Étienne – the money changers never gave their last names. This little hunchback lived in Épeule and trafficked in gold. The man gave him a 50 percent premium. He claimed he unloaded the gold at the pubs. Whatever he did with it, the pretext was sufficient for Wendiével to consider his conscience clear. Then early one day the Germans arrived without warning. What they sought he did not precisely know ... A hidden spy or perhaps a radio set or some object of overlooked value. Once more his house was put to the sack! And in the basement, behind a cask, a policeman with a keen nose uncovered the bag of gold. More than 50,000 francs in coins and 15,000 in bills from the Bank of France still remained.

"It's mine!" shouted poor Wendiével.

"We'll give it back to you."

In the meantime they took it all away. The Germans were honest after a fashion, an honesty that did not help Wendiével. They quite scrupulously gave him 65,000 francs – but in local currency. He thought he would die of a stroke.

Everything was expensive: sixty francs for a bottle of mediocre wine, a hundred francs for a skinny chicken, a hundred francs for a loaf of white bread, eighty francs for a litre of salad dressing – prices such as Danglars had known in the famous prison of the count of Monte-Cristo. But here this was real! A single commodity had seen a marked discount: prostitutes. One could get girls for next to nothing: a mouthful of bread alone, a plateful of cold meat in a tavern, a chocolate in a pastry shop. It was a golden age for lady's men, with this hunger torturing the world. But Wendiével refused to pay twelve francs for a chocolate éclair or forty francs for a glass of Cointreau, just for the beautiful eyes of Lisette.* Among other concerns, the inflation was a source of great anxiety regarding the stockpiles of fabric he had hidden. He had concealed a thousand bolts of worsted wool in the bottom of his factory smokestack. He would have preferred to liquidate them, turn them into cash. He knew that the Germans – certain Germans at least – were offering large sums under the table, so they could profit from the resale in Germany. Cloth back there was in short supply; everything had been requisitioned for the army. And a few resourceful individuals, taking advantage of opportunities in occupied France, had gotten in touch with certain traffickers and dispatched what they found on behalf of German department stores. But on the other hand, Wendiével was terribly frightened of dealing with the enemy: first of all the fear of being duped by these powerful people, who could at any moment break an agreement and act as masters, and above all fear of the postwar era, of the dreadful accusation of trafficking with the invader, of treason ... No, decidedly, he wanted to hear nothing of trading with the enemy. He had to uncover a means to liquidate everything such that none could reproach him, find anything blameworthy. Confound it! Some fellows were doing it, gradually selling off enormous stockpiles, without anyone raising an objection, without having contact with the enemy. Villard, Gayet, and many others ... It was well known that everything was dispatched to Germany, but it was not openly acknowledged since the Germans were not making the purchases. In theory the cloth was sent to Holland, and appearances remained intact. Wendiével thought of Barthélemy David, the demolition contractor. It was rumoured that this mercenary type was buying entire warehousefuls and paying cash. Wendiével had decided to contact him. The arrangements had been difficult. Wendiével, first of all, had been terrified to see David come into his factory with a German officer. David had to explain to him at length that

*"Lisette" is a reference to one of the main characters in Pierre Carlet de Marivaux's play *Le Jeu de l'amour et du hazard* (1730).

Krug, the officer, was acting in a private capacity, as the representative of a consortium of department stores, and not on behalf of the military authorities.

Then they haggled over the price. Wendiével wanted to sell by the metre. David offered 300 francs a bolt. Wendiével, in a fury, almost strangled him. He called him a thief, a Jew, a cutthroat. But he was forced to give way, to accept David's humiliating terms. Finally they broached the question of removal. Here again, the deal almost collapsed when David indicated that German trucks would come pick up the merchandise.

"German trucks!"

"But of course ..."

"No! I won't hear of it! I'm not fond of getting myself shot!"

It was necessary to draw up a sales contract in good form, to indicate that all aspects of transport, shipment, and delivery were incumbent upon David, and that Wendiével would not be involved.

David was accustomed to all of this maneuvring. People were fully aware that everything they sold him was bound for Germany via Brussels. But they wanted to save face, to stay within the confines of the law. He was mulling these things over while going up boulevard de Cambrai. His big felt hat cast a shadow on his irritable and weary features – those of the adventurer, the enthusiast – and lent a little something romantic to his appearance. Tall and ungainly, he walked with even footsteps, fists closed, flaunting an insolent diamond in his tie and enormous rings on his fingers.

"Good day, Mr David," said those he passed. For a ready generosity had earned him the affection of the common people.

"Good day, good day," he replied in familiar fashion.

Without admitting it, he relished the acclaim of being someone, a powerful figure, after having lived so long outside the law. It was from the bygone days of his youth that he had retained the taste for pretense, gold, jewellery, and pomp. He had been in a position to appreciate the weight mankind accords to appearances. Later on, time among the middle classes had not altered his opinion.

Barthélémy David was fifty-five years old. He had done a little of everything: street peddler, door-to-door salesman, huckster at the fairs, strongman on the stage. In his younger days he had run a seedy cabaret, smuggled contraband, gotten six months in jail for a brawl, and fulfilled his

military service in the African battalions. Old regulars of the cafés round
the train station even claimed to remember a time when David had been
a pimp ... In any event, he was the sort to have done it. By dint of shady
dealings, he had become a demolition contractor. Within a decade he had
amassed a handsome fortune. And as one needs money to make money,
he had been able to take advantage of the industrial expansion of the
Nord, speculating on the purchase and resale of old equipment and factories slated for demolition. With the riches, respectability slowly had
come to him as well, without his having sought it. People cultivated such
a powerful connection. They invited him to their homes. They asked him
to join the Cercle Pierre in Roubaix in spite of his six months in prison
and the record of his indiscretions tucked away somewhere in the department of criminal investigations. He went along without surprise, masking
his contempt. He played for high stakes with total indifference, helped the
sons of poor families with money from his own pockets, paraded handsome horses, pretty women, ostentatious jewellery. And since he had black
hair, brown eyes, and an olive complexion, he had a bit of the air of a
Spaniard or a South American, what with his big felt hat, his sideburns,
his jewellery, and his customary cigar. He was proud of his physical
prowess. Even now he would sometimes get into a bout with a stubborn
worker and bring him down. He took up all challenges. It seemed that the
carny, the fighter in him, had never completely disappeared. And even
among those who made fun of him, the luxury and the display of strength
were imposing.

When the war broke out, Barthélémy David had engaged all his liquid
assets in the purchase of an enormous factory in Calais. He ended up in
occupied Roubaix, without resources. But the situation did not frighten
him. He began by trafficking in a little of everything: butter and wine, coal,
foodstuffs, cloth. Then chance put him in touch with a certain Lieutenant
Krug, a former buyer for a big ready-made clothing firm in Hamburg.
Despite incessant searches in their factories, French manufacturers still had
enormous quantities of cloth that no one in Roubaix could afford and that
the owners did not want to forsake to the enemy. And now the German
population was starting to run short as a result of the blockade. Krug
thought of having David, his friend from prewar days, procure the stockpiles of cloth for resale in Germany. David thus served as a middleman for

the conclusion of transactions whose true nature was best kept secret. From German brokers, he then bought products that abounded in Germany: sugar, coal, and meat originating in Denmark and Holland. He sold them to the rich and, by inclination as much as calculation, gave of his huge profits to the poor and to charitable institutions. A trainload of livestock did not arrive but that a dozen cattle were butchered for rations. He distributed sugar and coal. He supplied hospices. His pity, it must be said, was totally sensory, visual. A shock, some painful or distressing sight, was what moved his heart. He was one of those people who empties his purse into the hands of a poor wretch. He could not see a child at the window of a pastry shop without taking him inside and stuffing him with cakes. His charity was a little over the top, dramatic like he himself, but which nonetheless came from a sincere compassion for unmerited suffering.

His mansion and his estate stretched between rue des Villas and Grand Boulevard. His home was a sumptuous structure, of a gaudy opulence, which elicited laughter but also jealousy. David, better than just about anyone, understood the mysteries of credit and the art of dazzling others.

He did not travel all the way to Barbieux. On boulevard de Cambrai, David stopped in front of a tall house, enormous and sullen, squeezed between the neighbouring buildings, and which had as its only garden a narrow forecourt. He took a key from his pocket and went inside.

The vestibule was solemn and chilly, floored in black and white marble. A servant in a lace bonnet arrived.

"Madam's upstairs? Good, I'll go see her."

He climbed the stairs to the second floor and pushed open a door.

The room was rather large, sombre, heavily shaded by enormous, oppressive blue curtains concealing the window. There was a strong odour of benzoin and pearl essence. In a deliberate disorder, the entire parlour was encumbered by armchairs in phantom-like dust covers, pedestal tables, stands, bric-a-brac, a Louis XV secretary, a desk of the same era – of a quite lovely design, though diminished by the milieu – some cushions, and a Récamier sofa. On the mantle, in antique green marble, was a very pretty tortoise-shell clock. In front of the window, in the narrow strip of daylight that passed between curtains of brocaded blue silk, stood a statue in Carrara marble, the image of a crying child. The stone took on a delicacy, a transparency, an almost moving hue of milky white in the beam of light which bathed it against the shadows. A chandelier of intricate Baccarat crystal hung from the ceiling. Seated before a mahogany Empire-style card table, a woman, her back to the door, was counting stacks of cards and winning a game of solitaire.

"Is that you?" she said without turning around.

"Phew!" responded David as he let himself fall into a creaky wing chair.

The woman gathered the cards, packed them into a leather-covered box, and got to her feet. This creature was forty years old, very tall, very slender, her face almost taut, strained, and her eyes fiery. She wore a remarkably elegant dress, and her rings, too large for her thin fingers, stood out.

"Your cigar stinks!" she said. "When will you drop that habit? ... Look at the ashes on my rugs! Couldn't you smoke somewhere else?"

"But that's precisely why I come here," said David, "so I can smoke in peace."

Albertine Mailly had been David's mistress for twenty-two years. The daughter of a vegetable merchant, she had run away from home at seventeen to follow him. They had worked the markets and the fairs together. She had seen his beginnings in the demolition business, when he had been a mere worker in the big Florens firm. She had taken advantage of his surprising ascent. She was at once ambitious and greedy. At David's expense, she had amassed a respectable and parasitic fortune, which she managed quite skillfully. She had had him buy her this house, the jewellery, the furniture. She would have liked to entertain, to play the grand lady, and secretly fumed at her inability to gain access to the rigorously closed circle fashioned by the "great families" of Roubaix. But David had always refused to marry her. Any chain lay heavy upon him. In certain respects he had remained a rebel, a lover of illegality. Albertine found consolation in receiving old friends whom she dazzled with the spectacle of her riches, in tyrannizing her household staff, in establishing a reputation as the most extravagant and the most exasperating of customers in the shops of Roubaix and Lille. For David paid the bills. And Albertine had supplied herself with a royal wardrobe that she rarely had occasion to use. But in her eyes, all of this had still been "taken from the enemy." And in her closets she hoarded sable coats, ostrich hairpins, bird of paradise clips, Japanese silks, furs and fabrics, spectacles of silver and gold, dress pins of jade, coral, ivory and onyx, elegant hats, lace from Mechelen, Bruges, and old Valenciennes, just as she kept utility and bank securities in her strong boxes.

In the midst of her splendour, she had grown bored. She missed her youth, the maternal handcart of apples and oranges, the alleyways, the cheap hotels, the nighttime dances in the cabarets, the life of the common people. Often, in moments of sadness, she went down to the kitchen, drank coffee with the maids, talked to them of David and the humiliations he inflicted upon her, told their fortunes, and passed a splendid afternoon. But the following day her natural inclinations resurfaced and she again proved harsher, more despotic, more disdainful of the pains of those who served her – she, the former little vegetable merchant – than the haughtiest, most pampered descendant of the Nord's feudal industrial lords.

David kept her nonetheless. He was aware of her scheming. He was one of the types who lets many things slide and for whom a long contention ends suddenly, all at once, with an outburst. He understood the nature of Albertine's affection, the elements of greed, hatred, resentment, and fear that figured into the love she had for him. She was bit like a caged animal, which avenges itself slyly on its keeper, as it is able. He recognized the fortune she had seized along the way, appropriated at his expense. He knew she had cheated on him a few times. But he had arrived at that time of life when one begins to love individuals more for oneself than for them, for what they represent in terms of memories and habits.

Change frightened him. Albertine and he understood each other, knew one another's past lives. With her, he could take off the mask, the armour. He again became Barthélémy the peddler, the fighter, the adventurer, the man of the people who remained one of "the people." Say what she might, with her he put himself at ease. The black looks of the world weighed heavily upon him. He threw them off, smoked foul smuggled tobacco, had his clay pipe, relaxed without her daring to lose her temper in front of the servants. He was the man to remind her, in anyone's presence, of the day when they had pushed their cart together.

And then, she knew everything about him: his adventures, his trouble with the law, his mercenary lifestyle, his violent instincts. With her he was at ease. He did not hesitate to speak openly. The man with a long, sordid past, a horde of memories and secret thoughts – and tragedies – adopts the habit of silence, of constant vigilance about himself. David spoke little, weighed his words, his actions. Albertine was his relaxation. He could only be himself with children or the common people whence he came. And that was what made him popular in Épeule. People overlooked his mansion, his carriages, and his mistress because he knew how to speak patois, gladly accepted a pipe of Belgian tobacco, and appreciated Wambrechies gin. With Albertine too, he could feel comfortable letting his guard down.

Ironically, he also stayed with her in part because of his indifference to her. She no longer roused his passion. With her there were no surprises, no dramas. For this man smitten by adventure, a lover of women and risk, incessantly involved in some intrigue or a dangerous scheme leading to weariness and disillusionment, she provided repose, respite, tranquility. Thus do many such men like to find peace of mind and spirit at home.

Between them was a long history of violent passion, disgust, dangers, victories and defeats, hatreds, fighting and mutual heartache, betrayal and resentment, which bound them in spite of themselves and which Albertine cunningly made him pay for by robbing and exploiting him. For Albertine, it was almost hatred that tied her to him, that occupied her existence, to the point that she would have found herself surprisingly alone, bored and almost lost had she not been able to fill her life with this mass of bitterness, jealousy, strife, triumphs and secret acts of revenge, this constant battle to conquer and exploit that David was to her.

"Anything new?" he asked, dragging on his cigar.

"Nothing ... Oh, yes, some people came collecting for the hospitals. They're organizing a committee. All the big names ... Yet another thing I should've been part of!"

He laughed.

"You can laugh! The fact remains that in our world ..."

"Don't talk about 'our world,' would you? Leave your black looks for others."

He had gone to the cupboard, searching among the empty bottles.

"All the same, you're lucky I'm so naïve. Someone else ..."

"That's strange, there's a little port left."

"Yes, yes, change the subject. The fact remains that if I hadn't been so stupid ..."

"My heart's bleeding!"

He lit a second cigar with the remnant of the first.

"I don't know why I ever attached myself to a man like you!"

"I do, I know why."

"Why?"

"To profit!"

"Imbecile! And first, please put out that cigar. My curtains stink of tobacco. I've had enough ..."

"It's good for the moths."

"Get rid of that cigar!"

"Never in my life!"

She came up to him, tore away his cigar, and threw it into the fireplace.

"Albertine!"

She had stepped back, defying him. She had the tongs in her hand. Again they had arrived at fighting, as in the old days. He snatched the weapon from her, put it back where it belonged, shrugged his shoulders, and left the room quietly as he lit his third cigar. He yawned, stretched, shrugged his shoulders once more, and went down to the kitchen. He grumbled, "To think that I wear myself out making money, for all this happiness!"

In the kitchen, he found the two maids pretending to be busy: one at the stove stirring a non-existent stew in the bottom of a saucepan, the other dusting the interior of a sideboard. But David had been a butcher's assistant and knew the habits of the servant type.

"You're working? Good, good, very good! But gosh, it smells like cognac here."

He bent down, pulled two little glasses of brandy from beneath the table, and sniffed them.

"You've done well!"

"The last bit of a bottle ..." whispered the cook.

"A good bit isn't bad. Carry on, my dears, enjoy it while it lasts ... Oh, someone's in the cellar?"

"The laundress, sir."

"What's she doing down there?"

"The washing ..."

"But in the cellar? What a house!"

David went down to the basement. There was hardly any light. Electricity was unavailable during the daytime. The Germans wanted to save on coal. Near the cellar window, a woman, her back to David, was scrubbing linen in a little tub.

"What're you doing down here? You've nowhere else to wash?"

The woman turned toward David in surprise. She was a young girl – eighteen or nineteen years old – blond, haggard, her eyes strained with weariness, a black shawl wrapped round her neck. She coughed in the cold dampness. A huge apron of rough linen gave her an awkward appearance, and from her torso sprouted two bare and lanky arms – surprisingly thin and red, a bit like the legs of an insect. She reminded one vaguely of some giant ant. She whispered: "There's no courtyard, Mr David. Also ..."

"Also what?"

"Also, the cook doesn't want the kitchen to get dirty ..."

"So you use the cellar?"

"Yes."

During the war, many bourgeois houses did not have a place for doing laundry, which, before the conflict, had been sent out. Women were now being brought in to do the washing in the basement.

"Good, good. Well, carry on ..."

She went back to the laundry. He looked at her sharp, lean, meager face, her slender and reddened nose, her poorly combed hair, and her long skinny arms ending with a beetle in each hand.* She stamped her feet. Watching her, David – who had been a factory worker – guessed that she was suffering from stomach cramps, like so many young girls condemned to work standing up. It's exhausting for a woman. She was neither pretty nor desirable, no. In spite of himself, David could not see a woman without thinking of sex ... But this one, truly, with her look of a wet cat, made him sick at heart. He softened his voice.

"You're the one they call Annie?"

"Yes, Mr David, Annie Mouraud."

She had finished scrubbing, paused, and straightened up. She wiped her forehead with a wet hand, leaving a bit of quivering white foam in her hair. And she grabbed the handle of the wringer. She began turning it, guiding the linen between the rollers with a hand reddened, bleached, softened, and pained by the potash in the water. As she leaned over the handle to push each time, David saw the poor muscles of her arms stretch and the bones of her thin spine bulge under the wet and clinging dress. Such things turned his stomach. Suddenly, he threw down his cigar, which

*Beetles were wooden tools used to beat linen.

went out with a sizzle in the puddle of soapy water. He took off his jacket, rolled up his sleeves.

"Give it to me ..."

"What?"

"Together ... Get some fresh water, old girl. You'll rinse, I'll wring.

"Mr David!"

"Let me do it. Let me ..."

He grabbed the handle with his sturdy paw, turned it with a strong arm, making dirty water squirt from the linen.

"Those women up there!"

But he did not call for them. An odd pride prevented him from ordering them, making them help. Even if it meant firing them, he preferred to do the job himself if they would not.

"Mr David ..." timidly protested the young girl, almost frightened.

"Rinse, rinse, and don't worry about the rest. And then you'll come drink something in the kitchen as well, my dear, with the two who're having a good meal upstairs, at my expense ..."

Chapter Three

One morning Alain had gone to a neighbour's to whitewash the kitchen ceiling. He still had no identity card and no longer left the house without extreme precaution. Usually, when he did go out, Félicie stayed home so he could come right back in the event of danger and hide. This day she was called away by an argument that had just broken out at the Duydts' between Zidore and his father. Zidore's mother had fallen ill, and little Marcel and Armande were crying for help. Félicie ran to intervene. It was at this moment that Alain returned. The ceiling was still yellow. Alain had gone home to get a little bluing to mix with his whitewash. As he reached the door, he saw a green devil at the far end of the cul-de-sac. The man held his bicycle in one hand and the chain of a prisoner he had just corralled in the other. The pair came up the street. Alain knocked frantically on the door. No one answered. He turned round to flee. And the green devil was upon him.

"Papieren."

Alain rummaged in his pockets. He had several old cards but none that was good.

"Papieren," repeated the German.

"Mein herr, papieren inside," explained Alain, pointing to the door. "One minute ..."

He hoped to get in, escape through the courtyard, and disappear. But this German was no novice. "Komme!" he said. And he calmly slipped his revolver under Alain's nose. Dirty, smeared with whitewash, having the look of a hooligan, Alain was bound in chains and followed the policeman across town, tied to a companion who came from some hovel or other and who was sporting a red belt, espadrilles, and sideburns. People stepped aside and watched them pass. The policeman's dog, a big Alsatian, trotted at their heels.

Alain was worried. He feared the fake cards would be discovered and wanted to get rid of them before going into the police station. With a skillful maneuver, he managed to slip his hand into his pocket, grab the bundle of cards, and let it fall. Then he felt himself go cold. The dog had stopped and was sniffing the bundle on the sidewalk. He picked it up in his mouth and took a few grave steps at his master's side. The German was distracted and did not notice. The dog dropped the cards. Alain could have kissed the flithy beast.

Alain and a group of captives were taken from the police station to the prison on rue de l'Hospice. Three soldiers accompanied them. They had bound the older men in chains. The younger ones, Alain and a few others, were left with their hands free. "Don't run," cautioned one of the Germans, "or you kaput ..." He pointed to his gun. They promised to go peaceably. But the Germans made the detainees open their jackets and cut their suspenders and the half belts of their trousers. The cortege set off with the men in chains out front and the rest following along and holding up their pants with both hands. By way of rue Saint-Georges, they soon stood facing the prison on rue de l'Hospice. There, suddenly, Alain's neighbour – a tall, young, blond man – dashed off toward rue de l'Espérance. A terrible scene unfolded. A soldier swore, took aim. There was a crack. And the runaway, struck between the shoulder blades like a rabbit, fell in a heap as he turned the corner and remained lying facedown on the sidewalk. Everyone rushed up. A moment of confusion ensued. The Germans collected the body. The one who had fired pointed to the corpse and his gun, explained what had happened to his comrades, and cried as he regarded his victim.

· · ·

The prison was set up in the former warehouse of a wholesale cloth merchant. It consisted of a series of rooms from which the shelves had not even been removed. Each cell held forty odd prisoners. Alain was on the third floor in a room ten metres by five. It was smoky, replete with dust and noise, absolutely filthy, with walls stripped of plaster and covered in graffiti, the ceiling black, the floor dotted with spittle and miscellaneous garbage, and the whole looking onto rue de l'Espérance by two little windows half covered with boards. Some of the men were lying on straw mattresses and sleeping or smoking. Others were sitting on the ground and playing cards. Still others were reading, singing, laughing, or arguing. There were nearly fifty of them in this overcrowded room, one on top of the other, and making a frightful racket. Shouting, laughter, bawdy songs, threats and insults, the dreadful smell of a zoo, a thick suffocating dust, and an impenetrable bluish haze instantly grabbed one's senses of sight, sound, and smell. But Alain had found a friend on the inside: Zidore Duydt. Zidore had been arrested a few days before Alain and was serving a four-month sentence. This connection might not have seemed like much. Yet for Alain, who felt so isolated, it was a priceless treasure. Because Zidore – long familiar with all these scoundrels and served as well by considerable physical strength and a thorough understanding of boxing – enjoyed great prestige among the prisoners, and his opinion mattered. Here the mob ruled.

There were a few good men in this vulgar herd, and for them the most disagreeable part of their sentence was being forced to serve it in such company. The underworld exerted indisputable sway. He who had neither the flexibility to submit to it nor the strength to hold his own against it, like Zidore, was its victim and plaything. Brutal, coarse, of an unimaginable boldness, with surprising skill at wrestling and boxing, accustomed moreover to placing little value in their wellbeing or that of others, these fellows threw themselves headlong into battle, unafraid of giving or taking violent blows. And they literally denuded the civilized man. They in no way hesitated to make him empty his pockets, hand over his tobacco, his money, his toiletries. The individual who had nothing to give was beaten or manhandled and tormented. Among the good folks – aghast, stunned, crazed by indignation and fear – there were some who went screaming to the German sentry for help. But the roughnecks were not afraid of the Germans either. They seemed quite at home here. The morning of Alain's arrival, he saw the sentry come in to stop a brawl. And the bandit at whom he took aim turned round and presented his backside, shouting "Here!" to the accompaniment of laughter and cheers. The German shrugged his shoulders and left.

"Transports" – convoys of new prisoners – arrived every two or three days. Each occasion was a source of great entertainment. The newcomers were surrounded, the scapegoats of the group immediately identified. And their pockets were emptied, they were pushed around, had repugnant tasks forced upon them, were left to sleep on the floor, had their foreheads set alight with crumbled cigarette papers – carefully positioned while they slumbered at night and resulting in painful burns. Live mice were slipped into their clothes. And if the persecuted showed signs of rebellion, they fell into the hands of fellows accustomed to footfighting who struck them in the pit of the stomach or below the belt, grabbed them by the balls, sank fingers into their eyes. The good man was unprepared to deal with such rabble. But even here money and a name retained their power. In one room was a certain Roblet, a regional manufacturer whom the Germans had thought it witty to inflict with companions of this sort. But Roblet was not so much to be pitied as one might have thought. Distributions of cigarettes and money and above all the prestige of an eminent name of industry, which in the Nord is akin to that of a great feudal lord, mollified the fiercest. There were still a few diehards who spoke of robbing Jules in his turn ... But others came to his defense and formed a bodyguard. One never knew, it could well be useful to have been of service to a Roblet.

Several hooligans offered him their straw mattresses or their lousy blankets. They reserved the most spacious rack for his bed. From the outside, by way of prisoners in the work gangs, he soon received choice items: cold chicken, wine, bread. He shared such fare with others. His largess charmed all and sundry. Money remains a great power, no matter the circumstance.

Those who did not have the luck of sporting a famous name by and large submitted to the tyranny of the crowd. Some wretches demeaned themselves, singing, whistling, playing the fool or the clown for this vulgar mob. Whoever had a talent capitalized on it. There was even an artist, a gifted caricaturist, Sassenet, whose disrespectful sketch of Commander Hoffman had landed him here. Sassenet, understanding that among the masses the artist still does not have the same renown as the manufacturer, had found a way to popularize his talent. He offered first-rate portraits to one man after another. His skill quickly won him a reputation. Most did him the honour of asking for their profiles. Then some fellows had him design ingenious tattoos and sign his creations. In the crowded room one soon saw a display of bare, hairy, filthy chests on which the artist – armed with a copying pencil – was sketching the patient's choice of musketeers, airplanes, naked women, or symbols of hope. Next a big hooligan, his own skin so tattooed that not an inch of free space remained, permanently tattooed these designs with a bundle of three needles tied together and dipped in India ink. He went slowly, from prick to prick. The blood oozed from the bare flesh. And the patients – motionless, in the midst of a circle of onlookers – made it a point of honour not to flinch. The outline complete, the surgeon liberally smeared the skin with a flood of ink. And for a week redness and swelling remained. Some prisoners exhibited amusing designs. One had giant handcuffs tattooed on his wrists, another a cop on his buttock as a sign of contempt, yet another a large face on his stomach which he made laugh, cry, or grimace by writhing comically, to bursts of laughter from an impassioned audience. These burlesque scenes drew the Germans, with guns in hand, to watch from the doorway.

Sassenet was now held in high esteem. His fellow prisoners paid for their tattoos with crackers and cigarettes. Here, at least, art sustained the artist.

And then there was Doctor Diedrick. He was a fat old man of considerable height, with the sensual, cynical, and weary face of a Silenus.* He was well known in the underworld for openly providing abortions as well as medical certificates for workplace accidents or for trials on assault charges. Here he enjoyed a certain celebrity, which he maintained by organizing well-balanced matches of dodge ball played with a rag rolled into a ball, games of leapfrog, or riotous free-for-alls of unbelievable brutality.

The contaminated food caused dysentery. The inmates went down to the lavatory by way of a staircase besmirched with human excrement. There was neither door nor paper. They relieved themselves in full view of the others, squatting over the hole, chancing a fall. The walls were dotted with brown streaks. For several days the corpse of the young man the Germans had killed lay on the ground. The prisoners defecated right beside his body.

But the strangest fellow in the prison was Chabot. It must have been a nickname.† Chabot was an old man. He had seven children. So, he explained, he had made sure he stayed in prison. While he was here, his family received his share of rations and ate a little better.

---

*In Greek mythology, Silenus was the oldest and most inebriated follower of Dionysus, the god of wine.

†A "chabot" is a type of bullhead fish. Because "Chabot" is also a common family name in France, it has been left as "Chabot" rather than translated as "Bullhead."

This wretch was not bitter. He had eventually gained the trust of the Germans, who employed him as a sweeper. He alleviated misery, tried to rally the prisoners, and collected food that was thrown out – the soldiers' leftovers – to supply famished inmates. At nighttime he went on his rounds. He knew how to recognize the most exhausted at a glance. He approached them: "You're hungry?" Oh, that look! "Here, eat!"

Some people shed tears at receiving this bowl.

In a cell he found a French prisoner of war consumed by lice, in dreadful condition. He took him something to eat, clean underwear, some clothes ...

Alain watched Chabot and was amazed. He was the first happy man Alain had ever encountered. Chabot was certainly a fool, a simpleton. He never read. He was not intelligent. His mind was not elevated. But he had a big heart. And Alain began to wonder if this were not the standard by which people ought to be judged.

· · ·

At the end of May 1916, Jacqueline Laubigier, Alain's little sister, took the catechism exam and was permitted to receive communion. She was ill. Even so she dragged herself over to the prison on rue de l'Hospice, where she could see her older brother through the window and shout the good news up to him. Then she returned, occasionally leaning against the walls of houses along the way. For months she had languished for want of food and fresh air.

It was an odd communion, at once funny and sad. This day is important for a child. Despite the prevailing sorrow, Félicie had done her best to put a little dignity into the occasion. She herself sewed the white garment. Mrs Hennedyck gave her the long veil. Félicie found some canvas shoes and bleached them to imitate suede slippers. There were no church candles. Félicie made one from a broom handle, cut down and sharpened to a point, which she painted with white enamel. All the communicants had such candles. A nail driven into the top represented the wick.

The dinner was one of those composite meals such as people still managed to put together: a soup from canned vegetables, a platter of lentils and American bacon, a rabbit with raisins alongside lettuce and fries. For salad dressing, Félicie had had to replace the oil with melted lard and the vinegar with the last bit of a bottle of sour wine that her sister-in-law Flavie had miraculously discovered.

The dinner began sadly. Félicie thought of Alain, Flavie of her eldest, who was in the war. They had just started carving the rabbit when Alain arrived with a German soldier. What a surprise! Alain explained that he had been allowed to come but that he had had to bring along a sentry and promise to return peaceably. From that moment, it was a real party. The rabbit disappeared. A cerealine pie followed. They had set a place at the table for the German, who did not look like a bad sort. He ate all that remained of the rabbit, plus a huge piece of pie. Félicie had even brewed beer by letting boiled oats ferment with sugar and a few hops. What a celebration! The good soldier was in seventh heaven. During dessert, he insisted on singing in German. They applauded politely, even though they could not understand the lyrics.

After dinner, they had to leave for vespers. Everyone went together, the communicant in front with little Camille, then Félicie and Flavie with the children, and finally Alain with his bodyguard and cousin François. The soldier was clutching a bar of soap that Félicie had offered him and from which he refused to part company. Soap fetched huge prices back in Germany. The soldier stopped in front of Épeule's Bac à Puces cabaret. Vespers did not mean much to him. And the music of the cabaret, the noise of the dances, the voices of the women called to him like siren song.

"You come back quickly," he said to Alain. "Me wait here." And he went into the Bac à Puces with his bar of soap while the others headed to vespers.

The church was full. In the crowd were many Germans watching the communicants. It must have also been the time for first communion in Germany. Never had folks seen so many soldiers in church. When Jacqueline entered, immaculate in her ingenious outfit, a German near her fell to his knees, took the hem of her long white dress in both hands, and kissed it as he cried.

Chapter Four

Around five o'clock in the afternoon, Isidore Duydt was hurrying toward the Bac à Puces cabaret. It was summer 1916. A few weeks earlier Zidore had escaped from the prison on rue de l'Hospice, where he had only spent a couple of weeks in the company of Alain Laubigier.

Zidore walked along, dragging his tattered espadrilles, his cap at an angle, his hands in his belt, and his stomach empty. From vanity, and though he hardly felt like it at the moment, he affected a swaggering gait, spit to one side, and cast impudent glances at the girls. People turned to look at his pale and round little face – a childlike, headstrong, obstinate countenance lit by two very blue eyes and dotted with the golden whiskers of a poorly trimmed blond beard.

This boy had started out courageously enough. He had not wanted to imitate his brother, who sold gold to the enemy. Zidore had refused to enter his name on the headcount lists. He had run contraband, stolen from the camps, pilfered German wagons. Then the frequenting of "runners," thieves, and hooligans had corrupted him. At bottom he was a bit a victim of his own heroism. And there were many like him.

Zidore had not eaten for two days. Last night there had been a card game at the Pou-Volant cabaret. He owed Pumpkin fifty francs. He had come back drunk and sick and had slept in till three o'clock in the afternoon. He had gotten up and searched in vain for something to eat amid the bric-a-brac of his father's shop. Old Duydt did business in a variety of merchandise. Positioned side by side on the shelves were a bottle of olive oil – a true rarity – schoolbags, books, lard-burning lamps, a litre of Pernod, a prosthetic leg for an amputee, condoms, herbal teas, potatoes, gas mantles, and stationary – an improbable jumble of cloth, old furniture, rags, tattered volumes, and battered saucepans – all things that were no longer manufactured, that were in short supply, that Old Duydt had hunted out, remnants from before the war, precious vestiges for which people had begun to wrangle. Old Duydt employed his two youngest children in smuggling and running contraband – moving goods across the border – even stealing. His older children had rebelled against him. Étienne and Léonie had left long ago, and hungry Zidore was working on his own account, having come to understand his father's unimaginable greed.

That day, Zidore and Old Duydt had exchanged bittersweet words. The old man knew quite well that Zidore, when rummaging like this in the shop, was in reality looking for his bread so he could cut off a slice. And Old Duydt had not left his side. For each member of this family stole food from the others. Zidore had had to give up his quest and left the store. He needed a hundred francs. First of all he was starving. And then Georgina, his mistress, needed money.

He had met her at a boxing arena. Short, stocky, and brawny, Zidore enjoyed remarkable physical strength, and since he frequented dark cabarets and milieus where force was king, he was soon feared and sought. Amateurs, old professionals fallen from their game, the whole shady crowd that revolves around wrestling and boxing arenas – all counseled him to fight. They taught him the basics, introduced him in the ring. He was surprisingly tough, this pale and stubborn little fellow accustomed to hard labour in the mines. He scored a success, made some money, won the admiration of women, and was intoxicated by a ready popularity, which his reputation as a rebel enhanced still more. At eighteen years of age, he was not a bad boy, with his round, childlike face, his naïve blue eyes, and a short golden beard too rarely trimmed. He sang pleasantly and played a bit of the accordion with his friend Olivier. He got girls for nothing. With the women, he even began accepting a little money, letting them pay for a round of drinks or a room ... He took it all in stride. Then he met Georgina, a cunning thirty-eight-year-old woman. And with this one he was truly smitten. It was above all for her that he had combed the streets today. He had promised her a hundred francs. He had been trying to find the money for a long time. His brother Étienne the hunchback, the moneychanger, had refused to give it to him. Étienne was an influential man. He lived on rue de l'Épeule, in a big house that he had converted into an office. The copper plaque read: *International Bank*.

And beneath it was a handwritten sign marked with the imperial seal: *This establishment is registered with the German Authorities.*

Such a talisman rendered the house inviolable. Étienne had even thrown out the Roubaix police commissioner, who had claimed to be executing a search warrant. Under the aegis of the German authorities, Étienne used his house as a base for all kinds of trafficking: buying gold, draining French assets, and passing them to the Germans for their foreign purchases. He was rumoured to make huge sums of money. Humpty was a name of the past. He had become Mr Étienne. Short, deformed, his complexion pale, with a ratlike face and surprisingly sparkling and inquisitive eyes, he went about town in high fashion, his hump concealed beneath the fullness of a raglan coat. He was shrewd, ingratiating, furtive, and invariably secretive. He carried a briefcase everywhere he went. The entire Duydt family regarded the hunchback – who had so quickly discerned the road to riches and become a power – with astonishment and pride.

Zidore had not understood the best strategy for approaching Étienne. Rather than talking to him about his wife Alice, who had run away and who still haunted the hunchback's thoughts, Zidore had simply named an amount ... Étienne, the miser, had coldly shown him the door.

But Zidore had found salvation at the home of his sister Léonie. Her house, on rue de Dammartin, was stately. It was ludicrous to see such a girl in this dwelling. Big wool merchants had inhabited it before the war. They had left for Paris. Léonie's lover, a captain attached to headquarters, had generously accorded the usufruct to Léonie – the daughter of miners, barely literate, rough and uncouth – who was living here in grand style. Her case was not singular. Since the start of the war, thus had many prostitutes treated themselves to the illusion of achieving the eternal dream – of being kept up in princely fashion.

A servant opened the door. Zidore – in his espadrilles – stepped onto the Persian rug of a rocaille parlour. And Léonie hurried to greet him. She was a tall, thin, plain-looking girl, her face pointed like Étienne's, illuminated by two fiery and restless eyes that transfigured her. Léonie consumed life, squandered it partying, impassioned, unbalanced, but even so good at heart. She welcomed her "little brother" with open arms. Léonie had reared him – slaved away like all the eldest children of poor families – and retained a maternal tenderness for Zidore. She showed him her furniture, pressed sherry on him, and borrowed a hundred francs from her servant to give to him. She did not have long to enjoy this lifestyle. Tuberculosis was eating away at her.

Zidore headed back toward Épeule and the Bac à Puces. He had not eaten. But he was so pleased that he forgot his hunger. He walked quickly. He thought of Georgina, of the hundred francs he was bringing her. He owed Pumpkin fifty. But she was waiting. His stomach rumbled as he neared a pastry shop. But Zidore restrained himself. Break the bill? Oh no! Georgina would be so pleased to have it whole.

He had met her after a boxing match while dancing at the Bac à Puces cabaret, a popular hangout for the women of Épeule. She was twenty years older than Zidore. She fell in love with his pretty little face, his youth, his strength, and the element of naïvety that still made him charming despite the beginnings of the conceit, the bragging, and the vainglory brought on by his success as a boxer and a wrestler. She found it amusing to steal the innocence of a child so fresh, so young. Zidore, immediately enthralled, obsessed, frantic with passion for this lecherous woman, fell madly in love with her and grew jealous for her attention.

He talked of keeping her up, rented a room for her, had her to himself for three whole weeks. Then he ran out of money and she left, returned to the streets. He got her back for a fortnight, began the same story two, three, a dozen times – crazy, mad with jealousy and pain, forced to take it all as a "joke" in front of others, and suffering silent agony for this creature prematurely aged, worn out by a risky, empty, wasteful lifestyle, and irreparably corrupt. Soon he began beating her. He cheated on her, but not with relish. She mocked him openly, made him see that she did not give a damn about men. She was decidedly too clever for him. He came back more subdued, more passionately in love after each separation. All his money went for her. And once he had run out he tried to keep her by force. He would have killed to hold on to her. Conscious of this love, she ruthlessly abused her grip on him.

"Make her work for you," said Pumpkin.

But Zidore did not know how.

A hundred francs! A week! A week to have Georgina to himself! He hurried, broke into a run toward the Bac à Puces. He was dying of hunger. His stomach pulled at him. He sucked on an old quid of bitter tobacco to hold it at bay. A hundred francs! A nice, even sum!

Zidore had grown accustomed to suffering and hunger since coming to know Georgina. He had quickly begun to deprive himself for her, to endure a three-day fast without complaint so she could have her money, so she would remain his for a week. He had almost fashioned a mystique, an ideal – a frightful ideal – out of Georgina. For her, he resigned himself to suffering, deception, cheating, stealing, betraying friends. She had become his morality. That which benefited Georgina was his good, that which harmed her, his evil. In his degradation, this mystique somehow afforded him a sombre joy, a touch of pride. To die for something, even a Georgina, was exhilarating! An ideal, yes, the folly of youth that, for lack of an ennobling object, finds one such object – however dreadful – at any price.

The Bac à Puces, on the upper end of rue de l'Épeule, flooded the street with the noise of its dances and the song of an accordion. Zidore pushed open the lattice door.

The cabaret was big, ugly, furnished in whitewood, with an oak bar in the rear where a Gambrinus sat enthroned on a barrel.*

Perched on a tabletop, Big Olivier – romantic-looking with his dangling lock of hair and a cigarette butt in his lips – was playing a doleful accordion. Some women, a handful of ruffians, and a few Germans were waltzing, making the floorboards sway to the rhythm of the music. At the bar, Mélie Nauserais, the owner of the Bac à Puces, was pouring mugs of beer that Otto, her German – a character in blue cotton pants and a black wool vest, who had somehow managed to stay with her since the start of the war – was distributing to the patrons. Among these bandits, Otto had the look of the accomplished type. It was rumoured that he had deserted and was hiding from the German police. In any event, he never left for the front and only used his uniform when he marched over to the army depot to cart away food and coal for Mélie. He was remarkably skilled with false keys.

With an air of indifference, Zidore passed through the group of waltzers, ignoring Georgina, whom he clearly saw dancing with a Bavarian. Pumpkin was playing cards with a soldier. The former was a fat little man with a swollen round face beneath an old greenish bowler, lending him the gourd-

---

*Gambrinus was a mythical Flemish king popularly regarded as a patron saint of beer.

like appearance to which he owed his nickname. Morlebaix and Red were watching. From Pumpkin's strained, feverish look, his uncertain glance, his rapid movements, Zidore could tell that he was cheating. The German, for his part, was agitated, beside himself, furious at losing like this without understanding why. Beneath the bench he had set down a basket of fresh meat, which Morelbaix, another of the cabaret's customers, was eyeing.

Morlebaix and Red welcomed Zidore to the table. He was flattered. They knew him to be a good and generous fellow. He had a tab at Mélie's. He ordered mugs of beer from Otto. They watched Pumpkin, who was almost done fleecing his German. Then Georgina came over, having finished the dance, called Zidore "my little man," sat on his knees, and threw her arms around his neck. Beneath the table, with a skillful maneuvre, he slipped her the bill. He felt himself blushing with joy and pride. But he caught the glance of Red, who was staring at him and chuckling. Zidore was ashamed and quickly put his hand back on the table.

Pumpkin finished the card game and tucked the proceeds of the pair-royal in his pocket while his victim, the German, went to console himself at the bar. Pumpkin was sweating. This old-school pimp was loath to strain himself, and nothing exhausted him like cheating. In one gulp he swallowed a special drink mimicking a mêlé cassis, which Otto had brought over.

At this instant shouting erupted. The German had gone to retrieve his basket of meat and could not find it. Stolen! Meat for the officers! The poor devil, he was not cut out for the front. He cried, yelled. He had not noticed Morlebaix's sudden disappearance. He grabbed Otto by the throat when the barkeeper tried to toss him out. Red jumped up and ran to the rescue. The German pulled a revolver. Shrill cries, women's tears, a sudden uproar filled the Bac à Puces.

Behind the bar, Mélie wailed, "My cabaret! My cabaret!"

Zidore had gotten to his feet. He headed straight for the German, pushing aside Otto and Red, who, both pale, had stepped back when the man had drawn the gun. Inside Zidore, at moments of danger, there was a strange excitement, almost a desire to show others how to put themselves in the line of fire. He shouted: "Get out!"

"Damn!" swore the German, rushing at him like a bull.

He caught Zidore with a blow to the mouth, but it was the only hit he scored. Zidore had moved back. He ducked, avoiding the terrifying swing of the German, then landed an uppercut beneath his chin, followed by a head-butt to the chest and a quick blow to the stomach. The German groaned, lurched backward, bent double, and staggered away to lean against the wall. Otto and several women grabbed his shoulders and pushed him toward the courtyard, to bring him to his senses.

Zidore, his mouth bloody, had gone into the kitchen, where Mélie gave him some water. He was in pain, suffering from a broken tooth and a split gum. He gargled with alcohol. From a distance, as he was heading back to the main room, he spied Georgina and Red in a corner, furtively kissing each other mouth to mouth while they danced.

The sight shocked Zidore more than the blow he had just received. "That lout!"

He marched over to Red, took a mug of beer, and threw it in his face. Red looked up, distraught, livid beneath his shock of red hair, ugly with his grey, sleep-encrusted eyes distorted by fear. For a minute they stared each other down. Red dared not move a muscle. He saw reason slowly return to Zidore's eyes. He realized they would not fight. Reassured, he shrugged his shoulders and left the building.

Zidore had turned toward Georgina, who was sobbing loudly. It was almost more than he could do not to beat her like an animal. "Get up!" he shouted.

She got to her feet.

"March!"

She marched outside. He followed her. The door slammed behind them. Pumpkin's voice broke a terror-stricken silence: "Not even a kick in the ass ... What an idiot!"

In the gathering darkness, Zidore and Georgina headed toward the Pou Volant cabaret, where Georgina was renting a room. This establishment was Mélie's chief competitor. Georgina walked straight ahead. Zidore followed behind her. She continued whimpering. They used the private entrance – fetid and slimy, and which reeked like a urinal. Georgina's room – right below the rooftop, furnished with an iron bedstead, a little stove, and a wardrobe – stank of cheap perfume, sweat, and mustiness, mingled with the scent of food and burnt fat. The disorder and the fake luxury of prostitutes – all ribbons and awful trinkets – dominated the scene.

Meek, still frightened – she had really thought she was in for a beating – Georgina started taking off her clothes. A little drunk, his stomach empty, Zidore felt confused, his head heavy. He instinctively unlaced his espadrilles and unwound the scarf that served as his belt. She saw that he was undressing. She considered herself forgiven, came up to him, and pressed her body to his, insidiously twisting them together.

"My little Zidore ..."

He felt himself mellowing. He had tears in his eyes. Like a child, he whispered, "Why'd you do that, Georgina? Why'd you do that?"

She shrugged. "We were joking. For a laugh ... It happens at the end of a dance ..."

"You shouldn't have done it ..."

"I didn't mean any harm. You're silly to make such a big deal of it! I swear I wasn't thinking, I swear! I'll never do it again. Just let him try! He actually disgusts me, the little redhead!"

She clung to him more lovingly.

"My little man, you know I didn't want ... Come, go, that's right, my dear ..."

She lured him, at once perverse and motherly, a mixture of protective tenderness and sensuality exactly as he wanted, child that he was. She drew him to her bed, her arms and legs already entwined with his.

Georgina fell asleep, forgiven, reassured, triumphant. She occupied the whole bed, splayed out. Zidore himself could not sleep. His broken tooth was aching. The candle had been lit. He watched the shadows dance. He gazed at this somnolent creature, this mound of flesh at his side. She repulsed him. He vehemently recalled her body, her skin, her smell. He scrutinized the wilted face, the eyes wearied by debauchery, the mouth with its sordid laugh, its vile kisses, its shameful words. For her, for this prostitute's flesh, he had stolen, fought, lied, suffered ... He was confusedly aware of the power he was wasting, of the irreparable blindness that led him to squander a storehouse of energy, courage, and youth for this creature. Zidore was alarmed to think of all the good, useful things he could have done and which, because of her and for her, he would never accomplish.

He slid out of bed feet first, slipped on his socks and his pants. His mouth was bleeding. He spit blood. Without a sound, he tiptoed away from the bedstead. The animalistic smell of this sleeping woman turned his stomach. He spent the rest of the evening in a chair, near a window cracked open to the pure breeze of the night.

II

"I won't do it," repeated Zidore.

They were in a corner of the Bac à Puces cabaret: Zidore, Pumpkin, and Red. They were talking, leaning toward each other over the sticky table because of the noise of the dancers and the din of the accordion that Big Olivier was playing near the bar. Zidore shook his head feverishly. Pumpkin, his typical bowler on his head, said nothing. Red, his eyes gummy, his complexion pallid, let his cigarette butt hang from his lips, with a contemptuous look on his face.

"Why're you chicken?" he said.

"I know you," responded Zidore. "I know you, and ... he's my brother, damn it! I just can't."

"You're being sentimental," said Red.

"No, I'm not!"

Pumpkin raised a flabby and greasy hand, his pinkie adorned with a huge signet ring. "I swear to you, your brother won't be hurt! No! Nothing of the sort! Rob him, that's all ..."

"I won't do it ..."

There was a respite. All three turned round, sat up in their chairs as if this battle had worn them out. Red emptied his mug. Pumpkin pulled out his pack of cigarette papers and turned down one corner with a flick of his nail. Zidore watched the dancers without really paying attention. His cheeks felt hot from having argued so much.

In a last whirlwind, a flight of skirts, the waltz came to a close. Olivier ended with a grand flourish on his accordion, unhooked the strap with a sigh of content, appropriated a mug, and stood up, heading toward Pumpkin and Zidore. He offered Zidore an enormous paw: "How's it going? You didn't come with Georgina?"

"No," said Zidore curtly.

Big Olivier could not have hit on a worse subject. Zidore had not seen his mistress for more than a week. Business was going badly. They had not managed to run any contraband across the border. Zidore was broke, and Georgina, smelling poverty, had cleared out, disappeared again with one or another of her casual customers. In front of the others, Zidore tried to laugh it off, but at heart he was suffering.

"It's not the first time Georgina's left you high and dry, is it?" replied Olivier, who was not the sharpest fellow.

"You're getting on my nerves about Georgina!" shouted Zidore.

He usually took such comments as a joke, but this time he really was at the end of his rope.

"Okay, okay, it's all right, don't make a big deal about it," said Olivier calmly. And without the least bitterness he sat down beside Zidore.

Pumpkin and Red were still debating, returning to the plan to despoil Étienne the hunchback. Zidore heard them without listening. He bit his nails. His disconsolate thoughts turned toward Georgina. He had looked for her everywhere, in all the bars, the dives, the cheap hotels, the soldier's nightclubs. She was impossible to find. She must have come across some imbecile to keep her up for a couple of weeks, or worse, a pimp to run her. Zidore chewed his nails till they bled. To think that a little money, one bill, almost nothing, would suffice for her to come back to him, of her own volition, magically! She was like a divining rod, magnetically drawn to money.

"And not bills," said Pumpkin. "Gold. That's worth double. What an opportunity's going to pass us by, eh!"

It was Zidore who, of his own accord, reentered the debate. He did it as if his words were the result of a long internal reflection. "First of all, these moneychangers, there're lots of them! We could rob another one ..."

"The others are on their guard."

"Étienne is, too. He's armed. He has two pistols. I've seen them."

"Yes, but with you he won't be suspicious. You could get him to go wherever you wanted."

"And then," said Pumpkin, "it's not worth trying if we come across a guy without a penny on him. We know Étienne carries his gold in a money belt. He prides himself on it. It's a sure thing. A done deal."

"Me, I wouldn't put up with the situation," said Red. "Here's a guy who's rolling in it, who jerks you around, who won't give you a red cent, who leaves you suffering like this, and you're chickening out? Well, I never!"

"You'd do it to your brother, then? Risk hurting him? What if he defends himself? What'll you do? I know exactly ... No, no. Pick somebody else!"

"I'm telling you we won't touch a hair on his head," said Pumpkin reassuringly. "You bring him to us somewhere or other, in a quiet spot, which we can figure out. We grab him, take his belt, rob him ... I swear, Zidore, we won't touch a hair."

"And if he puts up a fight? He certainly won't let himself be done like that!"

"What'd you think he could manage against four of us?"

"Four?"

"You, me, Red, Otto the deserter, and Olivier."

"That actually makes five," said Otto, Mélie's German, who had come to listen.

Olivier was surprised. "Me, what'll I do? What's this about?"

"Shut your ugly mug," said Pumpkin. "You'll see when the time comes."

"Okay, fine," said Olivier obediently. And he began rolling his cigarette, licking it with his tongue, completely at ease. One could manipulate this big hulk like a child.

"I won't do it," repeated Zidore obstinately. "Someone else, whoever, I'm in. But not Étienne!"

"All right, all right."

They talked no more about it. Pumpkin had the mugs refilled. Otto the German had gone to wait tables and pour beer alongside Mélie. Red had taken a dice tray and two throwing boxes from the window sill. He began a game of Zanzibar with Big Olivier, and the dice rolled on the sonorous wood.

"Six and four is ten and three is thirteen ..."

"Whoa, what a lucky guy!"

And then came the oily, dreamy voice of Pumpkin: "Thirty thousand francs. It's rumoured he sometimes has 30,000 francs in his money belt ..."

"Without counting his briefcase, which often has banknotes inside ..."

"He keeps it on a chain, like a collector. That proves it!"

And again came the distinct and noisy rattling of the dice in the tray.

Zidore made an abrupt, angry movement. He stood up, rejected the obsession, chased away the haunting idea – the slow invasion of his conscience – with a sharp word.

"Now you're all pissing me off! No, no way! Forget it!"

He emptied his mug in one gulp, slammed it on the table, and left.

• • •

"Is it much farther?"

"Five minutes," said Zidore.

Étienne and Zidore walked side by side beneath the hunchback's umbrella. It was raining. Night was falling. No one was on the streets. A sad wind wailed, driving the cold raindrops and lashing at their faces. Wearing only a jacket, his overcoat on his arm, Étienne was oblivious to the conditions and hurried on.

They headed up boulevard de Cambrai. They passed behind the hospice, skirting a long brick wall toward Place du Travail.

"Where is it?" asked Étienne again.

"At the end of rue Ma Campagne."

"Let's move fast."

And he pulled along his brother.

That morning Zidore had paid a visit to Étienne the hunchback. He had told him, "I ran into your wife. Alice wants to see you again. Tonight I'll take you to the home of some friends, if you want to go with me. She's afraid of you. She doesn't want to give her address."

And from that moment, Étienne the hunchback had waited in feverish expectation. Ever since his wife had fled and abandoned him, this nervous man had been obsessed with finding her.

They arrived at rue Ma Campagne. They traversed the sidewalk of an immense factory that stood empty and dead. Across the street were a few silent and sleeping houses and then some fields. At the end of the factory was a big derelict cabaret, seemingly abandoned, with all the windows shut. Farther on lay an empty lot encumbered with garbage and scrap iron. Above, in the twilight, was the grey, sombre, turbulent sky and the cold glitter of the rain.

They arrived at the door of the cabaret. Harried and feverish, Étienne noticed neither the dirty panelling nor the moss lining the threshold. Besides, at present all Roubaix had this bleak appearance. Zidore and Étienne approached the private entrance. Zidore hesitated.

"It's here?" asked Étienne.

"It's here."

Étienne knocked. A distant murmur responded from within. They heard footsteps, a click, and the door opened. A towering man stepped forward.

"My wife's here?"

"Come in, friend," said Olivier.

He let Étienne and Zidore pass and closed the door behind them.

In the darkness of a long, sombre, chilly corridor, Étienne moved toward a red glimmer visible at the far end, through a glazed door. He pushed open this door, entered the kitchen. And on the threshold he stopped in alarm.

There was no furniture, nothing but a miserable table abandoned in this desolate, high-ceilinged room with wet, mildewed, peeling wallpaper. There was a patch of soot under the draw hole of the chimney. The place had the atmosphere of a mausoleum, the smell of a mushroom bed, and the hollow and sinisterly echoing sound of a deserted house. On the table, a candle flickered amid a mass of shadows.

Étienne must have understood. He stepped backward, abruptly spinning toward the door. But three men, emerging from the darkness, already surrounded him.

He said nothing. He had gone white. He looked at Zidore with a strange expression of rage and sorrow. Otto, from behind, pushed him toward the middle of the room. Étienne stood there motionless, puny and deformed, with sombre eyes in his pointed face, which had turned impassive and impenetrable. He stared at Otto and Red. Behind him, seated on the table, Pumpkin was swinging his leg. In the angle of the doorway, Zidore had remained with Big Olivier.

Slowly, Red moved toward Étienne. The cripple grew frenzied. With an unbelievably quick movement, he reached toward his hip pocket. The same moment, from behind, Pumpkin's scarf swept over his face, pressing on his mouth and his throat. Tilted to the rear, upright, arched, with Pumpkin's knee in his back, the hunchback uttered a stifled howl. His feet beat the air with terrific kicks. He hit Red full in the chest.

"No nonsense!" whispered Olivier, wrapping his two enormous arms round the chest of a panicky Zidore.

It all happened quickly. As Pumpkin and Étienne had started to topple, Otto had thrown himself on Étienne's feet, grabbed his two legs, and pinned them. Toward the hunchback's chest – arched, bulging, offered up – Red brought his hand and the slender kitchen knife that he held like a parer, point first, with his thumb on the blade. He pressed slowly, firmly ...

"Not that!" sobbed Zidore, "oh, not that!"

But Olivier still overpowered him. One could see the fabric of Étienne's jacket bend beneath the blade, grow taut, give way. The knife sank in a single stroke.

Irresistibly, dragging Oliver despite his strength, Zidore moved toward Étienne. He gazed at the face – the ratlike, pointed, livid countenance – tragically illumined by the red flame of the candle, and which gradually took on a cadaverous appearance. Gagged, tilted backward, his feet held by Otto, the weapon sticking in his chest, Étienne stared at Zidore till the end, with a strange, darkening expression that slowly assumed a terrible fixity.

Otto released Étienne's legs and stood up again. Pumpkin unwound his scarf and put it back around his neck. They laid the enervated body on the table.

"No nonsense, Zidore, no nonsense," repeated Olivier.

Zidore, bewildered, no longer stirred. It was Red who opened the jacket of the deceased. He unbuttoned the vest, the suspenders, rummaged under the shirt, lifted the body, searching for the belt buckle on flesh that was still warm. Suddenly, he withdrew his hands, smelled them, shook them, and wiped them on Étienne's jacket.

"The bastard shit himself!"

Red thrust in his hands again.

They divided the gold on the table, right beside the body, amid a foul stench. There were 27,000 francs. Olivier put Zidore's share in the young man's pocket.

Red left the room, went as far as the front door, and came back.

"Not a sound. We can clear off."

Pumpkin blew out the candle. They left. Nothing remained but Étienne on the table, his stomach bare, his ratlike face directed toward the ceiling, and his eyes wide open.

Hardly were they outside when Pumpkin, Otto the deserter, and Red disappeared at full speed into the darkness and the rain. Olivier stayed with Zidore, dragging him like a child.

"Come on, Zidore, come on ... It's dangerous around here. Come on!"

But Zidore stopped. He leaned against the wall. He heaved, vomiting so dreadfully that he doubled over. It was as if he needed to get everything out. He moaned. Olivier supported his head, helped him.

Zidore straightened up laboriously, drained and panting, his face dripping with sweat and tears. He staggered. Olivier took him by the wrists, hoisted him onto his back, and vanished into the darkness with his human load.

III

For a few weeks, Zidore led a strange, unbalanced life, an existence that resembled a perpetual flight from solitude, silence, and thought. He craved noise, commotion, the crowd. He needed the overpowering atmosphere of seedy pubs, shady bistros, the Bac à Puces – the stimulus of alcohol, the delirium of drunken binges and orgies. In merely a week, he spent 2,000 gold francs on a wild spree.

Then he fell ill. Poisoned by alcohol, his body rejected the toxin, expelled it. Despondent, exhausted, miserable, unable to drink, unable to avoid obsession with what he had done, Zidore lived in a state of physical depression, his mind lucid and his body stupefied. As soon as he recovered, he again fled solitude, drank still more, and tumbled anew into a raging madness, succeeded by a second phase of depression.

Georgina eventually grew frightened of him. He was becoming ferocious, terrifying. She wondered if he were losing his mind. He beat her, kept her secluded with him for days at a time, then rejected her in disgust, chased her away like an animal. She repelled him. She horrified him. What! It was for her – this thing, this soulless creature, this dog in heat – that he had committed fratricide, this dreadful act, the thought of which tormented him each and every night? With a terrifying lucidity, he weighed her, judged her. It seemed that his crime had opened his eyes, enlightened him on his mistress and on himself, so that for the first time he understood her, saw her for what she was. In the end she ran away, taking all the gold she could carry. Thus did Georgina disappear from Zidore's life, without him attaching any more importance to her departure than to a passing shadow, one of the chimerical and abominable figures that aroused and consumed his nightmares. This woman for whom he had killed, who had been his whole life, who had possessed him body and soul, no longer mattered – drowned, smothered in a concern infinitely larger, more absorbing, more haunting. He no longer understood himself when he thought about it all.

Zidore dragged along. There was not much money left. He hastened to free himself of it, to get rid of it, as if the memory of his crime had remained attached – tied – to this gold. He had hardly taken advantage of it himself. Before the murder, he had often daydreamed when he came across tempting items, window displays, luxury. *If only I had some money!* But what he now had he foolishly wasted on others – buying rounds, giving it, throwing it away, leaving behind a stream of gold. He had thought he would realize his dreams. He had tried to buy stuff for himself, to have a good time. He treated himself to a white silk scarf, a horseshoe tie pin, a watch. Then suddenly these items gave him a sense of horror mingled with fear. He hid them, destroyed them, furtively tossed them into a latrine as if they were dangerous, incriminating things, as if one could have recognized them as the products of a crime. In vain did he reproach himself for this madness, call himself a fool; he could never get a grip on himself.

Other, more specific concerns assailed him as well. What had become of Étienne's body? Had the crime been discovered? Were the culprits being sought? Since the murder, Étienne's house had remained shut up. Zidore dared not return to his father's. Whether the crime had been uncovered or not, his family must have been distressed, his mother at least. How could Zidore put on his odious act in front of her? Even in his moral depravity, Zidore had retained a bit of tenderness and pity for his mother. What must she have thought of Étienne's disappearance?

Zidore gradually became obsessed with these questions. He would have given his life to find out if the murder were known, if the body had been located – a curiosity to no end, dangerous and pointless, and which was all the more consuming. He yielded to it. He went to prowl about Place du Travail – two times, three times, like a wary cat dawing closer each day to the deserted house at the end of rue Ma Campagne. A chance encounter would make him run and hide. It was amazing that such behaviour did not raise immediate suspicions.

In the end, he dared to walk by the cabaret where the crime had been committed. He noticed nothing peculiar. Everything was still closed, silent, dead. Except for one thing: under the door, in the keyhole, and in the cracks of the shutters was a blackish and living swarm. Zidore stopped to take a closer look. It was flies, millions of flies. A cold sweat came over him when he understood.

He returned the next day and the day after that. The thought of the flies haunted him. He lingered, roamed around the area at night. One day when the weather was overcast and darkness fell early, he could no longer control himself and slipped between the fence wires that closed off the empty lot beside the cabaret. He crossed the field with its rotting garbage and heaps of rusty scrap iron. Laying hold of the kitchen wall, he jumped astride it and dropped into the little courtyard of the deserted house. He paused, his heart racing. There was nothing, no noise, only the silence and sadness of the night. This muddy little courtyard was sinister – foul with the stench of an open privy, littered with old cans and rubbish, unbelievably dirty and black.

On tiptoes, as if someone could have heard him, Zidore approached the French door to the kitchen and leaned his forehead on a hazy, blurry pane.

The kitchen was replete with shadows. The only thing he could see – just barely make out – was the terrifying form on the table.

Outside, the wind started blowing, giving rise to a distant murmur, a great sad voice in the night ... Zidore shuddered in terror and scampered away from the door, scaled the wall in a single bound, and fled. He would have died of fright had something held him back.

That night he again envisioned Étienne: his pallid features, his black eyes, his pointed head set between tall, misshapen shoulders. What lay behind his final expression? What had he wanted to say as he was dying? What had been his last thought? What disgust, what hatred, had drained away the ultimate beats of his pierced heart? What fearsome curse? At present, for all the world, Zidore would have chosen something else, another lie with which to lure his brother. That he was dead, yes, but not having hoped ... This expression, what a fearsome curse it must have signified!

Sometimes Zidore felt a frenzied desire to confess. A remnant of childhood reminded him of the freshness of spirit, the alleviation, the inexpressible relief he had once experienced during reconciliation. To rediscover this sense of deliverance, of renewal, to confess, to admit his guilt at any price! But to whom? A priest? Zidore no longer believed. Georgina? She had run away, taken up with Red. Zidore felt nothing but repulsion and hatred for her anyway. His mother? Go tell his mother, "I killed my brother Étienne, I killed your son"? What curse would she not heap upon the parricide? His sister Léonie? No, he could no more go to his sister and say, "I killed my brother." Such words cannot be uttered. Would she read it, see it on his face? It would be too awful, the exact moment when she understood that Zidore had killed Étienne.

The body was discovered. Olivier told him. Zidore asked no more about it, wanted no more news. He holed up, incapable of doing anything, not knowing if he should go to his parents' house, attend the funeral, continue feigning ignorance, or just disappear. Go to the funeral? They would read the guilt on his face. Not go? They would be suspicious. Whatever he did, they would undoubtedly know that he had assassinated Étienne ... Zidore started drinking again.

Soon he had the strange, inexplicable impression of being followed. He felt tracked, hunted. There was no physical indication, nothing. It was a certainty that seemed to come from his subconscious and assert itself. Perhaps it was only his imagination, but he was more afraid of it than a real danger.

He was actually relieved when the threat took shape, when – in the cheap hotels, the seedy pubs, at the Pou-Voulant, at the Bac à Puces – people began warning him that the cops were after him, that his name had been posted on the housing registers. He moved three or four times in a row, changing cabarets and hotels. His money ran out. He went hungry, loafed around, and roamed the city like a vagrant, sleeping in random garden sheds. He would have liked to do a little "running," smuggle contraband across the frontier so he could make some money again. But he lacked the means to purchase merchandise. He saw enemies everywhere. He had crazy fears – of a hand placed suddenly on his shoulder, of a footstep behind him, of a persistent gaze. He was afraid to emerge unarmed from the wretched room he had finally rented, for thirty cents a week, in a sordid bar of the Guinguette neighbourhood. He went about with his hand in his jacket pocket, gripping the handle of a pistol, ready to draw it, to fire at the slightest provocation. He was liable to end up killing someone. He dared not drink. Alcohol overexcited his delirium, raised abominable images of decay before his eyes.

He grew ill and confined himself to the vile hovel that he now called home. Zidore lay in bed, suffering for three straight days – feverish, thirsty, turning back and forth, and thinking so intensely that the time seemed short.

He relived his whole life, from the beginning, under the tutelage of a harsh father and a submissive mother. The mine, the coalfields, the hard but happy work, the horses, the buddies and the gals with whom he had enjoyed a hearty laugh in the evenings while returning from the pit, exhausted and filthy though they all were. It had been a healthy and almost radiant life, viewed from the present. Then had come the war, the Battle of Charleroi, the destruction of the mine by the Germans, the tons of canister shot and iron tossed with dynamite into the pits, the agony of the horses at the bottom of the galleries, the flight of the population, and then Roubaix, the runners, the boxing ring, the prison, the debauchery, and Georgina ... With her had come downfall, hunger, cold, misery endured on her behalf, with a stupid and obstinate stoicism. And all of this to lead to that deserted house one night ...

At what moment had he gone astray? At what moment had he been guilty? Where was the turning point? At what instant had he clearly become responsible? It had all happened slowly, insensibly, outside himself.

What had he lacked? Determination? He had had it. Courage, perseverance, fortitude? He had had them, he had exhausted stores of them for Georgina. *What could I have done?* thought Zidore. *What might I have become, applying the same effort to different ends? What did I lack? What support? What insight? Why did chance deprive me of it, and to what degree am I culpable?*

He lived these three days as if in hell.

The fourth day he got up, weakened, drained, but comforted and his spirit almost a little more lucid from having reflected deeply on his ordeal. He managed to wash up, though he had no desire to shave, and devoured a crust of stale bread that he found lying about. Hunger gnawed at him. He thought of Olivier, who also lived in Guinguette. Dragging his feet, Zidore went to see him. The air cheered him. People turned to look at his round, poorly shaven face, bristling with faded golden whiskers and marked by suffering and hardship.

Olivier was in his room. He gave Zidore a superb piece of meat, a good pound at least. Since there was no stove at either Olivier's or Zidore's, the young man ate part of it raw. He wrapped the rest in a piece of paper and set out toward Épeule and the Bac à Puces.

Mélie welcomed him. She let him go into the kitchen, as she did for good customers, and gave him a frying pan and the use of the stove. Zidore browned some lard, then put the meat on to fry, and ate it. Since he had no money, he was afraid to ask Mélie for bread. Comforted, his senses dulled, heavy with sleep, he leaned his elbows on the kitchen table and nodded off.

IV

Since the beginning of the invasion, Roche, the police detective, had lost much of his power. He had no weapons, first of all. His revolvers and billy club had been taken away. The prestige of the green devils eclipsed his own. In the seedy cafés, among the shady clientele round the train station, he was no longer feared. His voice had lost the confidence, the authority that had once assured him of his absolute domination over the underworld. Armed only with his fists, he came up against fellows carrying loaded pistols in their hip pockets. One cannot imagine how naked an ordinarily well-armed man feels when he has suddenly been stripped of his gear.

Roche's assignments were now limited to trivialities: pursuit of petty thieves, investigations of alleyway disputes, searches for manpower on behalf of German headquarters. From time to time, the Germans would send orders to Police Central, "We need five masons, three coopers, and two harness makers."

Roche and his deputies were put on the search. They came back empty handed: a courageous way, all things considered, of continuing to demonstrate their patriotism.

Roche had also made some friends among the German police. They had the same tastes, the same respect for muscle, the same stories of arrests and pursuits and women, the same somewhat foolish vanity characterizing the regulars of dodgy locales. And then the strength, the speed, the strictness of the German administration and its police – this marvelous machine of command – inspired Roche's admiration. With them, no protest was possible. One felt governed. The Frenchman in Roche fumed, but the policeman stood in awe.

Roche was the one who investigated Étienne's murder. The body had been found a month after the crime, thanks to the flies. Going down rue Ma Campagne, some people had noticed a long, swarming string of flies on the threshold of an empty cabaret. The police commissioner had had it opened. And the cops had discovered Étienne, eaten away by insects.

Roche pursued his inquiry. He was acquainted with the Duydts. He knew that Zidore had gone on a wild spree in the cafés of Épeule. He had been seen using gold coins. And Roche was well aware that Étienne was a moneychanger.

Roche initiated a search for Georgina. She came to Police Central, very much against her will. She had already left Red a week ago.

"My dear," said Roche, "you have a reputation, and not a good one."

"If that's why you called me here!"

"No. You had a little romantic fling with Zidore, Zidore the boxer."

"I'm no longer with ..."

"That doesn't matter. He's spent a lot lately. In gold ..."

"Yes ..."

"Right. Then he disappeared, all of a sudden. Well, honestly, I need a little ... If you help me find him, we'll leave you alone. If not ..."

"If not?"

"You're still not registered, and you don't want to be. I'll make sure you're added, my darling. There you have it. The choice is yours. Either Zidore or a visit to the clinic each week."*

He saw Georgina every two or three days thereafter. The case dragged on. Roche was starting to get irritated when one morning – as he was in his office reading some reports – Guilhem, his deputy, arrived with a look at once gleeful and anxious.

"Zidore's at the Bac à Puces!"

"What?"

"He's been there at least a quarter of an hour. I saw Georgina."

"Quick!" shouted Roche, "we should nab him before he leaves."

"Yes, but he has a gun. And it seems he's determined to use it ..."

Roche stopped dead.

"He's got the edge on us, then!"

"That's right!"

"We oughta speak to the chief. Get a move on!"

They bounded down the stairs to the commissioner's office.

"Zidore Duydt's been spotted."

"Arrest him!"

"He's armed!"

"Damn!" said the commissioner.

"Any chance we could get some guns from the Germans?"

"Let's at least try."

---

*In France at the time, licensed prostitution was legal. Prostitutes were required to register with state authorities, submit to regular inspections for venereal disease, and confine their operations to brothels. Unregistered prostitutes were liable to prosecution.

Police Central was next to German headquarters. They ran over, found an officer. He refused to give them weapons. But he offered to have the two detectives escorted by three German policemen. They left a quarter of an hour later. The three policemen teased the detectives: "French, little boys! French always scared!"

Ruprecht, a great big fellow with a fine rosy complexion, who had a huge Ulm mastiff on a leash, tapped Roche on the shoulder: "Oh, you French policemen!"

Annoyed, Roche and Guilhem protested: "You're good, you three! With pistols on our hips, we'd go, too!"

Ruprecht laughed. "Pistol? We no need, no need ..."

This policeman had a reputation as a good-natured chap. Six feet four inches tall and broad as a door, he had a peculiar understanding of his duty. He never took miscreants to jail. Toward curfew, he could be seen striding along the deserted streets with his huge Ulm mastiff trotting by his side. If he saw a stray silhouette, a straggler going home in haste, Ruprecht would run, grab the delinquent, give him a good shake, and send him packing with a final kick in the rear. In reality, people were quite content to get off so easily. Ruprecht even brought to the job a certain fairness, a sporting decency. He ran like the wind, had enormous legs. He concluded that folks who escaped his terrifying pursuit deserved to be left in peace.

Ruprecht had stopped counting his amorous conquests. He was a handsome boy, naïvely proud of his commanding appearance. He plastered his hair with oil, wore his beret very flat, over his ear to one side, and always had a bold expression on his face.

The group headed down rue Saint-Georges. Roche and Guilhem had gradually taken the lead, none too proud to be escorted like this by German policemen. Passing by the horse pond, they turned onto rue de l'Épeule. And they stopped a few metres from the Bac à Puces cabaret. There was dancing inside. The sound of music spilled onto the streets.

"What're we going to do?" said Guilhem. "We need to block the private entrance."

"You two over here," Ruprecht ordered the detectives, pointing to the passageway. "We over there." And he pointed to the entrance of the cabaret. "Quick."

And the three Germans advanced on the cabaret. The two detectives slipped into the passageway. Detectives on one side, policemen on the other, they burst in with the dog.

"Halt!"

The dancers froze. The heavy footsteps of the couples on the sandy and squeaky floor came to a full stop. There was a thick smoke, an opaque dust. One could hardly see toward the rear, where the two detectives had stationed themselves to guard the doors. No one said a word. Amid general consternation, the phonograph continued playing a lively polka, in a great din.

"Papieren!"

Individuals took out their papers. There were about fifteen prostitutes and a few roughnecks who were the terror of the neighbourhood. Not one of them moved. They were familiar with the brutality of the German police. The green devils would crack your skull at the least sign of trouble.

Ruprecht took the cards. The men were put on the right, the women on the left, at the back of the café.

"Pretty, pretty young ladies!" said Ruprecht as he pushed them toward their corner.

Guilhem and Roche had walked over to the bar where Mélie Nauserais was waiting, a little pale and barely shuffling about.

"So tell me, mother, the little boxer – Zidore, the little blond – is he here?"

"No," said Mélie in a loud voice.

But over her shoulder, her thumb was pointing at the French door to the kitchen.

Roche understood. Cautiously, he stepped toward the door. He was just putting his hand on the porcelain knob when a pane shattered with a sudden crack merely two inches above his head.

"Christ!" said Roche, jumping back.

Roche and Guilhelm had gone white. In the other corner, keeping the group of hooligans at a respectful distance, the Germans were watching. Ruprecht shrugged his shoulders.

"French policemen!"

He came forward in turn. He had grabbed one of the big wooden panels that served to shut the windows at night. He raised it at arm's length, took a spring from the middle of the café, and threw the panel like a battering ram. The French door staved in, falling with a crash to the kitchen floor. And two gunshots rang out. Inside the kitchen one could see the ceramic table upended. Zidore, kneeling, had taken cover behind it. From time to time, he raised the top of his head with lightning speed.

Everyone had withdrawn to the cover of the wall, round from the bar.

"Go, go, now," said Ruprecht to the French policemen.

"Asshole!" shouted Roche in furry, "you're mocking us!"

"Go" repeated Ruprecht, holding out his pistols with a derisive expression.

Roche hesitated, having had a near miss just a moment before. Guilhem did the same.

Ruprecht shrugged his huge shoulders.

"French, little boys! You see ..."

He set his pistols on the bar and grabbed a chair. He raised it to eye level. And behind this shield he moved toward the kitchen, to crush Zidore.

Zidore was still kneeling. He no longer thought about what he was doing. He saw but one thing: this man coming at him. Kill or be killed ... Unintentionally, Zidore had already stepped past the point of retreat, of withdrawal. Destiny was fulfilling itself as if beyond his control.

Above the edge of the table, he ever so slightly raised his bony, pale, hollow little face. The golden whiskers of his poorly trimmed beard sparkled. With the concentration of a wild beast, he watched Ruprecht advance. It seemed as though he were playing some terrible, impassioned game in which the question were not one of life and death but simply one of material skill. Focus, determination pushed to the outer limits, obscured the revulsion of his conscience.

Two steps from Zidore, Ruprecht had insensibly lowered his chair to take a look. Zidore fired. Ruprecht staggered, as if from a heavy blow, and fell backward, a bloody star on his forehead. His gigantic body gave a brief spasm.

There was a rush. Without anyone giving the order, Ruprecht's big mastiff sprang with a howl. The beast must have understood. Zidore rolled beneath the dog. Then Roche, Guilhem, and the two Germans flung themselves at the table. Fury and shame had chased away their fear. There were several gunshots. A bullet destroyed a windowpane. Chunks of plaster fell. Zidore was quickly pounded like an animal beneath their heels. One kick from a boot made his eyes burst. Another ripped all the flesh from his countenance in a single stroke. A German crushed his nose, his teeth, and his face with the blows of a stool. Feet and fists ruptured his stomach. Bones could be heard breaking.

They stopped, having exhausted their stock of energy and hatred. From the pile of human flesh at their feet arose an animalistic moan. German soldiers were already invading the Bac à Puces.

They picked up Ruprecht's corpse and laid it on a table beside Zidore's body, which seemed tiny next to the colossus. Zidore's heart was still beating. A sack was thrown over his bloody face.

Someone had called a doctor, who arrived shortly. He was an old, phlegmatic practitioner. Even so, he recoiled when he discovered Zidore's face, a mass of bloody pulp with exposed jawbone, teeth, and fragmented nasal cartilage. Zidore's smashed eyes had popped from their sockets. The doctor covered this spectacle with the sac again and examined the body with a stethoscope.

"It's over! Ten minutes ..."

Isidore Duydt was no longer in pain. Scarcely could he still hear the distant voices. To die, so this was what it was like to die. How easy, what relief!

Already detached from earthly concerns, he contemplated the image of the puerile, incoherent, wretched being – composed of passions and suffering flesh – that had been Isidore Duydt. He observed this figure with tenderness and pity, as if it had not been him, this derisory product of chance, of a chaotic destiny. And besides, it was not important ... He saw himself from a great distance, far removed. Not even with scorn. Only a vast piteous indulgence for this poor, sad, and terribly weak body, which had expended so much courage, willpower, and energy to no end, and for whom life had been nothing but turmoil and sterility, lacking a purpose, an invigourating ideal. This creature was not responsible.

Final images of the world, faint apparitions, came to him ... His sister Léonie, his mother, Georgina ... He watched with indifference as they faded and disappeared. He regretted nothing. The memory of Étienne alone stirred a vague dismay in him ... But there was no hatred on the pale, narrow face, at present calm and seemingly stripped of bitterness. Only immense pity, immense mercy ...

Toward this shadow, Zidore made a desperate effort.

• • •

"What'd he mutter as he died?"

"Something like 'Étienne,' I think," said Roche. "Take him by the feet, Guilhem ..."

Chapter Five

I

Almost every week now, Samuel Fontcroix went to see Antoinette and Édith in Roubaix.

The women had left Lille. Samuel could no longer bring them merchandise. The Germans had sealed the Belgian frontier, and all trade had become impossible. Édith, who did not lack a certain flair in matters of business, had rented a little shop in Roubaix, on rue de Lannoy, where she had begun selling groceries again.

The store was in Old Roubaix. It was a tiny, squat house with narrow windows like small portholes, a big support post in front of the door, and ceilings within arm's reach – crossed by huge beams – that dribbled a perpetual stream of plaster and clay. The building was full of rats, mice, fleas, and ants. The enormous vaulted cellar was flooded with water. Floating on the surface were frothy, velvety things covered in white and green mould. Antoinette, such as she was, adored this house precisely because it was odd and quaint.

Édith's business was rather like that of Old Duydt, and of all commerce during the war, when nothing was certain or regular, when one sold what one came across with no chance of restocking, when scarcity made the price of goods rise in unbelievable fashion. A pair of new shoes cost 700 francs, used ones 150. A kilo of beets sold for 10 francs, coffee for 90, a cake made with white flour for 300. An industrial transmission belt was worth a small fortune because shoe soles could be cut from it. Everything was in short supply, and manufacturing had ceased. People eventually bargained for remaining items on the spot, anticipating that nothing would soon be left. Édith thus purchased a little of everything and made her whole house into a pawn shop, encumbered with fabric, clothing, bags of rice, cans of food, pharmaceutical products, old leather, tools, books, and musical instruments.

Lots of folks frequented her shop, and even many Germans. They came to her place looking for items for their families, for things that could no longer be found in Germany. When the troops went on leave, they would take home a scrap of cloth, a bit of leather, a piece of canvas. The soldiers were the ones who kept the rear in supply. Édith sold them whatever she wanted: old tablecloths and sheets for making shirts, napkins to be cut into handkerchiefs, and badly stretched blankets from which German women made outfits for children. The poor chaps, overjoyed, carried off these precious commodities. By speaking a gibberish half-German and half-French, client and shopkeeper eventually understood each another. The Germans explained to Antoinette the joy of their loved ones back home at receiving these princely gifts, the destitution of the German people, the shirts filled with holes, the paper-thin undergarments, the faux leather, the synthetic wool – a distress greater than that of the occupied French. Among these German soldiers, one found long-suffering, good-natured types who did not protest the conditions they faced. Certain ones nonetheless stole, and stole shamelessly. They brought Édith liquor from their canteen, sugar and wheat, oats swiped from the stables, and cases of crackers and jam. They were unbelievably audacious. One day some guard troops, in collusion with their noncommissioned officers, hauled in a wagon with 1,000 kilos of brown sugar hidden under telephone wire. Since they had no horses, they had assembled a dozen men and pulled the wagon through the streets, as if they were leaving for some sort of job. They carried off the stunt several times. Some of the Germans were true rogues. They got along best with the smugglers, the runners, the hooligans who occasionally came to Édith's to sell their merchandise, too.

Putting up with such characters was a necessary evil. They alone had the daring to risk their necks going to search for wheat and meat in Belgium. And then there were the prostitutes, the officers' friends, the "femmes à Boches" who came to cash in on their gifts in kind or the fruits of their plundering. It was a brutal, cynical, greedy environment in which Édith maneuvred with boldness and skill. But Antoinette – young, still naïve in many respects – was struck with an alarm, an astonishment, a disgust that she had difficulty overcoming. Above all, by consorting with the Germans, one ultimately acquired a reputation as a traitor, a turncoat, the type who came to terms with the enemy and was without basic principles.

Antoinette, being intelligent, quickly understood the looks, the innuendos, the hurtful way people stared at her and avoided her. As a result she felt a certain shame and then, in reaction, a disdain for the others, a complete disregard for "what they said," even a pretense of audacity and offhandness, a way of going about her business, dressing, acting, and thinking that bordered on impudence – a completely natural reaction of youth, but one that exposed her to even greater spite.

She felt all the more outraged and indignant at the malicious remarks as she saw most people around her in a way satisfied with official charity – living off allowances distributed by the commune, rations, handouts of food and coal – and doing nothing useful. Her mother and she were at least working, killing themselves to make a living. For what could they be reproached? They had done nothing reprehensible. They were a help to others, procuring food for people who could find nothing for themselves, undergarments for those poor wretches of German soldiers who were just as long-suffering, goodly, and miserable as French troops. The women tramped around the shop from morning till night, carrying sacks, moving crates, beating clothing, scrubbing, cleaning, running about, toiling to the point of exhaustion.

Édith, who was robust, bore this enormous task without strain. But Antoinette grew thin. Samuel occasionally worried about his daughter. He thought she looked tired and pale. She protested. She did not feel bad. The only repercussion that the excessive fatigue and hardship had yet had on her was a worsening of temper, anxiety, and irritability.

Even so, her father's concern eventually influenced Antoinette as well. She sensed that, in every respect, she was leading a reckless life. She began to recognize the wisdom of her father, who had wanted to leave her in school a while longer, to spare her the hard knocks of life. She could tell that Samuel was rearing Christophe differently than she had been. And this realization threw her into great uncertainty. She began doubting her mother, wondering if all that was right indeed lay on Édith's side.

In any event, her little brother was happier than she was.

What might she have become if reared like Christophe by her father? Something completely different than she was. In sum, after years of free living under the lax tutelage of her mother, she found herself disillusioned, disgusted by premature acquaintance with a corrupt environment, exposed to life and its ugly realities, terrified when confronted with the hideousness of the world. At the age of sixteen, she had no more illusions about men and love. She had no hopes, no dreams, only a premature cunning whose meanness she exaggerated, a feminine skill at manipulating her mother, flattering her, exciting her jealousy, getting her to hand over the money, the clothing, the trinkets she desired. Antoinette was beset by an almost total ignorance, the result of arbitrary readings and an insufficient fund of education and instruction. And she had earned a deplorable and unmerited reputation. Antoinette would have liked to pull herself together, to reestablish some measure of balance, and despaired at not knowing how to go about it.

More and more, she turned anxiously toward her father. Perhaps salvation rested with him. She began studying her father, scrutinizing the way he was rearing and guiding Christophe. She ended up feeling ashamed of what she was when she stood before him.

This was one of the times in her life when her mind worked the most intensely. Plunged into a sort of mental darkness, surrounded on all sides by ugliness and vulgarity, she made a desperate and surprising effort to escape, to break free, to elevate herself by her own scant strength to a higher intellectual and moral plane.

What should she do? And to what end? She did not know. She simply felt that she had to educate herself first of all, though without clearly understanding where to start. She relied on fortune, on whimsy. Shame prevented her from asking her father for advice. She began by learning Spanish and violin at the same time, haphazardly quenching the thirst for knowledge so characteristic of youth. She also read anything, no matter what, gathering the odds and ends that she came across in the crates of the shop, devoting herself to them with heart, reviewing what she did not understand – persuaded that she was doing useful work, increasing her sum of knowledge.

Édith and the friends of the shop – all these good, naïve fellows, these soldiers and scamps who made up their clientele – were astounded by Antoinette's behaviour. Édith swelled with pride. In their presence, Antoinette also seemed tolerably pleased with herself. But on her own she sensed that her studies were incomplete, incoherent, and uncertain. She recognized that this was not true learning and that she had nothing but fragmentary, confused, and ridiculously embryonic elements of understanding. She was unacquainted with history or geography. Spelling and grammar were tricky subjects for her. She would have had to start over, begin anew. But the immensity of such a task was frightening to her youthful mind. Besides, she had to work for a living. She could not count on going back to school. She was too big, too old. And all alone, without the support of a guide, she felt overwhelmed. Above all, she knew life. She had earned her bread, battled, employed cunning, known the bitterness and joys of the struggle. And such things hinder learning. One no longer knows how to apply oneself to fractions, to conjugations, when one has fought to survive and seen how easily one does without such things since they all have such a distant relationship with the world, reality, money. It was thus that, once more, she looked to her father, whose wisdom she admired and missed, remembering that in former times he, for his part, had wanted to leave her in school, to have her continue her studies and improve her mind.

And the eccentricity in which she had so recently delighted now seemed infantile and unbecoming. With all her strength, she tried to return to normal, to behaviours, gestures, clothing, language that were sober and reasonable. But sometimes she was annoyed that the task was so difficult. She tossed it all aside, threw herself headlong into new eccentricities, and alarmed rue de Lannoy by decking herself out in an old fedora set off with a bird of paradise. Charming and ridiculous, she brazenly defied the stupefaction and reprobation of the crowd.

She would have gladly turned toward a religion, a hope, an ideal. She had the dull, confused intuition that life could not be limited to what she knew of it, to this sterile and stupid battle for the sole object of perpetuating a meaningless existence. But not at the age of seventeen, and unaided, does one arrive at a doctrine, can one go beyond rituals to reach the spirit. She was taken with a sudden fervour and frequented Saint Elizabeth's Church across from Édith's shop. But it did not last. Poor Antoinette knew too much of life. She had seen too much of the world, of reality. No longer could she simply believe. There was something withered, dead inside her. Prayer did not seem useful to her. She could not determine the degree to which she was responsible for her mistakes. Sometimes she judged herself innocent, other times guilty. She abandoned a church that was so complicated. She went twice to the Protestant church, attracted by the contrast of its austerity and simplicity, but soon grew bored with it. Then she visited the Antoinistes but did not return to them either ...*

Nonetheless, there had to be *something else*. She could feel it, sense it. Life could not be restricted to the horizons she knew. Others had, if not a religion, at least an ethic, an ideal that ennobled them. She caught a vague, confused glimpse of the whole problem of the conscience and moral nobility, much as she caught a glimpse of science and knowledge, from a great distance, and in a haze ...

II

Samuel himself still lived in Épeule, in his big house on the cul-de-sac behind the convent. He was starting to run short of cash. To sustain little Christophe and himself, he had to devise expedients. He gradually sold what he had left of leather, fats, and old tools. Everything went, everything had assumed enormous value. Harnesses were used to make ankle boots. Axle grease was burned in lamps. From one month to the next, Samuel Fontcroix and his brother Gaspard drained away their assets, barely making enough to get by. What they did not sell, the Germans carried away little by little. Carts, horses, equipment, sacks, scales – everything made of metal, wood, or combustible material – it all evaporated. Samuel even experienced rage at seeing French workers – people like Decooster the butcher – come themselves with the wagons and the German soldiers to take the last sacks he had hidden in a shed, and whose location had been revealed by jealous neighbours. In the end, so he could profit from his own ruin more than the enemy, he undertook the total destruction of his warehouse. He spent months, hatchet and saw in hand – like a butcher – pulling down beams, chopping, cutting, demolishing the entire framework. He gradually burned all of his sheds, yet content in his wretchedness at least to be able to warm himself.

---

*Antoinism – a religious movement positing a belief in reincarnation – was established in the 1890s by Belgian miner and metalworker Louis-Joseph Antoine. See Régis Dericquebourg, *Les Antoinistes* (Turnhour: Brepols, 1993).

He spent the rest of his time cooking meals for himself and for little Christophe, doing laundry, keeping house, and periodically going to see Édith and Antoinette, all in the tireless, patient, and painful hope of the end, of victory ... Victory! He spoke of it with his brother Gaspard, with Mr Feuillebois the teacher. In the one he found pessimism and discouragement, in the other optimism and confidence.

They met regularly, almost every evening, for the communiqué. Samuel received the newspaper published under the supervision and inspiration of the German government – by Frenchmen no less. It was called the *Gazette of the Ardennes*. This paper rather cleverly preached immediate peace, Franco-German understanding, and placed entire responsibility for the war on England. French communiqués were published in it with a month's delay and certain retouches. But this modified truth, this watered down news, still captivated them. Each evening Samuel, with his brother Gaspard and Feuillebois the teacher, used a pencil to mark maps with the advance or retreat of the Allies. And they measured, they calculated, they hoped or despaired. Occasionally, Feuillebois also received the underground newssheet *Loyalty*. What a precious little paper! Fresh information, certain truths! Or at times an airplane would drop a handful of French newspapers. Perilously, from the very rooftops, the friends would retrieve a copy, and for a couple of weeks a ray of sunshine would warm their hearts.

Samuel's evening cartography session was religiously attended. Free from prison, Alain Laubigier was there as well as his cousin François, Big Semberger, and a number of women who did not know much about maps but who nonetheless came to draw a little courage and confidence from the atmosphere. And then, to attract readers, the *Gazette of the Ardennes* published a daily list of French soldiers from the Nord whom the Germans had taken prisoner. One might always run across the name of a brother, a friend, a son.

It was here at Samuel's that the opposing natures of Gaspard Fontcroix and Mr Feuillebois confronted each other.

Gaspard Fontcroix, Samuel's brother, was afflicted with a rather mysterious spinal ailment. Till now he had been able to take reasonably good care of himself. At present, like Samuel, he saw poverty and destitution on the horizon. Medical supplies in the occupied Nord were also running out. There no remedies, no available treatments. Gaspard's illness was gradually clouding his vision. He could feel himself going blind. For a while he had been able to delude himself with hope, trying injections, drugs, electrotherapy, anything that would provide relief for a few weeks or a few days, and at least nurture hope. This ultimate consolation was currently denied him. It was impossible to find medications, even at high prices. And besides, he was short of cash. He had been rather well off prior to the war. The sale of a large grocery store, before he went into business with his brother, had left him 40,000 francs invested in Russian securities through a Belgian notary. None of it was worth much anymore and was not even at Gaspard's disposal. He lived in the home of his sister, Joséphine Mouraud, and paid board. Once he had cut the figure of the rich relation, the uncle with a legacy. The Mourauds were of modest means and deprived themselves to ensure the education of their youngest son. They had hoped Uncle Gaspard would leave the children part of his fortune. But now things were different. Gaspard had squandered most of his assets and paid his rent irregularly. There was no telling what might be left with his Belgian notary. He was turning into the poor relation.

And where could he go without money? Here he was at least with his family, who would not dare throw him out on the street. He led a wretched life, the life of a man who was slowly declining. In times past he had been well-dressed, respectable, embodying the man of comfort, prosperous and happy. At present he could hardly see, dressed himself with difficulty, was even running out of undergarments and clothes. Henri Mouraud, his brother-in-law, stole his shirts and belongings, since Gaspard could not tell which were his. And Gaspard himself sold here a suit, there a jewel, a ring, or a tie pin to purchase phials of serum at forty francs apiece – remedies that poisoned him and completed his physical ruin. But he remained strangely, naïvely obstinate and confident. His obsession, his mad desire to get better, to escape the darkness, led him to credit all manner of stories, to collect advertisements and notices, to jot down the address of every bonesetter, specialist, surgeon, and electrotherapist who had relieved or cured unfortunates afflicted with his ailment. But he was short of money and had to wait. If this war would end, surely he would get better. Science works miracles! While biding his time, lost in his impossible dream, he felt the shadows drawing ever nearer from day to day.

The final outcome – total blindness – was only a matter of months away. His eyes were clouding over. He could barely see where he was going and no longer recognized faces. He came to Samuel's to eat a bite, warm himself, and talk. For the Mourauds harassed him and made him miserable. He knew that Samuel was low on funds. He was afraid to ask for money for himself. And the situation bothered Samuel as well. He was unable to comfort his brother and like him ended up doubting the purpose of the war, victory, everything.

Fortunately, the regular visit of Mr Feuillebois, for the communiqué, brought them a whiff of optimism and almost a flood of confidence.

Mr Feuillebois was a large, bilious fellow – olive-skinned, broad-shouldered, and routinely clothed in an ample morning coat. He walked swinging his arms, his fedora cheekily tilted to one side, his biceps bulging from his body like an athlete making his way to the arena. And in all weather he was armed with an umbrella, a huge umbrella of greenish fabric, capable of sheltering a half-dozen mortals of normal size.

Mr Feuillebois was a teacher. For him, life's path had always been smooth and easy. He was the incarnation of the happy man in the eyes of those around him and even in his own. From his parents he had inherited a modest allowance. He earned a reasonable livelihood from his beloved vocation as a teacher. As he was approaching thirty, he had married a well-bred young girl with a pretty little face, an agreeable personality, and a considerable dowry. She had given him a boy – a single, sturdy boy – who had enjoyed a brilliant career at the engineering academy. Mr Feuillebois's whole life had been nothing less than a chain of favourable circumstances and happy events. Endowed by heaven with the best of health and a stomach of steel, satisfied with himself and with others, satisfied with everything that came his way and everything that did not, Mr Feuillebois exuded the most pleasant optimism.

Since the war, however, Mr Feuillebois – a descendant of the generation of 1870, a teacher impregnated with the cult of patriotism – had suffered the worst humiliation. Being subjected to the Germans, watching them impose their rule even in the schools, chase him from his classroom, forbid him from teaching, restrict him to the simple role of babysitter – for him it was all intolerable. For thirty years he had molded hundreds and hundreds of young minds, had religiously taught them his own gospel: patriotism, revenge. These things had become part of him. The superiority of France, its destiny as a chosen nation: so long had he preached such ideas, inculcated them in his students, his children, that he – the old teacher in the style of yesteryear – had come to believe them himself, blindly, as matters of dogma. They had penetrated his skull, entered into his thought process, to the point that they were no longer subject to reason. In his eyes Victory was inscribed in the book of destiny.

Besides, unfailingly happy till now, favoured with his wealth, his family harmony, and his progeny by constant good fortune, Mr Feuillebois – like many happy men – had come to consider this fortune as part of himself, as inalienable. To see it fall short one day seemed to him impossible, ridiculous, much as if the earth had suddenly opened beneath his feet. The defeat of France would undoubtedly have given the most dreadful lie to this perpetual prosperity. It was thus impossible that France should be defeated. It did not make sense, could not be conceived. The same unflinching optimism had comforted Feuillebois when his son had left, among the first to be mobilized. This happy man could have no doubts regarding his good fortune.

His faith had nonetheless encountered some rude shocks. He had had no word from his son. Aside from a Red Cross postcard that reached him in 1915, with a six-month delay, and that only said, "Paul Feuillebois in good health," Mr Feuillebois had remained in the most frightful uncertainty. And then the war had dragged on, the Germans settled in as masters. One learned of victories here, defeats there, with no headway, no movement. People grew discouraged, spoke of a half-baked peace, even of defeat. Day after day one received the most grievous, the most disheartening news.

And yet Mr Feuillebois's spirits did not give way. It was he, during the review of the communiqué, who dispelled the doubts of Samuel and Gaspard. His son would return. France would triumph. He did not distinguish between the two things, the two conditions essential for his happiness. He gathered every favourable rumour no matter how spurious, and at least once a week brought Samuel word of a French victory, a German defeat, citing the number of cannons and prisoners taken. Outright contradictions did not discourage him.

Never did one see him doubt. Even at the darkest hours, at announcement of the most dreadful news, he did not reveal the slightest apprehension. His face looked a bit more gaunt, his complexion more sallow, but when Samuel, Gaspard, and he had discussed events and considered probabilities, Feuillebois would conclude, "Yes, yes, that may well be ... But wait till the end!"

Once this optimism almost led to a quarrel between the Fontcroix brothers and Feuillebois. As usual, he had announced some fabulous victory. A week later, he arrived distraught, his complexion blotchy, his hat over his eyes, his umbrella between his legs, to report a disaster in the Gallipoli Peninsula.

On the spot, an irritated Samuel blurted out his misgivings: "We obviously lend credence to too many false reports! I don't want to believe any more of these stories! If we're to know victory, we'll see it when it gets here. But at the rate we're going, it seems to be taking the long way round." And suddenly he added: "See here, Mr Feuillebois, you still believe in it, do you, in victory?"

At that moment, in front of Samuel and Gaspard, the man was transfigured. He straightened up to his full height. His eyes shone. His hat appeared to set itself crooked. And the umbrella – raised skyward by a formidable fist – seemed like the invincible sword of the angel of death. He stammered: "If I believe? If I believe? As I believe in my own existence! As in the sun that shines! You doubt, do you, by chance?"

"Mr Feuillebois," said Samuel, "I've shared your faith, your conviction. But when I recall the disappointments, when I observe events, the privileged position of the Central Powers, their long preparation, their united leadership, I wonder if we're not witnessing a useless bloodbath from which each side will come away with bumps and bruises as the only reward. In short, and between us, why is France sure to be victorious?"

Samuel was almost sorry for his audacity. He thought Feuillebois would hurt him. Feuillebois forgot all moderation. His free hand crashed down on Samuel's shoulder, making him stagger. And Feuillebois shouted: "What? Victorious? Why will she be victorious? Ah, good God, because ... because she is France!"

Perhaps it was absurd. It made no sense, this puerile cry, this exclamation of fanaticism. And yet it denoted such an irresistible power of conviction, such an absolute and blind faith, such a love, such a lifelong ideal of this old teacher, that the Fontcroix brothers found nothing more to say.

That evening Gaspard Fontcroix returned to the Mourauds'. Night was falling. As he went along, Gaspard was mulling everything over in his head: victory, the end of the war and of this disease in his eyes. He dreamed of a new treatment, of an electrical machine with coils. But it was expensive. He had been afraid to ask Samuel for money. There was also a

bromide medication that a pharmacist from Croix had told him about. It
was much less expensive, certainly ... If only this war would end! If only he
could have taken care of himself! He trudged down the uneven sidewalk,
stumbling and bumping into things, uncertain, with his hands a bit outstretched. He was still not accustomed to the darkness in his eyes.

The whole situation had come about senselessly. Before going into business with his brother, Gaspard had owned a big grocery store. While carrying a barrel down to the basement, he had fallen and struck his back on
the stairs. Since then he had had spinal problems and gone progressively
blind, without anyone being able to pinpoint the precise cause. Gaspard
felt sad. Now that he was no longer surrounded by the continual and captivating spectacle of the world, as he sank increasingly into an indistinct
greyness, he was ever more the victim of his imaginings, abandoning himself more completely to their obsession. He walked with the hesitant steps
of a drunk and talked to himself, absorbed and making gestures. Behind
him he heard some people laughing. He worried, felt himself over. His
brother would have warned him of anything foolish ... But it was so dark
at Samuel's ... No, he had forgotten neither a gaiter nor his tie. And nothing was hanging behind his back. They must not be laughing at him. He
resumed his meander through a universe of haze and indistinct shadows,
meditating aloud about the effectiveness of this bromide and occasionally stopping to affirm his thoughts with a gesture.

The Mourauds' house was on rue de Thionville. It was an old house, vast
and humid, modestly furnished, and which smelled of laundry. Joséphine
Mouraud, Gaspard's sister, was a laundress. Henri Mouraud, her husband,
was a mechanic. Before the war, Gaspard had rented their front room,
where he had had his office, and the finest of their three bedrooms. He had
been the rich relation. Now that he could no longer pay, he had been gradually dispossessed and forced to sleep in the attic. Joséphine had not
opposed this abuse at the hands of her husband, who had always envied
his brother-in-law with the misplaced jealousy of the workingman. She
undoubtedly had a certain affection for her brother. But she had dedicated
the greater part of her capacity for love to her youngest son, little Georges.
Joséphine wanted a bright future for him and worked herself to death so
he could complete his studies in chemistry. She demanded the same abne-
gation of her daughter Annie, who helped her with the laundry. There was
something shocking about this maternal love. It applied above all to boys,

and more especially to Georges. For him, Joséphine sacrificed her daughter Annie without any remorse, without even realizing what she was doing. Somehow, a relic of antiquated ideas seemed to have survived in this woman for whom women hardly seemed to count.

Gaspard returned home. He entered the kitchen, discerned the shapes of little Georges seated at the table doing his homework and of Henri by the fireside. In the scullery, Joséphine was doing some ironing. Gaspard said good evening. Henri Mouraud had an irrational hatred for his brother-in-law, was now taking advantage of his power over this wretch ruined by the war, and inspired in Georges the same sentiment toward his uncle.

Gaspard moved toward the stove. He was hungry. The smell of coffee tempted him. He bumped into the outstretched legs of his brother-in-law.

"Oh, excuse me ..."

Henri Mouraud grunted. And little Georges, who insisted on the entire family's absolute silence while he did his homework, clicked his tongue in annoyance. Gaspard gave up on the coffee. He turned toward the cupboard. He opened the door, doing his best to keep it from creaking, in consideration of Georges. Feeling his way, he began to rummage among the plates, searching for the bread and the lard, and fearful of making a racket. There was something painful at the sight of a big old man moving about like this, with immeasurable precaution, in terror of a child.

He found a loaf and kept looking for the lard. He knocked off the lid by accident, unintentionally digging in his fingers as he felt around.

"My lard!" shouted Henri. "That's really disgusting! You don't run your paws over other people's food like that!"

Henri had stood up. He snatched the pot of lard from Gaspard. The blind man returned the loaf to the cupboard and went to sit in a corner, renouncing his quest for food.

He unlaced his ankle boots. He was accustomed to the task, could do it quite well without being able to see them. He got back up to look for his slippers. He went about in his socks, feeling here and there the moisture of a rivulet on the tiles. He groped under the sideboard, the stove, the table, once again disturbing Georges, who pulled back, avoiding his uncle's touch with obvious disgust. Gaspard resigned himself and, in his socks, returned to sit on a chair in the angle of the doorway. Round about him, Henri and Joséphine came and went without taking any more interest in him than in some lifeless object.

The door to the courtyard banged shut. The blind man almost sensed a glow, a ray of sunshine. Annie Mouraud came in: Annie – the older sister of little Georges – who for Old Gaspard replaced the fading clarity of his eyes. She was pausing to eat between doing two loads of laundry.

She wiped her arms, her thin and sinewy arms. She approached her uncle: "Well, Uncle Gaspard, are you doing all right?"

"Yes, my dear, yes."

He felt better already. He forgot his troubles.

"And your slippers?"

She looked for them, found them under her father's chair, gave them to Gaspard. She felt his feet: "You're wet. Your socks ought to be changed."

She took some clean ones from a drawer and gave them to him. Then she went to the sideboard to cut some bread for herself. And she noticed the fingerprints on the cups, the traces of lard, the mark of a big finger. She could tell what had happened.

"Have you eaten, Uncle Gaspard?"

"Not yet."

She cut him some bread, poured him some coffee. And while he ate, she furtively wiped the dirty dishes and put them away.

Gaspard was busy with his meal. He ate in such a slovenly manner, letting crumbs fall, compelled to use his fingers to retrieve his bread from his cup. And Georges grew annoyed. With an air of disgust, he eventually picked up his notebooks and marched off to the other room. For a long time now, Gaspard had resigned himself to this spiteful behaviour and was no longer startled by it.

He finished off the last bites. Then he got up, took the box of shoe polish from beneath the sideboard, and began clumsily polishing his shoes. Annie, who was eating, turned around. She constantly watched over him. He did so many silly things! She shouted, "What're you doing, Uncle Gaspard?" And she took the shoe from his hands. He was about to apply black polish to yellow leather. "You went out with this on?"

"But of course."

"Well, you put on one black shoe and one yellow one!" She could not keep herself from laughing.

"So that's why they were making fun of me," said Gaspard in dismay.

He was pained. He still had pride. The humiliation brought tears to his eyes. Annie reproached herself for having laughed.

She had finished his shoes and was getting back to her washing. She could tell that he was smothering in this atmosphere of hostility, so she said to him, "Come help me, Uncle Gaspard."

"Help you?"

"Yes. I've left the big jobs for you."

He stood up immediately, following her. She gave him a pair of sabots, and in the laundry room she showed him the tubs of washing and the buckets to empty, rinse, and refill with fresh water. He threw himself into the work with all his heart. This large blind fellow was ruddy and still surprisingly strong. She knew it pleased him to set big jobs aside for him in such fashion, giving him the impression that he could still help with something. And she left him logs to saw, coal to bring up, tubs to decant. Annie was the Mourauds' only daughter. Joséphine first and foremost loved her boys, the sons, the males. Henri, Annie's father, was hard-bitten, little prone to tenderness. They had used Annie to realize their ambitions, to elevate their sons. She had already laboured on behalf of the eldest, Gaston, who was in the war. Now she was doing it for the youngest. Annie was bent to the task. She had grown accustomed to sacrifice. She had had to quit school, which she loved, to do the washing with her mother, the housework, the cooking, and serve Georges. From this experience, she had developed a spirit of devotion, the habit of underestimating herself and working herself to the bone without much hope of gratitude or affection. Her father was perhaps fonder of her than her mother. When Annie had come down with chorea as a child, he had cared for her, bathed, washed, and cleaned her. At heart, Joséphine Mouraud was rather inhuman.

In this disagreeable environment, the tenderness of Uncle Gaspard, who was more loving and perceptive than Annie's own parents, had at first surprised and then comforted her. She had retained a secret and profound gratitude for his affection. He had been the most beloved figure of her adolescence.

Then Gaspard had lost his vision – slowly, so slowly that Annie, no less than the others, had failed to understand the horror of his tragedy. Such a gradual decline is not really striking. And then, the initial symptoms had seemed rather comical. Absent-mindedness, clumsiness, a tendency to talk to himself, a somewhat infantile aspect to his disappointed but perennial hope of a cure with each new remedy, each new endeavour ... Annie understood that Georges laughed at these things. Gaspard's blindness was a matter of a semi-darkness, not a total one. Gaspard came, went, continued living like everybody else. By the time he was reduced to guiding himself by feel, seeing nothing but blurry images, recognizing nothing but voices, those around him had gotten used to it, did not realize the severity of the problem, because – in some respects – there had never been a shock.

By chance was Annie enlightened. One day she noticed a child, a little neighbour boy – undoubtedly remembering the schoolmaster's morality lesson – who was helping Uncle Gaspard tie his shoelaces. Annie was struck by the scene. It was a revelation, this stranger's assistance to Uncle Gaspard. She realized that right beside her, and without ever having suspected it, was great misery – a suffering similar to those in works of fiction, in books – with which she had somehow coexisted unawares. The daily grind tends to make one oblivious to drama, to sorrow, to the tragic side of life that compels one's pity. Annie felt remorse and set herself guard over Uncle Gaspard. Her family laughed at her, but she persisted in her mission.

Gaspard finished emptying his washtubs. He went down to the basement, brought up coal, worked himself hard. Annie completed the rinsing and the wringing. Her weary arms and tender hands pained her. She had spent the entire day doing laundry in people's cellars: that morning at the house next door, that afternoon at the home of Madam Albertine, Barthélémy David's mistress. The work at Madam Albertine's was difficult, but Annie was well paid. Barthélémy David occasionally went down to the basement to see her. Today he had fussed at Madam Albertine for ordering Annie around too harshly. He often defended her in this manner, without her understanding why he was doing it.

"I'm done," said Gaspard.

"Let's go back."

They returned to the kitchen, which was warm with steam from the ironing. Henri Mouraud had gone to bed. Georges had returned with his notebooks to the table, and his mother was ironing in the adjacent room. Annie ate in her turn. Uncle Gaspard had dried his hands, and now he was pacing back and forth, from room to room. He was in his shirtsleeves. His suspenders trailed behind him like a long tail. His pants had slid down and his shirt had puffed out, pulled free of his belt. Thus seen, he appeared at once ludicrous, huge, and wretched. He shuffled around in his old slippers with a small, regular, irritating noise, disappeared into the darkness, and stepped back into the light with hands behind his back, head down, eyes on the floor, murmuring, crying out, shaking his head, heedless of those around him. He was figuring, reckoning. Twelve treatments at a hundred francs and perhaps he would be healed. This bromide, these drugs were not as good as electrotherapy. Unless the remedies were combined ... Improvement with a multi-course regimen. Improvement! To see a little, to escape from the void! He was thunderstruck at contemplating such things. Lost in his ruminations, he stopped and said aloud: "I must have these twelve treatments."

A nasal echo reverberated close by. He tumbled back to reality, realized that little Georges was mocking him. He felt at once humiliated and furious at having thus forgotten himself, betrayed himself, revealed his anguish, his suffering, his hopes in front of this brat. He lashed out in anger and pain.

"Wicked boy!"

And he marched off, trundled up the stairs in his slippers, and headed toward the attic, where he had his bed.

"Oh, he gets on my last nerve," said Georges, affecting schoolboy slang. "He's dirty, he drools when he eats, he makes little noises with his false teeth, he runs his fingers in the butter and the shoe polish alike."

"Georges, you'll pay one day," said Annie, who could not believe that one could commit such acts of cruelty and injustice with impunity ...

"That's enough, that's enough," intervened Joséphine, their mother, who was heating the irons and upon whom this threat made a vague impression.

"Oh, you!" teased Georges, "we all know Uncle Gaspard's your sweetheart ..."

"My sweetheart?"

"He pays for your dresses, your jewellery, your shoes ..."

"What! I'd like you to show them to me, these dresses and these shoes!"

"Because he doesn't have a dime anymore! But in the past ..."

"Well, I've never asked him for a thing. If he did, it's because he wanted to."

She felt at once angry and embarrassed. It was true. For as long as he could and as much as he could, Uncle Gaspard had helped and succored Annie, buying her little dresses, bits of cloth, small pieces of jewellery, thereby reestablishing equilibrium, compensating for the injustice of Joséphine and the unequal treatment benefiting the boys. Her old sweetheart, yes ...

"If you're well-behaved and nice enough, maybe he'll marry you after the war," continued Georges, needling her.

"Keep going and I'll give you a slap, you little imbecile!"

"All right, that's enough," interjected their mother, sensing that the dispute was turning bitter. "Georges, do your homework, and Annie, you grab the irons. We've got enough work to keep us busy till midnight."

Gaspard had gone up to his attic. When he could no longer pay his rent, his bedroom had been taken away. He lay down. His bed was below the skylight. The heavens were right above Gaspard's head. But for a long time – to his weakened eyes – the sky had been nothing more than a vaguely illuminated rectangle set against the black mass of darkness. Gaspard could not sleep. He tossed and turned. From afar came the eternal, monotonous, and dull roar of the cannonade, of the battle that had lasted for two years. This sound constantly reminded people of the war, the oppression, the martyrdom being suffered here. How much longer, how many more years would one hear it – the dismal, bleak rumbling? Deliverance ... no, it would be too wonderful. Folks knew that the Germans were here to stay. They were building, planning roads, railroads. What agony, what a harsh experience, for two years now! Gaspard had come to understand his fellow men far better than before. To suffer their every wickedness, he had had to fall into poverty. He thought of money. He had again asked Samuel for some, but he had none. It was one more humiliation to add to all the others. There was no more money. How would he continue taking care of himself? He felt discouraged. He cried for a moment, wiped his eyes with his sleeve. Come now! One could not give up. One had to hope, to hope anyway, and in spite of everything, to have confidence in this dim, perpetual, rumbling work of the sappers, which had continued over there, to the thunder of the guns, for years now, which advanced slowly, so slowly, which wore down, ate away, gradually eroded the wall of iron, ceaselessly ... How long would it last, this immense and unrelenting toil? Would he see the liberation? Or would the last ray of light evaporate first, leading to absolute darkness, endless night, even death? There was nothing for it but to wait ... To wait desperately, till the end.

III

From day to day, however, a shadow cast a lengthing pall over Mr Feuillebois the teacher. It was the thought of his son. He had invested all his affection, all his ambition, all his hopes in this young man. Disillusioned with dogmas, Feuillebois's craving for a faith had fallen upon his son, whom he had transformed into a veritable object of worship.

Since the beginning of the war, this much-loved son had vanished from his daily life. The cherished image had become ever more distant and indiscernible, disappearing against the horizon, in a bloody haze amid the mass of victims. He had received a single Red Cross postcard and then nothing more: no address, no information. By means official, by means clandestine, Mr Feuillebois had tried to get in touch with his son and had failed.

For a while he held out hope. A neighbouring woman had obtained permission from the German authorities to return to her native town in southern France. She had promised to do her best to find Mr Feuillebois's son and send word to the father. Then the days, the months had passed without news. And round this father's heart had grown the imperceptible, inescapable shadow of human suffering in which this happy man had not heretofore believed. And ever so slowly his sturdy confidence in himself, in his unshakeable destiny, began to waver. He, the inveterate optimist, began to doubt his luck. And his troubled thoughts showed in his expression, his gait, his words. Samuel and Gaspard, though lacking confidence themselves, tried to reassure him from time to time. They did not succeed. They did their best, but he only nodded his head, not responding, not wanting to contradict an argument that still resonated so well, in spite of everything, with his deepest hopes. After two years, Mr Feuillebois was left in complete despair. He had tried everything, put all his resources into action, but in vain. And now Samuel's old friend, worn out by this never-ending wait, weary of counting the hours one by one, crushed by the ever increasing mental strain, was no more than a shadow of his former self. His hair had turned white. His cheeks were hollow. His hunched shoulders, his uncertain steps gave him the appearance of an old man. This colossus was pitiful.

And at present an obsession ruled him. After having long conflated his destiny with that of his country, after having surrounded them with the same radiant perspective of happiness, he had been forced to separate them, with God knows what heartache. And since he would not for an instant accept the defeat of France, and in contrast was witnessing the collapse of his own hopes, he – this fetichist – thought that his happiness must be the price of victory for his country. He convinced himself that there is a level of joy that man cannot attain, that no more than others could he double his luck – his with his country's – and that the fall of one would compensate for the ascension of the other. Samuel could not convince him to abandon these strange ideas.

Events were to lend a shade of credence to his imaginings and his fancies. Samuel and Gaspard Fontcroix went some time without seeing Mr Feuillebois. They were beginning to worry when he returned one evening at the appointed hour for the communiqué. Immediately, at first sight of their friend's face, Samuel could tell what had happened. Feuillebois must have received the terrible news. This sixty-year-old man appeared to be eighty. His face was lined with furrows of suffering and disappointment. His eyes had lost their sparkle. His long, wavy hair gave him a look of carelessness and neglect. And his ample morning coat – now too large for his emaciated frame – hung in long, unsightly wrinkles. He shook their hands at length, his gaze lost in some distant preoccupation. Then he said simply, as if it were something natural, expected, necessary: "My son is dead."

They remained silent, stunned.

"You're ... you're sure?" whispered Gaspard at last.

"I've just heard it through the Red Cross. He fell at the close of 1914, on the front in Champagne ..." In a low voice, he added, "I wonder why it took two years to let me know ... So much suffering ..."

"Feuillebois," said Samuel, "Try to pull yourself together. You know how life goes. Sooner or later, we all have to meet an end ..."

"Yes," said Feuillebois, responding to himself more than to Samuel. "Yes, it makes sense. It was necessary ..."

He looked at the maps scattered on the desk, pinned to the wall, the newspapers, the communiqués, everything that had captivated him for so long, everything that had sustained his painful wait. He whispered, "Victory ... Victory ... It was the price, wasn't it? It was necessary, I've accepted it. Now then ... Now then ..."

He wiped his eyes, raised a martyr's brow toward Samuel and Gaspard: "My sacrifice is complete ..."

For several weeks they saw their friend regularly enough, but he spoke little, showed interest in nothing, seemed as though his mind were lost in painful contemplation. And Samuel sadly reflected, *Poor Feuillebois is finished.*

He was not mistaken. A week passed without seeing him. Samuel was about to go to Feuillebois's to check on him when he received a mortuary notice. Using the typical phrases, it announced the death of the teacher Jean-Louis Feuillebois.

Samuel went to see him on his deathbed. Mr Feuillebois lay there, out-stretched and huge, dressed in his morning coat – the austere black morning coat of the old teacher of yesteryear. Samuel touched his hand, a hand heavy like marble, on which traces of the schoolmaster's black and red ink still remained. He thought of Feuillebois's odd imaginings, this sacrifice of his happiness, fancifully thrown into the hands of fate for the salvation of France. Strangely, everything had unfolded, come to pass, as if someone from the other side had agreed to the bargain. And Samuel, contemplating the stern, peaceful countenance by the light of the candles, felt the need to whisper to him: "Thank you, Feuillebois ..."

As if it had been true, as if Old Feuillebois's sacrifice had served a purpose.

• • •

The death of Feuillebois had a profound effect on Gaspard Fontcroix. He had taken a liking to the man. Gaspard regarded Feuillebois's passing as a bad omen and let himself fall into a state of discouragement that worried Annie. He delivered increasingly vehement soliloquies to imaginary beings, grew despondent, exaggerated his taciturn habits. He believed himself the victim of poisoning, anthrax, kidney disease. Annie had to care for him, rub him down, apply warm poultices that only provided temporary relief. She slept in the garret, next to the attic where he had his bed. Each night she heard him dreaming aloud, continuing his monologues, talking of money and remedies and drugs, calling for Samuel, begging him, cursing him because he could no longer give him money ... Financial concerns visibly gnawed at Gaspard. Soon he could no longer pay for his share of rations. Even so, Joséphine and Henri were afraid to let him starve to death. They continued allowing him to come to the sideboard, to cut himself some bread, to help himself to a little rice and beans at the table. Joséphine did not say much. But Henri, her husband, grumbled and complained. Gaspard was slighted and snubbed. He was accused of being a freeloader, of eating the others' bread. He realized they were stealing from him. Georges took his electrical equipment to conduct experiments. Henri, Georges's father, rummaged in Gaspard's pockets at night while he slept and made off with the remnant of his tobacco, his ties, his collar studs, and his cufflinks. He took advantage of Gaspard's creeping blindness to switch their ankle boots. Gaspard's life became a nightmare in which Georges and Henri Mouraud played the role of tormenters. He was afraid to go out and spent all this time rummaging around, feeling in his pockets. He was ashamed to eat within sight of the family, waited to be alone to steal a drop of coffee, a bit of soup, groped about hurriedly, took the wrong saucepans, made everything fall and raised a ruckus. They began insulting him, saying that he was becoming a dirty thief, reverting to childhood, turning into a vicious rogue. And it was a little true. He was dying of hunger. He spent his days near the kitchen stove, sniffing, filling his nostrils with the meager smells of the grub, hoping a crumb would fall his way. Joséphine served him his food. Gaspard was forbidden to touch the saucepans and – for a man with such a hearty appetite – found himself treated to pathetically small morsels. Consumed by hunger, Gaspard one day took advantage of the distraction of his brother-in-law to steal a potato from his plate. Henri Mouraud slapped him. The blind man had a sudden burst of desperate pride and confined himself to his attic for three days without eating, without coming down. Then he capitulated, returned to take up the position of misery permitted him by the stove. He was so famished that when Joséphine put on the lard and brought the bacon to a sizzle for dinner, he could be seen trembling with desire and shaking, his nostrils quivering, his mouth salivating. He gave a shudder, uttered a genuine sob, in throwing himself upon his plate. He lived surrounded by hatred. These domestic resentments sometimes resulted in real cruelty. Annie did what she could for him, but she could not manage much. She brought him a little food that she received in the bourgeois houses where she went to do laundry. She continued her efforts to ease his pain, bathing him on Saturdays, massaging his upper and lower back. He became a little like her child. He stood naked before her, shamefully abandoning all restraint, wretched, miserable, compelled to set modesty aside. She looked after him like a mother, without unease, without disgust, quite naturally. She did not suffer from the situation. She was not even bothered by it. Georges sniggered. Her parents were indignant. They thought Annie and her uncle were not behaving properly, that it was inappropriate for this old man to allow himself to be cared for and seen by a young girl. He acknowledged it, apologized humbly, one day refused the assistance of his niece. Then he was again afflicted by one pain or another and had to seek her help anew. Yet he continued hoping for a cure, doctoring his eyes, always believing he could restore the clarity that was fading away. He washed his eyes with hot water, salt water, boracic solution. He scraped the bottom of containers and flasks of medicine, and prepared ridiculous mixtures. Of late his vision had deteriorated altogether. He could see nothing of the world but a dim pallour. He went once more to eat at the home of his brother Samuel. Gaspard was ashamed of his decrepitude. He brushed up as best he could. He had a good meal, ate his fill, so moved, so overwhelmed that he cried. They had red cabbage and potatoes.

That day, when he returned, he climbed mysteriously up to his attic, carrying a big package in his hands. Georges, who was listening through the keyhole, heard the sputtering of an electric machine. The Mourauds were outraged: "So, he still has money to waste on gadgets!"

Three days later, they received the bill. In his obsession, his mad hope of recovering, of restoring his sight at any price, Uncle Gaspard had put the machine on their account. Henri Mouraud went wild with rage. He turned the entire attic upside down, found the device, and stomped it to bits in front of the distraught blind man. When he had gone down again, Uncle Gaspard picked up the pieces like a child gathering a broken toy ...

He continued using strange treatments. He resorted to concoctions, crazy remedies that he made for himself. He had collected the fragments of his electric machine in a box. He tried to put them together, stole a lamp battery from Georges, kept at it, groped about, proceeded by trial and error, screwed and unscrewed, readjusted the parts with clumsiness and inexpertise. Then he went to plug the machine into the gas pipe.

"He's mad!" sniggered Georges, who – reveling in his elementary understanding of physics – followed his uncle's endeavours with pity and scorn.

Gaspard abandoned his efforts, giving way to an increasing, overwhelming sense of grief. His whole back tortured him. Shooting pains radiated from his spinal column. At present, he was hardly eating anything, sat dozing in his chair, only rousing from his eternal daydream for Annie, whom he recognized, blind though he was, without even having to open his eyes.

One night around eleven o'clock, Annie was awakened by a noise in the attic. She listened. Someone was talking, writhing, thrashing about. She got up, lit the lard lamp, and went into the attic. Standing near his bed, half-naked, in his shirtsleeves, Uncle Gaspard was struggling to get dressed, trying to pull on his waist coast in place of his pants. He was hurrying, growing agitated, muttering a ceaseless stream of words: "No ... Yes ... You must be joking! A medication for fifteen francs? Yes, yes, right away ..."

"Uncle Gaspard!"

He turned to her with an apoplectic face, dripping in sweat.

"Uncle Gaspard, are you okay?"

"Yes, yes, I'm fine. I'm just fine! But I'm hot ... God I'm hot! I'm getting undressed, you see ..."

He flung off his waistcoat, ripped the buttons from his shirt, tore it up.

"I'm hot! I'm too hot! And my head! Oh, my head!"

He took out his dentures, tossed them to the middle of the floor. Naked, terrifying, he ran his hands through his grey hair, huffing and puffing, wild-eyed and distraught.

"Oh, Samuel, you're here! And the money? A hundred francs! I need a hundred francs! A brother, you'd refuse your brother? Oh, thank you, Samuel, thank you! I know ... No, no, don't worry, he won't find it. I'll hide it, I'll hide it ..."

He thrust his hand into an imaginary pocket, hiding the money, the money, the money ...

"Georges would take it ... Or Henri ... I need it for my equipment ... My equipment ... Oh, it relieves me, it relieves me. You'll see, Annie, jewellery, real diamonds, yes, yes, when my eyes ... But this money, first I need to find this money ..."

He rummaged in his pockets, turned over his mattress, rent his jacket, hurled himself toward the wall with a terrible cry: "Oh! Thief! Thief! He's taken it from me! Mouraud's taken it from me!"

This behaviour lasted all night.

In the morning Henri Mouraud hastened to army headquarters to request a German transport that would take the madman to Lille.

The family dressed Uncle Gaspard. Joséphine looked for his oldest outfit since it would remain at the hospital. He was left in his torn shirt and without a tie. He had the look of an old vagabond. Mouraud rummaged through Gaspard's pockets. There he found Gaspard's purse with a big silver chain and three francs. Joséphine gave the money to Annie because she had spent the night watching over the invalid. Annie had tried to give her uncle back his dentures. Her father was opposed. He had always been jealous of this device. He no longer had a single tooth in his mouth but had never had the means to purchase false teeth. And his brother-in-law's dentures irritated him.

"We can't leave this for the asylum," he said. "It's made of gold."

He removed Uncle Gaspard's dentures and put them in his pocket. Gaspard, stupefied, did not interfere. He put up no resistance when they led him to the German transport. They did not even have to resort to the traditional lie, the pretext of a walk or a trip to the doctor.

Annie visited Uncle Gaspard in Esquermes. He spoke to her. He wanted to leave. He cried, complained of hunger, asked for his teeth because he was unable to eat. He said that he had a niece, yes, Annie, a good girl. But he no longer recognized her.

She paid a second visit to the asylum, but she was not allowed to see her uncle. He was delirious, they said. And when she returned a third time, she was met with a terrible reception.

"But your uncle, he's dead! And even buried!" she was told. "Oh, yes, we're familiar with such things! You didn't want to pay for the coffin! And now he's in a pauper's grave."

She was ignorant of her father's position, if he had kept the news to himself to avoid the burial expenses.

That night, when Annie arrived at home, she noticed that her father was speaking oddly and seemed uncomfortable. He had teeth in his mouth, teeth that had not been made for him ... Uncle Gaspard's dentures. It made a strange impression on Annie, thus seeing the dead man's teeth in her father's mouth ...

Chapter Six

One morning in June 1916, at dawn's first light, the imperial guard invaded Épeule, woke the residents, and began seizing young people.

Two soldiers came looking for Annie herself and forced her out into the street with her pack of food and undergarments, which had been standing at the ready for a long time.

It was still dark. A crowd blocked the roadway, people of all ages, from every walk of life, and above all youth whom the Germans pushed, pulled, dragged from their homes, separated from their families with brutality. From each open doorway, folks could be seen spilling out like this, in a continual stream. In some spots painful scenes unfolded: a boy whom the parents were trying to keep by force, mothers throwing themselves on the Germans and driven off by rifle butts, fathers shaking their fists, crying, shouting insults, a tall young man being led away with hands bound while his parents, following behind, tried to defend him and were pummeled by the troops. So moving was this final scene that it reminded Annie of the arrest of Christ by the Jews. Some women kitted themselves out, set off with their daughters, refusing to abandon them. Others seemed to go mad and called down curses. Still others dropped in tears at the soldiers' knees, held them by their tunics, clung to them, clasp their hands, moaned, begged, "My son, my daughter, for pity's sake, leave me my child ..."

The Germans remained impassive. The imperial guard had been brought expressly for this prupose.

Some comical indicents occurred as well. One woman, who had appeared spry and healthy just the day before, came armed with crutches.

Others dragged themselves along the walls, pretending to spit, cough, swoon away ... On one house a clever fellow had affixed a stolen red poster, a typhus warning. And the soldiers avoided the contaminated residence like the plague. Anger, rage, sorrow, tears, screaming, swearing, cursing – all were to be heard alongside rapid orders and the metallic clatter of weapons. Folks were in mismatched clothes, loaded with crude bundles wrapped in hand towels, wearing old coats, blue aprons, clogs, worn-out shoes, most people bare-headed and looking like a herd of cattle on the move ... Round about stood the guard troops – rigid, muscular, armed, helmeted, imperturable. Haversacks were being thrown, wives and mothers slipping in again for a last word, a final kiss. Open doorways revealed the interiors of houses where Germans were coming and going, issuing commands, and manhandling the inhabitants. One was left with an impression of rape and rapine, a neighbourhood handed over to pillage and plunder, amid tears, moans, supplications, and imprecations ... And overhead was the dull and grey sky of early morn ...

The retinue set out, a slow exodus of wan, haggard people, their eyes swollen, trembling from emotion as much as the morning cold. Already, though, courage awoke among these youths. They pulled themselves together, got their bearings, realized that they at least had each other in their misfortune. Anger at the soldiers also mounted, leading to insolence, mockery. Deliberate laughter erupted, aimed at the Germans. Some of the kids in the lead began singing to show the Boches they were not afraid.

The group arrived at rue d'Avelghem. There stood a huge factory whose looms the Germans had removed. They penned the herd in the workshops, men on one side, women on the other, separated by ropes. And then began the wait, all morning, all afternoon, till evening. Frightful rumours circulated. The Germans were taking everyone to the front ... They were planning to attack, to take the offensive by using innocents as human shields ... Or the lot was being sent to Germany to serve as hostages because the French were bombarding German cities ... A thousand absurdities. Some of the men were sitting on the floor and playing cards. Some of the women, the prostitutes – hookers from the district round the train station and rue des Longues-Haies – were laughing, enjoying the novelty, flinging dirty words or invitations at the Germans. Annie – alarmed, tired of shuffling about – listened in amazement and felt drained, nauseated, and stupefied. She had brought along a little case, like a soldier's pack, which held her undergarments and some crackers. The whole bundle had been set aside for months. Every household had been living in constant expectation of this show of force. She was sitting on her case, looking round in exhaustion.

• • •

Fifty people had rushed to Barthélémy David's. He was well known among the working classes. People were aware that he trafficked with the Germans, but he was such a decent fellow and did so much good that they forgave him. In present circumstances, each family had thought of him and gone running: "Mr David, my son ... Mr David, my daughter ... For pity's sake!"

David rushed to German headquarters. There he found Lieutenant Krug.

"This is really despicable!" David told him.

"I agree, and so do the rest of us here," responded Krug. "We didn't hide our opinion. But we're soldiers, Mr David, we obey."

"Well in any event, I want to get a few poor devils out of this fix. Let's go, Krug, come with me. I'm asking you for fifty chaps."

"That's a lot!"

"Bah! Think of your family. Consider the plight of these unfortunates, Krug. The bourgeois houses weren't targeted! Let's go, come on."

He took him to rue d'Avelghem. In the spinning rooms David saw many of his acquaintances, Roubaix mill owners who were coming to look for their protégés. They pleaded, argued, demanded. Finally the Germans gave in. One more fortunate escaped their clutches, dashing away happily with his pack on his shoulder.

David marched boldly through the passageways, a man sure of himself, going along the ropes, shouting to Krug that the entire ordeal was revolting. In every "pen" he came across familiar faces: former employees, smugglers, roughnecks, acquaintances from the old days and people from Épeule, a whole host of folks whom he could not have identified by name but who saw him arrive like a Messiah, who called to him, begged him, implored him.

"Mr David! Mr David ..."

He was submerged, inundated. Outstretched hands, anguished looks, groans, pleas – the enormous cry for help left him overwhelmed. He did not know which ones to grab first.

"Fifty," said Krug, who knew his friend David.

And David steeled himself with impassivity, squelched his pity, attempted to read the imploring faces for evidence of the most dire, most urgent circumstances: the sick, the elderly, the frail, and those in whom an inner anguish – some gnawing concern – left the harshest and most strained features. These he pulled from the row.

"You ... You ..."

He selected young women whom he – the old observant playboy – could tell were virtuous, shy and wretched boys worn down by bullying, all the weak ones, all those whom he sensed would soon be crushed. Some of the women kissed his hands. He rebuked them roughly, overwhelmed, hiding his unease beneath a pretense of ill humour.

"Okay, okay, that's enough, get out of here, go, quickly now ..."

With surprising accuracy, at a glance, this man who had himself experienced so much, endured so much, picked out the long faces, the secret pains. He focused his energies on them. He preferred to set friendship aside, to alleviate only true suffering, real misfortune ... Round him came pleas: "Mr David ... Mr David ..."

It was thus that he suddenly discovered Annie seated on her case. She was almost hiding, ashamed to go beg him like the others, perhaps too proud as well. She said nothing, looking round with a weary and resigned expression. Abruptly she saw before her the tall, muscular silhouette, the heavy, gruff, coarse, and powerful face.

"You, too? You, too, my dear! Who'd have thought!"

She had stood up awkwardly ...

"And you didn't come, you didn't call me?"

She blushed, fumbled with the edge of her blouse.

"You don't want to get out of here? You'd rather stay, then?"

In a hushed voice, she murmured, "Mr David ..."

And she began crying, distraught from having already seen so much in these few hours, from having suffered, consumed her strength, been subjected to insults, laughter, contact with prostitutes and the dregs of humanity, the brutality of the army rabble. She would have liked to say yes, to beg, to ask to escape from this abyss herself. But she was crying too much and like the others could only blurt out: "Mr David ... Mr David ..."

"Let's go, this one, too," said David, turning round to Krug.

"Again!"

"Of course! You don't think I'm going to let my laundress be taken from me? Go on, my dear, clear off, get home quickly ..."

She fled without saying a word, frantic, crying, sobbing with joy, dragging her pack, wild with happiness. Her heart seemed as though it would burst. She whispered the name David to herself over and over, as one repeats a prayer of gratitude, of thanksgiving ...

On his way out with Lieutenant Krug, David went into the factory courtyard. Krug laughed.

"The girls'll make fun of you, Mr David ..."

"I can't help it, what'd you expect!" responded David.

But he carried the joke no further.

• • •

The same day Alain Laubigier had also been led away by the imperial guard and taken to rue d'Avelghem. There he was confined with François van Groede, Big Flavie's son, and a multitude of adolescents and adult men. A year younger than Alain, François was terrified. Alain, who had already endured imprisonment and encountered the mob, was less frightened and tried to comfort his cousin.

They were with a band of youth who had segregated themselves and were standing apart from the others. At nine o'clock they were joined by forty odd newcomers: fifteen- and sixteen-year-olds wearing schoolboy caps. They were students from the Institut Turgot whom the Germans, after having promised to spare them, had taken all the same, and at the school no less. These youngsters looked petrified.

All day long, there was unbelievable commotion at the huge factory: the buzz of the crowd, laughter and tears, arguments, wailing. One fellow was eating, another laughing, still another singing, yet another gesturing to women. One group started quarreling with the guards, others talked of escape. Many begged the soldiers, presented excuses: a sick child, a crippled mother. Still others offered money.

The Germans stood their ground.

From the outside, help soon arrived for many of the captives. Favouritism, patronage, string-pulling were again in evidence. Anyone who had a friend, an acquaintance capable of intervening with headquarters, suddenly remembered it, jotted a note, dispatched an appeal for help.

Families made arrangements from their end, too. Officers, women of ill repute, shopkeepers with ties to the enemy, traffickers, money changers – one hastened to beg them, to grovel at the feet of these influential folks. The result was that, from dawn till dusk, a parade of visitors and incessant appeals reached rue d'Avelghem. Names were called out. The chosen left the crowd, took off, frantic, not daring to believe their luck, beneath the jealous gaze of the others. Seeing so many escape, one ended up having hope. "Why not me after all? Who knows?"

François spent the entire morning with his eyes on the door whence arrived news from the outside ...

"Mamma will do something," he told himself. "You'll see, Alain, you'll see. She won't leave me here."

His hope had such conviction that he eventually undermined Alain's willful indifference.

"Who knows? Perhaps ..."

In spite of himself the young man started to hope that his mother, too ... He would soon hear his name shouted amid the tumult, would he not? To leave, to go home, to escape the nightmare. But what could be done by a miserable woman like Félicie Laubigier, who had no money and was not "in" with the Boches?

At the factory one saw many rich people – mill owners, gentlemen, well-dressed ladies. They came to claim a maid, a servant, a protégé, the son of a foreman, of a worker, of a wretch who had run to beg them. The entreaties of the wealthy still carried some weight with the authorities. Their intentions were commendable, charitable. And yet many inmates resented their intervention. That morning, at the time of the roundup, the Germans had noticeably refrained from grabbing youth of bourgeois origin. And then, one routinely saw these types – the German officers and the wealthy French – interacting differently than soldiers and "commoners." They greeted each other graciously. The German officers bowed before the ladies, with the somewhat stiff but extreme politeness of the well-bred German.

"Captain ..."

"Madam ..."

In their relationship one sensed a civility, a mannerly courtesy that was surprising and infuriating. The crowd pent up in the factory did not understand, could not accept it. Well what then, shake hands like that, smile, speak politely with the Boches? One noticed in amazement how, among the wealthy, between representatives of the dominant classes, the war had retained something courteous, conventional, "refined." There was no mistreatment, no blows, vulgarities, or reciprocal insults. No visible hatred, revolt, or vehement refusal to compromise. Instead there was the urbanity of civilized people, something that again recalled the old order of things – the gentleman's war, the panache, the mutual fairness. It was normal, logical, between people of similar culture and education. But something was still troubling about it. One had the all-too-distinct impression that war and hatred – like work, hunger, suffering – were made above all for the lowly, the masses ...

In the meantime Alain and François ate a little of their provisions and listened to the stories of the companions around them. One roughneck was worried about his mistress, who had been arrested at the same time as him, and was busy searching for her. Another man was absolutely furious, telling anyone who would listen that it was his wife's fault if he were here. She had a lover, a German officer. So she had found this means of ridding herself of a cumbersome husband. Still another boy was in tears, having been ripped from the bedside of his dying father. When the order arrived to release the students from the Institut Turgot, some comical incidents ensued. Fellows of every age and every stripe filed among the schoolboys, hoping to leave with them. François, who was just seventeen years old, also snuck into their ranks. But the Germans looked at his hands, which were hard and calloused, and threw him back into the room with a kick in the rear. The soldiers gradually conducted a selection, choosing among the inmates, retaining only the fittest. The Germans inspected identification cards, allowing fathers of four and individuals with grey hair to leave. People argued as their heads were examined, asserting that they did in fact have grey hair and quarreling with the troops.

The day was thus spent in confusion. Toward evening the Germans brought some straw mattresses. Fights broke out. The strongest alone got one. People slept as best they could.

The following morning the Germans distributed some murky coffee that smelled of camphor. In anticipation of a voyage in which women and men would be jumbled together, the authorities had used this means of slipping an anti-aphrodisiac on the herd. Then numbered labels were hung round the prisoners' necks, as if they were cattle. The crowd was forced out onto the railroad siding adjoining the factory. Lines of freight cars were waiting. Everyone had to climb aboard. Alain found himself in a baggage car with six other young men and twenty-eight women, all of them bewildered, already exhausted, and consumed with anxiety. Bumpers collided, cars lurched as the couplings engaged, and an indescribable bustle unfolded on the platforms. A quarter of an hour later, their train started off slowly, heading toward Lille.

The captives were both dazed and on edge. They were awaiting the adventure. Everyone, in every car, was at the doorways. They were peering round, shouting, many of them singing in an effort to defy the Germans. The train plodded across the rich, level, populous plain that it overlooked from the embankment. In Alain's baggage car were seven or eight prostitutes, some mill girls, and two or three young women who seemed more well bred and much more frightened, too. In one corner was a fifty-year-old woman with her two daughters, whom she had refused to abandon. The presence of this older woman of respectable appearance helped maintain an air of decency in the car. Even so, people were agitated. They hurled insults at the German sentries guarding the tracks. They broke into patriotic songs. No one wanted to reveal their anxiety and distress. Each put on an act of indifference. Along the route, some bystanders were waving their handkerchiefs, calling out goodbyes and encouragements. The train crossed Lille. Everywhere it passed, people were standing at their windows, motioning farewell, shouting. And at the back of a small courtyard in the Fives district, a man had planted himself, facing the rail line, heroically waving a huge tricolour flag with both hands! The passengers could not believe their eyes. They cried, they yelled ...

For hours on end, the excitement of the departure fired their spirits. Hanging in clusters round the doors, they greeted each village with a clamour, whistled at the Germans, sang the "Marseillaise." Everyone had a little something to eat and drink: synthetic brandy, water, crackers, lard, condensed milk, honey. They drank, for they were dying of thirst. The excitement went to their heads, intoxicating them like alcohol. Cheeks burned, voices cracked, one felt on the verge of tears and laughter and irritation all at once. These conditions persisted for a long time while the train rolled along at a slow, regular, monotonous pace across the flat, wooded countryside dotted with villages of brick and tile, going God knows where.

Toward evening the most fanatical piped down – exhausted, drained, their nerves frayed. Silence overtook the cars one by one. People ate as they were able, tried to get some sleep, but a pressing need soon tortured everyone. They had drunk too much and were suffering for it. Sleep was impossible. They hoped the train would pause at some station so they would have time to run to the washroom. But it kept chugging along relentlessly. Soon men were urinating at the doorways, onto the tracks below ... One girl spread out a newspaper and relieved herself. Shouting erupted – they were not animals, after all! It was nauseating. Women, feeling like they were getting sick, began crying in despair. In the end, the men had to hold them by the hands, one at a time, so they could pee above the tracks, hanging from the doorway. It was an appalling humiliation, driving many to tears.

The following evening, as night was falling, the train arrived at a village deep in the Ardennes. It was in the hollow of a valley. One could make out the surrounding hillsides, wooded and dark beneath the blue firmament. Bright rays, the revolving beams of spotlights, passed overhead. The Uhlans drove the herd into a barn. No more than sixty of the detainees remained. At each station along the way, the Germans had dropped off a car, which had been uncoupled and left behind with its entire human load. But new groups arrived from other directions. Soon there were more than 150 men, women, and children.

The barn was huge, dark, barely illumined by a few lanterns. On the ground lay wood shavings, and above hung beams where round, agile shadows were wavering – rats. Round this barn, one side of which let onto the village square, peasants were congregating and gawking. One could hear them arguing and worrying. They took the group for a band of French convicts brought by the Germans to do forced labour!

The captives were cold and hungry. Some men collected woodchips. Outside the barn they built a huge fire round which people warmed themselves. Alain, who had a little money, asked a peasant for beer and bread. The man returned with a loaf and some cider. Alain shared this fare with François and the women from his car. Soon others began imitating him. They rushed to the peasants, who brought litres of cider. People drank to their hearts' content. The cider sparkled, it roused and cheered them. Alain found the cider exquisite. He bought more. François did likewise. Soon they were quite tipsy. This sweet and deceptively strong drink went straight to the enervated brains of the whole lot. Someone who had an accordion started up a dance. They began capering about. In a short time there was an orchestra of flutes, harmonicas, and accordions making a hash of the popular waltzes. People danced, drank, sang. The merrymaking quickly devolved into drunken carousing. A good half of the women came from seedy cabarets. The men were no better. And these types influenced the others. The fatigue and exhaustion of the past two days disappeared along with the sorrows and anxieties. The revelers danced to the din of the instruments and the drumming of wooden planks, amid the red glow of blazing lanterns. Each individual squandered his savings, buying cider for strangers, forgetting tomorrow's needs, intoxicated by the noise, the alcohol, and the dancing. The gathering rapidly took on the hue of a dissolute orgy. Alain's young cousin, François van Groede – enthused, liberated, half mad with drink, excitement, and sensual fervour – dragged Alain along, screaming, shouting, dripping with sweat, kissing the girls: "We're men," he shouted, "we're men. Come on!"

And Alain let himself be swept away, danced, sang, and drank like the rest, and found it all delightful. In a corner of the barn there was one group of frightened and terrified young girls who were soon the butt of jokes. "Virgin's corner," it was called. Everyone else – women and men alike – waltzed, got drunk, did the cancan. From time to time, however, some folks were seen stepping away to vomit or to relieve themselves, for the cider was freshly brewed and promptly turned their stomachs. The nausea put the finishing touches on the crude charm of the festivities.

Alain grew weary and stopped dancing. He felt hot, feverish, beside himself. He watched with indifference as François, sweating and drunk, rifled through the blouse of a girl who was squirming and laughing. Why was he not shocked, more upset by the half-naked women, the obscene language, the frenzied atmosphere of the entire spectacle? He realized that he was drunk, on the verge of stupid mistakes. He stopped himself from emptying the mug of cider that he had just grabbed to slake his terrible thirst. He wandered off, left the square, avoiding the couples and going to cool his forehead in a ditch full of water. He could feel the beginning of a headache and of a dissatisfaction with himself that he could not quite fathom.

He spent half an hour dipping his handkerchief in the water and dabbing his face. Then he went back toward the glow marking the barn and the big fire of wood shavings. Rediscovering this mob sickened him. He skirted the barn to find a hedge and lie down. He stumbled over the body of a sleeping drunkard, disturbed some squatting women in the grips of a dreadful ordeal, and passed a few men leaning against the wall and vomiting. He was making his way toward the hedge when he heard moaning. And in the darkness he bumped into his cousin François, who was heaving up his cider.

"Are you okay, François?"

"A little better," he moaned.

François cast a feverish, stupefied, dazed expression toward Alain. From afar came the clamour of the party and the glow of the blistering fire. Alain pulled his cousin toward the hedge. François stretched out to sleep on the ground, resting his head on his hands.

For a moment Alain remained standing, his head in pain. He was haunted by the thought of his mother and his sister Jacqueline. He blushed at the idea of what he had done. For all the world, he wished he had never given in to this madness. A peel of laughter drifted toward him, increasing his remorse and his disgust. All of a sudden he heard crying. He stooped down. It was François.

"You're sick?"

"No," said François, "no."

"Well what then?"

"I was thinking of my home ... my mother ... oh là là!"

Poor François, he was no longer concerned about his manhood. He felt vaguely threatened by a danger that had undoubtedly touched neither his body nor his health, but which, without fully understanding, he perceived as no less terrible. He began crying like a little boy, the little boy from whom he had seemed so removed only moments before. And Alain, who tried to comfort François, was himself on the verge of tears. Never had he felt so young, so weak, so defenseless. He was humiliated by his actions. Such madness on account of a single day of liberty! Oh no, they were not yet men ...

II

The valley was deep, green, filled with shadows and running water. It was dominated by tall, dark, wooded hills, forests of black fir, oak, beech, and silver birch. The sky above – a high, delicate, blue arch – fell to each side of the hollow, far beyond the hills. There was almost no wind. The weather was drier and warmer than in Flanders. And the pure air smelled of sap and resin. In this isolated valley of the Ardennes, one had the impression of being a thousand miles from the war and the world.

The village, at the bottom of the little valley, stretched along the river, a shallow river, unbelievably clear and rapid, which murmured as it washed pebbles of flint onto the golden sand. The houses were built of grey and white stone and had roofs of slate, absent the brick – the ugly red brick – that for Alain and his compatriots from the Nord had become an expected sight, like the flat monotony of the plain.

After several weeks of amazement, Alain, like many others, had grown tired of the hills, the limited vista, this wall forever set against the horizon like a barrier. He missed the plain as sailors miss the sea.

Alain was quartered with the adults in an enormous cowshed outside the village. They received worse treatment than the youth, who had been left in the village itself, crammed into a big house, an abandoned mansion. This residence had been surrendered to the herd. Alain paid frequent visits to the house because his young cousin François had remained there. Alain went to seen him, to help him, to take him food. This huge building and this band of youth made for a colourful sight. The Germans, of course, could not make use of them. These boys and girls, too weak and too unruly, had been left to their own devices. But every week they were given a sack of peas and some bread, bacon, and potatoes. They lived like savages, in wild confusion, around fifty of them squeezed into the bedrooms, the parlours, the kitchens – pillaging, smashing, destroying, stealing from each other, fighting over the spoils. They broke up the floorboards and the furniture to cook their meals, each preparing his own food, one in the garden, another in the middle of the vestibule, still another in the attic ... Fires broke out dozens of times. It was astonishing that the whole place did not burn down.

Each week, within two days of the distribution of foodstuffs, they had devoured, wasted, ruined it all in frightful attempts at cooking, or traded it for marbles and tops in the village stores. At that point they would liquidate a few of their remaining assets – money, luggage, undergarments, clothing – selling items to each other or to the villagers. Soon a good half were living in an almost naked condition, without shoes or jackets, and occasionally without dress or pants. They no longer bathed. Wrapped in loin cloths, they went to pilfer, pillage, lay waste to the farms. A tribe of savages! They fought each other for food, struck up romances, corrupted each other with startling rapidity, infected each other with illnesses, were soon teeming with vermin, and subjected a few scapegoats – targeted because of some physical or moral flaw – to incredible bullying.

This band had become the terror of the local peasants. Chickens, wheat, fruit, vegetables – they plundered it all. If Roubaix and Tourcoing were destroyed, as was sometimes rumoured, or if the victorious Germans left the region in anarchy, then these urchins – reverting to a state of savagery – would subsist like a pack of wolves.

Alain looked after his cousin François, who was mixed in with this bunch. François got into brawls, took some nasty hits, wasted his supplies, and suffered from hunger like the others. Alain managed to get the Germans to entrust François to him. Alain found François a job at the Bricards' farm, where he was put in charge of tending the cows. Alain had become friends with the Bricards. He had won their support by doing them small favours. Thanks to their precious friendship, he was not at all unhappy. He was staying with them. They gave him supplies: bread, meat, even undergarments. And old Mrs Bricard did the young man's laundry with that of the farm. Despite the war, a certain abundance prevailed. They had wheat bread, milk, butter, eggs, potatoes. The farmers, each in turn, killed a calf, then a pig, then a sheep. Meat was not in short supply. To Alain, life here seemed opulent compared to Roubaix.

During the day, Alain went with the men to fell trees for the Germans. It was hard, healthy, almost joyous work deep in the forest. They were well fed. Each managed to add small extras to the standard fare. Some, like Alain, had easily won the friendship of the country folk. Others had found a makeshift lover, come across a meal, a bed, and all the rest in the home of some bored woman. Still others who spoke German or had some particular talents – like singing, playing the accordion, or doing card tricks – showcased their skills for the officers and noncommissioned officers, and collected leftovers from the canteen. There was even one fellow, a certain Morlebaix, an old Bac à Puces regular, vaguely familiar to Alain, who had gained the special favour of the commander, Hauptmann von Reinach, thanks to his wide array of tall tales. Von Reinach was a potbellied colossus, the caricatured stereotype of the German, with shaven head, protruding nape, brick-red complexion, and bulging eyes. He did not understand a word of French. But Morlebaix's anecdotes were translated for him. Von Reinach had gotten a taste of Gallic wit. And now, on his rounds through the forest, he had Morlebaix follow behind, along with an interpreter who scrupulously translated Morlebaix's stories. It was a cushy job, as good as any of its kind, and one that brought Morlebaix all manner of advantages. Since he was cunning, he even profited from his good relations with the bigwigs to ship packages of meat, bread, and butter to Roubaix. Morlebaix made a tidy profit. Thanks to him, Alain managed to get provisions to his mother on several occasions.

In the end, there was little cause for complaint. At times the German supervisors acted zealous, appeared demanding, but it was mostly for show. Unfit troops and convalescents had been assigned to the forest. These guards attempted to make the duty hard enough to avoid being sent back to the front. But they were not too tough about it.

In the evenings, after work, folks were free till curfew. They met up again in the huge barn of wood and slate where they were quartered together. Fires were lit for soup and coffee. People ate on the grass, some here, some there, along a hedge, beside a ditch, on a stump. Then the dancing began. The festivities took place regularly each night.

Alain distanced himself from the group. He climbed back up to the woods, to the top of the peaks that were so confining and troubling to the eyes of the lowlander, and – beyond the unmoving sea of hillsides and little valleys – contemplated the infinite run of green and black forest stretching to the greyish horizon. Far past the haze where the sky met the earth lay Roubaix, his mother, his house. Perched up here, Alain day-dreamed for hours on end, at once sad and happy. He had ultimately inclined toward fatalism. He worked, lived, did his best. For the rest, there was nothing to do but wait ... He was tired of worrying. He had suffered too many shocks, heard too many exciting or distressing rumours. Roubaix liberated, Roubaix in flames ... Germany defeated, Germany triumphant ... Alain refused to believe any more such tales.

It was in the course of these meanderings that he came across Juliette Sancey. He already knew her. He had occasionally seen her in Épeule. She was the daughter of Mrs Sancey, the big drapery merchant. The Sanceys were tradespeople, rich folks. Mrs Sancey was an inflexible widow renowned for charity and austerity. She had several well-bred, educated, and obedient children. Juliette was her eldest. The Germans had snatched

Juliette from her mother, and she had travelled here in the same car as Alain. They had taken a liking to each other, a product of the inexplicable magnetism that sustains youthfulness and sincerity in the world against all the odds.

Juliette Sancey was suffering in the base and uncouth environment into which she had been plunged.

Upon arrival, she had rather foolishly and unwittingly displayed her naïvety, her simplicity. Her alarm, her astonishment, her suffering, the humiliation and ridicule of which she had been the object had upset Alain, who was not a child of the bourgeoisie but who had nonetheless understood the pain of this girl, brutally ripped from a pure and rigid environment to find herself among bargirls, pimps, smugglers, even the insane. There were two or three of the latter whose fits and fainting spells delighted the most uncouth. Flirtatious remarks from Germans and Frenchmen, beds squeezed together, mattresses filled with vermin, shocking quarrels overheard during the midday siesta or round about at nighttime, public nudity, weekly communal baths in the river – to the accompaniment of laughter, cat calls, evidence of burning admiration from the male spectators – and the moral degradation, the girls gotten pregnant by French or German men and sent home each week: all of it had terrified Juliette. Like Alain, she had fled, taken refuge in solitude as much as she could. But it was more difficult for her than Alain because she was not as strong and because the others gave her a hard time and treated her like a prude. She had been grateful to find this young man to protect her, talk to her, understand her sorrows, her alarm, her grief, her desire for escape and isolation. To hold onto this support, she had put up with the mockery, the insinuations, the accusations of his companions: "The little Sancey girl's sleeping with Alain ..." Thinking of Roubaix, of her mother, of the normal life to which she would somehow return one day, she occasionally reproached herself for this familiarity with a person she hardly knew, with whom she risked compromising her reputation as an upright girl. But, on the other hand, to fall back under the dominion of the others would have been intolerable for her now. Alain had eventually given her his place at the Bricards'. He went back to sleeping in the communal barn. At present Juliette had at least a bed, a small space where she could be alone and free.

Clarity on the circumstances eluded Alain himself. Obviously, many of his companions already assumed that Juliette was his mistress. The subject provided material for little more than wanton allusions, without the least astonishment or reproach. Even for the Bricards, who were a bit coarse, Alain's relationship with Juliette was the object of friendly banter, the Bricards professing rather free and easy morals, especially in regard to the children of others.

This environment had an effect on Alain. Something accepted as so normal must be without consequence. He eventually wondered if he were not being foolish to prolong the situation. Young people will do stupid things to avoid looking silly. Some of the women, profligates who were older than Alain, understanding what was going through his mind better than he himself, did not pass up the opportunity of needling his young male pride: "She takes you for an idiot ... She's making a fool of you, she's toying with you. What're you waiting for to make her yours ... ? Can't you see you're being a sucker, my dear?"

They were filled with the jealousy, the hatred of the fallen woman for one who has remained pure, the desire – the loathsome and secret hope – of making her stumble in turn.

All the same, Alain hesitated. At bottom he could discern the path of wisdom and justice. After all, it was certainly not evident that Juliette was mocking him and taking him for a simpleton. On the contrary, perhaps she really was just as he thought: truly innocent, oblivious, and trusting. What a disappointment, what a rude awakening for her, if he suddenly appeared in a new light! The idea revolted him, and the more so since it in no way tempted him. He was untroubled in this regard, not at all obsessed with thoughts of sex. Much to the contrary, these things repulsed him a bit. He had been careful not to admit it to others, but he was not subject to such cravings. More than most would admit, young men are just as innocent as young women. Alain sensed that his friendship with Juliette was a beautiful thing, delicate and precious. To spoil it solely to comply with the mindset of others seemed to him stupid and sad. And yet it appeared necessary, like a custom. At bottom he regretted that, in the general opinion, they could not remain as they were. In the end he nonetheless resigned himself to try his luck.

But good Alain had nothing of the seducer in him. His first moves had a singular result. Juliette did not protest, seemed to consent, but as one consents to a self-sacrifice. She began shedding naïve, innocent tears, the tears of the young girl who does not know how to defend herself, is incapable of defending herself, and who realizes she is giving in, tying herself down ... Most often these tears hardly count for a man. Who stops for such things?

Alain stopped. His young age, a certain natural candour, the thought of his mother, of his sister, a lack of vice, and a sort of inexplicable apprehension prevented him from going further. He was disgusted with himself and with the others, deemed himself a rogue, a boy without heart, without nobility, and recalled his little sister Jacqueline. He was furious with everyone who could urge him toward such baseness. Too bad! He would pass for an imbecile, but he would do what he wanted, what he considered best, most just. Having taken this resolution, he felt true happiness, immense solace.

Alain and Jacqueline thus spent the rest of their time in platonic fashion – two city kids discovering together the boundless splendour of the Ardennes forest, the water, the cloudless sky, and marveling at it all. They found something extraordinary in foraging for blackberries, strawberries, and nuts, in watching hares bolt, pheasants and partridges take flight, a stocky boar cross a distant path in the heart of a thicket, in discovering a circle of green and tender grass in the midst of an arid heath – an area of coolness round a spring – like the remains of a fairy dance ... Each minute spent in the countryside is a revelation for city folk. Everything surprises them. They recognize things they have only seen, only known through pictures and books – mossy banks, the taste of wild fruit, ants carrying their larva, frogs beside pools in the evening, swelling their throats and unleashing one croak after another like a series of bursting bubbles. It was a grander, purer life, which misfortune had imposed upon them and which, despite the miseries accompanying it, would later leave them with a vague nostalgia, a longing for these first moments of affection amid a beautiful land of hills, rocks, and forests.

· · ·

After harvesting the wheat and the sugar beets, the Germans sent back a portion of the youth they had taken from the Nord at the start of the year. Through Morlebaix, the commander's jester, Alain managed to have Juliette and he included in the group that was repatriated.

They left the Ardennes in early November 1916. The sugar beets had been brought in quickly because of exceptional weather.

The trip home, oddly enough, was sadder than the outbound journey had been. The passengers had grouped themselves according to affinity, among people of similar taste, similar disposition, but they were too depressed for banter. They were thinking, wondering what they would find back in Roubaix – home, hearth, family. Such uneasiness, which follows long absences, detracts from the longing to celebrate.

Alain was in a car with Juliette Sancey. They did not speak much. As they neared Roubaix, they could feel themselves growing apart. Normal life was already taking hold of them again, with its conventions, its social distinctions, its obstacles of every nature. It was as if they were waking from a dream and coming back to reality. The Ardennes, which they had left only hours before, already appeared unbelievably remote, indistinct, like a distant fantasy. Alain could sense these emotions in both of them. Juliette was getting a grip on herself, pulling herself together. He hardly spoke to her, and she was grateful for it.

They spent an entire day en route. They arrived in Lille around six o'clock in the evening, vaguely recognizing the city and its environs amid the gathering darkness. And from that moment, with great emotion, crowded round the doorways of the railcars, the passengers peered at the shadowy landscape, screaming and shouting – "Lion d'Or! Fives! Grand Boulevard! Croix station! The Pont des Arts!" At this point many started crying because they were no more than 500 metres from the station in Roubaix.

They jumped onto the platforms and rushed outside. On Place de la Gare, people were waiting – whole families – somehow informed of their arrival. Juliette Sancey found her mother and threw herself into her arms. Alain, for his part, walked about, searching for his mother or Jacqueline, and seeing neither in the darkness.

He suddenly heard his name being called. Juliette, from behind, had grabbed him by the sleeve – "Sir," said Mrs Sancey, "I am truly indebted ... Juliette told me ... Thank you ..."

"Madam," stammered Alain, "Madam ..."

"Yes, yes," said Juliette. "He was good to me, Mother, and brave. Without him, I would've been absolutely miserable!"

She would have liked to describe it all, to explain everything he had done, the support she had found in him, but such things cannot be expressed in a single stroke. Words are not enough. She could find nothing but hackneyed phrases, repetitive clichés in which she herself sensed the emptiness and which embarrassed her all the more. No, none of it could convey anything of the devotion, the energy, the tenderness with which Alain had surrounded her. She could tell that her all too simple, brief, and spare words could not really speak to her mother. In spite of everything, this boy remained a stranger, an unknown for Mrs Sancey. She was appreciative – profoundly no doubt – but she did not, could not feel for him the burst of warm affection that Juliette had hoped for. Mrs Sancey expressed her thanks, she spoke of lasting gratitude ... But it was too polite, too cold. There was no heartfelt emotion to give her remarks warmth and sincerity. In reality the wretched woman was also in a hurry to be off with her daughter, to get home again, to drive away the odious memories and return to the good old days before Juliette's departure.

"You'll come see us, Sir," she said. "I'll be pleased to receive you, to thank you again ..."

Alain promised and set out. He tried his best, while heading toward Épeule, to drive the whole experience from his mind, to think only of his mother, his sister, and his little brother, of their delight, of the happiness they would find in seeing each other again, in living together, but the effort was in vain: without understanding clearly why, half the joy of his homecoming had evaporated.

· · ·

Alain's first desire, after several days of readjustment, was to escape from the Germans and their forced labour once and for all. In the Ardennes, he had learned how to maneuvre and manage on his own. Hardly had his little cousin François returned than he had gotten himself hired as a lock keeper on the Roubaix canal, to avoid working in the fields. And François made for a singular lock keeper, always at home, abandoning the canal for days at a time, and leaving the German bargemen to work the sluicegates for themselves. The green devils were constantly coming to harass him. He was only faithful to his post on the days scheduled for coal barges, which he pillaged liberally. Alain, for his part, soon found a job as well, thanks to the intervention of a friend from the Ardennes whose father worked at city hall in Roubaix. Alain was entrusted with what were called the S.C.'s and with a census of available beds in the event of an influx of evacuees.

The S.C.'s, or "special cases," were so called by the municipality to mislead the Germans. In reality these were rebels, folks who – like Alain himself at one time – had refused to submit to headcount and registration. Having no legal existence in the eyes of the enemy authorities, these fellows could not leave their homes or touch their rations. Alain was responsible for enumerating them so they too could get some food. It was a thankless job. Everyone mistrusted him. The people, the masses, did not draw much distinction between the municipal authorities and German headquarters. Alain was most often taken for a spy and given a cold reception. In addition, he had to count available beds and bedrooms in each house to prepare for a sudden arrival of evacuees.

Never had he seen such destitution. Alain came across rebels hidden in cellars and cramped in nooks beneath rooftops. He discovered ruined interiors, stepping into homes where suffering had banished every remnant of humanity, where starving residents fought over bread and other foodstuffs. He witnessed desperate attempts to survive, to hold on, to subsist – garrets crammed with chicken coops and kitchens packed with rabbit hutches when no courtyard was available, even goats and geese penned at the far end of cellars. He also uncovered an astonishing underground industrial network, things that left him flabbergasted: one house where residents brewed beer in the cellar, using boiled barley, hops, barrels, and tubs; another basement that had been turned into a textile mill – a real mill – with hand-powered reeling machines and old Jacquard looms whose shuttles were passed by means of large pedals; a butcher shop, too, a sausage factory where barely recognizable animals – sheep or perhaps big dogs – were being chopped up. The carcasses were deboned, mixed, ground in a press. And the meat came out the bottom, stuffed into translucent intestines like a skin. The repulsive filth, the odour of putrefaction, the sight of three butchers busy molding dead flesh in a cellar – it turned Alain's stomach. Elsewhere he discovered a mushroom bed, a candle factory, a sweetshop, a whole concealed, secretive, subterranean life that went on unbeknownst to Germans and French alike. The first few times Alain entered this world, he was met with threats and suspicions.

"Watch it, you! If we run into trouble, you'll pay!"

In the long run, however, people grew accustomed to him.

He had had no news of Juliette Sancey. Several times he had been taken with the thought, the temptation of going to see how she was doing, since her mother had invited him to come. He had never dared. He felt he was turning into a stranger again, almost an unknown. He would undoubtedly reawaken a mass of painful memories in Juliette. And besides, for her as for him, their shared experiences must have now seemed so distant, almost unreal. Mixed with this notion was pride, self-esteem. He had been useful, of service. It was not for him to go begging in a way for a reward. They should come to him.

And would he really be happy to see her again? All the differences separating them – education, money, family – so meaningless in the Ardennes – had been abruptly resurrected since their return to Roubaix. How awful it would be for them to come face to face with evidence of the gap between them, the necessity of parting ways. And because he had been unconsciously happy with his existence in the Ardennes – with the wilderness, the sunshine, the indifference toward poverty and riches, abiding in radiant and natural equality – he had come to miss the lifestyle – the toil, the openness, the simplicity – that had given him a glimpse of a vast, peaceful, and glittering land, an escape from real life, what the world ought to be ... Thinking about it in these terms increased his sorrow. He was beginning to understand his own feelings. He had truly loved Juliette in spite of their differences. He had dreamed of more things than he cared to admit. He began to equivocate, to make excuses, to lie to himself. A meeting, after all, a simple chance encounter, one could still hope for that ... A stroke of luck, of good fortune, was all that was needed. It would avoid any sense of sought-for reward on the one hand, of obligatory gratitude on the other.

Almost in spite of himself, he began trying to increase his luck. Several times he passed in front of the Sanceys' house. Huge, always shut up, the Persian blinds lowered over the big windows of the shop, the building looked hostile to Alain. He would have liked to ask the neighbours but was afraid to approach them. Two weeks running, he persisted in hoping to bump into Juliette. But he never saw anyone. One day he finally summoned his courage and questioned the neighbours under the pretext of information needed for city hall.

"The Sanceys? But they're not here anymore," said the tavern keeper. "They're gone."

"Gone?"

"Why yes, to France, a month ago. Mrs Sancey was too scared the Germans would come back for her oldest daughter, who was sent to the Ardennes for a while. So she managed to have her family evacuated. They're in France now, yes indeed. What luck, right, Mister?"

"To be sure," said Alain.

He was stunned. He thanked the obliging neighbours and set off in bewilderment. Gone! Gone to France. He would never see Juliette again.

He could not accept the thought. In spite of himself, hope was already returning: after the war perhaps ... He rejected the idea angrily. After the war! As if Juliette would remember him, would think of him again! And then, would the war actually end? Here people had come to envision an everlasting war, a world stabilizing this way, split into two hostile camps. And anyhow, even if it ended, the Germans would undoubtedly remain in the Nord. They were too strong, too well-entrenched. They would never be driven out.

Could he leave, too? A man? The enemy would never let him go. And besides, where could he find the Sanceys, where in France would he start looking?

From this day forward, Alain became even sadder and gloomier. He hardly spoke at home anymore. He was prone to long silences, an involuntary melancholy bordering on unsociability. At times he regretted his behaviour. He could tell that he was worrying his mother. But he could not help himself. Young though he was, he felt marked, broken by sorrows, just like everyone whose energy had been sapped by this long war. Félicie noticed the transformation without daring to say anything, attributing all the problems to the suffering her son had endured in the Ardennes, and sadly resigned herself to thinking, *Those Germans have changed my son.*

In fact he had become more callous, more sullen. He had lost the fine patience, the sweet and constant cheerfulness, the helpfulness, the graciousness of old, which had made him such an agreeable boy. He was quick to be suspicious, ready to doubt, approaching others with a certain mistrust and intransigence. He had aged. The pain of his fellows moved him less. He steeled himself to sympathy. It seemed that he was attempting to drive from his heart the magnificent and dangerous burst of altruism, the blossoming of charity and devotion that the spectacle of the prison on rue de l'Hospice had fostered in him. For one so young, his language was bitter and pessimistic, surprising those who had known him beforehand.

He continued his census for the municipality. From this angle, at least, fortune was smiling on him. Each week so many youth from the neighbourhood were taken to the Ardennes, or even the front! One morning as he was about to leave for city hall, a green devil arrived at his house on the cul-de-sac. Alain opened the door. The green devil asked him for his identification card and took him away immediately, chained behind his bicycle. He led Alain to the officer's post.

"You're Alain Laubigier?"

"Yes, Lieutenant."

"You're eighteen years old. You don't belong in Roubaix."

"I'm employed by the municipality."

"You ought to be working for us in the Ardennes or elsewhere. You leave tonight."

"But I'm employed, I'm of use here, and I have my mother, a sister, a younger brother. I'm needed ... Please, Sir ..."

The officer shrugged his shoulders.

"There's nothing I can do. Here, see who's at fault."

He held out a paper, an ugly, miserable, anonymous note.

"Dear Commander, It is my privilege to inform you that one Alain Laubigier, who ought to be working for the Germans, given his age, is still in Roubaix ..."

A jealous neighbour had denounced Alain.

He made a gesture of revolt and disgust, turned the letter over, searched for the missing signature, tightened his fists in rage. But what could be done? He had to reason with himself, to make use of his newfound skepticism, his new and bitter philosophy: *You know what people are like, Alain. Why're you surprised?*

The officer looked at him. He slapped him familiarly on the shoulder.

"It's not our fault, you see ... Ah, the French, the patriots!"

The Germans at army headquarters were in a good position to judge such matters. Each day they received anonymous letters by the dozen. In the end they had posted all of them on the door of Roubaix's city hall, on a huge board nailed below the entrance on rue Neuve, and which carried an inscription on the pediment: *How the French treat their fellow countrymen.*

It was a lamentable display of hatred, jealousy, and treachery. The panel featured denunciations of every sort. One person was accused of concealing wine, another wool, another chickens ... Still another of spying or smuggling goods from Belgium ... With the scornful Germans looking on, the crowds came to read the postings like newspaper articles, pieces at once humorous, entertaining, and filled with malice and invective.

That afternoon Alain was once again shipped off to an undisclosed location.

Chapter Seven

I

Toward the middle of 1916, the inter-allied information bureau in Holland, which was the main centre for espionage and communication with the occupied Nord, was rather skillfully burglarized by German agents. This was the cause of numerous arrests in Belgium and occupied France. And the Germans finally identified the publishers of the newspaper *Loyalty*, whom they had been seeking for a long time.

The abbé was arrested quite suddenly one morning. He only had time to write his sister Lise a couple of lines, which he entrusted to the caretaker at the lycée. He was shipped off to Loos and confined to a cell.

The abbé underwent a series of grueling interrogations that left him completely drained. Anyone who has ever been accused of a crime is familiar with the feeling of emptiness, bewilderment, exhaustion left by a long battle with policemen or an examining magistrate.

One thing reassured the abbé. Of his equipment, the Germans had found nothing but some porcelain insulators, a few bits of wire, and an old bicycle pump that he had used for a variable capacitor. His prudence was rewarded. This evidence was insufficient to prove that he had received messages. But the Germans had been informed by other means. One day, in the course of an interrogation, a policeman – irritated by the abbé's denials – exclaimed that he was stupid to persist in this manner, that they knew everything, and that Hennedyck had been arrested.

All was lost: Hennedyck, the paper, the printing press! The abbé had dragged everyone into the disaster and felt himself responsible. He had been arrested first, the radio components discovered in in his home! He returned to the lockup, his spirits crushed.

The preliminary investigation lasted a month and a half. For the trial the abbé was transferred from Loos to Roubaix.

He was imprisoned in the Roubaix bathhouse. That day, despite the discomfort caused by a cramped cell and teeming vermin, he found a source of great joy. A prisoner was going from cell to cell distributing the midday bowl of soup. When this fellow opened the door, the abbé recognized Clavard the typesetter. The man had never been very nice to the abbé. But he was thrilled to see him, as if he were a saviour. Clavard was serving a two-month sentence, which would be over the next week, for stashing some copperware at his house. He explained that Hennedyck was also in the prison and that he saw him quite often. The abbé entrusted Clavard with a letter for Hennedyck. He wrote: "My Dear Patrice, I don't know if it's my fault that you've been locked up like me ... If I'm to blame, I beg your pardon with all my heart ... I can never sufficiently atone for my recklessness ..."

This confession gave him tremendous relief.

He did not see Clavard again. From the prisoner who took Clavard's place handing out the bowls, the abbé learned that Clavard had been released. But he was unable to determine if his letter had reached Hennedyck.

• • •

One morning the guards finally came to get him for the trial. The first person he saw in the hallway was Patrice Hennedyck. They embraced.

"Have you forgiven me?"

"Forgiven you? For what?"

"Clavard didn't give you my letter?"

"I haven't seen Clavard since he was released ... But what'd you have to say?"

"The Germans found a capacitor and receiver components in my house ... I thought I was responsible for your arrest ..."

"My poor chap," said Hennedyck, "I was arrested the same day as you. They knew everything in advance, you see. You didn't have to tell them a thing. They broke into the inter-allied information bureau in Holland. And besides, didn't we run the risks together?"

"So who's responsible for this disaster?"

"No one, thank God ..."

"And what's become of little Pauret?"

"Gilberte? No news."

"And the others? Félicie Foulaud, Françoise Pélegrin?"

"You don't know? Everything's been broken up. The spy centre's been destroyed, shattered. Jeanne Villien and Pauline Bult – you know, the ones who smuggled letters and newspapers – were lucky enough to be in Holland. They'll not be back. Félicie Foulaud's hiding somewhere or other. Little Pélegrin was caught a week before us, that's right, between Brussels and the frontier ... I saw her here two days before ..."

"Before what?"

"Before they shot her, the poor dear ..."

He recounted Françoise Pélegrin's adventure. One evening, accompanied by Félicie Foulaud, she had left for Holland again, with notes concealed in the lining of her coat. It was dark. She had thought it funny, amusing, bold, to stop a passing German transport so they could hitch a ride and gain a few kilometres. Despite the pleas of Félicie Foulaud, she had signalled to a motor truck. It had stopped, they had climbed aboard. But an officer was present. Their rather pure French accents surprised him. He asked for their papers, saw that they came from France, had them searched. No one knows how Félicie, jumping from the truck at full speed, managed to flee into the darkness, disappear, avoid the consequences of their mistake. Little Pélegrin, the twenty-year-old leader of a spy centre, was left alone to bear the enormous burden of responsibility. In alarm she suddenly realized the magnitude of the adventure she had embarked upon. Until then she had not understood. For this girl who was barely seventeen years old at the start of the war, the whole gigantic struggle had simply been a source of amusement, of excitement ... A type of big game – for her, that is what it was.

She had been tortured first at Loos, then in Lille. She had suffered dreadful humiliation, been spared nothing. She had endured appalling physical and moral pressure. The Germans had taken advantage of her youth, her weakness, in the crudest fashion. They had gone as far as interrogating her naked, stripped bare, like a martyr from early Christian days, cast before the army rabble. They had hurled vile threats at her. She was too young, too weak. She did not have the strength to fight the German police. She had yielded, given way like Joan of Arc had given way. In the end she had cried, humbled herself, begged for mercy, signed appeals, confessions, everything they had wanted, in an effort to live, to avoid the terror of this horrible death of which she was constantly reminded, like a haunting thought. She died with courage, said the soldiers who executed her, as if at the last minute she had regained her self-control.

Hennedyck and the abbé were able to talk in the hallway for almost half an hour. They were left in peace. When the guards came for them and led them out, they passed a band of troops returning with rifles on their shoulders. The last two soldiers each carried a handful of bloody old clothes – a shabby jacket and a workingman's brown cloth cap – that had been stripped from a wretch executed at dawn. Coming at this instant, the sight was particularly shocking.

They attended a parody of a trial, rigged like Gaure and Théverand's had been. There was a dumbfounding counsel's speech, which was little more than a confirmation of the indictment, and a defense outlined by Hennedyck, to whom no one listened. Then the judges retired to deliberate. "Death," said Hennedyck. The priest was speechless.

The judges returned. Hennedyck and Sennevilliers stood when their sentence was pronounced. They were each condemned to ten years in prison. They were stunned. They had expected to be sentenced to death. But Hennedyck's titles, the importance of his industrial position, and multiple interventions – including David's – had put pressure on the judges.

Hennedyck and the abbé were led toward the door, between two rows of soldiers with fixed bayonets. They walked as in a dream, without yet understanding their new position, if they should rejoice or despair. They could not see what this verdict had in store for them. Only one thing counted: it was not death.

On the steps of city hall, an enormous throng was teeming, restrained by soldiers. The multitude wanted to see the two men, ignoring the presence of the enemy. In spite of the Germans, in spite of everything, Roubaix bore witness to its admiration and gratitude for Hennedyck and Sennevilliers. People stretched their hands toward them, shouting: "Bravo! Long live *Loyalty*! Long live Hennedyck! Long live Roubaix!" They grabbed the abbé by his cassock, cut pieces from it, shook their fists at the soldiers. A clamour mounted from the square. A riot was starting to unfold. The overwhelmed soldiers swore, bracing themselves, vainly crossing bayonets against the crowd, the folks who were besieging them, smothering them. Some women brought flowers, boughs. These fell at the feet of the prisoners as if it were Palm Sunday. People offered them food, books, momentos. Faces of friends, strangers, men, women, and children confusedly surrounded them, shouting words they could not make out. They moved forward, nodding their heads and crying along the length of this triumphal way. The crowd had to be held in check at the prison doorway. The mob's tidal din broke against the facade for a long time, bringing the two prisoners the last goodbyes from their native land and the French people.

They were shut in their cell again. Hennedyck, in the midst of his distress, felt beset by a veiled anxiety, which outweighed the rest of his anguish. He had not seen Émilie's sweet, sad face in the crowd ...

II

Patrice Hennedyck had been arrested one morning at the factory in Épeule. The doorkeeper rushed straightaway to tell Mrs Hennedyck. Émilie came running. She was aware of the perilous work Patrice had undertaken. He had tried to conceal it from her. But she had quickly found out. For a long time, she had been anticipating this disaster, like something destined, ineluctable. A certain fatalism was one of the dominant features of her morbid and pessimistic personality.

Most of the factory lay in ruins. Only the entrance buildings, where Émilie had set up her hospital in 1914, were occupied by the Germans, who treated the wounded there. Émilie went into the office of the head doctor and asked that he be called.

Von Mesnil finished dressing a wound. He arrived without having taken time to remove his big, white smock, which was covered in bloody stains.

"Émilie!"

He came toward her. She pushed him away ferociously.

"You see! You see what I said! It's over! Everything's over! They've arrested Patrice ..."

"Really?"

He stepped forward. She pushed him away again, savagely.

"Oh! Go away! Go away! Don't touch me!"

"Please, tell me ..."

"Patrice has just been arrested, right here."

She burst into sobs.

"It was inevitable," whispered von Mesnil. "One day or another, it was certain to ..."

"That's all you have to say?"

"What'd you want me to say ... What ..."

"But don't you understand that it's your fault, our fault, our joint penance? Heaven's punishing us, yes, punishing us! My God, my God, what've I done! What infamy! What shame!"

"What'd you want me to do about it?" said von Mesnil ...

"Go, hurry, do something ... Patrice must come back, Rudolf. You must set him free ..."

"And how can I do that, Émilie?"

"Do I know? Go, hurry, search, do something ... Give me back Patrice! He must return, he must live ... He's my husband, Rudolf. It's Patrice! I love him. He's my husband ... Go, go, quickly ..."

She was terrifying, eyes bulging, pale as death, with an air of madness ... Von Mesnil, almost forcibly, grabbed her by the hands and restrained her.

"Émilie, please, be quiet, calm down! People can hear us, you know. Your husband's been arrested? I'm ready ... I'll do whatever you ask ... But what would you have me do? There's nothing I can do, nothing."

"What? My husband's been arrested by your people. My husband's going to die, and you can do nothing? You're refusing to act? You're abandoning him? So you only knew how to lie and cheat? So there was nothing in your soul but ..."

"Émilie!"

"No, no! Go away! I hate you! Go away! Goodbye! Goodbye! You'll never see me again!"

She pushed him away, left the room, and took flight.

It was how things were bound to happen. She had foreseen it, sensed it, since the moment of her downfall. Weak, impressionable, ill, she had been subject to von Mesnil's powerful influence. He had nursed her, healed her ... Long hours of familiarity had tied them together ... Hennedyck, absorbed by the newspaper and the struggle against the enemy that had ruined his factory, had left Émilie in dangerous moral isolation. Hers was a feeble spirit, without cunning. The conquest of this sickly child had been a game for von Mesnil, one of those half-sincere fellows who charm all the more skill-fully as they are not far from believing – when desire calls – in the truth of their passion, their promises. She had fallen into the crime naïvely, like a girl of fifteen, in the course of a two-month stay in the countryside where von Mesnil had had her taken for her health. Since then she had remained trapped, incapable of betraying her husband with peace of mind yet equal-ly incapable of freeing herself from the tyrannical hold of a man like von Mesnil, whose domineering personality subdued her. He had embarked on the adventure skeptically, without deluding himself about its likely outcome or its duration. It was a wartime love that would end with the conflict ... Still, he had to admit that the breakup, when it came, would be more diffi-cult than he had first thought. No heart could remain unmoved by affection such as Émilie devoted to von Mesnil. But he had the immense advantage of having already had many lovers and of understanding that one always recovers from such heartache. In sum, it was a love in which, like many men, he had received ten times more than he had given. Skeptical to the core, von Mesnil believed no more in women than in nations.

• • •

Émilie suddenly found herself abandoned on all sides. She had hoped to do something, to make use of Hennedyck's connections, to call out the economic powers of the region. All shut the door on her. Her transgres-sion was known to many, though she had not suspected it was so. After Hennedyck's arrest, what had only been a rumour exploded like a bomb-shell. Everywhere she was rejected, turned away. The bourgeois world excommunicated her. She was subject to the anger of the masses. People from Épeule recognized her on the street and insulted her. They made up songs about her, the types of ballads that emerge spontaneously from the popular imagination. Rocks shattered her windowpanes. Some hooligans jumped over the garden wall so they could throw stones as far as the ter-race, and pilfer the estate. The staff, the servants – indignant or frightened – had quit her service. She was afraid to leave the house. Army headquar-ters had to provide protection for her as it did for a good many of the offi-cers' mistresses. Two sentries were posted at Émilie's door. She lived more than a week in this manner without daring to budge, famished, surviving on scraps, all alone, terror-stricken and desperate, like an outcast.

When, after more than a week, she finally saw von Mesnil – who till then had been afraid to return – she threw herself at him, gave herself to him again body and soul, wholly, as if he were her only help, her only salvation from unilateral abandonment.

She left the enormous Hennedyck house, fleeing by night to avoid recognition. Von Mesnil had found her a little apartment in one of the dreary, lifeless, bourgeois streets that give certain parts of Roubaix, an industrial city, the appearance of an old-fashioned provincial town. Émilie lived there under a pseudonym, alone and seldom seen, avoided and feared, like every woman known to be associated with a German officer.

Chapter Eight

One morning Lise went to see her brother in Tourcoing. She found out that he had been arrested and would soon be tried and undoubtedly shot. The caretaker from the lycée had attempted to take the abbé a few undergarments. The Germans had responded, "Don't bother, soon he won't be needing them anymore."

In a state of shock, Lise returned to Herlem. She crossed the square like a sleepwalker. Some people greeted her, but she made no response. She would have preferred to be home already, to reflect, to collect her disordered thoughts, to find some help, some salvation for Marc. She encountered several Germans. She had to stop herself from giving vent to her hatred. Never had she sworn such fierce vengeance. Never in her eyes had they so incarnated the enemy race, the cursed race, as on this day.

She cut across the village, left the last of the houses behind, and made her way through the fields toward Herlem Hill and the quarry. When she was halfway up the hill, within sight of the house of her brother Jean, she caught a glimpse of her sister-in-law Fannie and her nephew little Pierre, who were just coming out. Fannie was holding her son by the hand.

Since Fannie's infidelity, the two women had had no contact. They had avoided each other. Lise's fury and indignation, and Fannie's shame, had irreparably divided them. For a while, little Pierre had continued visiting his aunt and his grandmother. Then he must have understood. He had avoided them in turn, forsaken this vast, rugged, and picturesque quarry, which had been the Eden of his childhood. A subtle pride, a notion of other's feelings, had made him dig in his heels, shut himself off. He fled whenever he caught sight of Lise, and this was not the least of her concerns. But she recognized what was going on with her nephew. She respected this wildness, this fierce childhood pride, and did nothing to pull him back to her by force. She also sensed that for both Fannie and herself, it was best to remain at arm's length. Lise could not have controlled her anger.

But this time she did not avoid her sister-in-law. On the contrary, she marched toward her like an enemy. The despair and furry made her forget everything. Fannie had paused in apparent dread, standing hand-in-hand with little Pierre and watching her approach.

"Lise ..." whispered Fannie in a strangled voice.

Lise had halted in front of her and was staring at her with a harsh and sullen look.

"Lise, is it true ... is it true that ... ?"

"That what?"

"That Marc ... That your brother ..."

"Was arrested? Yes, it's true! Jean's dead and Marc's going to die! And it's your fault."

Lise had come face to face with Fannie and was heaping scorn at her: "It's people like you who've betrayed us, sold us! Judases, turncoats! You've accepted the Germans, you've lent them your support, you're to blame if victory isn't ours, you're the one who's killing our men. Boches' whore! Spy! You've sold yourself! Yes, you're a traitor, you're the one who killed your husband, my two brothers! And I curse you, curse you, curse you!"

Fannie's drawn, blotchy, yellowed features were distorted. She had taken the anathema straight in the face, as if Lise had spit on her. Fannie was livid, haggard. She raised clapsed hands toward Lise, begging, "Not that ... Not that ... Lise, if you only knew ..."

But Lise pushed her aside, drove her off with a merciless gesture: "Go away! Go away! May evil be upon you! Go away!"

Fannie stepped back. A simple-minded girl, she was devastated, crushed by this imprecation. She moved her lips as if to speak, to beg, but could not. For a moment she looked at Lise with fright and then set out painfully, dragging along little Pierre, who was terror-stricken and crying.

• • •

A few days later Paul, the German who lived at Fannie's, began fretting and talking about the front. He was a good man, already close to forty years old, who had nothing of the warrior about him. Until now he had managed to live peaceably enough, working at Donadieu's blacksmith shop, where he repaired farm tools. But the Germans were short of men. At present a relentless search was underway for shirkers in the rear. Paul felt targeted and threatened. He talked about it every evening and began sadly readying his rifle and his weapons, his packs of bandages, his sack, his undergarments. He did it all reluctantly, on the verge of tears like Fannie. This big, peace-loving boy was completely lacking in vainglory and bellicosity.

He received orders to depart. Paul left crying like a child, aware of his weakness, of his inexperience, knowing he was better fit to forge plowshares and than to kill people. He hardly understood how to handle his rifle. After two years of service in the rear, he felt terribly removed from the other troops, the comrades who had served in the trenches and been under fire. For him it was an unknown world that he approached as a novice. He sensed he was destined for the slaughter.

• • •

Little Pierre had fallen ill just before Easter 1916. He was unable to return to Mr Sérez's schoolhouse until the end of July. He had not seen his classmates in four months. And Paul had left for the front a week ago.

Pierre arrived in the schoolyard on his first morning back. The yard was rather large, covered with a layer of dross, and dotted with mighty chestnuts whose wild pods were prized for making pipes or Indian necklaces. A barricade of green-painted boards separated the yard from Mr Sérez's henhouse. This henhouse encroached upon the yard, providing a nook in the rear that served as prison, fortress, station, or stable at recess time, according to the imagination of the actors. Pierre had stepped into this nook to watch Mr Sérez's rabbits, for the schoolmaster had stopped raising chickens when the Germans began requisitioning eggs. Pierre was joined by an entire group of boys whose curiosity was aroused by his return after such a long absence. There were Antoine and Fernand Guégain, the barber's sons, Jules Humfels, the deputy mayor's son, and Léon Hérard, the ration delegate's boy. Humfels and Hérard had pockets full of ration crackers and derived great prestige from this affluence. There were also Robert and Arthur Mietz, the Mietz girl's children. They were staying with an aunt for the moment because their mother, who was subject to the army's medical inspection program, had been shipped off due to a syphilitic infection contracted in the line of duty and was undergoing treatment with the other "Princesses" in Tourcoing. A natural indifference and a belligerent disposition had spared these boys the mockery and bullying of most classmates. As for the "Princesses," such was the name given to syphilitic women whom the German authorities sent to a big factory in Tourcoing, where they were treated and whence they were sent home in a state of remission but saddled with the infamous label "back from Tourcoing." It was a designation sentencing them to the regular visit of the German doctor.

This particular group of kids surrounded Pierre immediately, with signs of the keenest interest.

"How's your mother?"

"And her lover? Is it true he's gone?"

"What?" said Pierre. "What'd you want from me?"

Until now he had been left in peace. The matter was little known in the village. Some kids, like the Mietz boys, had had to fight; others, tormented, had quit school and no longer dared return, having suffered too much there. Pierre had not been subjected to such cruelty.

He had turned quite red. Pierre had understood immediately. His surprise above all concealed an embarrassment, an inexpressible unease, the fear of a hunted animal searching for a means of escape. Long had he dreaded the pain of the question. The time had come. He stood there, his throat dry and his stomach tied in knots.

"Yes," Humfels replied, "your mother's lover, Paul the German, he's gone, eh? He left for the front ..."

Pierre had turned crimson.

"My mom doesn't have a lover," he said.

"He's not your mother's lover?"

"My mom doesn't have a lover ..."

"But," sniggered the elder Mietz, "hasn't that Boche replaced your father! Where's he sleeping, first of all? In your father's bed? With your mother?"

"I don't know ..."

"You're afraid to say, but you know!"

"What about it? What's it matter?"

There was a burst of laughter all around.

"What a wet rag! How stupid! We've never seen the like of it!"

"So," continued Humfels, who was determined to elucidate the point, "he's sleeping with your mother, and he's not her lover?"

"I'm telling you that my mother doesn't have a lover!" shouted Pierre, red with anger and shame, and feeling tears of rage welling in his eyes.

"So who knocked her up then?"

"Knocked her up?"

All of a sudden, a delighted clamour arose: "He doesn't know his mother's pregnant!"

"You're all crazy!" shouted Pierre in his fury. "Let me be! I'm leaving!"

And he pushed them away, shoved them aside to distance himself, but the Mietz boys held him by the arms, forcibly.

"So," resumed Humfels, proud of his young science, "you know nothing, you've seen nothing? You still don't know how a baby's made? You've never seen a nanny goat with a billy, or even a buck rabbit with a doe?"

"What about it?"

"What about it? It's the same thing, idiot! With people, it's the same thing ..."

"You're crazy," murmured Pierre again, flabbergasted, still not comprehending.

"You're the one who's crazy. Why'd your mother sleep with that Boche? Why's she getting bigger? Where'd this baby come from? Why ..."

"Dirty animal!" screamed Pierre, landing a violent blow with all his might between Humfels's eyes.

Both of them rolled to the ground. The others jumped on top of Pierre, kicking and punching him, though he remained insensible to the abuse. He had become as ferocious as a wild animal. He bit, scratched, tore at the face of his adversary. He groped with clawed fingers for the eyes of the other boy ...

Mr Sérez, the schoolmaster, came running. He put an end to the scuffle, pulled the two combatants apart, separated them, holding back Pierre, who was trying to grab Humfels again!

"Sennevilliers! Cut it out! Sennevilliers! Calm down! A thousand lines for both of you! What's going on! Who's plagued me with such madmen!

Sennevilliers, you're the one who started it! Answer! What'd you do? What's this fight about?"

Pierre said nothing, shaking, maddened by anger and shame.

"Well, answer ... Humfels? Sennevillers? Say something, you little ass!"

"They insulted my mother," whispered Pierre, bursting into tears.

Sérez understood. He had known of the affair for a long time. He felt a painful combination of powerlessness and compassion and chased away the mischievous brats with a gesture toward the schoolhouse.

"Go, all the rest of you! Everyone in class. Five hundred lines to anyone still outside thirty seconds from now! And you, Sennevilliers, go wash up, dear boy. And return home. You can't stay at school today ... You ear's all torn. Go on, dear boy ..."

Pierre returned home, sullen. He said not a word and went to sit in his little chair beside the stove.

"Where'd you come from?" asked Fannie in surprise. "What about school? Let me look at your ear. You're bleeding."

"I fell," said Pierre.

"Is it bad? Come let me see ... I'll wash it with fresh water ... It's swollen ..."

"No," said Pierre. "Don't bother."

"You don't want me to?"

"Not really ..."

"You're not sick, are you?"

"No."

He left again, set off to plod along the roadside ...

He wanted to get away from his mother. He did not know why, but he felt the need to be alone, to think, to deal with the enormous turmoil inside of him.

• • •

Pierre did not manage to regain his balance for a long time. He had received an enormous shock. Such a crude, hideous, and revolting discovery had plunged him into confusion, uncertainty, and disgust. It was too loathsome, really, too dreadful, too sordidly bestial. When he thought about it, when he tried to fathom what he had learned, to take things to their logical conclusions, he felt a repugnance, a repulsion that approached nausea, true horror. Such ignominy, such degradation of beloved, sacred, revered beings to the level of animals left him appalled and revolted, as if his idols had been desecrated in the most abominable fashion. No, certainly, these things were impossible, inadmissible, unimaginable. Humfels, Mietz, and the others – they were crazy. He himself was crazy to spend even one second worrying about such outlandish nightmares.

And yet there was a certain logic to the monstrosity, the horror. He sensed a seemingly frightful likelihood, an obviousness in such ideas. Animals, yes, animals ... Pierre, reared in a rural environment – amid the animals, the chickens, the rough simplicity of the fields – noticed a parallel in spite of himself ... He had seen puppies born. He knew how animals reproduced ... So where did children come from? He thought it through, recognized the similarity, recoiled with fear and sadness. His mother, his mother reduced to that, demeaned like that? No, no, it was not possible. His youth rejected such a tragic and hideous truth.

He lived in anguish. He would have given anything to know for sure. He sensed the truth and at the same time refused to believe it. He felt disgust for everything and for himself. He could no longer see his mother without thinking about it ... One day, in a terrible discovery, he realized that she was getting heavier, that his classmates had been right. He heard words slip, noticed preparations, as if his mother really were expecting a new baby ...

His personality changed. He became sullen, taciturn, sought solitude, seemed pensive and preoccupied. He no longer wanted to return to school. When Fannie tried to make him go, he simply skipped. The same ideas continually obsessed him, haunted him. He kept mulling over a question that was just too much for him, something that youth already prepared by their changing bodies acknowledge painfully enough but which a nine-year-old child finds too burdensome, too disheartening, and would like to reject with every ounce of his being. Pierre spent his time probing, pondering, reviewing details, conjuring up Paul and his mother, clenching his fists, and crying to himself in fury and despair. That! To have consented to that, his mother! Impossible! Impossible, like a repugnant and grotesque hallucination! And yet it all had an appearance of truth ... And then there was this child she was expecting. So there had to be something to it ... And Pierre tumbled back into the never-ending round of questions.

He arrived at a sort of hatred regarding his mother. He held her responsible. It was her fault, after all, if the boys at school had assaulted him to make him see the truth. She should not have exposed him to such suffering. He no longer spoke to her. His contempt for his mother was paired with constant invocation of his father's memory. Pierre had hardly known the man, but his reaction was now to cherish him with all this heart. He suddenly understood the enormity of his mother's transgression. He would have liked to vocalize his hatred and disgust for her. He felt relieved and almost avenged when they learned that Paul, the German, had been killed at the front by a bullet to the head and would not be returning.

• • •

Fannie accepted the blow with fatalism, submissively, as an expected punishment long overdue. She was now living in true poverty, deprived of everything – food and fuel, money and clothing. Paul had left her about a hundred marks, which lasted two weeks. In times past Paul had brought food from the canteen and potatoes from German storehouses. At present they had nothing, and Fannie had never dared to go sign up for rations, for fear of being jeered by the villagers.

It was September. She had a couple of potatoes and a few vegetables left in the garden. They were quickly consumed. Fannie was frightened to think of the child she would bring into the world amid such distress and who, starving before birth, would not even have a scrap of clothing. She had to cut diapers from the sheets.

Pierre, for his part, loafed about like a little vagabond. He never showed his face in town. Sometimes he still went to hang around the quarry, the big, wild, chimerical quarry of his childhood, and passed by the house of Lise and Grandmother Berthe. He would have liked to go inside, to ask for something to eat from these two women who loved him, as he certainly knew. But he was afraid and ashamed. He scurried away as soon as they appeared. Here and there he found a few beets to eat as well as some apples and pears that he pilfered at the risk of his skin, for the Germans stood watch over the orchards.

One afternoon at the end of September, Fannie returned home bruised, her face swollen and her cheek lacerated. Tired of going hungry, she had ventured to sign up for rations. And she had timidly hazarded the distribution, arriving a little late. A long line encircled the school where the food was handed out in an unused classroom. She had stood at the very end, among the women and the elderly. People quickly noticed her, recognized her.

"It's Fannie, Fannie Bauduez, Jean the lime burner's wife, Sennevilliers's wife, the one who's in with the Boches."

The women started speaking louder, taking digs at her. The men looked at Fannie, shoved each other with their elbows, and laughed. People who had lost a son or a husband were annoyed by her presence. Others were delighted with it. They said, "Oh, oh, she's lowered herself to come here at last. She's no longer too proud ..."

Fannie, red with shame, remained standing against the wall and took these withering insults. She was afraid to respond. She would have liked to slink away. But she felt her legs trembling from hunger and weakness. She had to stay both for herself and for Pierre, who had not had a hot meal in two days. She pretended not to hear, let herself be jostled and knocked about without saying a word, as if her resignation and passivity would mollify the crowd.

"So," one man said to her, putting his fist beneath her chin, "your Boche ditched you, or is he dead now? Answer, answer, you whore!"

"In any event, he got you pregnant before leaving, eh?" said another.

"You can feel, friends, it's not fake ..." said a third, reaching toward her bodice as she pulled back in fright.

And an old woman, stretching a clawed hand toward her face, more terrifying in this gesture of controlled hatred than if she had struck her, said in a calm voice, a voice of inexpressible, cold fury: "Just you wait, girl, till the war's over!"

Others shouted, "That's right ... Wait till they're gone, we'll tear the little Boche from your belly, we'll eat him alive ..."

"Me, I'm not waiting for the end of the war!" shouted a woman as she rushed at her.

This woman had just learned that her son was dead. She thirsted for revenge. She grabbed Fannie by the wrists, irresistibly.

"Boches' whore! You're the one who killed him!"

Fannie was scared to death and stood there motionless, like an adulterous woman about to be stoned. She had only one thought in her head: this curse, Lise's curse, which had been shouted at her again today, the same words that seemed to mark the child she was carrying in advance.

"It's your fault!" screamed the woman. "Your fault! Oh, but you'll pay for it!"

In vain Fannie tried to drag herself along the wall, to escape. The other woman had already picked up a rock and, using it like a weapon, struck Fannie's face with the jagged edge. Fannie groaned and shielded herself with her hands, hunching over, while the other woman tore at her scalp with the rock. Fannie had to plunge into the crowd to get away from the shrew. Fannie wound her way through the mob, hunkered down, hands on her head, amid jeers, insults, kicks to the legs, blows to the back and the head. They even hit her from below, aiming at her face, which she covered with her hands. Suddenly she broke free of the crowd, cradling her face with blood-stained fingers, her entire visage a sticky mess. A warm liquid ran down her sleeves. A rock hit her on the back of the neck and threw her headlong like a stout punch. She was dazed for a moment, then got up and set off again. Jeers mounted behind her. A shower of stones fell on the street around her. With each step a dozen rocks landed on her back and her skull. Her head felt as if it would explode.

A pack of children trailed her in this manner, ushered her all the way home. She had to shut the door against a final volley of bricks. Rocks smashed the windowpanes and fell on the table and the bed. She had taken shelter in a corner, watching the pebbles roll, listening to the increasing ridicule, and thinking of but a single thing: if only it would end, if only they would leave before Pierre returned ...

The riot lasted a good half hour more. And when there was not a sole windowpane left to break, the kids got bored and departed one by one.

Fannie remained where she was, dazed. She was not crying. But she was nearly sick. Her head seemed terribly heavy. She ran her hand gently round the back of it and moaned – less from pain than from fright – upon feeling a large, deep wound on her scalp, like a bloody hole. Her cheek was bleeding, too. She thought of her husband Jean. He was dead. He was lucky. She would have liked to die as well, but there was this child inside her ... Two lives destroyed at once. Could she do it? Undoubtedly, yes ... Why allow a being destined for such misfortune to come into the world? But there was also Pierre to consider – Pierre who did not deserve to suffer, who still knew nothing, who would soon understand his mother's crime ... She remained prostrate, so downcast about the situation that everything seemed useless, even tears.

At that moment she heard steps outside. Pierre was coming. He was hurrying. He had seen all the pebbles and rocks on the roadway and the broken panes in the window. He burst in, looked for his mother, and found her sitting in a corner. She was dishevelled, her clothes soiled and her face bloody, her appearance completely wretched. He was stunned.

"What ... What, Mother ..."

He could find nothing more to say.

She rose painfully to her feet and whispered, "I'm okay ... It's nothing."

She wanted to get going, to get moving again. She woefully dragged a bruised leg, a heavy stomach, and leaned on the table, exhausted.

Pierre watched her in silence and understood. He recognized his own ordeal in what he saw before him. She must have gone to the village, too ... How she must have suffered! He recalled his own sorrow, his own humiliation. He was still watching his mother. She became his mother again ... He slowly forgot his hatred. He could not despise her anymore. He could feel nothing but pity, a boundless pity surging inside of him like a new wave of rekindled, impetuous love that washed away the past, overwhelming him and choking him with emotion.

Fannie had gone to the window, was looking outside, hiding her shame, hesitant to glance at Pierre. Her face was that of an old woman. Pierre noticed her grey hairs for the first time. And her blue eyes, with their lost look, had something confused and uncertain about them. Though she had grown old, her features and her expression had retained something strangely childlike – akin to a painful astonishment at the world's harsh realities – which united her with Pierre.

He was still watching her. What had they done to her in the village? Had she endured – suffered – what he had suffered? He felt remorse welling within him. There was no more hatred, nothing but infinite pity that drove away all his anger, his resentment, his whole odious obsession, his nightmarish ideas. He whispered, "Mother ..."

She did not hear him, did not move. He said louder, "Mother ..."

She cast a weary glance at him.

"Did they hurt you?"

She instinctively put her hand to her cheek, her flayed cheek. She was too worn out to think of lying. In a dismal and toneless voice, she said, "They hit me ..."

And in misery and sorrow she began crying.

He had come up to her. He ventured to say, "Don't cry, mother ... I'm here, we'll manage somehow ..."

She slowly shrugged her shoulders, shook her head: "My poor dear Pierre, you can't possibly know ..."

"I know ..."

She shuddered. Pierre's low, firm tenor had startled her. She looked at him, shocked, almost fightened. She was afraid she had understood him, read him right. She had turned livid.

"What are saying, Pierre? You're saying that ..."

He repeated slowly, seriously, "I understand all of it. Don't beat yourself up anymore. I'm aware, and I realize ... Don't cry, Mother. It's not entirely your fault ..."

She let herself fall back into her chair. Pierre thought she was dying of grief and shame, and ran to her.

"Mother, Mother!"

She took him in her arms, frantically. She had no way of knowing the extent to which he had had to conquer his passions – to master himself – in order to return to her. She simply considered herself absolved by the only being who could still accord her absolution. She kissed him, smothered him, frenzied, teary-eyed, wild with gratitude and despair. She moaned loudly, invoking her dead husband: "Jean, Jean, forgive me ... !"

As if the forsaken man himself had granted her mercy through the voice of their son.

• • •

Fannie gave birth on the night of 2 October 1917. It was the seventieth birthday of Field Marshal Hindenburg. In the shed beside the kitchen were fifty odd Germans who had made a bonfire and who were drinking, eating, and singing.

Fannie fought the labour till eleven o'clock. Then she could no longer keep herself from groaning, waking Pierre.

"Go, dear, look for help," she wailed. "Go, quickly ... I'm in too much pain ... I can't stand it."

Pierre dressed hastily, left the house, hesitated a minute. He no longer knew anyone in town he could ask for help.

He made a quick decision and ran through the darkness toward the quarry. All was quiet at his grandmother's house. He knocked on the shutter, and Lise came to let him in.

She understood immediately. She tucked Pierre into her own bed, pulled on her dress and her coat, and set out, taking the road that wound toward the hilltop. She had not carried the lantern to avoid being spotted by the Germans, for curfew had passed. She had her ears open, ready to jump into a ditch at the slightest sound, at the first silhouette of a German glimpsed along the roadway. But all was well. There was no one in the countryside. She quickly felt reassured and walked more fearlessly beneath an unfathomably dark and bluish sky riddled with stars. There was no wind, no clouds, no moon. Even the guns, by some miracle, had ceased firing. The world was shrouded in a mysterious silence beneath the cold, starry splendour. It was a solemn night, a fitting night for nativity.

Lise rushed, despite the immense peace. She reached the hilltop. The roof of Fannie's house came into view. It was a tall thatched roof, high-pitched and dark, set against the boundlessness of the star-studded sky. Lise kept moving. A distant murmur reached her ears, growing ever louder: the din of men's voices shouting, laughing, and singing. It was coming from the shed. Around fifty men were inside, milling about in the straw and the hay, busy eating and drinking, hollering, arguing, laughing, numbing themselves, forgetting the horror of their ordeal in a wild orgy. Lise remembered that today the Germans were celebrating Hindenburg's seventieth birthday. Quietly, a furtive black shadow, Lise slipped like a phantom through the area of red light spilling from the open doorway and headed toward the house. There silence reigned. Through the window she could see a flickering, dancing glimmer, a speck of crimson light amid the shadows, like the light that guided the shepherds to the stable. It made for an almost tragic contrast, this humble flame trembling in the silence, set against the conflagration in the shed, the inebriated, raucous, and discordant clamour of drunken men striking up the "Gloria" in honour of Old Hindenburg:

Glory, victory,
With heart and hand,
For the Fatherland.
The birds in our forests,
How sweet is their song …

Our Fatherland, our Fatherland,
One day we'll see it again.
Yes, we'll see it again ...

Concealed by the shadows, Lise pushed open the door and entered the cottage.

Inside it was almost completely dark. On the table was a terracotta vase in which a wick was burning, like a lamp from ancient times. In a corner stood the bed. On it lay an indistinct, white shape, a tortured form, which was groaning painfully. At the bedside two men were bustling about, two young German soldiers of only eighteen, in shirtsleeves and stockinged feet, tramping through the blood, their sleeves rolled up, their arms sticky and red to the elbow, like butchers. They were sweating, swearing, doing everything in their power, the poor boys. With pallid and distorted faces, alarmed, distraught, terrified, they had come running, attended to her in a generous burst of human pity, and for the first time helped bring a child into the world ...

· · ·

It was a little girl. She was named Jeannette. Lise came every day to look after her and care for her. Lise felt bad that she had been so hard on Fannie. Lise said nothing to her, but she did the housework and brought over food. Pierre was now frequenting the quarry again. His grandmother, Old Berthe, saw him arrive each morning. He came in, sat beside the fire, and searched for an opening: "What's in this pot, Grandmamma?"

"Rice."

"Ah! Rice ..."

There was a pause.

"And you're having rice for dinner?"

"Yes."

"Ah!"

"And at your house, Pierre?"

"At our house? Oh, today we don't have much ..."

"Well then, you'll eat with us?" Berthe finally said.

He turned red with pleasure, could not keep himself from beaming.

"If you'd like, Grandmother, I'd be happy to ..."

Fannie, for her part, did not rebound. Winter came, and with it the cold. Fannie spent her days in bed, huddled up, covered with a blanket, her knees at her chin. Lise did all the chores at Fannie's house. Fannie remained indifferent, distracted. She hardly ate and took little interest in her new daughter, whom she was unable to breastfeed. It was as if Fannie were no longer among the living. She rarely slept and talked to herself all night long, frightening Pierre. It soon became evident that she was losing her mind. Pierre would have liked to take her to the quarry, but Fannie refused to leave her bed, even for an hour. Lise started to fear for Pierre and the child: one never knows what tragedy might be lurking in the back of an unbalanced mind.

Fannie vanished one morning in January. They looked everywhere for her. She could not be found. They had to accept the idea that she had left on a whim, searching for God knows what – her dead loved ones perhaps – or that she had killed herself in some forgotten hole. They had resigned themselves to her disappearance when a chance happening revealed her fate. It was in February 1918. The cold was terrible. The pond in the quarry was nothing but a block of ice. Some children came to go skating and had set up a slide along the banks. To cut the branches of a willow growing from the side of the quarry, near the very top, one of the boys began scaling the rocky ledge ... He reached the willow. He leaned over to see his pals and the pond from above. And it was in this manner that he just caught sight of a long shape imprisoned in the mass of translucent and frozen crystal, its face skyward, with long blond hair flowing behind. The ice, in petrifying the hair, had preserved the supple flowing wave ... It was a royal casket, like some enormous diamond, at the bottom of the white and wild quarry where Fannie had finally found everlasting peace.

Lise and her mother attempted to remove Fannie. They tried to break the ice but only succeeded in smashing two of the dead woman's fingers. They had to wait for the thaw to pull her out.

Lise adopted the two orphans.

PART III

Chapter One

Rheinbach prison was built in the shape of a star, after the standard plan. Five storeys of superimposed cells radiated from a central axis where the hallways converged. At the centrepoint, a single guard could keep watch over the entire prison.

Daniel Decraemer occupied cell 381, sector D, fifth floor, at the end of the corridor. It was a privileged location, nearest the light and farthest from the guard. The cell was small, high-ceilinged, painted in yellow, paved with blue tiles, lit by an elevated fan light, and actually rather cheerful. It contained a table that unfolded into a bed at night, a chained stool, a little armoire, and a ceramic flush toilet.

Decraemer had been in Rheinbach since the beginning of 1916. Convicted, sentenced to five years imprisonment for the burning of the factory, he had travelled by rail to Aachen and marched across the city as Germans taunted him, calling him a "Spion" and spitting in his face. He had spent a few days in jail before taking another train to Rheinbach, where he had endured the humiliation of photographs, fingerprints, and measurements of every sort. Then he had been stripped of his clothes and his name.

He had been in Rheinbach fourteen months. The village of Rheinbach is nestled in a little valley surrounded by wooded hillsides. A railroad passes through the town. Near the station is the prison house.

Incarceration had left its mark on Decraemer. His every faculty suffered from it. It obsessed him, lay siege to his thoughts, his vision, his hearing, even his sense of smell. Nothing failed to remind him at each and every moment that he was in captivity. Even the fetid odour of hospital and zoo wafting through the hallways was to be found nowhere else. For 410 days he had been in the grips – the clutches – of solitude and hunger. He spent hours trying to appease a frightful desire for freedom, a craving for escape and open space, and the torture of a body devoured by starvation. The daily allowance was often no more than a bit of gooey, paper-thin bread and a bowl of boiled rutabagas – akin to oversized turnips. Decraemer ate the bread for dessert, making it last for hours. On occasion, for variety, the inmates were given raw sardines on the verge of spoiling, or even rutabaga leaves instead of the roots.

Then again sometimes, around noon, a frightful odour – a smell of acetylene – spread through the hallways, raising howls of protest from the prison cells. This odour announced "carbide soup," a sinking, fetid, brownish liquid that smelled strangely of acetylene. Through his guard, nicknamed "Cheat Death," Decraemer had learned of the recipe. In German cities, the inhabitants had orders to divide household refuse into two piles that were collected separately: first inorganic waste, then animal and vegetable matter. The latter was dried in special ovens and reduced to a powder. Then, diluted in hot water, it served as the prisoners' soup. But dehydration produced complex chemical reactions that were the origin of the extraordinary acetylene smell. Such a broth did irreparable damage to the intestines. Ever since he had heard about the recipe, Decraemer had not managed to swallow it and contented himself with his bread.

At times the inmates also received an herbal soup, a greenish brew plainly covered with a layer of cooked, blackened insects that had to be skimmed off. It was nauseating. Decraemer could not force himself to eat on these days either. He was ecstatic when the arrival of a package from Lille – stuffed with crackers, chocolate, and canned goods – allowed him to enjoy acceptable fare. But most often the packages arrived with a hole in them, a hole the size of a hand, through which the largest part of the contents had escaped. Every now and then the packages were totally empty, containing nothing but derisory crumbs. And hunger gnawed at Decraemer.

On this diet the stomach shrinks, the body retracts, adopting of its own accord a vegetative existence, an avaricious effort to conserve energy. Instinctively, Decraemer remained squatting in a corner of his cell, his blanket wrapped around him, all huddled and curled up, preserving his breath, hoarding his body heat inside his blanket, like a precious fluid, and his mind lost in a hideous void. He risked additional punishment if he were discovered in this position. At any instant, a guard could pass by on rounds, cast a glance through the peephole, and cart Decraemer away to solitary confinement. For it was forbidden to use one's blanket during the daytime.

This peephole, this vigilant spy, this unblinking eye was for Decraemer one of his greatest agonies. Such constant observation is torture. The prisoner no longer feels like a man, no longer moves naturally. He senses, he feels he is being watched. In spite of himself, the inmate becomes anxious, cautious, deceptive. Lying becomes part of his essence. He experiences a clear loss of human dignity and grows accustomed to duplicity.

The only form of relaxation was walking, which was done collectively in a huge earthen courtyard encircled by a raised platform. The prisoners rushed there tumultuously, like a pack of unleashed hounds, fools, madmen, with shouts, gesticulations, outbursts that the guards could not contain. Once calm had been re-established, the inmates began walking one behind the other, at five-metre intervals, circling the huge courtyard interminably beneath the watchful eyes of the guards. It was a strange procession of shorn and shaven convicts in grey smocks, of fellows in caps, coats, and straw hats, of chaps in grey, kaki, or black overalls, of priests in cassocks, of workers in fatigues. The men shuffled along, approaching one another gradually to exchange a few words and take a little heart. Then a sharp, barking command from the guards would force them back into line.

"Abstand!"

Some rutabagas grew in the middle of the courtyard. The prisoners eyed them, tried to get close to them. With a furtive kick of the foot, one of the inmates would loosen the root in its shroud of clay. On the next pass, in an unbelievably swift movement, he would stoop and pick it up, hiding it against his chest, pressed to his skin, like a piece of himself.

Alongside Rheinbach's political detainees were common criminals, men with beastly faces exuding crime, guys whose laughter, voices, and very looks were horrifying. There was a sacristan who had slit his father's throat, a bailiff who had hung his benefactor to inherit an estate, bandits, thieves. The political prisoners lived side by side with this lot, rubbed shoulders with them, and the guards mistook one class of inmate for another. Decraemer felt his human dignity gradually slipping away. "Cheat Death" – a ferocious jailer who owed his nickname to a near miss on the battlefield and who had retained a livid and frightful visage from his ordeal – came a hundred times a day to spy on Daniel through the peephole. At four o'clock in the afternoon he would open the door, demand the prisoner's clothes, and leave him in his nightshirt, numb and shivering till the following morning. There had been a fight between a prisoner and a guard. Forks and spoons were taken away, to leave no weapons for the detainees. Decraemer had to eat his turnip soup with his fingers and lap up the liquid like a dog. Living in such conditions, man is demeaned and reduced to the level of a beast.

But worst of all was the solitude. Decraemer slowly felt his brain turning to mush. At the outset of incarceration, the prisoner has a whole mass of memories to draw upon, emotions to sort out, internal order to reestablish, new adjustments to make. Said tasks are completed rather quickly. Boredom soon takes hold. The inmate seeks to live on his store of knowledge, recalling family, work, acquaintances, books, everything he has loved, hated, encountered. Then he realizes that all these things have become progressively distant and uninteresting, and almost foreign. He becomes detached from them, witnessing this mass of recollections blur, cloud over, drift away. He no longer has mastery of them, fails to evoke them with clarity. He has neither photos nor letters nor papers, no scaffolding to set these remembrances upon. At a certain point he realizes that the faces of his kin have faded, are less distinct, can no longer be summoned at will. And to replace this mass of memory that slowly sinks into a motionless fog, there is nothing. The mind acquires, stores up nothing new. Fresh layers of memories are no longer superimposed on those vanishing and disappearing into a horrible darkness. The captive is frightened, exasperated, clinging to himself, holding onto that something – the personality, the self – thought to be so permanent and suddenly understood to be fleeting and transient, like a phantom. In the emptiness he makes an enormous effort, fathoming the conscience, rummaging within, tormenting himself, castigating himself to reawaken the numb, dying mind. And he grasps only emptiness. There is nothing, and he wonders in terror if the mind, the soul, the personality even exist, since they seem to be little more than the product of sense perceptions. In prison a man registers nothing new. Each identical day brings the same emotions, the same sensations. And the mind becomes a torpid body of water, a stagnant and dead pool in which the regular and unending trickle of a drop of water, at long intervals, stirs a dismal and brief ripple.

Decraemer was horrified to think that he had only been here for a year. It seemed a lifetime. The first winter had dragged on for an eternity with its fifteen- and sixteen-hour-long nights barely interrupted by a brief interval of light, this endless life in darkness, in solitude, barefoot and in his nightshirt, without clothing or food. Then summer had come, the light, long days, a ray from the setting sun filtering through the bars for a mere a quarter of an hour, like a kiss of life for the prisoner. Now winter was returning. Standing on his table, hanging onto the windowsill, Decraemer watched through the fanlight as autumn gradually ripened the golden harvest of the forest on the hillside. Another winter, another night of almost two hundred days was near at hand. Never had the fleeting beauty of things appeared so poignant and desirable. In the middle of a courtyard at ground level, low on the horizon and quite far off, there was a tree, a beautiful tree, solitary and robust, a shimmering cloud of splen-did copper green. Decraemer would have traded ten years of his life to go sleep under that tree with hands folded beneath his head, to inhale its fresh vigour and lose himself therein. A tiny, fluttering dot, a butterfly swept by the wind, filled his heart with a sense of distress, a grievous yearning for life, for freedom. When on rare occasions a bird perched on the windowsill, he stood stock still, contemplating it with fervour, whis-pering to it a prayer, a plaintive invocation. He was reminded of St Fran-cis of Assisi, who had charmed the birds, and was almost moved to tears. Decraemer no longer recognized himself. It was as if his heart had soft-ened like that of a tiny child.

The most grievous thought that came to him was of his loved ones, his son and his wife. Would he see them again? What would become of Jacques without him? And Adrienne? He envisioned her – desirable, tempting, like a beautiful, sensual fruit. Memories of passion roused and burned within him. He recalled their ardour and – in the soulless desert that is prison – was subject to heartwrenching daydreams. He missed her like food, like physical nourishment. The memory of her spirit called to him with all its power, and the memory of her body, too. He thus suffered a double anguish, a double heartache. At these times he threw himself into a task, something to do, anything. He scrubbed the floor, polished the bottom of the bed, began washing his undergarments, a handkerchief, a shirt, started over two, three, a dozen times, slaved away at a stupid, useless job to wear himself out, keep himself busy, provide sustenance – something to consume – for this strange beast filling his head and known as thought.

He latched onto anything and everything. He counted the floor tiles stupidly, mechanically, one by one. He dissected flies, surprised that with the naked eye one could see so many things he had never noticed before: the marvelous action of the proboscis, the ribs of the wing, the hairs of the abdomen and the tarsus, the intelligent, logical movement of the legs smoothing the wings and brushing the head when he set a stunned insect free on the tabletop. He contrived games, tried playing checkers and doing calculations and complicated multiplications in his head, invented short stories and themes for novels and plays. All these activities wore him out quickly without him ever managing to get very far. He made no progress. He wandered from the point for lack of a pen, a scrap of paper, and lost heart. He sensed that his brain was nothing more than a tool, a machine to grasp reality, to process it and store it for reconstruction as memories. Without nourishment, without external impressions, the brain becomes useless, like a mill without wheat. And Decraemer had the impression of watching, observing as his brain got rusty and came irreparably unhinged. Always seeing the same four walls, the same environment, caused him physical pain. The eye, it is said, needs a certain variety of images. For Decreamer these were lacking, and he felt their absence. His vision deteriorated. And his mind suffered from an analogous deficiency, growing ever weaker.

The only time there was any sort of communal life was in the evening, after the last round of the guard. The inmates knew the schedule. By the thousand regular sounds of the world around him, the prisoner understands the passage of time as if by clockwork. When the guard left, the captives squeezed their heads outside, through the fanlight, to talk to each other. Idle chatter, prison gossip, absurd reports on the war, impending freedom – these were the sole subjects of conversation. Decraemer's neighbour to the right was Arthur, a big Belgian policeman who addressed him familiarly, called him Daniel, and seemed as foolishly optimistic as he was preoccupied with his stomach and his digestive tract. He explained to Daniel how to ameliorate the ordinary fare by making a soup with crackers, thinning it down with oil from the sardine tins, and thus ensuring regular bowel movements. Such talk exasperated Decraemer. To his left was Vlaems, a lawyer – an intellectual really – but a downcast fellow, sadly pessimistic, full of apprehension, moaning about his loved ones and himself like almost all intellectuals and rich folks in this environment. Vlaems's soliloquies managed to drive from Decraemer the last shred of courage remaining him. Farther afield, the conversations of the other prisoners were nothing but "doorman's gossip" and stupidities, to the point that Decraemer had quickly begun to despise this lamentable distraction from his solitude and leave the others to chatter through the fanlights in the evenings without joining in the conversation. Decraemer missed mankind. He obviously felt himself ill-suited for this isolation. And then, he found men in these conditions even more debased than in normal life. Suffering appeared to degrade them, to bring them to the level of the beast. They became savage. Hunger rendered them inhuman. The veneer of civilization peeled off, giving way to instincts. Occasionally the authorities received American ration crackers for the prisoners. The Hausvater, or warden, had them distributed in the courtyard during the promenade. For these scraps of food, for a broken cracker, a bit more accorded to one than another, bitter recriminations and fierce arguments ensued. The prisoners insulted each other, would have fought each other over a missing morsel, a fragment wrongfully taken, and this with the Germans looking on. A banker, a notary, a lawyer insulted each other like street-porters because one had had a tad more than the other. In fact they battled over who would be served last, to get the crumbs ... And then finally, a whole world of temptations, ignominy, bestiality – a sexuality exacerbated by solitude and continence, by frightful secrets traded from prisoner to prisoner, by the perverse echo of imaginations depraved in cells where two young men were locked up together for want of space – ultimately distanced Decraemer from his fellows, causing him to withdraw into seclusion. At the first sight of a feminine silhouette glimpsed down a hallway or in a courtyard, the recluses would invent impossible romances, chimerical affairs, idylls or brutal dreams of satisfaction, according to their temperaments and their instincts ... For many of the inmates, such dreams became a quasi-madness, an obsession.

In sum, so debased were his prisonmates that the few dealings Decraemer could have with them did nothing but increase his confusion and discouragement, disgusting him with such vile humanity. With all his might he groped for something more, refusing to accept this state of affairs. He did not want to admit that he had made his sacrifice, resisted the enemy, burned his factory for a species such as this. There had to be more to life or everything would just be too dreadful – to have come here to die for nothing. In times past he would have accepted a world so meaningless, a philosophy so dark, so devoid of hope. Now he no longer could. His first sacrifice had raised him above his old self. He refused to have made it for nothing. And without finding the remedy, without discovering a way out of the darkness in which he was struggling, he rebelled with every ounce of his being against this confinement, this sterility. His mind, more than his body, lacked oxygen and seemed threatened by suffocation.

II

It was at this very moment that the Abbé Sennevilliers and Hennedyck arrived at Rheinbach.

Decraemer recognized them by chance, from a distance, at the promenade. He was unable to speak to them. He returned to his cell flabbergasted, waiting in nervous agitation for his next opportunity.

The following day, as the inmates were leaving the prison house for the promenade, he managed to let his friends pass him by, pretending to stop to wipe dust from his eyes. In this manner he watched first the abbé and then Hennedyck move ahead of him. He called to them. They turned round, hesitating a moment upon recognizing him, unable to conceal their dismay at his condition. The three men had just enough time to give each other furtive pecks on the cheek.

Soon, through one of the prisoners who distributed food twice a day, Decraemer learned that the abbé had won the favour of the administration. He had quickly secured a certain freedom, small privileges. He was employed in the office, handling the delivery of packages sent to the prisoners by their families.

The first thing the abbé sent Decraemer was a book. The prisoner on fatigue duty (such inmates were referred to as "caulkers") snuck it in, saying he would return for it three days later. Decraemer hid the book under his straw mattress and spent the morning in feverish excitement, waiting in mad impatience for rounds and mealtime to end. Finally, after a last glimpse through the peephole, the guards retired for a few hours. Then

Decraemer was able to grab to his book, open it up, devour it like one devours bread. It was a rather dull tale, the account of a missionary's travels in Tibet, but it made a strong impression on Decraemer, who found it touching and powerful. He would have consumed anything with the same passion. His famished mind craved sustenance. He read hungrily and avariciously, line by line, savouring it, relishing it, picking it clean, missing not a letter, in a way gathering the crumbs of this spiritual nourishment and feeling life within resuming, his brain assimilating new building blocks, new material.

He returned the book, received another, realized that a type of covert library was operating inside the prison. And with the books came a veritable stream of life wending from cell to cell. The books were of various genres: a few novels, a smattering of science texts, a collection of *The Correspondent*, some children's stories.* He poured over each with the same ardour. These readings left a mark of extraordinary intensity upon him. Nothing penetrates, nothing takes hold like material read in the depth of a prison cell.

Winter set in. Suffering from the cold and the interminable night began all over again. Daylight started waning in Decraemer's cell at three o'clock in the afternoon, and the darkness oppressed him, besieged him till daybreak around seven o'clock. One noonday, when the soup was being distributed, the prisoner on duty gave him a box. Inside Decraemer found a glass tube, a cotton wick, some matches, and an inkwell filled with kerosene. There was also a short note from the abbé: "Make sure you block the window. Take heart. [signed] Sennevilliers."

A lamp! Decraemer, who was in the habit of seeing nightfall as a torture, waited excitedly for the darkness today. At last the guard made his final round. Decraemer blocked the fanlight by covering it with a blanket, set the box on his table with the bottom of the container facing the door, put the tube and the kerosene-steeped wick inside the box, and lit the wick. The box served as a screen. Through the peephole the guards could see nothing. And in its niche, the small, quivering flame burned like a star. Decraemer contemplated it, worshipped it. It was so beautiful that he did not even think of reading. The flame sufficed: the flame, fire, a small piece of life stolen from the enemy, miraculously recovered. He invoked the

---

Le Correspondant was a Catholic magazine published from 1829 to 1937.

flame, addressed a sort of silent prayer to it as if it were an animate being. His was the soul of a primitive tribesman before the man who works the magic of fire. He did not understand how the abbé had managed to obtain the tube, the kerosene, the matches. It was extraordinary. And Decraemer felt less isolated, strangely comforted now that he had a friend close at hand, a friend he could not see but who nonetheless found the means – in a solitude and distress as great as his own – to improve the lot of those around him.

For a time the abbé had undergone a crisis of despair, homesickness, and depression similar to Decraemer's. Inactivity was killing him, he had soon realized. Like the others he had quickly sought to avoid this slow death. Well read, accustomed to mental work, he had the means and an exceptional ingenuity. And he had found a way to take his mind off his worries. He had begun studying German. Scraps of German newspapers lined the shelves of the little armoire, to protect them from dirt. The Germans had been careful to provide only the advertising pages so the prisoners would have no news of the war. But it was precisely these that suited the abbé best. For here he found sketches and pictures of objects with a varied and extensive vocabulary. The abbé's understanding of English and his familiarization with the German accent, which he had heard so often in the Nord, helped him as well. He learned a few words. He hazarded saying them to the guard by naming objects in his cell. The other was surprised, smiled ... The abbé showed him his advertisement clippings, the crude lexicon he had patiently assembled. The man must have been touched. A few days later he brought the abbé a little dictionary, then a grammar.

The abbé was saved. He began working on German. His guard assisted him with his still uncertain accent. The abbé no longer suffered from loneliness.

He occasionally received a letter from Lise. The envelopes were addressed to "Herr Doktor Sennevilliers." The title impressed the Germans. The Obermeister, the prison sergeant, rather pleased to have among his detainees a man of this calibre, and alerted by the guard of the abbé's efforts, came to visit him from time to time. As the abbé advanced in the study of German, the Obermeister suggested that he work in the office and act as an intermediary between the administration and the French prisoners. For the Direktor, the prison governor, the abbé would serve as a trustee, or "Vertrauensmann."

Thus did the abbé find himself faced with an enormous task – and widespread distress – which prevented him from thinking of his own troubles. There was a nucleus, a small stock of books that a few of the more fortunate prisoners shared. The abbé gathered ready funds, had some books purchased – whatever was available – and organized a covert, circulating library. The money came by way of the guards. It was procured by selling them chocolate or preserves from the inmates' packages. The abbé developed this system of exchange. He asked the richest prisoners for a tithe from their packages, made a collection on behalf of the poorer ones, and spread a little cheer. He obtained denatured alcohol from carpenters who worked at the prison, made a few stoves out of food tins, and sent them to Hennedyck, Decraemer, and others. In the pharmacy the abbé found test tubes to make little lamps, fashioned wicks with thread from his clothing, and drained kerosene from lamps in the hallways by using a wick as a siphon. It was thus that Decraemer had light and kerosene on a regular basis.

The abbé also provided moral support for many of the inmates. He comforted Hennedyck, who had grown distressed at receiving care packages without letters, concluded that his wife had left for France, and now talked of escaping and rejoining her by way of Holland. The abbé found the sick, the weak, the cowardly, even willful loners, as well as young men who had been crammed into the same cell for lack of space and who were plagued by odious physical urges ... To the latter he brought the only remedy – work – offering to get them started on Latin or the sciences, ensuring that they had paper and ink, and obtaining new books for them. Work alone removed temptation from these fellows and saved them. And the abbé, seeing this result, worried what would happen to mankind when machines condemned people to idleness and, beyond the problem of comfort, glimpsed a second problem even worse, one that few people give much consideration.

Daniel learned of all these projects from the "caulkers" and took heart. He soon discovered that the abbé was trying to get together with him. The abbé had asked to visit Decraemer in his cell for a couple of hours each week. After securing permission from Berlin, they were authorized to visit one another twice a week, for an hour at a time.

Decraemer felt as if he had been resurrected. Life became bearable for him again. A little food, a book, a light – and this occasional visit – provided him with unspeakable relief. Henceforth he could follow the abbé's contributions from afar, see him working, see him happy even in prison, for the abbé suffered infinitely less than the others. He found joy in this environment, took an interest in everything, and retained a zest for life – the idea, the anticipation of tomorrow – perhaps precisely because he had placed this future in the hands of Another. Even here, where most men sank into inactivity, he had found a boundless field of action and managed to see time as too fleeting! Daniel envied him, considered him enormously rich, rich with a religion, a support, a faith, happy because he did not seek happiness for himself but in the happiness of others – the only place one can find it. Decraemer wondered in amazement at the grandeur, the dignity of a man great in himself and whom an ideal and a faith raised still higher, who acquired new strength each day, found new sources of excitement, recognized the possibilities of ennoblement through prayer, through critical examination of himself. And from the abbé's attitude came his determination, his pride in remaining a man, abdicating nothing of his human dignity, in big things and little things alike. Even with the guards and the administrators – the Obermeister and the Hausvater – the abbé remained true to himself and superior to them, without effort, quite naturally. The greatest injustice, outrage, or insult threw him into neither anger nor tears as they did other inmates. When the abbé's compatriots launched into complaints, hurled their food bowls through the fanlight, rebelled against the noisome fare, he accepted it, ate it, finished it like a duty, starting with the worst to end with the best. He was thereby rewarded with more satisfactory physical health. He treated his body like his spirit, with discretion, like a good, useful tool, and not like an object, an end in itself, an item of worship and adoration. And because the body was for him only a means, the sufferings embittered him less, caused him less moral anguish.

At the same time he remained human, accessible. If he reached skyward, he also remained grounded, sincere, anxious for humility, in no way wanting to appear better than he was. With Decraemer and the others he was open about his weaknesses. He did not deny his perpetual battle with the beast. One sensed that for him sanctity was not a given but a struggle. All this virtue was not innate, otherworldly. The abbé remained a man and, desiring to humble himself, he thereby seemed all the nobler. He too was hungry, selfish, suffered from deprivation and the wretchedness of the food. He admitted his temptations, the desire to keep everything for himself and devour it when he chanced upon a package of choice items. He experienced times of weariness – when constantly dealing with the problems of others and shouldering their burdens became too much for him, when he had to make an effort to overcome despondency or certain aversions. He confessed to a subtle pride. He acknowledged the pain of being deprived of his cassock – his weighty habit – and having to don the rough prison uniform. To accept the humiliation, he had had to remind himself of the derisory royal mantle of Christ. And now he felt guilty about his resistance. Struggle, struggle, his whole life was nothing but a struggle, a constant effort at improvement. As deprived of reading material as he was, he refused certain books dangerous for his moral synthesis. He rejected the *Gazette of the Ardennes* – the only newspaper the Germans allowed in the prison – which was nothing but a web of lies. He gave first to others what he himself craved the most. All his friends had their little lamps while he still had no light. He forced himself to help the prisoners he liked the least. In sum, this man who did not have the right to love a woman seemed to have transferred his capacity for devotion, love, and sacrifice to humanity as a whole. And Decraemer, witnessing this battle, this veritable struggle for sanctity, came to wonder if the celibacy of the priest were not a good thing after all, if it were not precisely this ultimate sacrifice that allowed him to devote an unemployed need for affection to all mankind.

Words are not attractive; examples are. Decraemer was captivated by what he witnessed. At present, for all the world, he would have liked to be a Sennevilliers. And that is why he was astonished to realize that this man, who was for him an inaccessible example, admired him in turn.

"Decraemer, you do more than me," said Sennevilliers. "You've done more than me. I have nothing on this Earth, neither position nor family. I was risking nothing, I'm still risking nothing. But you, you had fortune, wife, children. You've sacrificed everything. I'm the one who admires you … Someone must have big plans for you to have sent this much suffering your way."

Decraemer was stunned by the notion. "It's true," he admitted, "it's true …" He himself recognized that his gesture was inexplicable, that his situation had favoured concession to the Germans, handing over his stockpiles, even working for the enemy. Why had he resisted? What force had impelled him? Was he meant to derive some benefit from the experience? He saw everything in a different light. Now he glimpsed a purpose in his adventure, a potential reason: his own betterment. He thought deeply. He realized in astonishment that the abbé was right, that he had already improved, grown since his confinement. He had become detached from money, from possessions. What could penury do to him now? Poverty-stricken freedom would be heaven compared to Rheinbach prison. At present he knew his strengths, his weaknesses; he knew himself. He had learned to relish the joys and the beauties of the world sensibly, humbly, to exult in the paltry flame of his lamp, a wild daisy plucked in passing from the prison courtyard, or steeping his wick in an old inkwell ... Yes, there had been a real purpose in this ordeal, an invisible hand of great wisdom.

It is an idea to which man willingly surrenders himself – that Providence would watch specially over him, use him for great ends. The concept appealed to Decraemer. Though still confusedly, he sensed that he was orienting himself toward a doctrine of hope.

• • •

Hennedyck, for his part, remained a man of action, even in prison. He was plotting a jailbreak.

His cell was on the fifth floor, in the same part of the building as the abbé and Decraemer. In the evenings he communicated through the window with his neighbours by means of an elaborate system of correspondence that he had helped establish. Utilizing ropes running along the facade, the prisoners could exchange food and scraps of paper on which they scribbled messages with little bits of lead. Distributed by a prisoner who worked as a plumber, these tiny pieces of lead would make black marks on the paper and served as pencils. Verscleven, a prominent Antwerp industrialist – a linen manufacturer whom Hennedyck had known before the war and whom the Germans employed in the laundry – had stolen some clothes lines and passed them to the others.

Hennedyck, Verscleven, Deraedt the plumber, and another young man – Hennedyck's neighbour in the cellblock – collaborated on the escape plan. They would take the abbé and Decraemer and try to reach Holland. Verscleven spoke fluent German and would be a valuable resource for the little group.

The prison was enclosed by a high wall. Between this barrier and a second, even taller wall was the guard path. One could access the latter by means of a door from the laundry room. They would have to get the key to this door. The outer wall was very high. A hook and a rope ladder would be necessary.

Hennedyck got the hook by cutting a spring rail from his table-bed. These rails were attached beneath the top pannel. Deraedt gave him the metal saw blade. Verscleven stole a coil of strong rope. Whenever American ration crackers were distributed, the partners removed a few crossbeams from the cases. They made holes on both sides of these boards and strung the ropes through, giving them a ladder to which they attached the hook. The Germans assigned Deraedt the plumber to maintenance of the prison's water lines and gas pipes. One day Verscleven, taking advantage of the inattention of the Werkmeister who supervised operations in the laundry, grabbed his keys from the table. Verscleven pressed the key that opened the door for the guard path into bit of soft bread, cut this morsel in two along the axis of the key, and thereby obtained an impression that he gave to Deraedt. The young man poured a mixture of tin and lead into the mold. This gave them their key. The whole process was long, difficult. But they had a sole, compensatory advantage: time.

Hennedyck received frequent packages. He sold his canned goods to the guards and purchased some maps and civilian clothing. Everything was ready. They decided they would leave on Sunday at mealtime, when the kitchens would be open and when they could take advantage of congestion in the hallways. The guards were much less numerous on Sundays. Breakout would thus be all the easier.

It was at this moment that Decraemer fell ill. He had been getting weaker for some time. While he was in his cell one day, he was taken with fainting fits and bouts of fever and delirium. The abbé thought Decraemer was going to die and refused to leave him behind.

On Sunday at noon, while the prisoners were heading into the hallways, Hennedyck and the three others slipped toward kitchen, rushed inside, and ran at full speed to the laundry room. Concealed in the basement, they watched through the cellar window till the sentinel passed by on the guard path. As soon as he was gone, they came back up, opened the door with the false key, and stepped onto the guard path. They threw the rope. On the third attempt, the hook caught on the top of the wall. They hoisted the rope ladder, climbed up, and, without taking the time to pull up the ladder and lower it down the other side, jumped to the ground and rushed headlong toward the forest crowning the distant hills. Hennedyck, who had twisted his ankle, was in the rear. He started losing ground. They tried to take him by the shoulder. He refused, not wanting the others to be captured because of him. The alarm had already been sounded, the bell of the cellblock was ringing, and the distant murmur of yelling and emergency orders was drifting on the wind. In five minutes a pack of hounds and men would be at their heels. Hennedyck later found out that a German prisoner, remaining by chance in the laundry room, had seen them scaling the wall and given the signal.

They ran for several kilometres, nearing the wood. In the distance some thirty armed guards were coming at full speed. Hennedyck could tell that he would not reach the forest. He stopped running, sat down, and waited for the guards while his comrades plunged into the first thickets of the wood.

Hennedyck was brought back to prison and tossed into solitary confinement. The Germans left him there for two weeks. Then, half-dead from hunger and exhaustion, he was put on a train and sent deeper into Germany.

III

As for Decraemer, he came to his senses after a week of delirium, but he was still quite weak. The abbé had been granted the favour of seeing him each day and spoon fed him condensed milk as if he were a child. Only later was Decraemer aware of the danger he had been in.

He felt a surge of boundless gratitude when he realized that the abbé had sacrificed his freedom for him and thereby saved his life. For he would certainly have died in his cell. Detainees were left to expire without the least humanity. And Decreaemer recalled having listened all night long to the death rattle of a young twenty-year-old who had passed away the next morning – in the cell right below Decraemer's – without anyone having been able to help him. Hundreds of men, in their tiny chambers, had stood by in like fashion – powerless in the face of this death agony – yelling, screaming, vainly shaking their doors, and thinking they would be driven insane.

Decraemer owed his life to the abbé. This was the shock that gave him the final push. He felt a burst of gratefulness. His determination crystalized. With all his soul, he wanted to be a member of this elite, to follow the abbé, to be part of this group of men, of this better humanity that the priest represented and whose charity had conquered him. Inadvertently, without having thought of it even for an instant, the Abbé Sennevilliers had thereby effected this strange conversion – an evangelist all the more persuasive for never having intended to evangelize.

. . .

The surprising ascension of Daniel Decraemer could be traced to these events. His detachment from the world was complete. The last threads had been broken. His body, mortified in the extreme, no longer reacted. In spite of himself his mind had grown accustomed to the idea of uncertainty about the future. He did not know where he was going, how it would all end. War, victory, death, freedom, so many enigmas. Detached by the force of earthly things, his thoughts turned toward God. And the sight of men – in their selfishness, their baseness, their passions that exploded and clashed even in this hell – altered his perspective still more and encouraged the change in him as much as the diet and the disciplinary regime. If philosophy dictates lifestyle, lifestyle in turn dictates philosophy. It was Maurice Maeterlink who once set forth the striking idea that every attempt of man at ennoblement almost always begins with the adoption of a diet rich in vegetable matter.* From Buddhism to Pythagoreanism, from Christianity to contemporary Antoinism, the religions recognize the impact of the physical on the mental and the peace of mind brought by balance of the humours. Moreover, it seems that man feels a certain pride in abusing his body. A healthy Pascal would probably not have written the *Pensées*.† In essence, the atmosphere of prison is akin to that of the cloister. Remarkably a discipline – whether desired or imposed – has almost the same impact on the human spirit. In ordinary life, Decreaemer would never have had the

*Maurice Maeterlink was a Nobel-prize-winning poet, playwright, and essayist associated with the Symbolist movement. For Maeterlink's thoughts on vegetarianism, see *Le Temple enseveli* (Paris: E. Fasquelle, 1902).
†Blaise Pascal's *Pensées* was published posthumously in 1669. Pascal was seriously ill for much of the last decade of his life. He wrote the *Pensées* under these conditions.

energy to place himself in such a harsh environment, away from the world. Imposed by a will not his own, it affected him all the same. He understood. He came to see in events – in this ordeal, this confinement – the purpose and will of God. It seemed that Someone, as the abbé said, had had extraordinary intentions for him, plans beyond the ordinary, that He had put him to the test in this manner and watched over him with a firm hand. In the *Imitation* Decraemer had found a sentence that seemed to capture this mystical idea. And he had written it at the front of a little notebook that the abbé had given him: "Here therefore are men tried as gold in the furnace ..."*

Yes, God wished it; God had chosen this ordeal especially for Decraemer so that he would emerge tempered. The war was truly the furnace. Base metal would not withstand it. Gold, noble hearts, proved in the crucible of suffering, would assume their true value, emerge purified. Perhaps a great mission awaited Decraemer. He had been chosen. With this thought in mind, he took great comfort, great pride in his wretchedness. The enormous role overwhelmed him and excited him at one and the same time. He in his turn would be the sacrifice. He had been called here to be a living example, like Christ of old, like the Abbé Sennevilliers today – that the sight of immense suffering bravely and resignedly endured would be of help to those around him, that it would remind them of the divine element of the human soul that everyone has within, that facing the ugliness of the world they could later say, "Even so, this isn't all there is, there's a Decraemer!" just like he himself had said, "There's a Sennevilliers," and that memory of him would reconcile them with mankind. This old idea returned to him, that he could take action, be the Leaven of the World – the infinitesimal bit of living yeast that moves the mass. Near at hand was the Abbé Sennevilliers and his immense influence. The abbé's example strengthened Decraemer in the idea that one could accomplish something, bring men back toward goodness. He did not realize that the prison atmosphere affected others in like fashion, prompting such mysticism, such conversions, which would not have been as sudden, as simple

---

*The Imitation of Christ, a devotional book penned in the early 1400s, is typically attributed to the German priest Thomas à Kempis. For this and subsequent quoted passages, William Benham's 1905 translation has been used. See Thomas à Kempis, *The Imitation of Christ*, trans. William Benham (London: George Routledtge & Sons, 1905), book 1, chap. 17, no. 3.

in a normal world. Had he had an inkling of the routine nature of his experience, he would have dismissed the notion. He rejected doubt with all his might. He felt like a new man living in a transformed universe. Things had taken on new meaning in his eyes. Readings like the *Imitation*, which he had not understood in times past, transported him. Previously, such a doctrine of asceticism and humility would have led him to shrug his shoulders. The other Decraemer who, deluded about himself, his wife, and his family, had made the acquisition of money his ideal and had loved Adrienne for what counts least – the body, beauty, finery, sensual delights. The other Decraemer who had reared his son as a pure materialist, stupidly attached to providing the boy ease, luxury, and wealth, preparing him for a life of useless accomplishments, ignoble joys, sadness, and regret. And all of it, in reality, out of selfishness. Because Decraemer had loved his family for himself. Through them, too, he had stoked his pride, his desire for domination, "this deceitful, covetous curious nature, which looketh upon all things in reference to herself ..."*

But at present all that had changed. He would know how to love others in their own right and not for himself. His love for his wife, wonderfully purified by time apart, by the demise of every sensual element – of everything contributing an element of corruption to human affection – now went beyond preoccupations with beauty, grace, and luxury. Now he would love her for what she had suffered, for the agony she had endured with him when little Louise had died. He would love her even in her sorrows, her weaknesses, and her transgressions. His son he would first and foremost arm with a faith, a belief. He would find a career for him and lead him toward a life in which money would be a secondary concern, a life in which Jacques would above all derive immense moral satisfaction from devotion, from meaningful work ... Decraemer even saw his enemies in a different light. He owed his ascension to them, to the hardships they had subjected him to. He refused to hate them. He owed them gratitude for what they had allowed him to learn about himself. In the end he abandoned all animosity toward the Germans and arrived at a sense of internationalism. Both sides should come to terms, compromise, end this war at once without concern for territory, money, or prestige, and begin a new

*A compilation of passages from *The Imitation of Christ*. See Thomas à Kempis, *The Imitation of Christ*, book 3, chap. 54, nos 2, 8, 10, 16.

era of permanent peace. He went to the extreme of denying the right to resistance, insisting that the French ought not to have defended themselves, that it would have been better to let the Germans invade the country and conquer them by way of resignation. The abbé, almost frightened by this mysticism, scared of the heights to which his friend had thus acceded, reproved him timidly: "But we can't let ourselves be slaughtered like sheep."

Decraemer had a decisive response, though, turning the abbé's own weapons against him: "You're a man of little faith, you doubt. And even if we must be slaughtered, our example will serve the cause of peace more than our resistance. There are basic principles ..."

He put his doctrines into practice. Through his passivity he wore down the senseless cruelty of "Cheat Death," his guard. He thereby achieved a sort of triumph that silenced the abbé. "Cheat Death" had a son at the front. He was killed. Decraemer learned of it. During the promenade, as he passed by "Cheat Death," he stopped right in front of him and in bad, laboured German said, "I'm sorry, dear fellow."

The gesture drew a tear of despair from "Cheat Deat" when after a moment of astonishment the brute had understood. From this instant, Decraemer seemed to have vanquished his ferocity. "Cheat Death" treated him better, expressing a certain pity, perhaps even remorse ...

These experiences bathed Decraemer in immeasurable serenity. He reached a height, an exaltation that the abbé found disquieting and worrisome. Decraemer sought out grief, invoked it like the bread of life. His diary reflected this mysticism, borrowing otherworldly invocations from the *Imitation*: "Thanks be unto Thee, because Thou has not spared my sins, but hast beaten me with stripes of love, inflicting pains and sending troubles upon me without and within. Smite me again and again ..."* For Decraemer, Pascal's Wager no longer existed.† He wrote, "By betting on eternity, I in any event profit, since in self-denial I am certain of the only possible earthly happiness." He had penned his last will and testament and

---

*Thomas à Kempis, *The Imitation of Christ*, book 3, chap. 50, no 5.
†Pascal argued that rational individuals should live as though God exists. If the latter is real, then they will win eternal life (an infinite reward). If God does not exist, then they will lose only a finite number of forbidden pleasures in which they might otherwise engage during life.

given it to the Abbé Sennevilliers. For Decreamer's strength was fading. He thought he would never see Adrienne again, and he wanted to enlighten her, to convert her to his new mode of thinking, even if from beyond the grave. He wrote, "This adventure has been the great good fortune of my life. I await suffering in peace, ready to welcome it as a boon, the special sign of God's solicitude for me, unworthy though I am. My cries of sorrow are the most beautiful hymn, the most beautiful song to the glory of the Godhead. If like me my beloved wife learns to extract the precious essence of truth from the bitter fruit of suffering, then my agony and death will be an immense blessing for the both of us. I have faith in that communion of souls which I long rejected as an injustice, and my suffering will benefit others like a salutary rain ... Here I will die in true happiness."

Happy, yes, he undoubtedly was. And in total contentment. Physical distress no longer affected him. He had adopted the saying of Saint Thomas: *Cella continuata dulescit ...** He found a monastic peace in his cell. In the silence of this solitude everything took on a moving aspect. And Decraemer's physical exhaustion enhanced still more the intensity of the rare glimpses he could get of the outside. The least of books, even a children's story, made him cry. Clinging to his window, he managed to gaze at the snow, the wintry whiteness spread across plain, hill, and woodland, at the virginal immensity. And all of this white purity drew tears from his eyes, without his quite knowing why. He relished the least joy. A word of affection from the abbé, the smallest touching phrase, reverberated in him for a long time, providing sufficient spiritual nourishment for days on end. He was afraid of too strong a shock, like eyes accustomed to darkness, which the least bit of daylight would damage. Above all, he was happy to have finally found a certainty, a peace, the assurance that skeptics never recover from having lost. There was no doubt, no hesitation, no hatred ... Hatred, that disease that poisons the soul. In place of these disquieting notions was the certainty of living on, the prospect of interminable, radiant light at life's end, the possibility of joining the spirits of the dead – his parents, his little Louise – and at long last a solution to the social problem, to the chaos of our civilization: an infinitely simple solution, that of love and charity. For Decraemer had long been one of those

---

*The Latin original of Thomas à Kempis, *The Imitation of Christ*, book 1, chap. 20, no. 5. Benham's translation is: "Retirement, if thou continue therein, groweth sweet."

rich men who questions the legitimacy of his wealth and for whom luxury retains a bitter taste. He had sought a means of organizing society on a
more equitable basis, even flirting with socialism. Nothing had satisfied
him. Now, in Christianity, he saw the means. What does the type of political system matter? One variety will be as good as another from the
moment men love each other, when each person adopts this simple line of
conduct: "For me what is necessary, for my neighbour the rest." And for
the future – a future that he awaited dispassionately, in great detachment
– Decraemer developed plans: a city of God in miniature right at the gates
of Lille ... A ventilated, clean factory, affordable houses with gardens, light,
and air – and without demanding that the worker abdicate his freedom in
exchange. An abbreviated and lightened workload. The liberation of
women by virtue of a stipend for each married wife, an allotment that
would belong to her alone and free her from the factory. A bilateral contribution from employer and worker through which the latter would pay
off his house in twenty years and assume ownership of it immediately.
With the backing of manufacturers, a bank operating along these lines
would easily find long-term capital. Abandon the myth of the worker
attached to his alleyways, his cheap hotels, his slums. And provide education not only free but truly obligatory, in the sense that a council of teachers would determine the advisability of further schooling for each child,
without the desire of parents to see the child employed presenting an
obstacle. Lasting longer, schooling would start later. It is pointless to spend
two years teaching a tiny tot what a twelve-year-old boy can learn in three
weeks. It is senseless to instruct a sixteen-year-old in philosophy, to intro-
duce him to Pascal or Racine. It would be much better to train the body
first, between the ages of six to ten, then to start on the humanities, study
of which could be prolonged until minds are mature enough for true
understanding.

The world needed employers who would be true to the name, in the
old-fashioned sense in which the wealth of the industrialist would accord
with his responsibilities, his obligation to furnish jobs, a healthy life, and
an example of devotion to all and charity for all.

When he looked at himself, when he compared the person he was
before the ordeal to the person he had become, Decraemer was left with
an impression of enormous enrichment. He felt more of a man. He was

able to understand things he had never understood before, to comprehend the misery of others. And now he truly grasped the philosopher's meaning: *The man who has suffered much is like he who knows many languages, and is able to understand all men.**

---

*An adaptation of the following quotation from the Russian writer Anne-Sofie Swetchine, often referred to as Madame Swetchine: "Those who have suffered much are like those who know many languages: they have learned to understand and be understood by all." See Anne-Sofie Swetchine, *The Writings of Madame Swetchine*, trans. H.W. Preston (Boston: Roberts Brothers, 1870), Airelles 7, no. 18.

Chapter Two

On this particular day, Annie was still doing laundry around four o'clock in the afternoon, scrubbing the whites on a strip of canvas tied to her wrist. It was cold in the basement. Outside, it was frigid. Steam from the washing froze to the walls. Standing in a pool of water, a sharp pain in her side from having tramped about in this dampness, arms numb, hands worn to the point of bleeding, Annie could not go on. She went back up to the kitchen to catch her breath for a minute before starting on the colours. She unpacked some slices of bread and ate, chewing her food slowly and rubbing the painful joints of her hands and wrists to massage them.

It was at this moment that she saw Bathélemy David coming down the stairs. He had returned a few minutes before, looked everywhere for his girlfriend, and found no one at home. Albertine Mailly had gone out, and the maids had taken advantage of her absence to clear off. David was not happy. This man was afraid of solitude, afraid of having a spare moment to reflect on his life and the vanity of the enormous effort he was making in his struggle for power and riches. He swore. He was surprised to find Annie alone in the kitchen. He had only seen her two or three times since he had rescued her when the young folks had been sent to the Ardennes. On each occasion they had chatted. He had asked her about her life, her parents, her Uncle Gaspard who had died. And she had responded with a somewhat naïve simplicity, revealing an almost affectionate confidence in him.

"Oh, you're here! Where're the maids?"

"I don't know, Mr David ... Madam Albertine'll be out till this evening ..."

"Women! Here I am all alone. And I'm hungry!"

He opened the cupboards, found some bread, put on the coffee.

"Well, we're going to make us some coffee, eh? It'll remind us of the good old days, of our youth ... And you, Annie, how're you doing?"

"Fine, Mr David. It's just too cold, though ..."

"Do you want some coffee? Real coffee, with real wheat bread and real butter? Come on ..."

He poured her some coffee, brought her the bread and butter, watched her eat. She dared not refuse and ate awkwardly, bashfully while he looked on. He thought of the other day on rue d'Avelghem, recalled how frightened she had been, hesitant to come to him, hesitant to believe in her deliverance, and then running off without even remembering to say thank you, as if she were crazed. He chuckled to himself. She amused him, the little dear. She evoked his sympathy, his compassion, and also a bit of curiosity. What did she think of him? How did she see him? Was she virtuous? Had she never wondered about his friendliness toward her? David knew that he had a reputation for being a lady's man. And he had always been skeptical of virtue. Her behaviour – the timidity, the bashfulness, the bewilderment – could well be nothing but pretense. What exactly did she expect of him? In reality, wasn't she flirting with him, simply playing a cleverer hand than the others? Perhaps she took him for a waverer, a fool? He didn't like to pass for a fool. He found her case decidedly interesting.

He realized that this long silence was a little unnatural.

"How's it going at your house, my dear?"

"Okay. But I miss my uncle a lot ... I don't know if I'll ever get used to the idea that he's never coming back. It's funny ... In truth, he was my best friend. He kept me going, you see, Mr David ... You could say it was a little like having someone I had to defend, to fight for. Like a having a child ..."

"Bah, you're young, you have the future ahead of you ..."

The hint of a melancholy smile passed across her face. "The future?"

"But of course, you'll get married, yes, and have children ..."

"Me, get married? That'll be the day ..."

"A pretty girl like you ..."

But she had not heard him. She continued, "I'm not rich, am I? I do laundry, I'm not what you'd call attractive. Do you really think some

well-bred, educated man'll come looking for me? And then, I'm too
difficult ..."

She laughed at her own confession, naïvely, heartily. She repeated, getting serious again: "Too difficult, yes ... I never want a marriage like the
ordinary, to live like everyone else, like ... like animals in a barn, in my
opinion. Really living, that must be something else, right Mr David?"

"Certainly," said David.

He thought to himself, *This girl's definitely putting on a show ... Really
living ... Something else ... Oh, of course ...*

Now she really piqued his interest, inspiring his curiosity anew, and quite
different from the start. The womanizer in him came to life, got his bearings, at last recognizing the adversary, always the same ... He was almost
reassured by it. At bottom, this exception was troubling. Well, she was like
the others, and it was for the best. No one likes to find himself suddenly
faced with a phenomenon, a marvel. She was still talking. But he was no
longer listening. He instinctively dreamed of conquest. He devised a plan,
imagining exactly where, in the worst-case scenario, this adventure might
lead. Abruptly he asked, "Are you done eating?"

"Yes."

"Wait, then."

He left, returned with a bottle and two crystal glasses – tinted goblets.

"First-class Napoléon," he announced. "There's not much left in
Roubaix, my dear ... We'll try it, you and me."

Without waiting for an answer, he filled the glassses.

"Go on, have a taste. And tell me if it doesn't warm you."

She took a sip, made a grimace, choked.

"Oh, it burns, Mr David."

She laughed. And suddenly, with a cry, she dropped the glass, which fell
to the floor and smashed to bits. David, from behind, had taken her in his
arms and was kissing her neck.

She pushed him back savagely. Standing up, she remained facing him,
stifled, distraught, pallid, as if she had not understood, not realized. She
whispered, "Oh, Mr David! Mr David!"

She broke into sobs, ran toward the hall, and fled.

"Hey there, hey! Annie, Annie! What a bitch! What a little beast!"

He stood there flabbergasted, looking at the bottle, the broken glass, the
puddle of liquor giving off a strong scent from the floor. He realized – and

his pride suffered in consequence – that he looked like a fool now. If Albertine returned at this moment and caught him ... The thought brought him back to reality. What would he say? It was an awkward situation: Annie's disappearance, the liquor on the floor, the broken glass, the laundry half finished ...

"The little snob. She forgot her coat!"

He grabbed it and hurled it furiously to the back of a closet. Then he picked up the pieces of glass, tossed them in the ashes, and wiped up the liquor from the tiles. On all fours, absorbed in this manner – picking up the chips of glass, swishing the cloth back and forth – even he had to laugh at his ludicrous position.

"I don't know how I'll get out of this one. I certainly can't finish the laundry by myself."

He got up, hesitated for a second. In reality he was unhappy with himself, none too proud. He shrugged his shoulders: "Oh, to hell with it! Let 'em think what they want!"

He left everything as it was and took off.

· · ·

In the days that followed, David mulled the situation over. At first he dismissed it casually. The little whore – she'd played a fine game, she'd been pulling his leg, that was all! More cunning than the others ... *Watch out, old man,* he thought, *these types are dangerous.*

But his nonchalance was hardly genuine. In Annie he had sensed sincerity, rebellion, a real burst of indignant pride. There was no mistaking it. He came to recognize that his assumptions had been flawed. He reflected more deeply, more sincerely. He remembered Annie's words, her distress, her sufferings sparingly recounted – the simple confessions, the question of marriage that she had raised so naïvely, in an amused and somewhat disappointed fashion. He recalled her appearance at that instant: the slight, rather sad smile, the eyes raised toward his – young, weary, moving ... She had confided, yes, confided in him. She must have wanted his friendship, his support, perhaps hoped to find a refuge. He thought of the role he had played on rue d'Avelghem. He thought of it with both pride and shame. Then he had done well; then he had met her expectations. And now he had behaved like a scoundrel. What disenchantment, what heartbreak for this girl!

David began to feel genuinely ill at ease, ashamed of himself. He would have liked to dispel the idea. It returned in spite of him, haunted him. An image harried him, the memory of Annie wet, soaked, weary, scrubbing laundry on her worn wrist, the way he had so often seen her in the cellar. A poor wretch! And here he had undoubtedly increased her misery. David's compassion was entirely instinctual. Hunger, cold, and misery upset him. He did not pride himself on philanthropy. Along the way he had brutally crushed troublesome adversaries, but the sight of material misfortune turned his stomach, caused him actual physical discomfort. Within this skeptical and coarse individual lay a whole secret, unsuspected mass of emotions that would have surprised most people. None felt more remorse, had more scruples, more internal struggles than this man – who jogged along with such apparent determination, without hesitation, without equivocation. Most often he suppressed his feelings, reconciling his conscience by compensating with generous donations, distributions of clothing, princely gifts to the welfare bureau. But this time nothing of the sort was possible. Annie would refuse money. The only way to make amends, to keep her from suffering, was by going to find her and apologizing, so she would return to work, so she could earn a living. The very idea offended him. He was revolted and reacted like a person facing a disagreeable task. He tried not to think about it, but it began turning into an obsession, an insidious obsession, ruining his leisure activities, preventing him from enjoying any peaceful pleasure. It was stupid and annoying. And he sensed that he would only free himself from it by going to Annie's, by setting things straight.

He resigned himself to the humiliation. One morning he set out for the young girl's house. He was carrying the infamous coat – wrapped in papper – which he had gone to retrieve from the closet.

He arrived at Annie's house. It was in Croix on rue de Thionville, a sordid street, empty on account of the cold. He knocked on the peeling door of the big, black, sombre house. Joséphine Mouraud, the mother, came to answer. She immediately recognized David, whose face was well known in Épeule. And her greeting reassured him: "Mr David ... Well, now!"

She stepped aside, showed him into the dark hallway with its musty walls and replete with the smells of washing and ironing.

"I'm embarrassed to let you in, the house's full of laundry ... We're washing."

"Don't worry, I've simply come to return Annie's coat ..."

"You're too kind."

"And to ask if she couldn't do the laundry at Madam Albertine's again."

The mother's expression indicated regret: "It's a real pity, Mr David, but the girl's decidedly against it."

"She wasn't well paid?"

"She was very well paid, Mr David, but I don't know, the last time she came back early, saying she was sick, that she'd been way too cold. And ever since she's wanted no more of it. I'm really sorry, believe me ..."

"Would you call her? Is she here?"

"Yes, I'll call her ..."

Joséphine disappeared into the back of the kitchen. A minute later she returned, alone.

"She doesn't want to come out, Mr David, she's ashamed, says she's too dirty. It's true that we're in the middle of washing ... She says it's not worth it, that she doesn't like working at Madam Albertine's anymore. She's stubborn, you know."

"All right," said David.

He set out, muttering to himself: "Little prude! There's a snob for you! I come to see her, the young lady, and she wants to lead me up the garden path, really force me to pay! It's no use making amends if she's trying to blackmail me! Well, it won't work, she's wasting her time!"

But deep down he knew he was making excuses. None of it was true, merely serving to divert his attention from the loathing, the disgust he felt for himself and which only surprised him all the more.

II

Ingelby was waiting patiently in David's parlour. It was a sumptuous room. But Ingelby – whose study boasted a Boule writing desk, antique Persian rugs of coarse, thin, and hard material, and dirty, coal-blackened Ruysdaël and Memling curtains – looked with indifference upon the somewhat gaudy luxury in which David delighted. To the blazing symphony of garnets, reds, and golds of the parlour, Ingelby preferred the bluish mist of the estate's far reaches, the redness of the thickets, the dense and spindly network of dark branches set against the greyish background of the sky, the tarnished, withered green of the frozen lawns where the

whiteness of rigid blocks of snow lingered in spots, like froth on the sea.
A pale and sickly sun, vaguely yellow, sitting low on the horizon behind
the bare and shriveled tops of great trees, cast sidelong shafts of light
through the veiled atmosphere, the pale sky, the great wintry silence.

Ingelby was fifty-five years old. None could boast of truly knowing this
phlegmatic, austere, and taciturn individual. Of modest birth, very learned, very well read – though apparently self-taught – he had first stirred
public interest by wedding Miss Bargerel, the only daughter of big cloth
merchants. He brought nothing to the marriage. She received a dowry of
700,000 francs. He used the money not in some woolen trade more or less
directly connected to the business of his in-laws, as one might have anticipated, but to set up a bottling plant for lemonade. It later came to light
that he had once worked for a similar concern in Brussels. He had retained
careful knowledge of operations and techniques. He began manufacturing
a clear yellow liquid, the colour of champagne, with a sugary flavour,
which tasted rather like mandarin orange and bubbled in the glass, producing a rich effervescence. Wide publicity, original labelling, the public's
dreadful appetite for these noxious, artificial soft drinks, and a well-
chosen name quickly launched the "Golden Bubble with the Orange Twist,"
as the advertisements put it – all the while boasting of the tonic, diuretic,
and stomachic properties the "Golden Bubble," with supporting medical
certificates. In the space of a few years, Ingelby had contributed to the
incurable ruin of thousands of digestive tracts and made some three million francs.

He bought an enormous piece of land between the canal and the railroad, in the Guinguette district. He took out a huge mortgage, found a
silent partner to cover what he lacked. And work began on the big brewery of his dreams. It nearly ruined him. The land was marshy and unsta-
ble. Twelve hundred concrete pilings had to be sunk. This doubled the
estimated cost of construction. Ingelgy let the work proceed and then
refused to pay, blaming the contractor for failing to forsee the added
expense. The lawsuit dragged on for years. Ingelby made clever use of
appraisals, counter-appraisals, arbitrations that settled nothing – every
judicial maneuver liable to delay the advance of the case. After four years,
the contractor went bankrupt. Ingelby knew how to cultivate the goodwill
of the receivers, compromising with the mass of creditors for a settlement
at 60 percent.

Then began the struggle with his partner. Ingelby did not like to share. He had had a clause inserted in the partnership agreement stipulating that any breach of honour liable to undermine the prosperity of the enterprise would result in full legal exclusion from the company, with the co-partner required to reimburse the guilty party for his share of the business. The firm purchased saccharine from Dutch smugglers for its pomegranate and lemon cordials. One day Ingelby announced that he had just leaned of this activity, exhibited a loyal indignation, and called for application of the exclusion clause. The resulting scandal was enormous. Ingelby's partner fired two shots at him, missed, and was given a suspended sentence of two years.

Ingelby was in full control of the business. Next he waged a campaign for the cabarets. In the Nord, breweries only sell beer to an establishment to the extent that they control its capital resources, from which payment is deducted. The big breweries direct their efforts at cornering the market in this fashion and imposing their beers, cordials, liqueurs, and wines, without even giving the cabarets a rebate at the end of the year. The war on this front has been so inveterate that an "independent" cabaret is a rarity nowadays.

Ingelby set himself to the task with the patience of a tunneling miner. The man had a feel for popular trends, could tell where tomorrow – the future – lay. He offered free installation of pressure dispense taps for serving draught beer. At first he distributed low-pressure, German-style beers: brown beers tinged with caramelized sugar and fortified with spirits. Then he thought of monopolizing refreshment stands in movie theatres. To businessmen who would assign their capital to him, he subleased premises below his own cost. To anyone putting up a new building, he would offer shares in the brewery in exchange for a lease. He established a subsidiary for the purchase of corner lots and the construction of cafés. He took advantage of his license to poison the public by adding excessive amounts of carbonic acid to his beers, rendering them supremely agreeable and injurious. From year to year, the size of the brewery along the wharves grew ever more, as did Ingelby's hold on the region. He had made a huge fortune by the time the war broke out.

The conflict did not halt this ascension. Ingelby was no longer brewing beer, but he continued with lemonades and cordials. There was virtually nothing left to drink. Folks imbibed whatever was available. Ingelby raised prices while lowering quality. His competitors were no longer operating. He had had the luck of holding reserves of sugar, chemical products, and coal. The discovery of stockpiles here and there, at regional producers, allowed him to keep going for a year. He nonetheless saw a day coming when he would have to shut down. Everything was in short supply. And he was not the sort to run straight at danger like David. Ingelby's weapon was prudence. He knew that, if France triumphed, his bargaining could cost him dearly. Fortunately for him, the Franco-American rationing program started at the beginning of 1915.* Here Ingelby was in his element. He knew lots of people – mayors, deputy mayors. He soon had sugar and coal. In the name of the commune, arrangements were made for the provision of supplements that Ingelby then took into possession. He also obtained licenses for the importation of Belgian potatoes and beets, which he distilled. He paid upon receipt, always in good order, insisting upon the paperwork, keeping the books. If anyone sought to accuse him later on, he would bring down quite a few resounding names with him.

He started brewing beer again, or at least a cloudy mixture that passed for beer. He continued with the lemonade. He sold coloured wood spirits in lieu of brandy. He produced wine by pressing swollen raisins. He even manufactured synthetic champagne.

Ingelby made an enormous sum of money. He was the most discreet, the most polite, the most austere man imaginable. He did not smoke, did not drink, had neither mistresses nor horses. He lived on mineral water and milk, rusks and boiled vegetables. He referred to himself as a vegetarian. He attended performances of classical music at the Société industrielle de Lille and collected antique furniture. A fellow like Barthélémy David – coarse, cynical, lavish, connoisseur of women and fine food, gambler and enthusiast – displeased and offended him. They rarely associated with each other at the club. Between them was the type of rivalry one

---

*The Comité d'alimentation du Nord de la France, which operated under the auspices of the Committee for Relief in Belgium, connected French citizens in the occupied territories with relief supplies originating primarily from the United States. The CRB functioned under Hispano-American sponsorship, with Rodrigo de Saavedra y Vinent, the marquis de Villalobar, and Herbert Hoover playing the leading roles. When the United States entered the war in 1917, the Netherlands replaced the United States as co-sponsor. See Philippe Nivet, *La France occupée, 1914–1918* (Paris: Armand Colin, 2011), 154–63.

encounters with upstarts. Only imperious necessity had prompted Ingelby to come see David.

Ingelby was running low on sugar. He was awaiting a shipment bound for a nearby village, through the ration program. Ingelby had reserved his share. But the canals were frozen. Several barges were stuck in the ice between Zelzate and Ghent, waiting for a thaw that seemed a long way off. Ingelby had thought of getting enough sugar from Lacombe, the mayor of Herlem, to keep going for a few weeks. But since a recent incident in which Marellis had challenged Lacombe in front of the entire municipal council, the mayor had felt the need for caution, at least for the time being. Ingelby had resigned himself to visit David.

Ingelby was still looking out the window. From behind he heard Barthélemy David enter the room. Ingelby turned round slowly.

"I'm sorry," said David.

"No worries, no worries ..."

Outward appearance revealed the contrasting temperaments and characters of these two men. David was big, tall, spoke loudly, affirmed his thoughts with gestures. Ingelby – short, thin, and erect, his complexion rather pale, his cold eyes set behind an imposing pince-nez – had the look of a grammar teacher, but the quick and decisive movement of his hands indicated a domineering personality. The furrowed brow affirmed his determination. Despite a deliberate impassivity, the agitation of his skinny fingers and a certain flair of the nostrils denoted emotion, pride, and deep internal passions. He had a way of shutting his eyelids, hiding the dull look of his grey eyes as if to conceal his thoughts, not let slip what was really running through his mind.

"Look," he said, "I need sugar."

"I guessed as much," smiled David.

"And I thought you could ... First I have to tell you that I want nothing to do with the enemy ... It's agreed that I'd only have recourse to you.'"

"It's agreed," said David. "You'll have your sugar. But you know my terms. I've got to pay in merchandise. The Germans don't need our paper money. They need cloth."

"I'd thought of that ..."

"Perfect ..."

"Yes, Villard, the manufacturer, has a stockpile of worsted wool in his cellars. We're in business together."

"Very good, we'll make a trade. My sugar for your cloth. I'll come to Villard's to inspect the material. Have a few parcels opened."

"The bolts are in crates. They've been buried ..."

"Okay, fine," said David. "And I ought to remind you that I charge eighteen francs per kilo of sugar."

"That's a lot," said Ingelby.

"Not at all! I know what it would cost you elsewhere ..."

He laughed. Ingelby remained impassive.

"All right," said Ingelby. "As for the cloth, you can make an offer when you've had a look. You're responsible for transport, of course."

Ingelby, always phlegmatic, let fly a parting shot, though one could not tell if it were intentional or subconscious: "I know you have special means for that ..."

David did not glance up.

"Agreed."

• • •

The February sky hung heavy upon the earth. It was a low, grey sky, laden with snow, swept by a powerful northeast wind. Beneath this tumultuous and rolling expanse, the frozen, dead canal wound its way, coursing like a bed of ice toward the Pont Morel, the slums of the Vigne and Basse-Masure districts, and the cemetery. The huge, deserted wharves, with their rusty rails and their cobblestones cemented with packed snow, lay bare before the icy gusts. Clouds of biting snow flakes twisted in whirlwinds. All along the two banks stood the snow-flecked walls of warehouses, longshoremen's cabarets, and workers' crowded, shabby, peeling houses. The vista was grey, wretched, uniformly sad. And suspended above this gloom – this dead and seemingly petrified city – the tall, black, skeletal cranes, the gantries, the booms of steel latticework, the cables, and the X-shaped girders presented a colossal tangle of monstrous, rusty, and lamentably useless machines. The lock, a little beyond the Pont Morel, obstructed the receding and whitish prospect of the icy canal, erecting a distinct fortress of stone and steel with its high walls and its bolted gates. In the distance, the railroad bridge – a metal structure with coffers painted in grey – spanned the wharves, casting a dark shadow upon them. The whole scene – stippled, accentuated by remnants of frozen snow, bathed in a diffuse and murky light – took on a bleak, disenchanting appearance, the inhuman look of an artificial creation made by man for his well-being but only oppressing him with immeasurable ugliness, relentlessly imprisoning him in stone, iron, and hopeless toil.

Toward the middle of the wharves, on the right-hand side, a solitary gantry was in operation, alive, amid this congregation of dead machines. Positioned on four tall and skeletal supports, it trundled along slowly, moving back and forth, letting its open-jawed scoop drop from above to the bottom of the canal, through a large hole in the ice. Ensconced in a cabin, the fellow maneuvring the gantry was out of sight. And the machine had the look of an enormous beast occupied by some enduring and colossal task. It collected a dripping black mud from the canal bed, dumping it in a warehouse. Through the open door of this building, one could see a huge courtyard where a crowd of unfortunates, tramping about in the cold water and the black silt, were loading sacks and wheelbarrows.

The whole thing was Barthélémy David's idea. The warehouse and the gantry belonged to him. He understood the population's distress in this Siberian cold of winter 1917. He had generously distributed money, meat, wheat. He had gotten a dozen freight loads of coal from the German authorities. Then, recalling that in times past he had seen poor kids searching for coal in piles of dredged mud, he had thought of scraping the bottom of the canal with the shovel from his gantry. Every day now a crowd came to fetch batches of the combustible mud, slowly formed by pits and pieces of coal tumbling off barges over the years.

From his office, David was watching the colourful mob. There were few men in their prime. It was mostly women, old folks, and especially children, kids whose feet were swallowed by oversized boots lashed to their ankles and swinging to and fro like misshapen things. Other people were wearing worn-out slippers. Still others were barefoot, cutting their heels on the ridges of ice. There were women draped in old coats, rain jackets, or canvas tarps, their legs wrapped in grey paper, their hands and sleeves pulled through old, cut-off stockings. One saw boys in petticoats, dressed like girls, and old men muffled with curtains or furniture tapestry, their heads crowned with cat skins or rabbit hides, like Eskimos. People wound string round their wrists. And they had stopped bathing, jealously guarding the paltry animal warmth barely furnished by their malnourished bodies. On their faces David recognized the usual signs, the marks of hunger and cold: runny eyes, scorbutic gums, boils, carbuncles, polyps. And on their hands were blisters, bluish chilblains that the frost made burst and bleed. It was a mass of unmerited suffering. The youngsters still managed to laugh, holding onto the gaiety of childhood amid the hard labour, tramping about in the water, the mud, and the ice. The old men and the women could no longer laugh. Their zest for life had been extinguished by three years of waiting, privation pushed to the outer limit of human endurance, the absence of sons and husbands, the dead, the oppression of the conqueror. They kept struggling only for their children, for whom they were responsible and whom they could not simply abandon.

Every few minutes the scoop returned with its load of black sludge, dropping it from on high. Water streamed and pooled on the grey cobblestones, where it quickly turned to ice. Armed with coal shovels, rakes, and makeshift tools, people dashed forward, collecting the half-congealed mud in pails, pots, and bags. They waded into the muck up to their knees, even their elbows, emerging with arms and legs covered in black. They filled sacks and buckets set in wheelbarrows, hand carts, strange contraptions fashioned from a crate and two makeshift wheels, or even baby carriages, while other folks simply headed off with the burden on their shoulders, their backs sprinkled with a coal-coloured liquid that froze to their clothing. Above all this commotion was the merciless sky, still heavy with incipient snow. And in the far distance one could hear the eternal, rumbling murmur of the artillery.

Some day soon, thought David, *I'll actually have to bring myself to have the big trees on my estate cut down.*

He left his office and plunged through the crowd, heading for the covered warehouse. He was waiting for the German army transports that were to bring him the cloth from Villard's. They arrived in quick succession, entering at the back of the warehouse, near the railroad branch line, where the crates of cloth were being loaded onto freight cars. As he was nudging aside women and children in a familiar manner, to make his way through the mob, he suddenly found himself face to face with Annie Mouraud. She had come pushing a little baby carriage, in search of a bag of mud.

With David, shock was revealed by little more than an imperceptible inflection of tone, something a trifle less assured in his expression. He could control himself, master his emotions, easily force a smile, an attitude, a joke upon himself. So it was only in a voice a trifle hoarse that he calmly said, "Hello, Annie! And what're you doing here?"

She had hidden her mud-covered hands behind her back. She appeared frightened. She stammered, "Nothing, nothing, Mr David ... I ..."

She made a vague gesture and found no more to say. He looked at her. Deep inside, at this instant, he felt a twinge of remorse, a strange suffering, a distress that came from something different, something more than simple pity for this poor wretch with gashed and frozen hands and a bluish face.

"So what're you doing here?" he repeated.

She showed him a bit of dripping coal.

"Come," he said.

"Come?"

"Yes, to the office. I'll have it filled for you, your stroller that is ... A sack of coal nuts or anthracite ... Come on, hurry up."

She looked at him, standing motionless.

"Well, what're you waiting for? Get your stroller."

He was already reaching for the handle.

"I won't, Mr David," whispered Annie in a low but firm voice.

He stopped and gazed at her in astonishment, without understanding.

"You won't? You won't do what?"

"Take any coal."

"Who'd have thought it! And why not? You're too warm, perhaps?"

"I can't ..." repeated Annie, barely audible.

"But why not? Because of that silliness the other day? A joke, a gesture of no consequence? Is that the reason!"

He got annoyed, raised his voice.

"This is absurd! I've never seen such behaviour! You're making a fool of yourself, my dear! I'm not asking you for anything, I'm not trying to ... Hell, I'm not a monster! You're cold, I'm offering you a little help, next to nothing, to you the same as anyone else. It's within my rights, isn't it? Why can't I do a favour for you like for the others? Answer, but answer me now, you silly girl!"

She stubbornly shook her head without saying a word.

"So, you won't have any?"

She said nothing.

"All right then," shouted David, "get going! You're a little idiot, a conceited little girl! I'm not a monster, after all! To hell with you and your coal, go get soaking wet as much as you like. I'm not in the habit of begging people to accept gifts. Goodnight!"

He dug his hands in his pockets, turned his back on her abruptly, and marched away. He headed toward the back of the warehouse, to the spot where the covered platform ran alongside the branch line from the railroad. There some Germans in faded blue fatigues were loading freight cars with the crates of cloth from Villard's factory. David watched, still furious, inattentive, brooding on his anger. All the same, at one point he noticed something like sawdust falling as a crate was being transferred.

"Halt!"

He came closer, scooped up the yellowish dust.

"Moths! Open this crate."

Nine of ten crates were affected. David fumed and blustered. He had the freight cars unloaded, removing all the material that had just been put onboard. And he went back toward his office, prey to a black fury, an amalgam of the afternoon's two disappointments, though he could not clearly distinguish one from the other.

III

Arriving at the club around six o'clock in the evening, he found Ingelby and Villard seated at a table with Old Wendiével. They were playing poker. Very few people were in the parlour. David went straight up to Ingelby and Villard. And clapping them on the shoulder, he said, "So tell me ..."

"One moment," said Ingelby, pointing to his pack of cards. "I'm in. Fifty to hold ..."

And he finished the hand. Then, getting to his feet, he turned to face David.

"Well?"

"Your wool's full of moths. Take it back and pay for my sugar."

"Moths?"

"Don't play dumb, you knew what you were doing, Villard and you, by selling to me based on sample and inventing that story about the crates. And it almost worked ... Who'd have caught the blame? David, of course, that rotter David ... It's downright crooked! I'm returning your wool. Now pay for my sugar."

"It's no business of mine," objected Ingelby. "The cloth was Villard's. You examined it, accepted it ... I don't at all see ..."

"You're going to claim that I accepted moth-infested cloth as payment?"

"I'm claiming nothing. I'm only saying that the bargain was struck, signed with all due process, that you accepted the merchandise in its present condition ..."

"'And taking account of deterioration resulting from prolonged exposure to moisture ...'" concluded Villard, who had stood up as well. "It's all spelled out."

"That's a bit much," shouted David. "See here, Villard, you knew better than anyone that I understood that clause to mean the running of colours, the yellowing of fabrics, things like that. But certainly not moths!"

Villard raised his eyebrows, making an expression of polite regret.

"The agreement is binding on the parties. I'm sorry."

"Well, it won't be binding on me!"

"You don't expect the courts ..." murmured Ingelby with a slightly mocking smile.

David turned to face him.

"I don't give a damn about the courts, and lots of other things besides. I'm powerful enough to exact my own justice. And with or without the courts, you'll take back your cloth, Villard, and you'll pay for your sugar, Ingelby, or I swear you'll both go to prison ..."

"To prison!" laughed Villard.

"We have judges in France, David," whispered in Ingelby, in his cold and ever calm tone. "You're not yet Caesar."

"The Germans have prisons too, Ingelby," retorted David.

There was a silence. Villard had turned white. A general consternation struck everyone else listening to the argument. Only Ingelby remained cool.

"So," continued David, "you said to yourselves, 'We'll dupe David, unload our moths for his sugar ... They can make do with that in Germany, and if they get upset he's the one who'll take the blame. And in any event, with a proper agreement, we'll have the law and the prophets on our side ...' Well, no, with or without a contract, come hell or high water, you'll give me my due, or you'll be off to Germany!"

In his furor, he had shouted these words at the top of his voice. People looked at him in alarm.

"Not so loud!" whispered Old Wendiével.

"I don't give a damn! Do you understand, Ingleby?"

"Oh, I understand," said Ingelby, in his cold voice, "I understand that you've just confessed, in the presence of these honourable gentlemen, to singular relations with the enemy and to patronage that's more than a little suspect ..."

"Relations? And what about the rest of you? You have no recourse to the Germans, you and your buddies? But you know quite well where it goes, your cloth that is, when you come to sell to me. And you beg to sell it to me! 'We don't sell to the Germans, we sell to David ... Let him run the risk, let him take the fall ...'"

"What! You suspect ..."

"Don't make me laugh, Villard. You burned your stockpiles like Decraemer? You didn't establish a 'Brussels Department' at your company, with employees who know Flemish? I'm okay with it, you have to make a living, I don't object. But I'd prefer a little more candour and not so many wry looks. You're hypocrites. You demand principles and hatreds from the common people that you yourselves don't countenance. There're two wars for you – one for the poor and another for the rich, and you preach morality without abiding by it."

Some of the men around him reacted with astonishment and anger, others with satisfaction – those who had kept their hands clean and who felt avenged by this remark. *That's what it means*, the latter reasoned, *to have agreed to this trafficking.*

Villard, furious, sensing the reprobation of the earnest ones, shouted, "You forget yourself, sir. A man like me, who has refused to work for the enemy ..."

"Because you were kept from doing it! Because Hennedyck ..."

"And *you* have the nerve to reproach *me*. You, David, who openly associates with the enemy, who leaves for Germany each week, who helps the German people survive, who prolongs the war ..."

"And?"

"Ah, so you admit it!"

A murmur of triumphant indignation engulfed David.

"We knew it!"

"He's never seen without their officers ..."

"German transports are the ones carting away merchandise ..."

"He was wearing a Boche officer's uniform at the train station in Lille ..."

"That hits the mark!"

Above the tumult, his grey hair bristling, David yelled, "Yes, I go to Germany! Yes, I sell cloth there! And I'm not hiding it. I work, I do business. I have the courage to rise above your petty decrees and your petty morality. And I help people over there survive just like I do here. Where's the crime in it? They're starving like the rest, they're no different than us. I sell them wool, and I do good for all and sundry! The Boches, the Boches! You're unbelievable, you fellows, with your Boches, their poison gas, their submarines, their atrocities ... And what about us? And the blockade? We don't wage war on women and children? Don't you know that thousands over there are dying from hunger and cold every day? It's fairer, perhaps, than leaving a passenger liner keel up? Don't make me laugh! No, there're no morals, no conscience when war is waged. Each side does whatever it can! And you're not a traitor because you do business with people you'll trade with again tomorrow. A smuggler's not a thief. The State's not my conscience! Leave me be!

"Besides, do you want me to tell you who the real bastards are? They're the ones like you, Ingelby! Me, I traffic, I buy, I sell. I'm useful. Thanks to me, people eat. Because of your lot, they starve. Where does the sugar come from? The coal? The rice? The barley? How're you able to keep your brewery up and running? Where do you find everything you need? Not in Germany, no, that's too dangerous. From the rationing program! Because you know how to scheme with people in high places. You don't deal with the Boches, but I'd much rather deal with the Boches than have the weight of your sins on my chest!"

He panted, flushed with anger. A surprising expression of energy and ferocity rendered his heavy, square, and oily face striking – a wrinkled, sybaritic, and massive face, like Wallenstein's.* At this moment he lacked only the iron breastplate and the basket-hilt sword. Ingelby, impassive and pallid, stood facing David, fixed him with an icy look, and said not a word.

---

*A reference to the portrait of Albrecht von Wallenstein by Michiel Jansz. van Mierevelt. Wallenstein commanded Habsburg forces during the Thirty Years War until his assassination in 1634.

"There you have it," concluded David. "Now, I'm waiting. My money in three days or else Germany. Good evening."

He left amid an uproar.

• • •

David had his money the following week, but friends told him that Ingelby intended to make him pay dearly for his victory when the war was over.

Chapter Three

I

Toward the end of 1917, Félicie Laubigier fell ill. Privation, hunger, the terrible winter cold, anxiety over this seemingly endless war, worry at seeing little Jacqueline slowly weakening and Camille – her youngest – roaming the streets for lack of school and getting into mischief with the neighbourhood brats: all of it wore away at Félicie. And above all she had had no news of Alain. He had left for the front with the forced labour gangs – the "red armbands" – and had never returned or provided any indication that he was still alive.* Perhaps he had died without his mother's knowledge, without anyone having gone to the trouble of informing her. The uncertainty was killing Félicie.

The winter of 1917 was dreadful. It had seemed like it would be a hard one from the start, and all the more so given the prevailing hunger. The wretchedness in Roubaix, particularly in Épeule, was unimaginable. The city looked like an abode of the dying. One saw nothing but haggard expressions, pallid faces, weary eyes, frightful emaciation. The elderly were perishing. Tuberculosis was ravaging children and adolescents. At the cemetery, one gazed in astonishment at the innumerable tombs of eighteen-to-twenty-year-olds. People who had not seen each other for a few weeks would meet up again and recognize each other with alarm. In the Nord, before the

---

*German authorities required forced labourers to wear red armbands. Members of these work gangs quickly became known as "brassards rouges." See Annette Becker, *Les Cicatrices rouges, 14–18: France et Belgique occupées* (Paris: Fayard, 2010), 181–90.

war, there were lots of beer drinkers, men with huge pot bellies and flushed complexions. These fellows made for an especially pitiful sight. Without generous amounts of beer, their girth had melted away, and this sudden retraction had left them empty, flaccid, incredibly aged. Big Semberger, who lived behind Félicie's place, was in sad shape. His flabby cheeks drooped and sagged to his throat. He wore his skin like a loose and baggy outfit. He himself described this phenomenon vividly. "Your spare skin could serve as a washcloth," he would say.

People somehow managed to survive. From the rationing program came dried vegetables, carrots, juliennes, and dehydrated potatoes that had to be steeped in water. Such fare was practically inedible. The American bacon was rancid. Milk and crackers were in short supply. Roasted barley sufficed as coffee substitute, and butter was a distant memory. Corn flakes, called cerealine, were used to make gruels, soups, stews. Bread was strictly divided. A whole family at a time would go to Old Duydt's to weigh out shares on his scales. Foodstuffs – a slice of bread, a knob of lard – became the objects of usurious loans, even between brothers. A system of barter prevailed throughout the neighbourhood. A cup of ground coffee would buy a packet of salt, a cube of artificial honey a kilo of rice. Félicie's waffle iron made the round of Épeule, along with her sister-in-law Flavie's coffee roaster. Animal breeding came back into vogue. Each family had a rabbit hutch, a chicken coop. Entire days were spent alongside the canal and the ditches, searching for grass to feed the rabbits. People ripped up pavers from courtyards so they could put in four or five potato plants. They transformed rain gutters into compost bins. And they grew peas, cabbage, and lettuce in jars, trays, or old pots. Not a bit of ground was left empty. Every vacant lot was divided into workers' gardens. People organized the common defense, the night watch. For it was necessary to guard cabbage patches like treasure troves. Folks had thus built shacks where a lookout armed with a club would spend the night. Amateur gardeners achieved miracles of patience to maximize land and seed. Time was on their side. They turned and improved rocky soil and counted seeds one by one. Some people planted wheat in jars, one grain at a time, and engaged in Chinese-style transplantation and earthing up, which consists of surrounding the base of each stalk with a mound of soil to encourage the proliferation of secondary stalks. In this manner, with seven or eight cycles of transplantation and earthing up, one could achieve extraordinary yields. The Germans encouraged these techniques, taught them, spread them. They publicized the method of transplanting potato eyes. To do this, one lets a potato sprout in the open air, cuts along the length of the white eyes, and transplants each portion as an individual plant instead of the tuber itself. One potato can thereby furnish as many as forty stems. A limitless ingenuity – stimulated by boredom, by inactivity – produced wonders. People reverted to savagery, to a primitive civilization, in which each – according to his preferences, his knowledge, his means – produced, exchanged, ate whatever he could. Some, like Old Duydt, made cider from rotten potatoes. Others boiled barley and sugar to arrive at a type of beer. Decooster, the former butcher, used his pork processing machinery to blend fats and produce an oily mixture that he called soap and sold at high prices. Félicie combined soot and burned sugar with melted lard to make shoe polish. A mixture of lard, cerealine, condensed milk, and an egg yolk yielded a yellow and oily paste that, spread on bread and with much imagination, gave the illusion of butter. People used all kinds of "substitutes," contrivances, imitation products. The question of shoes remained an insoluble problem, like that of fuel. In the midst of the Siberian cold, families had no more than ten kilos of coal per week.

All of these concerns fell to the mother, the one in charge of day-to-day affairs. Food, fuel, lighting, clothing, little desserts on feast days – the essentials of existence, of family life – rested on the matriarch's shoulders, making her the real victim.

"When the mother gives up," said Félicie, "the whole house is sad, no? ... You just can't ..."

And like all the other women, she rushed about, gave of herself, worked tirelessly so her family could retain a sense of life, an impression of home and hearth, of an existence that was still bearable.

Aside from these material concerns, and aside from the anxiety she felt regarding Alain, Félicie was worried about little Camille. Ill herself, frequently laid up in bed, she kept less of an eye on him, unable to supervise his playtime and his outings. Jacqueline was only thirteen years old, still lacked in authority. And Camille, though certainly not malicious, fell under the influence of neighbourhood pals and took to stealing, wandering, rude behaviour. There were no more schoolhouses. The Germans had requisitioned them for hospitals. Class was held two hours a day in a little cabaret furnished after a fashion with tables and benches. The students had neither heat nor books nor notebooks. They scribbled in old account registers, and if the weather were too cold the teacher turned them loose. For coal was in short supply and the ink froze. Camille hung around with the two youngest Duydts, went to pilfer transports and German camps, and pillaged abandoned houses. It was a merry and entertaining life that had no drawbacks other than the premature elimination of all moral sensibility. Félicie suspected he was stealing, discovered tobacco, pfennigs, cartridges, and gunpowder in Camille's pockets, and took fright.

The example of the "clever" types – of those who survived by unscrupulous means and enriched themselves – also discouraged the most tenacious. Folks saw prostitutes, money changers, and voluntary labourers associating with the Germans, making lots of money, and taking home food. One man worked for the enemy as a gardener and returned each evening with a bag full of vegetables. Another manufactured sandbags in one or two of the factories still in operation, stole cloth, and sold it, making handsome profits for himself. A third drove the German motor trucks that were carting machinery away from the mills. Others, like Decooster the butcher, bought animals, meat, and sugar from the Germans, or obtained official licenses to import merchandise from Holland. This Decooster made a fortune. For two years his wife had been the girlfriend of a captain attached to the office of army headquarters, and Decooster had gotten whatever he wanted through this channel. Still others, women like Clara Broeckx, using the same means to different ends, profited from their relationships with the bigwigs to take possession of fine furniture, carpets, knickknacks, and paintings stolen from abandoned mansions on boulevard de Paris. Thus did Clara Broeckx – in the absence of her husband – furnish her house in princely fashion and without spending a dime. When the war started, Clara Broeckx was living with her mother in one of the little houses in the cul-de-sac. She had gotten married the Saturday of the mobilization.* And since her husband was due to leave, neither mother nor daughter had wanted to hear talk of a wedding night. There was no sense in being a widow with a child to support, was there? The husband had thus been forced to depart, neither very satisfied nor very proud. Since then, Clara Broeckx had managed for herself quite skillfully. Her boyfriend was an attaché at headquarters. She had started by

---

*The French government initiated mobilization at 4:00 p.m. on Saturday, 4 August 1914.

taking advantage of this influence to move right into one of the nicest of the abandoned houses in the neighbourhood. Then with his assistance she had asked to install an officers' mess – what was called a Kursaal – in her home. The Germans had been searching for a location for their Kursaal in Épeule. She offered her house. And at present she was deriving invaluable benefits from it: plentiful and first-rate cuisine, decent wines, and small gifts that those whom she graced with her favours deposited upon leaving.

These examples demoralized the populace.

In spite of it all, though, the vast majority remained loyal to their attachments, to the memory of the missing and the nation. People like Flavie, Félicie's sister-in-law, persisted in fierce hostility toward the Germans. With one son at the front and another constantly harried by the enemy, with no money or possessions left to lose, with nothing to restrain her hatred of the enemy, Flavie was merciless. She did not even consider the Germans part of humanity.

Flavie had no dealings, no contact with the Germans. She had already been to prison – and suffered there – only to emerge more defiant, more unyielding. This resolve sometimes resulted in injustice, cruelty. Only a tormented mother like her could reach this level of vindictiveness. She would have killed had she not had the children to keep in mind.

And yet the Germans were no longer the tough and arrogant invaders of the early days. They were suffering, starting to experience misery – a terrible misery – in their homeland, too. There were no more strong, healthy, dashing fellows in brand-new uniforms. The troops were old, crippled, one-eyed, lame, short-sighted, men gone grey, stooped, and worn out, or – most distressingly of all in this war – kids, youth of sixteen, seventeen, or eighteen years of age: beardless, frail, sickly, still pale from the enclosed atmosphere of school and study, and terrified at the horror of the abyss into which they had let themselves be cast headlong, blindly. They returned from the front stupefied, caked in mud, half-crazed, blackened, dragging their feet, incapable of staying in formation, and stopping piteously along the sidewalks to catch their breath, despite the goading of their corporals. The cavalcade went on like this for hours on end, entire days even, splitting the district in two with a continual stream of men, cannons, baggage wagons, ambulances, caissons, and men and more men ... All in a dull, confused rumble, the sound of iron, boots, horses, artillery on the move, above which the shrill music of fifes was occasionally heard ... Their chiefs urged them on, called for the playing of the "Gloria," ordered parade march in an effort to mask the despair of the German army from the occupied population. The soldiers sang the refrain for a minute, fell into line, clicked their heels ... Then despair gripped them again. They started lagging behind and stopped singing one by one. Some were so exhausted that they forgot all shame. They paused, leaned against a wall, asked the women for a sip of water.

"To hell with you," said diehards like Flavie.

But others brought a bowl of fresh water without concern for public reprobation. One day a soldier whom some women had refused a drink dropped dead in the middle of the street. The incident made a lasting impression on the crowd.

• • •

One evening Félicie was serving supper to Jacqueline and Camille when a great big German arrived, dirty and worn-out. He had come for a billet at the Laubigiers'. He sat by the fireside – modestly, as a man who knows he is intruding – while Félicie and the children ate. She had used cerealine and melted lard to make greasy, heavy fritters which they were eating with a bit of brown sugar: a meal at once filling and inexpensive. It smelled good. The German inhaled the aroma of the warm grease right beside him and said nothing.

A little embarrassed at eating without offering him anything, Félicie ultimately motioned to the dish of fritters on the table, after long hesitation.

"Please help yourself ... Have something to eat ..."

He understood immediately. He sat down at the table and pulled the dish of fritters toward him. He ate with both hands, with frightful speed, harldy chewing, devouring them. The poor fellow must have been starving. The fritters vanished, disappeared into his mouth one after the other, much to the dismay of Camille and Jacqueline. He was sweating profusely. He swept the remnants of fried dough and sugar from the bottom of the plate into the palm of his hand, tossed them into his mouth, and turned a flushed, sweaty, and contented look toward Félicie.

"Oh! That good, Madam!"

He had such a pleased expression that Félicie was not too upset at going to bed without supper.

She showed him to his room, a sad garret furnished with a cot. The accommodations were wretched. Everyone reserved the worst they had for the Germans. But this man, like all the ones coming from the front, was not difficult. He was merely afraid of being a bother, of introducing his filth and his lice to this tidy home ...

He slept at the Laubigiers' and set out the following morning. But he returned around eleven o'clock with a sack of coal on his shoulder and an enormous pot of potatoes in his hands.

"Me cook, Madam. Me cook officers' potatoes here."

He lit Félicie's stove, put on the potatoes, let them boil for barely ten minutes, took them off, gave Félicie a dozen, and carried away the rest.

"But they're not done!" shouted Félicie.

"Yes, yes, just right. Not mashed ..."

He disappeared. Félicie put her potatoes back on to finish cooking.

He turned up again for lunch. He brought a dixie full of leftovers: sauerkraut, sausage, lentils, and marmalade. He set it all on the table.

"Good, good, eat ..."

He did not have to beg. They joined him in consuming these rare and delicious items. He seemed delighted. In a gibberish half-German and half-French, he explained that his name was Krems, that he was Bavarian, that he had been in the war from the beginning. He had found a good posting in the kitchens, attending in particular to the officers' meals for the Kursaal at Broeckx's house. He had three children and a well-loved wife who was heartbroken without him. He passed around their photos. And Félicie showed him one of her son Alain. They commiserated. Jacqueline asked him why he did not cook the potatoes longer. He explained that the officers wanted them whole and that he would be sent back to the trenches if they were too soft.

These gentlemen were actually rather demanding. They were set up in luxury at Broeckx's, had had carpets and armchairs installed, collected fine wines, and smoked banded cigars, which Krems discretely sampled from time to time. They lived like bureaucrats: going to the office, returning for lunch and dinner, gambling, smoking, and gossiping, or playing music in the evenings. They required choice and exquisite cuisine and had built a huge henhouse in Broeckx's yard to ensure a supply of fresh eggs. They had even installed a library and hung paintings on the walls. Other officers occasionally arrived from the front; their wrath and indignation were aroused by all this comfort, this regular and peaceful life. And several times fierce arguments erupted at the Kursaal between officers from the rear and those from the trenches.

Krems spoke of these things without astonishment or resentment. He simply wished for a few things in exchange: to cook his potatoes al dente, never go back to the front, and get home to his wife and children after the war, if it ever ended.

He returned to Félicie's each day at mealtimes. He brought the officers' leftovers and divided them with the Laubigiers. It was an agreeable arrangement. They grew accustomed to these tasty extras. Soon Camille and Jacqueline were waiting for Krems to arrive before eating. In the end the family no longer dined without him, lingered till his return, and sat down with him at the table. His place was set. He gradually blended into the family, became part of daily life. The Laubigiers grew fond of him. He was a good man who had a handsome face with lean cheeks, greying hair, and rather innocent, bright-blue eyes. Living with him bred a progressive familiarity. They no longer saw him as a German, an enemy. He became a man like any other, with affections, laughter, gaiety, attachments. He was not just a soldier they were billeting; he was Krems now. He busied himself with little tasks and played his role in the household, cutting wood and hauling coal. He would have been missed in the evening if they had not seen him smoking his pipe at the stoveside.

Félicie, who had been ill for quite some time, was bedridden a month after his arrival. One morning she could not get up. Krems climbed the stairs to her room. She cried, she had so much work, so many things to do. He reassured her. He went down to do the dishes, scrub the floor, light the fire. He woke Camille and Jacqueline, made them get ready for school, and attended to the preparations for lunch.

That afternoon he came back early. He was worried. He went up to see Félicie, took her some herbal tea and a warm brick, suggested she eat an egg that he offered to fetch from the Kursaal. He even proposed ridiculous things like helping her bathe or fixing her hair, with such a sincere and devoted expression that she could only smile. He made supper for the children and put them to bed. And he got up four or five times at night to see if Félicie wanted anything.

She was laid up for weeks. Krems played nurse to her, moving her from the bed to a chair, turning the mattress, and heating beverages for her.

He devoted particular attention to Camille. He knew the youngster had homework to do and was prone to avoiding it. Jacqueline herself was not old enough to have much authority over her little brother. Krems intervened. With considerable difficulty he learned how to decipher Camille's homework assignments. He made sure Camille finished them, checked his work, and went over his lessons with him. He took charge of Camille's behaviour, too: forbade him from going out and wandering, scolded him when he saw him loafing about and smoking with the scamps. Krems lectured him: "Above all, never smoke ... Tobacco bad ... Germans big, strong, solid. Little kids never smoke in Germany! French tiny, sickly, drink a lot, smoke a lot!"

For he was still prey to a type of chauvinism, that pride of race, that arrogance of being of German blood that had been inculcated in the German people for so long. But he said it with such naïvety, such sincerity, he acted from such an honest desire to make others – the poor French mired in ignorance – take advantage of his experience and benefit from it, that he was not at all unpleasant.

Camille soon feared and obeyed him. He was much more frightened of Krems than of his mother. Camille was seen less often in the streets of Épeule. A certain correctness became evident in his homework and his language. Félicie and Jacqueline were delighted at the change. And Krems carried on faithfully in his role as nurse and educator.

Sometimes Krems came home sad. He would tell Félicie, "It's bad, lots of meat ..."

For it had been a long time since the Germans had enjoyed the abundance of the war's first year. Rutabagas, beets, bran bread, and nettle soup comprised the typical fare, especially for ordinary soldiers. When Krems saw meat show up on the menus, he interpreted it as a bad sign. Departure – the front – were not far off. From that moment he spent his evenings swearing at length to himself, sighing, rereading letters. Then one day he disappeared, only returning four or five days later, muddy, consumed with lice, exhausted, dazed. He spent the night washing, cleaning himself up, picking off fleas. He remained for a time in a state of stupefaction, as if the trenches had stunned him, drained his spirit. Then slowly the innocent and funny Krems, the good man, reappeared.

What caused him even more grief were the letters, the posts from home. He received a few of them every other week. The correspondence provided news from the rear, from Germany, where people were suffering as much if not more than in the occupied territories. Hunger, cold, illness, lack of clothing – he discerned all these things behind the resigned accounts, the half-truths with which his loved ones no doubt continued to mask their distress from him. He read each letter ten times over. And once more he spread out the old photos from his wallet, gazed at them, absorbed every detail, and cried and lost heart. It was this, the bad news from the rear – more than the trenches, the suffering, the defeats, and the privations – that discouraged and demoralized the German soldier. As long as the rear held out, the soldier stood firm. He gave way from the moment he understood the wretchedness of those he was defending.

And yet Krems remained a German, a Teuton. Germany was still the great country, superior to the others, the martyred fatherland crushed beneath universal injustice. The Kaiser remained the great man, untouchable. At the end of this long, tortured road lay victory. And the German race deserved to rule. He did not see these qualities in his own person. He was not of course trying to point to himself or his comrades or anyone around him. All of these fellows were ordinary people, no different than the French. But above the commoners, he thought, there must be superior beings representing this ideal. He bore an unbelievable hatred for England, as if it had personally done him the worst harm. And often at night, Flavie van Groede and he – these two spirited opponents, these two incarnations of the popular patriotic mentality, having embarked for reasons they could not even fathom upon an adventure of which they were the first and the most pitiful victims – would argue about those responsible for the war – Poincaré, England, or William II – with heroic attachment to their respective causes ...

Krems went on leave in January. He was overwhelmed by his good fortune! He talked about it the entire week beforehand and made costly purchases: soap from Decooster's, cloth, chocolate, a piece of leather for ankle boots. Félicie gave him two jars of rhubarb jam for his children. He set off beaming with joy.

He returned twelve days later, looking sad. He set some small, unassuming packages on the table: a tiny cake, a rabbit pâté, paltry things whipped up with scarce ingredients. He did not touch them, encouraging Camille and Jacqueline to eat them.

"Krems, is everything okay?" asked Félicie.

"No, no it isn't ..."

"Is something the matter with your family?"

"My wife, very scrawny, very sick."

He did not elaborate, took refuge in his corner beside the stove, and forgot to light his pipe.

In the days that followed he was pensive, sad, distracted. Several times he let the potatoes boil and was reprimanded by the officers.

Then he received a letter. That evening he read it several times by the fireside. He cried. The family understood why he remained silent. He went to bed without eating. Before going up, he kissed little Camille.

That night, from her bed, Félicie heard him pacing back and forth, going downstairs, looking for things. She grew concerned, called out, "Krems, are you sick?"

"Nein, nein, not sick!"

She heard nothing more, but in the morning she found him hanging in front of the window, his face the colour of tanned leather, his body cold. He had hung himself discretely, with Félicie's clothesline. He had hesitated. His loaded rifle sat nearby. But he must have feared making noise, waking the family, disturbing them. He had chosen a more unassuming end.

Two officers came to certify the death. A crowd surrounded the house. People knew a German had hung himself. Such suicides had become increasingly common. The French onlookers interpreted it as a good sign and were quite pleased! Through the bedroom window, the officers could see this rabble. They spoke to each other in angry voices. And one of them shook his fist at the dead man and cursed him in German.

• • •

With Krems dead, the misery at Félicie's house became dreadful. Now they had no help, no food or coal. Félicie, sick as she was, had to make herself – force herself – to get up, to hustle and bustle, just to find a bit of food and fuel for her children.

Hunger prevailed, a despairing, resigned hunger without anger or fury or revolt. It was as if people were in the clutches of an enemy too strong. Above all, they felt famished, hunted, desperate. Not a house, not a family remained untouched by this famine, this stupefying emptiness of stomachs and minds, a bleak and apparently endless suffering without hope.

The rationing program was in bad straits. The canals were frozen. And the excessive level of corruption diverted a quarter of the best food en route. What remained was hardly edible, and, since it had to be paid for, people most often continued to do without. There was no money. Four individuals divided rations meant for two.

The Germans had set up their mess halls in old factories scattered about the city. At the gates, lines of pitiful beings – women, the elderly, gaunt and famished children – awaited distributions of leftovers, the charity of scrapings from a dixie.

At home people made unidentifiable stews, mixtures of whatever was available: goulashes of beets and dried fish; gruels of various types of flour blended with water and lard; whole buckets of crepes that kept good for a week, congealed in the stomach, and replaced hunger with indigestion; waffles made of barley, rye, buckwheat, or corn meal ... A waffle iron was worth a small fortune, a kilo of beets went for eight gold francs, or forty francs nowadays. Whoever managed to buy or steal some beets ate them raw. If he by chance disposed of a little fuel, he put them on to boil and ate them with a make-do vinaigrette – melted lard in place of oil, lemon juice in place of vinegar. Or, if he had a cache of lard, he treated himself to fried beets. They were sugary, insipid, and greasy.

Old Duydt sold potato peelings for six francs a kilo and, by fermenting the pairings with lemon juice, was now making a drink that tasted like firewater. Decooster openly sold dog meat, harvested from big animals purchased here and there, and which he himself slaughtered in his courtyard by beating them to death with a hammer. People rummaged through piles of garbage in the streets. One saw folks gathering dead rabbits, chicken innards, even old poultices – to eat the flax meal they contained.

Starting in February, the cold became unbearable. The winter of 1917–18 – a frightful disaster in its own right – added to the wrongdoings of mankind. It was twenty below zero. The sewers, which were no longer flushed on a regular basis, had gotten clogged in a number of spots. And the streets had flooded and turned into solid sheets of ice. Children skated in the roadways, sledded down the hills on rue de l'Alouette and boulevard Montesquieu. Ink, wine, and beer all froze. The threshholds of houses splintered. Trees soon cracked and split, and people froze to death in their sleep.

There was no coal, no cloth. The Germans had taken an inventory of all clothing and "requisitioned" what was fit for use, to such an extent that people used blankets for clothes and walked the streets dressed like Arabs. Others spent entire months in bed. For Félicie, the mornings – each morning – presented the agonizing problem of fuel. She rose early, around five or six o'clock, and set out in the darkness and wind and terrible cold to look for something to fire her stove. She wandered the city haphazardly, like a primitive tribesman in the jungle. She left her children Camille and Jacqueline in bed till she returned. There at least they were not too cold. Félicie herself – numb, stiff, crying in pain – scoured the streets for twigs, paper, a scrap of coal, often till the middle of the afternoon. People burned whatever they could find. The trees were pruned, and Félicie went to collect the branches and dead leaves, just like all the other residents. Then every other tree was cut down along the avenues and boulevards. People bought tar, sprinkled it on old paper, and made pellets from the mixture. These nuggets produced an appalling odour when burned.

The mountains of refuse blocking the streets – piles sometimes reaching to the second storey, as behind Saint-Sépulcre – had been combed through time and again. Men and women wrapped in sacks, their heads covered with scarves, looking like Eskimos, were contintually working through the heaps, searching them once more. People destroyed empty houses, attacking dwellings abandoned by emigrants. The buildings were laid waste, sacked. Nothing was left but bricks. Anything wooden, even the frame, was ripped out. These sinister skeletons were to be found on every street. Some people went after fences and the wooden stakes lining the railways. At nighttime other folks were seen going to pry up railroad spikes, so they could abscond with the wooden ties. Sentries fired on these poor wretches. Several were killed. Toward evening Félicie herself tramped out with a hatchet and attacked the fence around a warehouse, to pull off a few boards. The cache provided two hours worth of fuel, enough to cook rice or cerealine. People hurried to swallow their gruel, shivering, with feet on the lukewarm pot, to gather the bit of heat remaining. Then they went back to bed, and the rest of the time they stayed there, the whole family together, in a heap, buried under a mound of old clothes. Or else the youngsters headed down rue de l'Épeule to Hennedyck's factory. The wall of the factory faced south. One could soak up a little sun there. And since the hospital kitchen was on the other side, its heat warmed the wall. Some people spent the whole day in this position, flat against the wall, glued to the bricks, absorbing the heat. And they argued over choice spots along a twenty-metre stretch of the facade.

Soon families were tearing down their own homes, sacrificing a chair, a stool, an old table, a trunk, a linen chest. Then it was the beds. Everyone slept together anyway, so burning the bedsteads would only keep them warmer. The frames were cut into small pieces for cooking. Next sideboards, wardrobes, armoires, picture frames, and armchairs were broken up. Then people attacked the house itself. They had respected it till the last possible moment. They still feared the landlord. The house was sacrosanct. But in truth they were just too cold. They felt that beyond a certain level of misery one could no longer insist upon strict respect for legalities, that the first duty was survival. Folks began timidly by dismantling stairway banisters, attic panels, the unnecessary, the accessory: cupboard shelves, racks in the basement where food was stored. Then came the outhouse door, the planks, the seat, the roof. One could do without the frills ... Window shutters, rabbit hutches, tool sheds, coal bins ... A few weeks more and they had to set upon the bedroom doors and the attic floor, the gutters and the spouts. People ended up living in strange houses that would no longer shut, that were nothing more than a few naked walls with a straw mattress on the ground and a fire in the stove. People like Flavie even demolished their staircases, taking down the whole frame to burn it, and climbing a ladder to go to bed. Each bit of the house stirred memories. This rack in the basement, the husband had nailed in place. This armchair, the son had given to his mother for rest in her old age. The wood was burned and the fabric reverently safeguarded. Perhaps later a similar armchair could be reupholstered.

All these happenings signalled the end. People could not last much longer in such conditions. It was simply impossible, or Roubaix would die altogether. They no longer had the strength to move about. They shivered, frighteningly thin, beneath mounds of tattered old clothes. Their days were spent trying to elude hunger and cold, cutting up paper, crowding under blankets, while awaiting the brief and delightful moment when the fire would be lit, when food would be eaten. They cooked rice and beets in the evening so they would be a little less hungry and a tad bit warmer, and could fall asleep with water from boiling the vegetables in a bottle at their feet. People were so weak, so drained that after eating they felt a warmth in their bellies, a burning sensation, as if all of a sudden the newly filled stomach had begun to spread an invigourating heat throughout the body. They took advantage of it, going to bed immediately to fall asleep in comfort. And what else could they do? They had no desire for other activities. How could one read, talk, entertain oneself when one was cold and hungry? There was no tobacco, smoking was out of the question. There was no heat, no light. Folks could not bring themselves to burn lard for light and preferred to live in the dark. There were no books, no newspapers, no reading material of any kind. And besides, people's vision was deteriorating. They were turning short-sighted, their eyes weakening. There were no mattreses or blankets or clothes. Family members huddled together on pallets of eelgrass, their carcasses warming each other in the shadows, while outside the artillery continued growling, in this immense battle that had lit the horizon for a thousand nights without the lines budging a single inch.

Airplanes often flew overhead as well. Searchlights swept the black sky, cannons fired shards of shrapnel. Lead and iron tumbled onto the housetops, breaking roofing tiles and windowpanes. People no longer sought refuge in their cellars. They had developed a certain indifference, a sullen fatalism.

Disrupting the occasional silence, the fleeting nocturnal peace, was a dull rumbling, a sound more tragic than all the rest: the grinding of trams, trucks, and trains setting out for the front with their loads of men or bringing back the wounded and the dead while Roubaix slumbered. The Germans hid troop movements from the inhabitants. People listened to these echos in anxiety. When would it end? Would they be liberated one day? And if by some miracle the French returned to Roubaix, would anyone be left alive to tell their story?

I I

Along a narrow, sunken road, between two muddy ice floes stretching across the fields, Annie Mouraud and her cousin Antoinette Fontcroix were returning from Mont-à-Leux to the border, to "run" goods back across.

Annie was working on her own account. For a long time now, misery had killed the family spirit at the Mourauds', just as in many other households. Each individual lived for their own self-interest, transforming existence into a fiercely singular and egotistic pursuit. Doing laundry brought in almost nothing anymore. Georges Mouraud, Annie's younger brother, continued going to school, ambitiously pushed by his mother, who sacrificed herself for him. And Annie, forced to manage for herself, got by as best she could, doing a bit of sewing and "running" merchandise that she would then sell.

Antoinette, for her part, did "running" for the shop. Édith could no longer find anything to buy or to sell. At this point a kilo of potatoes going for twelve francs in Roubaix could be had for twenty cents in Belgium. Tempted by gain and above all by the danger and attraction of a new experience, Antoinette had begged her mother until Édith had finally given her consent. To Antoinette, sneaking past the guns of the sentries was little more than a game. She felt as if she were in a real-life adventure story.

Antoinette wanted to return to France by passing between Mont-à-Leux and Wattrelos, in the spot where the border is formed by a muddy stream (called a "babbling brook" in the Nord). It was February, and the thaw had at last begun, a diluvian thaw after the dreadful frost of winter 1917. It had been raining for four days. An unrelenting gusty wind, as dense as a physical mass, was pounding like a hammer from the northwest. The dull, grey landscape unfolded before the two hikers. In the distance one could make out a few hamlets, a winding railroad, a brickworks, a factory, and then again the plain, a damp and clayey plain in shades of brown and green, cut by rivulets, drenched, saturated, inundated with water. The sound of lapping waves rose from the four corners: the echo of all this water falling, running, spreading, drowning the world. And overhead stood the sky, a cataclysmic sky – obstructed, invaded by an accumulation of tumultuous, compressed, heaping clouds, driving their battalions of vapour pell-mell toward the troubled horizon beneath the blast of the storm, bursting, dissolving, unleashing scattered downpours, which in the far reaches looked like thick black torrents falling on the countryside. From up above a dim light peaked through, the pale light of the Flanders sky in February. And the eternal rumble of the distant cannonade harmonized with this apocalyptic setting, this epic sky that would have set a Ruysdaël to dreaming and exaltation, and beneath which – indifferent, accustomed, oblivious – Antoinette and Annie moved along, tiny, solitary silhouettes on a brown dirt road whose two parallel ruts – two furrows of rippling water with a dead, pewter-like reflection – rolled on endlessly.*

They had been walking for half an hour in the open fields when a hamlet appeared on the distant horizon, a mass emerging from an otherwise indistinct straight line between two greyish expanses. A chimney unleashed a strand of fine, black, tortured smoke, so quickly elongated, dissipated, and swept away that it seemed to enlarge and intensify the sombre hordes, the sinister parade of clouds in the sky. The village lay along the border.

They took back ways in approach, through the yards of little houses. At the kitchen door of one of these shacks, a woman asked them for twenty cents and let them come inside. The inhabitants of the borderland made their living this way, by exacting a tithe from those who sought refuge with them while awaiting a favourable moment to scamper across.

In the kitchen a crowd had already gathered: a few old women, three young hooligans who were smoking cigarettes and prating in colourful dialect, some kids between the ages of ten and twelve, a big athletic fellow – a veritable Hercules with red hair, poorly shaven, bestial, who was looking through the window and watching the German sentry from afar – and a woman in her thirties with her little boy.

Antoinette and Annie threw their sacks on the ground next to the others. The whole kitchen floor was littered with bundles. Antoinette had wanted to take too much. Her sack weighed over forty kilos. She claimed it was not heavy, that she could have run with the load. In truth she had welcomed the chance to set it down. Upon arriving at the shack, she had begun to feel a sort of tremor in her legs, a sign of fatigue. They waited a good quarter of an hour. From time to time the three hooligans interrupted the silence with a few brief comments.

"You got some taters?"

"Yep, my bag's full ..."

"I've got butter ..."

"And I've got rye flour ..."

---

*Jacob Isaacksz van Ruysdaël (c. 1629–1682) was a Dutch painter best known for his landscapes.

In the meantime the rain continued in its monotonous murmur. And occasionally the wind howled. Night was falling rapidly. The woman had set her little boy on her knee and was sighing as if depressed.

"How're we going to get to the other side?" whispered Antoinette.

"Across the brook."

"Should I take off my ankle boots?"

"No, you'd get hurt, there's glass ... and then afterward, you have to be able to run ..."

"We'll get drenched?"

"We'll dry off as we run ..."

The red giant who was watching through the window suddenly let the curtain drop.

"Here's our chance!"

He grabbed an enormous sack, a bale of wheat weighing at least eighty kilos, picked it up as he turned with a jerk, and landed it on his shoulders with a grunt! He tried to get his balance, secured the load with a slight lurch, hesitated for a moment, then plunged headlong outside.

Behind him the others dashed into the rain in disorderly fashion.

A rather steep slope lay before them. At the bottom flowed the swollen, muddy, rapid brook. A fetid steam rose in the twilight, marking its course. Farther afield was a little bridge. For the moment there was no sentry. They rushed down the embankment. From every house in the hamlet emerged groups of "runners": men, women, children bending under the weight of their loads and dashing toward the brook. Antoinette, in her state of excitement, had pushed beyond Annie, feeling light, fleet of foot, running quickly in spite of her burden, as if her over-stretched nerves had doubled her energy. In the lead ahead of her was the redheaded man, recognizable by his beastly stature and his enormous bag set like a mountain on his shoulders. Just behind him was the woman with the little boy, running and pulling the child by the hand.

They reached the brook. It was an open sewer – serving as an outlet for sludge from Roubaix and Tourcoing and joining the waters of the Scheldt by way of the Espierre Canal – a black torrent at ground level, running rapidly, muddy, putrid, lashed by large drops of rain, dotted with bubbles, shimmering with oil and gas, so foul-smelling, so greasy, so fetid that the rain seemed to be struggling in vain to purify it. They rushed into the muck, wading through it with great splashes. In front of Antoinette, the woman had taken the little boy in her arms so his feet would not get wet and was tramping through the water with her double load. Antoinette followed her. The slime oozed beneath her feet. She sank into it. The water was up to her stomach before she was even a third of the way across the brook. She kept moving forward, feeling the oily, stinking water rise and encircle her in an icy embrace. She was afraid of losing her footing. The current was pushing her, making her drift off course, forcing her to lean forward, fight it, throw her entire weight against it. Water was up to her armpits now. And still she had not started climbing the other side.

Suddenly shouting broke out around her, a great clamour that she found puzzling. But she felt a hand bending her head and recognized Annie's voice saying, "Get down!"

She obeyed instinctively, squatting more than bending, almost touching her nose to the water as her feet stirred the bottom, making pestilential bubbles rise to the top. On her right there was a crack, then another. She raised her head, saw the woman ahead of her stumble, heard a voice cry "Mamma!" And everyone surged forward in a mad dash. They reached the French side, left the water. The woman in front of Antoinette went another twenty metres, fell to her knees, and raised her arms.

"Sir, Madam, for pity's sake ..."

She had latched onto the coattail of the redheaded man ahead of her.

"To hell with you!" he panted. He wrenched himself free and rushed headlong again, like a mad bull.

"Sir, Madam, for pity's sake ..."

The wave of "runners," fleeing in panic, swept round the woman. She reached out, trying in vain to grab onto somebody. And her little boy was dashing from person to person, screaming, "Sir! Sir, for pity's sake ..."

Antoinette had stopped. She hesitated for a split second but was shoved from behind.

"We can't! Quick! Quick!"

Annie pushed her by the shoulders, hurried her along. They pressed on again, with this desperate cry ringing in their ears but growing ever fainter and more distant. They reached the shelter of a hedge. Antoinette had already stopped, breathless.

"Quick! Quick!" shouted Annie. And she hurried her along once more.

But for Antoinette the race became too difficult. The ground rose as they moved away from the brook. They sank up to their ankles in the clay.

With each stride, they had to yank their feet from the mire. Antoinette grew weary. The odd thing was that it was not her shoulders that hurt, though the entire load rested upon them. It was actually her back, her stomach, where she felt strange new pains – stitches, aches. The muscles of her neck were strained as well. She had the impression of a sluggishness, a gradual oppression of her whole being. Her breathing became short, laboured, painful. A vice squeezed her sides. Her vision blurred, her heart palpitated, everything swirled around her. She ran a few more metres, pitched forward, and tangled her feet. Her sack pulled her down heavily. She fell headfirst.

The ground seemed to swallow Antoinette. Clay covered her, imprisoned her. A mask of gooey muck enveloped her face, her entire chest. Only her legs remained free. The weight of a mountain was crushing her shoulders.

Stunned, checked, held in place, she needed a couple of seconds to realize what had happened, to recognize the power of this earthy embrace and the weight on her neck. And all of a sudden she was short of air.

Instinct stopped her from opening her mouth to breathe. Her arms were pinned beneath her body, her head buried under her sack. She made a terrible effort to extricate herself, free her arms, push up on her hands, get some air. She managed to raise her load halfway, pull her face from the muck, and remain for a few seconds with back arched, muscles tensed, straining frantically. Then she gave way, fell down again as if her shoulders carried the weight of the world. Buried alive, she began to smother. A storm broke inside her. Her heart beat with astounding speed. Unconsciously, in a spasm, she opened her mouth, inhaled. A wave of dirt and pebbles flooded her nostrils, her mouth, the back of her throat, tearing at her, suffocating her. She made a few dreadful convulsions. And the tumult within her subsided.

Annie was still running. She was by herself in the lead. The rest of the smugglers had spread out. There was nothing but an enormous silence filled only by the sound of the rain. The sentry was out of reach. She stopped.

"We made it, we're safe, Antoinette ..."

She turned round and saw no one.

She immediately assumed the worst: Antoinette had been caught, killed. Annie felt responsible, it was her fault. She scanned the veiled horizon with an anxious look. Nothing. Then she dropped her sack at the foot of a willow and headed back toward the frontier.

After a long search, she found Antoinette lying on the ground, flat on her stomach, with her sack on her head. She was no longer moving. Annie grabbed the sack and threw it aside. Antoinette remained where she was, face down in the clay, motionless. Annie turned the body over, knelt beside it, and wiped the dirt-encrusted face, which had retained a layer of sticky clay, like a death mask. She cleaned out Antoinette's nose, her mouth, her eyes, pressed on her chest to force out a breath, slapped her cheeks, cried, pleaded ...

Something indiscernible stirred in the long, immobile body between Annie's arms – a breath, life returning. Antoinette opened her eyes. And Annie felt herself reviving as well.

"Can you walk? Can you stand?"

Antoinette did not respond, laboured to get up, clung to her cousin. She whispered: "Don't say anything to Mamma ..."

It was a long time before she could stand up straight. She staggered. In a weak voice she asked: "What about my sack?"

"Leave it. We'll split mine."

Slowly they started on their way again. Antoinette leaned on Annie. They went a few hundred metres in this manner.

"We've been caught!" said Annie.

The silhouette of a German, a tall green devil escorted by a big dog, was emerging from the fog. Close at hand, one could see the glimmer of his brass, crescent-shaped gorget.

"Papieren!"

They gave him their cards.

"Komme."

They accompanied him on four or five errands, from one hamlet to another. For he was on rounds. Antoinette was at the end of her strength. It was eleven o'clock at night when he finally led them onto rue de la Fosse-aux-Chênes in Roubaix, where they entered a huge building, an old factory. They had to climb to the second floor and were pushed to the end of a long corridor, into a pitch-black room that smelled like a stable. A soldier gave them a straw mattress. They lay on it side by side, surrounded by a darkness apparently replete with sleeping inmates who were snoring and moaning.

The two girls had kept on their clothes and their ankle boots. Soon Antoinette began coughing. Drenched, soaked to the bone, she felt as if she were bound in a shroud of ice. She cuddled up to Annie without managing to get any warmer. They stayed awake for a long time, shivering and consumed by bedbugs. Only toward morning did Annie fall asleep, to the muffled sound of Antoinette's incessant coughing.

• • •

They were in an old mending room, high-ceilinged and dirty, littered with straw mattresses, old clothing, papers, garbage. Forty-five women were incarcerated here. A few old busybodies taken from their homes for hiding a copper saucepan or a bit of wool – and seven or eight rough-spoken "runners," whose coarseness belied their decent characters – constituted the wholesome element of the population. The rest was composed of bargirls picked up by the police, prostitutes, and two or three "princesses" escaped from the lazaret before the end of their term and sentenced to three months imprisonment for running away. These women often went about half-naked, washed together shamelessly – there was just one communal basin – spent the rest of the day lying about in breeches and untucked shirts, and slept together at night. One of the "princesses" was in possession of an old phonograph that she had had brought in with the complicity of a guard. The vile mechanism was set up, and she butchered old-time dances: "The Black Stockings," "The Wooden Leg," and other tunes. And the women danced in couples. The windows were covered with wire mesh and nailed shut. But one of them had been pried open. And through it the women waved outside and tossed notes to hooligans in peaked caps who were constantly loitering on rue de la Fosse-aux-Chênes, near the prison. The governor of this establishment was a former prostitute who had become the mistress of a high-ranking officer. She visited her detainees, and since she had a special fondness for other women, she took out the ones she liked under the pretense of having them do sewing or other work at her house. Some prisoners also received visitors from the outside. Several times a week, three "princesses" – dirty, smelly girls, loudmouthed and malicious, dressed in unsavoury cheap finery, and whose cropped hair indicated their recent visit to the lazaret – welcomed the woman who owned the bar where they had officiated before their "workplace accident." The proprietor was on good terms with the authorities and the prison governor. She thus brought her girls wine and chocolate, and dazzled all the wretches confined to this hell with gaudy outfits, furs, and rings. Even at the worst moments of the occupation, traffickers in human flesh made a comfortable living.

These visits were the only ones allowed.

Fortunately, from the window, Antoinette was soon able to catch a glimpse of her mother, who came each morning to see her from afar.

The guards were the masters. Through their offices alone could one receive a package, some sheets, or a letter from the outside. A few of the prisoners tried to seduce these Germans, bearing their breasts to them.

In the midst of the depravity, the shouting, the insults and the bullying, Annie and Antoinette discovered little Yvette. She was a child, not even fourteen years old. She lived in an alleyway of the Fontenoy district. Wearing only her nightshirt, she had been caught one evening, two minutes after curfew, while running to a friend's house right next door. The policeman, delighted at playing a nasty trick, had not let her get her things and taken her to prison just as she was, in her long dressing gown. Yvette was alarmed by what she witnessed in the prison house. She was the laughing stock of the others because she was wearing her nightgown and was afraid to stray from her straw mattress, because she was ashamed to use the common toilet, because she cried and did not want to eat. She had already been here six days and had yet to swallow anything more than a little water, driven to despair by the absence of her mother and refusing all food. Yvette had been instinctively drawn to Annie and Antoinette. She lived in their shadow, never leaving their side, a little phantom in her long, haggard, dishevelled, and ugly grey nightdress, her features distorted by sorrow, anguish, and misery. She took refuge behind them, cried, incessantly asked the guards if she would be allowed to return to her mother soon. Some of the prisoners laughed at her and pushed her around. Others, touched by her situation, ultimately took up her defense. There were fights on her account, terrifying her. Her immediate release would have required payment of the hundred mark fine imposed on .her. But her mother was too poor. Yvette had to serve thirty days in jail.

Each morning her mother came to rue de la Fosse-aux-Chênes. Yvette saw her from above, waved to her, and cried. Yvette had grown terribly thin. Some of the inmates gave her chocolate and crackers from their packages. She did not want any, she wanted her mother. In due course even the most callous was moved by her plight, fearing that Yvette would let herself starve to death. Antoinette suggested taking up a collection for the hundred marks. Only fifty-five were to be had. The prisoners searched again, rummaged in the bottom of their pockets. Thirty marks were still lacking. Yvette died before they had managed to collect ninety.

The guard came to remove her and carried her off in her nightdress like a big, light-weight doll. Stationed at the window, several prisoners kept watch for her mother. They saw her coming at the far end of the street. She raised her head, waved her fingers: "Four! Four!" She had collected four more marks. They dared not tell her and shut the window. She would learn the news in the afternoon. That was soon enough.

From this moment, Annie began to worry about Antoinette. Since the beginning of their incarceration, she too had refused to eat, repulsed by the inedible gruel served to the prisoners. Regardless, she was not hungry. She had caught cold from being drenched all night long, at the time of her arrest. She had remained feverish, shivered constantly, never managed to get her clothes completely dry. From the outside, Édith had sent several parcels. They had arrived three quarters empty, pillaged by the guards. Twenty days of their sentence still remained.

Yvette's death had frightened the two cousins. Antoinette coughed, spit. She cried. Eventually she confessed her fears to Annie. There were pink streaks in her spittle. People began looking askance at Antoinette. The most intelligent, the most compassionate, tried to reassure her: "It's nothing, it's not bad. I myself've coughed up tons of blood!"

For others had noticed the spitting. The masses are terrified of tuberculosis. Some of the women, disgusted and scared, in a burst of animal selfishness that left them afraid of infection, said to Annie: "Your friend's got TB, admit it! Keep her out of our spot! The rest of us don't want to catch it!"

Or they said as much to Antoinette herself.

She took fright. Not sleeping, not eating, crying, coughing, shuddering with fever – this would not end well. Sensing Annie's concerns increased Antoinette's alarm. She counted the hours. She would have given anything to get out of this prison, where she felt destined to die like Yvette. But nothing could be done or even hoped for. It was useless to offer money, to beg, to point out her misery. The Germans took no pity on "runners" and left the girls in prison.

It was thus that the idea of calling on Barthélémy David for help gradually dawned on Annie. She would never have wanted or dared to solicit his assistance for herself. But there was Antoinette to consider. And Mr David did so much good for everyone in Épeule.

She hesitated for a couple of days. The money collected for Yvette had been split up again. Annie had thus come across a few marks. She gave them to a guard, along with a letter for Barthélémy David.

• • •

David was waiting at the gateway of the big entrance hall. He had received the note and rushed over. A hundred marks to the prison office, a box of cigars for the non-commissioned officers, and he had reached his aim. David's name – and the signature of certain officers from army headquarters – opened all sorts of doors in Roubaix.

He was standing there, curious and pleased, happy to see Annie again, satisfied with his success and yet hardly at ease. He rubbed his big, ring-studded fingers impatiently and did not even feel the cold.

A door slammed. He heard rapid footsteps; Antoinette came into view, frightened, unkempt, pale but beaming, dragging Annie behind her.

"Go quick to the office!" David shouted to them. "Sign your paperwork and get out of here."

"Thank you, Sir! Thank you!" cried Antoinette.

And she pulled her cousin along.

Annie had come to a stop. "Go to the office," she told Antoinette. "I'll catch up with you."

And she remained in the corridor, standing before David, while Antoinette took off like a bird in flight.

Annie was rather pale and could feel a lump in her throat. She had to thank David. It was necessary. But it was difficult. She approached him.

"Mr David," she whispered, in a barely audible voice, "I'm very happy ... You came so quickly ... You've been kind, yes, and I beg your pardon. I didn't always understand ..."

He felt bad that she was so uncomfortable.

"It must've been difficult, eh, to lower yourself?"

"It wasn't, because it was for someone else."

"Still stubborn? Still proud?"

"I'm not proud ..."

"No, but you refuse to owe me anything, to have any obligation toward me. I wonder if one day you'll forgive me, for owing me your freedom."

"I didn't think I'd owe you my freedom, too ..."

"What? Bah! I'd bet you had in mind to get your cousin out and stay in prison yourself! Well? Admit it!"

She laughed, afraid to acknowledge that such had essentially been her idea.

"Come on, Annie," continued David. "What'd I do to you? You've dug in your heels out of pride, most certainly! You refuse anything I offer, you reject any debt to me as if it would be an unbearable burden! You hold it against me? You're afraid of me? I'm asking nothing of you. I did it on my own account, for the sake of friendship. I've been paid in advance. I won't tell you that I enjoy doing good. It would look like I was playing the generous type, and that would bother me. Plus it would look like charity. No. It's just that it pleases me. It gives me joy to create a bit of happiness for you, simply because you're brave, because you deserve it. It's because I've watched you slave away ... I'm like that. Why do you refuse? I do good all around, for so many others! I don't keep count, I give money to people I hardly know, I buy ten francs worth of cakes for the first kid I see drooling in front of the window of a pastry shop! And then there's you ..."

"I can't, Mr David," said Annie. "I can't. Think of it. It's impossible."

"But why?"

"You're rich. Me, I have nothing. My sole fortune is my virtue, my reputation as virtuous. It's the only chance I have of future happiness. My virtue, it's my dowry, yes. And what would people say, what would they think of me? Forgive me if I'm hurting your feelings, Mr David. The day people knew you'd helped me, that you were looking after me? To dismiss the gossip, no doubt, we'd ... we'd have to love each other ... so ..."

She did not know what else to say. She repeated a little awkwardly, "So, that's why ..."

She looked at him. He averted his gaze. His brows were knit together, his eyes fixed on the ground, his expression sombre. He raised his head slowly. He took her hand. Something embarrassed, almost anxious, showed on the heavy, massive face of this adventurer with a passion for pleasure and struggle. His eyes were red and burning, bloodshot. In a strange voice, low and hoarse, sheepish, trying and failing to maintain a lighthearted tone, and revealing something like a vague, unconfessed hope, he said, "And ... of course, I'm too rich, too old for you to love me, right ..."

"Those things don't matter ..."

"Well then, what'd stand in the way?"

"Nothing. I don't know. Of course, in any event, Mr David, it's not a man like you that ... After all ..."

"Too old? Too rich?"

"You're not too rich. You're ..."

She thought for a moment, hesitated, searching for the right word.

"You're too happy ..."

"Too happy!"

The word left him stunned – him, the dissatisfied, the unsatiated, in perpetual search for novelty, change, constantly fleeing moral solitude, boredom, the emptiness of an ostentatious and purposeless existence. In her choice of words he saw an irony that she had not intended.

"Too happy! Really! And besides, I don't see why ..."

"Yes. All this happiness, it stands in the way, prevents me from loving you. Essentially, I'd hope to bring a lot to a relationship, but there's nothing I could bring that you don't already have. That would pain me, hurt me. At the very least, I have a feeling that I could provide devotion, courage, strength to the one I love ... That's worth something. But a man like you would never recognize it. You don't understand me?

"I had an uncle, Mr David, perhaps I told you about him. He was blind. He died. I did a little bit of good for him. I comforted him as best I could ... Well, I'd feel closer to a wretch like him than to you. It's silly, right? I realize it ... But someone for whom I'd be everything like that, who'd see me as my uncle did, to whom I'd provide comfort, help, happiness, who couldn't do without me, who'd be like my child almost – that person, I think, I'd be able to love with pride and joy. And I could never love someone I could give nothing to. That wouldn't work.

"No, I'd never think of getting involved with someone like you ... After all, Mr David, why would you want me to love a man like you? I could give my all, but I'd feel like I'd done nothing but take. And you'd think so, too."

He made such a singular expression that she had to smile.

"Well," he said, "good heavens, it's the first time being rich has put me at a disadvantage with the ladies. What a strange circumstance! You'd gladly toss people into the water for the pleasure of fishing them out again!"

"Oh! I don't wish you any harm ..."

"That's a relief! So, in any event, we can still be friends, eh?"

"Oh, yes, Mr David."

"You've forgiven me for that silly business, that dust-up ... You know?"

She smiled, a little embarrassed.

"Yes, yes, let's not speak of it anymore. I'll never think of it again."

• • •

David headed back toward the square. He walked with his head down, at once morose and pleased. Too happy! The phrase had astonished him, shocked him – David, he who was forever unsatisfied, for whom life had cooled but not quenched his thirst for something more. Several people passed him as he went behind Saint Martin's Church. They greeted him, bid him good day. He was well known in Roubaix, with his face as bilious, heavy, and smooth as a bronze statue, his harsh and insolently bold expression, his poised and calm demeanour, his rounded shoulders recalling the weight of the longshoreman's pack and the smuggler's harness. David responded to these greetings with a gesture, a grunt. He ruminated on Annie's words. He could not regret his riches, his strength, his power, could he? He loved domination better than anything else on Earth, did he not? And yet it was nonetheless possible that this power impeded him from knowing everything, deprived him of a whole slice of life, a huge range of sentiment, of passion, of an existence remarkably new and enticing. Was not that precisely what he had been missing – true tenderness, access to devotion, to sincerity? What relief to finally encounter such sincerity, to be able to reconsider the sombre, bitter estimation he had so long had of humanity as a whole! Might he not find therein the appeasement, the satisfaction, the true joy in pursuit of which he had so long exhausted himself with enormous, fruitless struggle?

It would have been exciting, thrilling, to start over in such a direction.

III

By winter's end, Félicie Laubigier thought she was about to die. She was on the last of her strength, could no longer get out of bed. Her little girl Jacqueline was taking care of her. Every night Félicie raved, thrashed about in delirium, and attempted to grab at her daughter, who had to flee to the courtyard and call her Aunt Flavie for help. There was no food, no real life in the Laubigier household. Camille wandered the streets, stole from the Germans, had once spent three nights in a prison where the green devils had set him to the task of pulling grass from the courtyard. There had been no news of Alain, the missing son. If the family held out, Camille and Jacqueline would soon be old enough to work for the enemy in their turn and would have to go, too. And Félicie would die, leaving them all alone. And the war would never end.

Evacuation to France seemed the only option. Many folks were pulling up stakes this way, quitting the Nord, abandoning everything to return to "France." For here they no longer thought of themselves as living in France. Félicie resigned herself to letting Camille and Jacqueline depart. Jacqueline was thirteen years old. Félicie entrusted her with her little brother.

They left one day in March at five o'clock in the morning, after tearful goodbyes. There was no hope of seeing each other again. Jacqueline and Camille walked toward the station, entering it on rue de l'Ouest. Many people were inside, a herd of evacuees laden with bags and suitcases. It was chilly. They were corralled in a big train shed. Few spoke. The huge, lifeless station had a sinister appearance.

The evacuees underwent a detailed medical exam. They had to strip from head to foot, hand over all printed materials, all letters, all items made of gold. "You'll get them back after the war," promised the Germans.

Following this step, they were allowed into the station lobby, where each person received a big loaf of bread. A German came by, placing a lanyard with a numbered card round the neck of every evacuee. Outfitted in this manner, they proceeded toward the platforms, where a line a carriages awaited, their doors open. Some Germans arrived, accompanying French women and saying their goodbyes to them. There was one woman, clearly pregnant, who clung to her lover, a tall young Bavarian. She sobbed, cried, begged to stay. He had to push her toward the carriage, tear himself away from her, and took off crying. Another woman joked with two soldiers and told them cheerfully, "Yes, yes, after the war ..." She was supposedly going to France to rejoin her husband. The rest of the herd – a group of emaciated and grief-stricken women, sickly children, a horde of half-starved individuals wearing misery and suffering on their brows – watched these scenes in silence.

The evacuees climbed onto the train. Little Camille was filled with wonder. It was the first time in his life he had ridden on a train. The carriages were comfortable, for in the last year of the war the Germans, less certain of victory, treated evacuees much better than at the beginning. They no longer gave them cattle cars but second- and third-class carriages. After a minute to find seats and stow bags, the train slowly pulled away. It headed toward Tourcoing. Along the siding, hanging from the fences, squeezing onto the parapets of the Pont de l'Alma, a multitude was waving from afar, shouting to those who were leaving, "Goodbye! Goodbye ..." The train went down into the big cutting along rue de Cassel, and the parting came to an end.

The first hours passed quickly. There were lots of things to do: parcels to arrange, dispositions to make for the journey. Camille was running from window to window and suddenly shouted in surprise. Jacqueline recognized their neighbour, Big Semberger – who had managed to have himself evacuated on account of "illness" – sitting in a corner of the carriage. The others looked askance at him. He was suspected of paying the Germans handsomely for the privilege of leaving. For they did not easily release able-bodied men. They could only be persuaded with gold. Semberger was thus held in suspicion. People said, "A big strong man like him! He'll get it when we arrive in France!"

He sensed the hostility. He did what he could, made himself useful, hoisted suitcases up to the racks, handed out slices of German sausage in an effort to make amends. Soon he struck up some songs, his entire repertoire. Folks joined in the chorus. The atmosphere even became rather cheerful once they had eaten and sung for a time. The afternoon was spent in this manner as the trained rolled along, uncoiling a trail of dirty smoke across the vast plains of bare clay, where the first shoots of oats and wheat were budding.

Toward evening the passengers fell silent, one by one. The saddness of nightfall invaded the plains and their spirits. They were weary. Jacqueline and Camille, dejected without realizing it, watched through the carriage door. Camille's eyes were fixed on a big white cloud that the setting sun was turning pink. He pointed it out to Jacqueline.

"Look at that cloud," he said, "perhaps it's over Roubaix ..."

He started to break into tears. His contagious despair infected everyone. Only at this moment, it seemed, did they realize the strange adventure they had emarked upon, this exodus, this exile from their native land, which they would undoubtedly never see again. Tears flowed freely. To chase away the gloom, Big Semberger had to intervene once more and strike up his tunes in the loudest voice. The passengers perked up. The lamps had been lit. But folks were singing more from obligation than real enthusiasm when the soldiers guarding the train entered the compartment. They explained, "We're putting out the lights. The train is passing near the front. Talking and lights are forbidden."

A minute later they were plunged into blackest night. The train slowly trundled through the darkness. The sound of the cannonade could not be heard, only a red line seen on the left, close at hand, where bombs were bursting, the big muticoloured flashes of rockets. People whispered: "The front, the front ..."

And, with lumps in their throats, they watched the nearby horizon, the hell of thousands of men.

The procession continued for a brief half hour. Then the train moved away from the front and disappeared into the shadows. The lamps had been relit. People got ready for bed. The children were put to sleep on the luggage racks. The sick were given benches so they could lie down. Semberger, still full of zeal, made do with a seat in the lavatory.

The following afternoon they arrived in a village of the Ardennes. The good Belgians were awaiting the French evacuees with enthusiasm. How could the inhabitants of an isolated hamlet have known that two unaccompanied children were in the convoy? But somehow they knew. Everyone at the station clamoured for "the two little orphans." At first Jacqueline did not understand that they were talking about Camille and her. The children and the rest of the company received a warm welcome at town hall. They were given potatoes, meat, and other extraordinary things to eat. In the midst of dinner, Camille thought again of his home and his mother, was taken with another fit of crying, and drew tears from everyone else.

The group spent a month in the village. The Germans imposed this delay on all evacuees to prevent them from providing any useful intelligence upon arrival in France. Rations were distributed. Jacqueline went to get them like the adult women and sold the lard to earn a little money. Each evacuee was housed with a resident. It was strange; people had already grown accustomed to each other, found friends and lovers. The woman who had set out to rejoin her husband – the one whom two Germans had accompanied to the station – was living with an old farmer. She had immediately seduced him. She had taken care of him, washed him, brushed him up. She stole loads of his money, taking advantage of this short interlude with remarkable zeal. Others flirted with the Germans. Jacqueline and Camille were staying on the second storey of a cabaret where dances were held on Sundays. In the bedroom floor was a hole for tossing down pigeon rings on race days.* Through it, Camille watched the women dancing with the Germans. The tall young Bavarian had even rushed over from Roubaix to spend a few more days with the pregnant woman who had made the desperate goodbyes. And he returned to see her quite often.

The month came to an end, the evacuees headed off again joyfully, and yet it was another wrenching departure for more or less all of them. Mankind puts down roots so quickly.

They only travelled at night. During the daytime, they were cooped up in some village station or other, waiting once more for nightfall. The authorities did not want for them to see much of Germany.

---

*To time a racing pigeon, a trainer attached a rubber ring – bearing a serial number – to the bird's leg. On race days, pigeons were taken from their roosts to a central starting point and released. When a bird returned to its roost, the trainer removed the ring and inserted it in a special clock that marked an internal ribbon with a time stamp. To determine a winner, competitors took their clocks to race headquarters, where officials unsealed the clocks and calculated and compared the average speed of each bird. Because timing clocks were expensive, racing club members often pooled their resources and shared them. In the cabaret described above, the second floor undoubtedly served as a roost for several pigeons. When the pigeons returned, the trainers removed the rings and – to save time – dropped them through a hole in the floor to a club member who inserted the rings in the timing clock. See Martin Johnes, "Pigeon Racing and Working-Class Culture in Britain, c. 1870–1950," *Cultural and Social History*, 4, no. 3 (2007): 364.

The train went through Luxembourg, where the passengers ate some soup. They recognized Strasbourg at dawn. Passing over a viaduct, Jacqueline caught sight of a long wide boulevard at the end of which the tall and imposing cathedral rose into view. Then the train crossed a bridge over the Rhine. The convoy stopped a little farther on, because day was coming. The evacuees were assailed by a herd of Russian prisoners. They tossed leftovers to the Russians and saw some Germans fighting with them – hitting them with rifle butts – to get at the scraps.

Little was glimpsed of Germany, traversed like this in the darkness. The passengers dozed, only waking round two o'clock in the morning as the train was stopping in Offenburg. The rumour spread: "Switzerland, soon we'll be in Switzerland ..." They had to get off, undergo a final search. Then hot coffee was distributed. German women served it and acted friendly. Since the departure, on the whole, the evacuees could not complain about the Germans. It seemed they wanted the French to miss them. The train left again at dawn.

The evacuees crossed splendid landscapes: large valleys between distant ranges of steep mountains white with snow, forests, bottomless ravines, wild gorges, things that people from Flanders could hardly imagine. They arrived in Basel on a dazzling spring day, pulling into the concourse of a huge station, magnificently clean, decked out with French colours, and where an enormous crowd was waiting, brandishing little flags. The train stopped amid a clamour of joyous welcome. The passengers stepped off, were greeted with enthusiasm. As for the German soldiers, they remained on the train, whose doors were closed. A station master tied off the handles, sealed the entries. One now had the impression that it was them, the Germans, who were imprisoned within. The émigrés shook their fists at them, heaped scorn and insults upon them, took vengeance for four years of appalling tyranny.

The Swiss welcomed the French evacuees in grand style, with warm baths and copious, refined meals. The poor folks cried upon tasting such fare. They climbed back onto a luxurious train, not unlike a parlour on wheels, where they lounged while the procession of mountains, valleys, gorges, and lakes began anew. Swiss nurses onboard the train provided explanations. They pointed out French prisoners of war, saying, "They're poilus!"*

---

*"Poilu" is a slang term for the French infantryman of World War I. "Poilu" literally means "hairy one" in reference to the beards that men often grew during frontline service.

The word was shocking. The evacuees did not understand what they meant. The barrier was watertight. The expression would not reach the Nord till after the liberation.

The hospitality of the French toward their compatriots did not match that of the Swiss. The difference was noticeable from the moment of arrival in Évian. The bureaucrats charged with reception of evacuees were overwhelmed. They had seen too much misery, grown indifferent. Their initial emotion and enthusiasm had been blunted. Evacuees were no longer rare commodities. The convoy was received like all the others, coldly and without giving it much attention. Men were separated from women, boys from girls. It was for the best. But for Jacqueline and the others, it was an unpleasant experience. The Germans and the Swiss had been less severe.

The evacuees had to undergo humiliating, painful medical exams. It was to be expected. So many tubercular, mangy, even syphilitic cases had arrived from the Nord. Screening was necessary. But the ordeal was distressing for the poor wretches subjected to these minor harassments upon returning to the motherland, which they had so loved, so missed. Officials seized all of Jacqueline's money. It was local currency. She could not have used it in France. But the situation was no less upsetting. Her mother had stressed that she was not to part with her money under any circumstance. Then, at the hotel, some of the luggage was lost. There was such confusion that packages and suitcases disappeared. The evacuees recalled the Germans, their inimitable administration, their iron-clad organization. In spite of everything, they had not lost the luggage. People honestly began to recognize real virtues in the Germans. Denouncing Big Semberger was completely forgotten.

After a few weeks' stay in Évian, then in Lyon at the Parc de la Tête d'Or, the Laubigier children were placed with an old woman named Mrs Endive, from Belleville-sur-Saône.

Jacqueline, who wrote well, had found favour in the sight of the director of the refugee bureau. Thanks to him she had obtained a small job in the office. He liked her and protected her. Every day little Camille – who was miserable in the Parc de la Tête d'Or – came to see his sister, his scarf wrapped round his waist, his hair tousled, and his mood inflamed by a fight with one or another of the local boys. Jacqueline was distraught at failing in her duty, of her inability to watch over him.

One day she learned that he was sick and would not be coming. The Spanish flu was running rampant in Lyon. The director said that Camille was contagious, but in no danger, and could not come. Jacqueline was tormented by anxiety.

Around noon one day, a little old lady arrived at the office. She was wearing a pince-nez and very simply but meticulously dressed. In a high-pitched voice she announced, "I am Mrs 'Ondive.'"

The director went over to her, and Jacqueline, a little embarrassed, awkwardly rose to her feet.

"I've come looking for Miss Laubigier and her brother."

"Well, Madam," said the director, smiling, "here's your little protégé ..."

Jacqueline stepped forward timidly. The old lady looked at her in alarm: "An urchin! But she's an urchin! I'd asked for a proper young lady! What'd you expect me to do with this girl! I'm too old, and I can't ... And then what about her little brother?"

The director talked to her in a low voice. Whatever he said made an impression on Mrs Endive. She departed, saying that she would return for Jacqueline as soon as the director had reviewed her file and given his consent. For a serious inquiry was undertaken before assigning children in this manner.

· · ·

Little Camille had been confined to his bed and was delirious. He had held out till the last moment, resisted as long as possible, and continued going to see his sister at the office. Now he was no longer able. They thought he was dying. Mrs Endive went to see him. She was a good woman aside from the little eccentricity that led her to call herself Mrs Ondive, to avoid the absurdity of being named after a variety of lettuce. Her heart had been touched by this little boy whom she did not know and who was on the verge of death. She remained at his bedside the whole afternoon. From time to time, when the nurses stepped away, she pulled a little flask from beneath her petticoat and made Camille take a big sip. It smelled like brandy and burned terribly.

Camille always claimed that it was the brandy that saved him.

· · ·

The children lived with old Mrs "Ondive" in Belleville-sur-Saône. Camille went to school and got into fights with local boys who called him a "Boche du Nord." He tore up innumerable knee breeches, shocking Mrs Endive by his destructive tendencies. She had, in contrast, grown attached to Jacqueline. She would have liked for Jacqueline to remain with her. She had no children of her own. Old age would have been pleasant in the company of this dear girl who was good and brave. But Jacqueline and Camille did not forget their mother and Alain – whose whereabouts were unknown – and who were both perhaps dead. In the evenings they would retreat to a corner of the yard to talk between themselves about Roubaix and to cry openly.

Each week, in her capacity as "head of household," Jacqueline had to present herself to the authorities in order to receive the allowance and the rations for the two of them. Since she was so young, so little, the agent too had taken a liking to her, poked gentle fun at her, and called her "the householder"!

Chapter Four

The men were somewhere near Prémesques, on a little hill that had once been wooded, overlooking Armentières and the plain: in the runis of a château, in fact. At the foot of the hill lay a swamp. On the hillside stood what remained of a large wood: dead, metre-high tree stumps riddled with thousands of bullet holes. Pits, craters – some brand-new, still fresh, the clay sparkling yellow, others old and overrun by grass – were scattered about. Amid these relics was the forced labour camp. It overlooked the flat, grassy, waterlogged countryside – a perfidious marsh where water glistened between stands of wild vegetation and where little misshapen ponds indicated the locations of shell bursts. Bushes grew at random, together with clumps of grass and the dazzling flowers of abandoned fields. Huge and splendid butterflies – like those of ancient times – had suddenly returned. Barbed wire entanglements, big skeletons of dead horses, the carcass of a tank, half-filled furrows – the remants of trenches – put the finishing touches on the bitter desolation of the steppe. The front was less than four kilometres away. The forced labourers – the "red armbands" – had their base camp on the hillside. After work they went back up, a long line of skinny, tanned men, like a gang of convicts. The rags they wore revealed their distress: faded raincoats, velvet pea jackets, old hunting vests, bits of furniture upholstery, cloaks fashioned from threadbare carpets, and German army pants whose origin had been masked by dyeing them a greenish colour and ripping off the braids. A few rare men still wore the uniform of the "red armbands": a jacket and pants cut down the back and along the legs and restiched with big strips of yellow cotton, to make the detainees easily identifiable and thereby prevent escape.

Alain was working alongside the others. He had lost weight. His haggard features had bronzed and hardened. He wore a faded, tattered, hole-ridden vest of black wool, riding breeches with leather bottoms, brown canvas puttees, and espadrilles. On his head was a kerchief tied at the corners. Most of the men, like Alain, wore kerchiefs knotted in this manner – old madras rags in greys, reds, and blues – giving them the appearance of pirates. Poorly shaven beards seemed to have aged these fellows. The prickly, dirty scruff was on Alain's cheeks too, and weariness lent him a grimace marring his mouth and his features. The faces of Alain and his companions above all bore the bitterness, the cross and hardened expressions of men weighed down by an excess of misery.

The front was quite nearby. A loud and constant rumbling came from its direction, like the far-off din of an enormous ironworks. Alain's crew had been slaving away the whole day, finishing a dreadful project. They were digging a trench across the plain to bury an electric cable that the Germans wanted to conceal. An infernal sun blazed. The men were slopping about in water, which they had hit just a metre below the surface. As the ditch gradually advanced, two of them unrolled a big bobbin, laid the cable, and buried it. The sun baked their skulls. The labourers waded through the putrid, insipid water filled with rotting carcasses, and died of thirst in the midst of plenty. Sweat poured across their faces like rain. Their arms swelled. The pickaxe felt like it was made of lead, too heavy to pull from the soil, too exhausting to wield. They ceased making progress and had to work ten times harder. They could feel the veins in their arms bulging, ready to burst. And if they straightened up, panted for a moment, took the time to wipe their brows, a German came running.

"Faster! Faster!"

They protested, exhibited signs of revolt.

"Oh, fuck you!"

And immediately a baton was raised, a revolver brandished. They piped down, gathered their tools, and started up again. The water rose to their stomachs. They fumed like worn-out horses. They could actually see cramps forming – balls of tense muscle beneath the thin, lean skin. It was enough to bend a forearm or a leg to bring on a cramp in the calf, the hollow of the knee, the biceps – the torture of that variety of muscle knot caused by overwork. The men were not even allowed to leave the ditch to urinate. They relieved themselves standing up, producing an acidic and dark red liquid, the thick, cloudy, and painful urine of an animal wasting away, consuming its own flesh.

"Faster! Faster!"

They took up their spades and pickaxes again. The handle rubbed their hands raw. An oily liquid oozed from ruptured blisters, the skin peeling off in shreds. What saliva they had clung to palates and lips as if it were glue. And at times a shell would come hurtling from the front, making a great racket. They had to drop everything, run take cover under a road-mending wagon, wait for the explosion, and start over.

Finally, after eight hours of this agony, they returned to the camp. They passed by the canteen to get a dixie of soup. Then they went off to bed.

The hut that served as the canteen was overrun. Each fellow held out his dixie and received a ladle of oily water in which floated slices of beet and a scrap of boiled meat. Then he scampered off and found a corner of the camp where he could eat alone, like an animal, for the prisoners stole both food and dixies from each other. Large or small, the dixie was always filled to the brim. Here a big dixie was worth its weight in gold.

Alain was heading toward his shack, all the while fishing for slices of beet in his dixie. There were a dozen such huts – long structures made of wood and tarred cardboard, flimsy, rotten, half-inundated by the rains, half-destroyed by gales and shockwaves from the shellbursts – black, squalid, teetering heaps. Oil cloths and wire mesh covered the windows. Along the walls lay mounds of tin cans, rotting fabric, animal bones, broken glass, and other garbage. In the gathering twilight, a faint glimmer behind the oil cloths indicated an occasional candle or fire within.

The third shack was the one belonging to Alain's team. He went inside. It was a long, dark tunnel with a dirt floor and an A-framed ceiling traversed by beams. Ranged along the walls were two rows of iron bedsteads and piles of bags, clothes, rags, toolboxes, and old scraps of wood. In the middle of the room, in the half-light, was a smoky fire, black and red, sinister, rising in gaseous plumes and crimson tongues toward the roof, and escaping through a big, misshapen hole toward the sky. A few chaps were sitting around the fire, feeding it with bits of noisome tarred cardboard. A smell of burned pitch filled the air, mixing with the strong odours of a filthy, massive humanity and the wild aroma of a horse shank that had just been grilled over the polluted flames. The men had shared it out and were devouring the bits of flesh as they sat by the fire.

Alain went straight to bed so he could eat the rest of his soup while sitting on his layer of woodchips. The lodgers did not even have straw mattresses. They slept on boards arranged in tiers and covered with grass or sawdust. Alain's bed was very high up, right below the ceiling. Alain had actually engaged in a long struggle before obtaining this coveted spot. Here he was positioned above the rest. Neither wood chips nor garbage fell his way. Alain was still disgusted by memory of his first bed, which he had shared with Jules, nicknamed "the Rotter," a fellow suffering from a kind of oozing eczema called beard rash. Alain had abandoned him for the fellow on the tier below, an unfortunate type with a reputation for bed wetting. In the end, by virtue of his fists, Alain had conquered his present station. His bed buddy was Blaton. Blaton had died that morning after eating too much salt. He had been desperate to get home. He had told Alain, "You'll see, I'll stuff myself with salt, and I'll get lucky ... You'll see, I'll faint and they'll let me go."

That morning the men had not been alarmed to see Blaton tumble to the pavement. But when they picked him up, he was really and truly dead. He had eaten too much salt. They had returned his body to the shack. But during the day the rats had gnawed at his feet and his calves. He was buried the next morning. Blaton's was the second death that week. The day before, Alain had dug a grave for his friend Vlietz, who had been killed by the Germans for attempting to escape.

Alain contemplated these events while emptying the dixie he was holding between his thighs. Lice were crawling up his bare feet. He was scratching himself with one hand, instinctively, while continuing to eat. The lice were huge and grey, marked with a white spot on the back. Since this feature had a rather vague resemblance to a cross, folks said that the Emperor had decorated the lice too, awarded them the Iron Cross ...

Around Alain, the hubbub of the shacks went its usual turn, in an acrid and potent atmosphere smelling of animality, tobacco, and smoke from the pitch. Jules the Rotter, standing below Alain, his head level with the bed, was shaving with a razor blade held between his fingers, scraping his rough and inflamed skin. Bidart, called the Belly, was playing poker with Netje and three others. "Mussel," a Tourquennois who sold fish and owed his mollusklike nickname to this profession, was sitting cross-legged in the middle of the floor, with his back to the fire. He blew on a harmonica while a group of spectators clapped to the beat and encircled two pairs of roughnecks dancing strange numbers with lots of twists and turns, waltzing as they held each other by the neck, the shoulders, the hair, hopping on one foot while spinning round, or even down on their knees. "Mussel" nodded his head to the music, puffing away, making the harmonica move across his lips in lively fashion, passing from one tune to the next: "The Baby Waltz," "C'mon My Chick," "My Girl," and other samples of a surprisingly extensive repertoire. Donghe, a fellow of questionable morals, lay stretched on his bed, holding a sharp drill bit between his fingers, marking number holes on some dice in preparation for blackening them. Babin, squatting in front of the candle, opened his mouth as if to swallow the flame. A string of drool hung from this fetid hole, a maw like a redish cavern, whose entrance was guarded by a line of black stumps. Sitting across from him, his friend Foubert was boldly examining the chasm, risking a finger, gently wiggling an incisor. Babin was moaning incomprehensible words and unleashing copious amounts of saliva. He had an enormous lower abdomen distended by an inguinal hernia, which was clearly visible beneath his pants. He was known as "the Big Cock." And Donghe was known as "the Brute" for expressing his love of humanity, as the saying went, by quipping that his pregnant sister would be "calving soon." Here the men used a mixture of patois and slang that not even the troops could match.

Which of these men had denounced Vlietz? For he had been denounced; it was an everyday occurrence. These fellows – partners in misery – most of whom, like Alain, were here because of a betrayal, an anonymous letter, betrayed each other in turn, not permitting one comrade to have more daring or luck than another. Vlietz had made careful preparations for his attempt. He had saved up crackers. He had traded a hundred cigarettes and three bars of soap for Alain's ankle boots. He had managed to get hold of a compass, the only one in the camp. It had cost him an inflatable pillow, an accordion, and other rare items. All of the transactions must have alerted a jealous rival. Vlietz was sold out and captured immediately. He had made his escape on Sunday night. He had used wire cutters to snip the links of the fence that still surrounded the camp in a few spots, and which the sentries rarely kept an eye on. As he was heading into the darkness, he fell right into the hands of four Germans who were waiting for him. He was taken to the office. The other men, from their huts, could hear the screaming, the begging, the cries of agony. Then Vlietz was placed in solitary confinement. He languished there for two days. When the men walked nearby, they could hear his death rattle. He passed away on the third day.

Alain had buried him with the help of two Germans. He had bought the ankle boots from them. The compass had disappeared.

Alain had resolved to escape as well. Vlietz's adventure – such a striking incident – had decided him. He breathed not a word to anyone and made his preparations in secret. He had traded the remainder of his tobacco and soap for some crackers. He had used a big nail, whose head he had worn off and which he had fixed to a piece of wood, to make a weapon of sorts. He had sharpened the point and pounded it on a rock until he had approximated the shape of a triangular file. Alain's whole body shuddered when he thought of his house, his mother. He was afraid to dwell on such things for too long. Vlietz's attempt and death seemed to crystalize Alain's own decision. Everything would be over in a single stroke. He too would flee and either get home or die trying. Home ... To live there in seclusion, in the attic or the cellar, hidden away but with his family again, to return to his lifestyle from the early days of the war – what a beautiful dream...!

Alain dispelled the vision – so desirable it was painful – and forced himself to return to reality. Two gamblers situated below his bed, out of his line of sight, were having a row over a missing trump. Another fellow was delousing himself, still another counting the winnings from a game of poker, in hundred-mark bills. Even amid such appalling circumstances, these types had lots of money and played for high stakes, winning and losing hundreds of marks with soldiers from the front.

Near the dying fire, Mussel – squatting, waxing nostalgic in the presence of his audience – was still blowing on his harmonica, producing high-pitched, fast-paced music, mangling the favourite song of the lowlifes of Roubaix, which the chorus round him was singing softly, as if taking vengeance on the Germans:

Take off your slicker, Mein Herr,
We'll scrub you like a dish!
And smack your ugly mug
Just as much as you wish ...

It was one of the countless songs, epic poems in the style of Homer, born spontaneously from the popular imagination without any identifiable author, without ever having been printed or perhaps written down, and which were thus spread orally, by word of mouth. A few main topics – the femmes à Boches, the Germans, the political prisoners, the red armbands – inspired these chansons de geste, which disappeared with the war's end and which will never be recovered.

And then from the sky came a droning, a far-off droning – low, faint, and sinister amid the brouhaha of the shack, gradually obtruding, bringing the other noises to a stop for a moment, and – in the sudden silence – becoming monstrous.

"Fuck! Them again!"

"Netje, the candle, look out!"

The brusk extinction of the flame plunged them into darkness. All that remained was the glow of the dying and smoking fire. They fell silent, consumed by anxiety. The droning increased, drew nearer. There were at least ten of them – ten French planes. All of a sudden came a huge blast, an explosion that made the hut shudder, like a ship going down. Saucepans jangled, boards creaked. The men grabbed hold of their bedsteads. One could feel the timberwork groaning and swaying back and forth.

Two, three, four bombs burst. Anti-aircraft guns barked in anger, searchlights fell across the oil cloth windows, and clapboards began pulling apart. The French were aiming for the ammunition dump at the foot of the hill.

There was a respite. The men breathed again. Then came the oily voice of Bidart: "The bastards! If only they'd crash into the spire of the château."

"Good God, yes indeed!"

Such was the general sentiment. They were sick of the air raids! Every evening Allied planes flew in like this, targeting the ammunition dump. One day they would catch the men unawares. No, enough already, they would have preferred to be killed outright rather than endure this nightly agony. All patriotism was forgotten. At times certain fellows came prowling: civilians, French spies. They searched, asked questions, but the men were on their guard.

"Ammunition dumps, artillery batteries, here? No, no, nothing of the sort!"

Let them bugger off ... both of them, French and Germans, the ones doing the fighting. Here they were sick of it – the war of the others. These men wanted to live.

II

They were moving shells, unloading a transport that had just arrived. Teams of two carried each of the long, sinister, torpedo-like cylinders toward the sheds, stacking them carefully. The men were used to handling shells; it no longer made much of an impression on them. A soldier – an old man who was part of the "Genesung Abteilung" – was supervising.* He had been wounded and posted here to recover. He was walking about with his rifle lowered, leaving the men in peace. He was not accustomed to the role of prison guard.

Alain stopped working. He grabbed his stomach and motioned to the German, who understood and consented. Alain stepped away and jumped into a shell hole.

A minute later the soldier suddenly realized that the man had not come back. He turned round, searching desperately. Far off, already quite tiny, he saw a silhouette fleeing, disappearing. He had two or three quick, abrupt thoughts. An escape ... He would be sent back to the front, the trenches again ... The dirty scoundrel!

He raised his gun, fired, then threw it to the ground in despair and broke into tears.

Alain travelled through the fields under cover of darkness, for three nights in a row. He wandered about, guided by an elementary sense of direction he had acquired from spending so much time in the wilds. He ate oats, munching on the bitter grains and spitting out the husks. He arrived at Roubaix exhausted, staggering, weak from hunger and fatigue, trembling from nervous excitement at the thought of escaping from the hell of Prémesques.

He found Épeule shrouded in darkness. No one was home. He feared some misfortune, knocked at the door of his Aunt Flavie. And he learned from her and his cousin François that his mother was at their house, sick, at death's door, and that Jacqueline and Camille had left for France all on

---

*A Genesung Abteilung was a convalescent company.

their own. He could not stay here and hide. His mother would die of fright. He would have to return to Prémesques.

Alain let himself drop into a chair and start crying. He could not go on. So much effort, so much hardship – for nothing. He would never see his mother again! She would never even know he had come. He could not grab so much as a bite or a drink. He set off in despair – beside himself, unwilling to accept the situation – to give himself up at army headquarters.

• • •

There were seven men on guard duty, seven German soldiers, when Alain returned to Prémesques under the escort of two green devils. At the first blow of a rifle butt, he thought his head would split open.

It is unbelievable that an organism as fragile as the human stomach can endure such terrible shocks as flying kicks from steel-toed boots without being reduced to pulp. Trampled upon by two or three eighty-kilo men, intestines ought to rupture, ribs crack. A blow from an iron bar right in the face should make eyeballs burst from their sockets, teeth break. It is truly incredible that such a delicate machine can endure this sort of punishment, reconstitute itself, and start functioning again ...

Alain pondered these things during the four days when, left for dead, he lay sprawled out in the shack that served as a cell, and where Vlietz had died beforehand. Alain's mind was clouded, his body a mass of suffering. He no longer recognized the touch of his swollen and distended face. He spit up clots of blood, emitted murky urine, endured the inscrutable, agonizing work of the body reconstructing itself cell by cell, reestablishing connections, rejoining networks, draining discharge, expelling dead matter, slowly resuming normal rythms.

When he awoke on the fifth day, he realized in astonishment that he was hungry.

III

It was the arrival of François van Groede that saved Alain.

François, Aunt Flavie's son, had become a lock keeper. He proved to be such an odd civil servant – always absent, always missing, present only when coal barges were passing through – that the Germans had tired of him, offered him a short stay in the prison at the Roubaix bathhouse, and sent him from there to find a new direction in Prémesques.

Younger than Alain, less robust, less spirited, less capable of defending himself, François was in a matter of weeks reduced to a sad state. Stunned by the dreadful spectacle of the shacks, the camp, and the work, robbed, cheated, bullied, oppressed in every respect, unskilled at finagling or defending himself, the object of ridicule among his comrades and cruelty at the hands of the guards, he was soon completely dazed and exhausted. He got sick and sought out the army doctor, who sent him packing. François had to return to work and concluded that he would never see Roubaix again.

Alain had only run across him two or three times. François had given him news of his mother and his house, that was all. They did not live in the same hut, were not part of the same work gang. Alain had paid his cousin little heed.

Alain had changed considerably since his return to Prémesques. He had endured too much. He was sullen, bitter. He hardly spoke, had no friends, helped no one and asked for no one's help. Alain spent time only with a few Germans from the front with whom he smoked shag tobacco and drank rum and brandy. He had furiously rejected everything in which he had believed, arriving at a calm and silent despondency. He had seen too much of life's realities, the strong oppressing the weak, the wrong triumphant, a savagery common to French and Germans alike, envy, hatred, the selfishness of a herd of poor wretches who could not even manage to get along, to help each other out. He had no friends besides these soldiers from the front, who were much like him – numbed by life in the trenches, permeated by the same spirit of universal indifference. Alain and these fellows understood one another. They had long discussions, dawdling together in the only spot where one could find something approaching peace. On the far end of the camp was a latrine, a ditch at the edge of which lay a large beam. Alain and his buddies would sit there, pants down, talking, daydreaming, fraternizing. German soldiers returning from the front got along better with the prisoners than with the guard troops from the rear. The latrine had given rise to conflict. The prisoners were staying too long. The guards cut sharp angles into the beam. But the edges had been whittled down. The guards added angle irons whose ridges stuck into one's buttocks. But at present the men were taking along straw cushions.

Around noon one day, Alain had arrived late for work. He had been drinking the night before. Since he had put up a fuss and taken a swing at the guards, they had tied him to the "punishment post," where he had remained bound, hanging by ropes that cut into his flesh. Some soldiers from the front had arrived, quarreled with the guards, and released him. Such disputes were common.

Alain had returned to his pallet, his mind clouded, disgusted with himself and with others as twenty-year-olds often are, regardless of circumstance. On his arms and his face, he had noticed marks from beatings that he could no longer recall. When Alain rejoined his work crew, he learned that his cousin François was sick and wanted to see him. Bidart, who had spotted François, added that he had the runs, that he was white as a sheet and would soon be pushing up daisies.

When work ended, Alain rushed over to Barracks no. 2. The whole afternoon he had been prey to a sense of remorse, which was amplified by recollection of the previous night's binge.

François was huddled in a corner, weak, and "white as a sheet." On the ground beside him lay a dixie with slices of beet floating in water.

"You're not well?"

François opened his eyes, recognizing his cousin without surprise. He had already developed a certain worrisome indifference. He whispered, "Not very ..."

"What's the matter?"

"I can't keep anything down."

"What hurts?"

"My legs, my head ... I can't stand."

"Are you hungry?"

"Yes, but I spit up the beets."

Alain thought for a minute.

"Wait for me tonight. I'll bring you some meat."

"Meat?"

"You'll see."

• • •

"The horses are over there!" whispered Bidart.

Concealed by a stand of trees, the men were in a hollow near the edge of a clearing. Four of them – Alain, Bidart, and two Germans – had come to kill a horse some three kilometres from the camp. The vast clearing stretched before them, surrounded by the black shadows of the wood, and bathed in moonlight. Here and there, dark shapes lay in the tall grass. In the middle of the field stood the curbstone of a well, topped by a handle from which a pulley was suspended. There was no wind, only the light, steady rustling of the leaves in the trees and the magical peace of nighttime.

"Let's go," whispered Bidart. "Komme, too."

He slipped through the thickets, ducked under the barbed wire fence, and entered the clearing. The others followed him. The four of them moved forward, black vertical silhouettes blurred by the silver light flooding over them. They hesitated, then dispersed into a line, in a vague attempt at encirclement.

They had neither gun nor ax, nothing but two bayonettes and two knives. It was not much for such large game. They sensed the difficulty and advanced with visible uncertainty. For so long now, man has lost the habit of close-quarters, hands-on attack. Of the four of them, the most daring was Bidart, a real roughneck who knew how to strike.

They were in the middle of the clearing when the horses got spooked. The men saw them stand up, snorting. The animals had retained the ancient, wary spirit of the herbivore. They gathered together, sniffed the wind, moved as a herd toward the far end of the clearing, in a gentle, supple gallop that hardly disturbed the grass and that seemed as eerie as the moonlight, the setting, the entire atmosphere.

"Komme," called Bidart.

The men widened their circle. The elastic, living net tightened round the animals, pushing them toward a corner. The hunters had to run and jump, arms spread wide, to prevent the horses from slippling through. The guys stumbled, fell, started over. In the end they managed keep the horses together in one spot. Bidart and the others advanced slowly to avoid panicking them. Squeezed together, nervous, the animals pricked their ears, crowded in, made short gallops. One of them whinnied. They were clearly frightened by the apparent danger. The men halted. Only Bidart continued advancing, for he had once driven coal wagons and understood horses. He shouted, "Whoa! Whoa!"

The animals stopped, listened.

"There now! There ...!"

He kept moving forward. The human voice, the familiar words, reassured the animals and calmed them. They reverted to their obedient ways, their submission to man, the master. The horses let him approach. Bidart's shadow disappeared amid those of the animals. And he returned to his comrades leading a big chestnut horse by the mane and the nostrils.

The four men moved off with the animal. They instinctively avoided the middle of the clearing, the bare expanse illumined by the pure light. They headed back toward the edge of the wood, saying nothing as they walked single file. The horse flicked its tail, nodding its head and following dutifully, under the impression that it was heading for work.

They stopped at the corner of the field.

"There," said a German, pointing toward the shadows.

"Nein," said Bidart. "We need to see. Hier, here."

"Who's going to kill it?"

They looked at each other, then the beast. An animal like this one – it was too big. Where should one strike, where should one smite such a powerful creature? In the heart? On the head? It is easy to say. But a horse is strong. It has to be slaughtered in a single stroke. The horse waited peaceably, smelling the grass and huffing. Perhaps a certain insuperable pity clutched at the hearts of the four makeshift butchers. They made for an odd group, gathered round the tall animal in the bluish evening light.

"Hand me your bayonette," said Bidart.

A soldier gave him his bayonette.

"Alain, lower the head and hold the nostrils."

Alain made the horse lower its head. Bidart positioned himself to the side, felt the edge of the bayonette. The horse stretched its neck. And Bidart drew the bright metal weapon across the throat, toward him, slitting the neck with the ancient, sweeping gesture of a sacrificial priest.

Alain instinctively released the animal. It had raised its head in astonishment and jumped aside. It moved off in a great bound, kicked, took some long strides.

From afar, the animal watched them, standing motionless. It was starting to feel the pain. The men could not see the blood streaming over the brown coat of its legs.

"Wait," said Bidart.

They gradually approached. The horse craned its neck, slowly lowered its head. Closer up, they could tell that it was shaking. But its four legs were still braced, planted like stakes in the ground. A shudder passed across its hide, increasing from one moment to the next. It fell to its knees.

Its head swayed, rocking in slow motion. It rolled over gently, lay on its side. It raised its head one last time ...

"Let's take the hindquarters!" said Bidart.

They surrounded the animal. Bidart, squatting between the horse's enormous haunches, plunged a bayonnette into the groin, putting all his weight on the weapon, and opened the round, grass-swollen stomach. A flood of blue entrails poured out with a gush of air. The men tramped about in the muck, stepping on greasy elements, carving living flesh that slipped smoothly beneath the blade. Bidart, his bare arms buried up to the elbows in the horse's stomach, was feeling for the tendons of the femoral joint and cutting them, while the other three – grabbing the leg whole handed – twisted it, turned it, shook it like a tree branch, and ripped it off.

They went back through the wood, two pairs each shouldering a thigh, a long, furry haunch from which blood was dripping. The carcass – cut up, split in two at the stomach – had been left in the clearing.

The group halted a little before the camp. Footsteps were approaching. They dropped the meat and stood motionless. Suddenly Alain, who was in the lead, came face-to-face with two silhouettes. He made out green collars sticking above the greatcoats. Green devils! He stepped back, instinctively feeling for his knife. The Germans came forward. "You're stealing chickens, too?" one of them asked.

"No ... Uh, yes ..." said Alain, still sweating with emotion. "You're not policemen?"

They pointed to the green collars and opened their coats. They were two machine-gunners, whose uniforms had green collars like the policemen's.

Alain's group pointed them toward the remains of the horse. The machine-gunners plunged into the wood, and the others returned to the camp without incident. The rusty barbed wire, long since rent and smashed by the shells, no longer presented an obstacle.

They had built a fire in the middle of the hut. The skinned haunches were hanging from the ceiling, roasting at the end of long strands of wire bent into hooks. A smoky flame licked the dark meat, gilding it, browning it, adorning it with warm and splendid tones. Yellow fat sizzled, turned translucent, crackled as it trickled onto the flames and sent them spurting higher. The blackened bone was smoking. Greasy marrow seeped and overflowed, boiling. Heady steam from the roasting meat and burning fat filled their noses and their stomachs. The men were sitting round the red and black fire, gazing at the sumptuous, oily portions – dripping, bronzed, grazed by short and lively flames – the skin splitting open in spots, allowing congealed blood and precious juices to flow. The dancing, crimson flames lit up strained faces, an avid circle united in expectation of the feast. And everything else – bodies, clothing, and the distant and dark corners of the hut – remained in the shadows.

Each of them downed a bellyful of meat, without bread or wine or salt. Alain had taken a piece for François. He walked through Barracks no. 2. The smell of the meat roused the men as he passed, making their mouths water.

François was waiting. The scent alone revived his spirits. He grabbed the tender morsel with both hands and bit into it. Copious amounts of thick, warm juice squirted into his mouth, flooding it. He swallowed the liquid, practically inhaling it, squeezing and chomping at the meat as if it were a nipple. Life flowed into his veins.

· · ·

François ate meat for five straight days. His strength returned.

Alain made himself François's protector. Alain had become clever and strong, a wolf among wolves. He put these skills to use on behalf of François, purifying them, in a sense, by employing them for the benefit of someone else. Theft, pillage, and plunder – undertaken for the salvation of another – were once again justified by their ends.

François learned much from Alain. François had no survival skills. Alain taught him how to ensure that he could always start a fire by making a lighter from an empty cartridge and tinder from charred linen, and by begging gasoline from tractor drivers, who would drain their carburators for men at the camp.

When gasoline was in short supply, one could light a long piece of cotton rope, keeping it red hot. It burned slowly. And this little glowing ember was enough to produce a flame when touched to a bit of gunpowder. François learned how to steal tarred cardboard to build a fire, how to light wet wood on a bed of gunpowder. He became adept at bartering, at operating in the evening markets, where soap, cigarettes, and crackers served as units of exchange. Oats were traded for ankle boots, broad beans for a jacket, tobacco for a mandolin. The Germans purchased soap to send to Germany and strips of cloth that had been cut into puttees. In exchange they offered tobacco, crackers, and alcohol.

Above all François learned how to find food, get along with Germans from the front, and join them as partners in theft. These soldiers took pity on the prisoners, shared their paltry slices of bread, split small pieces of meat with their French comrades. At night French and Germans went together to pillage horse troughs. They brought back beans, the awful beans that caused indigestion but which one ate anyway, even though they were animal feed. Sometimes the men returned with oats. They could light a fire, heat a sheet of metal, grill the oats on top, and eat them. Hunger had dreadful consequences. The captives were wary of each other and marched to work with their bread strung on a rope and hung round their necks, for fear of thieves and rats. Alain and François made rat traps out of wire. But François could not eat rats unless they had already been skinned. Alain dressed them. Snails disgusted the cousins even more than rats. Once they found a frog on the road. They killed it by smashing it on the ground, cut it in half, and ate it.

After a while, François was allowed to return to Roubaix once every two weeks. But Alain was not. Since his escape, he had been classified as a troublemaker and the corner of his identity card torn off. At a pinch, this measure would alert the guards. On Sunday evenings, François returned with food – a dixie of rice and garden peas. They parcelled it out, made it last a week, counting the peas one by one, consuming twenty a day. Once they had a surprise, a real surprise. Toward the end of the week, in the bottom of a dixie of garden peas, they found a big leg of rabbit! They both started crying from the shock. A piece of rabbit!

François improved, became himself again. Support, protection – he needed nothing more to preserve and sustain him. He felt comforted, reassured. They suffered, but they survived. They could see the end of the war, felt certain it was approaching. In the midst of his troubles, and though the future still looked sad and bleak, Alain at least felt less dejected, less gloomy. And to his surprise, he began to realize that – however hopeless, however miserable one might be – one can still find happiness by setting aside one's own problems to help someone else.

Chapter Five

I

In Herlem, Judith Lacombe had come into conflict with Brook, the village policeman.

Judith had been completely disgraced. Germans went openly to amuse themselves at her house. The populace hated her, despised her, and yet still feared her. The influence of such women with the enemy was well known. When the villagers had need of something, they would even humbly seek her out, begging for a favour from army headquarters. Nearly half the village was indebted to her for help of this nature. No one in Herlem had done as much good as Judith the prostitute. But she did it with a certain indifference, asking for neither thanks nor reward. The strange girl had remained haughty in spite of her downfall. People went to see her and present their petititons, as if she were a power. She would intervene in the event of a fine, an illness, a requisition. The whole village had recourse to her. One day even her father, Lacombe, sent her mother to see if Judith could mitigate a fine of a thousand marks that had just been levied on him for hiding salted pork in his bakehouse.

Brook, for his part, had been the village policeman for six months. The old policeman had died. Lacombe, as so often before, had taken advantage of the situation by naming one of his puppets to the post without even consulting the municipal council. The war facilitated such license, which Marellis had again protested in vain. Brook – fifty-five years old, handsome, tall and strong, with jet-black hair and a becoming moustache – had been bursting with pride since donning the crossbelt and the kepi.

The dream of this narrow-minded, stubborn, and slyly malicious fellow had long been to hold a bit of public authority. He made tyrannical use of it. Vainglorious, the new lord of hill and meadow had proceeded to impose a cruel dictatorship on common citizens, terrorizing the lowly as he in turn licked the boots of the powerful. The big farmers and the Baron des Parges saw him as a servant, and ordinary folks – terrified by the threat of being reported for dirty ditches, stray chickens, or unregistered dogs – tightened their belts to grease his palm. The worst was that all of the tickets directly benefited headquarters, which collected the fines, and individual Germans, of whom Brook – ever the sly fox – had made himself a humble retainer. He saluted the officers, carried their luggage, stoked the fires in their offices, and ran their errands. Thereby elevated in his own eyes, adorned with the incomparable prestige of the uniform, Brook had imagined that Judith – on whom he had long had a crush – would be duly honoured by his advances. But the strange girl, debased harlot though she was, retained a singular pride: a fierce love of her independence. Brook was unceremoniously shown to the door. Judith had treated the overbearing representative of the public powers with contempt. Brook was shocked and infuriated in the extreme. He promised himself to have her registered as a prostitute after the war. In the meantime, he resorted to petty forms of vengeance. Judith had never been subject to medical inspection. Brook pointed this out to headquarters. Henceforth she could be seen each week among the women of ill repute whom headquarters monitored and examined on a regular basis.

Judith's shame touched Pascal Donadieu to the quick. It was painful for him to witness the downfall of this creature he had loved. He suffered all the more since he no longer considered himself beyond reproach. He had been working for the ration board ever since the streetcars had shut down. The underhandedness of his fellows, his own hunger, and his mother's distress had led him to commit some petty thefts, for which he felt a silent remorse. Above all, to retain his modest post, he had had to accept the humiliating terms of Mayor Lacombe.

Lacombe was rather vexed. He had received more than one letter of complaint about the deplorable management of the ration program. Lacombe kept these missives carefully tucked away. People had eventually tired of the situation and gone over his head by addressing themselves directly to the Committee. The Committee, duly alterted, had sent an urgent communiqué demanding the accounts and a detailed register of distributions.

Lacombe felt pressured. Above all, there was the business with Ingleby's sugar, a dozen freight loads that Herlem's villagers had never seen ... Lacombe, who had no gift for writing, had turned to Donadieu for assistance.

Lacombe had Pascal fill out two hundred ration cards with the names of people who had long since evacuated Herlem or who had merely passed through town. These cards covered Lacombe as far at the Committee was concerned. But the affair left Pascal Donadieu with the doubt, the self-loathing, the uncertainty and disgust resulting from an initial capitulation.

The only one who remained incorruptible was Marellis, the tax collector. He came to the distribution and served people with passivity, like an automaton. He had long since given up on the idea of bringing true justice to the situation. But he had refused to resign himself completely. He had suffered too much for his honesty, his righteous indignation. Even his home had been taken. Premelle reigned there as master, made use of the garden, and helped himself to the furniture while Marellis lived in a little room above the café on the square.

A new scandal had led Marellis to intervene, incurring the wrath of the entire ration board. The Germans employed local workers who were paid by the municipality. These men each received seven francs a day. The Germans had come up with the idea of increasing the wages by three francs a head and holding back two francs as a voluntary contribution to the war effort! It was an indirect way of forcing the municipality to pay army headquarters two francs a head each day. The workers had not protested, happy enough at making an extra franc. And Lacombe and Premelle had paid without argument. They knew that, if they refused, the Germans were more than willing to seize the assets of the farmers and the rich.

Marellis ranted, raved, threatened to alert the Committee. The others laughed at him, talked of excluding him from the board's deliberations. There was no recourse, no way around Lacombe's arbitrary authority. Weary, exhausted, Marellis let events take their course, placing his only hope in a victory as yet uncertain but in which he had to believe, despite everything, like some people believe in God – because otherwise it would all be too awful, too terrible. He sat silently through board meetings, mechanically fulfilled his duties as a ration distributor, and passively endured the insults, the derision, the barely disguised mockery of Leuil, Lacombe's pal, who took pleasure in ridiculing Marellis, motivated by an unreasoned hatred akin to that of the villain for the man of honour. Donadieu was a helpless witness to these scenes, which Premelle encouraged with his sniggering.

I I

Ever since Lise and her mother had adopted the two children of the dead woman, they had abandoned all pride, all determination at resistance and independence in regard to the enemy. What they had never consented to for themselves, they had resigned themselves to for the little ones: working for the Germans, coming to terms with them, buying from them and selling to them, accpeting their assistance, stealing from their carts or even from the farmers' fields.

For a time the two women had hoped to leave, to get to France. With Jean dead and the abbé a prisoner in Germany, they no longer had anything tying them to the Nord. Perhaps from France, on the contrary, they might be able to help the abbé again by sending him packages and assistance. They had presented their request for evacuation to the municipal government. The paperwork had gone missing, disappeared. They never heard anything of it. Lacombe had persisted in pursuit of his grudge against them, that spiteful peasant vengeance that holds onto its victims. He had made the files vanish. Lise learned of the situation from Pascal Donadieu, and there was nothing she could do about it.

The Sennevilliers also suffered from the general opprobrium of the village. Fannie's dishonour had rebounded on the women who had taken in the child. Besides, the villagers were not really sure what had happened. Herlem Hill was some distance from town, rendering it a secluded hamlet. Many believed that little Jeannette was Lise's own daughter. An insidious hatred surrounded the Sennevilliers, isolated them, and they suffered from it all the more as the villagers' intransigence so easily complimented the most shameful groveling before the enemy. People went with their children to gather strawberries, blackberries, and wild fruit from the forests of the château, to give to German officers. One day the Crown Prince passed through the village on his way to the front. Townspeople could be seen forming a line and taking off their caps in respect. It seemed that many folks had lost the true sense of things, accepting the idea that the Germans were here to stay. Preparations for a big offensive began in June. Wave after wave of troops, artillery, and materiel and endless convoys of cars and trucks passed through Herlem: an invasion of such magnitude that one would have thought an entire people on the move. And there were villagers who were delighted at the prospect, saying openly: "So much the better! If they advance, if they gain some ground, then we'll get a little relief. We'll be a little farther from the frontlines ..."

Lise would have liked some wheat. None was to be had. The farmers kept it for the Germans, who had reserved it in advance, or else sold it at ridiculous prices in Tourcoing. And Lise had no money. To get a bit of grinding scraps, she had to work in the farmhouses, kneading bread – beautiful wheat bread, yellow, firm, fluffy, with a golden crust, so beautiful that after having baked it she no longer recognized it when she saw it on the farmers' tables. She could not imagine having kneaded, baked, and produced such wonderful loaves! She was paid with bran and cheap flour. When she could manage it in passing, she would take an egg from the henhouse or butter from the cellar. She had reached the point where staying alive had become the top priority, trumping all other concerns. And then, like Donadieu, like many people, in fact, the deplorable example of those who took advantage of the situation ended up diminishing her own resistance and honesty.

Berthe Sennevilliers, the old matron, succumbed as well. These Germans who had killed one of her sons and taken the other, who had ruined her and pillaged the inn, at whose hands she had suffered in every respect – she ended up getting along with them, accepting them. She began to understand that most of them – the ordinary soldiers, a least – were simply victims like her. United by a common suffering, French and Germans inevitably started fraternizing, coming together.

Herlem is fifteen kilometres from Ypres. This part of the rear, so close to the front, witnessed the appalling wretchedness of the German army, the death throes of the imperial eagle. The villagers had to find room for all the troops, give them a place to stay. Berthe and her daughter long remembered a group of fifty men who poured into their home in the middle of the night. Fifty men – fifty boys, really – youths barely out of school, frail, thin, and pallid, whose features, behind the weariness and bewilder-

ment of their first taste of battle, still revelaed a remnant of the enthusiasm and the idealism that had cast them into the abyss. They came from
God knows what part of the line and were awaiting their return to the
front. They arrived en masse, flooded the house, invaded it, and spent the
night pealing off mud, picking off fleas, cleaning and bathing themselves.
They even apologized for the disruption. One could tell that they had not
yet acquired the habit of rudeness, the poor devils.

"We very dirty, Madam, but we good boys."

Lise and Berthe, awakened by the commotion, had positioned themselves by the fireside, no longer able to dream of sleeping, and watched the
men coming and going and bustling about. It was the first time Berthe
had seen such young, such frail boys weighed down by the heavy uniform.
She was aghast. Berthe, the die-hard patriot, ended up suggesting to Lise,
"We could make them a little drop of chicory."

When the troops saw that the dark, warm liquid had been prepared for
them – without their having asked, even as they had considered themselves vile intruders in this place – they were overwhelmed, moved to
tears. They drank the insipid water in gratitude and said, "Ah, Madam, if
only we could go home and come back after the war to thank you ... To
think that we're supposed to kill men, when we wouldn't so much as harm
a rabbit."

Accordingly, having received some potatoes the following day, they
called over Pierre, who was watching them eat, and gave him a plateful.
Pierre took his prize to Lise and Berthe, and from then on host and guest
shared everything they had during the unit's time in Herlem. Berthe had
taken a liking to these boys. She discovered that they too were disillusioned, had the same impression of being naïve – duped – like all honest
folks. They shared the same hatred of the bigwigs, the leaders, suffered
from the same endless privation, had the same longing for loved ones, the
same hunger, the same hatred of the police – the German police, the green
devils. In fact, Berthe had a hard time understanding their unbelievable
contempt for "Beanpole." They mocked him, sent him packing, took the
side of the villagers against him. They warned Berthe when they knew that
a perquisition would take place. They hid her scant victuals in their packs,
then watched with sardonic grins as "Beanpole" searched the nooks and
crannies of the inn. They had the same contempt – the same spite – for
the farmers and the wealthy. They went by night to plunder the haystacks

and the henhouses, returning loaded with victuals. Sometimes, under cover of darkness, they even killed a sheep or a calf out in a pasture and shared the meat with Berthe. Berthe developed a true fondness for the youngest boys. They told her about their families. They sensed her motherliness, confided in her, explained that they had quit school, were still young, had left their mammas behind, that they were sorry ... One could tell they had grown accustomed to being hated, treated as enemies by the occupied population – while still retaining an indomitable youthfulness of spirit that would surface at the first sign of trust and friendship, leading them to pour out their hearts and confide in others, almost too quickly. A friendly word, a sympathetic expression, and they would open up – touched, moved to tears like children drawn to an adult the moment one shows them a little interest and compassion.

And they were children, to be sure. There was Karl, good Karl, the son of ordinary folks from Bavaria ... He had gone home on leave before heading to the front. He had returned from Germany with a watch, a nickel-plated wristwatch. The numbers and hands glowed in the dark.

"This way, you'll be able to see it in the trenches at night," his mother had said when she had bestowed this princely gift upon him.

Karl was so proud of his luminous watch! The day he returned, Old Berthe must have followed him to the cellar a dozen times to admire the glowing dial and revel over it with him. He chuckled in wonderment.

Then there was Reynold, whose mother worked in the Essen munitions plant. He was quiet, pale-skinned. He had been studying to be an accountant. The war had interrupted this dream. He had taken a liking to little Pierre's pet white rabbit. The rabbit's name was Arthur. All day long, Reynold could be seen by the fireside or on the kitchen doorstep with Arthur in his arms. He scratched the rabbit's head, stroked him like a cat, played with him, kissed his muzzle, burst out laughing. And Arthur wiggled his tiny nose and moved his huge ears. There was a real affection between boy and animal.

Another lad, Wilhelm, was a little villager, sturdy and strong. He laboured from dawn till dusk. He dug, turned, sowed, and tended Berthe's garden. He cut the hedges, pruned the pear trees. He worked himself hard, wielding the rake, the spade, the shears, pushing the wheelbarrow, spreading manure, cleaning things up, and returned at night in happy exhaustion. One could tell that he had forgotten the war as he busied himself with such chores. It was unimaginable that these kids would be sent to the front, be forced to kill. One was afraid for them. How could one hate these poor, naïve youngsters? They reminded Old Berthe of her two sons. She could no longer think of them as Germans. She looked after them, washed and mended their undergarments, scolded them and loved them. With a certain shame, she admitted to Lise: "I can't help thinking of them as my boys!"

Other members of the company helped Lise with her trafficking, stealing bundles of cloth from trucks that passed through town, heading toward Roeselare. A bundle contained twelve bags stuffed into a sack. Fresh from the woolen mills of Roubaix, they were being sent to rot as sandbags in the trenches. Lise and her partners emptied the sacks and shared out the bags. Lise used them to make children's clothes that she sold in the village. The soldiers removed the stitches from their bags and sent the fabric to their families in Germany. Oftentimes they also accompanied Lise to Roubaix, where one could no longer travel without a permit. They provided her safe passage. Thus was she able to take vegetables to the city and come home with dry goods. Schumann, the liaison officer, went to Brussels by car once a week. He would bring back sugar, which Lise would then sell. She made a living from this exchange.

She also sold lots of potatoes. Every day a wagonload arrived for the soldiers. Lise had made friends with the transport guards. They managed to distract the driver. While one of them was chatting with him, the other would discretely knock a sack of potatoes into a ditch from which it was later retrieved. A good deal of the farmers' wheat was also stolen. The troops would slip into the fields, flat on their chests, and use scissors to cut ears of grain.

These Germans led a tough life. They drilled each morning for hours on end. Laden with full packs, they had to run through the fields. Many could not finish and collapsed in exhaustion. Beneath their enormous greatcoats, their boots, their massive equipment, they were still little more than children, with thin limbs and youthful faces on which the first whiskers had just begun to appear. Those who gave way too quickly were tied to a post for the rest of the day.

One morning the men learned they would be departing later that evening. They were afraid. At dusk they set off toward Ypres. They marched along the road toward the hilltop, passing the lime kilns. They sang the "Gloria":

Glory, victory!
With heart and hand,
For the Fatherland ...

Many of them waved to the Sennevilliers: "Goodbye, goodbye ..." And
Berthe waved back and cried, "Our soldiers! Our poor soldiers."

They had become "our" soldiers. She had forgotten her hatred.

III

Italian prisoners were now working at the quarry. The Germans had relit
the kilns and were using them to cremate men killed in battle. A railroad
had also been built from the front to Tourcoing, along with concrete shelters, blockhouses, and artillery platforms. Little by little, one gained the
impression that Germans were pulling back in the face of Allied pressure.
The railroad line passed by Herlem.

The Italian prisoners were in frightful condition. They slipped out in
the evening, jumped the fence round the camp, came to knock at the
Sennevilliers' door, and stayed at the inn for hours, warming up. The
women and their guests did not speak the same language, had nothing
to say to each other. All of them were risking terrible punishment, but
the Sennevilliers welcomed the Italians nonetheless, incapable of shutting their door, of refusing a little heat, steaming water, and light to these
unfortunates. Besides, Berthe and Lise had gotten into such a habit of
not having their house to themselves, of constantly seeing strange faces,
new fellows coming and going in their home, that the situation had
become normal.

Of the little German soldiers – the wretched "Marie-Louises" sent into
harm's way to support the final push, the last desperate attempt of the
Empire – not one had returned.* They had been too young, too green ...
From the others – the older ones, the experienced soldiers who came back
from the front – the Sennevilliers learned that the regiment had been
massacred.

---

*"Les Marie-Louises" was the name accorded to young men drafted into Napoléon's
forces in 1814 and 1815. The appellation is a reference to Napoléon's second wife, the
Austrian princess Marie-Louise.

The new arrivals were ferocious beings. Four days after they settled in, "Beanpole" was found along the roadside, strangled, a steel chain wrapped round his neck. As always, army headquarters accused the civilians, and the village was punished with two weeks of early curfew.

These fellows were akin to savages. They were eaten up by lice, frightfully dirty, afflicted by incurable dysentery, with nothing but pitiful scraps of underwear beneath their clothes. Stunned, stupefied, they sat in the sunshine playing endless rounds of cards and drinking "Goldwasser," asking only one thing – to be left here in peace, not to return to the front, not to be put in harm's way again. They had had enough of it. They no longer wanted to keep going. They were often called out at night for relief missions, or to take soup, ammunition, and supplies to the front lines. Or they were ordered into an emergency action somewhere. They refused. They stayed in bed, cursed, swore at Lise and Berthe who came calling them, begging them, screaming that they would be shot. The women had to drag them from their beds, push them outside ... They could not just stand by and let these men get themselves shot for disobeying orders. The soldiers set out angry, furious, or even crying like children.

Yet to these chaps, too, Berthe and Lise took a liking. One of them had such a complicated name that they could never remember it. So they called him "Cooper," after his profession. He made washtubs for Berthe and Lise and repaired their laundry bat. They literally had to struggle with him on the nights he was called up for relief missions. One evening he set off carrying ammunition bags and was killed.

Another boy, Max, had scurvy. He was a tall lad, blond and pale, as beautiful as a Christ. He bathed his disgusting, bloody, festering gums with lemon juice and olive oil. He howled in pain. He talked of deserting, crossing the lines one day or another and surrendering. His pockets were filled with leaflets signed by Lenin and handbills advocating a Republic. The third time he was sent back to the front, he never returned.

Julius, his pal, had trench fever, one of the new illnesses that was essentially a form of exhaustion. When it took hold of him, he would rave all night long. Though he dared not say anything, he must have had feelings for Lise, a vague, secret affection. In the yard he planted a tree in her honour, a chestnut cutting, something for her to remember him by. He was killed the first night he ventured on a relief mission.

And on and on it went ... Hundreds and hundreds passed through the Sennevilliers' guesthouse in this fashion. They would depart one night or other, and the women knew they would never return. The men gathered on the square, took the road up the hill, and passed by the inn. Some of their national pride still remained intact. Until they had left the last hamlet behind, they summoned the courage to sing their war hymn, the "Gloria" – grave and solemn, like a funeral march, cheerless, lackluster, heavily enunciated, perfect for the cadence of legions on the move, for men heading off to die.

Glory, victory,
With heart and hand,
For the Fatherland ...
The birds in our forests,
How sweet is their song ...
Our Fatherland, one day we'll see it again,
Yes, we'll see it again!
Our Fatherland, our Fatherland,
One day we'll see it again ...

In those tragic days, the folks who heard this tune, sung in dull tones by thousands of men making for the front at nightfall, amid the tramping of boots, the rattling of baggage wagons, and the rumbling of artillery over the cobblestones, would never forget its terrible grandeur. There was something moving in this desperate sacrifice of a people.

The misery of the Germans was frightful. They lived on rutabagas stolen from the French, who were themselves dying of hunger. All that remained of the once splendid army was a ruin, a caricature, batallions of tired old men and boys, or the rare survivors who had lasted four years and were teetering on the verge of insanity. In fact, many had gone insane. There was a huge camp for them next to that of the Italian prisoners. These deranged soldiers still had to work. They ran the kilns, cremated the dead, or mended the railroads under the supervision of the wounded or amputees. The villagers often saw these wrecks suddenly stop what they were doing and salute phantoms, or rip at their hair and moan. And these were the most manageable ones. Military police chased away people who came to gawk at them.

The equipment was as worn out as the men. All that remained were dilapidated, patched-up artillery pieces and gun-carriages – run down, fit for the breakers, rusty and dented scrap metal clattering along the cobblestones like janging saucepans. And then there were the uniforms – faded, discoloured, the shade of clay, riddled with bullet holes, removed a dozen times from the dead to serve the living. For the uniforms of the dead were salvaged. Toward the kilns stretched long lines of trucks filled with naked corpses – lashed together head-to-foot, in groups of four, fastened with metal straps like the ones used to bind bales of wool. The bodies were cremated in the kilns.

Cadavers from the battlefield arrived fully clothed, by way of a narrow-guage railway – known as a "Decauville" – that linked Tourcoing and its hospitals to the frontlines.* The dead were stripped and cremated and the clothing sent to Tourcoing.

The bodies of the officers were not burned. A little cemetery was set aside for them on the crest of the hill. The corpses arrived in pine caskets: light-weight, rectangular boxes like those used in hospitals. But, toward the end of the war, even the caskets were recycled as temporary abodes for the remains of others and the bodies buried in their natural state. Occasionally people from Germany came to the cemetery. Lise long remembered the visit of an old couple in deep mourning. To bring them here from Tourcoing, they had been given a soldier for a cabby and a cabriolet drawn by an old horse. The pair must have been wealthy. They laid flowers on the grave and afterward left in the little carriage with the soldier. The old woman was crying. From what part of Germany had they come, what frightful scenes must they have witnessed in crossing their country and occupied France, so they could cry at the foot of this grave?

· · ·

The end, the end ... It was drawing closer day by day. Autumn had arrived. Another winter would be unbearable. There were no more resources. The Germans had fed green wheat to their horses during the July offensive.

---

*Paul Decauville's railway equipment company, established in 1875, specialized in narrow guage products. Decauville rails and locomotives were widely used for military and industrial purposes.

Man and beast were dying of hunger. The horses were nothing but ridiculous caricatures, unbelievable nags, thin as rakes. The men refused to keep going. Entire columns sat along the roadside in protest. The military police would take them to a big, soggy meadow at the foot of the hill and leave them standing in water for an entire day. The leaders were forced up onto bricks and lashed to a post. Then the bricks were removed and the men left hanging by the cords. Officers arrived, made speeches, attempted to persuade the men. A few times beer was even brought. Not a day passed without witnessing such scenes: policemen dragging along mutineers who would sit down, laugh in their faces, refuse to keep going. There were too many of these fellows. All of them could not be shot. The excessive misery destroyed patriotism. The troops were too cold, too hungry. To get through the day, each of them had no more than a dixie of half-cooked turnips, a little synthetic fat, and a bit of artificial jam. The soldiers were ashamed to let the French see their paltry rations and went off alone to eat. There were no more clothes, no undergarments. Beneath the heavy uniform – that type of armour that till the end concealed all manner of wretchedness – the troops went around shirtless or wearing women's undergarments stolen here and there. There was no tobacco, no money, not even a ring on the finger, a gold wedding band. It had been given for the German cause. The soldiers wore nickel-plated steel rings – a sight astonishing to inhabitants of the occupied territories.

The end, yes, the end ... The closer it drew, the more frantic the pace of life became for these unfortunates. Troops were always on the move, always heading out – on work detail, on a relief mission – a pace continually accelerated without rest or repose. They returned from the front exhausted, bloody, caked in mud to the midriff. They bathed, dressed, started to wash their clothes. And immediately they had to leave again. An order would arrive and they would hit the road swearing and crying. The men slid bloody feet into their boots and put on damp clothes that dried as they trudged along. And yet, as downcast as they were at departing in this fashion, they still had to sing the "Gloria."

A perpetual stream, a flood of men passing by, marching off, and never coming back: that is all one saw. The army was melting away. It was frightful.

The troops were at the end of their tether and started blaming each other for the situation. The Saxon hated the Prussian who hated the Bavarian. The army was consumed by such accusations. As the Empire collapsed, distinct nationalities reemerged. Bavarians blamed the Emperor, Prussians the King of Bavaria. When a regiment of Saxons stationed at the kilns was transferred and learned that they would be replaced by Prussians, they laid waste to their encampment on the way out, smashing the brick furnaces, ripping up the fences, burying, burning, and sacking whatever could not be carried away. They preferred to give things to civilians – to the French – rather than their compatriots.

One also heard talk of a Republic. Leaflets, little handbills signed by Lenin and Trotsky, were circulating among the troops. They read:

Soldiers, brothers, the radiant example of your comrade Liebknecht and the revolutionary events in the Germany navy demonstrate that you are ready. Help us, rally to the banner of peace ... Long live peace, long live the Social Revolution. [signed] *Lenin, Trotsky*

There were also red, black, and yellow striped cards that proclaimed:

REPUBLIC

The following order has been given to the French armies: whoever surren-ders to the French and says the watchword "Republic" will not be treated as a prisoner of war ... All who so desire may work with us to liberate Ger-many. This war will only end when the Prussian spirit of the military and the Junkers is defeated ...

Toward the end, many soldiers deserted. First one and then another sold his modest belongings to civilians, took off at night – hiding near Menen and Ypres – and never returned. Sometimes they left in groups, ten or twenty at a time. Once, at the end of September, fifty or so made a sud-den appearance at the Sennevilliers'. They were pushing a cart filled with food and packs and leading an old white horse – of enormous stature and thin as a rake. The men laughed about the beast, hanging their berets on its two protruding hipbones. They washed, made some coffee, ate, and gave some food to the horse.

"War over, Madam. We leaving, we prisoners ... No more war, kaput!"

Toward ten o'clock at night, they reloaded their wagon, said goodbye to Lise, and headed toward the front with their big, emaciated horse.

The French were rumoured to be approaching Menen. The inhabitants of Menen abandoned the town, evacuated it. The residents of Herlem watched them pass through town. Each day the sad and comical parade continued, encumbered with wheelbarrows, baby carriages, old clothes, pigs, cats, and canaries in their cages. Old Berthe could not help chuckling at the sight. These people were crazy to take such things, so many trifles, so much foolishness ... Another column was moving in the opposite direction – groups of brash, insolent, rapacious rogues from Roubaix and Tourcoing who were going off to pillage Halluin. Hooligans and street urchins – boys and girls alike – knew that the city had been evacuated. They went to plunder the houses, returning with piles of sheets, linens, curtains, rugs and blankets, saucepans and dishes. Cities like Halluin were the victims of French civilians more than of the enemy.

At Herlem's town hall, officials were also beginning to consider evacuation. The front was drawing near. Everyone was leaving. Lise and Berthe were packing. Berthe piled up linens, momentos, filled enormous bags, then realized in despair that she could no longer lift them. She searched, sorted, and bewailed her inability to take everything, not recognizing that she was acting like those she had so recently derided.

Shells began falling on the village. Airplanes battled in the skies each and every night. Now the villagers could clearly make out the red glow of the battlefield and the shooting stars of the rockets, like northern lights of immense and bloody proportions. Folks returned to their packing. They buried anything they could not take, digging holes in their yards. The holes! During the war, so much time had been spent on them! Hiding, burrowing, burying. How strange it would be after the war – if it ever ended – not to have to hide things or dig holes, or communicate with signs and gestures ... The war had wreaked such havoc! People were so accustomed to gesticulating, motioning with their arms like deaf-mutes!

In the end, Lise and a soldier were caught smuggling merchandise to Tourcoing. Berthe ran to Judith's. Thanks to her, Lise did not go to prison, but she did have to work for the Germans by harvesting potatoes and beets. More than a dozen women laboured at the task, on the slope of Herlem Hill. Above them, a battery of howitzers was firing on Geluwe and Ypres. And English artillery was responding, shelling Herlem. The women took cover whenever a shell passed overhead. In the evenings, Lise went home with her blouse and pockets filled with stolen potatoes.

Under the supervision of German headquarters, all these vegetables were weighed, tallied, and sent to the rear. Till the bitter end, headquarters remained a rigid and unrivaled instrument of government and oppression. The army was disintegrating, ruin was clearly on the horizon – with the front drawing closer each night and revolution brewing among the troops. But the occupation authorities remained distinct, removed from the world of the front, the fighting forces. There had always been a gulf between them. They hated each other, even argued. The Roubaix commandant – a big Frankfurt banker – had paid dearly for the privilege of remaining in the rear, like his peers in towns of similar size. It was a well-known fact. And this disjuncture between the front and the rear was the reason why the occupation authorities continued functioning unperturbed – harvesting, organizing, issuing commands, mounting placards, constructing buildings, paving roads, preparing for sowing – even with the army in full retreat. On the eve of their departure, till the last moment, they were still posting notices: *The order is given ...*

So much was this the case that one did not know what to believe. Some said, "They're leaving." Others retorted, "They're staying. They're building, they're planting ..."

The uncertainty would linger even after the Germans had removed the last of their troops from Herlem.

The village was shelled. Plans for a general evacuation had been made. Many people had already left. Not even a quarter of the villagers remained. The Sennevilliers, for their part, did not want to go.

"How would I manage," thought Lise, "with an old woman, a boy, and a one-year-old baby?"

They shut themselves up in their house, listening to the shells and bombs flying overhead.

"It'll soon be over," said Lise. "It's the end at last, the end ..."

"It'll never be over," said Berthe, "since my son is dead. For me it'll never end ..."

Chapter Six

I

Antoinette fell ill upon returning to her mother's, following her stint in Fosse-au-Chênes prison. Édith took her to see an army doctor who was offering free medical care to French civilians. Édith was grieved by what she learned, but she said nothing to Antoinette. Samuel and Édith decided that Antoinette would return to Épeule and try to recuperate. A lung was infected.

Antoinette arrived at her father's in a state of exhaustion and lamentable anxiety. Sick, exasperated and weary, she felt nothing but sad confusion: suffering, revolt, and inexpressible disgust for all that her life had been. Mingled with this sentiment was an unspoken bitterness, first toward her mother for letting her fall into this condition, then toward her father for doing nothing to prevent it, and ultimately toward herself. She was completely bewildered.

But the old house made her happy. She had spent her childhood here. And the first days back were pleasant. There was nothing to bother her, nothing to trouble her. A bland diet, lots of rest, no work, a few occasional medicines, the daily visit of the doctor – that was all. She was spoiled. Samuel and Édith showed her infinite consideration, infinite solicitude. Her wish was their command.

Antoinette still had a bit of energy, felt no pain, wandered through the house, spent time in the yard, read, chatted, did whatever she liked. Aside from meals – which were an ordeal for her – she led an easy, almost carefree existence, lingering in idle repose, enjoying amusements as yet novel:

books; her violin, which she had taken up again; her beautiful garden, nature.

Samuel had a big yard. He kept up a good half of it, abandoning the rest to weeds. Tall wild raspberry bushes obscured the wall at the back. The tool shed, which became Antoinette's sanctuary, was hidden among the thick, light-green foliage. Little Christophe, lord and master of this domain, invited his buddies to play adventure games. Antoinette soon joined in, enriching their activities with all the resources of a vivid imagination.

She had made some friends: Abel and Cécile van Groede, the two youngest of Big Flavie, and especially Marcel and Armande, the Duydt kids, two disenchanted, filthy children ridden with lice and vermin, forever hungry, and as skeptical and nonchalant as little old humbugs.

The five children – including Antoinette's younger brother Christophe – constituted her entire universe. Without the least bit of revulsion, she scrubbed, scoured, and deloused the little Duydts and combed their hair. They submitted in astonishment. She enjoyed adorning them with rags, ribbons, and flowers. She gave them little bites to eat – food prepared for her that she could not get down. These kids quickly fell in love with Antoinette and hardly stayed at their own house anymore. Starting at seven o'clock in the morning, they would lay siege to the Fontcroix's door. Antoinette played tea party with them, invented all manner of games – which she enjoyed as much as they did – and organized parades around the big yard, with singing, foliage garlands, ribbons, and sprays of greenery and wildflowers. Behind these amusements, moreover, rested a vague hope, the thought that the supplications, the prayers of these little children for her recovery would not go unanswered.

But her illness was still not giving her too much difficulty. The amusements, the lack of cares, and the ignorance of her true condition left her feeling almost happy. She was awaiting the end of the war. She would go to the South, Nice, the sunshine, and there she would recover. She began packing her trunks with this purpose in mind. It was spring 1918. Soon, as in years past, the French would unleash a big offensive, and this time they were sure to win. Antoinette wanted to be ready to set out immediately afterward. From Lille and Roubaix she had brought back bits of silk, fabric, outfits, whatever pleased her, whatever was bright, shiny, delightful to behold. She sorted these items, envisioned herself dressing in whites and pinks beneath a cloudless sky, among palms and olive trees. She matched outfits, ensembles, scarves, dresses, and hats, every piece cheerful, every piece light-coloured and suited for a land of sunshine. She spoke of nothing else: "When we're in the land of sun and light."

She fastened her suitcases, moved her trunks, happily emptied her drawers, and sang.

It was thus that the first complication, the first warning sign appeared. After wearing herself out a bit too much one evening, she could not sleep, coughed all night long, and got up achy, worried, and uneasy. Several days passed, but she did not feel the least better. Never before had she been so ill. She wanted to rebel, got up by herself, went out to the yard, and fainted.

This time she was truly frightened. She agreed to use a chaise longue, resigned herself to doses of creosote, injections of arsenic, spoonfuls of cod liver oil. She swallowed a mixture of eggs and wine that merely succeeded in upsetting a stomach already weakened by the creosote. And none of it did any good. She continued getting thinner and weaker. She was alarmed to find herself so easily exhausted by the least effort. She began to wonder if she might be seriously ill and stopped thinking of her condition as a laughing matter. She had moments of revolt, refused to believe it, to accept it. No, none of it was true. It was the doctor who was making her sick. She was going to get up, play, read, eat. She tried, exerted herself for a quarter of an hour, and felt drained. It was as if she had squandered her entire youth.

What was wrong with her? Her parents had hidden the awful truth. They had called it pulmonary congestion. She attempted to find out more, questioned Samuel: "What do I really have, Father? It's not serious, is it? And I'm certainly in no danger of dying, right?"

Samuel reassured her. She asked only to believe. She resorted to a variety of capricious strategies to speed her cure. First she wanted champagne, which Samuel managed to buy from some friends. Then she demanded oysters, which a good German, at Édith's request, went by motorcycle to find in Ostend. And she kept requesting other things which were hard to come by, which required unbelievable search and effort. She drove her parents to the point of exhaustion, wasted items that were incredibly expensive at the time, and all to no effect.

She continued declining. Soon it was necessary to abandon both the creosote, which made her vomit, and the injections, which strained her kidneys and her liver. Yet these changes resulted in no improvement in sleep or appetite. She was not in pain, but no one could get her to eat. At this price she remained happy and calm, but she gradually weakened, coughed a little, spit up a bit of pus. Soon she could hardly walk and no longer wanted to leave her chaise longue or her bed. Then Fontcroix had to carry her back and forth between her bedroom and the yard. She could not support herself anymore.

After a few months, in reflecting on the stages of her decline, she realized that her life was slipping from her grasp, dripping by, streaming away without remedy. And one day, in the wake of a fit of coughing, she finally lost control, screamed, and shouted. She wanted to live! To live! Nineteen years old! What had she done to merit this fate? Why her and not others? She had toiled, struggled more than others, and this was her reward! What an injustice! What folly to have worked herself so hard! Why hadn't her mother watched out for her? It was her fault, this mother of hers, who hadn't realized how young she was, hadn't known to protect her from herself. This notion was more of a feeling than a fully formed idea, but it gradually crystalized as proximity to her father drew her closer to him.

For Édith had remained in Roubaix to run the shop and earn the money needed for Antoinette. Samuel no longer worked outside the home, caring for his sick daughter round the clock.

At first the relationship between father and daughter was a bit awkward. But the discomfort soon vanished. Samuel looked after her with such simple, paternal affection, with such obvious, total devotion, that Antoinette was soon at ease with him. Before long he had to bathe her, comb her hair, help her change her underclothes, carry her from the chair to the bed. She found his patience and concern touching. It was as if his sole purpose lay in devoting himself, giving himself to another. This dedication moved Antoinette. She began to see what her life had been missing: the observant tenderness that surrounded little Christophe, the peaceful and heartwarming atmosphere in which her brother was growing up. Life here was regular to the point of monotony. But Antoinette began to understand the importance of this uniformity of existence, of demeanour, the profound impact that it has on emotional balance, the economy of strength that comes with consistency, and the respectability that concern for a certain dignified way of living tends to foster. Samuel was open with Christophe about moral issues, sought to hide nothing. As a result he aroused no dangerous curiosities. In every matter Samuel appealed to reason, never corporal punishment, not even a threat. Édith did not use such tact, readily invoked divine vengeance, and was quick to strike. Samuel sought to influence only the heart and the mind. And this gentle approach produced extraordinary results.

Why wasn't I raised this way? Antoinette wondered.

And in contrast she reflected upon her own stupid life. So much stress! Haphazard meals, abbreviated sleep, violent and exhausting pastimes, the secrecy and lies of a woman who did not know how to enlighten her little daughter, or else sudden revelations that were overwhelming for a young and tender spirit!

So then, this mother of hers was clearly responsible! It was her fault if Antoinette – at nineteen years of age – had arrived at this lamentable condition of body and soul. Antoinette felt a burst of rebellion. She truly began to hate Édith. She would have liked to yell at her: "You're responsible for everything I've gone through! It's your fault!" And in reaction Antoinette vehemently rejected all the shortcomings Édith had identified in her father. Once more Antoinette went to extremes. She decided that none of it was true. The victim, the unfortunate one, was her father. She felt a surge of affection for him, of regret for her own past attitude. She accepted his care with overt gratitude and placed total confidence in him. His presence comforted her. She had forgotten all embarrassment, all shame. And, as if to prove her affection and regret, she relinquished her poor, sick body to his charge, without dismay, as if she feared no suffering at his hands. He was her only aid, her only hope. She was constantly summoning him: "Father, come. Father, I'm sick ..."

And Samuel would come running, go searching, do his best to find a remedy, a way to provide some relief. His presence alone sufficed.

"I'm better when you're here," said Antoinette.

Édith noticed these changes, and they saddened her. Antoinette's callousness and demonstrable ill will pained the wretched woman. But she could say nothing, dared not even get angry with a girl who was short for this world. Édith silently endured Antoinette's thoughtless cruelty, her spite, her injustice, the bitterness whose cause eluded her. *She's sick,* thought Édith. And she resigned herself, tolerated the irritability, the silences, the rebuffs of her beloved daughter. She came in the evenings, weary from working and weeping, at once fearful and happy at seeing her daughter again. And she found herself greeted by reticence and sullenness. Édith would have liked to know about Antoinette's day, to learn if she had been in pain or if she had fared a little better. Antoinette hardly responded, abusing the right of the sick and condemned to be tyrannical and cruel. Édith did not complain, toiled patiently, drowned her sorrow in her work, strove to the utmost, only to find this new sorrow, this new agony each evening. She carried back whatever she came across, whatever was good, interesting, entertaining – wine, champagne, a 150-franc cake, ribbons, a book ... Antoinette scorned these gifts, hardly cast a glance at them. And Édith – dejected and resigned – remained at her side, enduring this silence the whole evening through, yet happy for the poor joy that seeing Antoinette brought to her sorrow. Samuel felt bad for Édith. He called her to the kitchen: "Don't worry. She's tired. But everything's okay. She seems a little better today ..."

"Oh, the poor dear! I understand," said Édith, weeping and yet comforted.

Samuel figured out what was going on with his daughter and grew concerned. In the end he delicately broached the subject with her. Antoinette was taken aback. He was defending Édith? She could not restrain herself from blurting out, "But Father, you're not mad at her? She's made you suffer so ..."

"What do you want me to say!" responded Samuel. "Don't judge her. She had a wretched childhood. She's accustomed to seeing the world like a jungle, like an arena filled with wild beasts. And it is a bit that way! She's always struggled to survive. It makes you hard-bitten. And then, I'm responsible, too. I should've understood that we weren't made for each other. I took love lightly, like some sort of game. I thought I could toy with life. I should've considered things more seriously. I've been punished for my mistakes, and your mother along with me. And I should've tried to set things straight. But I did just the opposite ... We were both in the wrong. Your mother sinned out of ignorance, not because she doesn't love you. And I share the blame for your plight, since I knew better than she did ..."

He sensed that he had to stymie the mounting hatred within his daughter. She would need all of her composure for the ordeal to come. By the use of such stratagems, he gradually brought Antoinette round to her mother. And Antoinette admired him and loved him for it all the more.

II

July was hot. Antoinette dreamed of sunbathing. She had herself trundled out to the middle of the yard, where she sat in full sun for an entire day, surrounded by her little band of children. That evening she had a fever and could not get to sleep. Around midnight she was taken with a sudden bout of coughing. And a thick liquid gushed up from her throat. It had a nauseating taste and consistency. She sat up, lit the lamp, looked in her handkerchief. It was blood! She was so shocked that she passed out.

This episode produced a panic. In the middle of the night, Samuel ran to Clara Broeckx's house. An officer let him have a soldier with a lantern and a pass for a doctor. They set out together and returned to the cul-de-sac with the doctor in tow. The soldier walked in front, piercing the darkness with the light in case they ran into any green devils. The lantern, the procession through the shadows, reminded Samuel of bringing a priest for last rites.

Antoinette did not come round till morning. They thought she would die that very night.

After this incident, she never rebounded completely. It left her shattered. Above all, she had realized that she was going to die, that the term left to her was only a respite.

She spent her days at the far end of the yard in the clump of raspberry bushes and the shade of the tool shed. The children played in the grass nearby. She watched them and thought to herself. She had received a rude shock. The idea of death remained with her, deepening her sadness. Once again, but more intensely, more eagerly than before, she turned to this problem, this enigma of our purpose and the hereafter. Her illness, her detachment from all that her life had been, favoured this contemplation, this elevation. There was no more of the playfulness, the affectation, the vanity, the childishness of youth, only solitude and suffering. From her lonely retreat, she considered with detachment – from a new perspective – the foolish, incoherent creature that she had been, left to the mercy of chance. To think that she could have contented herself with that kind of life for so long. In any event, something else must lie behind man's time on Earth. She recalled readings, distant and confused aspirations toward an ideal, something better. She returned to the subject – drawn, stirred, secretly attracted by things she had not understood but in which she had sensed a hidden grandeur. Life had to have a meaning, an object, an aim. One could not accept such hideous, pointless, dreadful emptiness. With all her might, Antoinette groped for this meaning, this aim, this purpose. A purpose, yes, to find a purpose for this sinister adventure that had thrown her into the world amid a broken home for whose discord she had paid the price, that had abandoned her to the hazards of an unbalanced existence, and that was about to do her in stupidly, horribly, before she had even lived. By dint of searching and seeking – in the mysticism, the exaltation of a spirit relinquished to solitude, meditation, and suffering – she thought she had found this purpose, this task, and a magnificent one at that. She would have a mission. This death that had so infuriated her, which she had thought useless, stupid, and cruel, could have a point: to reunite her parents, to seal their reconciliation with her suffering ...

For she recognized how miserable they were. She was now neither angry nor bitter toward them. It was not their fault if she died. They had been more blind than culpable. She felt sorry for them, condemned to struggle, obliged to fight for her without being able to resign themselves as she had. Her mother's plight, especially, was dismaying – the miserable woman wandering in the shadows, so attached to material possessions, incapable of seeing beyond them, tied to her daughter by a love that was almost physical, bodily. Ought not she, Antoinette, attempt to prepare her parents for what was to come, to mitigate the anguish that her death would bring? Logically, lucidly, she considered what would happen after her demise. Samuel had little Christophe. Her mother would have no one. The compulsory union of the family, necessitated by her illness, must not be allowed to dissolve again after her passing. She reflected on the matter in calm reason. She would not permit a rupture: if she could last till the end of the war, her death would seem like less of a blow. An Allied victory would likely bring a stream of new life, a spurt of frantic activity, which would quickly diminish the pain of their loss. And there was Christophe who would bind them together. He would be their consolation, their hope. She already noticed that they were more anxious, more concerned about him now that he would soon be their only child. And Antoinette herself felt a deeper affection for him, forseeing the huge role he would shortly play.

But above all, more than anything else, she counted on herself and her memory to keep them together. They would love each other in memory of her. In life, she had not been a sufficient tie to unite them. In death, perhaps she would be. It was her destiny, her mission. Perhaps this was why she had to die. And in any case, she could make her death count for something.

She wanted to lay the groundwork, the foundation beforehand. She devoted herself to fashioning shared memories for them. She wanted them around her as often as possible, at her bedside, shoulder to shoulder, for she felt that so much time together, so much shared suffering, could never be forgotten. Antoinette hoped that memory of her deathbed, of the moments spent here gazing upon her in silence, would keep them permanently attached, allow them to love each other in remembrance of her, as Jesus's disciples had done in remembrance of him.

This idea, this parallel, increasingly rooted itself in her mind. She was undergoing her own passion for the redemption of others. She would triump through self-abnegation. She had changed to the point that she no longer recognized herself. Old friends came to see her again, reminding her of her former existence, and leaving her astonished that she had lived such a life. She felt sorry for them. She pitied them from her current position of serenity, a mindset favoured by a diet of fruit and water and above all by her total isolation, a universe restricted to her yard, her chaise longue, and her bedroom – a complete detachment from the outside world.

Sometimes she nonetheless felt a surge of rebellion, of horror. Her will weakened. She experienced a crisis of dismay. Living like this – her mind racing day and night, exhausting herself as she awaited death – it was just too much! And at nineteen years of age, while life still beckoned, still called! To live! To go, run, eat, sing, travel, play, drink in life! Above all, she was afraid. Aged, seasoned by the ordeal, she sensed the immense delicacy of a memory. Would remembrance of her triumph over time? Wouldn't her sacrifice be in vain? Wouldn't discord and hatred be stronger than she was, wouldn't they destroy the poor, fragile connection between her parents provided by recollection of her death? This idea in particular – the thought that her sacrifice would serve no purpose, that she would die for nothing – cast her into despair.

But these episodes were increasingly rare. Strangely, they decreased in number and severity as her strength diminished. The die, in all its horror, was already cast, and, as one's energy dissipates, one gradually loses one's attachment to life. Death is always less painful than one thinks. Antoinette slowly acquired this peace, this serenity.

Her life ebbed away in this manner, amid the large, primordial garden filled with foliage and sun and shade, and surrounded by her little flock of children, her disciples. She imparted a purified love to the little ones around her. In the beginning she had loved them for herself, a tad selfishly, for the distraction they provided. She had used them as a means of divine intercession, making them pray and sing as they circled the yard. Now she had come to love them for themselves. And she wanted to be of use to them, to abide in their spirits as an example of human dignity. Perhaps later they too could draw ennobling inspiration from memory of her calm resignation. She wanted to remain with them like a beacon, a presence, in the midst of this beautiful, wild garden ...

From the comfort of her litter, she continued organizing their games. She led them like her little flock, feeding the hungry ones, patching their old clothes, cleaning them up and tending to them whenever she had a bit of strength. It seemed that, as young as she was, and by a sort of mysterious instinct, she had miraculously divined the sole means of remaining alive in the hearts of men: being loved.

These children were mad about her. They were no longer happy except at her side. Marcel and Armande – the little Duydts – spent their days at Samuel's without their parents showing the least concern. Flavie van Groede, who was more cautious, restrained Abel and Cécile a few times. But they slipped out, hurried to rejoin Antoinette, only returning at midday to grab their meager portion and leave again. Two or three evenings, they were found hiding in Antoinette's yard, where they had planned to spend the night.

The youngsters lavished her with simple acts of kindness and consideration. The four of them ravaged gardens and hedgerows to gather her favourite flowers. They even searched the garbage pails, proudly bringing back half-wilted bouquets that she had tossed out and which she recognized without saying a word. Disagreements, rivalries, and resentments occasionally arose among the children over a semblance of favouritism, a preference shown more toward one than another. She was obliged to reestablish peace. They became fastidious and intuitive. For her, urchins like Marcel and Armande Duydt demonstrated a desire to please, a spirit of devotion inexplicable among beings reared in such a harsh, unloving environment. They would have shed tears if she had refused the old toys they offered her as gifts. They sensed her weariness and stopped shouting and dancing through the grass and along the pathways to come sit beside her like little courtiers, a charming flock of young disciples gathered round their delicate little queen – nineteen years old and dying ...

Autumn came. The big, primordial garden slowly shed its ornaments and died. Winter was approaching. Antoinette felt nature's great cold, its great silence, invading her as well. She abandoned her universe of sun, tall grasses, and wildflowers, and settled in the parlour of her house once and for all.

The atmosphere inside was unpleasant. Dried grass and leaves burned on the hearth. And the war was still not over. Antoinette suffered and waited. For her parents' sake, she had to make it till the end of this war. In the general renewal, the immense revival of life that would follow, her death would be less cruel for them. But the war continued. It was September 1918. For so long now, people had said the Germans were finished! And yet they were not leaving. Were they going to stay forever? People were afraid to deny it. Antoinette rationed the remainder of her strength. She would have like to see the French or English before she passed ... The only thing she feared was to hold out till the last moment and die on the threshold of deliverance.

All the same, one sensed that this really was the end. The artillery drew nearer day by day. Wave after wave of troops headed for the front. Germans were constantly arriving, searching for billets, men who were exhausted, worried about their families, and who were whispering, "Soon over! No more cannon fodder!"

But in the meantime there was the cold, the hunger, and the dreadful oppression of an inflexible general staff carrying on with its methodical work – putting up buildings, railroads, concrete shelters, as if telling the occupied inhabitants, "We're staying."

Antoinette refused to think about it. She needed all her strength, all her courage. She conserved them, curled up in her bed under woolen blankets. Her back ached in the hollow beneath her shoulder blades. She told Samuel, "Put your hand on my back, Father ..."

And she slept like this, with her father's hand between her shoulders, warmed, relieved a bit. Samuel feared to move and sat staring at her for hours, his arm numb and painful, yet unwilling to free himself.

Around the beginning of October, in parallel with Antoinette's decline, the Germans started withdrawing from Roubaix. They rigged the bridge piers with explosives. They ordered all civilian men to evacuate. Samuel was supposed to go like the others. He refused to budge. Antoinette was about to die. He had set a four-pound hammer behind the front door, intent on killing any policeman who came looking for him. The atmosphere was tense. But the last day arrived with no sign of green devils.

One afternoon they learned that the bridges were about to be blown. The city would likely be shelled. There was a big cellar at the Fontcroix's. They took Antoinette's bed downstairs. And toward evening Samuel carried Antoinette herself to the vaulted redoubt. The neighbours had asked for shelter. They filed quietly into the dark, smoky cellar, sinisterly lit by the sooty glow of a wick steeped in melted lard. They went to see Antoinette, who was lying on her mattress near the cellar window, beneath a rare draft of fresh air. Then they settled in a corner.

The night was spent in this fashion. The women said their prayers. The men slept. Antoinette neither prayed nor slept. As for Samuel, he had remained outside in the yard, at the risk of getting himself killed. But he wanted to be able to bring help immediately if the house collapsed.

Around three o'clock in the morning, after having brought a little fresh water to his daughter, he climbed back up from the cellar and went out into the darkness. The Germans must have left. Besides, he still had his hammer in his pocket. He leaned against a low wall that would not be toppled by an explosion. A vast peace reigned. The artillery had ceased. An immense silence surrounded him. There were no lights in the black sky. The city, shrouded in darkness, was waiting.

Samuel stood there motionless. The solemnity of this moment – anticipated for 1,500 days, 1,500 nights – filled him with poignant emotion. What was coming? Final destruction? Deliverance? He felt nervous, anxious. Then he suddenly remembered his dying daughter ... And none of it seemed to matter. Their rescuers were too late ... He broke down crying.

In the cellar, one could tell that dawn was breaking. Anxiety increased as daylight approached. Antoinette, in her resigned state, was waiting, her whole being transported in a final, serene vision of her calvary, a meditation so elevated that it was almost a prayer. Encircling her, in the smoky and heavy atmosphere of the basement, the shaft of white light passing through the cellar window created a magical radiance, like a sheer, luminous pathway toward the hereafter.

Then the explosions began. They continued for a long time. A terrific burst at the end, quite nearby, ellicited a cry of terror. The Pont des Arts and the railway had blown up. A red dust filtered through the cellar window. Little Christophe screamed, "Father ... Father ..."

For they did not know where Samuel was. A torrent of pebbles and debris shattered the roofing tiles. Then there was a long silence. Was it over? Or was the shelling just begining? They started whispering timidly, wondering aloud. What would happen? Another half hour passed in this fashion. Outside it was broad daylight.

Antoinette had sat up in bed, her back propped with pillows. She turned her emaciated face toward the cellar window. Suddenly she waved, "Quiet ..."

And outside they heard Samuel shouting through the cellar window, "It's over! It's over ..."

III

Félicie and Flavie had followed the Duydts, who had gone out to pillage and plunder. Rumour had it that there was still some coal at the train station. The bridges were being blown, but coal was worth the risk. They did not realize the war was actually coming to end.

They entered the station on rue de l'Ouest. It had been invaded by looters, the dregs who routinely put in an appearance for riots, fires, or catastrophies. Boys, girls, hooligans – rogues of every sort – were coming and going, kicking open the doors of shops, offices, and railway cars. The footbridge had collapsed, cut in two by dynamite. The station's dilapidated concourse – without a single floor tile and filled with garbage, straw, and broken glass – had a sad and ominous appearance. The canopies above the platforms had foundered. And amid this devastation people were roaming around, pushing wheelbarrows and carts, filling sacks, carrying off lignite briquettes, boards, old wooden bedframes, guns, scrap metal, a bit of everything. There were still lots of Germans who were looting alongside French civilians, mixed in haphazardly. People were fighting, knocking each other down, wrenching debris from one another's arms. The Germans dared not use their weapons. People sensed their hesitation, feared them no more, threatened to punch them in the face. From time to time, the distant explosion of a bridge hurled a black column of smoke into the air.

Around nine o'clock in the morning, a squadron of planes suddenly appeared, coming from the direction of Lille. They were flying low and fast, heading straight for the station. Black objects could be seen falling from their undersides. People scattered, hiding beneath railway cars, in the nooks and crannies of the buildings, anywhere they could find, French and Germans mixed together. The bombs caused great damage. When people came back out, they saw rails twisted and turned like unearthed roots. The French quickly returned to looting while the Germans abandoned the place, trudging along the rail line toward the Pont de l'Alma and Tourcoing.

Félicie and Flavie headed home with their bag of coal and lignite. The streets were still deserted. Most people were holed up in their cellars. Planes were flying over the city. As the women arrived in Épeule, they saw the occasional window open up. People questioned the two passersby: "Where're the Germans? Are they still here? Is it over?"

The women responded with a big sweep of the arm: "Gone ... Gone ..."

They said it without joy, with weary indifference. And people ventured outside, opened their shutters, hung out a bit of the flag, then pulled it back just as quickly, still reticent to risk anything. Even in their absence, these awful Germans left folks feeling terrified and submissive.

· That afternoon the women were back at the station when a big commotion erupted among the mob of looters busy at their task. People shouted, "The English! The English! There they are." And everyone rushed toward rue de la Gare. Félicie and Flavie followed the others, hurried with the crowd toward Grand-Place. Far ahead, barely audible above the ruckus, an army band was playing some tune. Thus did the women arrive at the square amid the throng.

Grand-Place was awash with people. All Roubaix must have been there. One could see an ocean of heads surging, seething, beating against the walls of city hall as if against the sides of some immense stone oceanliner. In the midst of this tumult, the English – a thin line of khaki – were making their way with difficulty. They were surrounded, bombarded, overwhelmed. Women were throwing flowers to them, kissing them. Everyone wanted to see them, touch them, carry them in triumph. Screaming, shouting, crying, a terrific clamour mounted toward the sky. A human wave crashed and broke against the doors of city hall. The frantic mob seized the huge placards where the Germans had attached their posters, where one could still read that symbol of oppression, *The order is given ...* People attacked the billboads, ripped off the posters, tore them to shreds, trampled them under foot. The panels were smashed to pieces, the fragments hacked to bits, reduced to smithereens, ground to dust. Folks were looking for things to destroy, to devastate. Fury seized the crowd. A procession of German soldiers, who had hidden in cellars so they could give themselves up, came from the direction of rue Neuve and headed toward the police station, escorted by the English and subjected to boos, jeers, projectiles of every nature, and outright blows at the hands of the French. A bristling sea of raised arms and outstretched fists shook in their faces. These fellows walked along, pale with fright, sheltering beneath their elbows. At the corner of rue Saint-Georges, a group of civilians had surrounded a woman, one of the "filles à Boches" whom neighbours were pushing and pulling, dragging by the hair, punching and kicking as she passed, tormenting with invective and abuse. They jostled each other to reach her, hit her, pinch her, tear at her skin, her flesh, her hair, make her scream, shout, suffer a little more. She was nothing but a moaning and bleeding heap of rags. One man opened his hand in pride, showing the mob a fistful of bloody hair dangling from his fingers. Near city hall a tense, breathless crowd was watching the ascent of a daring fellow on the exterior wall. Clinging to the stones like a bat, gripping the chinks, he slowly made his way toward the clock, grabbed the hands, and turned them back an hour, putting them on French time again. A roar greeted the symbolic gesture. Everyone was yelling something, to the point that nothing could be understood. At this stage the uproar was deafening. Mouths wide open, shouting at the top of their lungs, people could no longer detect their own voices. The screams errupted, colliding and blending into one another. On the front steps, just below the arch of the main entrance, a pack of frenzined men crowded together, climbing on each other's shoulders, pulling themselves up into a tottering pyramid, a human mountain, continually collapsing and reforming till finally – capped by a tall, thin boy with raised and outstretched arms – they reached the huge German flag hanging below the vault. One could hear the pole crack and break free. The men tossed the giant rag to the onlookers, who caught it, snatched it, tore it off the pole, ripped it asunder to a storm of laughter, crying and shouting, jeers and boos. And all of a sudden, spontaneously,

abruptly, rising from a corner of the square, mounting bit by bit, a boisterous, wild song – a muddled and indistinct "Marseillaise" – swelled, grew,
materialized, and triumphed, eclipsing and drowning out everything else,
taken up by 20,000 voices amid tears and delirium, to the accompaniment
of the final bells of Saint-Martin, whose great bronze peals resonated in the
chest, spread across the crowd in sonorous blasts, and draped this frenzy of
enthusiasm with something tragic, like a tocsin ...

Flavie and Félicie did not get home till evening. Épeule was in a state of
jubilation. The English took possession of the city. Time and again one
saw German troops coming out of hiding and surrendering to passing soldiers. As the two women walked by the Bac à Puces cabaret, they saw Otto
the deserter emerging, coming to give himself up to the English after
remaining hidden for four years.

• • •

In Herlem, the Germans left that same morning. English troops followed
close behind. Airplanes flew overhead and dropped bombs on the fleeing
enemy. The last inhabitants of the village had taken refuge in their cellars.
The two green devils from army headquarters were the last to leave.
Through the cellar windows, people could see them setting off on their
bicycles with their big dogs trotting beside them. The villagers would have
gladly run after them to settle scores, but they were afraid. They still found
it hard to fathom that the Germans were really leaving.

Around noontime the artillery barrage trailed off, then stopped all
together. People came outside. At the square they found a dead German
lying across the carriage of a piece of heavy artillery whose short, wide-
mouthed barrel carried the haughty Gothic inscription of the Hohen-
zollerns: *Ultima ratio regis.**

The English arrived two hours later. The municipal administration, led
by Lacombe, received them solemnly. Marellis, in disgust, had stayed away.

While some folks on the square gave themselves over to enthusiasm, others – thirsting for vengeance – scampered like a pack through the village.
They were brimming with pent-up rage. To satisfy his old grudge, the
policeman Brook had tossed out the name of Judith Lacombe, among others. Fifty odd madmen rushed toward the hill. But they found no one there.

---

*"The King's final argument."

Judith had been alerted. Pascal, moved by a remnant of pity, had warned her of the policeman's denunciation. Prison and inquest awaited her. She had abandoned her house to follow a column of Germans heading for Belgium.

She was not alone. Many women did likewise. And since their prospects in France were bleak, they hoped to forge a new life in Germany. There were seven or eight of this sort from Herlem who accompanied the troops. The Germans made fun of them. The women moved with the regiment, beseeching the men for food. They arrived in Courtrai in this fashion, lagging behind a horde whose insubordination was gradually increasing.

But in Courtrai there were units that had remained unaffected. Army headquarters – the authorities – were still in steadfast operation. They regained control of the troops, organized transport, evacuated the men in haste. The women were turned away. They begged and pleaded, threw themselves at the officers' feet, cried, explained that they would be killed if they went back to France.

"We don't need any more hookers in Germany!" they were told.

The women were expelled. Judith wandered for days and finally, at the end of her strength, returned to Herlem.

Brook arrested her the following day. She was taken to the fort amid the jeers of a crowd in which she recognized people she had aided and abetted during the war.

Judith was thrown into one of the cells at the fort. There she found other women, more than a dozen, the guilty along with the innocent. For the opportunity to settle scores had appealed to many. Among these women was Lise Sennevilliers, who was carrying Fannie's baby in her arms. People knew that little Jeanette was the child of a German. They had snatched Lise from her home because many claimed the girl was hers. They hardly knew the full story.

Folks came to shout insults at the prisoners and to hurl garbage and pails of water through the cellar windows and the loopholes.

IV

Antoinette knew nothing of this entire wave of passion, enthusiasm, hatred, and vengeance. She was already removed from the world, isolated and sheltered in her retreat at the back of the Fontcroix's gloomy and cheerless old parlour. There her earthly life drew to a close, untouched by

the outside world save a limited view – through the tall windows – of her
big denuded garden. She hardly spoke anymore, her thoughts turning to
vague and secret things for hours at a time, with her parents at her bedside and her little band of young worshippers around her.

She nonetheless realized one of her dreams. One morning Édith brought
in an Englishman, a soldier she had met in the street, and whom she had
managed to pull aside by speaking to him in a mixture of French and German. For out of sheer habit people were addressing the English in this
composite dialect to which they had grown so accustomed. The man had
come inside without understanding. He was shocked at the sight of
Antoinette. She gazed at him for a long time. She was at once happy and
sad. His presence heralded what she had so long awaited: deliverance and
the end ... She raised her hand toward him, touched his uniform, the copper buttons of his tunic. Then she closed her eyes and cried.

Antoinette lived for another six days. Her family no longer left her side.
Samuel cared for her like a little child. She neither read nor talked, living
in a dreamlike state. Coming to see her was akin to visiting a saint. One
found her in a calm state of repose, surrounded by her little disciples and
illuminated by an immense interior radiance, as if absorbed in contemplation of her sacrifice and her mission. Till the very end, a happy and
mystical obliviousness freed her from doubt. Only rarely did she have a
dreadful premonition of the probable uselessness of her oblation.

For above all she thought of her family. She was troubled by her impending demise more for them than for herself. She was aware of just how
much she absorbed their attention, how she took up their entire lives,
every minute, with the caregiving, the pain, the anguish of which she was
the eternal source. What emptiness there would be without her! "Poor
father," she said to Samuel, "all this suffering, you'll feel its absence so ..."

She also hoped that her death would be a lesson in regard to her little
brother, so her parents would spare him the mistakes that had led to her
tragedy. In the end, her death would be of use to him, too. She loved him
all the more as she was dying a bit on his behalf.

She wanted to leave behind the fewest possible tangible reminders,
things that her family would find later and that would revive the pain. The
ordeal gave her miraculous foresight. She had Édith reopen her trunks,
her suitcases, which she herself had packed for her departure to Nice and
the South. She rediscovered the bright fabrics – the straw colours, the vel-

vet and silk flowers, the stunning whites, all the happy things that she had hoped to make use of down in the land of sun and light ... She recalled the phrase. It took on new meaning in her eyes, a symbolic and poignant significance. And she broke down, cried once more for herself, for her youth, for this budding life that was slipping away.

It was her last moment of weakness. She remained at peace till the end.

On Sunday morning she had several fainting spells. She just barely came out of it, then fell into a sleep already akin to death. Édith held up a mirror a dozen times to catch the steam from her breath.

Antoinette reawakened toward evening, regaining a semi-consciousness. She felt confused, prey to anxiety of an almost physiological nature. It was as if she were returning from afar, emerging from an eternity of sleep and darkness. And to her the world still seemed obscure, hardly real. She already sensed herself slipping again toward an abyss of shadows. Her eyes closed once more. She had the distinct impression that she was about to die.

She let out a desperate cry, an instinctive appeal to those who had brought her into the world, protected her, defended her: "Father ..."

"Antoinette, Antoinette, we're here, we're right beside you!"

She felt them holding her hands ...

She reopened her eyes. She looked first at her mother, then at her father, with an expression that was no longer of this world. Her appearance revealed an intense longing, an ultimate distress, a poignant supplication that she could no longer express. She would have liked to remind them one last time of her wish, her ultimate desire, to tell them, she too, "In remembrance of me ... Love each other in remembrance of me ..."

But she cold only move her lips without speaking.

So, in a final effort, she touched their hands, united them, held them in her own with a silent and moving grasp, exhausting her remaining strength in clutching them like this. And one saw the light in her eyes slowly fade as she gradually slipped toward the darkness.

Antoinette never regained consciousness. She remained in the throes of death for two days, making a horrible sound, as if vile things had taken shape at the back of her pure, young throat. Her face had assumed a strange appearance. She seemed aged, to the point that she was no longer recognizable. The prominent, savage-looking jaw, the deep, hollow, forbidding eyes – her whole skeletal and sunken visage – it was as it she were readying her own death mask.

Édith and Samuel stood vigil. Antoinette's death agony, the culmination of her efforts, bound them together. Side by side, riveted to this body – the product of their own – they watched over her. Nothing mattered to them anymore except these seconds, the memory of which would preoccupy them for years to come. When Antoinette gasped for air, breaking the regular rhythm of her death rattle, they felt as if they were dying with her. They gave her something to drink again, forcing open her gritted teeth. And the tall, emaciated, frightful-looking creature that had been Antoinette clenched her jaws and bit the metal spoon, and seemed to be fighting again. Such scenes were endless torture for her parents.

Her little disciples spent these two days inside. The third day, at noon, they were with Christophe in the shed at the back of the yard when Samuel called to them, "Christophe, Abel, Armande! Come quickly!"

They rushed to the house in a panic. They found Édith and Samuel despondent, supporting the gaunt frame of a creature beyond recognition, a Christ with vacant eyes, long, radiant, flowing hair, arms crossed, and mouth open, as if she had uttered a terrible cry the moment she had given up her spirit.

v

Antoinette's sacrifice was of no use. Those whose thoughtlessness, dissension, or lack of foresight were partially responsible for her demise, and for whom she had thus consented to die, were unable to remain united. A few months later, Édith and Samuel separated again. A long history of conjugal hatred – which the pure visage of the martyr had not managed to eliminate – revived their bitterness, their intolerance, their selfishness, their violently opposed and stubborn natures. From the first argument, Samuel understood that the rift was still present and would reopen. They separated without delay to avoid further exasperating their suffering and misery from contact with one another.

Poor Antoinette had died for nothing. Compared to hatred, bitterness, selfishness, and life in all its harsh reality, what good was the sacrifice of one little nineteen-year-old victim?

Chapter Seven

I

Since October, Émilie Hennedyck had been staying in Brussels, where she had followed the retreating German army. She had abandoned the little Roubaix apartment where she had lived in seclusion, seeing no one but Rudolf and scorned and feared by her neighbours. Émilie had had no news of Patrice Hennedyck. She knew that he had spent a few months in Rheinbach, then in a hospital. Each week she had a package of woolens, undergarments, and food dispatched to him. But never a letter. Émilie avoided contemplating the possible return of her husband. She had drawn a curtain over the future, unwilling to reflect on it. She lived like more people than one might think – deliberately restricted to the present, resigned to let fate determine the path ahead, feeling incapable of making a decision, of determining which move would be for good or for ill. Her life was stupid, pointless, and slow, continually obsessed with the same thoughts, the same regrets, poisoned with insomnia, fainting spells, pains of every sort. She was terrified to recognize the influence of mind over matter, the impact of a troubled conscience on physical well-being. And von Mesnil noticed it too, in astonishment, and found himself forced to reverse his theories and to admit that if the body governs the health of the soul, the latter has significant influence on the former. He had embarked upon this adventure without much consideration, amused by the thrill of the chase, carried along by the automatic reflex of the lady's man who seeks seduction and gratification instinctively, without even thinking about it. He himself had gotten caught up in the game. This sincerity was now long gone, replaced by lassitude, even hatred as the war dragged on and the coming disaster became apparent. Germany's defeat caused von Mesnil, the skeptic, an almost unconscious form of suffering, which he endured without ever confronting head-on. He transformed these emotions into a muted hatred of everything French, including Émilie herself. And then, from the beginning, this affair had for him been marred by uncertainty. Even when he had believed himself in earnest, deep down he had always retained the doubt, the reserve, the skepticism of the man who has known many women, who understands from his encounters that even the most total passion cools and that – with a certain degree of experience – one never dies from love. As a doctor, he stepped back and observed his own behaviour, deciding that pure passions of the heart and soul must be nothing more than disguised sensual urgings of the flesh.

Von Mesnil had lost none of his foresight either. When the war was over – and the conclusion was drawing near – there would inevitably be a lasting schism between France and Germany. All cooperation, all contact would long be impossible. A breach between the two nations was inevitable, unavoidable. He did not admit as much to her, but he understood it, as did she. And this, too, prevented him from devoting himself wholeheartedly, forcing him on the contrary to withdraw a little more each day as the end approached.

As a matter of principle, he never mentioned these things to Émilie. She did not know where their affair was headed. This silence, this tacit agreement, left them a semi-happiness, without Émilie daring to ask him more about his intentions.

Émilie had come in a train full of women, arriving in Brussels at the beginning of October. Von Mesnil was supposed to follow a few days later. She awaited him for two weeks, meanwhile drifting like flotsam through the town and its foreign population.

She had written to von Mesnil. He did not respond but rejoined her two weeks afterward. She had rented a little room in a densely populated neighbourhood, on a humble street near the Palais de Justice. From time to time, von Mesnil met her there in the evenings. He had an enormous workload. The hospitals were overrun with wounded. The German withdrawal was turning into a rout. And, though unwilling to admit it, von Mesnil suffered in his German pride and took out part of his hatred toward the victorious race on Émilie. She understood what was happening. But she was already so happy, so grateful that he had come back to her that she forgave him everything and dared not complain. She lived a dismal, boring, hopeless life in Brussels, amid the bustle of a city in which impending victory had spirits running high. People here had not been repressed, crushed like those in northern France. The Germans had spared the Belgians, whom they would have absorbed into the Empire had they won. Food and clothing could still be found. The stifling atmosphere in the Nord did not exist, and a rebellious feeling was in the air, giving rise to audacious pranks. Caricatures of the German commandant von Arnheim were scrawled on the walls. It was rumoured that the Nord had been freed, that the Germans would soon be driven out. Even before the departure of the enemy, emotions were at fever pitch.

One morning in early November, Émilie had gone as usual to drown her boredom in the bustle of the downtown streets. Heading from the Palais de Justice toward the Palais du Roi and the Chambre des Représentants, she noticed the absence of sentries on rue de Louvain, in front of the Palais de la Nation. She headed up the street. The gate of the Palais stood open. In the courtyard, a crowd of German soldiers and Belgian civilians, mixed together pell-mell, was besieging the grand balcony above the main entrance. On the balcony, three men in uniform bellowed one after another. And the crowd was yelling, applauding. From the streets, passersby and soldiers hurried to swell the ranks of this tumultuous gathering.

Émilie approached. The three orators, each in turn, was repeating the same speech in German, French, and Flemish. They shouted, "Death to the Kaiser! Capitalists brought on the war! Long live the Revolution! Death to generals, death to officers!" The crowd roared in approval.

The multitude increased from minute to minute. Civilians outnumbered soldiers. People were clinging to the windows, the railings. Several carts had been transformed into grandstands. Men had perched themselves on artillery to see and hear.

Suddenly the crowd began to stir. Some folks started marching away. Everyone followed to see what was happening. Soldiers, civilians, women, and children were shouting all at once. An indistinct chant could be heard. Two or three thousand men were heading down rue de Louvain. They were pulling carts, pushing artillery by hand, with men still straddling the barrels. After crossing Place de Louvain, the turbulent stream narrowed, tightened, squeezed as if through rapids into the tiny rue des

Comédiens. The demonstrators dragged, swept, picked up anyone and everyone as they passed. The torrent swelled, rumbled, reverberated, moving haphazardly toward the boulevards without anyone quite knowing why. People were yelling, screaming, laughing. Red flags waved overhead. Shopkeepers closed up in haste. Street urchins rushed to join the throng. And the grinding of the artillery over the cobblestones filled the little streets with the din of a riot.

Thus did the crowd reach the Grands Boulevards. Émilie let herself be pulled along the sidewalk, intrigued, anxious to see what was happening. In the middle of the roadway, the monumental fountain of Place de Brouckère soon came into view. The big hotels, housing the officers, were closed. Émilie, almost in the lead now, watched. The procession had stopped. Two cannons were in the middle of the street. Some soldiers aimed them at the hotels, maneuvred the iron bars, chocked the wheels. On all sides, Belgian men and women observed the operation with curiosity. A few guys were still sitting on the barrels. An astonishing obliviousness immobilized the crowd, which seemed not the least concerned.

Émilie had instinctively turned her eyes toward the white facade of one of the big hotels. At that very moment she saw one of the Venetian blinds on the second floor rising, come up twenty odd centimetres. Something black slipped out. And in an instant everything changed. The sinister crackling of the maching gun spread terror all around. A clamour arose: the fearsome clamour of an insane panic. The canons were abandoned. One man astride a barrel raised his arms and screamed, tumbling off like a rag doll. People fled, knocking into each other, clinging together, jostling one another. A frenzied rout ensued. In ten seconds the street was empty. Two or three bodies lay twitching round the guns. With a dry sputter, a second tempest of bullets swept the cobblestones without hitting anyone else. Here and there, soldiers sheltered in doorways, firing shots toward Place de Brouckère. The machine gun fell silent.

Émilie had fled with the others. People sped past her, fighting to get in front. She was struck, bumped, pushed back a few times, shoved roughly against a wall. She fell to her knees, got to her feet again, dashed ahead. And in the midst of indescribable chaos – the violence, the shouting, the brutality of a crowd prey to savage and inhuman terror – she reached a street corner and threw herself round it, safe, breathless.

Émilie panted for a few minutes. She was disconsolate. There was hardly anyone left with her. She headed slowly toward rue Neuve, where she found a peaceful crowd, an extraordinary and reassuring impression of security, of tranquility, just a few steps from that dreadful boulevard! Gunshots could still be heard, but here people seemed barely concerned. They were not even paying attention. Émilie set out, headed back toward rue des Fripiers amid a crowd of people who were walking by, loitering around, talking, and laughing. Masses of onlookers and idlers were questioning each other. They knew something had happened, but none was aware that the shooting was so close at hand. They listened in surprise to the distant crackling now coming from the direction of Nord station and were not in the least alarmed. This fusillade, this revolution in one district of Brussels, was no more frightening than news of a big fire somewhere or other.

There were lots of Germans. In front of the post office on rue Neuve, an unperturbed sentry was still guarding the door. But near at hand, on every side, all along the sidewalks, soldiers were spreading their effects on the ground: weapons, bags, gas masks, packs of bandages, bayonettes, rifles, straps, cartridges. They were selling all of it, calling to the crowd, offering unbelievable things. People gathered round, picked through the items, bought a few souvenirs. This preposterous market stretched the entire length of rue des Fripiers, spilling onto rue aux Herbes. From afar the Germans could be seen brandishing their wares and hailing civilians. Officers were passing by, intentionally dishevelled and familiar with their men, laughing with them, encouraging the disorder they feared to restrain. At a street corner, however, Émilie saw one of the officers fighting with three big fellows. They were trying to rip off his Iron Cross and his epaulettes. A woman was attempting to pull him away, drag him off, crying as she called to him, "Komme, Karl, Komme ..." Shots rang out close by, though no one could pinpoint the origin. Troops were stomping on uniforms, epaulettes, buttons, insignia. A car – filled with officers waving a red flag – made its way through the crowd. Soldiers rushed up and surrounded them, shouting, "Revolution! Revolution!"

Farther on it was almost impossible to get through. A whole transport regiment was liquidating its equipment: horses, wagons, harnesses, feed. Some folks could be seen setting off with rifles on their shoulders, others examining bayonettes and helmets. One soldier offered Émilie a big officer's saber for ten marks, another a machine gun for twenty-five francs.

"Works well, very well," the man insisted.

The soldiers broke and smashed the things people did not want, splitting rifle butts on the pavement, snapping blades, trampling packs of bandages. The troops were like madmen. They fraternized with civilians. They would have kissed just about anyone.

"The war's over ... Revolution ..."

Some of the soldiers were crying, half crazed, dancing together. From upper-storey windows, straw-stuffed uniforms representing the Kaiser were already being hung in effigy. People leaned from their windows, holding copper saucepans and bronze objects – saved from the constant searches – as if they were trophies. And through this frenzied mob, a long convoy of trucks flew by at top speed, heading toward the upper city. Drunken soldiers were driving, with more standing in the rear, teetering round the curves, like a field of wheat bent by the wind. They were brandishing bottles, weapons, and scraps of red cloth, and yelling "Revolution! Revolution!" to everyone they passed.

Émilie made her way through the crowd, escaping with difficulty. She eventually reached calmer steets and slowed her pace, relieved, coming away from the adventure with the impression of having nearly been pulled into a vortex, unintentionally, in spite of herself. She now understood how one could participate in a riot almost against one's will and be crushed by it. Having extricated herself, she felt as if she had recovered a measure of liberty, a freedom of movement that she had not had just a moment before.

She got back to her house, the two little furnished rooms where she lived behind the Palais de Justice. Her lodging was on the fourth floor in a humble, almost shabby building. The tall and narrow window looked onto the huge transverse staircase flanking the eastern side of the enormous courthouse.

She had been home for half an hour when the bell rang. It was Rudolf. He wore a grey overcoat, had on his helmet, and carried a leather suitcase in his hand.

"So you've come at last?"

"Yes," he said, sitting down.

"What's the suitcase for? You're going somewhere? You're leaving? Answer me!"

"Yes, I'm leaving."

"Where to?"

"Back to Germany."

"Germany?"

"It's time. I think that in a couple of days ... besides, I have orders."

"So you're leaving? When will I see you again? Where will I meet up with you?"

He did not respond right away. He had pulled out his wallet.

"You can't stay here without money," he said. "I'll leave you a few hundred marks ..."

"Yes."

He set the money on the table. He stood there, hesitating.

"So," he said, "So ..."

She repeated, "Where will I meet up with you, Rudolf?"

He realized she did not understand. He whispered, "Meet up with me?"

"Yes."

"I ... I don't know ... Where do you expect to meet up with me?"

"What?"

"Where do you think you'll be able to meet up with me?"

She had gone pale. She said, "But how should I know, I ... Just tell me ... In Germany, wherever ... You know I'll go anywhere, just tell me ..."

He shook his head: "Émilie, don't you understand! We've been defeated, the war's about to end. For a long time to come, all ties between French and Germans will be impossible. It'll take twenty years to reestablish relations, exchanges. We'll keep on hating each other as long as the wounds are still fresh. A German in France or a Frenchman in Germany could not survive. I really don't see ... No, I don't see how ..."

She suddenly interrupted him: "Well! What's that supposed to mean? What're you driving at?"

"Émilie, what'd you want ... I came to say my goodbyes. That's right, we must say goodbye."

"Say goodbye? Part ways? You've gone mad! You're talking nonsense! I won't have any of it. I love you, I'm staying with you! I'll follow you, I'll go with you. I won't stay here without knowing when or where I'll see you again ... Show me, tell me where I should go! To Switzerland? To Holland? You talked about South America ... Tell me, answer, say something!"

She had grabbed him by his coat and was shaking him, clinging to him. He pushed her back gently.

"You know none of it would work."

"Wouldn't work? Well, what then?"

"Well then, I repeat, it's best if we say goodbye."

"You've gone mad!"

He said nothing.

"But everything you promised me, everything you swore! All the love, the tenderness, the plans! You couldn't have been lying to me the whole time! You told me, you promised me ..."

He shook his head, expressing his skepticism in a few simple words: "One promises so many things ..."

"What?"

"I never thought you could've believed it yourself ..."

She looked at him in astonishment. It was as if a new man stood before her, a strange face suddenly revealed. She whispered, "It's you telling me this? It's you ... Oh! It's not possible ..."

"Certainly, Émilie, you couldn't have hoped, could you, that a relationship so out of the ordinary would've ended any other way? You were married, after all. If you'd only thought it through, come down to reality. I'm not at all to blame. Oh, women's imaginations! Unbelievable!"

She kept looking at him in alarm. She suddenly shouted, "So you lied to me, you betrayed me, scorned me?"

He shrugged his shoulders.

"Could I have thought you'd take it all at face value! Words, vague promises – all of what constitutes a sideshow backdrop for happiness. Everyone knows it's contrived and accepts it as such. Perhaps I myself was in earnest, though. I must've gotten carried away. I've started down so many crazy paths! But I always stop at the edge ... It's as simple as that."

He paused for a second, then continued: "Yes, I thought you understood me. I thought I'd shown enough of my personality, revealed enough of myself that you wouldn't have expected anything from me ..."

She was still looking at him in disgust, hatred, and rage. She suddenly lashed out, "You're quite the German. Get out!"

He gave a start: "What'd you say?"

"You really are a cursed race that has called down heaven's fury, and will be made to pay!"

He had turned white with anger and shame. He grabbed her by the wrists and shouted, "Shut up!"

She wrenched herself free: "So, Rudolf, I've hit the nail on the head! Whatever you do, whatever you say, you still love something: your Germany! And thus will you be punished! By your pride! Yes, that's what'll make you suffer! If you'd won, you might've kept me. But since you've lost, you're pushing me away. Your pride makes me repellant. You can't help remembering that I'm French and that my people've beaten you! I've figured you out, haven't I?"

"Are you going to shut up!"

"No, no! And your pride will be your downfall. Go on, get back to Germany. Your dirty work, you've finished it, like the rest of your kind! The war, you waged it in your own way, bringing ruin, insult, exile. You stole my happiness, my life. You've brought shame upon me, sullied me to the very depth of my being! But you'll pay for your crimes, you and your race. You'll suffer in your turn, every reproach! You'll know hunger and ruin, the heel of the victors on your cities, your riches, the caress of our soldiers on your women! Ah, I can see your people at our hands one day, begging us for mercy, killing and destroying each other, and littering every road in the land with victims and outcasts. And you, Rudolf – you faithless, ideal-less man, you playboy, you soul sucker – I only wish one thing for you, one single thing: to see your cursed homeland burning, bloody, ruined, and for it to be the death of you! Get out!"

She spit in his face.

He stepped back. He slowly wiped his cheek. His face had a deathly palor.

She had left him standing there and fled to the bedroom in the rear. He approached the door. He called out, almost humbly, "Émilie, Émilie ..."

She did not respond. Instinctively, he returned to the middle of the room, wiped the sweat from his brow, straightened his officer's collar in front of the mirror, patted his cheeks to bring up a little colour. And he left, going back down the spiral staircase, with the furious curse still ringing in his ears.

He took a few steps onto the street, then suddenly stopped. Crossing an intersection thirty metres ahead of him was a unit, or rather a gang of dishevelled soldiers, most without weapons, pulling wagons by hand, singing, waving red flags, hauling off cartloads of loot in their defeat, and led by officers who were singing with them. It was a symbol of a Germany adrift, of a beaten people.

Von Mesnil stood rooted to the spot, motionless. And his heart broke. Tears of rage burned in his eyes. He rushed toward the officers. But a group of soldiers had seen him coming. They stopped him, surrounded him. A tall Bavarian reached a big, hairy hand toward his chest, to remove his Iron Cross.

"Comrade ..."

He got no farther. Von Mesnil had stepped back. Every element of latent faith, pride, and nobility – in this man who had affirmed and maintained his own skepticism – came welling to his chest. He moved quick as lightning. The barrel of his Browning touched the chin of the Bavarian. The gunshot shattered the man's jaw and blew out his brains.

Émilie had remained prostrate, lying on her bed, her face buried in her pillow. She had not heard Rudolf leave. Tears were choking her. She felt as if she were dying.

A gunshot in the street below gave her a sudden start. There was a clamour, more gunshots. She had a dreadful foreboding, opened the window, leaned out. At the end of the street, a crowd was gathered round something, and a bunch of Germans were singing as they left. She went down, took off running. The crowd was dense. She threaded her way through with difficulty.

"A German ..."

"He had it coming!"

"Poor chap ..."

She got to the front row. She instantly recognized the body on the ground. She threw herself down. Kneeling, sobbing, encircled by the hostile throng, she held the beloved head as she screamed, cried, moaned.

"Rudolf! Rudolf! It's me! Answer! It's me! Rudolf ..."

But he was already dead.

The mob gathered round her, indignant. People grabbed hold of Émilie, ripping her away from the corpse. They took her off, kicking, punching, shoving her about. The mob rumbled as it ushered her along, insulting her and abusing her, while others removed the body of von Mesnil – this man who had forbidden himself from believing in anything and who had died defending a symbol and an idea ...

I I

On 30 September 1918 Alain, Bidart, and François had left Prémesques with the rest of the camp's forced labourers. The Germans were taking all of the region's men with them in the general withdrawal. At the citadel in Lille, Alain and his pals thus joined an enormous crowd of city residents being forced to fall back toward Brussels. And the threesome embarked on an adventurous journey across Belgium, accompanied by four students they had met at the citadel. The group had a little German cart from which they had removed the registration number BKK6. Bidart, who fancied himself a poet, had rebaptized it "the swallow."* They had pushed the cart by hand for a long time. Then they had "found" a donkey. Other groups had French wagons, likewise taken from the citadel and still marked "43rd Infantry Regiment." The vehicles were hitched to oxen or even to men. Thus outfitted, the refugees set off on their quest toward Brussels, across the rolling and wooded countryside, teeming with game, which stretches from Ronse to Oudenaarde. In the beginning the Frenchmen had been given a warm welcome. But now they were in hostile territory. The inhabitants spoke Flemish. Communication was difficult. Looting had occurred. To find a place to sleep, the men sometimes had to seize a farm or a house by force. Alain, acknowledged as leader of the pack, had his six buddies with him. Together they were a strong bunch. Two or three times they had fought with peasants. Once a German policeman tried to requisition the donkey. He offered an ox in exchange. They refused. He had a revolver, but there were seven of them. He let them pass. Another policeman tried to take the whole group off to dismantle an airplane hangar. In the end, he too let them pass.

They finally reached Oudenaarde one evening. The little old town had been invaded by a swarm of emigrants. Alain searched in vain for a place to stay. He decided they would push on farther. And despite weariness and darkness they set off again. The donkey gave out. They had to pull the wagon by hand. At last they reached a village on the left bank of the Scheldt. Once again they had to force open the door of an inn, demand straw, and settle in like conquerors. They took turns keeping watch.

---

*A reference to the name of the coach that Emma Bovary takes from Yonville to Rouen in Gustave Flaubert's novel *Madame Bovary* (1857).

During the night, a flood of emigrants invaded the village in turn. And the next morning, as he was going to check on the situation, Alain learned that they would be getting some rations.

They stayed in the village for twelve days. By sharing their rations, they had eventually become friends with the innkeepers upon whom they had forced themselves. Then one morning the burgomaster posted a notice: "By order of army headquarters, all emigrants must leave for Brussels immediately."

Alain refused to go. His group remained hidden in the inn while all the other men headed out. And thus did they learn the next day that the Germans had issued no such command. The notice was a ruse of the burgomaster, eager to rid his commune of a band of troublesome looters.

Only three days later did the real order from headquarters arrive. This time there was no choice. Conditions were deteriorating, making further delay impossible. Alain's group decided to go but to make their way back up the Scheldt without crossing it, in hopes of meeting Allied forces. Alain had come up with the plan. On the morning of 25 October, they abandoned the wagon, took what they could carry, and travelled along the riverbank, walking slowly.

At noon they stopped to eat in a tavern run by a blacksmith-farrier. In the middle of their meal, some Germans arrived – a regiment beating a hasty, disorderly retreat. Alain, Bidart, and the others fled, hiding in a hayloft above the stable. It was boiling hot. They had to push up the roofing tiles to get some air. Through the cracks they could see the courtyard where a riotous scene was unfolding. The Germans had invaded the house, unloaded their carts, slaughtered an ox, and lit an enormous fire that they fed with bits of stolen furniture. They brought up a barrel of beer from the cellar, broke it open, and started drinking and dancing. In one of the wagons was a big upright piano, which an officer was playing with a vengeance. Quarters of ox meat were roasting. Soldiers fired rifles and revolvers into the air. They smashed carts and caissons, set fire to a motorcycle, and heaped uniforms, furniture, anything they could find onto the bonfire. They chased after the frightened residents of the house, kissing the wife and the daughters.

"War over, Madam! English here soon!"

And they forced them to drink and dance. The bonfire in the middle of the courtyard grew to an immense size. The revelry took on alarming proportions. Alain and his pals wondered if the stable would catch fire. But they were hesitant to come down. Madmen are just as likely to shoot you as to kiss you. The orgy lasted all night, amid infernal music, yelling, brawling, and dancing. New groups were continually arriving and fraternizing with the first comers. They threw down their weapons, greeted the others with a kiss, and began drinking, dancing, and shouting – officers and enlisted men mixed together haphazardly – amid a frightful uproar.

Toward daybreak the troops set off again, without having slept. They moved toward the Scheldt in a big herd, an unarmed, drunken, and disheveled mob. Only an hour later did Alain and his companions dare come down from the loft. And from a distance, as they were slipping away from the ruined tavern, they saw another group arriving, a German regiment retreating in good order, the men marching four abreast, with rifles on their shoulders, in rigorous formation, silently, and flanked by their officers. Here one found an undamaged cog of a marvelous machine that had been wrecked and destroyed. And the sight was striking – the discipline, the order, the rigidity of a regiment on the march – in contrast to the recent spectacle. One was left with the image of some gigantic organism in which a few parts remained healthy and alive while the rest of the body was decaying. Shells flew overhead. Artillery thundered behind the troops. And a blimp, high above, observed their movements.

The Germans passed on through. Alain and his companions ventured toward the artillery. They followed the Scheldt, crossing damp meadows, hedges of pollard willows, ditches full of gorse and green water. They ran for a line of trees and thickets. The sound of the artillery was growing louder and drawing nearer. Shells whistled through the air, though the men could not pinpoint the exact origin. When the din became too great, they hid in a ditch for a minute, then moved forward again, toward the big guns, in a state of mounting fright. In the end they were terrified. Alain and Bidart kept their composure. But François and the others wanted to flee and go back toward Oudenaarde. The firing line drew ever closer to them. The uproar, the din of crashing metal continued increasing. They kept to the ditch, running with hands over their heads, dropping all the bundles, the bags, and the satchels. The younger fellows' teeth were chattering with fear.

They were forced to stop. A few metres ahead, a plume of fire and earth had shot up from a ditch. They stayed glued to the dirt, huddled up. And then, breaking through a hedge, men in blue uniforms appeared, advancing with rifles in hand. Behind them raged the storm from unseen artillery.

"They're French!" shouted Bidart.

Alain had pulled off his khaki-coloured shirt. Standing up, he waved it with all his might, like a flag. Around him, the others were motioning, shouting, yelling, and crying. Something burst from a nearby thicket, a hunk of iron plowing through, ripping off branches, crushing the undergrowth like a buffalo. It was a tank. The machine came at them with a roar of the engine, hurtling up and down the ditches, so dreadful that they had to force themselves not to run. It stopped. A man jumped out, a French officer.

They surrounded him, grabbed his hands: "Lieutenant! Lieutenant! We're French! French!"

They fell on his neck, showered him with kisses, soaked him with their tears. He wrenched himself free, appearing at once pleased and annoyed.

"Yes, yes, okay, okay, but what on Earth are you doing here?"

They all attempted to explain at once, confusedly. He understood none of it. Round them flowed the thick, rapid, turbulent wave of the firing line – tanks, infantry, machine gunners. It moved like a flood, sweeping and pulling everything along, leaving emptiness in its wake. The troops faced no resistance. They were advancing twenty kilometres a day in this fashion.

Some trucks arrived, rolling across the fields, pitching like boats. The officer hailed the driver of a van. The seven young men were put onboard, and the vehicle turned about, heading back toward the rear. Inside two soldiers guarded the exit.

The vehicle came to a stop in a farmyard. The men stepped out and were led to a captain, who had set up his office in the farmers' dining room.

"A bunch of spies?" he said.

"Spies! Us?"

"Your papers?"

They had no papers. They searched their pockets but only found German cards, papers issued by German headquarters. For four years they had had nothing else.

"Oh, yes," said the captain, "I see what's going on here ... I'm inclined to have all seven of you shot."

"Captain," begged Alain, "wait a few days, check with our families, we swear ..."

They were terrified. To have endured so much, struggled so much, only to get themselves shot by the French! To die senselessly right at the end! All seven had started crying. They rummaged through their pockets, piling up evidence without convincing the officer. Finally, by some miracle, one of the students came across an old card from the Institut Industriel du Nord. It was dated 1913. This got the captain's attention. He announced, "Okay. I'm going to interrogate each of you individually, and without your being able to talk to each other beforehand. If the story of even one of you differs from the others, you're all done for!"

He had each of them locked in separate rooms and questioned them one at a time.

Alain, the leader of the group, went last. The wait had been excruciating. He told the truth. Never had he been so afraid of making a mistake, of forgetting something. One pays so little attention to the course of events! And now his life depended on it. He told his story like a confession, searching, plumbing his memory, and feeling the blood drain from his face when he stumbled upon a point on which he was fuzzy.

"Is that everything?" said the officer.

"That's everything."

"You're sure you've got nothing else to say?"

"I ... No, Captain, I don't see what else there is ..."

"You're sure your pals didn't tell me anything different?"

Alain broke into a cold sweat.

"Captain ... No, I've told nothing but the truth ... If my friends said anything different, they're mistaken ... My God, this is terrible ..."

And his courage failed him. He broke into tears.

"It's okay," said the officer.

He scribbled something on a piece of paper. He gave the note to Alain.

"You've had a close shave, my boy. Go on, clear out! Here's your safe conduct."

Never had life seemed as beautiful as it did along the road that led them back toward Avelghem, as free men. The countryside was empty, deserted, the houses pillaged, the wells marked with dire warnings: "contaminated." They had not eaten since the day before. They did not know what they would find back in Roubaix, in the Nord. But they had managed to cheat death. They felt alive. And the war was over.

A little before Avelghem, in the doorway of a house, they saw a French soldier. They ran toward him, surrounded him, showered him with kises.

"We're French! We're French!"

He bid all seven come inside. There they found a sergeant and a dozen men feasting on lamb stew and red wine. What delicacies! The soldiers shared their meal. The seven ate and drank till they were near to bursting, making up for four years of abstinence, four years without meat, potatoes, wine, or spirits. The troops encouraged them to eat up. All seven were soon beside themselves with excitement: singing the "Marseillaise" and hymns of praise, shouting in delirium. The formidable vengeance of long-repressed youth came welling up!

· · ·

The next evening Alain reached Roubaix. His excitement had already begun to cool. François and the others had not yet arrived, lost in Homeric celebrations. Alain, for his part, felt life taking hold again. What was he going to do now? What was he going find back in Roubaix? What had become of his mother? And his siblings? And what would become of him? What would life be like in the new world that men of good will intended to establish after the war? How would he find work? What kind? And would he one day be able to set aside the harshness, the savagery that four years of misery had built up inside him? Could he get readjusted, recivilized? At present he had almost turned into a bushman – tough, brutal, quick to resort to force. And if he did manage to readjust, to start over, how many others would remain forever marked, imprinted with such traits? It would be hard to recreate a peaceful world ...

With each step he took through the streets of Roubaix, a silent fear mounted within him. He found the city in a state of excitement, renewal, wretched and feverish, teeming with French and English soldiers, people running to and fro, transports bringing in food and new life. Stores were reopening on every corner, stands and bric-a-brac shops popping up all around, thrown together haphazardly, with signs reading *All goods bought and sold.* It was the disorder of the provisional, of momentous activity starting up again. Behind the hustle and bustle one sensed a frenzied need for renewal, recovery, and stimulation.

He reached Épeule. He recognized some faces, but no one recognized him. He had become a man, made more virile by the struggle. When he arrived at the entrance of the cul-de-sac, he felt something akin to foreboding tear at his heart. Suddenly he recalled that dreadful night, after escaping from Prémesques, when he had come seeking shelter and been forced to leave again. He mastered the emotion and moved on. The door to the house, absent its copper handle, opened with a string. He pulled on it and stepped into Félicie's kitchen, a room he hardly recognized: stripped bare, without furniture, wainscoting, or stairs. A ladder led to the second floor. There were neither doors nor shelves in the pantry or the cupboards. And the sideboard was gone.

He went into the courtyard and called out, "Is anyone home?"

He heard footsteps behind him, a weak voice, the voice of an old woman.

"Alain! My boy! My dear boy ..."

She had grabbed him, kissed him, showered him with tears before he even recognized her.

Nothing was lost after all! They would start over! They would bring back his siblings, reestablish hearth, home, happiness ... The bad times would be forgotten. The dark memory of their sufferings would fade. They would be happy again, yes, happy like before, happier even, now that Alain had striven and emerged from the ordeal as a man. And then there was the letter, the blessed letter that a beaming Félicie brought to her son, a letter in which Juliette Sancey, who had not forgotten Alain, told of her impending return.

PART IV

I

When he returned from Brussels, where he had been forced to follow the German army, Pascal Donadieu learned that his father had died. His mother had received two telegrams within two hours of each other.

"Simon Donadieu gravely ill."

"Simon Donadieu deceased."

The trip from Lille to Paris, by way of Calais, took Pascal thirty hours. It was an endless journey aboard jam-packed trains with broken windows, travelling across the front, the cursed no-man's land. One could feel the rails sinking beneath the cars into soil that had been all too recently disturbed.

As soon as he reached Paris, Pascal rushed to the hospital. But by the time he arrived, his father's casket had already been nailed shut. Pascal was merely given a bundle of papers and the address of the place where Simon had been staying. It was on rue de Flandre, on the seventh floor of a little hotel.

Pascal headed toward rue de Flandre. He went by foot. He was not familiar with the metro. And he did not have enough money to take another taxi. Around him, the seething and tumultuous city of Paris left him stunned, overwhelming him with its uproar, astounding him with an incessant, rapid, dizzying procession of trams, cars, taxis, buses, and wagons: the whole rushing along the roadway in a continual stream. The cafés were blazing, flooded with lights, crystal, mirrors, copper, and nickel. Crowds were sauntering, meandering, lingering, or fussing about, with eddies forming round newsstands, flower sellers, and metro stations. Women flowed past, so many young, attractive, festooned, laughing women, like the delicate ornaments of the world! Street hawkers were selling evening newspapers. Couples, idlers, pleasure-seekers were sipping aperitifs behind the huge bay windows of the cafés. Window displays were illumined, captivating, dazzling, with an abundance of lights and splendours, expensive jewellery, furs, perfumes, gloves, high fashions, and lingerie: all the luxury and splendour, all the bright, light-hearted, easy-going way of life, all the sparkling gaiety of an immense city of delights.

Pascal clutched the packet of letters in his pocket and hurried along. For a boy whose father was dead, the entire spectacle was nauseating. Four years of tense, joyless existence inspired nothing but disgust and revulsion for this fairyland. In spite of themselves, the people of northern France had turned into a bunch of ascetics. Amid the appalling and almost super-human contest, they had assumed a certain rigidity, a puritanical austerity. Artifice was shocking, offensive. They had endured too much to continue accepting a frivolous notion of life and the world.

So that's what it's been like, reflected Pascal, *that's what the war's been like for people here! How well they've lived! They've been so fortunate! While we* ...

He thought of Lille, Roubaix, Tourcoing: dead, funereal, depopulated cities littered with crumbling ruins, haunted by the dying with their pale, ghostly expressions. In his bitter sobriety, he developed a hatred for Paris – for the rest of France – which had been blessed, had not suffered, had not seen. He sensed that people from regions spared by the great tempest would never be able to understand the inhabitants of the occupied territories and that this lack of comprehension would quickly become a source of discord and injustice.

He found the hotel on rue de Flandre. It was a modest establishment: a jumble of mean and dirty rooms. The ground floor bore a semblance of luxury: a scrap of carpet, a banister with a copper knob, a sumptuousness that, starting on the second floor, gave way to dismal filthiness. Pascal had already begun heading up the stairs when the concierge shouted out, "Young man!"

"I'm Pascal Donadieu, Madam. I'm going up to my father's room."

"Simon's son! Come in, come into my place, young fellow!"

She pushed him into her lodging. She was a fat old woman with a wan, puffy face.

"He stayed here! Yes, indeed. His room's paid for. You can have it and collect your father's things. Ah, he was a good man. We were pals. We talked about you all the time. That's right, young fellow. I should've recognized you. You're all alone? Well then, you'll come to dinner tonight ... Yes, yes ... And I'll hold a séance. You'll see, we'll talk to 'him,'" she added, with a serious look.

Pascal realized that the old woman fancied herself a medium.

They dined together, along with her son and her husband. They had bread and sausage, cheese soup, and red wine. They talked about Simon, the war, the Nord. The family listened to Pascal. He tried to explain what he had done, seen, suffered, but he was unable to put it into words, finding only trite, worn-out clichés.

"We suffered. Oh, yes. We were starving, you see ... And the bombs and the artillery ... and the Boches. It was dreadful, I tell you."

He was astonished, to the depths of his being, that four years of martyrdom could not be expressed more forcefully, more intensely. He searched for the right words, trying to recreate for them the nightmare, the agony he had endured, and sensed that he would never manage it. No, it was pointless. He would never find a way. He had the clear sensation of failing to reach them. They nodded their heads in affirmation. The son said, "Yes, yes ... We went hungry here, too, we were bombed, too, you know ... And we just missed seeing the Boches in Paris."

Pascal felt revulsion welling inside him, the indignation one gets from being misunderstood. To compare this undamaged, merry, shining Paris – hardly touched by the war – this happy crowd, this abundance, this luxury, to the invaded, crushed, mournful cities with their dead industries, their tubercular, famished, freezing populations, their long streets overrun with grass and lined with crumbling, dilapidated houses whose interiors were without furniture, doors, or windows, without light or heat! No, these people would never understand.

He bid them all goodnight. He went up to his father's room, a little furnished garret with a fold-away bed and a trunk. The trunk was packed, sitting just beneath the skylight. His father had hoped to go home. He had thought of his family, loaded the bottom of the trunk with canned goods, wine, coffee, a few books, too – his whole collection – and a little dictionary in which Pascal found dried flowers.

Pascal had spread his father's papers on the lid of the trunk. There were hospital reports, lots of them. His father had done nothing but drag himself from one hospital to the next. There were also letters addressed to Pascal, and which had not managed to reach him. Pascal read them and cried.

In a big yellow envelope folded in two, the last in the bundle, Pascal found a paper scribbled in pencil, a sort of testament written in 1916, a sheet already old, faded, almost illegible – a compendium of advice, final words of wisdom, a bit naïve in their gravity but in which one could discern the anguish of a father, a man aged, matured, and who – sensing that he would be unable to pass on all his priceless life experience, all the wisdom that is so hard to come by – had attempted clumsily, awkwardly, and in a tragically solemn fashion to condense it into a final message from beyond the grave.

For my son Pascal, in the event of my untimely death ...

In life, my son, you must be brave and work hard ... The only way to secure a position is to make yourself indispensable. Educate yourself, especially in your best subjects. Never lie. Don't get involved in politics unless you make a career of it, but beware that it's a frightful business.

If Germany wins, don't stay. Learn a trade – mechanics or electricity – and leave with your mother for America, to join your Uncle Paul. You'll be happier there than in Germany.

Take care of your mother. A curse on this war that has separated us. Remember me as I have remembered you. [signed] Simon DONADIEU

Kneeling before the trunk, using the nub of a pencil, Pascal slowly – piously – traced over his father's faded handwriting. He could see his father penning this letter, perhaps right here, on this trunk, in this little seventh-floor garret, beneath the dark Paris sky ... He cried. He realized all that he had lost, just how much devotion, experience, and love his father could have imparted to him, and which this poor scrap of paper – despite Simon Donadieu's desperate attempt to pour his soul into it – could never replace.

II

Following his escape attempt, Hennedyck had spent four months under Streng arrest, in solitary confinement. He had almost died. His letters of protest had eventually moved the authorities. And – half-dead, suffering from a dreadful case of enteritis, reduced to no more than forty-eight kilos, a veritable skeleton through which the guards, chuckling to themselves, pretended to read their newspapers – he was finally granted a reprieve and admitted to the hospital in Beuel, a little city along the Rhine.

The local populace was not hostile and became increasingly favourable toward France as they sensed the Empire's impending demise. These Rhenish districts recalled their French past, during the reign of Napoléon. Many people talked to Hennedyck about it. In the pages of the *Gazette of Cologne*, he tracked the imperial collapse from day to day. He learned of the liberation of the Nord, the German retreat, the revolution in Brussels. On 9 November, the Kaiser abdicated. On the eleventh, the armistice took effect. On morning of the twelfth, the terms of the armistice were posted, written in chalk on a big blackboard at Beuel's city hall. A crowd filed past, read in silence, and headed off in dismay. One could hear people whispering: "That! They agreed to that!"

Hennedyck was immediately released and treated with the utmost respect. The change was abrupt. People were expecting to see the Allies arrive in Beuel. They feared mistreatment and reprisals. They begged Hennedyck to intervene. He took advantage of the situation to reclaim the bit of money left to him and board a train for Switzerland. He travelled with a hoard of drunken troops. They were stopped at the frontier. The Swiss feared communist revolution and had sealed the border. Hennedyck went back on foot toward the Rhine, crossed it at Saint-Louis, and reached Mulhouse. From there, a military transport took him to Belfort, where he located a train bound for Paris. On the evening of 22 November, he returned to Roubaix.

He rushed home, found the big family house empty and pillaged. People had broken the windowpanes. Looters had stolen the furniture. No one was there, not even a servant.

Filled with dread, Hennedyck went over to the factory. He entered the courtyard and was shocked by the extent of the devastation. The hospital rooms were nothing but a heap of ruins. The entire dye works had been brought down by the detonation of the railroad. The mill was inaccessible, the entrance blocked by a mound of rusty scrap iron that reached to the ceiling, as if bits of cast iron and steel from all of the city's looms had been piled up here. He did not have the heart to go down to the boiler room nor to the engine room. But he could see that the smokestack had been hit by a shell and split like a barrel, from top to bottom.

In the very back, he finally found his doorkeeper. The old man was harvesting Brussels sprouts from the railroad embankment, which he had converted into a garden. He was dismayed at the sad state of his boss. With difficulty, Hennedyck pulled out of him the tale of Émilie's adventure and her disappearance.

Hennedyck spent a week in anger and despair, half-crazed, wanting to flee, stymied by lack of money, not knowing where to stay, sleeping in a dilapidated office without furniture, dreaming of abandoning everything, selling everything – to anyone – simply for the price of the land, and disappearing. He would have spilled his own blood to learn of Émilie's whereabouts, to run insult her, beat her, kill her, or to find a way to return to Germany, track down von Mesnil in Berlin, and slit his throat. He felt a beastly rage, the need to inflict pain. He let out a cry of joy and hatred when he received the letter from Brussels.

It came from police headquarters. Some patrolmen had picked up Émilie – penniless, in deplorable physical and mental condition, half-disoriented, and dying of hunger. For three days she had refused to give either name or address. At present she was at Saint-Jean Hospital. The letter requested that her husband come see her or at least make his intentions known.

Henndyck's initial reaction was one of contented rage, the inner roar of gratified, satiated hatred. Vengeance! Vengeance was his! He need only leave Émilie in her present condition, forsake her, abandon her. She could die like a dog, for all he cared!

But at the same time, memories quickly resurfaced, images of a happier era, reminders of the timid and sickly Émilie whom he had so loved, so cared for. He was obsessed by the wretched end in store for her. She would die in that hospital. Or if not, what would become of her? Where would she go? She had neither money nor friend nor honour. She was done for. There was nothing left but the gutter, the street ... How clearly he could see her fragile body – which he had so loved, so revered, so cared for – sullied, prostituted, served up to the highest bidder ... He had flashes of memory, sudden reminders of a look, a word, a gentle voice – always a little quivering and muffled, as if trembling from constantly suppressed internal emotion ...

After all, what would be the harm in seeing her, just seeing her ... He would be making no commitment. He would not thereby be obliged to take her back. It would be better, really, to know exactly what had become of her. He rationalized. He sought justification for his present, imperious need to find her again.

On the third day, he set out for the train station, rented an automobile, and left for Brussels and that same Saint-Jean Hospital where Verlaine and Rimbaud had suffered.*

III

Deep inside their cellblock, Decraemer and the Abbé Sennevilliers learned of the victory in early November.

A delegation of soldiers and workers – sent from Cologne by revolutionary committees – came to Rheinbach with orders to release German soldiers imprisoned for desertion, treason, or refusal to obey orders.

The abbé, who was still the Direktor's "Vertrauensmann," or trustee, put the question to the delegates: "And what about us?"

"Do as you please."

The rumour had already spread through the prison, causing tumultuous excitement. The inmates spoke of revolt, of insurrection. The abbé – who had suddenly acquired new prestige and was now treated as an equal by a courteous and submissive Direktor – talked the matter over with him. It would be dangerous to let an exhausted, half-dead group of men set off on foot toward Beligum, guaranteeing that most of them would never see their country again. It would be best to arrange for railway transport, to take advantage of the convoys heading toward Belgium to salvage remaining German equipment.

In due course, the signing of the armistice further consolidated the abbé's position.

All political prisoners were to be set free. The abbé urged his compatriots to be patient. Three departures were organized. The abbé left last, on

---

*In July 1873 the poet Paul Verlaine shot friend and fellow poet Arthur Rimbaud in the arm, following a drunken argument. Verlaine and his mother accompanied Rimbaud to Sain-Jean Hospital, where Rimbaud received treatment for his wound. He made a full recovery.

the final train – a little like a ship's captain – accompanied by his friend Decraemer, who was at the end of his strength.

It was a dreadful journey, inordinately slow, in packed cars overflowing with men, so full that one saw clusters hanging from the doors and perched on the roofs. They sang, yelled, waved their arms. It was an extraordinary mixture of suffering, wretchedness, and enthusiasm. The mad exaltation ultimately sapped the fortitude of these declining men. For many of them, this final odyssey would remain etched in their minds like a terrible nightmare.

They ended up in Leuven, where no more trains were available. They had to wait several days. The abbé and Decraemer – who could no longer walk, who had to be supported and dragged along like a dying man – found lodging with a law professor and received a warm welcome in his home. The abbé tended to Decraemer, who once more owed his life to the priest. The abbé handled Decraemer with care, imposing a regimen of light fare for his companion's dilapidated constitution, which was incapable of sustained dietary struggle.

In the meantime, the abbé searched for some mode of transportation. He learned that a convoy of trucks was taking the sick and the wounded back to France. He thought of his friend, requested a place for him ... They said a tearful goodbye.

Three days later a train was finally arranged for Ostend and France. The abbé and his comrades left Leuven.

At Ostend they found some trucks, climbed aboard, and headed toward Dunkerque. But at the border, upon announcing that they were prisoners coming back from Germany, the abbé and his fellows were arrested. They were subjected to a humiliating interrogation. The authorities took them for spies returning under false pretenses.

At the station in Ghyvelde they were put on a train for Dunkerque, under military escort. The French soldiers guarding them told them about the camp where they were being taken: there they would undergo a physical and moral quarantine, be questioned, inspected, subjected to every imaginable precaution, injection, and medical examination. Men of all stripes were in these camps. The abbé – distraught, disgusted – was appalled and indignant. So this was the glorious return, the greeting of the motherland!

They got off at the station in Dunkerque and were herded through town, wretched and ashamed of themselves, as a crowd looked on. At a street corner, the abbé suddenly threw himself into the entrance of a carriage door and let the group pass by. He was free.

He asked a colleague in Dunkerque for money and a cassock. And two days later he arrived in Herlem, where he found his mother, Old Berthe, mad with joy and sorrow, along with little Pierre. For Berthe, the return of her son was a miracle.

She told him about the arrest of Lise, who was still imprisoned in Roubaix with little Jeannette, Fannie's child.

. . .

The cellar of Roubaix's city hall was near to bursting. People had been crammed into cells pell-mell. Without so much as the occasional recess, a military tribunal – composed of a French officer, an Englishman, and a Belgian – was trying all the men and women suspected of intelligence with the enemy.

Here one found prostitutes, traffickers in gold, informers, workers who had laboured for the Germans, café owners who had served an exclusively German clientele. And then there were all the innocents atoning for the hatred of a rival, a jealous neighbour. Each day a flood of anonymous letters arrived, inundating the officers' desks. This form of vengeance was convenient and discreet. Defamatory, slanderous letters poured in from the South of France, Paris, Lyon, Évian. Evacuees avenged themselves from afar. The sight of this cellar – this crowd of good people and scoundrels mixed together at random, this product of humanity's cowardice and maliciousness – left one sickened, disgusted with the victory.

Two days later, thanks to her brother, Lise was brought before the tribunal, pronounced innocent, and released.

The judges asked her what she planned to do with the German child accompanying her. Huge orphanages, special establishments were opening in Belgium, agreeing to take on these miserable children. But Lise wanted to adopt Jeannette.

While Lise was returning to Herlem, the abbé was escorting Judith Lacombe – whom he had also succeeded in having released – to a convent in Lille. She could not go back to Herlem. A hue and cry had been raised against her! She bore the weight of everyone else's transgressions. All the people she had obliged, assisted during the war, helped by way of her influence with the German authorities, had turned on her, as if they held it against her. Old Lacombe had disowned her. Her sister Estelle, whose husband Louis Babet had returned from the war, also had good reason for wanting Judith to stay away. The sight of her in the cloister was an atonement of sorts for the Lacombes' honour. She would find a refuge in religion, like many others.

For about this time a stream of women invaded the region's convents. Some were in earnest, driven to despair after the departure or death of a beloved German soldier, but others were only fleeing justice, anxious to avoid the dreadful "registration" held in store for them by the vice squad.

In Herlem, the Sennevilliers enjoyed peace and quiet, a necessary respite, and the distraction of their neighbours, of whom they had had quite enough. The village slowly returned to normal. Lacombe was nominated for the Legion of Honour. Put in charge of restocking the herds of the liberated districts, Humfels and he had just left for Argentina and were anticipating lucrative transactions. Marellis, pronounced dead by the Ministry of Finance, had found himself without a job, had an awful time proving he was still alive and having himself reinstated, and came up against the resistance of everyone with less seniority who had been promoted during the war. In the meantime, after a delay of four years, he finally received the evacuation order he had vainly awaited in October 1914.

As for Brook, the substitute policeman, he met a tragic end. This petty local tyrant, too old and too uneducated for a permanent position, had been forced to step down as soon as the first demobilized troops had returned. Brook had never gotten over losing his power, relinquishing his kepi and his badge, his authority over hill and meadow. He hung himself in his barn, preferring not to outlive his bygone glory. Every mind conceives an ideal, an ambition all its own.

The Sennevilliers' quarry was dead. It would not be brought back into production for a long time to come. Perhaps one day little Pierre would start it up again. For the time being, it was merely a destination for sweethearts and fishermen.

The Sennevilliers lived in the old cottage up the hill from the kilns.

Émilie Hennedyck, brought back by her husband, had taken refuge with the Sennevilliers, seeking to hide her shame and her wretchedness. And the abbé, through his affection for Fannie's children, had satisfied the paternal instinct that he was granted no other means of fulfilling – a need of the spirit more than the body. He had also returned to his cherished Latin translations.

Otherwise, nothing had changed. The farmers resumed their seasonal rythms. The country folks had survived, eaten their fill, sold their produce, hardly suffered, like all who stay rooted to the soil. Requisition vouchers were going to be redeemed for banknotes. Four years of harvests would thus be remunerated. And the prewar slump had given way to a need for activity, a tremendous demand for grain. A time of easy farm profits was at hand. And the old Baron des Parges, the great landlord, had become five times richer than before the war, thanks to the astonishing and automatic appreciation of land values, which the owner enjoys without putting forth any effort.

IV

Jacqueline and Camille Laubigier were still living with Mrs Endive. As soon as Roubaix had been liberated, they had sent a magnificent postcard featuring an odd group: Foche and Lloyd George, Clemenceau and Wilson, with Lady Liberty lighting the world and pronouncing the triumph of liberty and justice.

Félicie wrote back.

Alain was selling potatoes and had started making a little money. Work was getting underway again in the devastated department of the Nord. The family would soon be reunited. Jacqueline and Camille dreamed of going home.

Mrs Endive said nothing. She was an old woman. She did not care much for Camille, whose odd habits she found annoying. But she had grown attached to Jacqueline. Mrs Endive had lived by herself for a long time. Jacqueline had relieved her boredom, the emptiness of a solitary existence. If Jacqueline left, she would be lonely again.

Jacqueline waited several months. The authorities were reticent to send children back to the Nord, which still lay in ruins. The paperwork was complicated. Jacqueline proceeded with patience.

Mrs Endive grew sad. She had a plan but was hesitant to mention it. She finally worked up the courage and asked Jacqueline, "Wouldn't you like to stay here with me in Belleville? I'd see that you were educated. You'd be my daughter. And I have a few possessions. They'd be yours one day."

She did not know how to talk to children.

Jacqueline would not consent. Alain had written. He was anxious to see the household reunited, resurrected.

Departure required municipal approval. Jacqueline had requested it. The authorities summoned her and told her that her parents had refused because they did not have the means to support her. Jacqueline was stunned, refused to admit that it could be true, protested, fought back.

Only a few days later did the officials realize that the refusal concerned other Laubigiers who were living in Belleville-sur-Seine and not Belleville-sur-Saône.

Jacqueline and Camille returned together, making an endless journey to Paris, then across the Île-de-France and the front, gazing in horror at a wild and volcanic landscape dotted with bushes and steppe-like vegetation, which concealed the bareness, the devastation, the tormented and dreadful terrain. Then came Lille, the invaded Nord with its fields of sugar beets, green flax, wheat, and potatoes, and finally Roubaix, dark and gloomy, which they traversed on ruined tressels, crumbling embankments, temporary structures, bags of cement hastily stacked into piles and sprinkled with water. The footbridge at the train station had collapsed, and the windowless concourse lay in ruins.

They left the station and headed toward Épeule.

Little Camille no longer recognized Roubaix. It seemed at once enormous and crowded, dirty, sombre, smoky. His eyes were unaccustomed to the sight. Such ugliness, coupled with the difficulty and emotion of their return, left both of them feeling dejected. The residents were emaciated, like walking skeletons. The smell of oil, mud, and soot, the fetid plumes from the factories, the lingering odour of wool, suint, and chemical dyes drifting up from the sewer grates: it was disgusting. They noticed this stench for the first time, as well as the dark entries to the alleyways, the cutthroat aspect of the long, tortuous pathways, the squalid misery of these districts where an enslaved humanity had been stagnating for generations on end. Above the buildings, at the far reach of the street, a black keep stood against the bright background of a beautiful, pale green sky: a factory chimney wafting up smoke, like an extinguished torch.

At the corner of rue Watt, they came across Alain perched on a wagonload of potatoes.

That night there was a party at the Laubigiers'. They had invited the neighbours: Flavie and her children, old mother Duydt and her two little ones. Mrs Duydt was on her own now. Her two sons were dead. Léonie had left with the other women on the train for Brussels. And her husband, that frenzied old miser, had gathered all his money and cleared out just after the arrival of the English, leaving behind a weary wife and two children whom he had never seen as anything more than tools. The old woman, who had resigned herself to the situation, did not complain, accepted the ordeal humbly, merely speaking of the one thing – amid the general disaster – that she still found upsetting: her Étienne who was dead, her Zidore who was so good, whose childhood she evoked alongside his fatal destiny and his tragic end at the Bac à Puces cabaret. Of the two boys, oddly enough, it was the murderer who retained pride of place – a bit more affection – in the old woman's heart.

Flavie's eldest son was dead, too: killed at the front. A week after the liberation, the family had received a note from one of his pals. His head had been torn off by a shell. He was buried twenty-four metres northwest of Wood 19, in the Houthulst district of Belgium. His brother François had gone with Alain to look for the body. It was a distressing pilgrimage through Houthulst Forest: a haunting landscape studded with dead trees stripped bare as bones and ripped to shreds, a furrowed and rolling expanse like an enormous stretch of dunes invaded by vast, insidious pools of stagnant and treacherous water, cut by an impenetrable network of barbed wire and brambles, traversed by collapsed trenches transformed into ravines. Here and there, one would come across a huge, thickset mass: a tank painted in camouflage, dripping rusty liquid like brown blood, with gaping wounds clearly visible, big holes in its metal skin, marks of the shell that had killed it. The ground was littered with machine guns – blocks of scrap iron set in emplacements built of sandbags, concrete, or wood – and with cartridge cases, rifle butts, helmets, and horse bones protruding from the clay. One had the impression of treading on the grounds of a huge necropolis. Stretching toward the horizon, the vista was like an arid wasteland with a strong wind blowing from the sea and whistling through the waving grass. And in spots groups of Vietnamese – worrisome, stooping figures – were busy at some task or other. François and Alain felt they had to beware of them, that these fellows might easily resort to assault and murder just to rob them.

For two days François and Alain looked for the cemetery without success. The forest itself had disappeared. They had to come back later with maps. This time they found three bodies in a single grave. They recognized François's brother as the one missing a head.

François brought his mother a notebook discovered on the body. But it had to be burned. It had retained the dreadful smell of the corpse with which it had remained for so long.

Yet the family still had some momentos of the deceased. People who had billeted him on leave wrote to Flavie to convey their sympathies. He was a good boy. He had helped them with odd jobs, churned the butter, tended to the rabbits. They sent papers he had left behind. And by way of these odds and ends snatched from the void, Flavie reconstructed her son's life over the four years, resurrected it, envisioned it, eventually learned quite a lot about him. And this type of afterlife, the veiled existence that she penetrated and came to know little by little, left her with the impression that her departed son would keep on living, at least for a time. He would not be entirely gone as long as she could learn something else about him.

Each evening conversation at the Laubigiers' revolved around nothing but the dead, the war ... In almost every household there was a sense of disillusionment. People felt their suffering had been meaningless.

"We had it tough," said Flavie. "We resisted, we didn't want to 'take up' with the Boches. We went hungry. Why? I think that at bottom, we were stupid. I see the other women. They kept their sons with them. In my own case, François would've likely died in Prémesques if it hadn't been for Alain. Those other kids had meat and bread. They're big, they've got healthy cheeks. My children were deprived. They're sick and skinny."

"Or we had to send them far away," said Félicie, "and suffer still more."

Flavie replied: "You heard people say, 'After the war, they'll pay, the women who took up with the Boches, the men who trafficked, who made money. It'll cost them dear. We'll have our revenge.' But in the end a few windows were broken, a few women had a bit of hair pulled out, and it was over. They still have their money and their health. And their kids are strong and sturdy – the ones the Germans fed, the ones who didn't go hungry.

"And the husbands! You'd have anticipated all sorts of reactions ... Feared their wrath ... What would so and so do when they learned their wives had run after the Boches, jumped in the sack with them, had their fill ... Well, I tell you! ... I saw Clara Broeckx's husband come back. He was told, 'Your wife lived it up with the officers, she's a whore.' Yes, but then he went home, found handsome furnishings stolen from the mansions, drawers full of money, pleasant conditions, the easy life. He said absolutely nothing. He was too satisfied.

"And Decooster the butcher? He sold dog meat, trafficked with the Boches, let his wife party with the officers. Now he couldn't care less. He's got a car."

"We suffered for nothing," repeated Flavie. "I don't know why we stuck to our principles."

Alain and François laughed. Among the young, misery is quickly forgotten. Their grievous suffering was behind them. And the future before them seemed endless. They were at the age when time appears unlimited, when four years hardly seem to count.

But, of all of them, only Alain did not regret having gone through the war. The same ordeal that weakens one strengthens another. It had given him experience with life and his fellow men that he would never have had otherwise. The struggle had taught him much about himself and shown him the kind of happiness that he ought to seek: a free, expansive, active life, the independence he had tasted and that he could no longer do without, a wholesome career, loved ones to whom he could devote himself. That was how he would savour life's joys. He had abandoned the foundry, the gloomy toil amid dust and coal. Mrs Sancey had loaned him a little money, enough to purchase a cart and a few sacks of potatoes from Belgium. And Alain had fit himself out as an itinerant merchant. He already had a little wagon and a discharged mule purchased from the English army and still branded accordingly. He travelled to Belgian farms, buying up butter, eggs, and potatoes that he marketed wholesale. His business was prospering. And in three months he would marry Juliette.

Alain, ever the optimist, said, "Bah! We'll make up for it. We'll all be happy again, in spite of everything! Isn't that right, Camille?"

And he slapped his little brother on the hand.

Little Camille listened and said nothing. He was weary from his journey and vaguely sad, despite the joy of being home again. Deep down inside, he felt that something was missing. For months he had anticipated this homecoming with such intensity, such desire to see his mother again, that occasionally he had almost been frightened by the joy that awaited. But now he felt a little disappointed, a little sad ... He was not as happy as he had thought, as he had hoped he would be. He had suffered during his exile, not finding the tenderness, the kindheartedness, the affection of a mother in Belleville-sur-Saône. Mrs Endive was rather cold. His heart had hardened. He had almost become a little man. He was no longer interested in sitting on his mother's lap, in tokens of affection, in pecks on the cheek. And this change, amid the general enthusiasm, left him a tad bitter, as if he already understood – despite the words of his older brother Alain – that lost happiness is never quite found again.

V

Day in and day out, Annie heard nothing but talk of the David case.

For the past week, the newspapers had been filled with the story. It had started in typical fashion, with cautious openings: *Word has it that* ... and initials incriminating no one in particular. Then the rumour was confirmed. Trafficking, intelligence with the enemy, trade with the army of occupation ... Complaints had been lodged by several manufacturers. The prosecutor's office had had David indicted and incarcerated.

He had been arrested at home one morning. He had attempted to shoot himself in the head. The police had disarmed him just in time and transported him to Lille, where he had been greeted upon arrival by an angry crowd that called for his lynching. In Roubaix, the rabble had laid siege to his mansion the entire day, with the intention of setting it ablaze. In the space of three days, Albertine Mailly – David's mistress – had sold all the furniture, the paintings, the art objects, and the tapestries, which had been loaded onto wagons in the middle of the night. She had fled to Belgium. An antique dealer from Lille, it was said, had paid her 175,000 francs and made as much in the bargain.

At the Mourauds', as in all of Épeule, people spoke of little else. At bottom, they were pleased. David really was too rich. It was offensive. People's spiteful envy was satisfied. They invoked vague notions of divine justice. If he had remained as miserable as everyone else during the war, none of this would have happened.

Annie read the newspapers with anxiety. She did not understand much about the accusations. She merely saw a fearsome wave of hatred for David, as if all the responsibility had fallen on him alone, as if he had been chosen to atone for the sins of the many. When he had arrived at the Palais de Justice, the authorities had been forced to defend him from the crowd, surround him with a ring of policemen. A rock had hit him on the forehead. The situation pained Annie. She could envision David – so good, so humane beneath his harsh outward appearance – encircled by enemies, madmen, forced to take cover, hide himself, flee. She would have liked to have seen him, to have been there, to have shouted her support from afar, to have let him know that one person, at least, was on his side ... She would have given anything for such an opportunity. She wished for it, yearned for it, with a passion that included something more than simple pity.

Annie now spent days at a time doing sewing for the city's wealthy bourgeois – for she was a talented seamstress. One Saturday when work was less pressing, she took the Mongy streetcar to Lille. She knew that David would be questioned that afternoon.

• • •

David was called before the examining magistrate, Thavard, almost every day. He was held as "the accused" in the old prison of the Palais de Justice, for at this point in time only convicted criminals were taken to Loos.

More than a dozen people were standing in the courtyard, waiting to proceed to either a preliminary investigation or the criminal court. Beneath the rays of the sun, the vast square paved in grey cobblestones had the bleak, enclosed appearance of a fortress parade ground, surrounded as it was by tall buildings of dirty, brownish red brick with narrow loopholes blocked by rusty iron bars.

The accused were chained in pairs by the wrist. They made their way to the urinals in this manner, two at a time, and had to relieve themselves together, each man waiting till his partner had finished ... The policemen, dressed in ribbed kaki shirts, their throats bound by tightly bottoned collars, were wiping sweat from the inside of their kepis.

The complaint had been lodged by Villard and Ingelby. David was accused of intelligence with the enemy, trafficking in foodstuffs, importation of meat, butter, and merchandise from Holland by means of German permits, sale of raw and spun wool and cloth to the German army, and finally payments made in gold to the military authorities.

David had had a turbulent youth. He still had a long criminal record. In the business world he was known for the audacity, the forcefulness of a man determined to overcome any obstacle. The purchase of factories slated for demolition, of broken down looms, of scrap metal – all of this trade a bit outside the norm and in which the daring entrepreneur rapidly accumulates a fortune – provoked suspicion, as did the new stimulus enjoyed by his business immediately after the war.

Imprisonment spelled ruin for David. He had purchased enormous stockpiles in Calais: Willeme trucks left by the American army, woolen thread from England, raw cotton. All of it was in danger of spoiling. In Antwerp, four barges with thousands of tons of "firmly purchased" American wheat were fermenting and germinating. One boat had caught fire. A few days longer and all of it would be worthless. Ten other deals in the offing, pending options, contracts to salvage metal from the front, and the dispersion of David's workforce – recruited under the table by the competition – made his arrest a disaster, to say nothing of the enormous psychological impact of the ordeal.

He found himself completely alone. Witnesses recused themselves. Lawyers hesitated. It was still a time of overheated, hypersentive patriotism. To have come to terms with the enemy was tantamount to having the plague. David had great difficulty finding a lawyer to take his case.

David's vandalized mansion in Roubaix stood empty. He had learned of the flight of his mistress, who had vanished without sending him so much as a letter, a word of reassurance, like a rat abandoning a sinking ship. She had thought only of carting off anything of value, of putting the finishing touches on her hidden fortune – accumulated in slow, parasitical form over the course of twenty years. David had known her well, had no illusions regarding her, yet he was embittered by the desertion of this woman whom he had enriched and whom, after a certain fashion, he had loved. David, the skeptic, came to understand humanity a little better. He realized that he still had more to learn. It was a general abandonment, a stampede of everyone he had known, helped, succored, of everyone who had come to call and to beg at his door. He had become the leper renounced by all. "I know not this man ..."* The collective repudiation shocked David as much as the material ruin. And yet it is at just such times that a friendship – a sign of reassurance – assumes enormous significance ...

The police van had arrived in the courtyard. The journey was no more than a hundred metres, the prison lying adjacent to the Palais de Justice. But they had to take the street because the Palais was still partially blocked

*Matthew 14:71.

by a gallery that had collapsed in the bombardment. The accused were forced up into the van one at a time. The vehicle pulled out and reached the Palais by rue des Prisons.

• • •

The Palais de Justice opens by way of two doors set atop a staircase bordered by an iron balustrade. Standing along this balcony, squeezed among the crowd, Annie had been waiting since morning. She had come almost in spite of herself, and without knowing what she could do. She just wanted to see David, to show him that he was not totally alone. She did it instinctively, without realizing how much encouragement a gesture of friendship can bring to a prisoner at a moment like this. She was responding to a secret, unconscious urge.

Around her all sorts of people – constables, policemen, journalists, photographers, lawyers – were crammed in the doorway of the Palais and slowly pushed back inside by a teeming mass of onlookers awaiting David. The brand-new case had whipped up popular passions, grabbed the newspaper headlines. Kids were jostling each other. Old folks from the nearby Hospice Comtesse were smoking their pipes and chatting. And anxious women – the prisoners' wives – were shuffling about resignedly, holding little packages. Many hooligans had also come to familiarize themselves with the courtroom drama.

Suddenly the crowd began to stir. People were heading to the right and rue des Prisons. The police van had arrived. Folks ran toward it, escorting it. Guards had to push back the crowd so the rear door could be opened. The onlookers saw creatures in wrinkled attire and with gaunt, haggard expressions getting out one after another, chained together in pairs. Policemen immediately encircled them, establishing a shield and barrier to protect them.

Annie saw David as soon as he appeared, lowering his head to walk down the iron steps of the vehicle. Policemen were flanking him. He inched forward, pale and incredibly aged. Trudging beside him, almost touching him, was a great big fellow with dishevelled hair, a poorly trimmed beard, and the look of a smuggler or a vagabond. They went along at the same pace, forced to press against each other in the awkward, clumsy manner peculiar to prisoners shackled in chains. The authorities had maintained a rigid equality of treatment. In this instance the highest form of justice bordered on injustice.

The prisoners lumbered up the stairs to the accompaniment of jeers: "To Cayenne!* Death to the traitors!"

They passed right by Annie. She looked upon David in sorrow. She gazed intently at the face of the inmate, the face of the vanquished: emaciated, yellowed, aged, swollen beneath the eyes, exhausted by insomnia and distress. She was heartbroken by the anxious and worried expression of this harried, hunted man, and the sad and purified countenance, the new and moving appearance that intense suffering imparts to an individual's features. However debased he may be, a prisoner always acquires something of this demeanour. And for those who know how to read and understand it, this bearing invokes a compulsory respect and an outburst of pity.

David had not seen her. He headed toward the open doorway and entered the vestibule of the Palais. The police shoved folks aside to make a path through the crowd. Round the sad procession swarmed a mass of curious onlookers, angry protesters, reporters and photographers brandishing their equipment, women who wanted to hand a prisoner a child to kiss, a morsel of bread to eat. Driven back by this throng, Annie had to cling to a window sill protruding from the facade. And – submerged, drowned by the multitude – she shouted at the top of her voice to David, whose head alone remained visible above the others: "Mr David! Mr David!"

He turned round in astonishment. He saw only Annie, her arms raised above the crowd. And his face was transfigured.

"Annie!"

He moved toward her, unstoppable. Two policemen vainly attempted to push him back, hold him, force him inside, swearing and cursing: "Go on, get in there! God damn it ... Come on!"

But he pulled them with him, like a bear pulling dogs that have overtaken it, brushed aside the constables in front of him with the back of his hand, waded into the crowd and – tugged backward, half strangled,

---

*The reference is to the Bagne de Cayenne, the French penal colony on several islands – including Devil's Island – and portions of the mainland in French Guiana, not far from the capital of Cayenne.

suffocating, crying – he reached Annie. What followed was spontaneous, instinctive, like an impulse from the depth of their souls. She threw herself toward him, and he quickly kissed her on the cheek, the hair, haphazardly, eagerly, as if he thirsted for her, as if she had always been his.

• • •

The struggle between David and his adversaries intensified, assumed troubling dimensions. It was as if all wartime activity were on trial. David, for his part, went on the offensive. His initial despondency was followed by a fierce determination to defend himself, to sell himself dearly. He made counterclaims, threatened to prove that not only had he never operated on behalf of the Germans but that his services had been solicited, that certain manufacturers had made him proposals of their own accord, knowing full well the destination of the cloth he was purchasing from them. He had worked, trafficked, bought and sold. But everyone had done the same. One had to survive. And whoever had something in stock had been only too happy to convert it to cash.

If he had had recourse to Germans, it was not with the German authorities but with leading civilians. These transactions had remained in the realm of private affairs. If he had imported cattle and butter from Holland, it had done nothing but benefit the population. He had helped feed people while others had forced them to go hungry. This barb was aimed straight at Ingelby, who understood all too well. David must have had evidence of Ingelby's purchases of sugar rations from the mayors of certain communes near Roubaix.

Others, like Wendiével and Villard, had different reasons to worry. They had seen German trucks at their establishments, picking up the cloth sold to David. They could not have remained ignorant of the destination. Why had they not protested? And, above all, why had they cut subsequent deals of the same nature?

Furthermore, Wendiével was currently involved in a dispute with the War Damages Committee. He had thought it clever to include in his list of war damages some of the items figuring in his inventory from July 1914, but which in reality had later been sold to David. Shedding too much light on this situation would be quite dangerous for him.

Gayet, for his part, along with two or three others, recalled the early days of the war. For a few months, their factories had produced goods for the Germans. It had taken the protest of the workers, their refusal to manufacture sheets and sandbags for the enemy, to evoke a response from certain good-hearted men like Hennedyck and in a way force all of the region's manufacturers to resist. Gayet had complied, closed his factories like the others and headed to prison in Güstrow. But many people remembered his initial attitude. At the manufacturers' meeting, he had defended the idea of working for the enemy – he, Gayet, one of the most powerful local industrialists, who should have set an example rather than follow along. In short, the incident – if by chance mentioned in the course of the trial – could well lead to scandal. This possibility was even more bothersome since Gayet, tempted of late by politics, had just announced his candidacy in the upcoming senatorial elections and had a good chance of winning. Indeed Hennedyck – the partisan of resistance whose dramatic speech of faith and courage had carried the meeting – had been subpoenaed as a witness for David.

Many now quietly recalled David's threat: "If I have to go to prison, I'll make sure some of these gentlemen are there to carry my bags for me ..."

Gayet called for liencency and reconciliation. Forget the past, let everyone get back to work, pardon weaknesses ... The national interest demands unity ...

Ingelby withdrew his complaint. In the newspapers, *David the accused* became *Mr Barthélémy David*. The public prosecutor continued his suit. But the preliminary inquiry dragged on and passions cooled: time cast its shadow ... The case was expected to proceed to the criminal court for the October session. But it had been necessary to summon German officers, record their depositions, examine accounts. All of this took time.

David now had three Parisian attorneys who had come to plead his case before their colleagues in Lille. For it had become a major lawsuit, a cause célèbre, a huge trial. There was talk of sixty witnesses. All the manufacturers of the Nord had been subpoenaed. The case would arouse wide interest. There was not a single legal apprentice who did not dream of being chosen as a clerk by one of the renowned attorneys hired to defend David. The Palais was full of these young men. To have one's name associated with the David case: what a start for a new lawyer! And the wheeling and dealing and backstabbing proceeded apace.

The case was finally transferred to the criminal court and an initial hearing scheduled for June 1920.

VI

Following his return from Germany, Decraemer had spent several months recovering, attempting to restore his dreadfully compromised physical health.

His family cared for him, surrounded him, watched over him. His wife Adrienne was frightened by his thinness, his general detachment, the extraordinary mysticism at which he had arrived and that led him to live as if in another world. He sensed that she no longer understood him, could no longer identify with him. And so he forsaw a difficult task, an important mission for the future: to ennoble his wife and son, to help them attain the splendour and peace that he now enjoyed.

By spring 1919, Decraemer had recovered sufficient strength to return to the office and ease himself back into his business affairs.

His factory had burned to the ground. It was arson, and publicly acknowledged as such. The insurance company refused to pay the claim, which was within its rights. And all the other manufacturers – Decraemer's competitors – were already hard at work, feverishly re-equipping themselves. One or two factories were in operation. Others would soon be reopening. It was past time to jump into the fray again. Overcoming his disadvantage would already be quite difficult.

Daniel Decraemer set to work with a passion.

From the height of his idealism, thus did he tumble into the mad scramble. The experience left him dumbfounded. He witnessed a horde of greedy fellows dashing after money, merchandise, equipment: seizing hold of it, carving it up, devouring it. He knew of one little manufacturer, the owner of ten decrepit old looms before the war, who laid claim to sixty, took a hundred, and opened a huge factory. He saw the owner of an old jalopy from 1899, with a rear-mounted engine and a chain-drive transmission, obtain a half-dozen eighteen-horsepower De Dions. A wagon and a skinny old horse were transformed into two or three sturdy, five-ton Packard trucks, hand-picked from American stockpiles. It was a latter-day miracle of the loaves and the fishes! Old fashioned, unmarketable fabrics – dreadful, faded, hideous cotton stuffs, providentially "requisitioned" by the Germans – were reimbursed at top dollar, according to the current cost of living index. Some folks claimed that the enemy had seized merchandise that had actually been stashed away and sold in secret. All one needed were two witnesses and the affidivat of a marshal who had been duped. Money flowed. Germany would pay. One could file claims, collect payments, join the hunt. And splendid factories, new industrial parks – which would be demolished fifteen years later – replaced the old mills. Mansions of the nouveaux riches went up along Grand Boulevard. Roubaix would soon stretch to the outskirts of Lille. People hurried to pillage American stockpiles in Calais, to select and cart off looms, sacks, motors and automobiles, cement and earthenware, building stones, wooden trusses, and metal products. Signing a voucher sufficed. It was a sort of enormous free-for-all in which all sins were forgiven. Work, work, produce to replace was had been destroyed, produce to force people to consume, to stuff themselves so they could die from indigestion a decade later.

Men were coming back from Paris: rogues who had volunteered for the war, quickly found safe postings on the French side of the lines thanks to string-pulling or knavery, and made handsome fortunes by manufacturing shells and uniforms for the army, cement and concrete for the roadways. These rich fellows arrived like proconsuls dispatched to the provinces, with cars, tractors, equipment, horses, wool, and looms in tow. They set up shop, one in construction, another in spinning, still another in metallurgy. They enjoyed the friendship of politicians and the consideration of banks. And their appetites were unlimited, like the cravings of the others – the ones who had remained in the Nord. Invasion and suffering merited recompense, giving them the right to anything and everything. They worried about the negotiations for the Treaty of Versailles and wanted their voices heard. They dreamed of coal from the Saar, huge indemnities, a Germany dismembered like Austria and whose spoils they would divide – a river of gold, flowing from the other side of the Rhine, that would enrich them forevermore ...

Amid this mêlée, this mad rush, Decraemer sensed that he would be crushed if he did not defend himself like a wild animal. Such a struggle was of no interest to him. Anyone who has spent years in a prison cell no longer fears poverty. But he was not on his own. He had ambitions for his wife and son. And then, even for himself, he was not at all certain of having enough to guarantee a minimal degree of life and liberty.

He could count on no special treatment. Heroism has never sustained the hero. And Decraemer's sacrifice had long since been forgotten. As the saying goes, gratitude does not last long.

Decraemer understood that to avoid destruction he had to throw himself headlong into the struggle, take what he could, assert his rights by force, and mull things over later. He had no certificate, no requisition voucher. Insurance would pay nothing. If he waited for justice to be done, he would be left with little but his dignity. Slow-moving officials were taking forever to deal with his case. They recognized that he merited some recompense, that it would be unjust to refuse compensation to a man who had set an example of resistance while others had let themselves be bled dry without a word of protest. But tangible results of bureaucratic good will could be a long time coming.

Decraemer produced witnesses, proved that he had had a power plant before the war, rummaged through stockpiles, the warehouses where the Reconstruction Commission had its repositories, and helped himself ... Ensuring the well-being of his family took precedence. Later he could think matters through and reconcile his actions with his ethics. Never had the notion of "survival first" been so imperative.

Thus had he jumped into battle, struggled with others, carried off his share of booty. It was easy, no one was keeping track. Sometimes he thought he was taking more than his fair share. But so what! If he did not grab it, others would take advantage of the situation, grow stronger in the process, and crush him. "Don't be a sucker." This warning was heard repeatedly and symbolized the spirit of the times.

His employees pushed him in this direction. Reconstruction officials came to see him and, after beating around the bush, proposed certain arrangements, discretely asking for bribes. If he refused, they would surely go elsewhere, to his competitors.

Decraemer let himself be swept along, did like the rest, and convinced himself of the idea – the lie – that he would look to squaring his principles with his behaviour once his factory was running and his position secure. For the time being, if he wanted to avoid annihilation in the bitter contest, amorality and cruelty were almost a necessity.

Besides, all around him, competitors were building, growing, and infinitely faster than he was. Next to the others, he still felt so honest! This sentiment reassured him. Factories were opening, mansions and vast gardens were stretching toward the suburbs, stately old homes were being renovated in the wealthy districts. Automobiles, luxury, ostentation were rife. Moved by such examples, Decraemer went with the flow, obsessed by the fear of being submerged, of appearing weak, defeated in comparison to the others' success. Pride and self-interest demanded that he be their equal. The rich alone can obtain loans, especially from banks. The latter only do business with people who do not need them or at least do not seem to need them. Beyond these concerns was the trap he had set for himself, the bogus excuses he had made: *You have more right to this luxury – this reward – than the others. Your sacrifice paid for it in advance. You deserve it.*

Having himself reimbursed for old stocks at top dollar could also be justified. Who knows? These old-fashioned things might well have come back into style. And then, if everything had burned by accident, the insurance would have paid. The circumstances were similar. It is such unanticipated profits that make up for losses.

Each day brought new problems for Decraemer, confronted him with the necessity – forgotten in prison – of the thousand little compromises with one's conscience that are part of the life of the businessman. He had known them well before the war. And now he rediscovered them in their entirety: "tips," under-the-table commissions, prices cut to the last cent with the idea of making up for it on quality, selling high, buying low ... Profit in itself is legitimate, but how much? The Abbé Sennevilliers said that Decraemer ought to ensure a reasonable lifestyle in relation to his position in society. But what is a reasonable lifestyle? When does it become excessive? One is almost inevitably led to take what one can, all one can. The concept of legitimate profit varies according to profession, age, external circumstance, and individual. An economic system based on this principle creates a vicious and amoral circle, thought Decraemer. It would have been so simple, so pleasant, if each freely gave all his labour, his best effort, and were certain of living honestly in return! But as things stand, always unsure of what lay ahead, man – even the richest man – can only think of incessant acquisition, yet without ever finding safety or security regarding the future. Money, that constant, singular concern, seems so capable of ensuring tranquility, of guarding against old age, hunger, illness, the suffering of loved ones, that man is ultimately compelled to love it, to cherish it like life itself.

Decraemer surrendered. He set aside his moral considerations, his desire for a noble and elevated life for his family and himself. Ensuring their wealth and well-being took top priority. He would attend to other matters later. He did not realize that in building this fortune he might very well enslave himself to it and forever lose his capacity to be something more.

And so he was caught up, pulled into the system again. Each day he found it a bit harder to apply his noble principles to daily affairs, and his spirit waned a little further. His humanitarian preoccupations, his concern for workers and the poor already seemed so distant! The interests of worker and management stand in opposition. Even a saint could not change the situation. Prices determine everything. And competitive prices come at the expense of wages. One thereby arrives at the absurd conclusion that the most ferocious boss, the one who holds the strictest line on wages, will be the strongest, the most prosperous, the most stable, and will at least ensure his workers a wretched but steady wage – and ultimately serve them better than the others ... Alone against these odds, what could Decraemer do? When he had ruined himself with good intentions, when he had put seven or eight hundred workers out of a job, would the world be a better place? No, no, it was impossible. To apply the Gospel message in this environment was to condemn oneself to defeat in advance. One does not preach kindness to a tiger in the jungle ...

Thus did the spectacle of mankind revive his skepticism. In prison it had been easy to believe, to hope, to plan for a new and more spiritual life. In Germany Decraemer had been isolated, seen almost no one, and had gradually been able to craft his own image of humanity. Theoretical speculation leads the philosopher to imagine others after himself, after an exception, that is. He distances himself from reality. In the realm of business, Decraemer suddenly rediscovered this reality. He saw honourable folks swamped amid the crowd, isolated, oppressed, smothered by a mass so heavy that it could not be moved. The world of men appeared to run its course apart from every noble consideration. Human beings struggled for survival, grew to maturity, reproduced, and died haphazardly, like generations of trees in a forest or a pack of wild dogs. Mankind is no better than animals, than plants. And if one occasionally finds a good man, a man passionate about charity and justice, it is like sometimes finding a good dog, a loyal animal, for no apparent reason, mixed in with the others. The vast majority is removed from concerns with morality and personal improvement. For them, there is only one preoccupation: money. And the triumph of injustice and the power of the rich seemingly prove them right.

Decraemer found no solution to this problem. As time passed, mankind drifted toward a life of comfort. And humanity declines as leisure and the easy life increase. Suddenly raising.a worker's salary by 20 percent will not really help him, paradoxical though it may seem, and can even do him harm. Decraemer had proof of it before his very eyes. Operettas, revue shows, movie houses, and dance halls were all the rage. The consumption of tobacco, alcohol, and harmful substances was increasing alongside rates of divorce, crime, insanity, and pawnshop revenues. Amorality intensified at the same pace as wages or profits. Pleasure-seeking was endemic, among the bourgeoisie and the working class alike. An insidious salaciousness was on the rise, pandering to base instincts in novels and shows as much as newspapers and advertising. And the leaders, the bosses, the factory owners hastened this downward spiral, pushing for the production of cheap goods more than quality products. Fake luxury, pasteboard, mass production, special offers ... The age of artificial silk stockings was at hand. And it was impossible to fight against this current. In the streets, the theatres, and the cafés, the spectacle of a humanity unceasingly greedy, grasping, voracious, insatiable – absorbed by an endless desire for selfish enjoyment – prevented Decraemer from having any more hope for the future of mankind. And that was to say nothing of the sight of many Christians – of their formality, their selfishness, their inhumanity – that alienated Decraemer from Christianity. Everything had been so simple when Decraemer had been under the influence of the Abbé Sennevilliers! Ah, if only he could have remained with him, near him! Such men transform those around them. But how many of his kind can one find in the world?

It was thus that Decraemer gradually slipped down the slope, progressively yielded to the influence of his new environment. He felt himself reacquiring a taste for luxury and indulged himself. What was the good of making a useless sacrifice? And then, luxury is a necessity. One must keep up appearances, maintain one's position. And servants are needed to ensure freedom from material concerns, leaving the superior mind adequate time for reflection. One makes such excuses for oneself, speciously invoking a division of labour ... And the distressing feeling of Decraemer's first months back – his sense of shame at eating good things in front of his servants without sharing with them, of sitting idly by while they waited on him, of constantly leaning on others to spare himself – quickly vanished. Such habits are easily resumed.

Above all he was subject to the influence of his wife, Adrienne. She began living again with a frenzy, sensuously, as a ruddy, robust woman whose long-suppressed need for extravagance and the good life came surging back. After such a long period of grief, such a long time of suffering, she found life's charms intoxicating, dazzling, exhilarating. She was mad for luxury, clothing, jewellery, receptions, performances, soirées. She satisfied an eagerness for pleasure and parties, a craving for well-being. And she pulled her husband along with her. Unconsciously, Daniel Decraemer allowed himself to mellow, to yield to a life of ease, to begin sampling the delights of comfort, of a good table: the flavour of a vintage wine, the aroma of a fine cigar. He started with prudence, with moderation, but soon let himself go, drawn in spite of himself toward an endless pursuit of the strongest, most powerful sensation, the most refined delights. Insidious habit took hold of him. What was at first a mere pleasure gradually turned into a need. His long-deprived body took its revenge. And nothing reduces one to animal instincts like an excess of material well-being.

Adrienne neither perceived nor understood any of these subtleties. She loved Daniel the only way she knew how: tenderly, physically. She led him down this path. He indulged in the charm of her body, discovered and conquered anew. He was subject to intense impulses, the frenzy of renewed passion.

He felt his share of weariness, of disgust for his wanton, animalistic behaviour, sated with pleasure, reverting to selfishness. He again experienced moments when, his passion spent, he was left stupefied and empty-headed, prey to self-loathing. The first times it was dreadful, like the downfall of a saint. He had fits of remorse, heaped insults on himself, despised himself. He would not stumble again, would know how to impose discipline on his body, protect his love from the destructive seed of gratification, satisfaction, master the brute, respect the intellect in both his wife and himself ... But the flesh has a memory of its own. Pleasure becomes a need, the thought of it an obsession. The body craves sex once it has tasted it, like wild animals crave blood. Decraemer stumbled again and – by enjoying all his senses – became prisoner to his desires ...

When he looked back, when he considered the Decraemer that he had been, he no longer recognized himself. For all his prior concerns, life is a precious gift, a tasty, succulent fruit. How could he have renounced it, disdained it to such an extent? How could he have assumed that he would lose nothing and gain everything by choosing eternity? On the contrary, he would have lost everything! What is left beyond earthly pleasures? Only imaginings. He was alarmed to reread his notes, his prison diary, his meditations, his reflections on his readings.

"Thanks be unto Thee, because Thou has not spared my sins ..." "Always choose to have less rather than more ..."*

It seemed to him as if someone else had written these lines. No, truly, he no longer recognized himself.

The Abbé Sennevilliers had come to see him and returned this attempt at a mystical testament that Decraemer had written when he thought he was dying. And therein Decraemer rediscovered ideas so detached, so devoid of material concerns, so elevated, that he began to wonder if the person who had written it had been in full possession of his mental faculties and complete control of himself: "This adventure has been the great good fortune of my life. I await suffering in peace, ready to welcome it as a boon, the special sign of God's solicitude for me ... If like me my beloved wife learns to extract the precious essence of truth from the bitter fruit of suffering, then my agony and death will be an immense blessing for the both of us ... Here I will die in true happiness."

"Here I will die in true happiness ..." How could he have written such words, reached such heights, the pinnacles that now frightened him? But was it really an ascension, or was it rather a product of weakness, the breakdown of a brain deprived of nitrogen and phosphorous? Had he seen a clear vision of the supernatural or merely the chimeras and hallucinations of a sickly hermit? Still, it is hard to believe that a butcher's apprentice in his shop has more brain power than Pascal on his pallet ...

But then what a dilemma, thought Decraemer. *What a dreadful thing! Almost all mankind lives in ignorance of its true nature? The soul really is*

---

*Thomas à Kempis, *The Imitation of Christ*, book 3, chap. 50, no 5, and book 3, chap. 23, no. 3.

imprisoned? Our material existence would stifle it? One can only arrive at self-awareness through mortification of the flesh? In my cell in Rheinbach, was I mad? Was I enlightened? Did I see the truth or pure hallucinations, the ravings of a malnourished brain? I no longer know, I don't see how I can know ... I've had the impression, for quite some time now, of having been different, yes ... another Decraemer. Which is the noblest expression of myself? The man of yesterday? The man of today? Which is closest to the wisdom, the ideal toward which I ought to strive? I'll never know. Sometimes I think I'm talking nonsense, that reality is there, right in front of me: concrete, everyday life ... And at other times I'm afraid I've extinguished something magnificent within myself ...

He recalled the words of Christ before Pilate, the eternal question of a humanity torn by doubt: "What is truth?"*

Yes, what is truth? Who will ever manage to answer this question?

And yet, in this obscurity, one thing remained certain, clear to Decraemer: in his cell, in his physical misery, in the total renunciation of his old life, which went as far as inviting and blessing misery, blessing even his enemies, Decraemer had been happy ... He had experienced the only moment of perfect serenity he had ever known. And whether or not he had wanted it, whether or not he had been in his right mind, this period of his life was for him a little like a paradise lost. He now understood monks, Trappists, hermits, and he envied them. All these material things – money, luxury, sex, well-being, petty hatreds and jealousies, the endless pursuit of pleasure and gratification – would never provide the happiness he had known in his cell ... He had glimpsed heaven and then lost sight of it. His enlightened perspective had dimmed. There was no eternity, no resurrection, no certainty of finding the souls of the dearly departed in a new and better place. For Decraemer, it was almost as if his child, his little Louise, had died a second time. And he was left embittered by the experience, with the impression that – having climbed so high, having caught sight of this splendour and watched it slip away – he would never find consolation.

---

*Van der Meersch's reference is inaccurate. In John 18:38, Pilate poses this question to Christ.

VII

Patrice Hennedyck spent the first months after his return to Roubaix in utter confusion. Hatred, anger, sorrow, and shame mingled inside him, casting his spirit into indescribable chaos. He was fixated on his situation, totally preoccupied by it, taking a certain crude delight in aggravating his own bloody, wounded pride. He would have liked to flee, leave the Nord, seek refuge far away, find forgetfulness deep in a land where no one knew him and where he knew no one. For the moment, lack of money held him in Roubaix.

He stayed at the factory. Home would have been unbearable for him. He lived like a recluse, a true savage, away from people, feeding a fierce hatred of himself and others, nursing a merciless resentment, scorn, and contempt for his wife – that cursed creature. He laughed at himself. He realized how foolish it is for men to humble themselves in desperate adoration of a woman. So much courage, strength, talent, genius expended by the world and the centuries for such dirty, filthy beings! What folly on the part of man, and what woman could genuinely inspire that miraculous and semi-divine emotion of pure love? He wrung his hands, shed tears of rage, in thinking of the words he had once said to Émilie, of the affection he had had for her, of the way he had worshipped her. Now he scorned her, reviled her, despised her, muttering curses to avenge the shame of his humiliation, the sorrow, the pain of seeing another man preferred above him, and being forced to doubt himself. He was subject to singular, dreadful fits of rage. He was aghast to discover the sexual and impassioned nature of his love, which – after the first flames of desire had died down – he had long believed to be rooted in piteous affection for an ailing woman ... Sudden recollections made him jump from his bed, moan in rage and sorrow, scream, curse heaven. He relived passionate moments, times when – pressed against his chest – she had yielded to desire, almost in spite of herself, remorsefully, and in forebearance ... Once again he saw her pinched nostrils, her slight panting, the quivering of her closed eyelids, the strange and unusual expression that rendered her dearly beloved face strange and new, like an alter ego that one discovered only in this brief moment ... To think that she had given herself like this to another man, that he had seen her like this, held her like this. Hennedyck felt his head spin, would have shed blood so his rival could live again and die at his hands ...

He eventually decided to go see Émilie. She was living in Herlem, down the road from the Sennevilliers. Lise was looking after her, slowly nursing her back to physical and mental health. He made Émilie confess, tell everything, own up to everything, as torturous and distressing as it was. Each admission broke his heart. But he wanted to know all ... He was beside himself when he returned to Roubaix.

He dispelled his imaginings. Other memories, more affectionate, and perhaps more painful, haunted him: Émilie's songs, the lyrics, the reminders of celebrations and happy days, a simple roundelay from her younger days, a tune that she still loved to sing in her slightly cracked and quivering voice:

The lark is on the branch.
Jump, jump,
Little lark, little lark ...

He sang it to himself and broke into sobs.

My God! My God! To think that all these things, these times, this past happiness would never return, that something irreversible had occurred! He was seized by an insane despair when confronted with the impossibility of turning the clock back, returning to the good old days, or at least forgetting them, driving away the dreadful memories. But there they were, ruthlessly stamped on his brain forevermore. Nothing would remove them, nothing would alleviate them.

No distraction, no amount of sleep brought forgetfulness. He began to understand people who drank or used drugs. He could appreciate mental illness, especially split personality disorders, and yearned for something similar. If only his conscience, like the minds of so many others, could be rent in two, allowing him to cast aside the pain in his soul and start afresh! He looked like a wreck as he went about town, no longer attempting to conceal his grief.

All around him, the Nord was coming back to life. Factories were being repaired. The city was bustling with activity. In Épeule all the ordinary folks were nervous. Nothing was happening at Hennedyck's factory. The most well-informed claimed it would never reopen. Closed – the Hennedyck factory, which for almost a century had provided jobs in Épeule? People were dismayed, refused to believe it. Old weavers, good workers who had known Hennedyck's father, accosted Patrice in the street: "Say, Mr Hennedyck, when will we be up and running? When're we going to get to work? Huh, Mr Hennedyck?"

One could see the anxiety on the faces of these good people, the fear of remaining on the street, unemployed. He was moved by their questions, and a little ashamed. He was afraid to say no. He responded, "Soon, my friends, soon. Be patient."

And he trudged away in silent remorse.

He had dreamed of having the factory demolished, selling the land, and leaving. Now he hesitated. There were some folks who, in their rough language, found moving words that touched him: "Mr Hennedyck, we've been working for your family for thirty-five years ... We knew your father and your grandfather. Think how heartbroken we'd be ..." In the end he realized that he was betraying his duty as an employer. He felt ashamed of himself. All these good people had faith in him. Did he have the right to inflict misery on them so he could selfishly attend to his own affairs? And then he felt the silent desire to return to the struggle – the pride, the taste for the fight – reviving within him. Other manufacturers were starting up again. It looked like he had been defeated. The thought was humiliating. He decided to check into things, at least consider the situation, the requirements for a possible restart.

He was immediately engrossed. It was as if his mind had been starving for activity. Materials were in short supply. His enthusiasm increased all the more. He was confident that he had the know-how. Difficulty spurred him on. He was familiar with the sources of supply, the purchasing venues, where to find bricks, cement, iron, tools, looms, machinery.

He needed money. Before the war he had had a small spinning mill in Dunkerque. He realized that for a time the market for thread would be disrupted by fluctuating exchange rates. He sold this factory and used the money to set to work. The boiler and the steam engine had to be repaired, the cracked smokestack patched up, the destroyed workshops rebuilt. Hennedyck hired a team of mechanics who worked under his supervision. He obtained clay from land he owned in Leers, made sun-dried bricks the old-fashioned way, without a kiln, as Vauban had done for his fortifications. And he got hold of lime and cement in the Tournai region.

He was short of coal and means of transportation. The trains were running way behind schedule, and the canal was dry. The Germans had blown up the locks, and all that remained in the canal bed was a small stream where children went to trap fish in crude weirs. Hennedyck set about finding trucks. He bought six vehicles from a certain Villeblanc, an old cabby who had owned a worthless taxi in 1914 and had had the luck of finding a safe posting in the army motorpool during the war. This man, now acquainted with the officials overseeing compensation claims and the liquidation of American stockpiles, had made a considerable fortune by reselling 30,000 francs worth of chassis he had acquired for 600. He had just opened a huge garage in Lille and already had a dozen taxis, furnished under the auspices of war reparations to replace the single taxi of yesteryear. Hennedyck himself scoured the mining districts round Lens, Bethune, Mons, and Charleroi. He returned with coal. He had set up a foundry in a shed on the factory grounds. One of his foremen knew metal casting. They made the necessary charcoal and poured frames for the looms. Delicate spare parts came from England. Hennedyck himself had the Jacquard machinery built according to his own designs. For during his incarceration in Germany he had come up with an automated shuttle for the loom and a special scrollwork made by cards on the fabric to save on stitching.

He located some wool in Antwerp and Dunkerque, had it delivered by truck. He made arrangements with Gayet for the spinning. And he temporarily subcontracted the dyeing. Like everyone else, he was carried away by the excitement of reconstruction. The workers were also itching to get going again and badgered him with questions.

He started up on a Monday morning. It was a solemn occasion. All the employees had gathered. The boilers were under steam. Hennedyck moved emotionally toward the refurbished engine and turned the valve. Amid shouts of enthusiasm, the engine wooshed to life. Power once more flowed through the factory, along the cables, the camshafts, the pullies, the belts, in a tremendous roar.

Workers rushed toward looms and engaged the drives. And soon the tumultuous hum of the factory resumed: the metallic rumble made by the din of the looms, the thud of the beaters, the hasty rhythm of the Jacquard machinery, a familiar, instantly recognizable hubbub that had not been heard for five years. It was a call to work – tough, difficult work – but it had been so desired, so missed that many became teary-eyed upon hearing the sound again. The quick, lively, raucous shuttle in the network of threads, moving back and forth like a little torpedo between the two horizontal layers: that was Roubaix's true resurrection.

Reconstruction brought satisfaction to Hennedyck above all others. He had quickly realized that work absorbs and distracts, that it is the miraculous source of forgetfulness and joy, the sole remedy for every mental ailment. He had jumped in, immersed himself, and all else seemed more distant. One concern supplanted the other. Hennedyck began to think that his conscience was a mere ray of light, a tiny beam touching only a portion of his soul at any given moment, leaving the rest in obscurity. And thus did the immense preoccupation of work diminish and attenuate other considerations, reducing their importance. He began to see himself in a different light, to examine his situation from a calmer and more detached perspective. And he was surprised at his previous agitation, at the madness that had carried him away, the excessive nature of his obsession. He cooled down. He began to be less distraught in Émilie's presence. He had gone to Herlem only two or three times beforehand. At present he was going to see Émilie every week, in a friendly manner, finding in the short journey a certain charm, enjoying the respite it offered. He realized that he now awaited the weekend with a certain impatience. And on the other hand, his life in Roubaix remained incomplete. Amid all his work, something was missing. One day, hard on the job, the disappointing thought suddenly crossed his mind: *What good is all this effort!* Without Émilie his life was limited. He suffered when ordinary fellows and good-hearted women, with their somewhat rough simplicity, naïvely asked in passing about Mrs Hennedyck. He sensed that without her the "Maison Hennedyck" would never be definitively reestablished, that the project would always remain unfinished.

What peace of mind he might have had – and what new burst of energy – if he could have managed to forgive, forget, take back the miserable sinner whose suffering and regret left him filled with remorse. He recognized that this concern would always deprive him of part of his freedom of spirit, his capacity for action. Everything, and he himself, would always remain incomplete if he refused to yield, to straighten things out ... But how was he supposed to straighten things out? What solution was there aside from this pardon that repulsed him, that he rejected, and that nonetheless impressed itself upon him as a necessity? Separation, divorce, neither would satisfy him, neither would provide the mental tranquility indispensable for his work.

And then there was the name, this old, dynastic name that had to be kept alive ... In the depth of his soul, Hennedyck had long nurtured the unavowed hope – forever disappointed, forever undying – of perpetuating his name, of having a child, a son ... Perhaps it was not too late ...

But above all, compassion drew him to her. Here in Roubaix, he could still hate her from a distance. In Herlem, he had only to be near her again – to hear her voice – for her transgression to fade away. A mere glimpse at her was enough to understand how it had happened, to recall her immense weakness, her terrible lack of judgment. She was a sickly, nervous, highly impressionable woman who needed direction. He sensed her present wretchedness, her shame, her hidden suffering, her timid efforts to reconcile with him, her uncertainty. And this anguish stirred his own need to give of himself, to devote himself again, as in the past. Something was missing in his life: the gift of his person. Devotion had become a habit, a necessity. He had sometimes dreamed of a more typical woman: strong, balanced, a partner rather than a burden. Now he realized that this perpetual concern, this perpetual solicitude for a sick and anxious woman had filled and embellished his own life. In attempting to make her happy, to give of himself, he had made himself happy. An ordinary existence seemed dreadfully lifeless and mediocre to him. He rejected it.

Perhaps his own pride also impelled him. Within man there is always a small, subtle element of pride. One never works solely for oneself. Not showing Émilie the completed project – not having her present for the reopening – deprived his effort of its very meaning, its best reward. And then, forgiving her – looking past her offense – elevated him in his own eyes. It is immensely gratifying to see oneself as generous and noble. Pardoning her would have satisfied his own unconfessed need for self-esteem. The outbursts of anger and violence, the hatred, became less frequent. He suppressed these emotions, wishing to see nothing but the nobility and kindness of a gesture of mercy. And finally, deep down, he was forced to admit that his whole physical being also yearned for his wife, for the sensual pleasure that would be another form of renewal.

Hennedyck's managers came to see him in March 1920. The business would soon be a hundred years old. The centennial ought to be celebrated.

As Hennedyck organized the festivities, made arrangements for the banquet and the speeches, he recalled his family history and looked back over the long road travelled: the first factory with looms powered by a horse roundabout, the slow development, the expansion abruptly halted by the war, and the new page he had just turned. And more than ever he felt that

the finishing touch was missing. He thought of all the reopening ceremonies of late. Ordinarily it was the boss's wife who received the honour
of starting the steam engine up again: a charming, symbolic gesture contrasting grace and strength. This tradition, this sweetness, had been absent.

Hennedyck now understood that without Émilie all his efforts were
completely pointless. Without acknowledging it, without even realizing it
at the time, he was forced to admit that, ultimately, everything he had
accomplished, the entire uphill battle, had been for her.

In the beginning, Émilie's life at Herlem had been wholly passive, almost
instinctual. She was exhausted, at the end of her strength. She thought of
nothing, simply drifting from day to day, clinging to life itself. Patrice came
to visit her. She received him without shame, like anyone else, with the
distant gaze of the dying. The extent of her wretchedness forestalled any
other reaction.

As she recovered her strength, her adventure seemed increasingly remote, like a hazy dream, a terrible nightmare from which she was awakening. She could no longer imagine having lived the experience. Details
slowly came back to her, along with shame and remorse.

She had to endure her husband's questions. There were dreadful scenes
between this man mired in despair and this woman whose nerves were
frayed. Then things cooled off, as if the cyst had been drained. Patrice no
longer spoke of the past, maintained a willful silence regarding the whole
episode, gradually recovered his composure. At present his attitude
toward her was marked by a calm gentleness, a distant and almost reasoned affection, which caused Émilie more fear and shame than his bursts
of anger. What was he thinking? What was he going to do? What solution
did he envisage? She felt that deep down, behind his quiet demeanour, he
would never forgive her.

She fretted. She tried to figure it out. Soon she learned that he was getting back to work, rebuilding the factory. Why? For whom? He had not forgiven her, so he must have been dreaming of making a life without her. For
in the beginning he had talked of leaving the Nord and perhaps France. She
started to feel afraid in the face of his cold, intense determination, and to
admire it. Such courage was beyond her. Little by little, through the
accounts of the Abbé Sennevilliers, she came to grasp her husband's heroism during the war. She better understood his true character. He had calmly risked death, looked it head on, endured agony in Rheinbach. And com-

ing home to financial ruin, his happiness destroyed, he had set to work again, started over, clawed his way back up. And the factory had reopened. Without telling him, Émilie had gone to Roubaix to see it. She had been amazed by the sight. He really was one of the old breed, that race of bygone industrialists: the creators, the founders of dynasties. A parallel unexpectedly dawned on her. She recalled von Mesnil, the dead man. She remembered his pessimism, his caustic, sterilizing skepticism, his continual "what's the point," and his contradictions: the fiercity, the weakness, the duplicity of a personality at once passionate and enslaved to its passions, as he had demonstrated in Brussels at the tragic moment of their parting. With Patrice, there was none of this, only a deep, innate, robust optimism. Less reflection, less of a spirit of subtlety, but a bravery, an unshakeable self-confidence, a faith in work. Less art and elegance, more courage and resolve. Such a man was truly a man, a source of comfort and support. She had not understood Patrice until she had lost him. She despaired to realize what she had disdained, the happiness she had squandered.

What should I do? she wondered, as she walked through the loneliness of the quarry: a loneliness, a wild and sad setting that had dejected her at first but that she was beginning to appreciate. She thought about her husband, tried to get into his head, to figure out his secret plans. She would have liked to initiate a timid reconciliation. Being involved in his concerns, in his daily life, would have brought her such great joy. She questioned him awkwardly, sought to share in his affairs, took a chance ... Then she was seized by fear and shame, pulled back, retreated. How would he judge her? What would he think of her? And she started over again, more hesitantly than before.

He remained unaltered, consistently good, calm, like a man who had found peace. And this hurt Émilie even more. He was too tranquil, too steady. She detected too much intentionality, too much determination beneath his composure. She got the sense that he was rejecting her, pushing her out of his life. He brought her whatever she wanted: books, knitting material, fabrics, had her piano delivered. He made arrangements for her life, but apart from his own. She wept over the situation. She tried to look after him – his health, his laundry. He declined, setting up a barrier between them.

She began to take fright, to give in to despair. She thought of leaving: she would be happier elsewhere. Living near him like this, and knowing that she would never be anything more than a stranger to him, was too unbearable for her, as was seeing this nobility of spirit, this bavery, this moral dignity, these possibilities for happiness that she had foolishly wasted and which were forever lost.

• • •

She knew there would be festivities at the factory in honour of the centennial. He talked about it, seemed happy, recalled the work of his father and grandfather, and not without a certain pride.

"What's been built can't be allowed to disappear," he said. "It must continue."

His words alarmed her. What was he trying to say? Was he dreaming of a new life? With whom? How? Was he thinking of leaving her? Now that she had glimpsed this threat, oh how she wished for nothing to change, to leave everything as it was, to continue living a life that was not happy but that seemed surprisingly pleasant, considering the dramatic shift that she now anticipated. She often broke down in tears, frightening Lise.

One evening, four days before the festivities, Hennedyck suddenly arrived at the quarry, having warned no one beforehand, as was his habit. He seemed tense, preoccupied. He had brought packages, supplies, books. He set them on the kitchen table, went to say good evening to the Sennevilliers, and came back.

"Put on your coat, Émilie," he said.

"We're heading outside?"

"Let's go for a walk in the quarry ..."

She understood that he wanted to talk to her. He always took her outside to have a serious conversation. She put on her coat. She was shaking a little, nervous and her throat tight. She said nothing. Timidly she took his arm, and they stepped into the twilight. They wended their way toward the bottom of the quarry. A narrow path led down, suspended from the cliff of white stone and studded with tall clumps of grass. At the bottom were the still waters of the pond. The weather was pleasant. This was their favourite trail, deep within this big, isolated ravine stretching into the form of an echoing seashell. They did not speak, focused on watching their steps. He held her with a firm arm. She clung to him to avoid twisting her fragile ankles. They reached a platform, a terrace overlooking the pond. They strolled around it, following a path through the grass, and stopped. She heard him breathe deeply and cough two or three times, as he did when hesitant to speak.

"So," he began abruptly, "you know that this celebration will take place on Sunday ..."

"Oh?"

"Yes, a hundred years! It'll be a nice occasion, a nice family affair ..."

He paused, coughed again, making an emormous effort to continue.

"And naturally," he continued, his voice a bit hushed, "it's essential ... it's essential that, yes ... that you be there, you understand? That you be there ..."

She was overcome with emotion. After immense struggle, she managed to look at him. She could tell that she was not mistaken, that his words really did contain the deeper meaning she almost feared to discern. They struck her with a virtually physical pain, a shock, paralyzing her limbs. And she stood rooted to the spot, as after a big jolt, unable to speak, seized by dizziness. He saw her go pale. After such a long time, he recognized the twinge of the nostrils, the pallour, the dark rings that formed under her eyes when she was about to faint. He was suddenly afraid of seeing her die before his very eyes. She was not strong ... The emotion, the surprise ... The sight of her elicited the same physical response as in bygone days, the same attraction to her, the same bust of affection and tender pity. She was still his wife, his child wife.

"Émilie! Émilie!"

Anxiously, frantically, he had taken her in his arms, revived her, brought her back to her senses, showered her face with kisses and tears. He felt her recovering, slowly, with difficulty, pressed against his beating heart, as if he had once again infused her with his own energy.

Long afterward, they headed toward the pond. Émilie, exhausted, walked slowly, silently. She was still shaking, clinging to her husband, leaning against him. Her attention was focused on him alone. There was but one thought in her mind: Patrice. She felt the uselessness of words.

They sat on a rock at the edge of the pond. Still, limpid waters – bluish-green and flecked with ice – lay at the foot of the rock. The quarry – white and empty, quietly echoing beneath the vastness of the starry sky – imprinted their spirits with a doleful solemnity.

Émilie stared at the green water. Never before had it seemed so beautiful, in this place where Fannie had died. A slow familiarization, a patient love, had seemingly been necessary for her to recognize its poetic charm, the melancholy grandeur of this splendid jewel, hidden here at the heart of this enormous limestone seashell, like a magnificent product of silence and solitude.

With this strange chain of ideas running through her mind, she slowly looked toward her husband with an expression all the more anxious and tearful. He smiled at her. A deep peace permeated his plain, virile face, the calm assurance of the man who feels himself strong enough to pick up the pieces and whose happiness is found in his drive, his determination.

VIII

Hennedyck took his seat in the courtroom around four o'clock. David had had him called as a witness for the defense.

It was June 1920. The preliminary inquiry had lasted a year and a half.

The tall room with its coffered ceiling stood between the grand lobby on one side and a gloomy parapet of the old prison on the other. The heat was stifling, the atmosphere dense, permeated by the smell of a disparate crowd. Hennedyck recognized the familiar figures of manufacturers, wholesale merchants, and woolen traders seated on the witness stand or positioned alongside the lawyers in the courtroom. Behind them, in the section reserved for the public, a rowdy mob of sympathizers and enemies was milling about. Upon arrival, one had the sense of stepping onto a battlefield.

The trial had begun two days before. The case file was of monstrous proportions. Seventy-two witnesses had been summoned. The testimony of Ingelby and Villard, though called for the prosecution, had been noticeably restrained.

A number of manufacturers had testified, confirming they had seen David supervising the loading of goods while accompanied by German officers. David had also obtained permits for the importation of cattle from Holland. He had delivered sugar and coal shipped in from Germany. A turbulent crowd had greeted these accusations with a noisy response.

When Hennedyck arrived, the examination of defense witnesses was drawing to a close. There were many of them, and from all walks of life: industrialists and workers, rich and poor. Some had come for the sake of friendship, others in a spirit of equity, still others out of self-interest. It was almost as if the occupied territories as a whole were on trial. And people refused to accept this state of affairs. They were angry with those who, having abandoned the people of Nord, having left them to their own devices – handed them over to a ruthless enemy – now intended to put them on trial and condemn them because they had found a way to survive. And some said as much on the witness stand.

"Sure, David bought and sold wool and coal. But what of it! We couldn't let ourselves freeze to death, could we!"

"We're lucky there were a few like him," said others, "people who dared."

"If we're supposed to imprison everyone who traded with the Germans, we'll have to lock up half the population," some folks maintained. "No one let himself go hungry. And we had to survive. Anyone who had anything of value sold it and considered himself lucky. Anyone who got a loaf of bread or a jar of marmalade from a soldier said 'thank you' and walked away happy. But we never sold a thing to the German army, never worked for it, and that's good enough. As for the soldiers themselves, not a single store was closed to them, no shopkeeper could refuse them service. You have to distinguish between the German soldiers and the German army."

Testimony was offered by monks and nuns, Little Sisters of the Poor, the hospital director, nurses from the Red Cross clinic, administrators from the welfare bureau. David had given generously to all of them, deducting a tithe from each of his transactions on behalf of the sick and the elderly – magnanimity that was now repaid a hundred fold. From all of the proceedings one thing ultimately became clear: David had undoubtedly "trafficked," but just like many others ... Absolute intransigence would have been impossible. And then, punishing him would implicate everyone with whom he had cut deals, who had sold him their fabrics knowing the destination full well, who had not inquired further about the ostensible "Brussels delivery." In the end, whatever harm he might have done, he had more than made up for with good deeds. He had helped the populace survive. They would have died of cold and hunger without his coal and his meat. Principles are well and good, but those who had not been in the Nord could not understand what it was like to go without food and fuel for four years. Behind the testimony of witnesses, especially the humble folks who had come in droves to help their friend David, one sensed a certain anger toward his accusers. And at the back of the courtroom, a teeming mass – a crowd dominated by the common people – expressed its pas-

sionate approval and exacted its revenge by extolling David: a man who
had come from their ranks and had outfoxed the rich and the powerful.
Since the opening of the trial, a complete reversal of public opinion had
thus occurred. As the proceedings took a more favourable turn, the same
crowd that had at first wanted to lynch David would now have gladly carried him in triumph.

The audience sat in passionate silence as Hennedyck testified. He
embodied a century of Roubaix industry, an uncompromised reputation,
complete resistance to the enemy, and *Loyalty*, that great work of patriotism. Hennedyck recalled only that David had delivered his wool and his
fabrics to a person named Lieutenant Krug, not the army. This Krug represented a consortium of German department stores. So, indirectly, David
had sold to the German people. He had never paid in gold for sugar and
coal, but in marks or fabrics. Hennedyck placed particular emphasis on
the fact that David had energetically approved the closure of the factories
and the refusal to work for the enemy, and that his money had played a
considerable role in supporting *Loyalty*. David's intervention had also
spared Hennedyck and the Abbé Sennevilliers from the firing squad. His
testimony complete, Hennedyck returned to his seat, passing right by
David, amid a great clamour from the audience. David shook his hand
and cried.

The stream of witnesses continued in similar fashion. Slowly everyone
got the impression that the game was up.

When the session resumed, in an atmosphere a little more relaxed and
refreshed thanks to a slight breeze blowing through the big open windows,
the last witnesses presented their testimony. And when his turn came to
speak, the state prosecutor – pausing for effect – announced that he was
withdrawing his case against the accused ... At first people did not realize
what had happened. It took the applause of the most cognizant for the
crowd to finally understand. And then irresistible enthusiasm erupted,
drowning out the shouting of the bailiffs, the anger of the presiding judge,
and the efforts of the policemen to throw out the most frenzied members
of the audience.

The trial's momentum built up to a grand finale. After a short meeting
in private, David's attorneys in turn waived their defense plea. The judges
retired for a brief deliberation, returned a few minutes later, and the presiding judge announced the verdict amid sudden silence, the hushed and

almost solemn attention of the entire crowd. David, pale and sweating, seated in the dock, listened, straining ... When he was certain he had been acquitted, he leaned back with a great sigh of relief.

A tremendous din erupted – in the courtroom, the galleries, the hallways, gradually extending to the front steps and the square in front of the Palais de Justice. A human torrent invaded the tribunal. Friends, sympathizers, strangers, newcomers, all dashed forward, all wanted to see David, speak to him, touch him, congratulate him, add a little something more to the joy of this happy man. Surrounding the accused, pressed against him, four policemen were defending David in vain, struggling with a band of fanatics who intended to carry him straightaway in triumph to Bellevue.* They wanted him to come on out and heckled the policemen who were trying to put handcuffs back on him – because a convicted felon leaves the courtroom with his hands free, while an acquitted man exits it in chains, to complete the formalities of his discharge. The crowd had no patience for such details, called for David, assailed him, wanted to take him off by force. David himself – livid, his cheeks wet with tears – shook the hands of his sweaty, beaming attorneys, gestured to those calling for him, smiled with a sort of despondency at all the faces – the strangers and the friends – behind the sturdy wall of policemen. It is remarkable that a crowd of strangers, unaffected in and of themselves, can get so excited, for no apparent reason, about the good fortune of a single individual.

This tempestuous uproar surged toward David, but it did not satisfy him. It was not what he had been waiting for, hoping for. He was completely oblivious, unmoved by all the commotion. He sought only one face, one cherished form among the swarm of faces, the uplifted arms, the waving canes and hats. A sudden thought came to him, a hope. And all at once he caught sight of the woman he sought, far off among the crowd, engulfed, submerged by the others, shedding tears of joy but standing still, both hoping and fearing to be seen ... He shouted, "Annie!"

And he motioned to her, pushed through the multitude, moved toward her, waving at her in the thrill of victory – to this woman who had relieved his anguish with the comfort of her tenderness and who, now that fate and fortune were smiling once more on the conquering hero, was afraid to show herself ...

*A reference to the Bellevue hotel in Lille.

IX

Thorel, the managing editor of *The Lantern*, whose presses had for a time been used to print the resistance newssheet *Loyalty*, had returned to Lille immediately after the armistice. For much of the war, he had given talks in France on the invasion of the Nord and German atrocities. He had made quite a stir and created the illusion of serving a purpose. As soon as he came back, he started reorganizing *The Lantern*. At the same time, he undertook a sly campaign to monopolize credit for *Loyalty*. Thorel was ambitious. Politics, honour, and power tempted him. He wanted to go far. Having edited *Loyalty* during the war would carry weight, not to mention all the publicity and profit that would accrue to *The Lantern*, of which *Loyalty* would henceforth be portrayed as little more than a continuation. Appropriating *Loyalty* was worth the trouble, and Thorel tackled the project with considerable skill.

The Lantern published a series of articles on underground newssheets during the occupation. There had been a number of such papers. *Loyalty* was accorded a position of prominence. Thorel, *The Lantern*'s managing editor, was depicted as the founder, producing the broadsheet with associates from *The Lantern* and the assistance of a priest, the Abbé Sennevilliers, who had managed to pick up certain messages by radio. Through courageous articles, intelligence gathered from a variety of sources, and enormous sacrifices of money, Thorel had succeeded in lifting the morale of his fellow citizens. The abbé was cast as only a minor player in the affair. Hennedyck figured not at all. Clavard, the typesetter, who had sold Thorel his documents and his collection of *Loyalty* at a steep price, was given a role of prime importance.

The abbé was unaware of what was happening. Hennedyck, stunned by the series of falsehoods reproduced in a host of area newspapers, sent a letter of protest. Thorel ignored it. While Hennedyck considered filing an injunction, *The Lantern* began reprinting the main issues of *Loyalty*, as if the broadsheet had been its exclusive property.

Registered letters, summons, and injunctions flowed back and forth. Battles began in the newspapers, a series of claims and counter-claims that confused readers and took the shape of a polemic in which the truth was forever lost. Then it came to light that Thorel had been nominated for the Legion of Honour. Hennedyck was never concerned about the ribbon in

his own regard. He had enough influential allies in Roubaix and Tourcoing that it would be easy for him. One of the local bigwigs, Gayet, recalling his attacks on Hennedyck during the debate over working for the
enemy – and the ammunition Hennedyck thus held against him – had
turned into a real devotee, as had a number of others. Gayet was the one
who alerted him. Hennedyck decided that all three – the Abbé, Thorel,
and he – would be decorated, or no one would at all.

The files of Hennedyck and the abbé joined Thorel's. Apprised of the
situation, Thorel had displayed the most affable goodwill and promised
his support for the three nominations to be considered simultaneously.
The abbé, for his part, demured, sought to throw a veil over the whole
business, to remain in the shadows. They had done their duty, acquitted
themselves before their consciences. It would have been so nice if everything had remained anonymous and unrewarded! But Hennedyck, who
was more combative, refused to let a fortune-seeker claim all the credit for
his own benefit. He was as passionate about this as his other projects and
flung himself into the effort.

They were informed by Gayet that things would be much easier if they
were listed as veterans. Thorel already was, for his round of talks in France
during the war. So Hennedyck put together new files and, since he now
was living in Herlem, where he returned two or three times a week to be
with Émilie, he directed the requests for the abbé and himself to the head
of the Herlem veterans' commission.

It turned out that this fellow was a certain Thiermès.

Thiermès, a veterinarian, had left Herlem in October 1914. He had been
captured by the Germans and spent the war in a prison camp. Having
returned to Herlem, and not lacking in ambition, he had had himself
elected honourary president of a number of musical, sports, and recre-
ational associations.

Thiermès's reputation had grown. Hennedyck's arrival in Herlem offended him. With Thorel's influence playing an additional role, Hennedyck and
the abbé found their request denied. Civilians could not claim veteran's
status.

Hennedyck persisted. He proved that others besides him – including
women – had been recognized as veterans without having served in the
army. He went over Thiermès's head and appealed directly to Paris, invoking article 4: "Veteran's status may be attributed to individuals having par-

ticipated in wartime operations." The statute, he argued, ought to be interpreted in its broadest sense. He noted wrilly that two civilians could certainly be accorded veteran's status when the Legion of Honour had been
given to carrier pigeons, whose great act of heroism had consisted of
returning to their roots as quickly as possible. The national office posed
no objection to granting the two friends veteran's status. And for newspapers of the opposition, the occasion presented an opportunity for wise-
cracks and sarcastic remarks about the "unarmed zone" and cassocked
gunners, whom witty cartoonists depicted firing a cannon made from
a stovepipe.

Hennedyck laughed at such commentary. But the abbé was distressed.
As a man of thought, the squabble pained him. By jumping into this mêlée
– by getting mixed up with the bunch of ravenous, greedy, ambitious folks
chasing after honours – he felt a certain disgust and shame, as if he had
sullied his cassock. For in this regard, too, the race was on: the scramble
for medals, power, glory, a fierce competition in which the weak and the
dignified were mercilessly crushed. Heroes turned up everywhere. They
were practically falling from the sky. One fellow had refused to work for
the enemy, another had escaped from prison, still another had harboured
French soldiers, yet another had engaged in espionage or passed letters or
handled pigeons ... Grasping natures rose to the fore. Among this crowd,
two recognizable figures had reappeared: Jeanne Villien and Pauline Bult,
who had returned to Roubaix and received veteran's status. They were at
all the ceremonies, all the patriotic occasions, and embodied resistance to
the enemy. Showered with honours, they cut the figure of heroines, conveniently forgetting that they had only carried letters and newspapers to
enrich themselves – no different than smuggling tobacco. Such posturing
took nerve, an unmistakable panache, a feeling for skillful maneuvring
and audacity – gall, really. And they were not lacking in this respect, riding roughshod over those around them and taking sole credit for counter-
espionage work in the Nord. To hear them tell it, they alone had acted.
Françoise Pélegrin, the little martyr – in reality the true leader of the
women – was depicted as little more than a minor associate. Only protests
from the dead woman's family shed a bit of light on this ingenious ruse.
Fortunately, or perhaps unfortunately for the remembrance of the poor
young girl, who had been shot after a long ordeal at about the same time
as Gaure, a certain Planchart – an architect – latched onto her name like

a banner, a placard. He was ambitious, dreamed of politics. He wrote a series of articles on Françoise Pélegrin, then a fictionalized biography, then poems and brochures. He called for statues, a monument, commemorative services, posthumuous honours. He made such a stir about her that people soon recognized Planchart's name as much as Françoise Pélegrin's. He was featured prominently at every ceremony and in dozens of newspapers: Planchart, always Planchart. In the end, this outrageous publicity led many many to think more of Planchart than Françoise Pélegrin. It was a novel means of feeding off the dead. The battlefield was not the only place where bodies were stripped. Faced with this blistering attack, the other women had to restrain their zeal, curb their appetites. A tacit truce was reached. All were heroes. It was better that way. The cake was big enough for everyone to have a slice. It was better to come to terms and pat each other on the back – to shower each other with praise – than to dredge up uncomfortable truths and knock each other about. Novelists in search of material came out of the woodwork, made inquiries, took notes, asked for momentos. Twenty volumes on the heroes and heroines of the occupied territories were published: twenty paeans equally false, equally superficial. Anyone who discovered a bit of the truth took fright and shunned it in horror. Jingoism was all the rage, and the public was not to be offended. In the meantime, Pauline Bult, who was not lacking in imagination, became an editor at a daily newspaper. Jeanne Vilien married a rich American who was delighted with the idea of becoming the spouse of a recognized heroine, and Mauserel herself – the same Mauserel whom Gaure had once seen absconding with the spy network's cashbox – took clever advantage of the favourable circumstances, found some financial backers, and opened a banking and brokerage firm on rue Nationale in Lille.

Commemorative ceremonies, banquets, and celebrations went on and on. Bastille Day parades, veterans' funerals, monument unveilings, flag and medal presentations: it was all good, all served as a pretext to recall the noble deeds and civic virtues of all and sundry. It was like a stock of glory on which each intended to subsist. Such became a right. It appeared that, for a single act of bravery, one deserved to be seated in the lap of luxury. The thought of getting back to work was repulsive. The honourees were indignant and – crowned, praised, and recognized though they were – claimed to be the victims of ingratitude.

In this scramble for sinecures, the memory of Gaure and Théverand was lost, trampled underfoot. Théverand's wife was poor and ill educated, a humble homemaker. And Gaure had been a bachelor. No one had given a thought to the ones who, in the whole adventure, had been the most genuine heroes. But perhaps it was actually better that their memory was in no way associated with this horrid mess. As for Françoise Pélegrin's friend Félicie Foulaud, the mystic, she had come completely unhinged. One day in Lille, the abbé ran into her by chance. She was in her own world, leading the dreary life of a little seamstress, still haunted by memories of the adventures and dangers she had encountered alongside Françoise Pélegrin. No one had given her much thought either: this girl who had been heroic, who knew the truth about so many others, but who did not understand how to "handle" things and in any case would not have wanted to. She had waited for people to come to her, and no one had come. She was living in a little room on Quai de la Basse-Deûle, alongside a mass of workers who poked fun at her and thought her rather nutty, what with her crazy tales. They got her to talk, and she gladly told her stories, the only things that still interested her amid the dreadful and monotonous mediocrity to which she had been condemned. She would never get over living while Françoise Pélegrin had died, at having known this fantastic and thrilling life like a far-off dream and having tumbled back to reality. Now she was a sweet eccentric with a distracted look, haunted by her obsessions, living on passionate memories, as if forever lost in the past, chained to the war that would always preoccupy her. She would never readjust ...

· · ·

The processing of the Legion of Honour nominations came to a standstill. Hennedyck, suspecting something was up, had Gayet look into the matter. He uncovered some strange goings-on. Thorel was secretly continuing his efforts to exclude the others and monopolize credit for himself. When Thorel had acquired all of the papers related to *Loyalty*, Clavard had also sold him a letter that the abbé had written to Hennedyck in prison, a letter that Clavard – released early on – had never delivered to the manufacturer. The abbé, horrified that he had perhaps been at fault for their arrest, had begged Hennedyck's pardon. Thorel had had the letter included in the dossier, to make it look like Sennevilliers had been to blame for the Germans' discovery of the operation.

Hennedyck went to Thorel's. It was not a pleasant encounter. Hennedyck named his terms. Either the abbé, Hennedyck, and Thorel would be honoured together, or Hennedyck would reveal the whole sordid story of Thorel's maneuvrings with the newspaper: the removal of equipment, the threats to fire employees ... Hennedyck was willing to let Thorel claim credit for a role he had not played but not to let him steal the credit due others as well.

• • •

Three months later, at the headquarters of *The Lantern*, a big celebration was held in honour of the new legionnaires – the Abbé Sennevilliers, Hennedyck, and Thorel. For this formal occasion, the authorities had been anxious to bring together those who had been united during the ordeal. There were some very fine addresses fetting the brotherhood of arms and the heroism of *Loyalty*'s founders. Speaker after speaker referred to the men as "brothers in arms."

X

Long afterward, one quiet autumn evening, Patrice Hennedyck and the Abbé Sennevilliers talked these matters over.

They had gone to the quarry's edge to enjoy the cool of the evening. They were sitting side-by-side on a wooden block and were looking at the quarry, the gaping hole that lay before them, across which the moonlight cast a huge diagonal shadow, flooding but one side with a cool radiance. This glow lent a strange brilliance to the sheer cliff, leaving the pond at the very bottom shrouded in darkness. They could make out just one bank, a jumble of willows whose thin leaves had a magical, silvery appearance. The setting and the hour encouraged serious reflection, the sad contemplation of fate.

"In the end," said Hennedyck, "we were fools."

"You're bitter, Hennedyck."

"No. I'm not resentful. Let's admit it, what we did, we couldn't have helped doing, could we? We're simply made that way ... But all the same,

I wish this war had had some purpose. You'd think that after so much suffering the world would've acquired a taste for a certain wisdom, for moderation, for simplicity. Yeah, right! I had faith in the new Gospel of the
League of Nations. In principle, it's still a splendid thing ... And here, in
the occupied territories – as at the front, I've been told – French and Germans came to understand each other. We figured out that we're all nothing but poor devils in the hands of our masters. We should've come
together. But instead we've witnessed a harvest of hatred, a frenzied chauvinism! Germany's to be made to pay. Germans have been taken from
their homes and forced work here in Lille, and the newspapers are criti-
cizing them for the ninety grams of meat they're given each day ... We
shouldn't have set eyes on such things in the Nord! And our women! German women begged for mercy for their country. And our women said, 'No
mercy!' The official line's already eliminating any other possibilities. We've
watched it happen in our own case, we know what it's like. More than anything else, that's what leaves me such little hope of seeing the war serve
some greater purpose.

"We've been fools, Father! We've played into the hands of others. Free-
loaders have sponged off the work of honest folks. Those who did nothing are treated like royalty. They've take advantage of us. You know ... No,
I've kept it from you till now. Well, during the war, profiteers sold our little newssheet for twenty francs, fifty francs – made money off it! And lots
of ordinary people – workers – criticize me now: '*Loyalty* was a fine thing,
Mr Hennedyck ... But it was for the rich. We commoners, we never knew
anything about it!' Of course! Nine times out of ten, the people we gave
the paper to got scared and kept it to themselves. They undermined our
work, the circuit was broken right then and there. We risked our lives for
a bunch of selfish bastards. That – of everything about our paper – that's
what pains me the most.

"Yes, we were fools ..."

"I'm not so sure," said the abbé quietly, "not so sure. And anyhow, what
difference does it make? Blessed are the poor in spirit, blessed are the pure
in heart, for they will see God."

"That's cold comfort for some of us, Father. I understand those of you
bathed by the light, I get where you're coming from. But I also understand
the others, the ones who see no reason for hope. To them, humanity is
decidedly evil, loathsome. And now they can't even manage to look to the

heavens for this hope, this serenity, which the spectacle of mankind has destroyed for them. To you, I know, those stars up there are like a highway to heaven. And this beautiful firmament – the work of a sublime mathematician – retains a divine promise of eternity. But for others, for lots of other poor folks – and even for me sometimes – it's nothing more than a ruthless machine, a huge soulless clockworks that stirs no reaction. The heavens have lost their mystery. They no longer seem like much of a reason to believe ..."

"What difference does it make?" repeated the abbé. "The mystery remains, Hennedyck. And the ones who no longer understand how to fathom it in the heavens should do like me: try to find it around them, near at hand. For myself, I've always thought that however vile, however debased a man may be, a bit of the divine spark nonetheless remains within him. And I search for it, and I need only find it to love that person. On the most impassive, the most hostile, the most materialistic face, I like to evoke the ennoblement of suffering, the reflection of love ... And I always manage to think of a chap's features – oftentimes hard and uncouth – as embellished and transfigured by a humane sentiment: fatherly affection, pure tenderness, or even the anxiety over the future that affects all of us at one time or another. And then that fellow is transformed before my very eyes, and I love him for the eternal problem, the tragic drama that I thereby see in each and every one, as I do in myself."

He stopped talking. They sat quietly for a moment, thinking.

"It's true," said Hennedyck, "it's true. We must believe, hope, continue our task no matter what. For myself, in spite of everything, I don't want to doubt. I refuse to doubt. I've known skepticism, the pessimistic outlook on the world and mankind that's so tyrannical, so debilitating when it gets hold of your mind. And I reject it because I sense all too well that it would lead to sterility, the awful 'what's the point?' that paralyzes everything. There's a constant struggle inside me between Reason and Will. And I've chosen the latter! I want to believe, to believe in something, to believe in progress, in justice, in goodness, to have faith in the future of Humanity. That's the only way I can find a reason to act, a reason to live, and an ultimate feeling of peace. Otherwise, life would be filled with nothing but emptiness and despair.

"And then, Father, you're right. It must be edifying, comforting to find the mystery, the deep, total, abiding mystery written on people's faces ...

And like you, when I'm feeling down now, I think I'll manage to seek out certain faces – the faces of women, of mothers, which you see filled with devotion and self-sacrifice – for a reflection of the divine light that I can no longer seem to fathom in the heavens ..."

The End